Daniel O'Connell

The select speeches of Daniel O'Connell

Daniel O'Connell

The select speeches of Daniel O'Connell

ISBN/EAN: 9783337275501

Printed in Europe, USA, Canada, Australia, Japan

Cover: Foto ©Andreas Hilbeck / pixelio.de

More available books at **www.hansebooks.com**

THE

SELECT SPEECHES

OF

DANIEL O'CONNELL, M.P

EDITED, WITH HISTORICAL NOTICES ETC,

BY HIS SON,

JOHN O'CONNELL, ESQ.

In Two Volumes.

VOL. I.

DUBLIN:
JAMES DUFFY, WELLINGTON QUAY,
AND
22, PATERNOSTER ROW, LONDON.
1871.

PREFACE

.

It being the intention of Mr. JAMES DUFFY, the Publisher of this Volume, to bring out, at no very distant period, a "LIFE OF DANIEL O'CONNELL,"* written in full detail and with every advantage of access to family documents, correspondences, &c., &c., it is not thought necessary to preface or accompany the present Selection from his Speeches with any biographical sketch or detailed narrative. This Publication will therefore comprise nothing beyond the Selection just mentioned, and a brief statement of such facts and dates as may appear indispensable.

CONTENTS

SELECT SPEECHES

DANIEL O'CONNELL, Esq., M.P.

~~~~~~~~

Daniel O'Connell was born at Carhen, near Cahirciveen, in the County of Kerry, on the 6th of August, 1775. At the age of thirteen he was sent for a time to school near Cove, or as it is now called, "Queenstown;" a year or two later he was sent for greater educational advantages to the Continent, where he studied successively at Louvain, St. Omer, and Douai.

Driven from the latter place and from the Continent by the atrocities of the French Revolution and the evident approach of war, Mr. O'Connell spent the next two or three years in London preparing for the Bar; to which he was eventually called in the sadly memorable year of 1798

When thus fairly entered upon the world's wide stage, he had strong reasons for avoiding politics. No lawyer could then hope to rise in his profession, unless willing to be the parasite and slave of the Government; and it was not even safe, in Ireland at least, for Protestant or Catholic, but especially for the latter, to be found in opposition

For these and other reasons the leading members of Mr. O'Connell's family and circle of friends were very much indisposed to his putting himself forward in any public struggle, and he was himself of course fully aware of the disadvantages and dangers he must incur by so doing. But he could not be silent when he saw the Legislative independence of his country about to be annihilated, and when it had become clear that the minister sought to implicate the Catholics of Ireland in his crime. Overtures had already been made in private to some of their nominal leaders, and rumour said that they had not been unfavourably received; timidity, credulity, or corruption jointly or separately operating to produce this result. There could not indeed be a doubt that the great bulk of the Catholic body felt as Irishmen should on this occasion, and abhorred the idea of the Union; but they were entirely unaccustomed to acting in concert, or coming forward in their aggregate character. Some one was wanted to show them the way. Their "natural leaders," as the phrase went, hung back, or were inclined to acquiescence in the proposed measure The minister's designs against the good repute and independence of the Catholic body seemed about to be consummated, when just at the critical moment Daniel O'Connell stepped forward.

The first speech of his which we give in this collection—his first public speech of any kind—was that delivered on the occasion we have mentioned. The meeting at which it was delivered—a meeting got up mainly by his efforts—took place on the 13th of January

In the year 1800, in the hall of the Royal Exchange, Dublin. Ere it had well assembled a panic began to spread, at the rumour that the authorities at the Castle had come to the determination of suppressing the meeting, in the exercise of the arbitrary power they sti' hesitated not to have recourse to, although the alleged necessity for it had long ceased with the utter extinction, more than a year before, of the last embers of rebellion / Pre sently in confirmation of this rumour, the measured tramp of soldiery became audible and the redcoats appeared under the main portico of the Exchange, facing to Parliamen' street. The noise of their approach and the sudden halt, with the clashing of the muskets as they were grounded on the flag-stones outside, increased the fast-spreading panic, and occasioned a sensible diminution along the outskirts of the assemblage. However, owing to the exertions and exhortations of Mr. O'Connell and a few other gentlemen, the main body stood firm; and h'. then advanced to meet and parley with the officer in command of the com bined military and civil array. This was the noted Major Sirr, whose name occurs so fre quently in the dark records of the internal government of Ireland at that unhappy time. He inquired the objects, &c., of the assemblage: and evidently disappointed at the peace good order, and readiness to submit to the law, with which he was encountered, reluctantly suffered the meeting to proceed.

The following was Mr. O'Connell's speech on the interesting occasion :—

Counsellor O'Connell rose, and in a short speech prefaced the resolutions. He said that the question of Union was confessedly one of the first importance and magnitude. Sunk, indeed, in more than criminal apathy, must that Irishman be, who could feel indifference on the subject. It was a measure, to the consideration of which we were called by every illumination of the understanding, and every feeling of the heart. There was, therefore, no necessity to apologize for the introducing the discussion of the question amongst Irishmen. But before he brought forward any resolution, he craved permission to make a few observations on the causes which produced the necessity of meeting as Catholics: as a separate and distinct body. In doing so, he thought he would clearly show that they were justifiable in at length deviating from a resolution which they had heretofore formed. The enlightened mind of the Catholics had taught them the impolicy, the illiberality, and the injustice of separating themselves on any occasion from the rest of the people of Ireland. The Catholics had therefore resolved, and they had wisely resolved, never more to appear before the public as a distinct and separate body; but they did not—they could not then foresee the unfortunately existing circumstances of this moment. They could not then foresee that they would be reduced to the necessity either of submitting to the disgraceful imputation of approving of a measure as detestable to them, as it was ruinous to their country; or once again, and he trusted for the last time, of coming forward as a distinct body.

There was no man present but was acquainted with the industry with which it was circulated, that the Catholics were favourable to the Union. In vain did multitudes of that body in different capacities, express their disapprobation of the measure; in vain did they concur with others of their fellow-subjects in expressing their abhorrence of it—as freemen or freeholders —electors of counties or inhabitants of cities—still the calumny was repeated; it was printed in journal after journal; it was published in pamphlet after pamphlet; it was circulated with activity in private companies; it was boldly and loudly proclaimed in public assemblies. How this clamour was raised, and how it was supported, was manifest—the motives of it were apparent.

In vain had the Catholics (individually) endeavoured to resist the torrent. Their future efforts, as individuals, would be equally vain and fruitless; they must then oppose it collectively.

There was another reason why they should come forward as a distinct class—a reason which he confessed had made the greatest impression upon his feelings. Not content with falsely asserting, that the Catholics favoured the extinction of Ireland, this their supposed inclination was attributed to the foulest motives— motives which were most repugnant to their judgments and most abhorrent to their hearts. It was said that the Catholics were ready to sell their country for a price, or, what was still more depraved, to abandon it on account of the unfortunate animosities which the wretched temper of the times had produced. Can they remain silent under so horrible a calumny! This calumny was flung on the whole body—it was incumbent on the whole body to come forward and contradict it; yes, they will show every friend of Ireland, that the Catholics are incapable of selling their country; they will loudly declare, that if their emancipation were offered for their consent to the measure —even were emancipation after the union a benefit—they would reject it with prompt indignation. (This sentiment met with approbation.) "Let us," said he, "show to Ireland that we have nothing in view but her good; nothing in our hearts but the desire of mutual forgiveness, mutual toleration, and mutual affection; in fine, let every man who feels with me proclaim that if the alternative were offered him of union, or the re-enactment of the penal code in all its pristine horrors, that he would prefer without hesitation the latter, as the lesser and more sufferable evil; that he would rather confide in the justice of his brethren, the Protestants of Ireland, who have already liberated him, than lay his country at the feet of foreigners." (This sentiment was met with much and marked approbation.) With regard to the union, so much had been said—so much had been written on the subject, that it was impossible any man should not before now have formed an opinion of it. He would not trespass on their attention in repeating arguments which they had already heard, and topics which they had already considered ; but if there was any man present who could be so far mentally degraded, as to consent to the extinction of the liberty, the constitution, and even the name of Ireland, he would call on him not to leave the direction and management of his commerce and property to strangers, over whom he could have no control.

He then concluded by moving the resolutions, which being seconded, passed unanimously, and the meeting broke up.

The following were the resolutions passed at the meeting. They were drawn up by Mr O'Connell himself :—

"Royal Exchange, Dublin, January 13, 1800.

"At a numerous and respectable meeting of the Roman Catholics of the City of Dublin, convened pursuant to public notice, Ambrose Moore, Esq., in the chair—

"Resolved—'That we are of opinion that the proposed incorporate Union of the legislature of Great Britain and Ireland is, in fact, an extinction of the liberty of this country, which would be reduced to the abject condition of a province, surrendered to the mercy of the minister and legislature of another country, to be bound by their absolute will and taxed at their pleasure by laws, in the making of which this country would have no efficient participation whatsoever.'

"Resolved—'That we are of opinion that the improvement of Ireland for the last twenty years, so rapid beyond example, is to be ascribed wholly to the independency of our legislature, so gloriously asserted in the year 1782, by virtue of our parliament co-operating with the generous recommendation of our most gracious and benevolent sovereign, and backed by the spirit of our people, and so solemnly ratified by both kingdoms as the only true and permanent foundation of Irish prosperity and British connection.'

"Resolved—'That we are of opinion, that if that independency should ever be surrendered, we must as rapidly relapse into our former depression and misery ; and that Ireland must inevitably lose, with her liberty, all that she has acquired in wealth, and industry, and civilization.'

"Resolved—'That we are firmly convinced, that the supposed advantages of such a surrender are unreal and delusive, and can never arise in fact ; and that even if they should arise, they would be only the bounty of the master to the slave, held by his courtesy, and resumable at his pleasure.'

"Resolved—'That—having heretofore determined not to come forward any more in the distinct character of Catholics, but to consider our claims and our cause not as those of a sect, but as involved in the general fate of our country—we now think it right, notwithstanding such determination, to publish the present resolutions, in order to undeceive our fellow-subjects who may have been led to believe, by a false representation, that we are capable of giving any concurrence whatsoever to so foul and fatal a project ; to assure them we are incapable of sacrificing our common country to either pique or pretension ; and that we are of opinion, that this deadly attack upon the nation is the great call of nature, of country, and posterity upon Irishmen of all descriptions and persuasions, to every constitutional and legal resistance ; and that we sacredly pledge ourselves to persevere in obedience to that call as long as we have life.'

" Signed, by order,

" JAMES RYAN, Sec."

THE CATHOLIC COMMITTEE.

THE next speech that we shall give, was the first to be found reported of his public address in reference to Catholic affairs specially. In January, 1808, the "Catholic Committee," as the AGITATORS of the day styled themselves, assembled to debate the advisability of an immediate Petition to Parliament for the total abrogation of the Penal Laws. The negative was strongly urged by some of their number, supported, as was rumoured, by the opinion of the celebrated John Keogh, the Catholic leader of that day, who was however prevented by illness from attending in person.

His objection was said to be founded on the idea that it was beneath the dignity of the Catholic body to petition so repeatedly ; and that it would be more advisable for them to remain quiet, watching in "dignified silence" the course of events and the conduct of their parliamentary friends.

The other opponents of petitioning had less specious objections to offer, and in answer chiefly to them the following speech was delivered :—

Mr. O'Connell said he had not intended to address the meeting. His anxiety for the Catholic cause alone brought him forward. He entertained no apprehension about Catholic Emancipation, but such as might arise from the conduct of the Catholics themselves. He could not avoid asking whether the public time was to be wasted by childish and puerile objections—objections that could only manifest a spirit of division, a feeling of party, and a miserable ambition of leadership. With every faculty of his mind awake to the deplorable consequences of division, he should not cease to exert all the energy of his soul to stimulate their minds to unanimity. When an adjournment was proposed, he expected to hear it supported by some kind of argument ; had any existed, it would certainly have been put forward by the eloquent gentlemen who had already spoken ; that they had not condescended to reason was to him decisive proof that no plausible reason existed. No man was more ready to abandon his opinion to argument, but he could not agree to a measure fraught with mischievous consequences, merely because one gentleman made a motion, and another was pleased to second it. He would entreat of gentlemen to take a cautious view of the precipice which opened to them, shou d they suffer their good sense to be led away by any motives, to the adoption of the sentiments excited industriously ; but for no good purpose excited by those who would divide the Catholic body. Commor sense alone ought to be a sufficient protection against the insidious attempt. He begged to remind gentlemen of what had taken place at the last meeting. The generous feelings of Catholics had gained precedence of their interests, and they had given up the presenting of their petition, in the last session of Parlia ment, to their gratitude towards their political advocates. There was another reason for that sacrifice : a stupid and atrocious spirit of bigotry had been fomented in England, even by ministerial authority ; and the Catholics had generously withdrawn from the struggle, that they might deprive British intolerance of even the *shadow* of an excuse. He recollected with pleasure the splendid exertions of the ancient advocate of the Catholic cause (John Keogh,) upon that occasion. He it was that had urged the topics just alluded to, with irresistible force ; and had not an illness, now deeply to be deplored, prevented his attendance this day, division in the Catholic body could not be feared His powers of reasoning would have frightened away the captious objections taken to the resolution, and the Catholics of Ireland would have again to thank their old and useful servant for the preservation of their honour, and the support of their interests. Mr. O'Connell called the attention of the meeting to the resolution which had unanimously passed at the last meeting ; and by which the care of the Catholic petition was entrusted to the noble earl in the chair. It was committed to his sole management. Neither jealousy could suggest, nor folly express an objection to the resolution which had so committed it. It was unnecessary for him, and indeed he had not the powers to put in their proper point of view, the qualities that called for and justified that confidence ; and the presence of the noble lord restrained the effusions of public gratitude for his services, but the impression was the more deeply felt for being cherished only in the silence of the heart.—[Mr. O'Connell was here interrupted by loud and repeated acclamations:]—Well, to Lord Fingall you committed the sole management of your petition ; he accepted the office ; he was authorised to act for himself ; and it is attempted to be insinuated to this meeting that he has not acted consistently ; because, when he might have acted upon his own suggestions alone, he anxiously and industriously sought for the advice and assistance of every individual who had heretofore taken part in the Catholic question. This, under the resolution of the last meeting, was an unnecessary condescension ; but assuredly it was the more amiable and the less liable to objection. Yet what was the ground the supporters of an adjournment went upon ? It amounted to this : that Lord Fingall had done, with advice and deliberation, that which he might have done instantly and alone. Was the calling of the present meeting less the act of Lord Fingall, because the opinions and judgments of so many whom he had consulted concurred with him in its propriety ? To such absurdity were his opponents driven, that they must support the affirmative of the proposition. But it was said that there had been no notice given of the present meeting. It was strange to hear this objection urged by gentlemen whose presence seemed to admit that the notice was sufficient. However, what was the fact ? Had not that meeting been announced in all the Dublin papers more than ten days previously ? It could not be denied that it had been so announced ; still a pretext was left, and they had been gravely told that it was true the announcement of the meeting had been published, but that it was published in form of a paragraph, and not of n advertisement. Here then it stood admitted that it was not for substance, but mere matter of form, that the Catholic body was to be divided. One would imagine that division was a good thing, when so flimsy a pretext was resorted to, to produce it He trusted that the gentlemen themselves would abandon their opposition, when they saw the question put in this, its proper light. The Catholics of every part of Ireland had been consulted : their sentiments as to the propriety of petitioning had been required by letter. Numerous answers had been received from the most respectable persons in all the counties, who all concurred in this one opinion, that the petition should be forwarded without the smallest delay. In some parts the Catholics had already gone further—meetings had been held in the cities of Cork and Waterford, and resolutions to that effect entered into ; nay, the petition had not only the good wishes of our liberal and enlightened Protestant brethren of Ireland, but some of them had expressed their sentiments by a public resolution ; he alluded to that of the nobility and gentry of the county of Tipperary. Their conduct, patriotic as it was amiable, useful as well as benevolent, was the theme of general admiration. He regretted that he could not speak of it in terms according with the gratitude of his heart. It reminded him, however, of that affectionate attention and care for the rights of Irishmen, warmed, though not created, by the benevolent recommendation of our beloved sovereign, which has induced the Irish Protestants of the present generation to break the fetters of the Catholic, and totally to emancipate the Presbyterian—a wise and magnanimous policy, which would have long since restored the Catholic to complete freedom, had their cause and their country been left in the hands of Irish Protestants (loud and repeated applause.) Under those circumstances, nothing but disunion among themselves could ever retard the Catholic cause. Division, while it rendered them the object of disgust to their friends, would make them the scorn and ridicule of their enemies. He was ready to admit that the present administration were personal enemies of the Catholic cause ; yet, if the Catholics continue loyal, firm, and undivided, they had little to fear from the barren petulance of the ex-advocate, Perceval, or the frothy declamations of the poetaster, Canning—they might meet with equal contempt the upstart pride of the Jenkinsons, and with more than contempt the pompous inanity of that Lord Castlereagh, who might well be permitted to hate the country that gave him birth, to her own annihilation. He was also free to confess that he knew of no statute passed since the Union, which had for its object to increase the trade, or advance the liberties of Ireland ; but he thought it impossible, if the Catholics persevered, with undivided efforts, in their loyal and dutiful pursuit of Emancipation, that any administration could be found sufficiently daring in guilt to stand between them and the throne of their father and sovereign ; and most calumniously and falsely use his name to raise obstacles in the way of good subjects seeking to become free citizens. He did therefore, conjure the gentlemen to give up their opposition ; he respected their talents, and however convinced of their mistake, could not doubt the purity of their motives. They must see that their arguments against the resolution were confined to the ridiculous opposition, in fact, against the noble lord, for his having condescended to ask advice before he acted ; and to the equally frivolous difficulty objected to the form of the notice for calling the meeting. Was it possible that rational beings should govern their conduct by such arguments in the serious pursuit of freedom? They were sons, and might dearly love the parents who gave them birth—let them recollect that it was for their rights that the petition was framed : they were brothers, and

should, if they felt tne endearing impulses of fraternal affection
sacrifice party, and of course mere forms and ceremonies, in a
struggle for obtaining the rights of their brethren : they were
parents, and all the sweet charities of life, combined in favour of
the children who looked up to them for protection. It was the
liberties of those children the present petition sought—would
they postpone for an hour that sacred blessing ? Could they,
from any motive, thwart the progress of those who sought it ? He
knew that was impossible, and he hoped, therefore, there would
be no division.

The result of the debate was a withdrawal of the amendment, and the unanimous carrying of the resolution to petition.

AGGREGATE MEETING.

Not long afterwards, Mr. O'Connell had again an opportunity, most congenial and acceptable to his feelings, of coming forward upon a national question, and suspending for the
time all mention of the claims and wishes of a particular class or body, however numerous
or important in themselves. A movement was suddenly and most unexpectedly made in
the very bosom of the exclusive and deeply-dyed Orange Corporation of Dublin itself, in
March of the year 1818, against the Act of Legislative Union between Great Britain and
Ireland; and although the patriotic attempt—headed, we are glad to record, by the name
of one of a family known then and ever since as among the best and most considerate
employers of labour in the City of Dublin, the Hutton family—made no progress in 1808,
two years later a better success attended it.

Upon the 18th of September, 1810, the following meeting took place. The subject being
still of such interest, we give, in addition to Mr. O'Connell's speech, some brief prefatory
matter descriptive of the occurrence, including the remarks of some others of the speakers.

" At a meeting of the citizens, freemen, and freeholders of the city
of Dublin, at the Royal Exchange, on Tuesday, 18th September, 1810,
held pursuant to a requisition of several respectable citizens of Dublin,
to the high sheriffs, to consider of a petition to the king's most excellent majesty, and the imperial parliament, praying them to take into
their consideration the Repeal of the Act of Union—Sir James Riddall,
Knight, high sheriff of the city of Dublin, in the chair.

" On Sir James Riddall taking the chair, he addressed the most
numerous and respectable auditory that ever assembled in the city of
Dublin. He recommended to the assembly to maintain the utmost
order and regularity in their proceedings ; assuring them he had the
greatest hopes that if they conducted themselves with propriety, they
would finally succeed in carrying their point ; but by manifesting a contrary disposition, they would afford a pretext to their enemies to malign
their motives.

" The requisition, signed by a number of citizens, freemen, and freeholders of the city of Dublin, at the late Quarter Sessions Grand Jury

was read by Mr. Frederick Conway, who was appointed secretary to the meeting, stating, that on account of the depressed state of the manufactures in the county and city of Dublin, the citizens of Dublin pointed out as the only mode of radical relief which occurred to them was to present a requisition to the high sheriffs of the city of Dublin, to call a meeting of the citizens, freemen, and freeholders of Dublin, to consider of presenting a petition to his Majesty, praying a Repeal of the Act of Union.

"Sir James Riddal then said—In consequence of the requisition, I have called you, gentlemen, together this day. I am determined, impartially, to hear every one for and against the question; a patient hearing will be given to every gentleman who chooses to deliver his opinion on either side.

"Mr. Hutton then rose, and spoke as follows:—Mr. Sheriff, I am called upon to move a resolution, that a committee may be appointed to prepare and draw up a petition to the king's most excellent Majesty, and to the imperial parliament, to take into consideration the Repeal of the Union. I stand forth on this occasion an advocate of the Repeal of the Act of Union, and I claim your candid attention. I am aware of the inadequacy of my abilities on this occasion, but I appeal to your candour and goodness, and I appeal to every man that knows me, for the rectitude of my intentions. It has been asserted privately, that this assembly has been convened for improper purposes: the purport of this meeting is, to put down everything like disorder in the state, and present a petition to his Majesty, stating that we conceive it would be for the benefit of our common country, and to preserve our connection with England, and testify our loyalty to our king, by having the Act of Union Repealed. This wretched act has prevented our manufactures from having a fair competition in the market, and were it repealed, it would be of the utmost advantage to our manufactures, and give a new impulse to our commerce. The repeal of that measure, he contended, would tend to the best means to secure the prosperity and happiness of Ireland. At the time the Act of Union was proposed, it was held out to the people of this country, that persons possessing great British capital, would come over from England and establish manufactures in Ireland, and particularly in Dublin, our trade would be increased—that we should have the education of the poor in Ireland properly attended to. The Roman Catholics were told that they had a right to expect more benefits from the interference of the British parliament, than they could expect to receive from an Irish parliament. Sir, we have now had the experience of ten years, since the passing of the Act of Union, and let me ask have the Irish manufactures had a fair competition in the British markets? Have the manufactures of Ireland been protected and encouraged, or have those of Dublin flourished as we were promised? Let me ask, have the poor of the land had their education properly attended to? Every man that is a well-wisher to the prosperity of Ireland, will answer me in the negative. Have the Roman Catholics met with any acknowledgment of the justice of their claims? If they have, let any man who now hears me, stand forward and avow it.

On the contrary, the Catholics, in their rights, ever since the passing
of the Act of Union, have stood, and do stand at present, just where
they began. They have endeavoured to get their claims acknowledged
and acquiesced in ; but are they not at this instant precluded from holding any superior rank in the army ? I do not, Sir, speak of administration, but I contend that the welfare and prosperity of Ireland depend
upon the Repeal of the Act of Union. We, therefore, wish the parliament of Ireland to be restored to the same state it was in at the period
of 1782. A parliament in Ireland is the only means of restoring the
independence, promoting the happiness of our country, securing its
peace and prosperity. Sir, I feel myself inadequate to do ample justice to the business now before us ; I shall only say, I consider that the
Repeal of the Act of Union would tend to the advantage of my country.
My want of ability to do adequate justice to the great question, and I
expect that this business will be fully spoken to by these honourable
gentlemen who will take a part in the debates of this day, with whom
this business originated. I trust, Sir, that this day's proceedings will
show to the world, collectively and individually, our loyalty, zeal, and
attachment to our good king, and prove that our opinion is universal
and unanimous, concerning the Act of Union. I mention, Sir, that it is
by such a Repeal only, that the peace and tranquillity of Ireland can be
preserved. We should be indissolubly linked to Great Britain by such
a Repeal, and by such a one alone ! I move, Sir, that a committee of
nine persons be appointed to prepare and draw up an address to his
majesty, and to the imperial parliament, praying a Repeal of the Act
of Union.

" Ambrose Moore, Esq., seconded the motion.

" The resolution was read accordingly, and agreed to without one
dissenting voice.

" A committee of nine gentlemen was then appointed to draw up and
prepare the said petition. The names were, Mr. Hutton, Mr. Randal
M'Donald, Mr. Ashenhurst, Mr. O'Connell, Mr. Moore, Mr. N. Mahon,
Mr. Abbot, Mr. Hurty, Mr. Farrell. The said committee appointed to
prepare and draw up the petition, having prepared the same, they made
their report to the assembly at large.

" The petition to the king was then read and carried unanimously. '

Mr. O'Connell declared that he offered himself to the meeting
with unfeigned diffidence. He was unable to do justice to his
feelings on the great national subject on which they had met. He
felt too much of personal anxiety to allow him to arrange in
anything like order, the many topics which rushed upon his
mind, now, that after ten years of silence and torpor, Irishmen
began again to recollect their enslaved country. It was a melancholy period, those ten years—a period in which Ireland saw
her artificers starved—her tradesmen begging—her merchants
become bankrupts—her gentry banished—her nobility degraded.
Within that period domestic turbulence broke from day to day.

into open violence and murder—religious dissensions were aggravated and embittered—credit and commerce were annihilated—
taxation augmented in amount and in vexation. Besides the
" hangings-off" of the ordinary assizes, we had been disgraced by
the necessity that existed for holding two special commissions
of death, and had been degraded by one rebellion—and, to crown
all, we were at length insulted by being told of our *growing prosperity.*" This was not the painting of imagination—it borrowed
nothing from fancy—it was, alas, the plain representation of the
facts that had occurred—the picture, in sober colours, of the real
state of his ill-fated country. There was not a man present but
must be convinced that he did not exaggerate a single fact : there
was not a man present but must know that more misery existed
than he had described. Such being the history of the first ten
years of the Union, it would not be difficult to convince any
unprejudiced man, that all those calamities had sprung from that
measure. Ireland was favoured by Providence with a fertile soil,
an excellent situation for commerce, intersected by navigable
rivers, indented at every side with safe and commodious harbours, blessed with a fruitful soil, and with a vigorous, hardy,
generous, and brave population; how did it happen then, that
the noble qualities of the Irish people were perverted? that the
order of Providence was disturbed, and its blessings worse than
neglected? The fatal cause was obvious—it was the Union.
That these deplorable effects would follow from that accursed
measure, was prophesied. Before the Act of Union passed, it had
been already proved that the trade of the country and its credit
must fail as capital was drawn from it; that turbulence and violence would increase, when the gentry were removed to residence
in another country ; that the taxes should increase in the same
proportion as the people became unable to pay them. But neither the argument nor the prophetic fears have ended with our
present evils. It has also been demonstrated, that as long as
the Union continues, so long must our misfortunes accumulate.
The nature of that measure, and the experience of facts which
we have now had, leave no doubt of the truth of what has been
asserted respecting the future. But, if there be any still incre-
dulous, he can only be of those who submit their reason to authority. To such person, the authority of Mr. John Foster, Chancellor of the Exchequer for Ireland, would probably be conclusive ; and Foster has assured us, that final ruin to our country
must be the consequence of the Union. I will not dwell, Mr
Sheriff, on the miseries of my country; I am disgusted with the

wretchedness the Union has produced; and I do not dare to
trust myself with the contemplation of the accumulation of sorrow that must overwhelm the land, if the Union be not repealed;
I beg to call the attention of the meeting to another part of the
subject. The Union, Sir, was a violation of our national and
inherent rights—a flagrant injustice. The representatives whom
we had elected for a short period of eight years, had no authority to dispose of their country for ever. It cannot be pretended
that any direct or express authority to that effect was given to
them; and the nature of their delegation excludes all idea of
their having any such by implication. They were the servants
of the nation, empowered to consult for its good—not its masters, to make traffic and dispose of it at their fantasy or for their
profit. I deny that the nation itself had a right to barter its
independence. or to commit political suicide; but when our servants destroyed our existence as a nation, they added to the
baseness of assassination all the guilt of high treason. The reasoning upon which those opinions are founded is sufficiently
obvious. They require no sanction from the authority of any
name—neither do I pretend to give them any weight, by declaring them to be conscientiously my own; but if you want authority, to induce the conviction that the Union had *injustice* for
its principle, and a *crime* for its basis, I appeal to that of his
Majesty's present Attorney-General, Mr. Saurin, who, in his
place in the Irish parliament, pledged his character as a lawyer
and a statesman, that the Union must be a violation of every
moral principle. and that it was a mere question of prudence
whether it should not be resisted by force. I also appeal to the
opinions of the late Lord High Chancellor of Ireland, Mr. George
Ponsonby—of the present Solicitor-General, Mr. Bushe—and of
that splendid lawyer, Mr. Plunket. The Union was, therefore,
a manifest injustice—and it continues to be unjust at this day;
it was a crime, and must be still criminal, unless it shall be
ludicrously pretended that crime. like wine, improves by old age,
and that time mollifies injustice into innocence. You may smile
at the supposition, but in sober sadness you must be convinced
that we daily suffer injustice; that every succeeding day adds
only another sin to the catalogue of British vice; and that if
the Union continues, it will only make crime hereditary, and
injustice perpetual. We have been robbed, my countrymen,
most foully robbed of our birthright, of our independence—may it
not be permitted to us, mournfully to ask how this consummation
of evil was perfected? for it was not in any disastrous battle that

our liberties were struck down—no foreign invader had despoiled the land ; we have not forfeited our country by any crimes—neither did we lose it in any domestic insurrection. No, the rebellion was completely put down before the Union was accomplished : the Irish militia and the Irish yeomanry had put it down. How, then, have we become enslaved ? Alas ! England, that ought to have been to us as a sister and a friend—England, whom we had loved, and fought, and bled for—England, whom we have protected, and whom we do protect—England, at a period when out of 100,000 of the seamen in her service, 70,000 were Irish— England stole upon us, like a thief in the night, and robbed us of the precious gem of our Liberty ; she stole from us ' that which in nought enriched her, but made us poor indeed.' Reflect then, my friends, on the means employed to accomplish this disastrous measure. I do not speak of the meaner instruments of bribery and corruption—we all know that everything was put to sale—nothing profane or sacred was omitted in the Union mart—offices in the revenue, commands in the army and navy, the sacred ermine of justice, and the holy altars of God were all profaned and polluted as the rewards of Union services. By a vote in favour of the Union, ignorance, incapacity, and profligacy, obtained certain promotion ; and our ill-fated but beloved country was degraded to her utmost limits, before she was transfixed in slavery. But I do not intend to detain you in the contemplation of those vulgar means of parliamentary success—they are within the daily routine of official *management* : neither will I direct your attention to the frightful recollection of that avowed fact which is now part of history, that the *rebellion* itself was fomented and encouraged in order to facilitate the Union. Even the rebellion was an accidental and secondary cause—the real cause of the Union lay deeper, but is quite obvious. It is to be found at once in the *religious dissensions* which the enemies of Ireland have created, and continued, and seek to perpetuate amongst ourselves, by telling us of, and separating us into wretched sections and miserable subdivisions ; they separated the Protestant from the Catholic, and the Presbyterian from both ; they revived every antiquated cause of domestic animosity, and they invented new pretexts of rancour ; but above all, my countrymen, they belied and calumniated us to each other— they falsely declared that we hated each other, and they continued to repeat the assertion, until we came to believe it ; they succeeded in producing all the madness of party and religious distinctions ; and whilst we were lost in the stupor of insanity, they plundered us of our country, and left us to recover at our leisure from the horrid delusion into which we had been so artfully conducted.

Such then were the means by which the Union was effectuated. It has stripped us of commerce and wealth ; it has degraded us, and deprived us not only of our station as a nation, but even of the name of our country ; we are governed by foreigners—foreigners make our laws, for were the one hundred members who nominally represent Ireland in what is called the imperial parliament, were they really our representatives, what influence could they, although unbought and unanimous, have over the five hundred and fifty-eight English and Scotch members? But what is the fact ? Why that out of the one hundred, such as they are, that sit for this country, more than one-fifth know nothing of us, and are unknown to us. What, for example, do we know about Andrew Strahan, printer to the king? What can Henry Martin, barrister-at-law, care for the rights or liberties of Irishmen?— Some of us may, perhaps for our misfortunes, have been compelled to read a verbose pamphlet of James Stevens; but who knows anything of one Crile, one Hughan, one Cackin, or of a dozen more whose names I could mention, only because I have discovered them for the purpose of speaking to you about them ; what sympathy can we in our sufferings, expect from those men? What solicitude for our interests ? What are they to Ireland, or Ireland to them ? No, Mr. Sheriff, we are not represented—we have no effectual share in the legislation—the thing is a mere mockery ; neither is the imperial parliament competent to legislate for us—it is too unwieldy a machine to legislate with discernment for England alone; but with respect to Ireland, it has all the additional inconvenience that arise from want of interest and total ignorance. Sir, when I talk of the utter ignorance, in Irish affairs, of the members of the imperial parliament, I do not exaggerate or mistake ; the ministers themselves are in absolute darkness with respect to this country. I undertake to demonstrate it. Sir, they have presumed to speak of the growing prosperity of Ireland—I know them to be vile and profligate—I cannot be suspected of flattering them—yet vile as they are, I do not believe they could have had the audacity to insert in the speech, supposed to be spoken by his Majesty, *that expression*, had they known that, in fact, Ireland was in abject and increasing poverty. Sir, they were content to take their information from a pensioned Frenchman—a being styled Sir Francis D'Ivernois, who, in one of the pamphlets which it is his trade to write, has proved, by excellent samples of vulgar arithmetic, that our manufactures are flourishing, our commerce extending, and our felicity consummate. When you detect the ministers themselves in such gross ignorance, as, upon such authority, to place an insulting falsehood as it were, in the mouth of our revered sovereign, what think you can be the fitness of nine minor imps of legislation to make laws for Ireland. Indeed, the recent plans of taxation sufficiently evince how incompetent the present scheme of parliament is to legislate for Ireland. Had we an Irish parliament, it is impossible to conceive that they would have adopted taxes at once oppressive and unproductive—ruinous to the country, and useless to the crown. No, Sir, an Irish parliament, acquainted with the state of the country, and individually interested to tax proper objects, would have, even in this season of distress, no difficulty in raising the necessary supplies. The loyalty and good sense of the Irish nation would aid them ; and we should not, as now, perceive taxation unproductive of money, but abundantly fertile in discontent. There is another subject that peculiarly requires the attention of the legislature ; but it is one which can be managed only by a resident and domestic parliament—it includes everything that relates to those strange and portentous disturbances which, from time to time, affright and desolate the fairest districts of the island. It is a delicate and difficult subject, and one that would require the most minute knowledge of the causes that produce those disturbances, and would demand all the attention and care of men, whose individual safety was connected with the discovery of a proper remedy. I do not wish to calculate the extent of evil that may be dreaded from the outrages I allude to, if our country shall continue in the hands of foreign empirics and pretenders ; but it is clear to a demonstration, that no man can be attached to his king and country, who does not avow the necessity of submitting the control of this political evil, to the only competent tribunal—an Irish parliament. The ills of this awful moment are not confined to our domestic complaints and calamities. The great enemy of the liberty of the world, extends his influence and his power from the Frozen Ocean to the Straits of Gibraltar. He threatens us with invasion from the thousand ports of his vast empire; how is it possible to resist him with an impoverished divided, and dispirited empire? If, then you are loyal to your excellent monarch—if you are attached to the last relic of political freedom, can you hesitate to join in endeavouring to procure the remedy for all your calamities—the sure protection against all

the threats of your enemy—*the Repeal of the Union.* Yes, restore to Irishmen their country, and you may well defy the invader's force ; give back Ireland to her hardy and brave population; and you have nothing to dread from foreign power. It is
useless to detain the meeting longer, in detailing the miseries
that the Union has produced, or in pointing out the necessity
that exists for its Repeal. I have never met any man who did
not deplore this fatal measure, which has despoiled his country;
nor do I believe that there is a single individual in the island,
who could be found even to pretend approbation of that measure.
I would be glad to see the face of the man, or rather of the beast,
who could dare to say he thought the Union wise or good—for
the being who could say so, must be devoid of all the feelings
that distinguish humanity. With the knowledge that such were
the sentiments of the universal Irish nation, how does it happen
that the Union had lasted for ten years? The solution of the
question was easy. The Union continued only because we despaired of its Repeal. Upon this despair alone had it continued
—yet what could be more absurd than such despair? If the
Irish sentiment be but once known—if the voice of six millions be raised from Cape Clear to the Giants' Causeway—if the
men most remarkable for their loyalty to their king, and attachment to constitutional liberty, will come forward as the leaders of the public voice, the nation would, in an hour, grow
too great for the chains that now shackle you, and the Union
must be repealed without commotion and without difficulty.
Let the most timid amongst us compare the present probability
of Repealing the Union, with the prospect that in the year 1795
existed of that measure being ever brought about. Who, in
1795, thought an Union possible? Pitt dared to attempt it,
and he succeeded ; it only requires the resolution to attempt its
Repeal—in fact, it requires only to entertain the hope of repealing it, to make it impossible that the Union should continue ;
but that pleasing hope could never exist, whilst the infernal dissensions on the score of religion were kept up. The Protestant
alone could not expect to liberate his country—the Roman
Catholic alone could not do it—neither could the Presbyterian—
but amalgamate the three into the Irishman, and the Union is
repealed. Learn discretion from your enemies—they have crushed
your country by fomenting religious discord—serve her by abandoning it for ever. Let each man give up his share of the mis-
chief--let each man forsake every feeling of rancour. But, I
say not this to barter with you, my countrymen—I require no

equivalent from you—whatever course you shall take, my mind is fixed—I trample under foot the Catholic claims, if they can interfere with the Repeal; I abandon all wish for emancipation, 'f it delays that Repeal. Nay, were Mr. Perceval, to-morrow, to offer me the Repeal of the Union, upon the terms of re-enacting the entire penal code, I declare it from my heart, and in the presence of my God, that I would most cheerfully embrace his offer. Let us then, my beloved countrymen, sacrifice our wicked and groundless animosities on the altar of our country—let that spirit which heretofore emanating from Dungannon spread all over the island, and gave light and liberty to the land, be again cherished amongst us—let us rally round the standard of Old Ireland, and we shall easily procure that greatest of political blessings, an Irish King, an Irish House of Lords, and an Irish House of Commons.—(Long-continued applause.)

After Mr. O'Connell had concluded his speech, Sir James Riddall observed, that calumny or misrepresentation might be exercised upon Mr. O'Connell's expression of an Irish king, and he, therefore, was happy to give Mr. O'Connell an opportunity of doing justice to our most gracious sovereign. Mr. O'Connell ardently availed himself of the occasion to pay a very grateful tribute to the virtues and patriotism of his majesty, and observed, that if ever a monarch existed, abounding in every great and good qualification, calculated to make his people happy, that monarch was George the Third.

" Sir James Riddall then put the question separately, that the address and petition should stand the address and petition of the meeting, which was carried unanimously.

" Mr. Hutton then proposed that a committee of twenty-one be chosen as a standing committee to co-operate with the other meetings throughout the kingdom, which was unanimously agreed to, and a committee was appointed accordingly.

" Nicholas Mahon rose, and spoke to the following effect:—Mr. Sheriff, the respect I feel for the opinions of several gentlemen present, whose liberality I respect, and by whose exertions this meeting (which I trust will produce the happiest result) has been called, has induced me to undertake the task of subscribing to your two resolutions, which I hold in my hand, expressive of approbation of the conduct of his Grace the Duke of Richmond, since his appointment to the government of this country. I beg leave in making this motion, to be distinctly understood as not approving of the measures of the administration to which his Grace is attached, which I consider as most hostile to the welfare of those countries; but no one can deny his Grace the possession of many amiable social virtues, and that he wields the sword of power in mercy and clemency. Without further preface, I move you, Sir, that those resolutions be now read."

PETITION FOR CATHOLIC EMANCIPATION.

In the same year, 1810. Mr. O'Connell drew up the Petition of that year, to the House of Commons, for Catholic Emancipation. It ran as follows:—

"*To the Honourable the Commons of the United Kingdom of Great Britain and Ireland, in Parliament assembled:*

"We, whose names are hereunto subscribed, on behalf of ourselves and of others, his Majesty's subjects, professing the Roman Catholic religion in Ireland, humbly beg leave to represent to this Honourable House—

"That we, your petitioners, did, in the years 1805 and 1808, humbly petition this honourable house, praying the total abolition of the penal laws, which aggrieve the Catholics of Ireland.

"We now feel ourselves obliged, in justice to ourselves, our families, and our country, once more to solicit the attention of this honourable house to the subject of our said petition.

"We state, that the Roman Catholics constitute the most numerous and increasing portion of the inhabitants of Ireland, comprising an immense majority of the manufacturing, trading, and agricultural interests, and amounting to at least four-fifths of the Irish population; that they contribute largely to the exigencies of their country, civil and military; that they pay the far greater part of the public and local taxes; that they supply the armies and navies of this empire with upwards of one-third part in number of the soldiers and sailors employed in the public service; and that, notwithstanding heavy discouragements, they form the principal constituent part of the strength, wealth, and industry of Ireland.

"Yet such is the grievous operation of the penal laws of which we complain, that the Roman Catholics are thereby not only set apart from their fellow-subjects, as aliens in this their native land, but are ignominiously and rigorously proscribed from almost all situations of public trust, honour, or emolument, including every public function and department, from the houses of legislature, down to the most petty corporations.

"We state, that whenever the labour of public duty is to be exacted and enforced, the Catholic is sought out and selected, where honours or rewards are to be dispensed, he is neglected and contemned.

"Where the military and naval strength of the empire is to be recruited, the Catholics are eagerly solicited, nay compelled,

c

to bear at least their full share in the perils of warfare, and in the lowest ranks ; but when preferment or promotion (the dear and legitimate prize of successful valour) are to be distributed as rewards of merit, no laurels are destined to grace a Catholic brow, or fit the wearer for command.

"We state, thus generally, the grievous condition of the Roman Catholics of Ireland, occasioned solely by the fatal influence and operation of the penal laws, and though we forbear to enter into greater detail, yet we do not the less trust to the influence of reason and justice (which eventually must prevail) for effecting a full and deliberate inquiry into our grievances, and accomplishing our effectual relief.

"We do beg leave, however, most solemnly, to press upon the attention of this honourable house, the imminent public dangers which necessarily result from so inverted an order of things, and so vicious and unnatural a system of legislation—a system which has long been the reproach of this nation, and is unparalleled throughout modern Christendom.

"And we state it as our fixed opinion, that to restore to the Catholics of Ireland, a full, equal, and unqualified participation of the benefits of the laws and constitution of England, and to withdraw all the privations, restrictions, and vexatious distinctions which oppress, injure, and afflict them in their country, is now become a measure not merely expedient, but absolutely necessary—not only a debt of right due to a complaining people, but perhaps the last remaining resource of this empire, in the preservation of which we take so deep an interest.

"We therefore pray this honourable house to take into their most serious consideration the nature, extent, and operation of the aforesaid penal laws, and by repealing the same altogether, to restore to the Roman Catholics of Ireland those liberties so long withheld, and their due share in that Constitution, which they, in common with their fellow-subjects of every other description, contribute by taxes, arms, and industry, to sustain and defend.

"And your petitioners will ever pray."

CATHOLIC RIGHTS.

Tᴀᴇ next speech of any length (that we find reported) of Mr O'Connell's, was delivered to the "Catholic Committee," on the 2nd of February, 1811, upon the question of again peti-tioning the Legislature for Catholic rights.

The immediate occasion, however, of his rising upon that day, was a squabble that had arisen amongst some of the leading members, during which more than one insinuation had been thrown out against himself, of wanting to usurp the position of " leader."

In answer to this, and to allay the paltry bickerings that were growing, more and more frequent in the meetings of the Committee, and turn the general attention to the real business in hand, he is reported to have made the following address, which as usual we copy verbatim from the newspapers of the time :—

Mr. O'Connell began by expressing an anxious hope that the discussion of this day would be conducted with good temper, and terminate in harmony.   His object was to stifle every senti-ment amongst the Catholic body, that would militate against that cordial spirit of co-operation, which had hitherto animated the members of the committee.   Hitherto, at their meetings, a difference of opinion did sometimes, as it was quite natural, prevail ; but there was no intention of division—and, from this heartfelt unanimity, he had with delight beheld the dawning certainty of speedy and complete emancipation.   The Catholic cause was now too great and irresistible to be destroyed, even by the misconduct of its own advocates.   It had, indeed, been almost crushed in its infancy, by distrust and dissension.   Dis-sension had impeded it in every step of its progress, and was still the drag-chain that encumbered and retarded its movements. By division, the Catholics would be not only weakened, but degraded : if they quarrelled amongst themselves, they would disgust their friends and delight their enemies.

Could anything be imagined more agreeable to the Wellesleys and the Percevals, than to find the Catholics of Ireland involved in a wrangle amongst themselves—than to see them engaged in attacking and vilifying one another, when every faculty of their minds ought to be directed to concert one combined effort of all the Irish people to put down their enemies, and to procure, in a constitutional course, their Emancipation.   He did, there-fore, conjure the gentlemen who had brought forward the pre-sent question to revert to that subject, for which the committee had been originally framed, namely, the petition ; and to suffer *that* to proceed, without embarking in discussions that could not be productive of advantage.   He expected from those gentle-men, that they would, when they contemplated the triumph to our enemies, and the mischief to the Catholics, which must ensue from dissension, abandon that species of crimination and attack, which had been that day, for the first time, introduced into the committee. The charges that were made, even supposing them founded, could be obviated, if those gentlemen would, themselves, take the trouble of attending in future. But he must say, that the gentlemen who did attack the committee, were altogether mistaken. The fact was, that the committee stands high in the public opinion—and that this estimation was founded on important services and pure exertions—upon a painful sacrifice of the time and labour of the individuals—and upon the more painful exposure which they made of themselves, to every shaft of calumny and ridicule, from the mean, mercenary, and malignant hirelings of the enemies of the Catholics.

With respect to that part of the Irish Catholic bar, which took a part in the labours of the committee, he would not say a word in its vindication : for his own part, he should be most grateful if the bar were altogether to be excluded from Catholic politics—and it would be easy to exclude them. If the noble lord could spare time from his other avocations, to attend the affairs of the Catholics, he, for one, would rejoice at their being placed in such excellent hands ; and would then think himself 'ustified in devoting himself, exclusively, to his professional pursuits. All he wished to see was, that gentlemen would come forward, and take upon themselves the trouble of advancing the Catholic concerns; but it really was rather severe that gentlemen, who avowed that they themselves had not leisure to attend to the business of the Catholics, should charge those who, with a disinterested zeal, had made, and were ready to make a sacrifice of their time and exertions, with being animated with the pitiful ambition of leadership. No—that was a contemptible object; and he had no difficulty in calling on the all-seeing Deity to attest the truth of his assertion, that the conscientious discharge of duty to an afflicted country, was his leading motive to come forward; and that neither he nor his children should ever be reproached, with truth, for having committed the cause of the Catholics into any advantage of a personal nature to himself.

Neither did the committee deserve any part of the reproaches cast upon them ; on the contrary, they had done their duty well. The cause of the Catholic soldiery attracted their attention—they exposed to view the gross violations of the law, which were daily committed with respect to Catholic soldiers—the really patriotic prints of the metropolis joined in the cause—and the result has been, that even the Wellesley administration in this country have condescended so far as to recognise the law of the land in their military orders ; and now the Catholic soldiers in Ireland are allowed to serve their king, without being called on for any violation of their consciences. No petty tyrant, dressed in a little brief authority, could now indulge his vile bigotry, by compelling the defenders of their king and country to abandon what they conceived to be their duty to their God.

Was this no service ? Did the committee deserve no thanks for this ?—or rather, was it not an earnest of what the committee had still to do, and would do, in redressing other oppressions, if their cause was not impeded by division and dissension ? At all events, we had a right to call upon those who impeached the committee, to state in what respect *they* had done even so much for the Catholic cause. Let *them* state their services, and he would return them thanks, and not impeachment. But, Sir, the committee have not confined their exertions to this single subject. We have framed, in very firm and constitutional language, the petition which has been already signed by thousands : we have already procured illustrious personages in both houses of parliament, to take charge of it ; and it is now actually ready for transmission to England. There was another subject which engrossed much of our attention : it was the placing before the empire and the world, the present oppressed and degraded state of the Catholics of Ireland, in all its emaciating details. It appeared to him that the principal cause which had hitherto prevented the emancipation of the Catholics, was the strange ignorance of our situation, under which our warmest friends laboured. Even our best and brightest advocate, that ornament to Ireland, Henry Grattan himself, laboured under this mistake : Mr. Ponsonby, too, who has exerted himself so strenuously in the Catholic cause, appears to be equally ignorant. It is to me, therefore, not at all surprising, that the Edinburgh reviewers should have fallen into the same error, so that they stated more than once, in their late most admirable essay on the subject, that the Catholics were excluded from only about forty offices, besides the houses of parliament.

Notwithstanding this, to them almost inevitable error, theirs was a most admirable discussion—it was a specimen of that inestimable logic, that clear arrangement of the subject, and that conclusive display of proofs with which that work abounded ; but what would it have been if they were informed of our real situation ; my praise of those reviewers must be allowed to be unbiassed. I differ from them on the subject of the veto, and would undertake to convince any of them that I am right. I also easily see myself amongst those whom they style "bombastic counsellors ;" and I smile to see how happily they have described that fustian and rant, which I am in the habit, as at present, of obtruding upon your meetings. But, notwithstanding this attack, which I admit to be personal, I do most sincerely and cordially thank them for their exertions. It is not in the nature of popular feeling to continue long its gratitude ; but I have no hesitation in saying, that the Catholics of Ireland deserve to be slaves, if they ever forget what they owe to the writers of that article. Let me, however, repeat my regret, that its effect should have been weakened by the erroneous view which those writers took of our situation. It is strange enough, that when they contributed so considerably to the repeal of the slave trade, they were found to be perfectly conversant with the savage tribes of Raarta and Bambana ; and that they were able to give dissertations on the police of the barbaric cities of Sego and Timbuctoo, and yet are so deplorably ignorant of the condition of the white slaves of Ireland.

We have another excellent advocate in England—an advocate whom we could bribe only one way, with the justice of our cause— I mean William Cobbett. It is truly important to us that his exertions should not be paralyzed by ignorance of our wants. The moment we can show him the extent of our oppressions, we furnish him with materials to ensure our triumph—and it must be admitted that we could not have a more useful advocate. When he is right, he is irresistible—there is a strength and clearness in the way he puts every topic ; he is at once so convincing, and yet so familiar, that the dullest can understand, and even the bigot must be convinced. But what has deservedly raised him high in public estimation, is the manly candour with which he avows and retracts any opinion that he discovers to be erroneous. I can hardly conceive a greater proof of sound understanding and perfect honesty than such conduct ; but what has been his fate ? Why, he has advocated your cause, and is suffering under an atrocious sentence—indeed, in the history of modern times, a sentence so disproportionate with the offence, as to excite horror and disgust in the mind of every man who heard it—a sentence which actually has the effect of converting the object of it, from being the victim of just law, into the martyr of some unpopular, and therefore hated cause. What a besotted, benumbed people these English are ! They heard the sentence pronounced : two long weary years' imprisonment for a libel on the German legion! They saw the victim conveyed to his dungeon; the fountain of mercy was there, yet there was no address, no petition to the throne for its interference—neither has this subject yet been brought before either house of Parliament.

Upon this subject I confess I have been led away by my feelings; but as I have wandered, allow me to indulge in relating to you the fate of another public character. A certain landcalf, of the name of Sparke, pronounced and published, some two years ago, a dissertation in bad Latin, in which he strenuously advised that Catholics should be turned out of every civil situation; and that they should be expelled from the army and navy! Upon what grounds, think you? Why, as the enemies of everything human and divine! Here was a libel—a libel most admirably calculated to serve the interests of Bonaparte, by depriving us, at a single blow, of at least three-fourths of our army and navy. You imagine, of course, that he was punished—that the Attorney-General prosecuted him, and called for a vindictive sentence in the name of the army and navy, and that he conjured up the shades of the Catholics who bled at Aboukir and Trafalgar—who bravely fought and greatly died at Vimiera and Talavera, to scream for vengeance. You suppose that this worthy divine was sentenced to at least one fortnight's imprisonment. Oh, no, you are mistaken—he was only made a bishop, and he will soon have to give his enlightened vote on our petition to the lords. Mr. O'Connell entreated pardon for thus wandering from the subject—his object was to show the labours and services of the committee; and he had pointed out the state of ignorance in which our advocates were, with respect to Catholic privations. It was unnecessary to enlarge on the utility of giving accurate information on the subject. The committee felt that they had this duty to discharge, and they have, with no small labour, completed it. He held in his hand the volume of near two hundred pages, which they had compiled on the subject and if the meeting would suffer him, he would undertake to demonstrate that the committee had exerted itself with much attention and labour. If he was suffered, he would shortly state an abstract, taken from their report, of the offices of trust, honour, and emolument, from which the Catholics are excluded, and which even our friends estimate so low as about forty, but which, in truth, amount, when the influence, as well as the positive enactment of the penal code, is considered, to upwards of thirty thousand. If it did not weary the meeting, he would now g° into detail.—(A general cry of 'go on, go on.') Mr. O'Connell in continuation, said, being encouraged, he would proceed with the abstract. The first thing that offered itself was the parliament. From seats in both houses the Catholics were excluded, amounting to 900 ; next came the offices in corporations. We are, in Dublin, excluded from the

Offices of Lord Mayor and Aldermen,	24
Sheriffs and Sub-Sheriffs,	3
Sheriff's Peers,	38
Common Council,	96
Recorder,	1
Treasurer,	1
Town Clerks,	2
Masters and Wardens of Guilds,	73
Total	238

There are, I think, 86 other corporate cities and towns in Ireland, which, at the low average rate of 32 officers in each, from which Catholics are by law excluded, amount to 2752 ; giving a total, under positive exclusion of 3083. But if a more accurate view of the other offices in the gift of the corporation, or confided to them, be taken, it will be found that Catholics are, by the spirit and operation of the law, if not by the letter of it, excluded from those latter offices—as, for example, in Dublin—

President of the Court of Conscience, his Secretary and Clerk, (worth two thousand pounds per annum,)	2
Lord Mayor's Secretary	1
Police Justices,	12
Their Secretaries and Clerks,	12
City Officers, as Constables, Sword-bearer, &c., (see Red Book),	27
Cranes,	4
Pipe-water Board,	22
Public Money Yards, &c.,	3
Ballast Office,	16
Paving Board and Offices,	13
Grand Jury, with very few exceptions, and other public boards, offices, and clerks,	50
Amounting to	162
Add to those similar offices in the other 86 corporations of Ireland, averaged at only 32 to each, amounting to	2752
Total	2914

Thirdly—There are in the profession and administration of the law-officers, from which we are directly excluded :—

Lord Chancellor,	.
Master of the Rolls,	1
Law Judges,	12
Sergeants,	9
King's Counsel, (now)	28
Masters in Chancery,	4
Attorney and Solicitor-General,	2
Counsel to the Commons,	2
Chairman of Kilmainham,	1
Sheriffs of Counties,	32
Sub-Sheriffs,	32
Advocates in the Spiritual Court,	20
Proctors in Dublin,	9
Proctors in the country,	40
Notary Public,	56
Law Officers in the Spiritual Courts—the jurisdiction of these Courts extend over temporal matters,	109
Total	362

Add to those a number of Officers under the patronage principally of the foregoing; which, although the profession of the law is not unequivocally liberal, yet Catholics are almost uniformly excluded from such as Assistant Barristers of Counties, Assistant Counsel Coroners, Law Clerks in the Law and Equity Offices in Counties, (see Red Book,) amounting, at least, to . . . 700

Total	1058

The next class I shall mention is that of the officers in the army and navy. It is notorious that the Catholics contribute very largely in money and men, to those services. The number of officers may be thus estimated. In the army the regiments are thus :—

Life Guards,	2
Horse Guards,	1
Dragoon Guards,	7
Dragoons,	24
Foot Guards,	3
Foot,	101
Artillery,	3
Irish Militia, from several of the commissions in which Catholics are absolutely excluded,	28
Total	199

Several of the regiments have two, three, or more battalions, so that the entire may be estimated at 200 battalions, and must contain 7500 commissioned officers, from which deduct 100 for

Catholic officers in the Irish militia, it will leave 7400. And it is quite manifest that the proportion of 100 Catholic officers in the Irish militia, is a great exaggeration. Add the paymasters, commissariat department, the staff, storekeepers, contractors, &c. under the same patronage, amounting, at least, to 1600; amount ing, in the entire, to 9000. In the navy, the officers may be thus estimated :—There are in commission, about 900 ships. At a very moderate average there are ten officers to a ship, being 9000; admirals, &c., about 200; add the dockyard establishments, the companies of marines, the pursers, and the other officers dependent on the naval departments, amounting to 3800; amounting, in the entire, to 13,000. There are other offices of trust, honour, and emolument, from which the Catholics are excluded :—

Lord Lieutenant,	1
Lords of the Treasury,	8
Governors of Counties, (now)	38
Privy Councillors, including Duigenan,	90
Fellows of Trinity College,	28
Scholars of ditto,	60
Postmasters-General,	2
Teller of the Exchequer,	1
Chancellor of the Exchequer,	1
Keeper of the Privy Seal,	1
Vice Treasurer,	1
Auditor-General,	1
Custodes Rotulorum,	16
Secretary of State,	1
Secretary to the Lord Lieutenant,	2
Total	**251**

I am sure I can be reproached only with having too far diminished the dependent offices from which the Catholics are excluded under this head, when I state them only at 2060. Catholics are excluded from the following offices :—

	Directly.	Indirectly.
1. Parliament,	900	
2. Corporations,	3152	1829
3. Law,	358	700
4. Army,	7400	1600
5. Navy,	9200	3000
6. Other Offices enumerated,	251	2000

Thus giving a total of offices from which Catholics are excluded, by positive enactment, of   21,261

And of offices from which they are almost, with equal
certainty excluded, by the spirit and operation of the
law, amounting to 9,229

Amounting, in the entire, to . . . 30,490

Let it be recollected, that in giving this statement, we abstain altogether from the situations which belong, of right, to the Established
Church. We should be sorry to see any similar law created for our
clergy, and we most assuredly do not seek to disturb those that exist."

There is another important branch in the political economy
of this country, from which the Catholics are almost altogether
excluded ; it relates to the collection and distribution of the public
money. There are annually about six millions raised on the
Irish people—of these, it is said, that only four millions, or 13s.
4d. in the pound, reach the treasury. There are, besides, four
millions annually borrowed in England, for Ireland, and expended
in this country ; so that there seems, taken together, a sum, making altogether ten millions, is collected and managed, almost
exclusively by Protestants ; there not being, I dare say, at the utmost, twenty Catholics employed in such collection or management.
I am sure I should grossly exaggerate it, were I to say there were
twenty ; amongst other reasons, because I have already shown
that the far greater number of the offices attached to that collection and management, are by the law shut against the Catholics ;
so that we have ten millions yearly, the principal of no less than
six millions of which are raised from the inhabitants of this land,
and the interest of the entire of which is charged upon them and
their descendants in perpetuity. We have these ten millions
oppressive to all, and emolumentary only to a few of the Pro
testants. Let it also be recollected, that the four millions which
are paid into the Irish treasury, have a second operation, for of
course they are paid out again in discharge of the expenditure
of the state ; but the management of such payment is also in the
hands of the members of the Established Church ; so that, in fact,
we are thus excluded from the management, and all the advantages that result from the management of fourteen millions of
money annually, taking into consideration the second operation of
the four millions raised in Ireland. The committee have entered
into various details to illustrate and prove their statements ;
they do not omit to treat often of the insult that the parade of
Orange anniversaries, and the commemoration of ancient feuds,
excite and perpetuate ; but above all, they have investigated the
deplorable situation of the inferior orders of Catholics in the

towns, particularly in the north, on those days devoted to the celebration of Orange festivals ; when the lower order of those systematic oppressors meet together for the purpose, according to the phrase used by some of themselves, at a late trial at Omagh, " *of making Orangemen.*" The committee has remarked, too, on the degrading situation in which the Irish Catholic officers, who go to England with their regiments, are placed. *There, they* must quit the service, or violate their consciences, whilst they see *German* soldiers enjoy complete toleration in the Catho-.ic religion; as if the conscience of a German was declared by law to be worthy of respect, that of the Irish, of none ; why else do the pious Perceval, and holy Wilberforce, consent to allow Popery in the German legion, and persecute it amongst the loyal Irish ? It is our anxious wish that some of the class of hirelings who do the dirty work of the Wellesleys and the Percevals, shall have tne audacity to contradict the facts which our statement contains. We challenge them to that contradiction ; all we entreat is, that they will come to particulars ; but if they do not —if they protect themselves by general denials, we are ready with the proofs of each and every assertion. I entreat the indulgence of the meeting for this lengthened trespass on their patience. I hope I have shown that the committee has not neglected its duty; it has assisted to relieve the soldiery from the oppressions under which they laboured—it has prepared the petition, and made every arrangement for its presentation—and it has ready for publication, a detailed statement of the penalties and persecutions under which the Catholics suffer ; yet, whilst we do thus suffer—whilst the multiplicity and weight of our chains may affright even our enemies, we, wretched slaves that we are, instead of combining heart and hand to procure redress and relief, are about to engage in a miserable warfare among ourselves. The old curse of the Catholics is, I fear, about to be renewed ; division, that made us what we are, and keeps us so, is again to rear its standard amongst us ; but it was thus always with the Irish Catholics. I recollect, that in reading the life of the great Duke of Ormond, as he is called, I was forcibly struck with a despatch of his, transmitted about the year 1661, when he was Lord Lieutenant of Ireland. It was written to vindicate himself from a charge of having favoured the Papists, and having given them permission to hold a public meeting in Dublin. His answer is remarkable. He rejects with disdain the foul calumny of being a favourer of Papists ; though he admits he gave them leave to meet : " because, said he, " I know by experience that

the Irish Papists never meet, without dividing and degrading
themselves." I quote the words of the official despatch; I can
lay my finger on the very spot, in " Carte's Life of Ormond."

One hundred and fifty years have since elapsed, and we are
still in thraldom, because no experience can, I fear, cure us of
this wretched disposition to divide. He entreated of the respectable gentlemen who that day attended the committee, to consider that their mistakes, if they had made any, ought not to be
visited with so grievous a calamity, as that of creating dissension
amongst them. But in point of fact, of what was the committee
accused? Why, that they, having been expressly entrusted with
the management of Catholic affairs, had thought it prudent and
wise to consult, not the citizens of Dublin alone, but the Catholic inhabitants of every county in Ireland. Had not the counties of Tipperary, and Kerry, and Clare, and Carlow, and Kilkenny, as good a right to be consulted with, and heard, as the
city of Dublin; and he appealed to the good sense of every man
present, whether it must not have the worst effect on the Catholic mind, if any gentlemen shall continue to insist, as they did
that day, that an aggregate meeting in Dublin was all-powerful,
that it was " *the people*," and that the Catholics of the different
counties had no right to contribute to the foundation of the general committee. The objection in point of form to encreasing the
committee, would have weight but for the state of the law. The
managers of the petitions appointed by the counties were not
delegates, and could not act in a representative capacity; but
this was only because the law prevented the Catholics from
choosing delegates, and holding a representative assembly. It
should, however, be recollected, that a precisely similar objection
lay against the committee appointed by the aggregate meeting
for neither were they delegates or representatives. If they insisted on the country, they would only expose themselves to the
hazard of an indictment, with the certainty of being convicted.
This was the distinct answer to the maxim, the trite and quaint
maxim which no person disputed, that a deputy could not constitute a deputy. The fact was, that there were not, and could
not be any deputies in the committee. In the present state of
the law, we could only regret that delegation was forbidden—but
we should not be driven, even by this impeachment, to violate
the law, and expose the Catholic committee to a prosecution. It
assuredly could not be the intention of the gentlemen to drive the
committee into that predicament. It was impossible not to be
sensible that he had already consumed too much of the time of

the meeting; he should therefore rapidly conclude by moving
the order of the day, namely—"That the Catholic petition be
forthwith presented to parliament." He was anxious to place
that out of the way of dissension. Indeed the cry of no petition,
like a somewhat similar cry in another quarter, had, it was supposed by the country, been the watchword of party in Dublin.
it was strongly suspected by many well-meaning persons, that
such cry was used for the sole purpose of serving as a rallying
word; and this suspicion unfortunately justified in some measure by the change that had taken place in the arguments used to
oppose the petition. Formerly, gentlemen talked for hours in
praise of " dignified silence," and of " frowning upon their enemies," and of "muttering curses deep not loud." Now, indeed,
their faces were decked in smiles; they were smoothing their
whiskers, and putting them on the peace establishment; they
talked of delicacy, and with courtly air, entreated that we would
not embarrass our friends of the new administration. Sir, I
know but of one embarrassment in this nation—and that arises
from the state of weakness and distraction the empire suffers
from the political injustice inflicted on the Catholics. I know
but of one embarrassment to the Catholics, and that arises from
the state of inferiority and degradation in which the criminal
neglect of our just right leaves us. I know too, but of one
course to procure emancipation. It is the open, manly, and
constitutional right of petition. If you petition session after
session, you take away all pretext for intrigue and cabal amongst
yourselves; all rational hope of managing a party amongst us
from your enemies, and also from your falsehearted friends; and
for my part, my humble opinion is decided, that you should continue to repeat your demands for liberty, until every grievance
shall be extinguished, and every trace of religious oppression annihilated. It was, however, right to observe that if the country
differed with him on this subject, they ought in justice to be
heard. It was imperative on the committee to lay the petition
before parliament; but no discussion could take place upon it
till after the Easter recess; in fact, until the middle of next
May. In the interim, the managers for each county would be
able to ascertain the sentiments of their respective neighbour-
hoods; and should it appear to be the will of the majority of
the Catholics, that the discussion of our petition should be deferred for another year, why the example set by the English Catholics last session may be adopted, and the petition allowed to
lie on the table for the present. He must say that he would

regret any such determination, as our claims, if understood.
which they could be but by discussion in parliament, are really
invincible. But he never would set up his own opinion against
that of the majority, or even against that of any considerable
portion of the Catholic body.

He then concluded by reminding gentlemen, that every authority, human and divine, spoke trumpet-tongued of the evils of
dissension ; and he conjured the meeting, as they wished to be
true to their country, and to their God, not to divide, and distract fellow-labourers and fellow-slaves.

Mr. O'Connell finally prevailed, though not without a division, on which, however, there
was a considerable majority against Mr. Clinch's amendment.

According to a resolution of a previous meeting (on the 29th December, in the preceding
year, 1810), the petition was to be entrusted to Mr. Grattan, for presentation in the Com
mon

THE FRENCH PARTY.

A short speech of Mr. O'Connell's at the meeting just referred to—viz., that of December,
1810, may (without any more extended notice of the meeting itself) be here inserted, as
one of the many links of the chain of evidence we trust this collection of his public acts
will be found to afford, in proof of how undeviatingly he always, while working for Ireland,
looked to and endeavoured to serve the best interest of the empire at large.

Mr. O'Connell said, that what had fallen from the learned gentleman (Nicholas Purcell O'Gorman, Esq.,) who had preceded
him, required some observation. He (Mr. O'Gorman) had supposed that the French party, mentioned by Mr. Grattan, was, by
our enemies, alleged to exist among the Catholics of Ireland.
This was an assertion which he, Mr. O'Connell, said he must
controvert. There did not exist, even among the mean and
miserable herd of the adversaries of the Catholics, any man so
shameless as to assert that a French party could be found
amongst us. In truth nothing could be more obvious than that
the only genuine and effective *anti*-Gallican party in Ireland
was that of the Catholics—for their object is to consolidate the
strength, and increase the resources of the empire ; not merely
to contribute as they do, to every defeat which the enemy meets,
but to render it quite impossible that he should ever succeed,
by combining the entire nation in the defence of their king and
constitution. Our first desire, and the motives which govern
us, are to take away from France even the hope of success by

removing those excuses of *distrust, and dissension, and weakness in this country, which, at present, are really so many temptations* to the *enemy to invade us.* We would fain excite a NATIONAL and IRISH PARTY, *capable of annihilating any foreign oppressor whatsoever,* and devoted to the amelioration of this our native land. There is, indeed, a French party that *does* exist in Ireland —a party most useful to the views and designs of France. It is the *party of the present ministry—that party which exerts its vicious energies to divide, distract, and oppress the realm*—that loads the nation with the weight of ill-judged taxation, and employs the money, wrung from poverty and distress, in fomenting internal dissensions—in calumniating the Irish people to each other—accusing the Catholics of disloyalty, because they seek the rights of the constitution—charging the Protestants with bigotry, and yet encouraging them to become intolerant. It is, in fine, this party which desolates the country, and then talks to us of our growing prosperity.

Mr. O'Connell then proceeded to speak of Mr Grattan, and paid him the following warm and generous tribute :—

He could not sit down without entreating of his learned friend, Mr. O'Gorman, to withdraw his opposition to the present motion. Let not our enemies be able to boast that there was a single dissenting voice among the Catholics, upon the subject of Ireland's best and last resource, Henry Grattan. Surely that learned gentleman cannot be insensible to what that illustrious and genuine patriot has done and suffered in the cause of his country. If other evidence were wanting of his love for his devoted country, alas, poor Ireland ! the active hatred of his enemies, which he has so long sustained, would alone demonstrate it.

That greatest foe Ireland ever experienced—her first and deepest curse—the late Earl of Clare, honoured Grattan with his deadly hate. Can we forget it, how, under Lord Clare's auspices, a committee of the House of Lords turned itself, as it were, into a committee of assassination of Grattan's character, and, with monstrous effrontery, gave to the public, in their report, what they did not themselves believe, the assertion of a wretched informer, charging him with treason.

They did not themselves believe it, for if they had, not only their duty, but their strong and infuriate inclination required that they should prosecute him even to death.

At that melancholy period (and may heaven avert from Ireland the recurrence of such another) little evidence was necessary, when mere accusation could almost supply the place of guilt. Let this instance of the vain and impotent malice of the enemies of Ireland show the extent of his offence in serving his country.

There was one other consideration which rendered it imperative on the learned gentleman to abandon his opposition. Let him recollect that it was Henry Grattan "that watched over the cradle of Irish independance, and that he walked after its hearse!" Our country is entranced in the death-sleep of the Union; and I pity that Irishman who does not feel pleasure in repeating with me that Henry Grattan is alone worthy to "sound the glad trumpet of her resurrection!"

Surely it will not be said that Catholic ingratitude diminished his ardours. He, Mr. O'Connell, felt that the sin of ingratitude was heavy upon the Catholics, while they seemed to hesitate, but for a moment, on this subject. He would not, therefore, detain the meeting from passing, what he trusted would be, an unanimous vote.

UNANIMITY.

On the 9th of February occurred another of the occasions, now fast multiplying, to test Mr. O'Connell's abilities for leadership, in the important points of conciliating opposing sentiments, obviating the difficulties suggested by the timid, the silly, or the dishonest, and clearing away the obstructions wantonly thrown up to arrest or divert the popular movement.

In the current of this debate, as in that of the preceding debate of this month, there was strong evidence of a design, on the part of a few individuals in Dublin, to get into their own hands the exclusive management of Catholic affairs. Mr. O'Connell, while he entirely defeated this effort, and kept the Catholic Committee on its liberal and more popular basis, yet so managed matters as to have been appealed to by one of the chief parties in the debate to compose the differences that were agitating the meeting.

His speech for this purpose was as follows:—

Mr. M'Donnell's motion is for an adjournment for a fortnight, and the proposal has been offered on such reasonable grounds, that I give it my most cordial support. Let it not be supposed that I am actuated by any personal felling, or that I secretly indulge a hope of becoming one of the persons who shall be entrusted with your petition. High as I esteem the honour, I am not endeavouring, by any means, direct or indirect, to obtain it. I think not so highly of myself, and I must declare that it would be to me a most pleasing circumstance if there could not be found a more suitable individual than myself. I conjure my countrymen not to suppose that I would make the cause of my native land subservient to any idle or criminal ambition. I reject, with scorn, the foul imputation. I seek only for unanimity among Catholics, and I leave to others the glory of dividing the body. I do not wish to speak harshly; I have often been mistaken, but I cannot avoid saying that, unfortunately, I have witnessed in the discussion of this day, more violence than should have entered into the consideration of slaves. I do not suppose that the gentlemen act from base or unworthy motives; but I say that error has entered their hearts, and I lament its baneful effects in the division which it must inevitably cause among the Catholic body. When are our petty and miserable squabbles to have an end? Are we not allowed to go into open air? But must we decide on the impulse of the moment, with all the evil effects of division and distraction ; whereas by an adjournment of a fortnight, we would become unanimous. I do not give up my opinion of the necessity of delegation; but I would rather forego the advantages resulting from delegation, than weaken the effect of your petition by dividing the committee on the question The petition must go before both houses of parliament, and its merits must be discussed, but I will not, by pressing a division, afford an argument to your enemies to identify the sentiments of a few men in this committee, with the voice of five millions of persons.

It has been proved to you this day, that the sentiments of several populous and respectable districts are indubitably in favour of having their petition committed to the care of delegates ; but I will concede the point, for I would think myself criminal if I should divide the committee. My Lord Ffrench, I entreat you to consider, if it is not an evil of the utmost magnitude to divide us, as it will show to our enemies, who are secretly exulting at the prospect of division— that we are to the last a divided, and, therefore, a contemptible people—objects for the derision of our malignant enemies.

See the predicament we are reduced to. We are charged with having a faction amongst ourselves, and we ask for deliberation for a fortnight, which would render us unanimous. It has been said that I am anxious to become one of your delegates; I solemnly assure you that I am not. Some of my friends have often expressed their wish that I might become the object of your choice, but I did say that I could not have that honour. So impressed am I with the necessity of being unanimous, that I promise the gentlemen, if they consent to adjourn, that I shall, at the next meeting, vote against delegation. (Cries of 'hear, hear;' Mr. Keogh seemed to desire that ne and his friends consented.) I thank the gentleman for his concession : I hail it as a happy omen ; it is the voice, it is the heart, it is the support of his venerated father. (Hear, hear, hear.) We now are actuated by a proper feeling ; for it is by perfect unanimity alone that we can triumph. You no longer afford your enemies the malignant gratification of seeing dissension among you. It is thus you conquer the bigotry of your opponents; not by "*frowning* and *dignified* silence," but by heart-felt unanimity. (Hear, hear.) It is thus you put them down ; and let us no longer be a miserable or divided people, but a great and unanimous people, whose voice is justice, and must be law. (Loud applause.)

ADDRESS TO THE PRINCE OF WALES.

UPON the 8th of March the Catholics met in aggregate meeting, at the old Music Hall or Theatre—still standing—in Fishamble-street, for the purpose of addressing the Prince of Wales, upon his being called on to assume the office of Regent, in consequence of the second and final mental alienation of the still reigning king, George III.

The occasion was only intended to be made use of for the purpose of expressing the strong dissent of the Catholics of Ireland from the attempted designs of the Perceval administration to limit, most unconstitutionally, the powers and prerogatives of the new Regent.

Mr. O'Connell made two speeches on this occasion. The first was simply explanatory of the objects of the meeting, and introductory of an address drawn up in conformity with those objects. Its adoption was seconded by Mr. Shell, in a speech of great talent, and carried unanimously'; as was also a motion that the address should be presented to his royal highness by the following noblemen and gentlemen :—Earls Shrewsbury, Fingal, and Kenmare ; Viscounts Gormanstown, Netterville, and Southwell ; Lords Trimleston and Ffrench ; Sirs Thomas Esmonde, Edward Bellew, Hugh O'Rielly, Thomas Burke, and Francis Goold, Barts. ; Major-General O'Farrell ; Colonel Burke ; Messrs. C Bryan, R. M'Donnell, D. O'Connell, J. Keogh, Owen O'Connor, M. Donnelan, Edward Corbally, T. Wynne, J. Burke, Wm. Coppinger, Ambrose J. Roche, Edward Murphy, D. W. O'Reilly, George Browne, E. Taaffe, D. Caulfield, Esqrs.

The following is the newspaper report of his first speech :—

Sir Edward Bellew—At the suggestion of several members of the Catholic committee, whose wishes are considered by me as an imperative law, I rise to address you at this early period of the meeting on a subject on which universal unanimity prevails. Indeed, it were impossible, in Ireland, to procure among the Catholics, on the subject I shall submit to you, a single dissentient voice ; need I say that I allude to a dutiful and loyal address to his Royal Highness the Prince of Wales. I shall not

consume the time of this meeting, by entering into an explanation of our motives for presenting the address; and I feel it
would be a reproach to induce any argument to justify a measure
so anxiously wished for by the Catholics of Ireland. We owe it
to his royal highness to express, with heartfelt gratitude, our
unfeigned thanks for the many favours and benefits conferred on
us by his revered father, to whom we are perhaps indebted for
the privilege of meeting here this day. [Here Mr. O'Connell took
a summary view of the political state and incapacities of the Catholics at the accession of his Majesty to the throne]—when, he
said, they were excluded from every situation of trust, honour,
and emolument; when the then existing law sanctioned the breach
of every honourable principle; when there was hardly a grievance
or degradation that man could be subject to, that the laws did
not inflict on the Catholics of Ireland.

Thus stood the abominable code at the period of his Majesty's
accession, and such hardships and slavery did it impose, that the
mind cannot contemplate on it without recoiling with horror and
disgust. By adverting to this period of our history, he did not
wish to excite religious distinctions; he did not wish to re-
kindle hatred and animosity among his countrymen; his motives
were widely different: they were to lay before the meeting the
obligations we owe to his Majesty, for the many privileges which
the Catholics at present enjoy. Though we continue a degraded
race in our native land; though we still suffer, as we do, the exclusion from every situation of honour and of emolument, yet to
the kind interposition of his Royal Highness the Prince of Wales
he looked forward for the full and speedy extinction of our
slavery. The past conduct of his royal highness assures us that
those disabilities which distinguish the Catholic from the Protestant, can no long continue. Through life, on every constitutional question, he has given the nation a convincing proof of
the liberality of his enlightened mind. He has selected the
friends and companions of his private life from among the most
able statesmen that England ever produced. Who can forget
that Charles James Fox was the bosom friend of the Prince of
Wales? (Hear, hear.) Who can forget that the Prince of Wales
expressed his anxious desire that the constitutional principles of
that immortal patriot should be impressed on the mind of his
infant daughter? Among the confidential friends of the Prince,
let it be remembered that the Hutchinson family hold a distinguished place. And here permit me to remind you, that if there
be any class of people that owe that great and good family a

special debt, it is the Catholics of Ireland. He had almost omitted to mention the name of his illustrious countryman, Mr. Sheridan, who has long participated in the friendship of his royal highness; but he was ashamed for trespassing so long on an occasion like the present, when he found himself incapable of describing the grateful feelings of the Catholic people to his royal highness, to whom they were attached by every principle of loyalty and of gratitude.

He lamented that through the misguided folly of our rulers, the country had already suffered too much. It had been involved in deep calamity ever since the baneful measure of Union had been forced upon distracted Ireland. (Hear, hear.) At that calamitous period the argument made use of by the parliament of England, for withholding from the Prince his undoubted right, was, that by appointing him Regent, they preferred him to William Pitt. The offence given to the ministry of the present times seems to be, that the people prefer his royal highness to the usurper, Perceval. It is observable that the moment the Regent was appointed, W. W. Pole set off for Ireland, to misrepresent the Catholics and excite discord. He (Mr. Pole) seemed to fear that in the liberal mind of the Prince something would be found that would drive faction out of its fastness. He took the most decisive measure that his *little mind* could suggest. Although a general committee of the Catholics of Ireland had been established for almost eighty years, he had the audacity to issue his proclamation, declaring that it was an illegal assembly, and that the meeting was guilty of a high misdemeanour. He thus thought proper to pronounce sentence without going to trial; without the interposition of any judge. He said he acted under the advice of a judge, *who is not a native of this country*, and who is, therefore, ignorant of the Irish character. He admitted that the judge was an accomplished gentleman and an able lawyer, but Irishmen would not submit to be ruled by special pleadings and English technicality.

But to return to the subject of the letter. It appears that it was the first act of his royal highness's government in Ireland. It was the ill-advised measure of William Wellesley Pole, the secretary of all ages. We know it could not have emanated from his royal highness. As for Wellesley Pole, he was first secretary to the king, then to the usurping protector, and then to the regent; but his first act was for the purpose of putting up the Orange, and dividing Irishmen; but this was not the act of the Prince: his confidential friends' conduct, in both houses of par-

liament, is a sure pledge that what appeared as the first act of
his regency, was unknown to him. The Earl of Moira had disavowed the act, and he was not only a friend to his country, but
he was the friend of his Prince; he could not speak in terms
strong enough of the noble exertions of that great man in behalf
of his country; he was the true patriot, not like the men who
might vote for the Catholic petition. He would disavow them as
they voted at the side of Perceval against their prince—one member for the county he belonged to had done so, and he hoped yet
to meet him on the hustings, to express the contempt he felt for
such conduct.

How different was the conduct of the other member of that
county; he would not mention him by name, but his grateful
country felt his worth—the Knight of Kerry. [Mr. O'Connell
then adverted to the address he was about to propose] It had,
he said, the concurrence of the existing committee—it had the
approbation of that venerated man, Mr. John Keogh—in short, it
had been approved of by all the friends to the Catholic cause, to
whom it had been submitted. Mr. O'Connell then proceeded to
read the address, which was very concise, and to the following
effect: "We take leave to approach your Royal Highness, to express our heartfelt sorrow for the grievous malady with which
our revered Sovereign is afflicted. We remember, with gratitude,
the many acts of favour and protection which his Roman Catholic subjects have received during his reign." It then proceeded
to express their confidence in his royal highness, and how providential it was, that, at such a crisis, the nation had such a prince
to uphold the principles of the constitution, and to protect it from
its foreign enemies; and it assures his royal highness that every
hand and heart in Catholic Ireland are devoted to his support
It then proceeds to lament the hateful restrictions with which his
royal highness is encumbered, and that the Catholics of Ireland,
feeling the delicate situation in which his royal highness was
placed, would forbear to enter into a statement of their situation;
and it expresses an assurance that they know his royal highness
to be their friend'; and that, in a recent instance, they had experienced the favour and protection of his royal highness.

THE DUKE OF RICHMOND.

Mr. O'Connell's second speech on this occasion, was to compose a difference that had sprung up, relative to an amendment condemnatory of the Lord Lieutenant, the Duke of Richmond. This was proposed by Major Bryan, but opposed by many influential persons present, on the ground chiefly of expediency, though some went so far as to praise the conduct of as bad a viceroy as Ireland had a long time known. At length, however, the motion was carried in a modified shape, praying inquiry into what might be the circumstances justificatory of a circular letter written by Wellesley Pole, the secretary and that if none such could be found, that his royal highness should dismiss the latter, and his principal, the Duke of Richmond.

Sir Edward Bellew, I decare, most unaffectedly, that my feelings are much interested in the fate of this question. On the one hand, if the motion shall pass, it is to be feared that some of our best friends may take offence at it; on the other, shall it not be acceded to, it may encourage a supposition that we are prepared to submit to every species of insult without expressing our just indignation. A noble lord and two other gentlemen have spoken against it, whose hostility to any measure, in a Catholic meeting, must be considered as almost fatal to that measure; but in this case it will be forgotten, at a future day, what course of argument they pursued, when their opposition to the measure will be remembered. No gentleman has, however, thought of praising Mr. Pole, although some eulogized the lord lieutenant; none has been so bold as to attempt that which would rack and exhaust invention to make it palatable. No, Sir; it has been found necessary to squander the public money in purchasing the labours of hireling prints, and their depraved parasites, to bestow diplomatic wisdom on Mr. Pole, and military skill on the redoubtable Lord Wellington.

What man in this assembly shall be found voting against any censure of Catholics upon those men who came here under the conviction that they thus stand pledged against your claims, and must be prepared to concur in every measure of a no-popery administration? Any men who could accept offices under a Perceval ministry cannot be friendly to your emancipation. The Duke of Richmond came here as a military lord lieutenant, and I suppose Mr. Pole as a military secretary, expecting, in all probability, that a display of their talents might, at some time, be essential, and particularly amongst the Catholics, as if we could be hostile to an army composed entirely of such. The career of his excellency's life has been a harmless one; he is fond of amusement and the convivial circle; but I am not sure that the qualities are such as the government of Ireland needs at this moment; and I defy his panegyrists to produce any others. It has been said that the Orangemen are put down; but what proof have we for it? I have been informed that a new Orange constitution has been framed within the last eighteen months; if this be true, to what a state will not this country be again reduced. Nothing can be more deplorable than any association which has a tendency to divide Irishmen. Yes, there is, to us, one thing more deplorable; and that is any measure which may create division amongst Catholics.

Having said so much respecting the Duke of Richmond, it is but fair to observe, that there is no proof against him in Mr. Pole's letter; nothing can be deemed official from him but his proclamation. I do not mean to dispute about words, but let me concede what is right, and say that some more evidence of the duke's concurrence with Mr. Pole, is wanting to justify us in adopting this motion. Is it becoming the dignity of the Catholic body to censure without examination—to condemn without scrutiny? Is it worth our while to divide this meeting about a cabinet clerk? It is quite manifest, that if the honourable mover presses his resolution, a division will be the consequence. I think some middle course may be adopted, which may save us the necessity of dividing the Catholics. I am sure the gentleman who brought forward this motion, would not wish to insult the Prince, or the meanest individual in society; that gentleman I am proud to claim as my friend; his dignified and spirited conduct, in upholding your character, entitles him, very fully, to the confidence of the Catholics of Ireland. Whatever decision this assembly may come to, I shall, of course, assist to the best of my abilities, in furthering our common cause; but in the hearing of my countrymen I declare, that the passing of this resolution will provoke the enmity of a powerful party in our own body, with whom the Duke of Richmond is personally acquainted. The great objection to this petition is, that it demands what is impracticable; you address the Prince Regent to remove the Irish executive, and sure you do not mean to say that it is in his power to do so. See what comes of it—if you agree to this motion, you certainly insult the Regent, because you ask him to grant a favour which it is not in his power to bestow, and on his refusal you ay be tempted to say, that he will not do all he can to conciliate Ireland. I know the artillery had been prepared to intimidate a constitutional and unresisting assembly of gentlemen. I know the military were at new quarters to co-operate in the mighty plan. I know that the city of Dublin might be compared, on that day, to a place beseiged, but all these occurrences are not sufficient to justify a measure not well digested, and which will infallibly divide the Catholics once more.

Let me suggest, by way of accommodating the difference, an amendment; I am not prepared with one, but the substance of it would be, to refer this question to the next meeting of the Catholic committee, for them to consider the propriety of petitioning parliament on the subject; and if the committee shall take it up, and address for the removal of the lord lieutenant and Mr. Pole, there is no doubt but it will take place. I would leave the discussion of this question altogether to the committee; this course of mine may be not the best, but it is well meant; would it not be a cruelty to the Catholics to cause a division amongst them for the sake of Mr. Pole? I may be told, the gentlemen of the committee would be against the introduction of this question; if so, let them decide according to their judgment in the committee, but let us not persist in this miserable practice of counting noses at an aggregate meeting. Gentlemen may say the committee may be wrong, and an aggregate meeting right, and, therefore, persevere in causing a division; I think, although there may be a majority for the motion, the minority will be triumphant. We stand upon high ground at present, let us not descend from it by mean or vindictive measures.

I shall not detain you longer, than to entreat gentlemen to consider the fatal consequences of dividing the Catholics. By persevering and carrying this motion, you most certainly will insult the Prince, although unintentionally. See what a victory will be to your enemies to put one Catholic name against another when you divide. My God! are gentlemen so wedded to their own opinions as not to yield a little for the sake of unanimity? For my part I am always ready to concede any opinion or measure of my own, when a better may be offered; and I shall always do so when a doubt occurs to me that my own opinion may be correct. I earnestly conjure you not to leave it in the power of your calumniators to say, that you have proceeded beyond the bounds of discretion. I will now move, as an amendment to Major Bryan's motion, that the consideration of this question be referred to the members of the general committee at their next meeting.

PETITION TO THE PRINCE REGENT.

On the 20th of April, 1811, there was another discussion in the Catholic Committee, Lord Fingal in the chair, on the instructions to be given to the delegates who were to go to England with the Catholic address and petition to the Prince Regent. Mr. O'Connell announced the impossibility of his forming one of the number, owing to professional engagements; and supported a motion of Sir Edward Bellew for disclaiming, on the part of the Catholic Committee, "any right to control the delegates."

The base manner in which the hopes of the Catholics were excited, and the delusive nature of the assurances with which they were fed, of the good will of the Prince Regent towards them, will appear from a few sentences which we will quote from his speeches on this occasion.

He earnestly deprecated all division at a time when the Catholics of Ireland were so near emancipation—a moment when the accomplishment of their ardent wishes, the fulfilment of their longing expectations, and the reward of their unwearied labours were in view—when their emancipation was considered at hand . . . . Let them not fear that in going forward to present the petition with the address they would offend the Prince. Could he suppose such an event; he (Mr. O'Connell) solemnly declared, from the feelings of genuine loyalty in his heart to the Prince, he would give up any question sooner than incommode his royal highness. But it was not the case. The Prince has shown how he regards the true principles of the constitution . . . . . such a petition would give satisfaction, not displeasure to him, and so he would venture to prophesy; the delegates would find it.

"WATTY COX."

[LIBEL.]

The bigoted and pettifogging hostility of the ministry to the Catholic claims continued to betray them, during the course of this year, into several of those "mistakes" which, in matters of state policy, are held by those who assume to be authorities as to statesmanship, to be "worse than crimes;" both designations, however, apply to the acts of the English government in 1811, as unfortunately for poor Ireland, they apply to the acts of her English governors throughout the weary period of her subjugation.

Amongst the most ludicrous of those "mistakes" was the prosecution for libel of the individual who is known to fame in Ireland, as "Watty Cox," proprietor of a periodical of a strange rollicking character, which he entitled The Irish or Watty Cox's Magazine. One of Mr. O'Connell's speeches in mitigation of punishment, will give the reader some idea of the man and his publication. Cox was found guilty on two indictments, and sentenced to the pillory, and to imprisonment.

My lords, I am compelled to entreat your attention to a few observations, by the particular request of my unfortunate client. Had I merely consulted my own feelings and judgment, I certainly should consider anything from *any man* unnecessary, after what has been so powerfully submitted to your minds, by the talents of my eloquent and able colleague. I not only consider it unnecessary, but justly apprehend that it may prove injurious, by diminishing the impressions which his address must have created on this court.

My lords, attempts have been made to blacken my client's character, by describing him as a systematic and common libeller; I trust that insinuations of this description can have no weight on this court, or diminish the claim of my client on its mercy. If he has been a libeller on any other occasions, he is liable to be tried for such productions, and to be punished if convicted. It is, in truth, a libel on the law officers of the crown, to insinuate that they would suffer to escape from their notice such libels as could affect the safety of the state; it is, of course, the present duty of the court to dismiss from their minds every other blameable publication, and confine their attention to the publication immediately before them. This publication is written in a manner which must greatly circumscribe the range of its mischief—absurd and unintelligible, extremely vulgar, but extremely obscure—levelled to the language of the common people in its expression, but entirely hid from their undestandings by its incongruity. Thus it is unintelligible to those on whom the mischief could operate; and carries its own antidote to those who have the ingenuity to extricate any meaning from the wretched mass of absurdity.

That the production must be quite unintelligible to the common people, clearly appears from this circumstance :—The writer, when speaking of the abominable tyrant of France—I use the words of my client, in which, in his affidavit, he describes the present ruler of that country, I would be understood as incapable of applying such phrases myself to any man—the writer, I say, in speaking of that character, clothes him in trophies, emblems, and various adjuncts, not only very ridiculous but inapplicable, and in no place suitable or characteristic, quite unfit to unravel his enigma or develope his allegory, but well adapted to make it inexplicable and impenetrable. For instance, he invests the ruler of France with those naval characteristics only adaptable to a resistless naval power that rides on the wave the lord of the ocean; *how, when, where,* did he acquire trophies and honours of that kind? Was it at Camperdown, St. Vincent's, Aboukir, or Trafalgar? Few could understand the character under so awkward, so strange a description—few could know the man, when decked in attire so suitable to conceal or to mislead.

My lords, as to punishment by considerable fine, strictly speaking, punishment of any kind cannot affect him in a pecuniary way. His poverty protects him in a pecuniary way; but though a considerable fine cannot affect him in a pecuniary manner, it may affect him in a manner particularly severe, because it may, indeed, in effect it must, amount to the punishment of perpetual imprisonment. Perpetual imprisonment is unknown to our law; nay, it abhors imprisonment that is measured by *years;* and although such punishment has been sanctioned by the judicial severities of modern times, it was entirely unknown to the merciful wisdom of the law of our fathers—the common law of the land. The common law abhors a lengthened imprisonment, that melancholy, miserable, emaciating punishment, which shuts a man out from the fruits of industry, the comforts of society, the joys of his fireside.

The common law is slow in inflicting such a punishment; and that high crime of unjustifiable homicide—the highest of all crimes not punished with death—the wantonly sporting with and destroying the life of another, the common law considers as sufficiently punished by imprisonment for a single year. Punishment by fine in this case cannot operate against *income,* but may against *industry;* it cannot reduce competence to poverty, but may reduce poverty to want; his family are fed by his labour; exclude him by imprisonment from the opportunities of labour, and you will punish the children for the crime of their father, and decree that the innocent should suffer with the guilty. I shall not resume the same line of argument by which my learned colleague has established, that this is the same crime for which he has already suffered, and that by punishing him in this instance you punish him twice for the same offence. The two accusations form one crime or they do not; if they form one, he should not be punished, because he has been punished already: if they form two, the first should not be adduced to aggravate the second, because he has already suffered for the first. I shall not any longer detain your lordships' attention; I commit my client to the clemency of the court, in the confident hope that you will feel it to be your constitutional duty not merely to punish the incidental licentiousness, but also to preserve a free press: that invaluable blessing to which we owe the rights we enjoy—you

the dignified stations you fill; and our king the throne on which
he is placed !

VOTE OF THANKS TO EARL GREY AND LORD GRENVILLE.

On the 29th of February, in this year, another aggregate meeting of the Catholics took
place in the same locality as usual, the theatre in Fishamble-street, to "petition the
legislature, and to address his Royal Highness the Prince Regent."

The following resolution, amongst others, was passed at this meeting :—

Proposed by Mr. Burke, of Gilnsk, and seconded by Major Bryan, and resolved unanimously—"That the General Committee of the Catholics of Ireland, appointed by the
aggregate meeting, upon the ninth day of July last, are entitled to our thanks; and it is
requested that they will not meet, until the legality of their doing so is decided.'

A resolution, moved and seconded by the same parties, expressing the thanks of the
meeting to "our friends in parliament, Earl Grey and Lord Grenville," was spoken to
by Mr. O'Connell.

Mr. O'Connell came forward and said he did not mean to oppose the motion, nor was it necessary to use any argument in its
support. Since the commencement of the British constitution to
the present hour, no statesmen had ever stood higher than those
noble lords in public estimation. They had, with the purest
patriotism, refused everything that power could give; they had
rejected all the allurements of office, rather than sacrifice, or even
postpone the assertion of principle—a splendid instance of public
virtue, more brilliant for its rarity and for the contrast it afforded
to the subserviency of their adversaries.

It was unnecessary to urge the motion. Every Irish heart beat
responsive to the liveliest accents of gratitude. But he would
avail himself of that opportunity to make some observations on
the recent events—on those interesting events which had occured
since the last meeting of the Catholics. His observations should
certainly be made with the utmost good temper, because, in truth,
there was nothing in these occurrences to irritate, or much that
afforded unmixed consolation.

The first topic that presented itself was the late trial of Mr.
Kirwan. That trial had proved only what was already well known,
namely, that it was possible for the Irish administration, with all
its resources, to find a single jury to take upon itself to swear that
pretence means purpose. and that the man who was admitted, by
his prosecutors and judges, to be innocent in act and intention, was
in law and fact, guilty.

the numbers were altered ?—was it corruption ?—was it a miracle ?

I do still fondly hope, for the sake of law and of justice—for the sake of everything valuable to Irishmen, that this matter is not at rest ; but that the baronet or knight, or whichever he be, will yet have this matter seriously and solemnly discussed and examined by parliament ; that the entire transaction shall yet appear ; and that my lords the Justices of the King's Bench, may possibly, hereafter, think it their duty not to suffer so strange a fact to pass in review before them, unexplained and unexplored.

Allow me to say one word more, and I conclude, as to the late trial. The prosecutors insulted us, by excluding every Catholic from the jury ; they injured us, too, by excluding every Presbyterian. How I thank them for the compliment they paid, on this second trial, to the sterling integrity of the Irish Presbyterians, the very best class of men in any community. To all that is generous and warm in the Irish character, they add a firmness and a discretion, which improves every manly virtue. I do greatly admire the friends of religious and civil liberty—the Presbyterians of Ireland.

There is now another, and a different topic, to which I would lead you ; it relates to an afflicting circumstance which occurred since our last meeting. You will recollect that I then warned you against the machinations of your enemies ; I said that it was conjectured that there were schemes on foot to involve the lower classes of the people in some idle dream of disaffection ; I cautioned my countrymen against those schemes ; and I added, " that any person who suffered himself to be implicated in them, must be either a miserable dupe, or the hired spy of the Castle."

Little did I then imagine, that my prophetic fears would be so soon realised ; little did I then imagine, that I should be so soon placed in that most distressing situation in which I have since stood ; that I should be reduced to the necessity of feeling the abject humiliation of disclosing facts which might be fatal to some of my deluded countrymen, or be obliged to expose them all to the danger of becoming the victims of secret conspiracy, and to do what you all know to be impossible—to violate the solemn oath of allegiance, which I have repeatedly taken.

Let any man of feeling judge of my situation. I did feel as if I were degraded ; but I felt that I could not be untrue to honour, when I was in the company of your lordship, and my most estimable friend, Captain Bryan.

The affair was fortunately passed over; those who were arrested have been discharged:

"My bosom's lord sits lightly on its throne,"

when I recollect that those men have been restored to their families; but I must again indulge in anticipating hope—I must still hope to see, in this country, an administration that will offer pardon and reward to the proclaimed conspirator, Fisher, for the disclosures of who were his instigators, and with, or under whom he acted. .

I may be much mistaken; but I do expect, then, to find some vile and abominable scheme disclosed; a scheme to dupe the poor, in order to continue the vassalage of the rich.   Let me not be misunderstood.   I do not mean to accuse the administration at the Castle with any such scheme; it is of a nature too revolting to humanity to allow me to attribute it to civilised beings.   The secretary may, indeed, indulge his taste in juries, but he would scorn to deal in blood; the scheme is confined, if it exists at all, to some of the inferior agents—to some expectant place-hunter, or, rather perhaps, to some spy by profession, who, in the vacation between the terms, happens to be devoid of other occupation.   (Applause.)

I ought not, my lord, to detain you longer; but I am induced to request the attention of the meeting to a publication of a very strange nature : it imports to be a report of a speech in parliament, and it bears the name of Mr. Wellesley Pole——

| [Here Mr. O'Connell was interrupted by Mr. Francis Huddleston—by that Francis Huddleston who prosecuted the Catholic delegates—who wanted to address the chairman. Mr. Barnewall, Major Bryan, Counsellors Hussey and Finn protested against this attempt with great indignation, and were strongly supported by the entire meeting.]

Mr. O'Connell continued his address :—What that gentleman might have said in parliament, I am quite ignorant of, nor do I inquire; I have at present no right to reply to him here; and I entertain little doubt but that anything to our prejudice, or in his own praise—his favourite subjects, which he might have brought forward—was sufficiently replied to and exposed; my business is merely with a newspaper publication—a publication contained in a paper bearing, with a constant contempt for truth as its title, the sacred name of "*Patriot.*"

This publication is entitled "the speech of the Right Honourable W. W. Pole."   I cannot bring myself to believe that any man could pronounce such a discourse: the style is of the poorest order ; it talks of the magistrates having a row with the committee ; and there are a thousand other phrases in it which de-a demonstrate that no man of common education could have composed it. But it would be absurd to waste time in censuring more of this composition; it is the absence of truth and decency which distinguishes it, and entitles it to some notice amongst our calumnies.

Let me be pardoned whilst I delay you to expose its want of veracity. It is by calumny alone that our degradation is continued; if nothing were told of us falsely, if "nought was set down against us in malice," we should long since have been emancipated. My lord, I beg leave to confute these calumnies, not because they are talented or skilful, but simply to oppose the system of detraction.

I have selected six different assertions, which are either but partially true, or destitute of any the slightest foundation of fact.

The first I shall mention is one, perhaps, in itself, of little moment; but it will serve to show how incautious "this speech" is in its assertions. It does, my lord, assert, in speaking of the addition to our former Committee, in the beginning of 1811—

1st—"That the government intended to stop the elections, and did stop them. The ten persons which (I preserve the beauty of the original) were ordered to be returned from each county, in point of fact, never did assemble." '

In point of fact, my lord, we all know that the government never stopped any such election; that it never did interfere, save by sending forth the slovenly and ludicrous circular; and that in point of fact, the appointment did take place in most of the counties—every county that pleased—and the assembling of those persons was a matter as public, and as well known to the government, as any other fact which was entrusted to the daily newspapers; but there is certainly this happy colour for the assertion of the speech—that all the counties in Ireland did not appoint to the last Committee.

It is also asserted—

2nd—"That Lord Ffrench, in consequence of the violence of the members of the Committee, selected from them."

When shall I find time to express my astonishment at this assertion—an assertion directly, pointedly, and positively the contrary of the fact. Mr. W. W. Pole could never have said any such thing. Why, Lord Ffrench was in the chair, when Mr Pole sent his police-justice to disperse that Committee. Lord Ffrench entered into a correspondence with Mr. Pole to maintain that Committee. He lent his character, his rank, and his talents to support that Committee; and, in perfect defiance of Mr. W

W. Pole, he did support it. What becomes of the audacious assertion of his secession ?

I wish my noble friend, for so I am proud to call him, were allowed by his health to be here this day: how he would refute this calumny. He never seceded or deserted the Catholic cause ; and I can assure Mr. W. W. Pole, that there breathes not the man who would presume to tell his lordship that he seceded from the Catholic Committee or the Catholic rights. I know the reply which such presumption would meet and merit.

The next assertion which I shall notice is—

3rd—" That many of the counties in Ireland could not produce ten respectable persons of the Catholic religion, above the rank of farmers."

Where was the creature found who wrote this speech ? Is this ignorance only, or is it unblushing effrontery ? I shall not stoop to refute this foolish untruth ; it may serve a purpose in England ; in this country it is almost beneath ridicule.

We soon after find it gravely stated—

4th—" The meetings to appoint the present Committee were held for the most part during the assizes ; but they were conducted in such a manner, that it was almost impossible to find out what passed at the time."

Shame, shame upon this profligate speech-writer ! Why, all Ireland knows that these meetings were held with even ostentatious publicity ; that they were crowded by Protestants ; and that he who could make the assertion that I have just quoted, deserves not the trouble of contradiction. It may be supposed that it was impossible to exceed the absurdity of the last misstatement ; but, my lord, it has been exceeded, for I find in this speech these words—

5th—" The Earl of Fingal had also seceded from the Committee."

No, my lord, calumny more absurd was never invented ; assertion more destitute of fact was never written. [Lord Fingal declared his assent.] Yes, my lord, you are thus calumniated ; and the purpose of publishing these untruths only aggravates the guilt of him, whoever he be, that invented them.

There remains yet one calumny. I do not entreat the members of the Committee, so many of them I see about me, to restrain their indignation whilst I read it. It is this :—

6th—" Mr. Pole said, that if gentlemen would read the debates of this Committee, they would find *separation* was openly and distinctly recommended."

Mr. Pole said no such thing: the man does not live, suffi-ciently audacious to say any such thing. Why, my lord, this is a direct accusation of high treason; and he who would assert it of me, I would brand with the foulest epithets. No; a writer in a newspaper may be found to compose such a paragraph, but no man in his senses in the world dare to utter it aloud. But if it were said, I care not, while I proclaim it to the world to be unfounded as it is injurious—as false as it is foul; and I defy the slightest proof to be given of its veracity.

I have trespassed upon you too long, with this miserable pub-.ication; it deserves notice only, because having circulated among the English, who know us not, it may, remaining uncon-tradicted, be believed. In the six assertions which I have noticed, there is but one that has the slightest pretensions to any colour of being otherwise than being directly and palpably the exact reverse of the fact.

I am tempted to give you another instance of the stuff this speech is made of. It treats of the book called "The Statement of the Penal Law," and, as usual, it flagrantly misrepresents or absurdly replies. I have been done the great honour, by some persons, of having that book attributed to me. I should be proud to own it if I could, but I am incapable of writing so excellent a composition, or of sharing the honour with a gentle-man to whose pen the Catholics of Ireland are deeply indebted, for everything admirable that has emanated from him; and never were they more obliged than by the address and petition which you have adopted this day.

I do not choose to dilate on the resplendent talents of my respected friend; but in him Ireland possesses a model of clas-sical taste and refined judgment, devoted exclusively to patriotic purposes. His book has been criticised in this speech; and the law, which is the intervention of the commissioners of charitable donations, precludes the possibility of establishing a Catholic charity, with permanent funds, is palliated by endeavouring to show, that the rigour of the statute is softened by the mildness of the commissioners. It is alleged that they humanely spare many a popish charity, and allow the pious sin to be perpetrated in quiet. Instances of their forbearance are given; and amongst them we find the following, under date, 1810:—"James Baldwin, of Macroom, county Cork, left all his lands, in reversion, to Doctors Segrave and Moylan. in trust, to raise £400 per annum, for ever, to establish a school to instruct poor children in the tenets of the Church of Rome."

This is one of the instances of the lenity of the commissioners of charitable donations. Now, let me tell you what the value of their kindness is—Mr. Baldwin was married to a near relation of mine. I am his executor. It was I proved the will, so that I am authority upon this point. The fact is, that he had eight children, five of whom are married, and have, most of them, large and increasing families. He first devised his estates to his children, successively, and their issue, male and female ; then to two other individuals of his own name, having families, and their issue, male and female ; and after the decease of all those persons, between seventy and eighty in being, and all their issue, this £400 per annum, is bequeathed to endow a Catholic school, so that the vesting of this bequeath depends on the contingency of about eighty persons dying without issue, an event very little likely to take place in this country.

. Such is the wonderful forbearance of those commissioners—such is the happy art attributed to Mr. W. W. Pole, of furnishing proofs and illustrations. Yes, this article illustrates the active genius of the speech. Unfounded assertion, ridiculous argument, paltry self-sufficiency, and ludicrous quotation, distinguished the narrative of the parish clerk, whose situation, exposing him to public view, he has mistaken for elevation. I have to apologise for attaching so much importance to matters so insignificant.

I hasten to conclude by expressing my conviction that the Emancipation is certain, and will be immediate. The generous, the cordial support of our Protestant brethren, in Ireland, assures us of it. The petition—which is exclusively their measure, and with respect to which, every Catholic has scrupulously avoided the least interference—the Protestant petition has, at this moment, more signatures to it than were affixed to any petition of our own. It has been supported in every county by the wealth, talent, and rank of our affectionate countrymen, and I am proud to see amongst us this day, at the head of so many of our Protestant friends, a noble Lord (Glentworth) whose ardent patriotism entitled him to the gratitude of every class of his fellow subjects ; and whom we shall see met by corresponding patriotic exertions, and proudly placed in the first rank of the representatives of his native country. The voters of Limerick will not be blind to the insults they have received from other quarters, nor to their own interests and dignity, nor to the worth of the noble lord.

We have the Protestants of Ireland in our favour—the Protestants of England, at least the rational part of them, are not

opposed to us. No, in the two last discussions in parliament, the right and justice of our claims were conceded, even by those who opposed on the ground of the time; there was but one solitary exception—a single individual, Sir John Nichol, who was sent forward as the scape-goat of English bigotry, to revive ancient calumny, and to add some fresh ones; he was installed in the enviable office of successor to Dr. Duignan; but, good Lord! he is quite unfit for the employment. There was about Duignan, a sturdy, robust, unblushing effrontery, that enabled him to assert anything, and prevented the possibility of his retreating. This poor Nichol, however, was no sooner attacked and ridiculed, at every tide, than he explained one passage, softened down another, and gave up a third, until he himself abandoned, piecemeal, the web of intolerance, so that it really appears, that even the futile resource of bigoted calumny is at length exhausted.

Of the Prince I shall say nothing—uncertainty as to present circumstances—reliance on the past, and the lingering and dutiful affection in a heart devoted to the friend of Ireland, restrain me. To canvass the subject would appear to be the entertaining of a doubt.

Oh! but there is one objection still remains to our emancipation; it is quite novel and most important. Our enemies object to the tone which the Catholics use. This notable objection was struck out by the Earl of Rosse. He disliked our tone—he might as well have quarrelled with our accent—but that would rather be a strong measure in Lord Rosse (laughter). Seriously, however, the descendant of Sir William Parsons has an hereditary right to be the enemy of the Catholics upon any pretext, or even without one. I do not believe this lord has fallen into inconsistency. I have some faint recollection that, under the name of Sir Lawrence Parsons, he once enacted patriotism in Ireland—I may be mistaken, but I do not think he ever supported our claims; and I am quite sure I wish he never may.

But our tone is disliked—yes, my lord, they dislike the tone which men should use who are deeply anxious for the good of their country, and who have no other object. We are impressed with the sense of the perils that surround us, and of all the calamities impending on a divided and distracted people. We see our own resources lavishly squandered upon absurd projects, whilst our tottering paper currency is verging fast to bankruptcy—the fate of every other paper currency that has as yet existed. We see the private ruin that must ensue, the destruction, so prodigally hastened, of the funded system. We see the most formidable military force arrayed on the Continent. The Emperor of the European world is now busied with some quarrel on the Northern Frontier, which now extends to the suburbs of St. Petersburgh ; his fleet augments by the month ; who shall dare to say that we shall not have to fight, on our own shores, for the last refuge of civil liberty, in this eastern world. What blindness, what infatuation, not to prepare for that event !

We, my lord, assume the tone which may terrify the invader ; we use the tone of men who appreciate the value of civil liberty, and who would die sooner than exchange it for the iron sway of military rule. We talk as men should, who dread slavery and disgrace, but laugh to scorn the idea of danger. Shall it be asked, if the invader arrived—

> " And was there none—no Irish arm,
> In whose veins the native blood runs warm ?
> And was there no heart in the trampled land,
> That spurn'd the oppressor's proud command ?
> Could the wronged realm no arm supply,
> But the abject tear and the slavish sigh ?"

Why, yes, my lord, we are told if we had been servile and base in our language, and dastardly in our conduct, we should be nearer success ; that the "slavish tear," the "abject sigh," would have suited our dignity ; that had we shown ourselves prone to servility and submission, and silent in oppression, we should advance our emancipation ; and that by proving, by our words and actions, that we deserve to be slaves—we should ensure liberty.

MR. VERNER MOORE.

At a meeting of the gentlemen of the bar, held on Saturday, May 30, 1812, Mr. O'Connell delivered the following speech, as reported in the *Dublin Evening Post* of Thursday, June 4, 1812:—

He said that having had the honour of being called to the chair at the small meeting of the bar which had occurred in the vacation. he felt it to be his duty to state the object of those who called that meeting, and had adjourned to the present day for the convenience of the bar at large. The facts were, simply and without comment, these:—Shortly after the last circuit, Mr. Verner Moore had published, in the newspapers, a statement

purporting to detail a transaction which he asserted to have occurred at the last assizes of Omagh. It purported, as far as it
went, to be the report of a trial that had taken place in the public court-house, as personally interested Mr. Moore ; it was addressed to the Irish bar, and for the truth of the statement, Mr.
Moore solemnly pledged himself. It appears that, shortly after,
the benchers, as they are called, of the King's Inns, had a meeting ; they summoned Mr. Moore before them ; they required to
know if he were the author of the publication in question ; he
admitted the fact—he went further—he admitted that the mode
of publication of his complaint, in a newspaper, was an improper
one ; but he again repeated his solemn assertion of the truth of
what he had published, and offered to prove, beyond any doubt,
its perfect accuracy. He was then dismissed ; and the benchers
who had, before his personal examination, deliberated in private,
resumed their private sittings, and the result was, a vote of the
severest censure on Mr. Moore ; and another vote, that the censure should be read publicly in all the courts, on the first day
of the present term. Such were the facts. It stood thus :—
Mr. Moore had published a report of a trial, or part of a trial ;
if what he stated was true, misconduct of no ordinary kind
was attributable to one of the benchers in the exercise of his public duty.   .

The bench, including the personage thus accused, meet. They
do not investigate the facts ; they are incompetent to investigate any facts ; their meeting is held in secret, and they inflict
punishment for the publication of that which they do not accuse
to be a falsehood. Upon this subject he would not, for the present, give any opinion ; although he should be sorry any one
supposed he had not formed a distinct opinion on it. But he
would, for the present, concede that Mr. Moore was guilty of
some offence that deserved punishment. The question was,
whether the benchers had any jurisdiction over the offence. It
was a question of great importance to the bar in every point of
view. Their property, their characters, their honour, were all
involved in its consideration. No man could well consider himself safe in his professional pursuits, if any body of men assembled in a private chamber, without power to administer an oath,
or examine into a disputed fact ; without form of indictment or
mode of pleading ; without allowing the advantage of counsel,
or showing the grounds of decision, were entitled to vote away
the profession and the reputation of the Irish gentlemen who belong to the bar.

These were alarming considerations ; he was ready to admit the respectability of the persons who composed this secret tribunal ; it was not against the individuals he complained, it was against the existence of the thing itself. He could not see any the least necessity for its existence. The Irish bar composed, he was convinced, the first profession in the world ; it required no inquisitorial power to keep it within the bounds of the strictest propriety —nay, it possessed the most certain method of repressing misconduct among its own members, by the moral force of its own high character. The man who conducted himself in a manner unbecoming a gentleman would shrink abashed from their society, or, if he haunted the hall, he would be seen to glide through it despised and unnoticed, and solitary in the midst of a crowd ; and if greater delinquency should be found, it would meet with exclusion and expulsion from the entire society, who were alone capable to exclude, but who could never conspire against an individual.

This inquisitorial power could not be necessary for the protection of the judges ; it was ludicrous to suppose that it could ; the judges were armed with abundant power for their own protection—they could commit to the dock, they could force, they could imprison at their own discretion, almost at their caprice, for the slightest disrespect. All these powers existed, and were recognised by the law ; nay more, they were all absolutely necessary for the due administration of justice. To diminish any one of them would be to render it difficult, perhaps impossible to do justice effectually between angry litigants ; but those powers have been, by experience, found amply sufficient for that purpose. When, however, there is added to this, the natural effect which the disfavour of the judge must have upon the success of any individual barrister, it would be seen at once how unnecessary further securities were ; there was even danger of the other extreme, and servility to the bench, to which poor human nature afforded so many temptations, could be guarded against only by the high-mindedness of educated gentlemen, who rather condescended to belong to a profession, than to be the slaves of its emoluments.

Without the independence produced by this spirit, it would be impossible to be honest as an advocate ; for that advocate is not honest who, for his own sake, shrinks from the manly assertion of his client's rights, whatever may chance to be the impressions of the bench against it ; but at the Irish bar, where the very soul of honour was to be found, there was no danger of any tone being adopted but that which would dignify individuals and exalt a profession. It may, perhaps, be said, that although it is clear that the judges had sufficient means of making their authority respected in court, yet, that they wanted further grounds for contempts committed out of court, and the case of publication of a false and libellous account of a trial might be sustained. But this he was ready to deny, because there existed already abundant means of punishment for such contempts. There were attachments, informations, ex-officio or by rule of court, indictments, and actions.

Now, for example, this Mr. Moore might have been proceeded against in any of these ways if his publication were false. To an action he was liable, but there the truth would be a justification. An attachment or an information, by rule of court might be obtained against him ; but then an affidavit must be made of the falsehood of his statement, and he who swore the affidavit might be prosecuted in his turn ; so the information ex-officio, render truth or falsehood immaterial ; but in a case of this kind a jury would, in law, as well as in fact, be bound to acquit, if the publication were proved to be an exaggerated statement of what had occurred at the former trial.

It only remains then to see whether any person will be found sufficiently rash to assert, that this tribunal, called the benchers, was calculated to punish for the publication of the truth—of the truth of what occurred in the presence of the public—in a public court—at a public trial. It would be grossly to calumniate the respectable personages who composed that body, to assert that such was the jurisdiction they sought to exercise. It was important first to consider of the necessity of this species of tribunal, before any discussion arose as to the legality of its jurisdiction ; because if it could be shown to him that such a jurisdiction was necessary for either the honour of the judges, or the convenience of the suitors, he should not be very scrupulous in investigating its origin, on the foundation of its authority. But being deeply impressed with the conviction, that the contrary was the fact—that this tribunal was unnecessary—that, of itself, and placed in the hands of the best of men, it was unconstitutional and dangerous—that its immediate effect must be to crush the spirit and independence of the bar, and to convert an honourable and liberal profession into mere retailers of chicane, and servile slaves of authority.

With this impression upon his mind, he must solemnly protest against every exercise of power by this tribunal, even against a guilty individual, and conjure the bar, at once to ascertain their rights, and to trace the limits of this jurisdiction, so that it may be either ascertained to be a mere usurpation, or if it have a legal existence, that parliament may be resorted to for its abolition. For his part, he had given the subject all the attention in his power; he had investigated all the sources of information on this subject, and he had convinced himself, that the benchers of the King's Inns had no legitimate authority over the Irish bar. As a legal or corporate body, it was clear, upon their own confession, that they had no existence. In the late case which they had instituted in Chancery against a Mr. Caldbeck, an objection was taken to their legal capacity to sue; to this objection they had submitted, and their incapacity to exercise corporate functions was, therefore, matter of record. Prescriptive rights they could claim none; their history was modern and well known; charter they had at present none; about sixteen years ago they obtained one, with an act of parliament to confirm it; but this act, which had passed *sub silentio*, having been discovered, the bar remonstrated, and in the ensuing sessions the statute and charter were repealed. Such was the short history of this formidable tribunal; it had no chartered rights, no powers by statute, no claim to prescriptive authority. It was, indeed, mentioned in two more statutes, but merely to qualify it to take land for the purposes of buildings. Statutes that, so far from admitting its general corporate capacity, were direct evidence that none such was in existence.

But he might be told, that although the foundation of its authority could not be clearly ascertained, yet that facts proved its existence; and, in the absence of argument, precedents might be resorted to, a thing not unusual. There were, indeed, four instances of interference by the benchers with the bar; four instances in which men had been struck out of the barristers' roll upon their recommendation. In the two first, the cases of School and Brody, the profession had been disgraced by the commission of the crime, he believed, of perjury. The indignant Irish bar rejoiced at the expulsion of such men, and cared little by whom they were kicked out of the hall. The other two instances were those of Messrs. Arthur O'Connor and Thomas Addis Emmett. Those gentlemen had, in the year 1799, been, upon a similar recommendation, disbarred. But it should be recollected that they first stood convicted, upon their own confession, of being traitors—that they had forfeited their lives to the laws, and had actually, upon an agreement with government, submitted to perpetual banishment.

When he spoke of the crimes of those gentlemen, he could not but express the regret he felt at mentioning the name of one of them, with whom he had once the pleasure to be personally acquainted. Whatever might have been the political crimes of Mr. Emmett, those who knew him were bound to say, that a more worthy gentleman, in private life, never lived. But having abjured the realm, the benchers exercised the superfluous loyalty of getting them excluded from the list of Irish barristers. No person was interested to inquire into the authority by which so immaterial a result had been produced. Such are the precedents, the only precedents that can be alleged. What do they prove? Just nothing. But, perhaps I am mistaken; perhaps this jurisdiction does exist; you may not be willing, and you might not to submit to act upon my researches; yet I hope I have said enough to convince you, that an inquiry ought to be instituted, and that every man at the Irish bar may know upon what footing the preservation of his professional property and personal honour stands. This inquiry should be conducted in the most respected manner; no offence will be taken where none is intended; we would be bound to make the inquiry at every risk; but, in truth, the benchers themselves are ready to concede much to the general feeling of the bar. To this feeling they have already sacrificed the resolution to publish their censure of Mr. Moore. If the bar declares its conviction that no such inquisitorial authority does, in point of law, and that none such, in point of fact, ought to exist, we shall never again hear of the cause of our present alarm.

Mr. O'Connell moved, "that a committee, consisting of three of the gentlemen of the bar, be appointed to ascertain the authority of the benchers, either to censure or disbar a barrister."

The benchers not only gave no redress in the matter dwelt upon in the foregoing speech, but were guilty of the additional arrogance and injustice of not paying even so much attention the bar-remonstrance, as to acknowledge having received it

THE REGENT'S PLEDGES.

We are now come to the first general manifestation of feeling on the part of the Catholics, upon the disappointment of their hopes, after the assassination of Mr. Perceval. The extent and nature of that disappointment will be best gathered from Mr. O'Connell's speech. It was at this meeting that the resolutions were passed, known in the records of Catholic agitation as the "*witchery*" resolutions. In the third resolution will be found the allusion that supplied the designation. It refers to the shameful entanglement of the Prince Regent with Lady Hertford—an entanglement, by means of which, influence was exerted over him to entirely destroy what remnant of honour and good feeling there was yet in his cold and selfish heart.

The allusion gave great offence, not only in the quarter for which it was intended, but also to many of the timorous or deceitful "friends," as they called themselves, but gracious patrons, as they in fact assumed, to be, of the Catholics. By them it was strongly reprobated; but the bold and singularly-able compiler of these resolutions, Denis Scully, cared little for the offence, when seeking to give vent and expression to the mortified and indignant feelings of himself and fellows.

The Donoughmore family, then true to Ireland—as one of them has again recently proved himself—were not amongst those who disapproved of this semi-declaration of rupture with the Prince Regent, and their approbation of it was an additional reason for persisting.

The meeting took place at Fishamble-street Theatre, on Thursday, June 18, 1812—Lord Fingal, as usual, in the chair. After some preliminary matters, Mr. Hussey rose, and gave an account of the proceedings of the gentlemen who had been sent to London on the part of the Catholics. He stated that on applying for a personal interview with his Royal Highness the Prince Regent, they received a blunt refusal, and were informed by Mr. Secretary Ryder, that the address to his Highness, with which they were charged, should be presented at one of his public levees, "in the usual way."

Of course there was no option but to submit; and, accordingly, the address was so presented, and received, too, "in the usual way" of most addresses presented on such occasions, viz.: the announcement of its purport and origin being all that was allowed to be stated, and then the document itself being handed over to the tender care and entire forgetfulness of one of the lords in waiting.

"His Royal Highness," said Mr. Hussey, "was not pleased to make any communication on the subject to the Committee. What impression was made upon his mind was not known; what he felt, what he thought, are left to conjecture (it was not long left a matter of mere *conjecture*); but this melancholy fact is sufficiently understood, that his Royal Highness did not think fit to offer any recommendation to Parliament upon the subject; and it is notorious that the minister seemed to have acquired new zeal in propagating his old insinuations against the Catholic people, and in repeating his old experiment against religious liberty."

The resolutions agreed upon were brought forward by Mr. O'Connell, moved by Lord Killeen, and seconded by Mr. Barnewall.

A very able and excellent speech followed from John Finlay, Esq., (at present Assistant Barrister for Roscommon county), to whom the cause was much indebted for powerful oratory and useful exertions on many occasions.

The reference at the commencement of Mr. O'Connell's speech, which we are about to give, is to the gentleman just mentioned.

I have, my lord, much to say, but I shall say little: I cannot venture to detain you after my eloquent friend—after the brilliant display you have just witnessed of the talents and powerful eloquence of my learned and excellent friend, Mr. Finlay. We do, indeed, owe him much : I was about to regret that he was not a Catholic, I was so pleased with him, and so anxious that we might have the credit of such talents ; but when I consider, I think it is better that matters should be as they are ; for it must gratify every Catholic in Ireland to have Protestant talent such as his come forward to grace and support our assemblies ; and it is a new source of unconquerable strength to our cause, to have Protestant and Catholic equally ardent in the struggle in which we are engaged. His are talents which ministerial corruption would not purchase, for they are beyond all price.

My duty calls upon me to address you ; I may be mistaken ; but I consider it as my duty—upon a subject, painful in itself, yet as speaking upon it may be beneficial in its consequences, I will not shrink from, nor decline it : I allude my lord, to the public assertion of some of the many pledges which his Royal Highness the Prince Regent was graciously pleased to tender to the Catholics of Ireland, before any part of the executive authority of the state had devolved upon him.

I shall state but a few of them : I do it without any breach of confidence, or violating any honorary engagement, either expressed or implied. Without egotism, perhaps I may say, that no person will charge me with being guilty of either—and I defy my enemies, who are mine only because they hate or oppress my poor country, to insinuate the slightest doubt of the veracity of my assertions.

I shall bring before the public, for the present, but four of those pledges. I am sorry they were not formerly made generally public ; for if they had, no man could have been so profligate as to advise the Prince to anything tending towards a violation of them, and much of the anxiety and distrust which now distract the mind of the nation, might have been spared and avoided.

The first in rank, though not in order of time, is that communicated to the Catholics of Ireland, by his Grace the Duke of Bedford. He lives—my witness lives : what is said here will probably reach him through the public papers ; and I call upon him, publicly to contradict anything I advance, which is not literally warranted by the fact. Thus, then, do I state, that in 1806, about the commencement of the Fox administration, when the Catholics, flushed with hope at seeing their late advocates in power, were about to prepare petitions to parliament, the ministry used many means to postpone that measure. At that period, and as one of those means, his Grace the Duke of Bedford, then

Lord Lieutenant of Ireland, did communicate to the Catholics
of Ireland, the wish of his Royal Highness the Prince of Wales,
that the question should not then be agitated; and at the same
time, his decided conviction of the justice of our claims, and his
decided resolution to admit them whenever he should have power
to do so.

Perhaps I can state this pledge; but I see persons before me
to whom this language was held; and I am quite sure that the
Duke of Bedford would never, never have conveyed one idea on
the subject, if he had not his authority directly from the Prince.

Secondly, my lord, we have had in the same year, the same
pledge repeated to many Catholics, by the Chancellor of Ireland,
George Ponsonby.

The keeper of his Majesty's Irish conscience must be supposed
to have had a kind of reversionary solicitude for that of his Royal
Highness, the heir apparent. Mr. Ponsonby do I understand,
distinctly avow the authority under which he communicated to
the Irish Catholics, the promise of emancipation—when, in the
fulness of time, he whom we then cherished as the early friend
of Ireland, and the proudest hope, should have it in his power
to rouse the enthusiasm of an elective people round his throne.

Good God! what a prodigal waste has since been committed
—not of wealth, for that, comparatively, is no more than trash
—but of the cheerful and best defence of the monarch, the Irish
people's love.

The third pledge is a written one, and is in the possession of
a Catholic peer, not now present. I have not the honour to be sufficiently known to the Earl of Kenmare, to have applied to him
for it; but I entertained hopes of being able to procure it through
a friend of mine, and of his lordship. It is sufficient to say of
that pledge, that it afforded for years consolation to the Irish
Catholics; and the discretion with which it was communicated,
enhanced its value. I believe, my lord, I need not state to you
how little doubt it could leave of the firm decision of the Prince's
mind upon our question.

The fourth and last pledge, which, for the present, I shall
mention, was that given by his Royal Highness to a noble lord
now present. At the conversation I allude to, that noble lord
was accompanied by the late Lord Petre, and the present Lord
Clifden. After retiring from the presence of his Royal Highness, the declarations which he was so graciously pleased to make,
were from a loyal and affectionate impulse of gratitude, committed to writing, and signed by the three noble lords.

His Royal Highness did, I understand, offer something like an apology, for not having taken an active part in promoting the success of our petition, in 1805. He was pleased to say, that obvious motives of delicacy restrained his interference on political subjects, but that this delicacy was still more imperative on our question. However, he desired it to be understood that he had formed his opinion upon it, and would ever entertain them unaltered. They were, that concession to the Irish Catholics were required, not only by reasons of expediency and policy, but by the first principles of justice.

I will not add—I must not add one word more on this subject. These were the sentiments of his Royal Highness : we should have proclaimed them last year, and no minister would have been found sufficiently profligate to have disappointed our certain expectations of immediate relief : nor has his Royal Highness, to this hour, by any personal act of his—by any public declaration, or recommendation to parliament, retracted any part of these sentiments. Let us, then, fondly and respectfully hope that they are unaltered. Sure I am that no base minion will venture to assert, that the air of Manchester-square has infected the royal mind with *simples*, or that Lord Yarmouth has inoculated him with the theory or practice of excessive piety.

We may still hope. Hope, the last refuge of the wretched, is left us ; and we lately indulged it almost with the pleasures of certainty : a crime, the horrid crime of causeless assassination, had deprived England of her prime minister—for, my lord, everywhere but in Ireland, assassination is admitted to be a crime. Here, also, it depends on circumstances ; you have but to combine these circumstances. Let the victim be an Irish Papist—let the murderer be an Orangeman—and let a legal junta administer the government in the name of the Duke of Richmond. It requires no more to turn murder into merit !

The process in England is different. There they hanged and dissected the murderer, and transferred the advantages of the crime, if I may so express myself, to the victim ; it really and truly has been considered a merit in Mr. Perceval to have been murdered. The public men in England seem to think his death constituted not only an expiation for all his political sins, but turned his offences against his country into virtues.

For my part, I feel unaffected horror at his fate, and all trace of resentment for his crimes is obliterated. But I do not forget that he was a narrow-minded bigot, a paltry statesman, and a bad minister—that every species of public corruption and profligacy had in him a flippant and pert advocate—that every advance towards reform or economy, had in him a decided enemy—and that the liberties of the people were an object of his derision.

All this has not been changed by the hand of the assassin; yet I do, from my heart, participate in the grief and anguish which his premature fall must have excited within his domestic circle. The sorrows of his family have been obtruded on the public by ill-judging party writers, with something like ostentatious affectation; but I do not love the man—nay, I hate the man who could contemplate, coldly and unmoved, the affecting spectacle of the wife and children standing in speechless agony round the lifeless body of the murdered husband and father; it was a scene to make a stoic weep.

But are all our feelings to be exhausted by the great? Is there no compassion for the wretched Irish widow, who lost her boy—her hope, her support? I shall never forget the pathetic and Irish simplicity with which she told her tale of woe—"My child was but seventeen; he left me on Sunday morning, quite well, and very merry, and he came home a corpse." Are her feelings to be despised and trampled on? Is the murderer of her son to remain unpunished, perhaps to be rewarded? Oh yes; for Byrne was a Papist, and the assassin, Hall, was an Orangeman, nay, a purple marksman; and, recollect, that his Grace the Duke of Richmond did not pardon him until after a most fair and patient trial. Hall was defended by his counsel and attorney; he was tried by a jury of his own selection—I say of his own selection—because he exhausted but few of his peremptory challenges; nobody, indeed, would think of accusing honest Sheriff James of packing a jury *against* an Orangeman. Even had the list been previously submitted to the secretary at the Castle, he would not have altered a single name; Sir Charles Saxton might have reviewed it with perfect safety to the prisoner.

After a patient trial, and a full defence, Hall was convicted; he was convicted before a judge, certainly not unfavourable to the prisoner; he was convicted of having murdered, with the arms entrusted to him for the defence of the public peace, and in the public streets of your city, and in the open day, an innocent and unoffending youth. He has been pardoned and set at large—perhaps he has been rewarded; but can this be done with impunity? is there no vengeance for the blood of the widow's son? Alas! I am not, I trust, inclined to superstition, yet it obtruded itself on my mind, that the head of that government which had allowed the blood of Byrne to flow unrequited, might

F

have vindicated the notion of a providential visitation for the unpunished crime.

My lord, I have digressed: I meant to speak of Perceval's removal by the assassin, merely as that tragic event opened a near prospect of our emancipation : we should have been emancipated. At the moment I am speaking, the bill for our relief would have been in its progress through the legislature—we should have been emancipated this very sessions, unconditionally and completely emancipated ; but for what ?—I speak it in no anger, but in the deepest sorrow—but for Lord Moira.

Lord Moira is a name that I have never before pronounced without enthusiasm ; I am quite aware of his high honour, his unbounded generosity, his chivalrous spirit ; his heart has ever been without fear, his intentions have ever been, and will ever be, without reproach ; Ireland was justly proud of him ; where could his fellow be met with ? In the disastrous period that preceded the Union—at the time that measure was in preparation—when Foster and Clare banished Abercrombie from Ireland, because he was humane—when murders marked the day, and the burning cottages of the peasantry illumined the darkness of the night—when affright and desolation stalked through the land—when it was a crime to love Ireland, and death to defend her ; at that awful moment, Moira, the good, the great Moira, threw himself between his country and her persecutors : he exposed their crimes ; he denounced their horrors ; he proclaimed and proved their guilt ; and, although they were too powerful to be beaten down by him, he has left his country the sad consolation of beholding a perpetual record of the infamy of her oppressors.

Good God ! if his advice had been taken in 1797, what innocent blood would have been spared ; how many cruel oppressors would have been punished ; and oh ! our country would still have a name, and be a nation !

Can these services be forgotten—can those virtues be unremembered ? No, never ; but still the truth must be told. *This is Lord Moira's administration.* He it was that stood between some worthless minions and the people's hopes. He had to choose between them ; and he has given his protection, not to Ireland or the Catholics, but to Lord Yarmouth and his family. It is now confessed that a single word from Lord Moira would have dismissed the minions, and placed Earl Grey and Lord Grenville at the head of affairs. Why was not that fated word pronounced ? Alas ! I know not. Full·sure, however, I am, that the intention which restrained it was pure and honourable ; but I, at the same time, feel its fatal effects. We are, my lord, to continue slaves, because Lord Moira indulged some chivalrous notions of courtly romance !

It may be said, that as Lord Moira has interfered, the Catholics may reasonably expect some relief. Let us not be deceived. From the present ministry we cannot expect anything. Our best and boldest advocate, Lord Donoughmore, has, in his manly reply to our address, offered the best advice that ever was given to the Catholic people of Ireland. He has suggested the grounds of caution and jealousy. We know his devotion to our cause ; but this last proof of his zeal and vigorous integrity, has rendered it impossible that we should ever be sufficiently grateful. I am proud that your resolutions re-echo his sentiments.

But, in sober sadness, in whom are we to confide ? Are we to believe the word of Castlereagh ? My lord, I would not believe his oath. Already has he been deeply pledged. He was an United Irishman, and, as such, must have taken their test. It was then administered, I believe, without the ceremonies of an oath, but it had all the solemnity of that obligation. It pledged him to Catholic Emancipation and Parliamentary Reform. Again, my lord, upon the hustings of the Down Election, he was called upon, and he volunteered a similar declaration. It was a bond, solemnly given to his constituents and his country. But how has he redeemed those pledges ? Why, he has emancipated the Catholics by duping some of them at the Union, and uniformly voting upon every question against us ; and he has reformed the parliament by selling it to the British minister. May this Walcheren minister be suitably rewarded in the execration of his country ; and may he have engraved on his tomb for an epitaph—

" Vendidit hic auro patriam."

No, my lord, from us Castlereagh can obtain no confidence, nor can his colleague, Lord Sidmouth, expect that the friends of toleration can confide in his promises. Lord Sidmouth, who declared to parliament that he would prefer the re-enactment of the penal code to the extension of one other privilege to the Catholics ; Lord Sidmouth, who began his absurd career of persecution with the Dissenters in England ; that Lord Sidmouth (liberal and enlightened gentleman) has been selected for the home department ; he it is who is to regulate the motions of our provincial government ; he it is that is to cheer the drooping spirit of persecution in this country ; his natural allies are embodied here ; the group of " good men," as they fantastically designate themselves, who manage the legal administration of this country ; men who have worked themselves into reputation with ancient maidens and decayed matrons, by gravity of deportment and church wardening piety, but who, all their lives, have been discounting religion and the Diety into promotion and the pay and plunder of office—those men, together with *our friend.* (the Solicitor-General,) have a suitable companion in Lord Sidmouth, and we should, instead of concessions, be prepared rather to expect some other persecution, grounded, if possible, upon a pretext still more absurd than that " pretence means purpose ;" that assertion, which I defy an honest man, however credulous, to believe.

From this ministry we expect nothing ; let us be on our guard, and cautiously watch their progress. As Lord Moira has been their patron, they will endeavour to deceive him with a show of concession ; but their object is to give a change to the question. In its present shape it presses upon them with all the force of present expediency, and all the weight of eternal justice. If they could entrap us into collateral discussions ; if they could entangle us in the chicanery of arrangements and securities, the public attention would be distracted and turned from the principal object ; time would be wasted in useless discussions ; animosities would be created upon points of little real importance, and whilst the ministry practised the refinements of bigotry, they would give themselves credit for unbounded liberality.

These are not imaginary fears ; the nature of the subject must convince any man, that such was the design of an administration that had, for its only recommendations, intolerance and incapacity.

Indeed, the indiscretion of the party already betrayed itself. It is not twenty-four hours since a friend of mine had occasion to converse with one of those right honourables, who did the business of the Castle, who are always as ready to pack juries as to obtain pardon for an assassin, or to write paragraphs in the *Patriot.* My friend said, " Why, you are going, I find, to emancipate the Catholics at length." " We l" replied the other. " Oh, no ! Canning's motion will entangle the rascals completely ; we shall easily get rid of them without committing ourselves."

Of those men, Lord Donoughmore has advised us to be distrustful. I beg leave to say more. Let us utterly disbelieve

them. It is impossible that they can do anything for us ; they
would be false to themselves if they were true to Ireland. But
we are not without our resources ; we have them in ourselves ;
we have them in the liberality of our Irish Protestant brethren ;
we have them in the support of such men as the all-accomplished
Vernon, son to the Archbishop of York—as the honest and independent Robert Shaw. We have also a rich resource in the
eternal ridicule with which bigotry has lately covered itself in
the persons of its chosen apostles, Paddy Duignan and Jack
Giffard ; but, above all, we are strong in the justice of our cause
and in the unextinguishable right of man, in every soil and climate, to unlimited liberty of conscience. Let us, however, expect nothing from the mere patronage of courts and ministers.
The advice given by a noble advocate of ours, to other slaves, in
a poem, that it is impossible to read without delight, is not inapplicable to our situation :—

> " Hereditary bondsmen ! know ye not,
>   Who would be free, themselves must strike the blow—
> By their right arms the conquest must be wrought ;
>   Will Gaul or Muscovite redress you ?—No.
> True, they may lay your proud despoilers low,
>   But not for you will freedom's altar flame.
> Shades of the Helots ! triumph o'er your foe—
>   Greece change thy lords, thy state is still the same,
>   Thy glories all are o'er, but not thy years of shame.'

Yes, we must, after all, look to ourselves—to a perseverance
in a course of temperate, but firm exertion—to that blow which
we can strike on Prejudice by the force of Reason, and the unceasing exhibition of our meritorious conduct.

It is true, that after common sense has overthrown every pretence that there is anything in the Catholic religion hostile to
loyalty or liberty ; another ground has been long since taken,
and from time to time revived, by the unhappy dulness of one
pedant or the other. It consists in an admission that the Catholic
religion is quite innocent, and even laudable in other countries ;
but that it acquires malignity from the soil on its transplanta-
tion into Ireland. In short that other Papists are innocent or
good ; but that Irish Papists are execrable.

This precious doctrine has been dressed up anew, in sufficiently
bad English, and published in a pamphlet called a "Speech," by
that snug little Foster, who represents Trinity College in Parliament. It is added, too, with most admirable consistency, that
the mass of the Irish Papists are quite indifferent to the question

of Catholic Emancipation. But see what the fact is. Look to the history of the last six months for the contradiction of those vile assertions. Why, the Protestants of Ireland had only to show their wish to relieve us—they could do no more than express their inclination to set us free. The Union deprived them of the power to give us liberty; but they declared it was our right, and they joined us in demanding it. What followed? Why, in the first place, a season of unexampled scarcity and distress in both islands. In England there chanced to exist tumult, riot, destruction of property, murder, insurrection, and almost actual rebellion. In Ireland there was seen tranquillity the most profound, obedience the most perfect; pressed by famine and want, goaded by insulting prosecutions, by arranged juries, by the thousand other wrongs which I shall not name, the people of Ireland have found abundant consolation in the single liberality of their countrymen, and they have shown their sense of this liberality by dutiful and unbroken submission at those moments of the greatest peril England has as yet known. Not a feather is ruffled on the surface of our island. The Caravat and the Shanavest seem to have forgotten their quarrels; and every angry tone and turbulent propensity is hushed by the presence of the spirit of universal toleration.

In the meantime, the precious hours for peace and conciliation are wasted—the genius of Napoleon, the star of his imperial house, prevails. England, under the guidance of the venerated name of Moira, has appointed an administration first rejected, and then approved by parliament, for the appointment of which Napoleon would have given millions. How he must rejoice to see the parliament degrade itself by inconsistent votes—to see the Dissenters and Catholics insulted by the nomination of Lord Sidmouth to rule the Home Department—to see Walcheren Castlereagh conducting our war counsels; and, last and wonderful, to see Lord Liverpool prime minister! !

My lord, securities are wanting; they are wanting for the last refuge of public liberty—the only remnant of representative government in Europe, they are wanting for the throne and the people; they are wanting against the folly, the incapacity, the intolerance of the ministry—against the power and the talents of the French Emperor. He, to be sure, is absent for a season—he is gone to Petersburgh, to receive the submission of a vassal, or to dethrone an enemy. It is absurd to expect any other result; he will return with his hundreds of thousands to the conquest of Spain and Portugal. What can the unarmed bands of the one country, or our few companies in the other (though braver spirits than our brothers and kinsmen there never graced a field of fight)—what can they be able to do, overmatched by myriads? And then, my lord—and then, in what condition shal. those countries be found to fight the battle of our existence?

It is to prepare for that dreadful moment, which is so steadily on its progress, that all my anxieties are roused. I should fear it not, if a system of conciliation and mutual tolerance were once adopted—if justice were distributed by the hand of confiding generosity—if the persecutions ceased, and that the persecutors were removed—if Grey were prime minister, and Moira, then restored to the hearts of his countrymen, were lord lieutenant. Every village would produce a regiment, and every field serve for a redoubt. The Prince would then be safe and glorious: and the country, combined in its strength, would laugh to scorn the power of every enemy.

This is a vision ; but it might have been realised. And why has this prospect been closed? Why!—*to preserve the household!* Oh, most degrading recollection ! My feelings overpower me—I must be silent,

CATHOLIC EMANCIPATION.

On the 2nd of July, another aggregate meeting of the Catholics took place, to agree upon a petition to be presented in the ensuing session.

That some change had occurred in their prospects within the brief interval since their preceding meeting, will be evident from the extracts we are about to give from the newspaper reports.

Lord Fingal, on taking the chair, congratulated the meeting on their case "being before parliament, under the favourable consideration of the legislature, and certain of being ultimately triumphant. . . . The bringing of the Penal Code under notice was ensuring success to the Catholic cause; because it was impossible to consider its provisions, without having the mind coerced to assent to its repeal. He did not rejoice at their improved prospects because of any peculiar benefit to himself; he did not rejoice at it as opening new hopes and expectations to the friends he saw about him, or to those who were now fighting the battles of England in Spain or Portugal; his gratification sprung from another source—from his anticipation of seeing the whole empire feel, in security and prosperity, the benefits of equal rights and undisturbed tranquillity."

His lordship was followed by Randal M'Donnell, who spoke nearly in the same strain and strongly urged the necessity of continued and increased exertion on the part of the Catholics to back up the efforts of their friends in parliament.

He was followed by Mr. O'Connell, who is thus reported in the *Dublin Evening Post* of the 4th of July, 1812:—

Mr. O'Connell commenced by paying some very appropriate compliments to the merits and exertions of the secretary to the

Catholics of Ireland, Mr. Hay—a gentleman to whom we owed that tribute, as well from feelings of private friendship as from motives of public gratitude. Mr. Hay had devoted his life to the service of the Irish people, and refused to receive any other recompense than what was to be found in the barren praises of his countrymen.

After a panegyric on the public virtues of Mr. Hay, Mr. O'Connell proceeded. He said the Catholics were assembled at the most momentous period of their history. We have to contemplate a novel scene—the parliament of the United Kingdom, after nearly twelve years of neglect or rejection, had at length undertaken the consideration of our great cause. One branch of the legislature, by a triumphant majority, resolved to investigate the Penal Code of Ireland, with a view to its repeal ; and perhaps before this hour, a similar resolution has been adopted by the House of Lords.

The voice of the House of Commons was, at all events, certain. In it the Irish people had a distinct pledge, that the question of their freedom was to be taken into consideration, for the purpose of final adjustment, at an early period of the next session. The House of Commons was unequivocally pledged 'to some measure of Emancipation. The effect of this vote might perhaps be diminished, when it was recollected that, during the present session the same honourable house had, more than once, rejected all inquiry ; but times were altered, and we have now arrived at what appears to be the first great step in the progress to complete religious liberty. The preliminary to Emancipation is over ; and Emancipation itself, full and entire, is the natural, if not the necessary consequence.

Feeling, as I do, the great advance that has been made in this national cause, I cannot avoid declaring that I am happy and proud to concur with your lordship in all those sentiments of conciliation and confidence which you have so powerfully recommended. I rejoice, my lord, at our victory—not as the conquest of one party over another, nor with the view to any triumph over any other denomination of my countrymen, but because I look upon it as a victory obtained by the combined activity of all classes of Irishmen over their own prejudices, and over intolerance and illiberality. It is that species of victory that ought to endear the Irish Protestant to the Irish Catholic, because it has been obtained for the benefit of the latter—principally by the exertions of the former. It is doubly dear, because it holds but the prospect of mutual conciliation and mutual affection.

I, too, my lord, am ready to confide—I am ready with you to confide in the great and growing liberality of the British nation, in the pledge of the honourable house, in the promised vote of the lords, in the facility of the administration to abandon all former notions, and to comply with the temper of the times.— But let me conjure the meeting to place its first and principal reliance in the determined spirit and unalterable resolution to persevere until emancipation shall be complete, never to relax their efforts until religious freedom is established.

I may, without any allusion to its military import, which I dislike, remind my countrymen of the advice of Cromwell to his soldiers. The night was wet, and they as usual were engaged in prayer. "Confide," said he, "in the Lord—put all your trust and confidence in the Lord—but *be quite sure to sleep upon your matchlocks.*" (Laughter and loud cheering.)

Such, my lord, is the confidence we ought to entertain at present. In truth, every circumstance suggests caution—and he knows little of human nature who reposes with too implicit a belief upon the promises of any administration—and he has read history to little purpose, who does not doubt of the fair professions of newly-converted enemies. It is for this that history is useful. Its lessons may be neglected, and the consequence will be just what we see in the great affairs of the nation—distress, embarrassment, and permanent difficulty, produced by the miserable repetition of temporary expedients. The history of the Irish Catholics warns us to be cautious how we shall proceed. Within the last twenty years there were no less than three different periods at which the Catholics might have been emancipated, if a combination of exertion had been used.

Twenty years, however, have passed away, and we are still slaves. My days, the blossom of my youth and the flower of my manhood have been darkened by the dreariness of servitude. In this my native land—in the land of my sires—I am degraded without fault or crime, as an alien and an outcast. We do not, my lord, deserve this treatment. We are stamped by the Creator with no inferiority; and man is guilty of injustice when he deprives us of our just station in society. I despise him who can timidly and meanly acquiesce in the injustice. Oh, let us at length seize this opportunity of abolishing the oppression for ever.

To avoid failure at present, let us see whether we can discover how the Catholics failed before. The first occasion upon which, within these last twenty years, the entire Emancipation might have been obtained, was in the year 1793. In that year great concessions were certainly made—great boons were extorted from an adverse and very unwilling government; but the principle of servitude, and many galling and insulting restrictions remained. And why were they suffered to remain? Simply, because the Catholics were not sufficiently combined amongst themselves, and sufficiently determined.

I reproach none of the actors in the Catholic cause at that period; many names dear to freedom were amongst their popular leaders—treachery there was, I am sure, none—deceit there was, I am convinced, none; but leaving, as they did, so many weighty chains and oppressive restrictions, there certainly was a miserable failure of the one great object—the simple repeal of the acts restrictive of religious liberty. The Catholics, then, were supposed not to seek for the abolition of every penal law; they were supposed to be ready to consent to something short of that great measure; they were then, or had lately been, much divided amongst themselves, and the result was, that distraction in their counsels, and that dexterity in their enemies, which have ever since postponed the day of freedom.

The second occasion on which the Catholics might have been emancipated was the Union—but at that period, also, the Catholics were much divided amongst themselves—the reign of Robesperian terror still prevailed, and the voice of the Irish people was stifled. We thought and acted differently upon this melancholy subject, and, amidst the bitter anguish which the memory of my extinguished country excites, I have consolations both personal and public. First, because *the opposition to the Union was, (and I thank my God for it,) the first act of my political life;* and, secondly, I feel some comfort that the Catholics did not barter the constitution of their native land for advantages to themselves. I blame no person for the failure of emancipation on that occasion; on the contrary, I proudly rejoice that the Catholics, even those of them who supported that baleful and degrading measure, despised any idea of trafficking upon, or profiting by the miseries of Ireland.

My lord, all the Catholics are free from the guilt of having participated in the sale of their country; and this benefit results, that they are bound by no contract to continue their thraldom. *Nay, the existence of the penal code is soothed by the recollection, that in the efforts made to procure redress, a popular spirit is roused, which, if not soon laid by the voice of emancipation, may generate a determination to reanimate the fallen constitution!*

The third, and last period, at which the Catholics might have been emancipated, occurred since I had the honour to be an humble labourer in the Catholic cause ; it was the commence ment of Mr. Fox's administration.   The year preceding, Mr. Fox had most powerfully supported our claims in the House of Commons ; he supported them, not upon any narrow view of sect or party, but upon the great principle of universal toleration—on that principle, which, in our country, would repeal her test and corporations' act, and secure the uncontrolled freedom of religious worship and belief, in every climate, and to every cast and colour.

I believe, my lord, you were present at the liberal and manly declarations made by Mr. Fox, at a meeting of our delegates, some days previous to the introduction of our first petition to the imperial parliament.—[Lord Fingal said he was not present at that meeting.]   Well, my lord, Mr. Scully certainly was : we heard him say so no later than yesterday ; and when I mention his name, I know I can use no authority more likely to obtain the full belief and confidence of the Irish people. (Loud cheers.) Mr. Scully was present as a delegate at those declarations, when Mr. Fox proclaimed the restrictive code as a crime—religious liberty as a right.   "I cannot," said that enlightened man, "I cannot consent to become your advocate unless you are ready to concede to all other sects, the toleration you require for your-selves."   "We should be unworthy to obtain it, could we hesi-tate to accede to your terms ; we would gladly bestow on all mankind what we ask for ourselves," was the reply.

Upon this avowed principle, in 1805, Mr. Fox supported the claims of the Catholics : in 1806, that very Mr. Fox became minister.   What could have prevented that principle from being carried into action ?   The Catholics did not call for it ; a mis-taken confidence occasioned them to allow the only decisive mo-ment to elapse ; they did not press their claims.   If I am asked the question, why ? alas ! I cannot tell.   I was myself, one of the actors of the national drama, and yet I am quite ignorant why it was that we did not then insist upon the recent pledge being redeemed.   I can only account for it by drawing upon the unsuspecting credulity of the Irish heart.   The administration declared itself friendly, and we believed ; they made professions, and they obtained confidence ; the noble generosity of the Irish disposition could not bear to doubt where it entertained affec-tion ; or, perhaps, the very novelty of the voice of kindness had its charms.   The Irish had been so long used to obloquy and harshness, that they received as a boon, deserving of gratitude, the mere language of conciliation. The result was, that the favourable moment of compelling that administration either to emancipate or to resign, was passed by, and our servitude continues to this hour.

Let us profit by those lessons—from the errors of those periods ; let our present conduct be free ; our course is plain and simple. It consists not in relaxing, but in redoubling our efforts —in pressing forward again as a people should do who deserve liberty. Let us enter into no collateral discussions, no dishonourable stipulations. Under the banner of " The Simple Repeal," Ireland has already once gloriously triumphed. It is a word of good omen. Perhaps she is fated again to progress in the cause of her freedom, under the same standard. "The Simple Repeal" should be re-echoed from north to south, from east to west ; and should we again fail, we shall, at least, have the consolation to know, that we deserved success, and that the failure cannot be attributed to us.

But shall we fail ? Think you are we to owe our freedom to Lord Castlereagh and to Lord Sidmouth ? Let us, my lord, beware of raising too high the expectations of the country. In such a people as the Irish, the effects of disappointment may be terrific. They are too apt to believe that which they wish. They are too prone to rely ; and when the hour of political treachery has come; when the promised "graces" are withdrawn from light, the sudden violence of disappointed expectation is not likely to be controlled by the influence of reason. Already we have seen the effects of blasting the hopes of the Irish people. In the year 1794, Lord Fitzwilliam arrived in Ireland, with conciliation and Emancipation in his train ; he proclaimed our freedom as at hand ; the Irish parliament sung responsive ; there was not a dissentient voice; unanimity prevailed in both houses : the Catholic Bill was actually brought in under the most favourable auspices ; if it had passed, the Union was hopeless. Mr. Pitt, who prepared for that measure from a distance, saw the necessary consequence of abolishing religious dissensions in Ireland ; the promised liberality was withdrawn ; Lord Fitzwilliam was recalled ; and, in the space of one short month, that very parliament which bid the Catholics arise to freedom, and the country to concord, declared, that dissensions should be perpetual, and slavery eternal.

History relates the sequel. In a short time the land was deluged by native blood, and rebellion reared its horrid crest. My Lord Castlereagh interposed, and terminated the scene. Accord-

ing to the plot of the original projectors, by the Union. That
same Castlereagh again governs. Is it safe, my lord, is it prudent, to exaggerate the people's hopes, to give them anything
like a certainty, which may meet nothing but disappointment?
Let us spare our country from the horrid consequences of outraged feelings. This is the last resort of public liberty in Europe
—the only country where the sword alone, the tyrant's law, does
not prevail. I, my lord, for one, am determined not to survive
the representative system of government in this country. Surely
we ought not to endanger it, by rousing those angry passions which
must result from betrayed confidence. We should warn the people not to believe over much those who are hackneyed in duplicity and treachery.

The opposition to Catholic Emancipation has assumed a new
shape ; bigotry and intolerance have been put to the blush, or
covered with ridicule ; every body laughs at Jack Giffard and
Paddy Duignan ; and their worthy compeer and colleague in
England, Sir William Scott, does no longer venture to meet,
with adverse front, the justice of our cause. He may, indeed,
talk of setting our question at rest—he may declaim upon the
moral inferiority of the Irish Catholics ; but let him rest assured,
that so long as his children—if he have any—so long as the
swarthy race of his Scotts are placed, by law, on any superiority
to the Irish Catholics, so long will it be impossible to put the
question to rest. It never can—it never shall rest, save in unqualified, unconditional Emancipation. As to the moral inferiority, I shall not dispute the point with him, but I trust no
Catholic judge will ever be found in this country with such an
accommodating disposition as to decide the precise same question
in two different ways, as we are told that learn d gentl man has
done, with the question of " paper blockades." Let nim, I am
sure I consent, direct his sapient opposition, in his present prudent course of retarding the discussion of the right and justice
of our claims, by introducing other topics. The points of delay
—the resting places are obvious ; and when the present are exhausted, I rely on the malignity of our oppressors to invent new
terms for this purpose.

First, there was the Veto—that, indeed, was soon put down
by the unanimous voice of the Catholic people, who, besides
other reasons, really could not see, in the actual selection made
by the Irish government of persons to fill the offices belonging
of right to them, anything to tempt t m to confer on that
government the nomination of upwards thirty other offices of

emolument and honour. If hostility to the Irish people be a recognized recommendation to all other employments, is it likely that, in one alone, virtue and moral fitness should obtain the appointment? It was too gross and glaring a presumption in an administration, avowing its abhorrence for every thing Irish, to expect to be allowed to interfere with the religious discipline of the Irish Catholic Church.

Driven from any chance of the Veto, our enemies next suggested "the arrangement," as it was called; but this half measure had but few supporters. It was not sufficiently strong for the zealous intolerants; its advantages were not so obvious to the profligate; it was met by this plain reply—that we knew of no real inconvenience that could possibly arise from the present system of the government of our church; but if any existed, it were fitter to be treated of by the venerable prelates of that church, who understand the subject best, than by ministers who wished to turn every thing into an engine of state policy.

"The arrangement" was then soon forgotten, and now, my lord, we have new terms stated—those are "sanctions and securities." We are now told we cannot be emancipated without "sanctions and securities." What are "sanctions?" They are calculated, I presume, to do a great deal of mischief, because they are quite unintelligible. As to "securities," indeed I can understand that word; and I am quite ready to admit that *securities* are necessary; they are necessary against the effects upon a passive, but high-minded people—of continued insult and prolonged oppression. They are necessary, in a sinking state, against the domestic disturbances and organized disaffection which prevail in England—against the enormous and increasing power of the enemy—against dilapidated resources, expiring commerce, depreciated currency, and accumulating expenditure—against the folly, the incapacity, the want of character of the administration—against all those evils of which there is courage to speak—against that domestic insult, respecting which it is prudent to be silent —against all these, "securities" are necessary, and they are easy to be found—they are to be found in conciliation and emancipation—their rectitude and justice. The brave, the generous, the enthusiastic people of Ireland are ready to place themselves in the breach that has been made in their country; they claim the post of honour, that is, the post of utmost danger; they are ready to *secure* the throne and the constitution, and all they require in return is, to be recognized as men and human beings in this their native land.

Do not, then, I would say to any minister— do not presume to insult them, by attempting to treat them as maniacs, to be secured only by ropes and chains. Alas! their only insanity is their devotion to you. Tell them not that the more they are free the less will they be grateful ; tell them not that the less you have to fear from their discontent, the more strictly will you bind them. Oppress them if you please, but hesitate before you deem it prudent thus to insult their first, their finest feelings.

Having disposed of "Veto, arrangement, sanctions, and securities," there remains but one resource for intolerance ; the classic Castlereagh has struck it out ; it consists in—what do you think? Why, in "hitches." Yes, "hitches" is the elegant word which is now destined to protract our degradation. It is in vain that our advocates have increased ; in vain have our foes been converted ; in vain has William Wellesley Pole become our warm admirer. Oh, how beautiful he must have looked advocating the Catholic cause! and his conversion, too, has been so satisfactory—he has accounted for it upon such philosophic principles. Yes, he has gravely informed us that he was all his life a man detesting committees ; you might see by him that the name of a committee discomposed his nerves and excited his most irritable feelings ; at the sound of a committee he was roused to madness. 'Now, the Catholics had insisted upon acting by a committee, the naughty Papists had used nothing but profane committees, and, of course, he proclaimed his hostility. But in proportion as he disliked committees, so did he love and approve of aggregate meetings — *respectable* aggregate meetings! Had there been a chamber at the Castle large enough for an aggregate meeting he would have given it. Who does not see that it is quite right to doat upon aggregate meetings and detest committees, by law, logic, philosophy, and science of legislation? All recommend the one and condemn the other ; and, at length, the Catholics have had the good sense to call their committee a board, to make their aggregate meetings more frequent. They, therefore, deserve Emancipation ; and, with the blessing of God, he (Mr. Pole) would confer it on them! (laughter and cheers.)

But, seriously, let us recollect that Wellesley Pole is the brother of one of our most excellent friends—of Marquis Wellesley, who had so gloriously exerted himself in our cause--who had manfully abandoned one administration because he could not procure our liberty, and rejected power under any other, unless formed on the basis of Emancipation ; and who had, before this Luur in which I speak, earned another unfading laurel, and the eternal affection of the Irish people, by his motion in the House of Lords.   The eloquence and zeal and high character of that noble marquis seemed all that was wanting to ensure, at no remote period, our success.   He knows little of the Irish heart who imagines that his disinterested services will ever be forgotten ; no, they are graved on the soul of Irish gratitude, and will ever live in the memory of the finest people on the earth.   Lord Castlereagh, too, has declared in our favour, with the prudent reserve of " the hitches ;" he is our friend, and has been so these last twenty years—our *secret friend*—as he says so, upon his honour as a gentleman, we are bound to believe him.   If it be a merit in the minister of a great nation to possess profound discretion, this merit Lord Castlereagh possesses in a supereminent degree.   Why, he has preserved this secret with the utmost success.   Who ever suspected that he had such a secret in his keeping ?   The whole tenor of his life, every action of his negatived the idea of his being our friend ; he spoke against us—he voted against us—he wrote and he published against us ; and it turns out now that he did all this merely to show how well he could keep a secret.   Oh, admirable contriver ! oh, most successful placeman ! most discreet and confidential of ministers !

But what are his " hitches ?"   They constitute another " secret."   I think, however, I understand them.   In the morning papers of this day, there appeared a call upon the Protestants of the county of Sligo to come forward in support of the Establishment.   It looks like the tocsin of intolerance ; the name signed to it is John Irwin.   Who this person is I know not, and I have not had time to inquire.   If he be an Irish Protestant gentleman of independence, I respect, whilst I pity his errors and his prejudices ; I would apply no other remedy to him but the voice of mild reasoning and argument, shaped by the spirit of conciliation.   If he be an hireling of the administration, and that this is the first demonstration of the " hitches," I proclaim his miserable attempt to the contempt of the enlightened Protestants of Ireland—its fate is certain ; the government may give it a wretched importance, but they never can afford it strength : they may give it "sanction," but they cannot procure " security" for bigotry.   The Protestants, Presbyterians, and the Quakers of Ireland, have too recently evinced the noble liberality of their sentiments—their sense of our wrongs, and their sympathy in the sufferings of their brethren, who are, in their turn, ready to die in their defence.   The Irish

Protestants of every denomination are too just and too wise to be duped into the yell of bigotry. The result of the attempt is certain. Even in 1792, when intolerance stood in formidable array, a similar effort to stem our cause only covered the projectors and actors with immortal ridicule. Mr. Byrne and Mr Keogh proceeded then as we shall now proceed; and we have the advantage of being cheered by the great majority of those very Protestants whom the intolerants seek to dispose against us.

I said I understood Castlereagh's "hitches," and I proclaim this as one of them; I know, too, we shall have new persecutions. Our legal persecutors, who hunt us with a keenness only increased by their disappointment, and rendered more rancorous by our prospect of success—good and godly men—are at this moment employed in projecting fresh scenes of persecution. Every part of the press that has dared to be free will surely be punished, and public spirit and liberality will, in every case that can be reached by the arts of state persecution, expiate its offence in a prison. Believe me, my prophetic fears are not vain: I know the managers well, and place no confidence in their *holy seeming*. Again, England affords another opportunity of extending the "hitches," under the pretence of making laws to prevent rebellion there; the administration will suspend the habeas corpus, for the purpose of crushing emancipation here; and thus will illustrate the contrast between the very words which would require twelve simpletons to swear meant the same thing. The new laws occasioned by English rioters will pass harmless over their heads, and fall only upon you. It would be inconsistent if Castlereagh, the worthy successor of Clare and John Foster, used any other plan towards Ireland. The "hitches," the "hitches," plainly mean all that can be raised of venal outcry against us, and all that can be enacted of arbitrary law, to prevent our discussions.

Still, still we have resources—we have rich resources in those affectionate sentiments of toleration which our Irish Protestant brethren have proudly exhibited during the present year. The Irish Protestants will not abandon or neglect their own work; it is they who have placed us on our present elevation—their support has rendered the common cause of our common country triumphant. Our oppressors, yielding an unwilling assent to the request of the Protestants of Ireland, may compensate themselves by abusing us in common; they may style us agitators—Mr. Canning calls us *agitators with ulterior views*—but those Protestant agitators are the best friends to the security and peace of the co

try ; and to us, Popish agitators—for I own it, my lord, I am
an agitator, and we solemnly promise to continue so, until
the period of unqualified emancipation—until "the simple
repeal." As to us, agitators amongst the Catholics, we are
become too much accustomed to calumny to be terrified at it ;
but how have we deserved reproach and obloquy ? How have
we merited calumny ? Of myself, my lord, I shall say nothing
—I possess no talents for the office ; but no man shall prevent
the assertion of my rigid honesty.   I am, it is true, the lowliest
of the agitators ; but there are, amongst them, men of the first-
rate talents, and of ample fortunes—men of the most ancient
families, and of hereditary worth—men of public spirit and of
private virtue ; and, above all, men of persevering, undaunted,
and unextinguishable love of their country—of their poor,
degraded, insulted country—to that country, will I say of all
the agitators, with the exception of my humble self—

" Boast, Erin, boast them tameless, frank, and free."

Out of the hands of those agitators, however, the government is desirable to take the people, and the government is
right.   Out of the sphere of your influence, my lord, the people
can never be taken, for reasons which, because you are present,
I shall not mention, but which are recognised by the hearts of
the Irish nation.   (Loud cheering.)   But out of our hands the
people may easily be taken.   They are bound to us only by the
ties of mutual sufferings and mutual sympathies.   We are the
mere straws which are borne upon the torrent of public wrongs
and public griefs.   Restore their rights to the people—conciliate the Irish nation, which is ready to meet you more than half
way, and the power of the agitators is gone in an instant.   I do
certainly feel the alarm expressed at the agitation of the question
of Catholic rights as a high compliment ; it clearly points out
the course we ought to pursue.   Let us rouse the Irish people,
from one extreme to the other of the island, in this constitutional cause.   Let the Catholic combine with the Protestant,
and the Protestant with the Catholic, and one generous exertion
sets every angry feeling at rest, and banishes, for ever, dissension
and division.   The temptation to invasion will be taken away
from the foreign enemy—the pretext and the means of internal
commotion will be snatched from the domestic foe—our country,
combined in one great phalanx, will defy every assault, and we
shall have the happiness of obtaining real security, by that course
of conciliation, which deserves the approbation of every sound

judgment, and must ensure the applause of every feeling heart·—
we shall confer an honour on ourselves, and ensure the safety of
our country.

THE "NO-POPERY" CRY.

THE increased virulence of the "No-Popery" feeling about this time aroused the Catholic
Board to greater activity, and a resolution was passed to the following effect:—

" Resolved—That the Board do meet on the first and third Saturday
of every month till November, and that the Secretary do write circular
letters to all the members, announcing *their serious apprehensions that
a religious persecution is about to commence in Ireland, apparently
sanctioned by the administration ;* and inculcating the necessity of frequent deliberations, and constant activity on the part of the Catholic
body, in obviating the approaching calamity, and in the firm assertion
of their rights, at this fearful and important crisis."

The propriety of passing such a resolution was much questioned at the time, by those
who had installed themselves as "patrons," as it were, of the Catholics; but there is no
doubt that circumstances fully bore out its averments, and not only entirely justified it,
but even rendered it necessary, as a means of awakening to their danger, the threatened
objects of this new persecution.

The anticipated danger was not only from the chances of open, undisguised persecution
but from the design, now again revived, and confidently spoken of as about to be pushed
by the minister, of bringing forward some measure of state-interference with Catholic
ecclesiastical matters, either by the notorious " Veto" proposition, or some other equally
to be deprecated and resisted.

A stout response to the alarm-cry from Dublin was promptly returned from various
parts of the country, but especially from Limerick. On Friday, the 24th of July in this
year (1812), a large meeting of the Catholics of the city and county was held for the purpose, at the Commercial Buildings, George's-street, Limerick, at which Mr. O'Connell
then upon circuit, attended, and made the speech we are about to give. T. R. Ryan, of
Scarteen, Esq., was in the chair, and the meeting was opened with a speech from Mr. William Roche, the same gentleman who represented the city of Limerick, on Repeal principles, from the passing of the Reform Bill until 1841. After expressing general concurrence
with the proceedings of the Catholic Board in Dublin, confident hopes of the success of the
cause, in the next session of parliament — gratitude to its friends in that body — and
aversion to the idea of what were called " securities," being given in return for Catholic
emancipation, he read the resolutions that had been prepared, and moved their adoption.
We give the chief among them ·—

" Resolved—That however injurious the policy which laboured to sever
the Prince from the people, the recent declarations in parliament revive
our long-cherished hopes, that that illustrious personage will adhere to
those principles, which, by establishing the harmony and happiness of the
subject, would best ensure the stability of the throne, and the prosperity
of the empire.

" That at a time when continental Europe is yielding her last sigh, and all the rivulets of rational liberty are nearly lost in the flood of universal domination ; and when these countries, the last refuge of European freedom, are threatened with no less than total annihilation, we consider the continuance of political disabilities as tending to paralyze the energies of the state, and to further the views of our implacable enemy.

" And we, therefore, consider, that it would be a criminal apathy in us, at this perilous crisis, to cease our earnest application to the legislature, to embrace, within the protection of equal laws, all and every description of his Majesty's subjects.

" That having, with regret, observed a design to mar the progress of our just claims, by propositions intended solely to raise alarms against us, we feel called upon to declare to the empire and to the world—

" *That we will enter into no compromise for our rights, incompatible with the integrity of our religion.*

" That the best security we can give, is our attachment to the constitution, which we are solemnly and irrevocably sworn to defend—our proved invariable fidelity to the laws, guaranteed by our properties, our lives, and the very principles of the religion we profess.

These, with other resolutions, were seconded by Mr. A. F. O'Neill, and passed unanimously.

Counsellor O'Connell then rose, (adds the *Limerick Evening Post*, whose report we quote,) and delivered a speech, the most brilliant and argumentative we have ever heard. This accomplished and powerful orator continued for upwards of an hour to address the assembly as follows, and was cheered, almost at the close of every sentence, with loud and rapturous applause :—

I feel it my duty, as a professed agitator, to address the meeting. It is merely in the exercise of my office of agitation, that I think it necessary to say a few words. For any purpose of illustration or argument, further discourse is useless : all the topics which the present period suggested, have been treated of with sound judgment, and a rare felicity of diction, by my respected and talented friend (Mr. Roche); all I shall do is, to add a few observations to what has fallen from that gentleman ; and whilst I sincerely admire the happy style in which he has treated those subjects, I feel deep regret at being unable to imitate his excellent discourse.

And, first, let me concur with him in congratulating the Catholics of Limerick on the progress our great cause has made since we were last assembled. Since that period our cause has not rested for support on the efforts of those alone who were immediately interested ; no, our Protestant brethren throughout the land have added their zealous exertions for our emancipation. They have, with admirable patriotism, evinced their desire to conciliate by serving us, and I am sure I do but justice to the

Catholics, when I proclaim our gratitude, as written on our hearts, and to be extinguished only with our lives. (Hear, hear.)

Nor has the support and the zeal of our Protestant brethren been vain and barren. No, it has been productive of great and solid advantages; it has procured, for the cause of religious liberty, the respect even of the most bigoted of our opponents; it has struck down English prejudice; it has convinced the mistaken honest; it has terrified the hypocritical knaves; and finally, it has pronounced for us, by a great and triumphant majority, from one of the branches of the legislature, the distinct recognition of the propriety and the necessity of conceding justice to the great body of the Irish people. (Hear, hear, hear.)

Let us, therefore, rejoice in our mutual success; let us rejoice in the near approach of freedom; let us rejoice in the prospect of soon shaking off our chains, and of the speedy extinction of our grievances. But above all, let us rejoice at the means by which these happy effects have been produced; let us doubly rejoice, because they afford no triumph to any part of the Irish nation over the other—that they are not the result of any contention amongst ourselves; but constitute a victory, obtained for the Catholics by the Protestants—that they prove the liberality of the one, and require the eternal gratitude of the other —that they prove and promise the eternal dissolution of ancient animosities and domestic feuds, and afford to every Christian and to every patriot, the cheering certainty of seeing peace, harmony, and benevolence prevail in that country, where a wicked and perverted policy has so long and so fatally propagated and encouraged dissension, discord, and rancour. (Loud cheering.)

We owe it to the liberality of the Irish Protestants—to the zeal of the Irish Presbyterians—to the friendly exertion of the Irish Quakers; we owe, to the cordial re-union of every sect and denomination of Irish Christians, the progress of our cause. They have procured for us the solemn and distinct promise and pledge of the House of Commons—they almost obtained for us a similar declaration from the House of Lords. It was lost by the petty majority of one—it was lost by a majority, not of those who listened to the absurd prosings of Lord Eldon, to the bigoted and turbid declamation of that English Chief Justice, whose sentiments so forcibly recal the memory of the star-chamber; not of those who were able to compare the vapid or violent folly of the one party, with the statesman-like sentiments, the profound arguments, the splendid eloquence of the Marquis Wellesley. (Hear, hear.) Not of those who heard the reasonings of our other illustrious advocates; but by a majority of men who acted upon preconceived opinions, or, from a distance, carried into effect their bigotry, or, perhaps, worse propensities—who availed themselves of that absurd privilege of the peerage, which enables those to decide who have not heard—which permits men to pronounce upon subjects they have not discussed—and allows a final determination to precede argument. (Hear.)

It was not, however, to this privilege alone, that our want of success was to be attributed. The very principle upon which the present administration has been formed, was brought into immediate action, and with success ; for, in the latter periods of the present reign, every administration has had a distinct principle upon which it was formed, and which serves the historian to explain all its movements. Thus, the principle of the Pitt administration was—*to deprive the people of all share in the government, and to vest all power and authority in the crown.* In short, Pitt's views amounted to unqualified despotism. This great object he steadily pursued through his ill-starred career. It is true he encouraged commerce, but it was for the purposes of taxation ; and he used taxation for the purposes of corruption ; he assisted the merchants, as long as he could, to grow rich, and they lauded him ; he bought the people with their own money, and they praised him. Each succeeding day produced some new inroad on the constitution; and the alarm which he excited, by reason of the bloody workings of the French revolution, enabled him to rule the land with uncontrolled sway; he had bequeathed to his successor the accumulated power of the crown—

power which must be great, if it can sustain the nonentities of the present administration. (Loud and continued cheering.)

The principle of Pitt's administration was despotism—the principle of Perceval's administration was peculating bigotry—bigoted peculation ! In the name of the Lord he plundered the people. (A laugh.) Pious and enlightened statesman ! he would take their money only for the good of their souls. (Bursts of laughter.)

The principle of the present administration is still more obvious. It has unequivocally disclosed itself in all its movements—it is simple and single—it consists in *falsehood.* Falsehood is the bond and link that connects this ministry in office. Some of them pretend to be our friends—you know it is not true—they are only our worse enemies for the hypocrisy. They declare that the Catholic question is no longer opposed by the cabinet—that it is left to the discretion of each individual retainer.

The fact is otherwise—and their retainers, though not *com manded*, as formerly, are carefully advised to vote against us. (Hear, hear.)

The minister, Lord Castlereagh, is reported to have said in the House of Commons, that in the year 1797 and 1798, there was no torture in Ireland, to the knowledge of government! Is it really possible that such an assertion was used? You hear of it with astonishment. All Ireland must shudder, that any man could be found thus to assert. Good God! of what materials must that man be made who could say so? I restrain my indignation—I withhold all expressions of surprise—the simple statement that such an assertion was used, exceeds, in reply, the strongest language of reprobation. But there is no man so stupid as not to recognise the principle which I have so justly attributed to this administration.

What! No torture! Great God! No torture! Within the walls of your city was there no torture? Could not Colonel Vereker have informed Lord Castlereagh, that the lash resounded in the streets even of Limerick, and that the human groan assailed the wearied ear of humanity? Yet, I am ready to give the gallant colonel every credit he deserves; and, therefore, I recal to your grateful recollection the day when he risked his life to punish one of the instruments of torture. (Hear, hear.) Colonel Vereker can tell whether it be not true, that in the streets of your city, the servant of his relation, Mrs. Rosslewen, was not tortured—whether he was not tortured first, for the crime of having expressed a single sentiment of compassion, and next because Colonel Vereker interfered for him. (Hear, hear).

But there is an additional fact, which is not so generally known, which, perhaps, Colonel Vereker himself does not know, and which I have learned from a highly respectable clergyman, that this sad victim of the system of torture, which Lord Castlereagh denied, was, at the time he was scourged, in an infirm state of health— that the flogging inflicted on him deprived him of all understanding, and that within a few months he died insane, and without having recovered a shadow of reason. (Hear.)

But why, out of the myriads of victims, do I select a solitary instance? Because he was a native of your city, and his only offence an expression of compassion. I might tell you, did you not already know it, that in Dublin there were, for weeks, three permanent triangles, constantly supplied with the victims of a promiscuous choice made by the army, the yeomanry, the police constables, and the Orange lodges ; that the shrieks of the tortured must have literally resounded in the state apartments of the Castle; and that along by the gate of the Castle yard, a human being, naked, tarred, feathered, with one ear cut off, and the blood streaming from his lacerated back, has been hunted by a troop of barbarians!

Why do I disgust you with these horrible recollections? You want not the proof of the principle of delusion on which the present administration exists.   In your own affairs you have abundant evidence of it.   The fact is, that the proxies in the Lords would never have produced a majority even of one against Lord Wellesley's motion, but for the exertion of the vital principle of the administration. · The ministry got the majority of one.   The pious Lord Eldon, with all his conscience and his calculations, and that immaculate distributor of criminal justice, Lord Ellenborough, were in a majority of one.   By what holy means think you?   Why, by the aid of that which cannot be described in dignified language—by the aid of a LIE—a false, positive, palpable LIE !

This manœuvre was resorted to—a scheme worthy of its authors —they had perceived the effects of the manly and dignified resolutions of the 18th of June.   These resolutions had actually terrified our enemies, whilst they cheered those noble and illustrious friends who had preferred the wishes and wants of the people of Ireland to the gratification of paltry and disgraceful minions.   The manœuvre—the scheme, was calculated to get rid of the effect of those resolutions, nay, to turn their force against us, and thus was the pious fraud effected.   (Hear.)

There is, you have heard, a newspaper, in the permanent pay of peculation and corruption, printed in London, under the name of the *Courier*, a paper worthy the meridian of Constantinople, at its highest tide of despotism.   This paper was directed to assert the receipt of a letter from Dublin, from excellent authority. declaring, I know not how many peers, sons of peers, and baronets had retracted the resolutions of the 18th of June; that those resolutions were carried by surprise, and that they had been actually rescinded at a subsequent meeting.

Never did human baseness invent a more gross untruth ; never did a more unfounded lie fall from the father of falsehood ; never did human turpitude submit to become the vehicle of so "glaring" a dereliction of truth.   But the *Courier* received its pay, and it was ready to earn the wages of its prostitution.   It did so—it published the foul falsehoods, with the full knowledge of their false-

nood; it published them in two editions, the day before and the day of the debate—at a period when inquiry was useless—when a contradiction from authority could not arrive; at that moment this base trick was played, through the intervention of that newspaper, upon the British public!

Will that public go too far, when they charge this impure stratagem on those whose purposes it served? Why, even in this country, the administration deems it necessary to give, for the support of one miserable paper, two places—one of five, and the other of eight hundred a year—the stamp duty remitted— the proclamations paid for as advertisements—and a permanent bonus of one thousand pounds per annum! If the bribe here be so high, what must it be in England, where the toil is so much greater? And, think you, then, that the *Courier* published, un- sanctioned by its paymasters, this useful lie?

I come now to the next stage in the system of delusion; it is that which my friend, Mr. O'Neil has noticed. He has power- fully exposed to you the absurdity of crediting the ministerial newspapers, when they informed you that the member for Lime- rick had stated in the House of Commons, that the commercial interests of Limerick were opposed to the Catholic claims. Sir, for my part, I entirely agree with Mr. O'Neil; I am sure Colo- nel Vereker said no such thing; he is a brave man, and, there- fore, a man of truth; he is probably a pleasant friend, and he has those manly traits about him, which make it not unpleasant to oppose him as an enemy; I like the candour of his character, and our opposition to him should assume the same frankness, and openness, and perfect determination. He well knows that a great part of the commercial interests of Limerick is in the hands of the Catholics—that the Quakers of Limerick, who pos- sess almost the residue of the trade, are friendly to us, and that, with the exception of the " tag, rag, and bob-tail" of the corpo- ration—(loud laughter) there is not to be found amongst the men who ought to be his constituents, a single exception to li- berality. (Repeated applause.)

There remains another delusion; it is the darling deception of this ministry—that which has reconciled the toleration of Lord Castlereagh with the intolerance of Lord Liverpool; it is that which has sanctified the connection between both, and the place-procuring, prayer-mumbling Wilberforce; it consists in *sanctions* and *securities*. The Catholics may be emancipated, say ministers in public, but they must give *securities;* by securities, say the same ministers in private, to their supporting bigots we

mean nothing definite, but something that shall certainly be inconsistent with the Popish religion—nothing shall be a security
which they can possibly concede—and we shall deceive them and
secure you, whilst we carry the air of liberality and toleration.
(Hear.)

.And can there be any honest man deceived by the cant and
cry for securities?—is there any man that believes that there is
safety in oppression, contumely, and insult, and that security is
necessary against protection, liberality, and conciliation?—does
any man really suppose, that there is no danger from the continuance of unjust grievance and exasperating intolerance; and
that security is wanting against the effects of justice and perfect
toleration?   Who is it that is idiot enough to believe, that he is
quite safe in dissension, disunion, and animosity, and wants a
protection against harmony, benevolence, and charity?—that in
hatred there is safety—in affection, ruin?—that now, that we
are excluded from the constitution, we may be loyal—but that
if we were entrusted, personally, in its safety, we shall wish to
destroy it?   (Hear, hear.)

But this is a pitiful delusion : there was, indeed, a time, when
" sanctions and securities" might have been deemed necessary—
when the Catholic was treated as an enemy to man and to God
—when his property was the prey of legalized plunder—his religion, and its sacred ministers, the object of legalized persecution!
—when, in defiance and contempt of the dictates of justice, and
the faith of treaties—and I attest the venerable city, in which I
stand, that solemn treaties were basely violated—*the English faction in the land turned the Protestant into an intolerant and murderous bigot, in order that it might, in security, plunder that very
Protestant, and oppress his and our common country!*   Poor neglected Ireland !   At that period, securities might be supposed
wanting; the people of Ireland—the Catholic population of Ireland were then as brave and as strong, comparatively, as they are
at present; and the country then afforded advantages for the de-
sultory warfare of a valiant peasantry, which, fortunately, have
since been exploded by increasing cultivation.

At the period to which I allude, the Stuart family was still in
existence ; they possessed a strong claim to the exaggerating al
legiance and unbending fidelity of the Irish people.   Every right
that hereditary descent could give the royal race of Stuart, they
possessed—in private life, too, they were endeared to the Irish,
because they were, even the worst of them, gentlemen.   But
they had still stronger claims on the sympathy and generosity

of the Irish : they had been exalted, and were fallen—they had possessed thrones and kingdoms, and were then in poverty and humiliation. All the enthusiastic sympathies of the Irish heart were roused for them—and all the powerful motives of personal interest bore, in the same channel, the restoration of their rights —the triumph of their religion, the restitution of their ancient inheritances, would then have been the certain and immediate consequences of the success of the Stuart family, in their pretensions to the throne.

At the period to which I allude, the Catholic clergy were bound by no oath of allegiance ; to be a dignitary of the Catholic church in Ireland, was a transportable felony—and the oath of allegiance was so intermingled with religious tenets, that no clergyman or layman of the Catholic persuasion could possibly take it. At that period, the Catholic clergy were all educated in foreign countries, under the eye of the Pope, and within the inspection of the house of Stuart. From fifty-eight colleges and convents, on the Continent, did the Catholic clergy repair to meet, for the sake of their God, poverty, persecution, contumely, and, not unfrequently, death, in their native land. (Hear, hear.) They were often hunted like wild beasts, and never could claim any protection from the law ! (Hear, hear.) That—that was a period, when securities might well have been necessary—when sanctions and securities might well have been requisite.

But, what was the fact ?—what was the truth which history vouches ? Why, that the clergy and laity of the Irish Catholics, having once submitted to the new government—having once plighted their ever unbroken faith to King William and his successors—having once submitted to that great constitutional principle, that in extreme cases the will of the people is the sole law—that in extreme cases the people have the clear and undoubted right to cashier a tyrant, and provide a substitute on the throne—the Irish Catholics, having fought for their legitimate sovereign, until he, himself, and not they, fled from the strife— adopted, by treaty, his English successor, though not his heir— transferred to that successor, and the inheritors of his throne, their allegiance. They have preserved their covenant—with all the temptations and powerful motives to disaffection, they fulfilled their part of the social contract, even in despite of its violation by the other party. (Loud and continued applause.)

How do I prove the continued loyalty of the Catholics of Ireland under every persecution ? I do not appeal for any proofs to their own records, however genuine —I appeal merely to the testimony of their rulers and their enemies—(hear, hear)— I appeal to the letters of Primate Boulter—to the state-papers of the humane and patriotic Chesterfield. I have their loyalty through the admissions of every secretary and governor of Ireland, until it is finally and conclusively put on record by the legislature of Ireland itself. The relaxing statutes expressly declare, that the penal laws ought to be repealed—not from motives of policy or growing liberality, but (I quote the words,) "because of the long-continued and uninterrupted loyalty of the Catholics." This is the consummation of my proof—and I defy the veriest disciple of the doctrine of delusion to overturn it. (Applause.)

But as the Catholics were faithful in those dismal and persecuting periods—when they were exasperated by the emaciating cruelty of barbarous law and wretched policy—as they were then faithful, notwithstanding every temporal and every religious temptation and excitement to the contrary, is it in human credulity to believe my Lord Castlereagh, when he asserts that *securities* are *now* necessary? Now, that the ill-fated house of Stuart is extinct—and had it not been extinct I should have been silent as to what their claims were—*now*, that the will of the people, and the right of hereditary succession are not to be separated—now, that the Catholic clergy are educated in Ireland, and are all bound by their oaths of allegiance to that throne and constitution, which, in the room of persecution, gives them protection and security—*now*, that all claims upon forfeited property are totally extinguished in the impenetrable night of obscurity and oblivion—*now*, that the Catholic nobility and gentry are in the enjoyment of many privileges and franchises, and that the full participation of the constitution opens upon us in close and cheering prospect—shall we be told that securities are now expedient, though they were heretofore unnecessary? Oh! it is a base and dastardly insult upon our understandings, and on our principles, and one which each of us would, in private life, resent—as in public we proclaim it to the contempt and execration of the universe. (Great applause.)

Long as I have trespassed on you, I cannot yet close: I have a word to address to you upon your own conduct. The representative for your city, Colonel Vereker, has openly opposed your liberties—he has opposed even the consideration of your claims. You are beings, to be sure, with human countenances, and the limbs of men—but you are not men—the iron has entered into your souls, and branded the name of slave upon them.

if you submit to be thus trampled on ! His opposition to you is decided—meet him with a similar, and, if possible, a superior hostility. You deserve not freedom, you, citizens of Limerick, with the monuments of the valour of your ancestors around you—you are less than men, if my feeble tongue be requisite to rouse you into activity. (Applause.) Your city is, at present nearly a close borough—do but will it, and you make it free (Continued applause.)

I know legal obstacles have been thrown in your way—I know that, for months past, the Recorder has sat alone at the sessions —that he has not only tried cases, in the absence of any other magistrate, which he is authorised by law to do, but that he has solely opened and adjourned the sessions, which, in my opinion, he is clearly unwarranted in doing ; he has, by this means, I know, delayed the registry of your freeholds, because two magistrates are necessary for that purpose : I have, however, the satisfaction to tell you, that the Court of King's Bench will, in the next term, have to determine on the legality of his conduct, and of that of the other charter magistrates, who have banished themselves, I understand, from the Sessions' Court, since the registry has been spoken of ! They shall be served with the regular notices ; and, depend upon it, this scheme cannot long retard you (Great applause.)

I speak to you on this subject as a lawyer—you can best judge in what estimation my opinion is amongst you—but such as it is, I pledge it to you, that you can easily obviate the present ob stacles to the registry of your freeholds. I can also assure you that the constitution of your city is perfectly free—that the sons of freemen, and all those who have served an apprenticeship to a freeman, are all entitled to their freedom, and to vote for the representation of your city. (Hear, hear, hear.)

I can tell you more : that if you bring your candidate to a poll, your adversary will be deprived of any aid from non-resident or occasional freemen ; we will strike off his list the freemen from Gort and from Galway, the freemen from the band, and many from the battalion of the city of Limerick militia. (Loud cries of "hear, hear.")

In short, the opening of the borough is a matter of little diffi culty. If you will but form a committee, and collect funds, in your opulent city, you will soon have a representative ready to obey your voice—you cannot want a candidate. If the emancipation bill passes next sessions, as it is so likely to do, and that no other candidate offers, I myself will bring your present number to the poll. (Loud applause.) I, probably, will have little chance of success—but I will have the satisfaction of showing this city and the county, what the freeborn mind might achieve if it were properly seconded. (Here the eloquent and patriotic speaker was interrupted for some minutes, by thundering applause.)

I conclude by conjuring you to exert yourselves ; waste not your just resentments in idle applause at the prospect I open to you ; let not the feeling of the moment be calumniated as a hasty ebullition of anger ; let it not be transitory, as our resentments generally are, but let us remember ourselves, our children, and our country? (Hear, hear, hear.)

Let me not, however, close, without obviating any calumny that may be flung upon my motives. I can easily pledge myself to you that they are disinterested and pure—I trust they are more. My object in the attainment of emancipation is in nothing personal, save in the feelings which parental love inspires and gratifies. I am, I trust, actuated by that sense of Christianity which teaches us that the first duty of our religion is benevolence and universal charity ; I am, I know, actuated by the determination to rescue our common country from the weakness, the insecurity, which dissension and religious animosity produce and tend to perpetuate ; I wish to see the strength of the island —this unconquered, this unconquerable island—combined to resist the mighty foe of freedom, the extinguisher of civil liberty, who rules the Continent from Petersburgh to the verge of the Irish bayonets in Spain. (Loud and repeated applause.) It is his interest, it is a species of duty he owes to his family—to that powerful house, which he has established on the ruins of the thrones and dominations of Europe—to extinguish, for ever, representative and popular government in these countries ; he has the same direct intent which the Roman general had to invade our beloved country—" Ut libertas veluti et conspectu." His power can be resisted only by combining your physical force with your enthusiastic and undaunted hearts. · (Hear, hear.)

There is liberty amongst you still. I could not talk as I do, of the Liverpools and Castlereaghs, of his court, even if he had the folly to employ such things—I wish he had ; you have the protection of many a salutary law—of that palladium of personal liberty—the trial by jury. I wish to ensure your liberties, to measure your interests on the present order of the state, that we may protect the very men that oppress us. (Loud applause.)

Yes, if Ireland be fairly roused to the battle of the country
nd of freedom, all is safe. Britain has been often conquered :
he Romans conquered her—the Saxons conquered her—the
Normans conquered her—in short, whenever she was invaded,
he was conquered. But our country was never subdued ; we
never lost our liberties in battle, nor did we ever submit to
armed conquerors. It is true, the old inhabitants lost their
country in piece-meal, by fraud and treachery ; they relied upor
he faith of men, who never, never observed a treaty with them,
until a new and mixed race has sprung up, in dissension and
discord ; but the Irish heart and soul still predominate and pervade the sons of the oppressors themselves. The generosity,
the native bravery, the innate fidelity, the enthusiastic love of
whatever is great and noble—those splendid characteristics of
the Irish mind remain as the imperishable relics of our country's
former greatness—of that illustrious period, when she was the
light and the glory of barbarous Europe—when the nations
around sought for instruction and example in her numerous
seminaries—and when the civilization and religion of all Europe
were preserved in her alone. (Continued cheering.)

You will, my friends, defend her—you may die, but you cannot yield to any foreign invader. (Hear, hear.) Whatever be
my fate, I shall be happy, whilst I live, in reviving amongst you
the love and admiration of your native land, and in calling upon
Irishmen—no matter how they may worship their common God
-to sacrifice every contemptible prejudice on the altar of their
common country. (Great applause.) For myself, I shall conclude, by expressing the sentiment that throbs in my heart—I
shall express it in the language of a young bard of Erin,* and
my beloved friend, whose delightful muse has the sound of the
ancient minstrelsy—

> " Still shalt thou be my midnight dream—
> Thy glory still my waking theme ;
> And ev'ry thought and wish of mine,
> Unconquered Erin, shall be thine !"

This speech procured him from the meeting the following compliment :—

" Resolved—That our sincere thanks are hereby returned to Daniel
O'Connell, barrister-at-law, for his luminous and patriotic speech this
day ; as well as for his manly and distinguished exertions at all times, ir
the cause of his country.

* Charles Phillips, Esq., author of the poem entitled "The Emerald Isle," then at the
Irish, subsequently for many years at the English bar, and now one of the District Commissioners of Bankruptcy in England

The legal opinions delivered by Mr. O'Connell in this speech were ALL verified in the courts of law. The city of Limerick, from being a nomination borough, was, by means of legal decisions, thrown open to the popular control, as Mr. O'Connell had pointed out. The expense was enormous, but it was cheerfully borne by the patriotic citizens.* The popu-lous triumph was complete, and Mr. O'Connell had the delightful satisfaction to have roused the sleeper and presided over the victory

Various other Catholic meetings were held in counties and towns of Ireland during the summer and autumn of 1812, at which resolutions to the same general effect as those we have recorded of the Limerick meeting, were unanimously adopted. If in these and other demonstrations of popular opinion in Ireland, one sentiment more than another was pecu-larly marked, it was that of determined hostility to the proposition of giving in exchange for Emancipation any of what were insultingly termed "securities," especially and parti-cularly that of which we shall have soon to treat fully, the "veto" proposition.

Mr. O'Connell was enabled to attend the Cork "city and county" meeting, held on Fri-day, 21st August, at the North Parish Chapel, William Coppinger, jun., Esq., of Barry's Court, in the chair; but the Cork paper (the *Intelligencer*), which contained the proceed-ings, states that it was unable to report with *precision* his speech, and so passed it over entirely, with a few complimentary sentences

In the list of resolutions here passed we find the following:—

" 15th. Resolved—That our cordial thanks are hereby offered to our patriotic fellow-Catholic Counsellor O'Connell, as the tribute of our ad-miration and applause, for his unceasing and energetic exertions in the common cause ; and for his able and eloquent speech delivered here this day

It will thus be seen that the period of the parliamentary recess in the year 1812, was by no means a season of repose and quiet, either to the Catholics or their opponents. The events of the session just gone by had startled and effectually aroused both parties. At a moment when a ministry, generally known to be adverse to all concession, had, after the double shock of the loss of their head and a vote of want of confidence carried against them in the lower house, been suddenly reseated in office, with renewed power, and, as it was natural to sup-pose, unabated inveteracy, Catholic and anti-Catholic in Ireland had beheld, with equal astonishment, a motion favourable to the former, carried by a large majority in the Com-mons, and only lost in the Lords by a majority of one—a defeat in name, but virtually a triumph.

The probabilities were on the side of an actual and entire success in the next session. The grand object therefore, with the one party, was to advance this consummation during the recess by all the means in their power; and, of course, with the other party, to strengthen the old obstructions, and endeavour to create others anew.

The party of the bigots had, however, a fearful advantage in means, and were not deterred from using them by any scrupulosity. We have already alluded to the efforts at reviving the "no Popery" cry. But, successful as these were with the strongly-prejudiced public mind of England, it was determined not to trust to the mere chance of their influence re-acting upon the parliament. The latter was *doomed*—doomed, because of its one act of liberality—no consideration given to its many acts of an opposite nature, not even to the surprising cele-rity with which it had retracted and cancelled the vote of want of confidence before men-tioned

Accordingly, early in the month of October, 1812, the usual proclamation appeared of the dissolution of parliament, and writs were immediately issued for a general election.

----

* The father of the present mayor of Limerick, Mr. Edmund Ryan, subscribed £500; and another young gentleman, a Mr. Patrick Creagh, a similar sum. The Verekers were thrown out; but, alas! the people, in the excess of their enthusiasm, put Spring Rice in his place. What a practical blunder.

The struggle was now transferred to the hustings; and that it was one of no very gentle or moderate character may well be supposed. The government and its agents and supporters stopped at nothing to secure the return of men opposed to concession, and their efforts were very generally successful.

THE CITIZENS OF DUBLIN v. POLICE MAGISTRATES.

BEFORE coming to an occasion when Mr. O'Connell expressed his sentiments upo'. the results of the general election, there is an incident of his legal avocations to be noted.

On Monday, the 19th of October, he and Mr. Finlay appeared as counsel for the prosecutors in the matter of some charges made by a large number of citizens of Dublin against the city police-magistrates, and investigated into by Mr. Sergeant (the late judge) Moore and Mr. Disney, who were appointed by government for that purpose. There was a very crowded attendance to hear the case, being one of considerable interest to the inhabitants of Dublin at large; but, to the astonishment of all present, the commissioners announced that they had determined *not to permit the interference of counsel.*

"It was their impression," said Mr. Sergeant Moore, who made this announcement, "that it was much better to dispense with the assistance of counsel, and to investigate the charges by an examination of witnesses unperverted by colouring or exaggeration of any description. It was even a matter of question to them whether there was not an irregularity in the interference of gentlemen of the bar when the nature and constitution of the committee were taken into consideration."

Counsellor O'Connell observed, that he had no doubt either upon any of the points either of the *regularity* of the interference of counsel, their entire *right* to assist in the present investigation, or the actual and absolute *necessity* of their assistance.

He said that, as a member of the Irish bar, he was fully entitled and empowered to appear before any tribunal whatsoever, on behalf of his majesty's subjects, in any instance wherein their lives, liberties or properties were concerned; and if there was not, as there ought not to be, any question as to *his* title and his right to appear upon that or any other legal occasion, there could, of course, be as little as to the right and title, as well as certainly to the expediency and utility of his learned friend's appearance and assistance.

The fact was, there were the most heinous charges pending against individuals holding high and very important situations; the interests of the community were concerned, the lives and properties of the inhabitants of Dublin were deeply interested; nothing, therefore, ought to be left undone to satisfy the public mind, to make the investigation searching and complete. The whole matter should be sifted to the bottom, and every effort made to arrive at the truth; and for these purposes the attendance and assistance of counsel were imperatively required.

In truth, he considered it little better than a libel upon the bar, to say that its attendance was unnecessary. Surely, if the parties accused were innocent of the heavy charges brought against them, the exertions of a barrister could do them no possible injury. If they were really innocent, as it was asserted, they could not have anything to dread ; but if they were guilty, the exertions of an honest and zealous barrister were peculiarly needed to point out the extent of their delinquency, to leave no branch of their crimes unexplored, to allow no one particular of their misdemeanours to remain unrevealed to the world.

Besides, it was to be recollected, that those parties themselves enjoyed the advantage of legal aid. There were no less than six of the accused who were themselves capable of performing the duty he had undertaken ; and the rest of them possessed the advantage of an acquaintance with the rules of evidence and of an experience and practised dexterity, highly available to them in the conduct of their defence. It would be, therefore, absurd to pretend that they could at all be considered in the light of ordinary persons unskilled in legal proceedings and unfamiliar with them.

And when they were in possession of such advantages, was it not a palpable injustice to attempt to deprive his clients of what would no more than place them upon an equality? It was an absolute and gross injustice so to act. He would most solemnly and energetically protest against the foul play of not allowing the benefits of legal aid upon the one side as upon the other ; and until the commissioners should take it upon themselves to order him to walk out of court, he would not so much surrender his own privileges and his clients' rights as to cease his protest for one moment. He appeared in court as the retained counsel of the memorialists ; and if he were to be disbarred, he could not, of course, help it : but this he would most certainly do—conscious of the extent of his professional privileges, the necessity and entire regularity of his attendance ; if the court should decide against him, he would instantly throw up his brief and advise his clients not to attempt going one step further in this most necessary, most useful, most solemn, and most desirable investigation.

Without legal aid this inquiry would be fruitless—the truth could not be known, the intentions of the legislature and of the government (to whom praise was due for giving that opportunity) should be defeated, the country will be disappointed, the public-spirited individuals who had brought that important sub-

ject before the nation would have been making only a nugatory
effort at the attainment of justice—and he should therefore repeat. that if the court were against him he would instantly and
unhesitatingly throw up his brief, and advise those upon whose
behalf he appeared not to proceed any further.

Again, he would say, the present inquiry was most important.
The criminality it was instituted to examine into, deeply and in-
timately concerned the citizens of Dublin in their lives, liberties,
and properties. His instructions authorized him to declare, that
delinquency of the most enormous magnitude, perpetrated in the
guise and under the pretence of the administration of justice,
would be exhibited to the public in all its enormity. Curious
instances of imposition would be exposed to view. Penalties—
sometimes with ludicrous whimsicality—sometimes with inveterate cruelty. The investigation of such charges as these was a
matter of the most serious and highest importance to the community at large—they required the most serious pains-taking
and solemn attention—they demanded all the consideration of
the commissioners themselves, and (surely if the assistance of a
barrister had ever been found useful in forwarding the ends of justice, in protecting and vindicating the liberty of the subject) they
demanded also all the exertions of a professional man.

He, therefore, claimed to be heard as a barrister—he claimed
to be heard as a householder—as a citizen of Dublin. How
could the commissioner possibly resist this his just demand?
By what authority, and according to what precedent? In the
courts of law, high and low, of every degree, it never was held
or pretended that a barrister's assistance could be dispensed with.
The House of Commons admits that assistance. How, then, by
what authority, and according to what maxims of expediency or
justice could that Court, and that Court alone, reject?

Mr. Finlay, the other counsel for the citizens, followed with an able argument, but the
Commissioners were not to be moved.

AGGREGATE MEETING.

On Thursday, the 5th of November, 1812, there was an aggregate meeting of the Catholics
of the county of Dublin, held at Kilmainham, convened, according to the terms of the
requisition, "to take into consideration the propriety of petitioning parliament for the
total repeal of the penal laws affecting our (the Catholic) body," but, in fact, to afford an
opportunity of discussing the results of the elections just concluded, and the conduct of

particular parties in various localities during those elections; and, generally, the state and prospects of the Catholic cause. William Gerald Baggott, of Castle Baggott, was called to the chair.

When Mr Baggott had concluded his short address, on taking the chair, Randal M'Donnell, Esq., after some remarks in praise of the conduct of the poorer classes of the electors during the late contests, introduced the resolutions that had been prepared.

There were loud calls on every side for "O'Connell, O'Connell:" and, as the newspaper reports, "after a short hesitation, the Man of the people came forward and spoke to the following effect:"—

I could not be an Irishman, if I did not feel grateful, if I was not overpowered at the manner in which you have received me. Sorry, sunk, and degraded as my country is, I still glory in the title of Irishman. (Bursts of applause.) Even to contend for Ireland's liberties is a delightful duty to me. (Enthusiastic plaudits.) And if anything is wanting in addition to the evidence of such humble efforts as I have already been engaged in, for the restoration of our freedom and independence, to evince my devotion to the cause of my country, I do swear, by the kindness you have shown me now—by any I have ever experienced at your hands, and by all that I hold valuable, or worthy of desire, that my life is at her service. (Applause.) And may the heavy hand of adversity fall down upon me, and upon all that are dearest to me—the children of my heart—if ever I forsake the pure pursuit of the liberty of Ireland. (Cheering for several minutes.) Gentlemen, we are now arrived at a period, when we are not only struggling for the interest of our own religion, but for the liberty, security, and peace of our Protestant brethren, both here and in England. (Applause.)

We are arrived at an important crisis, when a serious profession has been made, on our behalf, by the English parliament. This is the first time that a declaration such as that to which I allude was ever made in the senate. It is the first time that the voice of religious liberty was really heard in the British parliament—the first time that men were allowed to judge for themselves, and to obey the divine precept, of treating others as they themselves would wish to be treated. (Hear, hear.)

The period is highly important, and calls for all the watchfulness, zeal, and assiduity of which we are capable. An administration (formed, heaven knows how!) have given us a specimen of their acting a neutral part towards us. They have promised that they shall not interpose their authority to interrupt the good intentions of any man. Some of them have even pledged themselves to support the Catholic question; and, probably half of them have given some earnest of their improved liberality.

will, however, give them little credit for sincerity ; I believe
they would not even pretend to lay much claim to our confidence
—they have too much modesty to expect to be believed by us—
(laughter, and cries of hear, hear)—we have, I believe, without
paying much attention to the professions of the Cabinet, arrived
at a most important crisis.   It behoves every man of us to do
his duty, and to take care that we shall lose none of the important acquisitions we have made.   This very administration of
whom I am speaking, notwithstanding all their fair promises,
have been busily employed in throwing new impediments in our
way since last session.   But those impediments shall do us little
injury if we do our duty.   They certainly are our natural enemies—they hate liberty—they have an inherent abhorrence to
freedom, and their hostility to us is particularly embittered by
our contempt for them (loud applause) ; yes, gentlemen, such
are the men whom you, in your resolutions, have justly termed,
"incompetent," and "profligate"—such are the men who now
command the destinies of those realms, and, probably the fortunes of Europe.   (Hear Hear.)

I am afraid, gentlemen, that I shall take up too much of your
time if I advert to some topics that are crowding upon my mind.
(Cries of no, no, go on, go on.)   The first I should be inclined
to allude to is, an address, lately published by a real friend to
religious liberty, and printed by Mr. Cobbett, a distinguished
colleague of his, in the exposure of public corruption—I mean
Lord Cochrane, one of the members for the city of Westminster,
than whom no man deserves better of every real admirer of
political integrity and patriotism.

This distinguished member observes, that he was once opposed
to the Catholics, because he disapproved of the slavish doctrines
which prevail "in the Romish Church."   It is some consolation,
gentlemen, that there is some person who can assure ministers,
there is no danger in granting us emancipation—we are not *too
fond* of liberty.   (Laughter.)   But, gentlemen, see the consistency and rationality of our calumniators !   At one time they
say we are agitating democrats, crying aloud for an unwarrantable portion of freedom : the very next moment they turn
round and tell us, that we have a marvellous propensity for
slavery !   (Loud cries of hear, hear.)   The truth, however, is,
that their accusations are false in both instances ; we do not go
to excess on either side ; we are partial to a legitimate and well-
modelled monarchy in an hereditary line, and we, at the same
time, reverence the majesty of the people.   While we bear a

true allegiance to the British constitution, we still say, that life
is not worth enjoyment, without the blessings of freedom.
(Reiterated applause.)   Lord Cochrane admits that he is converted from his original antipathy to Catholics, and he says he
is now ready to grant them all the immunities he himself enjoys,
if, in the first place, they accept the privileges of Englishmen,
and if in the second, they renounce the jurisdiction of the Pope.
I say, we are most anxious to obtain the privileges of Englishmen.   Let Lord Cochrane recollect what the first Irishman that
ever was born said at Newry.

[Here the learned gentleman was interrupted for several minutes by the acclamations of
the assembly.]

I am not surprised—continued Mr. O'Connell, when silence
was again restored—I am not surprised that you should feel the
most ecstatic emotions of the Irish heart, when I but allude to
the name of John Philpot Curran. (Renewed cheering.)   It re-
cals to us everything that is dear or interesting in our history
—it pronounces everything that we are proud to live with in
this age, and everything that shall be estimable in the minds of
posterity. (Loud applause.)   I know the name of John Philpot
Curran has conducted you back involuntarily to that most awful
era in our annals, when we were deprived of our independence,
and metamorphosed into the colony of a people, who were not,
and who are not, in the least, worthy of being our MASTERS.
But, my friends, if we are true to ourselves—if Protestants and
Catholics be alive to their commonest and most intimate interest, we may, profiting among other aids, by the assistance of
this very idol of ours, to whom you have just paid your affectionate tribute—we may, I say, become a kingdom once more !
(Thunders of applause.)

I had adverted to what my most venerated friend, John Philpot Curran, said at Newry.   I would take leave to remind Lord
Cochrane of it, assuming it to be the expression of Catholic feeling.   The Irish Cicero there observed, that Englishmen love the
privilege of being governed by Englishmen.   I would tell my
Lord Cochrane, that Irishmen fully as highly value the privilege
of being governed by Irishmen. (Long-continued applause.)

The second proviso of Lord Cochrane is one merely of a polemical description.   He wishes to destroy the jurisdiction of the
Pope.   I would ask of him in the name of Christian charity, ha
be not our solemn oaths to satisfy him ? (Hear, hear, hear.)   We
are degraded, excluded, and insulted, because we regard the ob-

ligation of an oath—because, for any favour, earthly power can bestow, we would not violate our consciences; and still, though this fact is clear and patent before the world, we are insulted, by being told that our oaths are not a sufficient security for our allegiance! It is most amazing how men will presume to play with our feelings. We show them that we would be willingly bondsmen to all eternity, sooner than violate our oaths; yet they demand, as a security, a breach of the precepts of our religion—not thinking even an oath from such people sufficient. (Hear, hear.) In the course of my professional pursuits, I have been one hundred times compelled to swear that I did not think it lawful to commit murder. (A laugh.) You laugh, gentlemen, but what I tell you is not a greater absurdity than Lord Cochrane's proposed pledge. But see how the imputation which such men would throw upon us, would operate as applied to an individual in private life. They demand a pledge of us, saying, by implication, that we do not value an oath. Why, if any man in the community had the audacity to tell me directly that I did not value an oath, either he or I should not long survive such a flagrant insult. But we are told we have predilections—we do not deny the charge. As for my part, I do not value the man who has not his predilections and resentments; but at the same time, Lord Cochrane may be as much afraid of our predilections for the grand lama of Tartary, as for the Pope of Rome. (Hear, hear.)

Those imputations upon our value for an oath evince only the miserable ignorance of our opponents, with regard to our principles and our uniform conduct. They bring to my recollection, again, the words of the great Curran at Newry, and serve to convince me still more of their entire justice, when he said "that they are unfit to rule us, making laws, like boots and shoes for exportation, to fit us as they may." (Long-continued applause.)

I have taken up much of your time, gentlemen, but I confess I am anxious that the people of England should know us. If Lord Cochrane was here, I do not think that we could fail to convince him of the mistakes he has fallen into. We are no deluders or traitors—we do not make promises to violate them. There is a long tribe of wretches who accuse us of treachery; if they, indeed, revived their slanders, they should not obtain a reply. This junta constitutes the worst and vilest herd of the community. Whenever the invader touches our shores they will be the first to join him; while we, the insidious and agitating demagogues, are ever most ready to oppose him. And why should they not sell their countr ?—surely they sell it to the minister. They may as well sell it to Bonaparte as to Lord Castlereagh, if they be proportionately rewarded. (Hear, hear. hear.) This tribe, I say once more, accused us of an insensibility to moral obligation. I would not condescend to answer them; but Lord Cochrn deserves a reply; he is a friend to civil liberty—a man whose bravery in the battles of his country is not more distinguished than his integrity in the senate; it is a useful occupation of time, to labour to disabuse his mind of prejudices adopted, doubtless, without consideration; his charges merit an answer, and if he were here they would, I trust, receive a full and satisfactory answer.

But, turning from the events and scenes that are taking place at the other side of the water, and contemplating what is going on in this country, let us examine what there is to interest us. The elections are in some places even still going forward. I am told the Catholics have considerably lost by the appeal to the people. (Hear, hear.) In one place they have lost, and lost to an incalculable amount, indeed. Christopher Hely Hutchinson has lost his election in Cork! (Cries of shame, shame, and hear.) I the more regret this misfortune, because it was not the efforts of a profligate minister that rejected him—not the anger that has followed his family, ever since one of them, with a patriotic and Roman-like resolution, drew the veil from the infamy that has kept you in slavery—from that nauseous luxury of enjoyment, in which the wine-bearer's voice is decisive, when he pronounces that you shall be still kept in bondage. (Applause.) He failed —Hely Hutchinson failed—not because the attendants at the Castle were despatched to uphold his opponents—not because our worthy Viceroy expended any of his private property in opposition to him—the profits of the coal tax in London, or the £30,000 he is allowed as a slave. Christopher Hely Hutchinson 's out of parliament, not because he is not a friend to the liberties of mankind, an ornament to his country, a credit to human honour and integrity, but he has failed because of the apathy of Catholics! (Loud cries of shame, and hear, hear.)

The negligence—the wicked and pernicious negligence of Catholics did against him what neither the frowns nor smiles of administration—the favour nor the anger of the Court, could do. Catholics neglected to register their votes in time, and thus they inflicted upon our cause, one of the greatest and heaviest calamities that could befal us. (Hear, hear.) With what contempt do they now look upon themselves! Do they not despise themselves

and their criminal negligence   But let not the lesson oe lost—
let it be proclaimed and spread as widely about as intelligence
can reach.   Let every man who hears me bear it strongly upon
his mind, and communicate to his friends, that the neglect of the
Catholics of Cork, in registering their votes, was the sole cause
of our losing the services of an admirable Irishman.   (Loud
plaudits.)

With the single exception of Cork the elections have been decidedly in favour of us. In Galway, indeed, there is not much
to applaud.   At the head of the poll is Mr. James Daly, a nephew to Mr. Justice Daly, who sits on the bench, because of
having voted for the Union. (Hear, hear.) The honest, manly,
and incorruptible Denis Bowes Daly ought to have been returned
without expense, and ought to have been in the place of the other
gentleman.   This upright Irishman has sat for thirty-six years
in parliament, without ever giving a vote against the interests
of his country ; and *we are* told that there shall be a dubious
contention between this well-tried patriot and a Mr. Eyre, a man
who never did anything, but who tells us that he will do something.   Meantime, the judge's nephew will be returned in spite
of fate.   (Hear, hear, and cries of shame.)   This instance of ingratitude is truly lamentable, and most discreditable to those
who are its authors ; and whilst other counties are exhibiting
the most cheering proofs of true public spirit, this falling off in
Galway should be proclaimed to the reprehension of the world.
(Hear, hear.)

In Tipperary, General Mathew and Mr. Prittie are at the head
of the poll. (Loud cheering.) All the efforts of Bagwell—all
that private friendship and public corruption could effect—all
that the influence of the Court could avail—all that favour,
traced to the foot of the Throne, could perform, were unavailing.
Catholics and Protestants stood and acted firmly together, and
Mathew and Prittie were triumphant.   (Loud cheers.)

Nearer home, however, we have not so pleasing a prospect of
popular success.   Mr. Clements, a decided enemy of yours, is
in ; and Mr. White, whom you have so justly thanked and applauded this day, is out ; but I trust there is still public spirit
enough to return him, and add him to the list of your friends.

In Wexford you have got too additional advocates.

In Downpatrick, even John Wilson Croker of the admiralty,
has, to use a northern phrase, been kicked out. (Laughter and
cheers.) I remember about six years ago, when this gentleman
and I were going circuit together, his Protestantism did not keep

my Popery much in the back ground. (Laughter and cheers.) If, however, he were not a Protestant, I verily believe he would have been doomed to drudge all his life at the bar, though he has been, since that time, in parliament, and is now rewarded with a situation in the admiralty.

In Drogheda we have got Meade Ogle, and have got rid of Foster. (Hear, hear.)

But, surely, in Trinity College, we have not only been emancipated from another Foster, but we have had an accession to our strength, in that credit to Ireland, that ornament to the bar, and that honour to human intelligence, William Conyngham Plunkett. (Loud applause.)

I need say little of Dublin, the corporation are involved in debt, and Jack Giffard, the police magistrates, and Billy M'Auley, could not muster votes enough to get up any man in opposition to Mr. Shaw, whose great crime it is to have acted honestly and conscientiously. The *"felonious rabble"* of the corporation, if I may use the delicate expression of one of its members, had not courage to produce one person to oppose Henry Grattan, who "watched Ireland's independence in its cradle, and followed it to its tomb !"

I have not called your recollection to the county of Dublin, where Mr. Hamilton, who had the credit of relinquishing his prejudices to you, was returned without opposition, because he discharged the trust you reposed in him faithfully and honourably ; and where that truly excellent Irishman, Colonel Talbot, was returned also without opposition. (Here there were the most enthusiastic acclamations which lasted for several minutes.) Gentlemen, I am sorry that Colonel Talbot is present, because I am thus restrained from saying what my heart dictates, and his merit demands. He speaks, acts, and thinks like a true and genuine Irishman. Register your votes, and let him be ever sent to watch your interests as he has been at this election—namely, without the vexation of any opposition. (Loud applause.)

Such is the state of the elections—such is the state of your cause. Is it not demonstrative, that if you had a Protestant parliament in Ireland, they would emancipate you ?

[The manner in which this sentence was received by Mr. O'Connell's auditory is described as having been enthusiastic almost beyond any former experience. The applause was taken up again and again, for many minutes, with unabated, and almost increasing warmth, and it was not for a long time that he was suffered to proceed ;

In the county of Clare, I forgot to say, the Chancellor of the

Exchequer is thrown out. The Catholics of this county have covered themselves with eternal honour. All the money of the treasury was without influence to seduce them from their duty. Relinquishing, as was the case with numbers of them, the closest ties of intimacy, friendship, and kindred, they nobly told the Chancellor that they had every good wish for his interest, but that their country had the first claim upon them and upon their votes. (The loudest applause.)

The Ponsonby family have succeeded in the north. If the north was disgraced by the return of a Yarmouth or a Castlereagh, there is sufficient consolation in the circumstance I have just mentioned, to make us well pleased with our liberal Protestant brethren, in that portion of Ireland. In speaking of Lord Castlereagh, I do not know how to select words to adequately express my feelings. I should become an old man in foaming out the torrent of hatred and indignation with which my bosom teems. He is not here at the present moment ; but I do not feel myself the less authorized to speak of him as an honest and injured Irishman should speak ; because there are people here, I am well persuaded, to convey to him the language I use. Mr. Wellesley Pole boasted of his having people behind the curtain at every Catholic meeting. His successors, I suppose, have imitated his wisdom ; and as there is, therefore, some spy, in all probability, lurking to apprise Lord Castlereagh of what goes forward, I have not restrained myself. Let the man who buried thousands of our brave troops in the marshes of Walcheren, and destroyed the springs of his country's liberty, know the feelings which are experienced by an Irishman, when his name is mentioned. (Loud applause.)

To counterbalance the gloom that is thrown over the mind when the success of an enemy to the cause of Ireland is contemplated, I might exhibit the prospects that are presented by the residence of the young Duke of Leinster amongst us. (Loud acclamations.) Inheriting such a load of the virtues of his ancestry, his promises are great. Indeed there is something in the name of Fitzgerald to cherish and console Ireland under th heaviest afflictions. (Loud applause.) Let us hope that those virtues only want an opportunity of action to prove advantageous to the empire. Let us hope that he is at this moment at the meeting in Kildare, commencing a career of glory to himself and usefulness to Ireland. (Cheering.)

I must now advert to the disgraceful efforts that have been made in the counties of Sligo, Leitrim, Roscommon, and Longford, by a disgraceful no-Popery faction, to agitate and disturb the public peace.   To those, however, is to be opposed that formidable and imposing document, the Protestant petition, signed by everything of wealth, respectability or talent that was to be found throughout the country.   As to the no-Popery agitators, we have leading them a Mr. Steward Corry, whoever he may be—a Mr. Owen Wynne, who is said to be a great encourager of fat pigs.   (Much laughter.)   He is also, however, brother to that important dignitary, the caterer-general of the Castle.   Then we have a Mr. Counsellor Webber, who was an assistant-barrister, or, in the words of the great Flood, who had availed himself of the "refuge for *tried* incapacity."   In one county an obscure clergyman was the author of a pompous string of anti-Catholic resolutions.

But the hypocritical affectation of liberality in those gentlemen was worst of all!   (Hear, hear.)   Catholics were their loving brothers!—everything that was sweet and delightful and sublime and affectionate!!   (Laughter.)   They love us—oh how dearly!—but they desire us to continue slaves!   They desire us to fight for them and to pay the taxes:—but they keep the rewards to themselves!

Mr. O'Connell then proceeded, at some length, to descant upon the necessity of agreement and unanimity of sentiment among all classes at the awful crisis now impending.   He said it would be much wiser for ministers, at this juncture, to enter into a treaty of amity with the Catholics of Ireland, than to lavish a subsidy of £80,000 upon Bernadotte—than to build hopes upon the insurrection in Paris—form alliances with a chieftain in South America—or conclude arrangements with the Dey of Algiers; and concluded amid loud acclamations.

JOHN PHILPOT CURRAN.

UPON the 14th of November, 1812, Mr. O'Connell was about to move that a dinner should be given by the Catholics to their Protestant supporters, when Mr. Lawless introduced a vote of censure on certain members of the Board, who had acted against the celebrated John Philpot Curran, at his then recent contest for the borough of Newry.

After some other gentlemen had spoken, Mr. O'Connell rose and said:—

He had very little to offer on the present occasion.   He had no doubt, and he believed the Board had no doubt, of the propriety of inflicting their great and heavy punishment of their censure on men who had yielded to the basest motives of betraying their country. It was not only the duty of every man who gave his vote, to pledge the candidate, not only to the support of Catholic Emancipation, but also to the exertion of every means in his power to oppose an incompetent administration, and to support the rights of the country. But he was sure that a meeting of Irishmen—of Catholics, and of gentlemen, would not confound the base and despicable betrayer of his native land, the shameless deserter of the tried friends of the cause, and the man who had acted from an impulse the most honourable to any man, that of redeeming plighted faith.

You seem to find it difficult to draw the discriminating line yourself; and how much more so will it be for the public. If an indiscriminate stigma of this nature were to be sent abroad, it would be easily converted into the instrument of private malignity. This air-drawn dagger which you sent forth to the world would be soon presented to the breasts of, perhaps, meritorious individuals, to gratify the purposes of malice and revenge. It would be made the weapon for avenging injuries committed, or supposed to be committed, upon individuals in private life, and thus, instead of carrying the weight and dignity of a censure pronounced by a great body after difficult evidence of its justice, it would dwindle into the petty, but mischievous character of a tool, which every ill-minded man might seize upon to satisfy his private resentments.

It was true there had been room for censure. But the Board should, at least, give those persons an opportunity of satisfying themselves before it inflicted punishment upon them ; it should hear before it decided. The censure involved the most serious consideration. It was one which would not only affect the individual, but would be handed down to the latest posterity. It should, therefore, be resolved upon with the greatest and most mature deliberation ; not when the assembly was heated by the remembrance of recent election contests, heated by a warm and protracted discussion, and doubly excited by description of the transcendant merits of John Philpot Curran—merits which it is impossible to do justice to. He would ask whether such was a moment to pass a grave and solemn censure, and to pass it in such a form that it may be applied to the very last man in the community to whom the Board would wish to extend it—a man who has ever been the most steadfast supporter of the cause, and who would freely lay down his life for it. It may be said he deserves it; if so, inflict it; but do it manfully, openly, honourably. Let

it not be said that you decided without trying—that a tribunal of
Irishmen would even risk the charge of visiting an Irishman with
injustice. It would be cowardly to rob a man of his character in
the dark. Those men may have cases to make ; they should be
permitted to make them.

With respect to the political principle, he conceived the Board
possessed the power. It would be impossible for many reasons,
for an aggregate meeting to inflict the censure ; and as to sending members back to the counties, that would be recognising the
principle of representation, which they denied in the most positive manner. The members of the Board were not representatives, but they contained within them the mere and unbought
feeling of Irishmen, and to that feeling he would appeal for justice to the character of a gentleman. You are now acting upon
ex post facto law. It is possible that reasons may have existed
for this conduct; and sure you are not to put those persons to the
bar of the Irish people, without hearing them. He would propose an adjournment for a fortnight. If gentlemen were right
in adopting the censure this evening, they would be equally so
this day fortnight, and it would come with double weight when
resolved upon coolly, without being inflicted by a panegyric on
the merits of Curran, of Hutchinson, of Mathew, or of another,
whom Mr. Lawless forgot, Prittie. The Board, by passing the
present resolution, will assist to shield the real delinquent, by
laying part of the blame upon worthy men. He concluded by
moving an adjournment, which was seconded by Nicholas Mahon ;
and, after a short additional discussion, carried, on a division, by
a large majority.

On Saturday, the 28th instant, the discussion was again revived, in a densely crowded
meeting of the Board. Mr. O'Connell called the attention of the Board to the unwarrant
able exercise of authority by certain individuals, who had taken upon themselves to issue
summonses to attend the adjourned debate on Mr. Lawless's motion. He also proposed a
further adjournment until the following Monday, to some larger place of meeting, where
there would be room for the immense crowds which had that day assembled, blocking up
the passages, and crowding even the street below. It was, however, determined to remain
where they were ; and the debate proceeded on Mr. Lawless's motion, put in the following
shape :—

" That such persons as had deserted the tried friends of the Catholics
at the last general election, were no longer deserving of their confidence."

After several very animated speeches pro and con, M. O'Gorman (Nicholas Purcell)
moved, by way of amendment, to add a sentence, approving the explanations offered by
Mr Laler, of Cranagh, and some of the others originally inculpated.

Mr. O'Connell supported the amendment, but not as an addition to Mr. Lawless's motion. The original resolution he consi

dered to be one of the most unjust, indiscreet, and inconsistent
that could possibly have been conceived. It would affect any
man and every man. It would sacrifice men who had ever
evinced the utmost anxiety and zeal for the promotion of the
Catholic cause. It would go to divide the body, and interrupt
that harmony which was acknowledged upon all hands to be of
the most vital importance. It would carry the broad inconsistency upon the face of it, of censuring persons who at the same
time were held to have satisfied public opinion.

One gentleman (Mr. O'Gorman) had told them he supported
it on the grounds of its having elicited the satisfactory explanation which they had that day heard. But, surely, it was unfair,
after acknowledging these vindications to be so entirely full and
complete, to send out to the world a vague and general censure
that might be turned against the best men in the community.

Another gentleman (Mr. Costigin) had said, "let those the
cap fit wear it ;" but it was not always the person whom the cap
best fitted that it was placed upon by the public. It seldom
happened that the individual whom the cloak of infamy best
suited would of himself put it on. Such a person was generally
far more disposed to throw it over the shoulders of the innocent,
and array himself in the garb of hypocrisy, and so elude the disgrace which he was so conscious of meriting. It was, to borrow
an illustration from scenes of horror that had been alluded to, a
pitch-cap of torture, that they were about to force down upon
the heads of unoffending men, and not a well-earned infliction
upon real and shameful delinquency.

It should be borne in mind that that Board was the organ, as
it were, of the Catholic people. Being so, its denunciations came
to be considered, and were, in effect, the denunciations of that
people. The Catholic Board should not forget those men whose
exertions, whose influence, and whose active patriotism had
worked up the cause to its present high position and momentous importance. It was no small triumph to observe gentlemen of the first rank and consideration in the country coming
forward to vindicate themselves to that Board. He well recollected a time, when men, possessed of their fortune, station, and
high respectability, cared nothing for any resolutions that might
be passed by meetings in Dublin. The Catholic Board, he would
again beg of gentlemen to recollect, had now arrived at such a
pitch of influence and importance, that their frown was sufficient
to cast dismay around any man they attacked ; but it behoved
them to prove that the moderation and justice with which they

exercised that power was commensurate with its magnitude.
Whatever might be the decision of that day, he would take upon
himself to assert, that no Catholic in the land would venture to
vote again in a manner that could subject him to their displeasure.   It was evident how unjustly the resolution might operate,
from the statement which a highly-respectable gentleman (Mr.
Burke) thought it necessary to make a short time before ; and
he begged leave to assure that gentleman, that if he had not
been present to advocate his cause in person, no efforts of his
(Mr. O'Connell) should have been wanted to ensure the justice
which was his desert.

He thought individual votes of censure, on every account,
highly reprehensible, and certain to be attended with the very
worst consequences.   It would be nothing less than transform-
ing the Catholic Board—which possessed the dear, invaluable,
unbought confidence of the Irish people—into a terrible inquisition.   If such a transformation were to take place—if an assembly, instituted for the advancement of constitutional freedom,
assumed to itself such inquisitorial privileges, there was an end
at once to the security of the best men.   No one, however conscious of his own innocence—however anxious to do his duty to
his country without a thought of personal advantage to himself,
could feel or could be safe.   He claimed for himself sincerity at
least ; and he was not conscious of ever having acted otherwise
than as he sincerely believed his duty to his country required :
yet if this system were to be established, he knew not how soon
he might be unjustly and summarily condemned.   Should a faction who could muster twenty or twenty-five votes have it in
their power to act in this manner, he knew not how soon they
might come forward and say, "Daniel O'Connell does not deserve the confidence of the Catholic people."

He prayed the Board to act with the dispassionate candour
becoming them as a great, deliberative assembly ; and concluded
by supporting the amendment, in so far as it expressed approval
of the explanations that day offered, and confidence in the gentle
men who had made them.

However the efforts to which Mr. O'Connell alluded twice in the foregoing speech wer
successful.   The room had been packed in favour of the vote of censure; and, after two
divisions—" one upon the amendment of approval, and the other on a subsequent amend
ment to adjourn—the censuring vote was carried."

TAAFFE *a*. CHIEF JUSTICE OF QUEEN'S BENCH.

THE case of Taaffe and others against the Chief Justice of the Queen's Bench, came now, November, 1812, again before the courts, after successive adjournments from the preceding terms.

Our concern is not with a detailed history of its progress; and we shall therefore give, without further preface, Mr. O'Connell's speech in this case, Friday, November 13, 1812, in the Court of Common Pleas.

The following is the report of the *Freeman's Journal*, in its number of Saturday November 14:—

"Mr. O'Connell appeared in court this day to make his reply to the arguments of Mr. Pennefather, as delivered on Tuesday last. The court was excessively crowded, and it may with truth be said, that no person who came for the purpose of enjoying a display of forensic powers, went away disappointed.

My lords (said Mr. O'Connell), I am highly sensible of the indulgence I have received from the Court on the present occasion. I feel no small regret at having consumed any portion of your lordship's time, but I shall be as brief as possible, while I endeavour, in discharging the only duty that now remains to me, to reply to the arguments of the gentlemen on the opposite side. And, my lords, in discharging this duty, I shall avoid imitating the example set me on the last day by one of these gentlemen, and (if I do not err) by the other on a former day, in travelling out of the direct course which the question before the Court prescribes. I shall leave unnoticed what has been called the "whimsicality," of introducing politics upon an occasion like the present, and confine myself to a mere question of law.

But though Mr. Pennefather, in describing the nature of the present action, takes a fancy to quoting one of the law books, and calling it "a bold attempt on the government of the country;" yet, in explaining what I conceive to be the law of the land in the case, I will not, even though I exclude political reflections, for a moment persuade myself that I ought not to speak my sentiments and those of my colleagues upon it, with the most unrestrained and unembarrassed freedom. The question involves great constitutional principles. It does not depend upon mere technical rules or technical reasonings, but must be decided upon consideration of the nature and extent of personal liberty in this country, and the sense judges have of the rights of the subject, and the redress they are entitled to avail themselves of for the injuries they suffer.

Little aid can be obtained from modern cases. The simple question is, whether there is a class of magistrates in this country entitled to issue their warrants without any information upon

oath, and without any crime having been actually committed,
and entitled upon such warrants to imprison any description of
the king's subjects, without having afterwards to make atonement and compensation.   If the Court decide with the defendant,
they establish this monstrous proposition.   See what the action
is : it is an action brought against the defendant for false imprisonment, and his justification is that he is Chief Justice of the
King's Bench.   This is the proper form of an action brought
against a magistrate who issues a warrant.   The case of Morgan
v. Hughes, in Term Reports, 225, proves that it is the only form
of action suited to such a case.   This was an action of trespass,
the defendant being accused of having issued his warrant, and
maliciously arrested the plaintiff.   There was a demurrer to the
declaration, and judgment was had that the action should have
been brought for false imprisonment.   What is the nature of the
present defence ?   The mere assertion, that the learned defendant
is Chief Justice of the Court of King's Bench, and the assertion
of the mode he adopted in imprisoning the plaintiff.   It does
not say that he despatched his menial servant with such commands as he pleased to give ; but it does say that he granted
his warrant with such recitals as his imagination suggested.
This is the real language of the plea.   It cannot be aided by any
intendment—no presumption can be made in its favour ; on the
contrary, the first principles of pleading require that it should
be taken most strictly against the defendant.   This is the rule
laid down by Lord Coke (Coke Littleton, 303-6); and to show
that this general rule of pleading most directly applies to justi-
cation, I beg to refer you to Cummins's Digest, E. 17.   Nothing,
therefore, can be intended beyond this allegation, that the defendant was a magistrate, and arrested the plaintiff by his warrant.   The Court cannot supply the allegation :—1st, that the
crime was committed—2nd, that the plaintiff was one of the
persons concerned in that crime—3rd, that the defendant knew
or suspected that the plaintiff was so concerned.   These are
clearly material and traversable allegations, upon which issue
might be taken, and the fact tried by a jury ; but no issue tried
upon this plea can bring any of these facts into controversy.
Upon the trial it would not be necessary for the defendant to
prove any of them ; so that it is clear, that if the demurrer be
over-ruled, the Court will establish a right in a class of magistrates, or in some of them, to arrest without knowledge—without
suspicion—without a crime—without a criminal act.
    The class to which I allude is, the Lord Chancellor, the Lord

Treasurer, the Lord High Steward, the Lord Marshal, the Lord High Constable, the four Judges of the King's Bench, and the Master of the Rolls. (1st Blackstone, 350.)

I now proceed to show—1st, that the plea does not state any matter sufficient to justify the imprisonment of the plaintiff, or, in other words, that the trespass is manifestly a false imprisonment, notwithstanding anything alleged in the plea ; 2ndly, that there is nothing stated in the plea sufficient to bar the action for false imprisonment against the defendant. If I clearly establish the first, I think I shall go far to induce the Court to decide the second proposition in my favour.

Now, as to the first, it seems unnecessary to go beyond the unrepealed clause of the great charter—namely, that " no freeman shall be imprisoned unless by the judgment of his peers, or by the law of the land." Here I may rest my client's cause, and call for that judgment of his peers, or that law of the land which dragged him, without the ordinary courtesy of summons or notice, from his family ; which associated him through the streets of this city, as if he were a felon, with the thief-takers of the police. Where is the judgment which condemned him to sustain this inconvenience and contumely ? There is none, my lords. It is not pretended that there is any. And for law we are presented with this warrant —a warrant, not only assuming, but creating all the facts, and fortified by nothing but its own allegations, commanding the arrest of the plaintiff—a warrant, distinguishing, it is true, between meetings for the purpose, and those held under pretence of petitioning parliament, but declaring guilt in either case. But can it be insisted that this warrant answers the description of the law of the land ? It seems to me to be a monstrous proposition to call it so ; and, indeed, it would be more absurd to call any man a freeman who was subject to such a law. He would be the abject slave of caprice.

I know, my lords, that a statute, the 37th of Edward the Third, chapter 1, has explained the words *legem terræ* to mean " due process of law." Here I wish it to be distinctly understood, that I, for the present, concede in argument, that which, in point of law, I could not admit, save for the sake of argument, that the supposed offence charged upon my client, is one for which any subject is liable to arrest before indictment. It is not a felony nor a breach of the peace, and, therefore, I do not think an arrest before an indictment was justifiable in this case ; but for the present I concede that it would have been justifiable upon " due process ;" and if this warrant be " due process of law," is the present question.   I have already shown that this warrant is not grounded upon any evidence, a suspicion either of an existing crime, or of the plaintiff's being a criminal · but to sanction an arrest, all these are necessary ingredients in ' lawful warrant, for no arrest can be made before indictment, except there be either first a direct charge upon oath, stating the existence of a criminal, and that the party actually is, or is sus- pected to be the criminal ; or, secondly, strong and rational sus- picion declared on oath, of the crime and criminal.   That this is the utmost extent of the legal doctrine of arrests—that these are the legal grounds to justify the granting of a warrant, appear from all the books—4th Blackstone, 289 ; 2nd Hale, 108, 110 ; 2nd Hawkins, 135–6.   Hale, in page 110, represents the neces- sity of examining the parties requiring the warrant upon oath, as to the fact of the existence of the crime and the criminal ; and Blackstone says, that " without such oath no warrant should be granted ;" and the same law is laid down by Sergeant Hawkins. By consulting these authorities, my lord, you will find that I am borne out in asserting that this is the very extent of the law ; for more ancient writers, as Lord Coke (2nd Institute, 51, 52) had asserted that, before indictment or presentment, no man could be arrested ; and all that Hale, Hawkins, and Blackstone contended for is, that Lord Coke is mistaken ; for that if there be a charge upon oath, a warrant to arrest may be granted be- fore indictment.   This point, namely—that a charge upon oath sanctions an arrest, is the utmost they contend for ; and Hawkins concludes his observations upon the subject in these words— " Yet, inasmuch as justices of the peace claim this power (that of arresting ·before indictment) rather by connivance than any express warrant of law ; and since the undue use of it may prove so highly prejudicial to the reputation as well as the liberty of the party, a justice cannot well be too tender of his proceedings of this kind, and seems to be punishable, not only at the suit of the King, but also of the party grieved, if he grant any such warrant groundlessly and maliciously, without such a probable cause as might induce a candid or impartial man to suspect the party to be guilty." (2nd Hawkins, 135–6.)

We have then got to the extreme of the law when we arrive at arrests by warrants, because of a charge established by oath ; and an extreme which has been resorted to, not because it has the sanction of any express law, but by means of its necessity, to prevent the escape of felons before they could be indicted, and from connivance at the long-used practice. It is not, indeed, in cases where it applies now, disputed, because, in addition to the authority on which it rests in the direct opinion of the " sages of the law," it has been recognized in some cases of felony by those acts of parliament, which direct the manner, in some instances, of giving bail upon such warrants. But there is no where to be found any case of any allegation of any law writer carrying the power of arrest further ; for I need not detain the Court by any comment on the passage in 2nd State Trial, 5, 6, which refers to Trogmorton and Allen (2 Rolle's Abi., 558.)

Mr. Perrin has, with the ability and learning he discovers on every occasion, shown you that Hale must be understood as meaning that the warrant of the justice is a justification to the constable who executed it, not that the justice could protect himself by his own allegation. This distinction is familiar to your lordships ; and, although Mr. Foster seemed to rely on the passage, to sustain the defence of the justice who issued the warrant, yet, Mr. Pennefather felt himself bound to admit that the passage is merely applicable to the constable ; and the case referred to, Trogmorton and Allen, is accordingly the case of a justification by a constable. There is, therefore, I repeat it, not even a solitary dictum in the books, and if there had, the research of the counsel for the defendant would have discovered it. There is not, I confidently repeat, a single assertion in any law book, that a warrant may be legally issued without a charge upon oath. It follows, therefore, of obvious and inevitable necessity, that this warrant was not legally issued.

It was not "due process of law." My client has been illegally and against the provisions of the great charter, deprived of his liberty. The defendant is guilty of false imprisonment.

This brings me to the second point ; for it is alleged, that though the arrest was unjustifiable, although the defendant be clearly guilty of a trespass and false imprisonment, yet he is not responsible in an action for damages. In short, that although he is not infallible, still he is inviolable ; but I trust, notwithstanding, I shall be able to satisfy the Court of my second proposition—namely, " that the matter stated in the defendant's plea is not sufficient to bar the action for this false imprisonment." The plea contains nothing but the fact which appears on the face of the declaration—viz., that the defendant is Chief Justice of the King's Bench, with all the authorities and rights belonging to that office, and that he, as such, arrested the plaintiff by means of a warrant. Upon this allegation, the counsel for the

defendant contend that no action lies, and conceding that a trespass has been committed, they say, that this is one of the instances
in the law where there is an injury without means of compensation, because the defendant being a judge of a superior court, no
action will be against him.

It is, my lords, readily admitted, that no action lies against
any judge for any judicial act whatsoever; but we insist that it
does lie against every judge for ministerial acts. This distinction
was taken by Mr. Perrin, and sustained with his usual force and
ingenuity. It was admitted by Mr. Foster, and though not expressly admitted, it was, as I shall show, distinctly recognised
by Mr. Pennefather, who, however, has announced a new proposition—namely, that no action lies for any act of a judge of the
superior courts, adding, in the meantime, any act done as a judge.
Now, if by acts done as a judge he means judicial acts, this is
conceded. If he includes ministerial acts, and that the judges
of the superior courts are in no wise responsible in actions, although for the same acts, and within their jurisdiction, inferior
judges would be responsible; this is not only denied, but the
charge of a "bold attempt" to subvert principle recognised in
every case he has himself cited, is retorted, and justly retorted
on the learned gentleman; for, in Hammond and Howell (2
Mod. 218) quoted by him, the Court expressly say, "though
they, (the judges) were mistaken, yet they acted judicially, and
for that reason no action could lie against the defendant." For
what reason? Not because the defendant was judge of any particular court, but because he acted *judicially*. And in Floyd *v.*
Barker (12th Coke, 23rd) also cited by him, this distinction is
expressly taken—"A judge or justice of the peace cannot be
charged for conspiracy for that which he did openly in court, for
the causes and reasons aforesaid."

The two next causes cited by the learned gentleman, not only
confirms the distinction we rely on, but illustrates its application
in practice. These cases are Barnardiston *v.* Soames (2 Liv. 114)
and Ashby and White (2 Lord Raymond, 938). In the first of
these cases it was held, that no action would lie for falsely and
maliciously making a double return to Parliament. Why? Because the judges were of opinion that the sheriff acted, in that
respect, judicially. In Ashby and White it was held, that for
rejecting the vote of a person qualified to vote at an election, an
action would lie against the sheriff. Why? Because it was
held, that the sheriff acted, in that respect, ministerially. And
this distinction is further recognised and acted on in the next

case cited by the learned gentleman, of Miller v. Seares (2 Black-stone, 1141), where an action was held to lie against the Commissioners of Bankruptcy, for improperly committing a man for not answering satisfactorily. It was held to lie, because their office was considered executory and ministerial, and not judicial. Let me add to these authorities the case cited by Mr. Perrin, and commented on by the gentlemen on the other side, in Green-velt v. Benwell (in Salk. 396 ; Lord Raymond, 467 ; and Cum. 77).) The Court will find the judgment of Lord Holt given very distinctly in Cummins—"And that no action will lie against any judge for what he does judicially, and of record ; but if a justice of the peace issue a warrant, and commit a party without cause, he may be punished, because the act is only ministerial, and the commitment only intended for process and not for punishment ;" and he cites, from 12 Coke, Nudigate's case. He was a justice of the peace, and though he recorded a circumstance falsely, yet, as he acted as a judge, that is, judicially, no action would lie. Now, compare the cases. If Nudigate had issued a groundless warrant for any act of violence, an action would have lain against him, because the act was ministerial ; but when he acted judicially and upon record, no such action could be maintained.

Thus, my lords, all the cases establish our distinction between judicial and ministerial acts, as well those relied on at the opposite side, as those cited by Mr. Perrin. But where is the distinction stated by Mr. Pennefather to be found? I have been unable to trace it in any of the cases ; and if you examine the authorities from which he has endeavoured to infer such a distinction, I think you will join me in considering that his inferences are unfounded, and his positions untenable.

And now having I trust, established that which is, indeed, a familiar distinction to your lordships, I shall proceed to show you that the issuing of the warrant by the Chief Justice was a ministerial, and not a judicial act. I admit that the Judges of the King's Bench are coroners and conservators of the peace throughout Ireland, and it is in this capacity of conservators of the peace that the present warrant was issued, or indeed could have been issued. None of your lordships, notwithstanding the dignity and extent of your judicial authority, could issue such a warrant, because none of you is a conservator of the peace throughout the different counties. But the conservator of the peace was, and is, a merely ministerial officer. In page 354, volume 1, Blackstone says, that his power consisted "in sup-

pressing riots, and taking securities for the peace, and in appre-
hending felons and other malefactors. This would appear to be
the full extent of the common law authority of conservators of
the peace. The Court is, of course, fully aware that the constitution of justices of the peace is widely different. The power
of electing conservators of the peace having been taken from the
people, and vested in the crown, by the 34th of Edward the
Third, chapter 1, they first got a judicial character, were empowered to try offences, and obtained the name of justices.—
(Blackstone, 350.) The justices of the peace are judges of a court
of record—the conservators of the peace are not so. This power
of conservator of the peace the Chief Justice of the King's Bench
holds in common with the Chancellor, the Master of the Rolls
and the other persons whom I have named; and if this be a
good justification for him, it would be equally so for the Master
of the Rolls, for he has closed in him the same authority in his
ministerial capacity. Then was the warrant issued improperly,
as it was, in itself, a ministerial act. For this I have the express
authority of Lord Holt; his words are, an action will lie for improperly issuing a warrant, because the act is only ministerial,
and intended for process not punishment; and I have the equally
explicit authority of all the cases from Windham v. Clue, (Cro.
El. 130) to Morgan v. Hughes, (Second Term Report, 225,) and
those cases which occur every day, in which actions are maintained against justices of the peace for issuing warrants without
legal grounds, although those justices are judges of the very
courts in which the offences specified in those warrants are triable,
although they have jurisdiction over the offence and the offender,
and although for their judicial acts in that very matter no action
would lie. This, then, is a ministerial act, done by a ministerial
officer, for which, whatever be the number and value of his other
high dignities, he is responsible to my client.

I shall now follow Mr. Pennefather in a few observations upon
some of the other points which he has laboured in this case; and
first, where he insists that this must be taken as a judicial act,
because it is averred to have been done by the Lord Chief Justice; and as we have not traversed the fact of its being so done,
and in order to sustain this proposition, he cited Eton v. Southly,
from Walker. I shall dismiss the case by observing, that all it
proves is, that an allegation "that A. B. having been possessed
as a tenant at will," is a sufficient averment that he then was
tenant at will—but we are not disputing upon averments in this
instance. It is sufficiently averred that the defendant was Chief

Justice. and as such, namely, by virtue of the office of conservator, which that dignity conferred on him, issued this warrant Can it be seriously contended, that issue should have been taken upon the title the defendant chose to style himself by, when he issued this warrant? What would the jury have to try? Certainly something very immaterial—the appellation the defendant chose to be addressed by at that moment. But the question is, whether this be a judicial or a ministerial act. Now, can the nature of the act depend on the name or title of the actor?—Is the quality of the fact to be changed with the dignity of the doer? But, really, it does not appear to me that I should be at all justified in detaining your lordships upon this part of the case.

The second point in Mr. Pennefather's argument, to which I have to entreat a few moments of your attention, is that part of the case in which, without admitting the distinction between judicial and ministerial acts, he still acknowledged its authority, by the pains he took to prove the granting of a warrant to be a judicial act. He first insisted that no action would lie for unjustly issuing a fiat, and then he compared warrants to fiats. Now, it may be conceded that no action would lie in the first case ; but if warrants be fiats as process to bring the party in, then the authorities and cases in which actions have lain against justices of the peace for issuing warrants are all mistaken, and a discovery is made that by comparing warrants to fiats, the defendants would have been entitled to non-suit the plaintiffs in those actions—a mighty discovery, truly!!! But if this be a point of non-suit only for a Chief Justice, this absolutely would follow, that if this identical warrant had been issued by my Lord Mayor A. B. King, who is a magistrate of great dignity, and I presume entitled to some veneration from the counsel at the other side—if the Lord Mayor who is also a presiding judge at the sessions had issued this very warrant, an action might have lain against him, because it was ministerial, though to the extent of trying and punishing this crime, he is as fully a judge as the present defendant.

It is contended that the superior quality of the Chief Justice alters the act into a judicial one—it becomes a fiat and not a warrant, and no action can be maintained ; but there is, really, no similitude between the two ; a fiat is only an order to the officer to make out a writ or process—a warrant is the process itself ; the writ issued on the fiat, must, of necessity, be returnable in the court out of which it issued—a warrant is not return-

able at all, and it is intended to force in a party to any court
having cognizance of the offence, within the territorial limit of
the officer who grants it. In Blackstone, 294, are these words:
"The warrant may be either general or special; general, to bring
the offender before any justice—special, to bring him before any
individual justice." So that this warrant is part of a case afterwards tried before the defendant, only because he chose not to send
the plaintiff to the sessions. It has, therefore, no necessary connection with the Court of King's Bench, nor indeed any other connection with that court, but what the defendant chose to give it.

Next, the case of the King v. White (Cases Temp. Hard. 37)
has been relied on. To prevent any controversy I have brought
the book to read it. [Here Mr. O'Connell referred to the book,
but it was thought unnecessary by the Court, and passed without debate.] Now, what does this case prove? Does it convert
any ministerial act into a judicial act? Does it alter or qualify
the authority of the cases I have mentioned. It proves nothing
but what is familiar in every day's practice, namely, that all officers of justice are under the control of the King's Bench. Where
complaints are made to that court of any magistrates or officers,
if the fact be admitted, they grant an attachment—if the fact
be disputed, they grant an information to have it tried by a jury.
In the King v. Reilly, (T. T. Rep. 204,) the King's Bench attached Mr. Reilly for calling a meeting of the county. Lord
Earlsfort there lays it down, that the Court of King's Bench has
a general control over all inferior courts and inferior officers, and
the power of punishing them by attachment for misconduct; and
it clearly follows, that an attachment might, upon these admitted principles, have been granted, if the constable had disobeyed
the warrant of any other magistrate. Thus the King v. White
proves nothing but what was not denied, viz., the power of the
Court of King's Bench to punish the misconduct of inferior officers as for a contempt of that court. The arguments drawn
from the cases of fiats do not apply; and if they did, they would
prove too much, and are encountered by all the cases in which
magistrates have been convicted on actions for issuing warrants.
The capacity in which the defendant acted is a matter of law not
capable of being tried by a jury, and not altering the nature of
the act. That act was a ministerial act, which is not protected
from actions, and not a judicial act, which is protected; and,
lastly, this arrest upon those pleadings is a false imprisonment,
for which the defendant is bound to abide the verdict of a jury.

I have now, my lords, argued the case, and have only to add

a word or two in reply to some general topics introduced by Mr. Pennefather—1st, he said that this was one of that class of injuries for which there is no remedy. He cited the case of Lecaux *v.* Eden, but it does not prove, by any means, what he would wish to establish. The aggrieved party here, though he did not get immediate redress, was told that an appeal to the Court of Admiralty would be efficacious. Mr. Pennefather talked of a case of felony in which the party had no redress by the recovery of damages, but it could not escape observation, that if he was not remunerated in money, he would in the punishment of the offender. He commented upon the expediency of suffering a private injury for the purpose of effecting a public good ; but though I admit, most cordially, the general principel, yet I deny its application in the present instance. He has bestowed some words upon the necessity that existed for the defendant's interference in the case of the Catholic delegates. I do not see this necessity. There were many persons who could, with the greatest propriety and delicacy, fill his place on such an occasion. But if, as Mr. Pennefather would contend, the Chief Justice acted in his judicial capacity in granting a warrant against my client, see to what a predicament he has been reduced. He has first judged my client; secondly, resorted to the mockery of a process to bring him to trial ; and, thirdly, judged him again ! And what would, my lords, be the consequence of suffering this extraordinary and monstrous power in a chief justice ? Why, my lords, if my Lord Ellenborough, the English Chancellor, or the Master of the Rolls, had conceived any malice to any of your lordships to-morrow, they might issue their warrants and drag you from your bench to answer a fictitious charge before them, and do all this, subjecting themselves to no penalty !

Mr. Pennefather has, lastly, told us, that the subject could resort to parliament, in the event of any unwarrantable proceedings on the part of the Chief Justice. Why, my lords, what a mockery this is ! If the Irish peasant has been aggrieved by a chief justice, it is a consolation for him to have the liberty of making a miserable passage to Holyhead, then walking barefoot to London, and, lastly, stating his wrongs to the imperial parliament, in a language unknown to them. My lords, I am confident you cannot—from a due consideration of the authorities I have cited, and the reasoning that has been advanced on our behalf—decide against us.

The Court signified that judgment would be given on Tuesday.
However, at the sitting of the Court upon the next day, Lord Norbury announced that

himself and brother judges were so far from having made up their minds on the point at
issue, that they "required more argument from counsel," and appointed the succeeding
Tuesday (that day week) for the hearing. Upon that day judgment was deferred till the
next term, and then decided against the Catholics.

VOTE OF CENSURE.

On the 5th of December, 1812, the Catholic Board again met, when Dr. Dromgoole revived
the subject of the vote of censure and in an able speech contended against its impolicy
concluding with a motion to the following effect :—

"Resolved—That, in order to meet the public and private calumnies
which the enemies of religious liberty have circulated, we feel ourselves
bound to declare, that the resolutions of last spring and summer, respecting candidates for parliament, could not be, and were not intended
to enjoin or sanction the violation of promises entered into at any time
previous to their adoption."

Mr. O'Gorman recommended the adoption of this resolution.

Mr. O'Connell said he was anxious to second the motion, as
well because he concurred most heartily in every thing that fell
from his respectable friend, Dr. Dromgoole, as from his wish to
take at length an opportunity of delivering his sentiments distinctly upon the subject which had caused so much of agitation
amongst the Catholics themselves. One would imagine that we
really were at a loss for enemies, so sedulous did we appear to
excite them amongst ourselves. One would suppose that Ireland was not sufficiently divided and distracted already, but
that division and dissension in the Catholic Board could be
afforded in addition and as a pastime. Indeed, the progress of
this unfortunate feud in the Board might have been arrested at
a certain period. Perhaps, I draw upon my mere vanity, when
I indulge the dream that I could sooner have terminated it; but
full sure I am, that I ought to have sooner endeavoured to do
so, but I was restrained by motives which, upon reflection, I am
unable to justify.

It is due to candour to state them :—in the first place, it was
impossible not to see, that your resolution, although dignified
with the appellation of an abstract proposition, was intended
first, and principally, not altogether, for a single individual. I
do not say that it was the design of the movers to use it as the
instrument of particular vengeance ; they have disavowed any
such design, and we are bound, as we are ready, to believe them.

The effect, however, was precisely what I have stated with the individual thus alluded to. I mean Mr. Lalor; I am proud to avow my conviction. I have the pleasure to be his intimate friend; I have the honour to be his kinsman; I boast of his friendship, because I have long known his worth in all the relations of private life, and in our public cause. I have seen him .n this Board, ever ready to adopt the most manly, spirited, and honourable course; he never spoke amongst us of entering into any timid compromise with our enemies; he never shrunk from danger. When we were menaced with any persecution, he was of the first to throw himself forward; his spirit rose with our perils, ay, and his determination increased with our difficulties. I loved him, because I saw that his views were confined to the good of his country—that he had not, and could not have any personal motive—that, with generous heart and open hand, he contributed to all your expenditures, and that his existence was ever at your service. I saw that every vote he gave in your board or committee, was precisely that which struck my humble judgment as the best calculated to serve your interests.

With those public and private qualifications, I was, and am proud of obtaining the friendship of my respected relative. And I now condemn that species of mistaken delicacy, which prevented me at an early stage of this business, from taking an active part in opposition to your resolution; I imagined that my opposition would be attributed to the zeal of private friendship, and not to that which, in truth, suggested it—the firm conviction of my conscience. There was another motive which also contributed to paralyze my resistance to the resolution of last meeting—I am ashamed to have yielded to it for one moment—it was this : Mr. Lalor's vindication, which has appeared in the public papers, was well known to have been written by me; it was known that I had written it, merely in the exercise of professional skill, and for the ordinary inducements of professional exertions. I did not feel myself at liberty to refuse drawing it in that capacity, but in none other would I have consented to do so. I may be much mistaken, but I thought that I ought not to lend myself personally to any part of that vindication. With all the facts (except a single one of no moment to the general question,) I was a total stranger; and in the controversy as to the then pending election, if I were *personally* to have interfered at all, it would most certainly have been in favour of the candidates who have succeeded. Having, however, once acted as Mr. Lalor's counsel, I am ashamed that I shrunk from

the base calumny which might have imputed to me the sentiments of profession, in resisting the general vote of censure—
it was unbecoming of me to yield to so paltry and pitiful an influence of delicacy. You well know whether I am a man likely
to be influenced in my conduct in this Board, by any other motives than those of honour and of conscience. I speak of myself
with all humility, yet I own I entertain the expectation that my
countrymen in general require not from me any defence against
the imputation of mean or selfish motives ; yet they were these
false delicacies that prevented my opposing the resolution of
abstract censure, as it has been called, determinedly and upon
principle.

For I could not see what right or authority you had to pass
any such resolution. If Mr. Lalor had forfeited the confidence
of the Catholics of the county of Tipperary, they might have
declared that he was no longer to be a manager of their petition,
as the Catholics of Newry did with respect to Mr. Jennings, and
from that moment he would have ceased to be a member of this
Board : but when you passed a vote of censure, you clearly
travelled out of your authority, and into the hands of the Attorney-General—you abandoned, for a moment, the conduct of
your petition, for which alone you are appointed, and you committed yourselves to the tender mercies of your friends in the
King's Bench. It is, therefore, fortunate that your resolution
passed, as I am ready, if necessary, to show, irregularly, and
after having been, in point of fact, negatived. I do not say this
to reflect upon, or to diminish the triumph of those who have
succeeded in that vote ; I introduce it simply to show you, that
we have a valid defence against any attack of the Attorney-
General upon this ground—an attack which, I am convinced, he
would have already commenced, but that he and your other enemies imagine that you are about to do their work for them, and
to destroy yourselves by your own dissensions.

There is an unhappy spirit broke out amongst us. It is the
inevitable consequence of turning this Board into a species of
mock tribunal, and destroying individuals with an axe, which
you call "abstract censure." In plain truth, how is it possible
we should judge with discretion or discrimination upon the motives that may impel private individuals ? Their neighbours in
their respective counties may be able to judge of them, and they
certainly are able to punish them by exclusion from this Board.
But how are you to summon witnesses or to examine them, to
form any estimate of facts ? I will tell you what the witnesses

are—public report—a liar to a proverb—and anonymous calumny—an assassin upon record. I myself, for example, have no less than five anonymous letters lying upon my table, which charge my estimable friend with every atrocity. I know of my own knowledge, that it is simply impossible that some of them should be true—I am convinced they are all false. Yet, how many members of this Board—how many excellent and truly honest men may not be influenced in their decision of Mr. Lalor's case, by communications which may have reached them in a similar way!

In truth, it would be most dangerous for us to usurp the power of judging of facts, which we want the means to investigate. But my great objection must be repeated : the discussion of questions of this nature, affecting particular individuals, must necessarily tend to excite personal animosity amongst us, and to produce irritation and rancour. I appeal to you, whether it has not already had this effect. Indeed, I need not make the appeal ; there is not a man in the Board who has not seen, with regret, a spirit of violence and of hatred—the very genius of personal malignity settling here, where all was peace, and unanimity, and cordiality.

And have we not enemies enough, and to spare? Have we not Lord Manners and his Grace of Richmond in front, whilst the Attorney-General and the Dublin Grand Jury hang on our rere? Have we not on our flank the bigoted Liverpool and that Castlereagh, long exercised in every dark stratagem of ruin, who would, for emolument, barter a seat in heaven, if he had any interest in that country. At this moment bigotry is awakened from the slumber into which Protestant liberality, in Ireland, had cast her—bigotry, at the command of power—bigotry, lured by the beloved voice of interest, has aroused in every part of the land. The first in station and in rank set the example of obedience to the command which they themselves issued. Every little village bigot in the land is animated with the hope of discounting his despicable malignity into the pay and plunder of some office. Mark the active rancour of their hostility: Hutchinson—the patriot Hutchinson—is opposed in Cork for being your champion. The opposition of the Castle stoops to all the meanness of personal animosity ; it disgorges its domestics and menials, from the highest to the lowest, against him ; the refined amusements of our refined government are suspended—even Cassino stood still, and the tea-table was unattended—everybody was absent—everybody was sent to oppose Hutchinson, because he was the friend of the Catholics.

The clergy, who sometimes have a most admirable instinct in discovering what is for their interest here, as well as hereafter, are many of them active against us ; they are easily marshalled under the auspices of a right rev. prelate of the Established Church—the son of Popish parents—the brother of a Popish priest, who has published a pompous pamphlet against us, of great promise and pretensions, but of little performance, save what it effects by the very difficult and novel process of repeating calumnies a thousand times refuted, and abjured, and contradicted upon oath, by every Catholic in Ireland. I should be content if we were at leisure to investigate the worthy prelate's motives, or that we even had an opportunity of printing, in the same shape with his pamphlet, another literary *morceau* of the learned and pious divine. It was, I believe his first attempt—a farce, called the "Generous Impostor!"—oh, the generous impostor! The theatrical dictionary informs us that this farce was damned ; a friend of mine who happened to have seen it, assures us that there was a warmth of expression in it—he would not for the world call it an obscenity, which in some quarters would almost atone for its dulness, but it was too dull even for the vicious taste of a London audience to preserve it for its seasoning. But, perhaps, this pamphlet is as great a farce, in the Fitzwilliam administration, as the silent exertions, if not the pamphlets of the divine were at the other side—oh, the generous impostor!

Look to the counties—see how you are calumniated. I have already more than once had occasion to remark, the principle of this administration is falsehood ; this principle betrays itself in all its acts ; it, therefore, unblushingly, circulates its calumnies against us, with the most thorough conviction of their total want of truth. Where it cannot procure the direct assertion of an untruth, it is content with an insinuation containing the same meaning. Thus, for example, a fraction of the county of Dublin Grand Jury could never have dared to charge the Catholics of Ireland plainly and directly with high treason, but they have had the meanness to insinuate it covertly and in bad English. We should thank them little for the prudence which taught them to avoid the direct assertion, when we meet the depravity that allowed them to make this oblique and unmanly attack on our characters. Where is the individual amongst them that would venture to make the foul and false insinuation of disloyalty to any gentleman of this Board? and if there were any individual so rash as to use the insinuation, I know the chastisement he would meet with and receive. But as a body, we are calumni-

*ted with safety, because we are idly busied in dissension and division amongst ourselves.

Take another example—one of direct falsehood—what Shakspeare calls the "lie direct;" and not, as in the case of the grand jury, the "lie by equivocation." An advertisement has appeared in the Dublin papers, stating that a meeting of the Protestant freemen, freeholders, and inhabitants of Dublin had taken place. Now, this means, and was intended to mean, a public meeting, at which every such Protestant might have attended. But was there any such meeting? There certainly was not. Everybody knows there was not. It is a falsehood—false as God is true—a falsehood signed with the classic name of Abraham Bradley King, Lord Mayor, but not the less unfounded. The noble, grand Lord Mayor just certifies an untruth. He might and probably had a parlour or dining room meeting, but it was no more what he says—a meeting of the Protestants of Dublin, than it was a meeting of the Jews of Frankfort. This untruth, however, is of advantage to our enemies. Why? Because we have left it uncontradicted—because we have been so busy in quarrelling with one another about Mr. Lawless's abstract censures, that we have not had leisure to mark with our public contempt the scandalous and impudent falsehoods with which we are assailed.

But let us return to our own affairs. Let us return to the consideration of the state of the Catholics' rights. Let us make peace amongst ourselves and carry on the war of words only with our enemies. All our vigilance, all our zeal, all our activity, are necessary for our protection. We cannot afford to squander or exhaust any part of them in a quarrel amongst ourselves. You have passed your vote of censure—be content with it, allow us merely to qualify it, by excluding the possibility of any person being deemed to come within it, who ought not to do so. Those are persons whose faith was pledged previous to your resolutions of last spring and summer. You admit that such persons are not the object of your censure. All we require is, that you should declare the fact to be so. If your sword afterwards be wielded by private malignity out of this Board, the declaration we require will serve for a shield, co-extensive with your censure, to those who are entitled to wear that protection.

I can assure you, that my esteemed friend (Mr. Lalor) desires no other, nor would any man be his friend who sought anything further. All he desires is for the honour of the Board itself, that it should not be said that you censured him for observing the promise in which he had pledged the honour of an Irish gentleman. By this means you will vindicate the Board from a calumny, not less actively circulated for being unfounded, and you will restore that harmony and good temper amongst us, which are so necessary for our preservation at this perilous junction. I do therefore conjure gentlemen, in the name of that afflicted country which has so many ardent and affectionate votaries in this room, to waive all matters of form, and let us now, at once, adopt a resolution of admitted truth and necessary conciliation. Let us think that poor Ireland, goaded and distressed, wants all our attention. Let us sacrifice every angry feeling—turn from the past with the temper of forgiving kindness, and to the future with all the firmness which will result alone from unanimity in our own body; continue divided and our cause is lost for ever.

This speech is reported to have made a powerful impression.

The result, after some explanatory speeches from persons who had supported the vote of censure, was the unanimous carrying of Dr. Dromgoole's resolution.

CATHOLIC ASCENDANCY.

The aggregate meeting, of which Mr. O'Connell had given notice, was definitively fixed for Tuesday, the 15th of December, on which day it accordingly took place in Fishamble street theatre.

The first six resolutions here passed bore reference to the preparation and presentation of the Catholic petition to both houses early in the next session; and also to the preparation of an address to Mr. Hely Hutchinson, expressive of Catholic feeling towards him.

The seventh, eighth, ninth, tenth, and eleventh referred, in indignant terms, and with strongly worded contradictions, to allegations in recent addresses of grand juries (city of Dublin, &c.) charging the Catholics "with disaffection—with entertaining disguised any secret views, and with an intention to obtain a Catholic ascendancy."

Then followed thanks to Sheriff Harty, for his conduct in his office; and, as usual, to the Protestants who had attended, in particular to Counsellors Finlay and Walsh, for their speeches.

On the resolution respecting Mr. Hutchinson being put from the chair, there was, as the newspapers inform us, "a loud and general call for Mr. O'Connell, and when he came forward he was greeted for several minutes with the most enthusiastic plaudits."

Mr. O'Connell commenced with a very warm eulogium on Mr. Hutchinson, and dwelt at some length upon the loss of his election. We take up the report of his speech, where he commenced to deal with the recent exhibitions of their enemies.

The meetings in some of the counties where resolutions, hostile to us, have been passed, cannot properly be called *Protestan* meetings. I say *properly*, because, although the parties who were there prominent assumed the denomination of Protestants, they were, in reality, of no religion at all, except, indeed, in so far as might give the means of carrying on a base traffic, and turning the profession of it into money. I shall not think it necessary to name the people to whom I allude, for I am quite sure you will agree with me that their names are of no very high importance. If one instance might be given, and one as insignificant as need be, there was John, Earl of Aldborough. (Hear and laughter.) His lordship was very active in defence of the church, and he was by no means to be blamed; on the contrary; he deserved the greatest commendations for having come forward so boldly, and offered himself as a martyr for the good of the church! Such men honoured the cause they supported (laughter), and the cause, in its turn, honoured them just as much.

In Dublin, the sixteen grand jurymen who had signed the resolutions against the Catholics might have been bought (he was going to say might, perhaps, be sold) by those worthier seven who have refused their signatures. But he was not going to waste time with the *men*, it was with their resolutions and petitions that he had more properly to do, although, in truth, it was little better than a waste of time to deal even with them. (Hear, hear.)

These resolutions and petitions displayed a glorious continuance of the system under which the ministry, which had fostered their rankness, had begun its career—the same barefaced and impudent falsehood—the same meanness and cunning. To that system the majority of one, which they had obtained last session in the House of Lords, was solely attributable. (Hear, hear.) They had, in their official paper, in the *Moniteur* of the ministry, published a falsehood—a foul and calumnious falsehood—imputing to the Catholics a conduct disgraceful and mean as their own; and by this had they operated upon the unsuspecting minds who would otherwise have voted with what turned out to be the minority. To the same base system recourse was had now. The London *Courier*, the same paper I have alluded to, has, in its last number, a paragraph, stating that the "Third Part of the Statement of the Penal Laws, aggrieving the Catholics of Ireland," had been received in London; and that it contained a full and faithful account of the views of the Catholic body. They already knew that this was a pure and mischievous falsehood; the so called "Third Part of the Statement, &c.," was a production of some of the hired writers of the Castle, and was only to be found in the shop of Jack Giffard, or some of his compeers in corruption and bigotry.

But to return to the resolutions of the meetings. They had

brought forward various accusations against the Catholics, and
to one of them I, for one, am perfectly ready to plead guilty.
They have said that what we once asked as a boon and as a
favour, we now demand as a right; and they say well. We do sc.
(Hear, hear.) I would take Emancipation in whatever shape
it came; if it was even held out as are the alms of a beggar, I
should accept it.   But should I for that the less consider it as a
right which was my due, and which ought to have been obtained
by insisting on it as such? Certainly not. I am glad from my
soul that they admit this—that they allow we consider it as a
right. · For when they allow that we demand it as a right for
ourselves, do they not likewise allow that we grant it as a right
to others? and they themselves do away with the foul calumny,
that our religion leads us to believe that no one should have
equal right with professors of it. If religious liberty is *right*
to one, it is a right to all. When we, therefore, say it is a *right*
to us, we allow that the same right belongs to the Quaker, the
Presbyterian, the Dissenter. We do not ask it as relying on
our numbers, our strength, or the wealth of our body; we come
forward on the broad principles, that political equality is the
right of men of all religions; and this our enemies allow; let
them not, therefore, shrink from the consequence.

But if they have said the truth in this instance, they have
amply compensated it in others by the most unblushing falsehoods. They have thrown out imputations in their resolutions
which, I am sure, they themselves are conscious of being grossly
calumnious, and which they would not dare, even in terms the
most distant, to insinuate in private life to any Catholic gentleman in Ireland.

They have said that the Catholics are disaffected. Yet how
often have these Catholics sealed their loyalty with their blood!
If the Prince Regent has forgot Ireland in his speech, his enemies might remind him of her by the respect which they pay
him in consequence of the resources he derives from her. Did
not Vimiera—did not Talavera and Badajoz give proofs of the
loyalty of the Catholics? at Salamanca, was it not felt in the
terrors of rout and defeat by every flying Frenchman? It has
been amply proved. And if Britain would know the benefit she
derives from the proof of it, she may have an idea from but one
solitary instance. Before the late removal of part of the Penal
Laws, I myself had no less than forty relations in the military
service of France, from an inspector-general of infantry down to
a lieutenant; I have now none: but in every victory which

graces the military annals of the British empire, I have to trem-
ble in perusing the Gazette, lest I meet among the lists of the
honourable dead, the name of some dear and respected relative.
Sixteen are at this moment serving in the Peninsula.   If such
be the case only in one instance, and resulting only from the removal of a part of those laws, what might not be expected to the
interests of Britain, were the same benefit extended to all, and
the hopes of our youth allowed, in every instance, to be bound
only by their merits?

They accuse us of a wish for Catholic ascendancy.   Their inconsistency in the accusation is glaring and ridiculous.   They
first blame us for asking Emancipation as a right; and they
then say that we are desirous of a Catholic ascendancy.   Does
not the demanding Emancipation as a right imply that an
equality of privileges is the right of every citizen, be his religion
what it may?   And does not the wish for a Catholic ascendancy
imply, that we think no man ought to be on an equal footing
with the Catholic?   The absurdity is manifest: they accuse us
of saying that an equality of civil privileges is the right of every
citizen, of whatever persuasion; then they accuse us of saying,
that there should be no such thing as an equality of privileges;
and they condemn us for both.

But their absurdities shall not be the ground on which we
shall defend ourselves.   The accusation is contrary to our feelings
—to our opinions; we have already expressed our disapprobation
of any connexion subsisting between government and the Catholic prelates; and I am free to say, that there is no event which I
should consider more fatal to the liberties of Ireland than what
they have called a Catholic ascendancy.   Our prelates would no
longer be the respectable characters in which we now revere
everything that is virtuous or respectable; they would, at least,
have more temptations to become otherwise; and whenever they
should degenerate into the tool of the minister, then should I
consider the doom of Ireland as sealed for ever.

There is, I am sure, no man of education who hears me, that
does not join in the opinion that I have offered; and there is none
who, even in the warmest moments of enthusiasm for the prosperity of those professing the same religion with himself, that
can be charged with having ever uttered a word inconsistent with
it.   I do not refer our enemies to the resolutions of our meetings;
but let them go to the most incautious speech that ever was delivered at any of them—let them scrape together words uttered
in the heat of debate, even then I defy them to find a sentence

that will bear them out in their accusations. It is not necessary for them, after being foiled in the search, to betake themselves to conjecture, and to build a conclusion, on their own suppositions, of our wishes; for well they know, that we have too much of Irishmen about us to conceal them, did we entertain them.

So far, indeed, from wishing for ascendancy, we do not desire that we shall be necessarily taken into any office or political employment whatever; all that we insist upon is, an enlargement of the prerogative of the crown, by which his Majesty may be allowed a wider range in search of virtue, talent, and respectability, among his subjects, in selecting the offices necessary in his government.

There is another circumstance of much importance, which I think it necessary to call your attention to. Every body recollects that the last parliament was pledged—solemnly pledged to the serious and immediate consideration of our claims. The present parliament is completely bound by the promise of the ormer; it is still the imperial parliament, though a few, and very few, indeed, of the persons composing it have been changed; I should hope it will recollect this; it would be a most truly gross and miserable chicanery if it were to attempt a recantation, knowing, as we do, that not even the whole of the new members amount to near the majority, which had the wisdom to decide on giving us a hearing. There is a solemn and deliberate treaty —a direct and unequivocal pledge; it is true, we have known treaties violated; and it is, unfortunately, full as well attested, and that to our own knowledge, that pledges have been left unredeemed. Let them recollect the terrible confusion that ensued when a former pledge was revoked. I shall quote an authority for them, and one which they will be likely to respect, that of Sir Lawrence Parsons, now Lord Ross, as to the probable consequences which he thought were likely to result from retracting that pledge—consequences far more dreadful than I shall either look for or suppose.

When Lord Fitzwilliam came over to this country as chief governor, he gave a pledge for the repeal of the penal laws, when by one of those changes, not unfrequent in the Pitt administration, the pledge was left unredeemed, and that patriotic earl was recalled. When the subject, however, came before the House of Commons, Sir Lawrence Parsons delivered his sentiments, and we have those remarkable expressions in the report of his speech. It is impossible to assert that it gives precisely his words, but if any report be correct, I should suppose this to be, for it seems to bear great marks of care and attention. The report states, that Sir Lawrence Parsons said in the House of Commons, "if a resistance to any thing would be productive of evil consequences, it was that against the wishes of the people, and the prospects which have been held out to them; that if the demon of darkness should come from the infernal regions upon earth, and throw a fire-brand among the people, he could not do more to promote mischief." I hope some one will remind him of this part of his speech at the King's County meeting, which I hear he is to attend to-morrow. He continues, "he had never heard of a parallel to the infatuation of the minister;" he may see one now; "and if he persisted, every man must have five or six dragoons in his house."

And it was true; for in many houses it was necessary for the owners to have five or six dragoons, and the whole country was thrown into confusion. I hope and trust that no such consequence will ever again occur, though sure I am that such is the desire of the British minister. He wishes (to make use of the words of Christopher Hely Hutchinson) that *you should draw the sword, to afford him an opportunity of throwing away the scabbard.* Certain he was, that at this very moment, there was a foul conspiracy to draw the warm-hearted, but unthinking people of Ireland into a sham plot, to give an opportunity of wreaking vengeance on her dearest sons.

Here he must warn his countrymen to abstain and shun, with the greatest caution, every inducement which might be held out to them for disturbances similar to those he had alluded to. Nothing would more thwart the progress of their cause; nothing, he suspected, could, for that reason, be more satisfactory to the ministry, than just so much of it as would give a pretence for a suspension of the Habeas Corpus act, and some other violences of the same description, together with a total refusal of the claims of the Catholics. Ireland had already been taught to beware; her lesson had been stamped in letters of the best blood of her children, and assuredly now she would avoid the snare which was intended for her.

That such was the wish of certain persons in power, he could not doubt. Keegan's plot was not yet to be forgotten; occurrences of the same kind had been discovered in Kilkenny and Limerick. What, too, was the reason that the garrison of Dublin was under orders to be in immediate readiness to march? Why were the matches kept lighted? Why preparations made for attack or defence? Was it not to inspire credulous people with the idea that there was danger of an insurrection; and to induce others, who thought their wrongs almost called for it, to believe that they might soon hope to be joined by others, as injured and more determined than themselves: keeping alive, on the one side, the fire of hatred, and on the other, the desire and hope of revenge.

But the people of Ireland have too much good sense to be misled by such phantoms, by such paltry contrivances. They see that a pretext is only wanting to crush them and their claims for ever, and cancel the bond in the best blood of their country; and they despise the nefarious attempts that are made upon them. They feel, too, that their cause is advancing; nothing can prevent its progress. Ireland, in the meantime, is tranquil, and awaits the result with confidence and hope.

The Prince Regent, in his speech from the throne, alluded to the disturbances in England. What a pity that he had not a Professor Von Feinaigle to recal to his recollection, that he had five millions of peaceable subjects in Ireland, who bore their oppressions with fortitude, and who could not be goaded into disloyalty, even by the foul and false calumnies which were heaped upon them. No; they had proved, and they would continue to prove, that the depraved and contemptible fabricators of those tales had mistaken their aim, and that they could no longer practise upon the credulity of their intended victims How much it is to be lamented, that his Royal Highness had not some person to remind him of Ireland; and to point out the contrast which so strikingly exists between the quiet and profound peace which reigns in it, and that tumult in the other island which he thought it proper to notice in his speech.

I shall now conclude, entreating your pardon for having trespassed so long upon your time, and returning you my grateful thanks for the many marks of your favour which you have been pleased to confer upon me; and particularly for the attention and kindness with which you have heard me this day. I also express my most entire concurrence in the resolutions which you are about to adopt. (The whole of this speech was received with the most marked applause. Mr. O'Connell was frequently interrupted by the cheering, and the acclamations continued long after he had ceased.)

HUGH FITZPATRICK—LIBEL.

[APPLICATION TO SET ASIDE VERDICT.]

Mr Hugh Fitzpatrick, publisher of Scully's "Statement of the Penal Laws," having, for an alleged libellous note in that work, been prosecuted and found guilty, Mr. O'Connell, on the sitting of the court the following day (Thursday, February 11, 1812), rose to make an application to set aside the verdict which had been obtained in this case, as originating from the misdirection of the learned judges who had charged the jury, and as being against law and evidence.

The Attorney-General just came into court, when Mr. O'Connell had proceeded thus far, and called on Mr. Fitzpatrick to appear in person.

Mr. Fitzpatrick immediately came into court, and the Attorney-General moved that he should then stand committed.

Mr. O'Connell observed that such a motion on the part of the Right Hon. Attorney-General was just what had been expected.

The court complied with the Attorney-General's motion, and ordered that Mr Fitzpatrick should stand committed.

Mr. O'Connell then resumed.

He said he made his motion upon the grounds alleged in the notice, which had been served on the other side. The first of which was the misdirection of the learned Judge who had charged the jury; and the second ground was, that it should not be permitted to stand, inasmuch as it was contrary to law, and against evidence.

He said that in case this motion should be refused, it was his intention to submit a further one in arrest of judgment, grounded on the pleadings alone; but as the two motions were perfectly distinct, and that the second one would not become necessary unless the first was refused, he should confine himself solely to that which he had for its object—the setting aside the verdict.

Beside these two grounds which he had mentioned, there were also two others—viz., that the defendant had been deprived of the benefit of a second counsel being permitted to address the jury, although he had produced evidence, which Mr. O'Connell contended was his right; and that the information charged the defendant with having libelled the Duke of Richmond, and his Majesty's ministers in Ireland, acting under his authority, when, in fact, if any imputation of the kind could be attributed to the note which formed what was termed the libel at all, it must have been intended to allude to those who had acted, not those who were now acting; for every person knew that those *nondescripts*, who were entitled his Majesty's ministers, had been changed both between the execution of Barry, and the publication of the book; and again, between the publication and the filing of the *ex-officio* information by the Attorney-General.

The information had been filed in Michaelmas term; it contained two counts, the second of which was wholly out of the question. The word *farmer* had been omitted; and in a prosecution of this nature the defendant was fully warranted in taking advantage of anything in his favour; when the point had been made at the trial, it was not contested. The second count was, therefore, wholly out of the case.

This information stated that Hugh Fitzpatrick being a person of a bad, malicious, and wicked disposition, &c., and desiring to stir up and create a rebellion, &c., did, on the 19th of June last, publish a libel, a false and scandalous libel, *of and concerning* his Grace the Duke of Richmond, &c., and of and concerning his Majesty's ministers in Ireland, *acting* under the authority of the said Lord Lieutenant, &c. It then recites the libel itself, which is of the following tenor :—

"At the summer assizes of Kilkenny, in 1810, one Barry was convicted of a capital offence, for which he was afterwards executed. This man's case was truly tragical—he was wholly.innocent—was a respectable Catholic farmer in the county of Waterford. His innocence was fully established in the interval between his conviction and execution, yet he was hanged, publicly protesting his innocence! There were some shocking circumstances attending this case, which the Duke of Richmond's administration may yet be invited to explain to parliament."

After the libel, close follows the *inuendo*, "meaning that the said Barry did not obtain pardon, because he was a Catholic, although his innocence was fully proved to the knowledge of the said Duke of Richmond, &c."

Such was the information which had been filed by his Majesty's Attorney, upon which a jury returned a verdict of guilty, and in consequence of which Mr. Fitzpatrick then stood in actual custody.

The first of these objections to allowing the verdict to stand, turned upon what was conceived to be the misdirection of the learned judge's charge, which had left it to the jury to decide upon the truth and applicability of the last *inuendo*, which was described, as the *meaning* of the passage, that the said Lord Lieutenant had been advised by his ministers to refuse pardon to a person where innocence had been made apparent after his trial and condemnation, and that such pardon had been accordingly refused in the face of a conviction of innocence, and solely because he was a Catholic.

This *inuendo* contained much new matter which had not been spoken of before.

Of all this, said Mr. O'Connell there had been no previous averment; the information contained only an assertion of the intention being to vilify. There was not a word in the libel concerning advice received by the Lord Lieutenant, or of any action of his in consequence of it; yet, that such averment was necessary there was the strongest authority to prove. In the case of the King against Home, where the opinion of the twelve judges of England was asked by the House of Lords, and was delivered by the Lord Chief Justice De Grey, his lordship states (reported, Cooper, page 683) that where a libel is of such a nature, either from its being ironical, or from having an allusion to circum stances not generally known, that the words in which it is given, do not, of themselves, convey all that is meant and understood, it is necessary that the things so understood and not expressed, should be laid before the jury; but that a jury cannot take cognizance of them unless they be upon the record, where they cannot be unless by an averment; so that either the charge of the Court, upon the trial of Mr. Fitzpatrick, must have been wrong, or the opinion of the twelve English judges, expressed by Lord De Grey, must be so. It could not be said that the *inuendoes* themselves were, in reality, averments; an authority (2nd Salkeld, page 315) was perfectly conclusive on this subject; an *inuendo* being there defined negatively as not being an averment, but on the contrary, a production, *id est*, &c.

It being thus ruled that a jury could not take cognizance of the matter contained in an *inuendo*, without there having been a previous averment, it followed that no evidence in support of the *inuendo*, in the present case, should have been allowed to go to the jury, or, if it had been so allowed, that the judge should have desired them to discharge it entirely from their minds previous to giving a verdict. This, however, had not been done; and, on the contrary, the Court had desired the jury to consider the information precisely as if the averments had been regularly made; it was universally allowed that averments were necessary to let in evidence of *meaning*, even where such evidence could be produced. But here, in point of *fact*, the Crown did not go into any evidence to show the meaning, or prove the *inuendoes;* and, with great respect, he conceived that the jury should have been told, there was no evidence in support of the *inuendoes;* and directing them to find the truth and applicability of those *inuendoes*, there being no averments, was travelling out of the limits prescribed by the law, and recognized by Chief Justice De Grey and the twelve judges of England, and, therefore, he conceived that

the charge of the learned judge had been erroneous, and contrary
to law.

The next ground to which he should call the attention of the
Court was, that there existed a material variation as to a matter
of fact, between the evidence given or admitted, and the information. The information stated, that the libel had been published of, and concerning the persons acting as his Majesty's
ministers in Ireland ; that is, of the persons so acting at the
time of the publication of the libel. Now, it was obvious that
this was an anachronism of the grossest kind. The circumstance
which gave an occasion to the libel had taken place in 1809; the
book had been published in 1812, and the ministers of these two
periods were entirely different. How, then, could the libel be
said to regard the ministry existing at the time of its publication?
It was impossible that it could not exist without entirely vitiat-
ing the information.

He now came to the third ground for the motion, and upon
that he should be still more brief than he had been on the other
two ; it related to the trifling advantage which he might have
derived from being allowed a counsel to speak to evidence. It was
very confidently relied upon, that there could not exist any doubt
as to the right of the defendant, evidence having been produced
on both sides. The objection upon the trial came from a quarter
to which no reply could be made, namely, the Court ; had it
been otherwise, it might have been easily and satisfactorily shown,
that the reason given for this decision did not apply.

Formerly, it had been the practice, if the defendant had evidence, to allow him the benefit of counsel to speak to that evidence. The judges of that court (the King's Bench), however
had thought proper to alter this practice; they determined that
no second counsel should be heard upon the part of the defendant, and they gave as the reason for coming to this decision,
that the defendant's counsel, in opening his case, speaks to the
plaintiff's evidence, and observes upon his own. It was also a
part of the rule, that unless the defendant goes into evidence,
the plaintiff has no right to be heard by a second counsel ; yet
the very Court he was then addressing, and which had made the
rule, had heard counsel for the crown twice in the case of the
King v. Kirwan, although there had been no evidence produced
by the defendant. It must naturally be supposed, that the
Court had determined, that in civil cases no second counsel
should be heard, but that criminal ones did not come within the
rule, otherwise it would be, in fact, granting to the crown an

additional and necessary advantage.   Lord Kenyon, in the case of
the King v. Abbington (1st Espina, 136,) condemns the practice.

Considering that the crown had the benefit of the great and
unrivalled talents of the Solicitor-General, who was to reply, an
advantage which nothing could have procured the defendant, and
which nothing within his power could balance, as the learned
gentleman who had opened his case could not be heard a second
time, and that it would have fallen to his (Mr. O'Connell's) lot
to have spoken to evidence, his client, certainly, had lost but a
small advantage ; such as it was, however, he had a right to it ·
but the Court had thought proper to over-rule that right, and
in doing so had referred to the case of the King v. Kirwan.
Coupling the decision in the case referred to, with that on the
late trial, it came to this, that the rule does apply to take away
the advantage from the traverser, and that it does not apply to
take it away from the crown.

This was a position which he was sure their lordships would
not think of establishing, and unless they did so, the right of his
client to the benefit of a second counsel was unquestionable ;
therefore, the denial of it by the Court rendered the trial faulty,
in respect to the manner in which it had been conducted, and
consequently the result of it nugatory.

He had now arrived at the fourth objection, and one of much
importance ; it was, that the jury had, upon the most material
part of the information, found the verdict without evidence, and
even contrary to evidence.   Mr. O'Connell here read over the
paragraph forming the libel, and contended that there had not
been sufficient evidence to connect any part of it as a libel with
the name of the Duke of Richmond.   This had been attempted,
indeed, by connecting the circumstance mentioned in the libellous note, with passages in the text to which a construction had
been given favourable to the inference wished to be drawn from
the whole.   It was first said that the passages thus read, stated
that government was influenced in granting pardon to criminals,
or in denying it by their religious persuasions ; and it was then
concluded that the note was intended to give an instance of the
partiality alluded to in the text ; and had the text been examined
more clearly, it would have appeared that the thing expressed
was, that Protestant criminals had a greater facility in procuring
attestations of previous good character, or of other circumstances,
such as usually entitle to pardon, than Catholics, and, consequently, that the Lord Lieutenant, so far from having been accused, was justified for granting pardon more frequently to the one

than the other ; the note, then, being an instance of what was asserted in the text, could not reflect, by any means, upon the Lord Lieutenant.   As to the concluding part of the note, which stated that the Duke of Richmond's administration might yet be invited to explain certain circumstances to parliament, it only meant that the documents for regular investigation, being in possession of the ministry, could not be procured without inviting its aid.

Had the trial been had before an unbiassed jury, it was very probable that the result would have been very different.   It was very likely that they would not have been content with the mere *assertion* of the Attorney-General, that the note which formed the subject of the libel was intended to vilify the Lord Lieutenant and his Majesty's ministers in Ireland, acting under his authority ; they might possibly require an explanation of *who those persons, called ministers, actually were,* before they convicted a respectable and honest man of libelling them, merely because the Attorney-General had thought fit to say they were libelled.

It was matter of Irish history, that when these state prosecutions were carrying on against a Catholic of this country, not one man of his own religion was suffered to remain upon the panel.

This had been stated by the respectable and learned gentleman who had opened Fitzpatrick's case, and was not attempted to be denied.   It was observed, indeed, that one Catholic name had happened to be put upon the panel through mistake ; this fault, however, was not intentional; it had occurred by accident, and no doubt the apology which such a trespass required was made.   He was not now stating anything improbable or unwarranted, for it was a well-known fact that the persons who had the appointment of the jury, had given a solemn and deliberate *pledge* of their dislike and hatred of Catholics ; and that it was to this avowed hostility to so numerous and loyal a class of his Majesty's people, that they owed their election.   Thus, in a case where a Catholic is tried upon a charge of asserting, that the Catholic subjects of this country have not equal justice done them, special care is taken that not more than *one* Catholic shall be put upon the *panel*, and that he shall not be of the jury, but that the accused shall be tried by *twelve* men. of a different persuasion from himself, and some of them, perhaps, strongly imbued with prejudices unfavourable to himself and his religion.   Had the question been one of property, such a disgraceful circumstance would not have taken place in the city of Dublin, where as many upright, wealthy, and respectable Catholics were to be found, as could be selected from the ranks of their Protestant fellow-subjects.

Mr. O'Connell now shortly recapitulated his arguments, and submitted to the court that he had made out a case sufficient to induce their lordships to set aside the verdict; and if Mr. Attorney-General thought it prudent to file a fresh information, that a new investigation should be entered into.

The Chief Justice said, that Mr. O'Connell had made much more of the argument than, in the beginning, he thought could be done.

Motion refused.

A suggestion was made that it should remain over till next term.

Mr. O'Connell—"But, my lord, Mr. Fitzpatrick is in actual custody, and it would be very oppressive that he should remain in confinement the whole of the vacation, when it is strongly relied upon that there are sufficient grounds to arrest judgment."

Mr. O'Connell prayed the Court that Mr. Fitzpatrick's recognizance might be immediately taken, in order to avoid his remaining in custody all night. He said that Mr. Fitzpatrick was a respectable man, and there was no danger but he would be forthcoming. He therefore presumed that his own recognizance would be sufficient.

Security—himself in £1000, and two others in £500 each—required.

Mr. O'Connell—"You were already offered to have that requisition complied with upon fair terms. The bail shall be immediately produced."

THE ENGLISH CATHOLICS.

The conduct of the English Catholics came under discussion for the second time this year, in the Dublin Board, on the 13th of February. On this occasion—

Mr. O'Connell rose to propose a resolution, on which he believed there would be but one feeling in the Board. It related to the gratuitous interference of a gentleman in England, and a Catholic, too. The Catholics had before suffered from the officious and unauthorized interference of persons, who had undertaken to act for them with, perhaps, the very best intentions in the world; and it had, therefore, become necessary for them to pay close attention to anything of the kind which was attempted, no matter from what quarter it came. If, as he had just stated, that individual interference, though accompanied by excellent intention, had produced unpleasant consequences, how much more likely was such conduct to cause ill effects, if it were the offspring of a contrary disposition?

Whether the intentions of Mr. Charles Butler were of this latter description or not, he should not then take upon him to decide; but this much was certain, that he had echoed the despicable and unfounded cant which the enemies of the body had been at such pains to propagate; he had complained of the intemperance with which the just demands of so many millions of loyal though oppressed people were urged. He had even gone farther; he had attempted to prove that the Board had been guilty of intemperance; but he (Mr. O'Connell) denied that he had proved any such thing; he utterly dissented from the charge and assertion.

It was not intemperance for men, who knew they deserved to be free, to wish for freedom; it was not intemperance for men, whom the gifts of nature and the advantages of rank and fortune, had combined to render eminent; it was not for such men to be charged with intemperance, because they panted to enjoy those common rights, which are the inheritance of every man in this community. When my Lord Aldborough, and my Lord Kiltarton, and such holy Apostles, assisted by others, whom motives of personal delicacy induced him to refrain from mentioning, wished to drown the Catholics in their inferiority—to force them to continue Helots—slaves—when they saw men endeavouring to perpetuate and sustain every sort of political profligacy, and to clothe that profligacy in the sacred mantle of Christianity—it was not to be wondered at if those who were the sufferers, should assert, with a manly, but constitutional firmness, the impolicy and injustice of perpetuating their degradation.

And was it for this that they were to be charged with intemperance, by such men as he had described? And how could Mr. Charles Butler satisfactorily account for lending himself to such a charge? He (Mr. O'Connell) proclaimed the charge to be a foul and malignant stratagem, invented by the enemies of the cause of Ireland and of the empire. Thank God! they could not say that the Catholics prostrated themselves at the foot of the minister, for the purpose of advancing their interest, or that they sacrificed themselves on the altar of dishonour, and bartered to become the slaves of corruption, instead of being the slaves of an unjust and impolitic penal code. Slavery, in the first instance would be infamy in themselves; in the other (although acutely felt by the victim), it reflected disgrace only on their oppressors!

He moved the following resolution:—

"Resolved—That from recent information, we deem it necessary to state, that no person has been, or is authorised to hold any communication with any member of the administration on behalf of the Catholics of Ireland as respecting their affairs, our confidence being reposed in the noblemen and gentlemen composing the delegation, and acting under the directions of the Board."

The resolution passed unanimously.

NO POPERY PETITIONS.

On 5th the of May, 1813, Mr. O'Connell addressed the Catholic Board on the subject
No Popery Petitions.

Mr. O'Connell rose, and stated that it was his intention to
move for the appointment of a committee to consider in what
manner most consistent with that delicacy which it was desirable to observe towards the real Protestant petitioners, the immense number of forged and fictitious names which had been
affixed to the petition, styled that of the "Freeholders, Freemen,
and Inhabitants of the city of Dublin," and which had been presented with such ludicrous pomp and ceremony, might be brought
before the imperial parliament.

He requested permission to take that opportunity of return-
ng his thanks for the high honour conferred upon him, on the
ast day of meeting, in his appointment as one of the Catholic
delegates.   He entreated also leave to excuse himself from the
apparent neglect of his duties as such.   Those who voted for him
ought to have recollected how entirely impossible it was for him,
at this period of term, to leave Dublin.   He was ready to make
every sacrifice for the common cause; he was ready to sacrifice
nis life to advance civil or religious liberty in his native land.
But he could not tamper with the interests of other persons at
that moment confided to his hands.   He, therefore, very gratefully and very respectfully tendered his resignation of the office
of delegate.

As to the plan which he should recommend for the exposure
of the forgeries, he could not have thought necessary to suggest
it at all, had the Catholic bill been rejected.   He was little disposed to desire the Catholics to alter their tone at any time;
but when the legislature evinced so decided a disposition to grant
and to conciliate, he did not think a corresponding spirit should
be wanted on their part.

The Catholics had at length arrived at that important stage of
their history, that a bill, intended to give them relief, was actually making progress in parliament.   The good intentions of
their friends in parliament were obvious; they intended to extend eligibility—all that was required—with considerable liberality.   What a deplorable circumstance it was, that, with such
excellent dispositions, they have not taken the trouble of acquir-
ing such information as would enable them to carry their good
intentions into practical effect!   The bill they had brought in

was a well-intentioned bill, but it was a slovenly bill! Slovenly in its recitals—slovenly and inaccurate in its details.

Before proceeding further, he wished the tenor and object of his remarks to be distinctly understood. There were clauses purely civil, and clauses that had reference to ecclesiastical matters in this bill. Upon the nature of the latter he should observe a total silence. The discussion of them was too well calculated to produce heats which it was his object to avoid. He should confine himself closely to the subject of civil rights; the Board was not called upon to entertain the question of religious security at all, nor, in fact, was it necessary to be introduced anywhere for the present. When it was seen that the legislature would grant *civil liberty*, then it would be time to let those whose province it was, consider of *religious security*.

As he had bestowed much attention upon the bill, and as he was anxious to serve his countrymen at home, when he did not perceive how he could do it by going to England, he had felt it his duty to lay before the Board the frame and plan of a bill for civil liberty, such as he conceived could not fail to satisfy the people. In submitting this frame, he would again repeat, that he gave the persons who had prepared and brought the bill now before parliament, the most perfect credit for the purity of their intentions. His objections to the frame of the bill, were, perhaps, but technical, still he thought them entitled to attention. There were phrases in the recital and enactment which were new and unknown to the constitution and law. Catholics were to be made participators in what was called *"Free Government."* What was the legal meaning of the word *government*? It was a term, the legal meaning of which was unknown and undefined. It would apply equally well to the government of Constantinople as to that of England. In the common meaning of the word here, we are apt to think of the government of the Duke of Richmond when the words were used, and the Catholics did not desire to have it understood that they wished to participate in his Grace's government. They felt no such inclination; their wish was to participate in the constitution—in the free constitution that had been framed by Catholics—by rigid Catholics—all of whose grand, but now neglected principles of popular power and popular representation, had been established before Protestantism had a being or a name.

It might be deemed trivial to criticise verbal inaccuracies; but let it be borne in mind, that these were the words of an instrument purporting to be a great state bond and compact between two nations, united in name, but kept separate by impolicy and injustice. (Hear, hear.) In this important act every word was of moment, for, upon every word would depend the liberties of living, and of yet unborn millions! (Hear, hear, hear.)

And sorry he was to say, that to defective recitals, still more defective enactments were attached. True it would, upon the condition of taking this vile oath, open the House of Commons and the House of Peers, and many an important office and honourable rank, and serve as a stage in the natural progress to the complete establishment of an equalization of civil rights. But it was slovenly as far as related to the peerage; it was defective as far as related to judicial offices; it was useless with respect to corporations; and it did nothing at all for charities, education, marriage, or landed property; and this was but a brief and amicable summary of its defects.

Such was the bill which was at that moment before the house. How different from what it ought to be—how different from what it might have been, if our excellent liberators had but condescended to consult the parties most interested. (Hear, hear.)

A draft of a bill has been prepared by my friend, to whose pen and to whose services the Catholics are so much indebted (Mr. Finlay). It has my warm approbation, because it is comprehensive in its principles—ample in its relief. It would abolish all civil and lay distinctions for cause of conscience, and open to every faithful subject a career unfettered by the trammels of persecuting laws. It would leave for merit what is now conceded to creed, and destroy jealousies and religious animosities by removing their causes. Such was the bill which, he trusted, would yet be brought before parliament. He begged permission, as it was short, to read it——

Upon this Mr. O'Connell was called to order by Mr. Baggot, Mr. Costigan, and Counsellor Bellew, who spoke at considerable length to show that the merits of the bill, or of any substitute for it, could not be relevant to the object of the motion before the Board.

After a good deal of discussion upon the point of order, in which Mr. O'Gorman and Counsellor Finn also took part, the chairman decided that Mr. O'Connell was certainly out of order and that the draft of the proposed bill should not be read.

Mr. O'Connell immediately submitted to the decision of the chairman, although he said he could show that what he had been saying bore directly upon the question then before the Board; before he proceeded, however, to the more immediate discussion of that question, he gave notice of his intention to submit, next Saturday, a brief abstract and skeleton of such a bill as he conceived was calculated to great real and complete Emancipation.

(Cheers.) I am now come (said he) to that part of the question which is included in the very terms of my motion. I am not confined to the history of the fraud and forgery of which I now complain. I shall not, I trust, be interrupted whilst I observe shortly upon its clauses. I allude not to the hostility—the rancorous but ineffectual hostility of the Richmond administration, in this country, to the rights of the Irish Catholics. That is scarcely worthy of investigation, and deserves little more than to be mentioned for the purpose, simply, of reprobation. The causes I advert to lie deeper; they are to be found in the great and continued success of which falsehood—unblushing falsehood—has already had against the Irish Catholics!

It was not in the field of battle that our liberties were cloven down! (Hear, hear.) No! Our ancestors when they fought, if they did not advance as victors, surrendered upon the faith of an honourable capitulation; but that faith was violated, and its violation was justified by calumny! (Hear, hear, hear.) The Catholics were accused of entertaining opinions which they have ever detested—of adopting positions and principles which they have ever abhorred. Charges were brought forward and repeated against them which could be aptly contradicted only in the broad vulgarity of Lord Ellenborough's language—*"Charges false as Hell!"* Charges—the falsehood of which was known to the very accusers themselves—were repeated, until the credulous were convinced, and the weak yielded. From the Press, the Stage, the Bar, the Bench, and the Pulpit, were opinions charged upon the Catholics directly the reverse of what they entertained, and articles of belief asserted to be theirs, which they always rejected and abjured. Those who were violators of their own faith with the Catholics in *fact*, accused the Catholics of being violators of faith in *theory*; and those men who persecuted the Catholics in reality, accused their victims of being persecutors in imagination and design! (Hear, hear.)

The accusation you feel and know to be utterly false, but it was repeated until it was believed, and the Catholic suffered the punishment, not of any crime of which he could, by any possibility be proved guilty, but of offences fabricated in the malicious fancies of enemies, and which were not only unfounded, but impossible. They were impossible, because so utterly repugnant to human nature, and contradicted by the stamp of his own divine image, which the Diety had infixed upon the human soul. (Cheering.)

Yet, it was by the assertion and re-assertion of those calumnies—it was by attributing to us opinions which, if they existed, I should be sorry a single Catholic remained in Ireland—I am quite sure I should not be one. It was by those false and foul imputations that we were degraded in public opinion, and then reduced to slavery, and since continued in bondage.

It was vain to protest against the untruths ; for near a century they maintained their sway, and new generations sprung up before the appeal of calumniated millions was heard, or their wrongs investigated. (Hear, hear.)

Falsehood having been so long successful, it suited well to the mischievous and malignant activity of the management of the Richmond administration to resort to its resources. Accordingly, the most impure and corrupt Press that ever disgraced any age was set at work, with plenty of present pay and of future expectation, to traduce, to calumniate, and to vilify the Catholics collectively and individually. (Hear.) Accordingly, all the ancient calumnies were revived, and every new calumny brought forward that could be invented by a very malignant disposition, but a very miserable intellect. The seven-times-sold apostate from every principle was purchased and arrayed against us, until all the force that malicious dulness could collect was brought into action, and commanded by a general better versed in the quibbles of the law, than in the tactics of the field. It was in pursuance of this government plan of imposition, that the "Third part of the Statement of the Penal Laws" made its appearance —that it was circulated in England as genuine, and given to the world as the sentiments of men, who held its contents and its authors in equal contempt !

Perhaps, so scandalous and impudent an imposition never disgraced the annals of bigotry. But the fabricators—have they been punished ? Oh, no ! Mr. Attorney-General has no terrors for men who would divide and distract ; he prudently reserves all his vengeance for those who dare to preach harmony and conciliation, and to call oppression and bigotry by their right names.

Next in order followed this petition, the signatures to which are the object of my present motion. It commenced in falsehood, it was conducted by fraud, and it was consummated by forgery. Yes, its commencement was in falsehood, for it was alleged to have been voted at a meeting of " the freemen, freeholders, and inhabitants of the city of Dublin." ' This allegation was printed in several of the Dublin newspapers for near three months, and to the assertion was affixed the name " Abraham Bradley King," and yet a more unfounded assertion was never made—an allegation more destitute of truth never insulted the patience of public credulity, than that signed and repeated for three months, under the signature of "Abraham Bradley King." I need not ask, when this meeting was called, or where, or by whom? I need not remind you, that there was no theatre suffi ciently large to contain such a meeting, if it ever took place ; nor need I revive the indignation which the miserable excuse excited, that, really, the exhausted remnant of a supper table at the Mayor's house, did vote itself, being full half a dozen in number, into the freemen, freeholders, and inhabitants of the city of Dublin, and then passed this petition! And yet, in sober sadness it must be admitted that no better justification existed for the Lord Mayor's assertion of a public meeting.

I said that it was conducted by fraud ; for this fraud, we are told by the uncontradicted report of the public papers, was re- sorted to. The mayor procured himself to be deputed—nobody knows by whom—to take the petition to London. Arrived there, he presented, we are told, the no-Popery petition, as the authorized delegate of the Corporation of Dublin. Yet, he had no such authority ; he was the simple messenger of a simple party of obscure individuals who, as this petition originated at a supper, sent him off from a dinner, after which the Duke of Richmond ludicrously graced him with a troop of horse to accompany his mock lordship thence to the Pigeon-house. His very journey to London was a fraud, because it held out to the English people the appearance of the first magistrate of a great city despatched by the constituted authorities of that city on public business. Under that pretence he presented himself in London, whilst it is shrewdly whispered that he attended for the purpose of en- deavouring to traffic upon the importance of his official station, in order to get the name of his son inserted into an appoint- ment connected with his lucrative employment. In short, the farce was just worthy of the legal managers that are at the bottom of every work of bigotry and persecution in Ireland, and of the inflated buffoon who was the principal actor.

The consummation of the petition was forgery, in the ordi- nary sense of the word, consisting of the affixing the names of individuals without their authority or consent ; forgery, equally, if not more culpable, in writing hundreds of imaginary names, and affixing them to this petition from a multitude. The Pro- testants of Ireland petitioned last year on our behalf. The wealth, the worth, the talent of the Irish Protestants—every thing that was noble, and dignified, and intelligent, and independent amongst our Protestant brethren united in that petition; their names have been printed, and it is with pride and with pleasure that we see those names constitute a large book, whilst every name speaks a volume of mutual affection and reciprocal charity.

This is, indeed, a proud display for Ireland; this was all she wanted from man, that her children should combine in conciliation and harmony. It would, really, have afforded a curious incident in the history of human frailty, if those who had come forward last year, under the banners of liberality and justice, had been seduced this year to join the blood-stained flag of Orange intolerance. (Hear, hear.) The experiment had been made; everything that the wealth and power of the state—that the ingenuity of the advocates, or the authority of the judges—that the exertions of the writer, or the intrigues of the courtier could supply, was brought into action, to seduce, to convince, to intimidate, to control, to cajole, and to deceive the Irish Protestants. But all these resources failed; the drunken orgies and the morning preaching intemperance of abuse, and the hypocritical lamentations of pretended friendship were tried, and tried without effect. The independent and enlightened Protestants of Ireland remained true to the liberality which they had professed, and rejected every attempt to bring them over to the ranks of our opponents. (Hear, hear.)

It was a matter, therefore, of much curiosity to discover who the 2,800 "freemen, freeholders, and inhabitants of Dublin" could possibly be: public curiosity has been gratified—gratified by the inspection of the names—gratified by the discovery that the dagger is air-drawn and imaginary, by which it was sought to assassinate Protestant character and Catholic liberty! (Hear, hear.) I have seen an authentic copy of this formidable petition, and I rejoice to be able to assure you, that it affords decisive evidence of the low state of intolerance. I have read this list, and, after the most minute inquiry, added to my own knowledge in this city, it does appear to me that there are not twenty names to this petition of persons of fortune and independence of mind, who signed it from mere motives of conscientious bigotry. This class of persons are certainly to be treated with the most respectful deference; they labour under a mistake, but they act from pure intentions, and I respect whilst I pity them. They had an undoubted right to petition against conceding, upon any terms, anything to the Papists; they had a clear right to pray the legislature to continue to be indiscriminate in laying on the burdens of the state, but partial in conferring its benefits. I admit their perfect right to sign this petition, and I request it may be understood, that I am incapable of applying any harsh expression to them, as I certainly also am of feeling any resentment against them. But, undoubtedly, in the number of twenty, I have given abundant room for the uninfluenced signatures.

I blush to tell you that this list contains three or four of the Irish bar. (Hear, hear.) I am ashamed to say that there are so many certainly as three—I fear four. The Irish people, long accustomed to find in the Irish bar the friends of every freedom, will hear it with astonishment, notwithstanding the acrimony, the native and the imported acrimony, towards the Catholics, cherished by the head of the law department. It will scarcely be believed that our profession, proudly distinguished, as it formerly was, for liberality and love of country, has so fallen as to afford even three signatures to an anti-Catholic petition. I regret, from my soul, the discovery. (Hear, hear.)

The number of clergymen of the Established Church who signed this petition is, I am happy to say, few ; nor, when we recollect what excellent and accomplished gentlemen those clergymen in general are, will it excite any surprise in the minds of the bigots of any sect, that the number of their signatures should be few. Of attorneys, there are, at least, eight or ten—I expected to find twice the number ; of placemen, there are many ; of pensioners, several ; many from the offices of the castle ; many from the police offices ; several from the custom-house : almost all the hired constables ; the judge, the registrar, and the proctors of the prerogative court, and as many of the wretched watchmen of Dublin as are, or pretended to be, Protestants ; there has been so much liberality exercised, as to admit poor Papists to the dignity of the nightly watch. (A laugh.) To these are to be added the "tag, rag, and bob-tail" of the corporation—numbers of those who hold its principal stations—all those who hold its lower offices, and are appointed and removable at pleasure. Add to these, writing clerks, dependents, and a small, but hungry group of expectants, and you have the entire catalogue of genuine signatures.

But there will remain near two thousand signatures to be still accounted for—near two thousand signatures will remain, for whom no owner can be found. (Hear, hear.) Of those there are some hundreds which purport to belong to individuals who have indignantly disclaimed them. There are, in short, some hundreds of forgeries. (Hear, hear.) Need we give a more

striking instance than that of Mr. Stephens? He discovered
that his name had been forged to this petition, and immediately
wrote to the Mayor, to inform him of the circumstance; the
Mayor did not condescend to give any reply, but took the known
forgery to England, and presented it to the House as genuine.
(Hear, hear.) When forgery was exhausted mere fiction was
resorted to. There was danger in giving names which, being in
common use, might be disavowed by individuals bearing them.
The fabricators of this petition set disavowal at defiance; they
produced names which no man ever bore or will bear—(Hear,
hear); they invented John Hedpath, and coupled him with John
Ridpath—they attached James Hedpath to James Ridpath; they
united the noble families of the Feddlies to the illustrious race
of Fiddlies; they created the Jonneybones, and added the M'Coo-
bens to the Muldongs; to the uncleanly Rottens is annexed the
musical name of Navasora—the Sours and the Soars—the Dan-
dys and the Feakens—the Gilbasleys and the Werrillas—five
Ladds and five Palks—the Leups and the Zealthams—the Huzies
and the Hozies—the Sparlings and the Sporlings—the Fitzgetts
and the Fibgetts—the Hoffins and the Phantons, and the Giri-
trows, and the Hockleys and Breakleys, the Russinghams, and the
Favuses, and the Sellhews, and the Mogratts and Calyells—all,
poor innocents, are made to combine against us, and to chime
with the Pithams and Paddams—the Chimnicks, and Rimnicks,
and Clumnicks, and the Rowings and Riotters; they threw in
the vulgar Bawns, and after a multitude of fantastic denominations, they concluded with Zachariah Diamond. (Great laughter.)

In short, a more tasteless group of imaginary beings was never
conjured up by the delusions of magic. To the tune of "Jonny
Armstrong,"—they gave us five-and-twenty Armstrongs, and
placed eighteen Taylors on the list—it ought to have been "four-
and-twenty tailors all in a row," there would have been some
pleasantry in it. In short, by these means, by the force of mere
invention, upwards of one thousand names have been added to
this petition, and one thousand children of the brain of those
worthy managers of intolerance appeared in formidable array
against us, at the bar of the House of Commons, covered with
the mantle of the Mayor for swaddling clothes. (Laughter.)

It is incumbent on us to bring these facts before the public
and the legislature; we owe it to ourselves and to our children,
to get rid of an obstacle to our liberty and theirs; we owe it to
the legislature to detect the imposition which has been practised
upon them; and chiefly it is due to the liberal Protestants of

Ireland to rescue the Protestant name from this additional imputation of bigotry which their enemies, no less than ours, would
cast upon it. (Hear, hear.)

There is, too, another motive, which, I confess, influences me
powerfully. The very men who have been guilty of those base
forgeries have, in a recent instance, foully tarnished the Irish character; an innocent person was accused—an innocent female was
accused—perjury the most foul—subornation the plainest and
most palpable, were used against her life, and, still more, against
her honour. We, Irish, often feel (it is part of the real character
of Irishmen) pity for the accused, it is said, even for the guilty;
but accused innocence excites our warmest sympathies; but
when female innocence stood accused, I thought for the honour
of my country. I thought that, without any poetical fiction,
thousands of Irish swords would start from their scabbards, and
that the wretch would be driven from society who checked our
manly, our virtuous indignation. But a set of beings, I will not
call them men, have been found, who, under the auspices of the
persecuting Castle, the pious and no-Popery forgers have been
found to refuse the poor and pitiful tribute of their approbation
to exalted virtue and dignified purity, escaped from calumny,
from subornation of perjury. These loyalists—these creatures
who call themselves exclusively loyal, because they are the ready
sycophants of every tool of power—(Hear, hear)—these exemplary loyalists, have refused to address the niece and the daugh-
ter-in-law of their King—the wife of the Regent—their future
Queen—(Hear, hear)—the mother of their future Sovereign,
though the triumph which her unassisted innocence obtained
over the vilest conspiracy ever disclosed, powerfully demanded
the expression of congratulation.

And what excuse did they give for this refusal? Why, they
scorned all mockery and delusion, and insisted that to address
the Princess was to insult the Prince; and would the Prince feel
insulted at such an address? I should hope two things of him
—first, that he means, hereafter, to redeem the pledge he has so
often repeated to the Irish Catholics (Hear, hear); and, secondly,
that he does not feel insulted when the triumph of the Princess
over her perjured and her suborned traducers is celebrated.—
(Hear, hear.)

But who are the men who have refused to address her Royal
Highness? Who are they who have no sense of justice—no abhorrence of calumny—no enthusiasm in defence of female innocence? They are our enemies; they are the fabricators of every

falsehood, and of every forgery that could injure or impede our cause; they are men who degrade the Irish name—the character of manhood. (Hear.) We are bound by every consideration dear to men, and sacred to Irishmen, to expose to the empire those wretches—to show them as they are—poor, paltry, and profligate—the ready slaves of every secretary—secretary's clerk. We are bound to show the British empire that it was not the Irish—not the mercantile inhabitants of Dublin—but the dregs of the fabricators of its frauds and its forgeries, that could refuse, under the pretext of not wishing to displease the Prince, an ad-dress of congratulation to his once persecuted, but now trium-phant consort. (Hear, hear.)

In short, I desire to succeed in my present motion, for this first and principal reason, that the meanness of the open enemies of the Princess amongst us, and of their titled and legal instiga-tors and prompters, may be put on record for ever. That will be done by bringing the question of those forgeries and fictitious signatures before the House of Commons. (Hear, hear.) To impose upon that House is, I presume, a breach of its privileges. (Hear.) Let us demand inquiry and investigation. Our asser-tion will be, that two-thirds of the signatures to this petition were forged, or simply fictitious; but we will not require an as-sertion to be credited without proof; we will challenge inquiry; we will show five hundred names without an owner (hear); and we will then point out the fabricators of this mean and dishon-ourable scheme to retard the progress of Emancipation.

If we are mistaken, our enemies can easily confute us; they have only to produce the individual. Mr. Riotter may head their party. I should be glad to see the gentleman. If he does not live in the city, this Riotter, I presume he is to be found in the liberties. After him our enemies can show off Mr. Wevilla, hand in hand with Mr. Navasora, and Johnny Bones, Esq., may appear with Fibgetts, gent., and even Mr. Knowing can be sum-moned to come forward in company with Mr. Dandy. (Cheers and laughter.)

But why should I fatigue with the ridiculous catalogue. If those men exist—pardon my supposition—if they exist, they live for our enemies; if they do not exist, then what is to become, in public estimation, of those our enemies—of those worthy allies of the traducers of her Royal Highness? Perhaps their spirit of loyalty may save them in parliament from punishment, but their fraud and forgery will consign them to the execration and con tempt of posterity.

Mr. O'Connell concluded. amid great cheering, by moving the following resolution :—

" Resolved—That a sub-committee of twenty-one members be appointed to take into consideration the most proper method of investigating, and respectfully submitting to parliament, the alleged forged and fictitious signatures to. the petition against the Catholic claims, to the House of Commons, by the Lord Mayor of Dublin."

Major Bryan seconded Mr. O'Connell's resolution, which was agreed to unanimously.

" Resolved—That the committee be directed to request the aid of such of our Protestant brethren as may be pleased to assist in accomplishing the object of their report."

CATHOLIC RELIEF BILL

On the 29th of May, 1813, Mr. O'Connell read, in the Catholic Board, the unanimous repudiation by the Catholic prelates of Ireland. of the then proposed "religious securities" in the Catholic Relief Bill of that session.

To this document, continued Mr. O'Connell, I was requested to call the attention of this Board, whom the authors have ever honoured with their esteem ; at all events I was desired to deposit it in the hands of the secretary. I have discharged one part of my duty, I perceive not without the approbation of the meeting ; I will now discharge the remainder, (handing it to the secretary,) troubling you with very few observations indeed. (Loud cries of hear, hear.) This communication is such as has been usually received at periods much less important than the present. It contains no assertion beyond the strict bounds of episcopal propriety. The only objection I can possibly see to its being received with respectful thankfulness and cordiality, arises from a consideration personal to myself, (hear, hear.) On the last occasion, two prelates condescended to attend here, and made in their own persons the communication of their brotherhood ; the task has this time devolved to hands much more incompetent and less entitled to consideration ; and I admit, that this undesirable circumstance might, if there were no justification for it, be a very substantial reason why you would not now feel so well pleased as before. But, gentlemen, there exists what you will, I am sure, think a sufficient justification for it. There was a distinguished prelate to whom the duty of waiting on this Board was delegated. From this most Rev. prelate—his Grace

the Archbishop, Dr. Murray—I had this morning the honour of
a letter, intimating his wish that I should appear here for him.
I wrote back to him stating that I should much rather see himself in attendance ; and I got an answer, alleging, as the sole
reason of his intended absence, a sufficient one, as I am quite
sure you all must at once allow, that he would be kept away by
avocations connected with the discharge of his sacred functions
too urgent to afford him leisure or admit of delay. (Hear, hear.
Enemies might have suggested that there was an appearance of
disrespect, or of some want of sufficient attention in the variance
from the formality that was observed on the last occasion, but I
flatter myself, it is now quite clear to every gentleman that it
was an appearance only. (Yes, yes.) The motion, then, which
I intend to submit, of a respectful vote of thanks to the prelates,
members of the Catholic Synod, for their communication, and
for the zeal and vigilance they always evince on behalf of the
Catholic Church, will, of course, have your approbation, and the
loud and unanimous concurrence of the people of Ireland. (Hear,
hear.)

Indeed, I may venture to say, that there was no motion ever
submitted to this Board, to which assent will have been so completely yielded as a matter of course.

The Catholic prelates of Ireland deserve your eternal gratitude. They have stood forward manfully and without disguise,
to assist you in getting rid of a bill which purported to be for
your relief, but which, in reality, would have perpetuated your
degradation and your slavery. (Loud cheers.) The prelates, if
they had given their countenance and support to this bill, might
have consulted and advanced their own worldly interests. But
the sacred calls of duty made them reject such considerations
with contempt. It is not possible to impute any motives for
their opposition to the measure, but such as must indisputably
have originated in conscience and a sense of duty. (Cheers.)

And they were right, clearly right. They were right—I take
it in the spiritual matter involved in the new regulations ; and
they were most manifestly right in its temporal operation. Nothing but mischief and degradation, nothing, I repeat, but the
heaviest mischiefs and the most utter degradation could have
resulted from the commission which was proposed in this bill.
For see by whom it was to have been formed and selected, and
of whom it was likely to be composed. It was to have been
the creation of the Duke of Richmond, of that man whose administration has been signalized by a sullen and sulky oppos-

tion to the Catholics of Ireland ; and whose most distinguishing characteristic as a chief governor is, that he continues bitterly to hate the Papists—he knows not why nor wherefore. (Hear, hear.)

Well, this hopeful commission, this "charter of emancipation," (laughter and cheers,) was to be framed by his Grace the Duke of Richmond, and upon whom is it likely that his choice would fall ? Recollect, however, that before his, before even his selection commenced, you were certain of having, as president of this commission, that ludicrous enemy of ours, who has got, in jest, the names he deserves in good earnest, of "*Orange Peel.*" (Hear, hear.)   A raw youth, squeezed out of the workings of I know not what factory in England, who began his parliamentary career by vindicating the gratuitous destruction of our brave soldiers in the murderous expedition to Walcheren, and was sent over here before he got rid of the foppery of perfumed handkerchiefs and thin shoes, upon the ground, I suppose, that he had given a specimen of his talents for vindication, that might be useful to the present and future administrations of Ireland ; in short, that he was a lad ready to vindicate anything—everything!

This special vindicator was to be at the head of the proposed commission.   And let me dismiss him for ever, by venturing to conjecture what he may hereafter be in our country.   But no; I will not—I cannot estimate his future qualities.   It is impossible to say what the man may be in old age, who, young—with the first impressions of nature about him—with a heart uncontaminated, at least, by much intercourse with the world—with any charities of his nature unsullied—with any milk of human kindness unexhausted—whose first step in life was the vindication of the most foolish and the most cruel—the most absurd, and the most fatal—the most useless, and the most murderous expedition that human insanity ever directed, or human depravity ever applauded.   (Great cheering.)

After this worthy president would have come—the chosen of his Grace—first, we should have had, I presume, my Lord Manners ! a gentleman, certainly, by birth, education, and in deportment; but, I can safely assert, quite as ignorant of the state of the Irish people, and as unacquainted with their wants, wishes, feelings, and dispositions, as he was the day before his arrival in this country.   Surrounded by, and pleased with those men only who are inclined and interested to deceive him, he has received their miserably mistaken opinions, and adopted their bigotry with a facility quite inconsistent with a sound judgment or an enlarged understanding—and still more, incompatible with a good heart.

In truth, he seems just such a man as bigotry would select as her choice instrument. Too decent to inspire any disgust—too polite to give personal offence—too weak to discriminate between the artful misrepresentation of bigotry and the plain language of truth, and with the natural propensity of a small mind to the practical details of intolerance. (Hear, hear.) He has no connection with this country—no interest in its prosperity. He has no stake in its lands, nor does he possess a habitation or a dwelling of his own in Ireland. He is a dry lodger—in furnished lodgings; and when the hour of his departure shall arrive—and may it soon come—he will only have to put his hat upon his head, to turn into bills his large savings on the ten thousand a year, which the poor people of Ireland pay him, and forget us as rapidly as we shall consign his name to oblivion. (Cheers.)

Next to my Lord Manners, we should have been sure to find upon the list of these commissioners, the Duke of Richmond's privy councillor, the Right Hon. Doctor Duigenan! he, who was so specially appointed by his Grace for ecclesiastical affairs, and for none other, that he was very aptly compared to the tanner's dog, kept chained all day, and only let loose at night. This religious bull-dog is particularly fitted for worrying Popish bishops, no tanner's dog ever hating a thief at night, as he does a Popish priest in the noon-day. It is not in the nature of the canine guardian, either of the tanned leather or of the ascendancy, to feel pity or show mercy. (Hear, hear.) Poor Popery would soon have been torn to pieces beneath his vile tooth.

Either Mr. William Saurin, the Attorney-General, a man after Doctor Duigenan's own heart (hear, hear), or Jack Giffard would have been the third commissioner. I suppose the choice would fall on Saurin; for although he is as either of the other two, and pretty much on a par with them in rancour, yet I will very candidly confess, I think him rather superior in other respects to Giffard. He would, therefore, be chosen; I take it for granted; and what a state this would be for Ireland?—the grandson of a French Huguenot sitting in judgment on the Catholic hierarchy of the land! A man, belonging, in fact, to the only sect of Protestants who, even under persecution, asserted the atrocious and unshaken principle of intolerance, and afforded to those who deprived them of liberty of conscience, the semblance of an excuse by avowing, that if they were themselves in power they would persecute in their turn! With what delight would Mr. Saurin hold his inquisitions, under the pretence of examining into the loyalty of the candidates for the mitre, but for the purpose of discovering and excluding the talent, the integrity, and the piety of our priesthood!

And, if these commissioners—if Saurin and Duigenan, Peel and Lord Manners, should not be sufficient to exclude from the prelacy all the piety, the integrity, and the talent of the Catholic priesthood, should they so neglect their duty, as to allow a single worthy man to exercise episcopal functions in Ireland, the Lord Lieutenant would, under the "*charter of emancipation*"—for I like the expression—have had it in his power to remove them from that office, and to substitute others who would carefully abstain from committing any similar mistake.

So that if this bill had passed into a law, some accident might, perhaps, have given us, at one time or the other, one respectable bishop. It would have been impossible that we could have had a second, or any other, save from among the most supple and pliant tools and slaves of the Secretary of the Castle.

I will not task you as Catholics, but I will boldly demand of you as Irishmen, whether you do not rejoice at having escaped from an act of parliament, the necessary consequences of which I have thus laid before you? (Hear, hear, hear.) Do you not rejoice, that the corrupt influence of the government is not to be extended to your church, and that there remains, and will remain, in Ireland, one spot free from ministerial pollution, and that your bishops are not to be degraded to the subserviency of gaugers and tide-waiters, nor your priesthood to the dependence of police constables? (Hear, hear.) If your feelings and opinions be, as your approbation of those sentiments proclaim them to be, accordant with mine—if you dread as Catholics, and abhor as Irishmen, the extension of the influence of the servants of the crown, an influence equally fatal to religion and to liberty, you will join with all your hearts, in the unanimous adoption of my motion. (Loud cheers.)

The bishops have stood between you and this bill; they have stood between you and the mephitic breath of ministerial corruption; they have stood in the front of the battle of Ireland, and they deserve that, without any regard to the event, the first praise and glory should be theirs. Recollect, too, that your refusal to adopt my motion, if it were possible you should refuse to adopt it, would imply an approbation of this most paltry and misconceived bill. To refuse your thanks to the Catholic prelates of Ireland, would be to declare that they deserve censure

If you think so, reject my motion; but no, no, it is impossible you could bear the name or form of Irishmen, and censure the rejection of this absurd and mischievous bill. (Cheers.)

I shall say one word more and conclude. Perhaps there are amongst you men who would confide in the liberality of your enemies. If such there be, let him, I entreat, but recollect the ruffian shout of English insolence, with which the declaration of the majority against the only valuable clause in this bill was received. Oh! may that be the last shout of English victory over poor, fallen, and degraded Ireland! (Hear, hear.) May the measure of English iniquities, and of English triumphs over us be full, and the day-star of Ireland at length arise. (Hear, hear, hear.)

But they have triumphed, they have defeated, and they have insulted us. Oh, fortunate Napoleon! it is thus the leaders of your foes have ever conducted themselves. Of little avail was your victory at Lutzen to you, compared with this victory! The men who defeated your legions at Barrossa and Vimiera, at Badajoz and Salamanca, are degraded although they are brave, and are insulted because of their fidelity. Their valour is disheartened by being refused its just reward, and their honour is insulted, and tarnished, and trod under the hoof of the yelling and triumphant spirit of English bigotry!

They defeated you, but you are now revenged; your English allies have defeated them, and added contumely and disgrace to defeat. Without a bribe or a subsidy from you, have these English fought your battles; and if these your most useful allies have been paid, it has been out of another treasury than yours. (Hear, hear.) I shall say no more—I cannot trust myself on this maddening subject. This last insult is indelibly written on mine and every other Irish heart. (Hear, hear.) There it shall live for ever; we may forgive it, but it shall never, never, be forgotten. (Hear, hear, and cheering for several minutes.) Mr. O'Connell then moved—

"That the most respectful thanks of the Catholic Board be given to the Most Rev. and Right Rev. the Catholic Prelates in Ireland, for their communication to us this day, and for their ever vigilant and zealous attention to the interests of the Catholic church in Ireland."

Major Bryan seconded the motion, and Mr. Byrne spoke warmly in its support.

Anthony Strong Hussey, Esq., rose to move an amendment It was to the effect, "that all the words after the word 'communication' should be omitted;" that is to say, thank the prelates simply for the communication they had that day made to the Board through Mr O'Connell, and to leave out that branch of the motion which went to thank them for

"their ever vigilant and zealous attention to the interests of the Catholic church in Ireland."

Counsellor Bellew seconded and supported the motion, in a long and able. t ut most discreditable speech

REPLY TO MR. BELLEW.

Mr. O'Connell rose and spoke as follows :—

At this late hour, and in the exhausted state of the meeting,
it requires all the impulse of duty to overcome my determination to allow the debate to be closed without any reply ; but a
speech has been delivered by the learned gentleman (Mr. Bellew),
which I cannot suffer to pass without further answer.

My eloquent friend, Mr. O'Gorman, has already powerfully
exposed some of its fallacies ; but there were topics involved in
that speech which he has not touched upon, and which, it seems
to me, I owe it to the Catholics and to Ireland to attempt to
refute.

It was a speech of much talent, and much labour and preparation.

Mr. Bellew declared that he had spoken extempore.

Well, (said Mr. O'Connell,) it was, certainly, an able speech,
and we shall see whether this extempore effort of the learned
gentleman will appear in the newspapers to-morrow, in the precise words in which it was uttered this day.   I have no skill in
prophecy, if it does not happen ; and if it does so happen, it will,
certainly be a greater miracle, than that the learned gentleman
should have made an artful and ingenuous, though, I confess, I
think a very mischievous speech, without preparation.

I beg to say, that, in replying to him and to the other supporters of the amendment, I mean to speak with great personal
respect of them ; but that I feel myself bound to treat their
arguments with no small degree of reprehension.   The learned
gentleman naturally claims the greater part of my attention.
The ingenuity with which he has, I trust, gratuitously advocated
our bigoted enemies, and the abundance in which he has dealt
out insinuations against the Catholics of Ireland, entitle his discourse to the first place in my reprobation.   Yet I shall take
the liberty of saying a passing word of the other speakers, before I arrive at him ; he shall be last, but I promise him, not
least in my consideration.

The opposition to the general vote of thanks to the bishops was led by my friend Mr. Hussey. I attended to his speech with that regard which I always feel for anything that comes from him; I attended to it in the expectation of hearing from his shrewd and distinct mind something like argument or reasoning against this expression of gratitude to our prelates. But, my lord, I was entirely disappointed; argument there was not any—reasoning there was none; the sum and substance of his discourse was literally this, that he (Mr. Hussey) is a man of a prudent and economical turn of mind, that he sets a great value on everything that is good, that praise is excellent, and, therefore, he is disposed to be even stingy and niggard of it; that my motion contains four times too much of that excellent article, and he, therefore, desires to strike off three parts of my motion, and thinks that one quarter of his praise is full enough for any bishops, and this the learned gentleman calls an amendment. (Hear, hear, and a laugh.)

Mr. Bagot came next, and he told us that he had made a speech but a fortnight ago, which we did not understand, and he has now added another which is unintelligible; and so, because he was misunderstood before, and cannot be comprehended at present, he concludes, most logically, that the bishops are wrong, and that he and Mr. Hussey are right. (Hear, hear, and laughter.)

Sir Edward Bellew was the next advocate of censure on the bishops; he entertained us with a sad specimen of minor polemics, and drew a learned and lengthened distinction between essential and non-essential discipline; and he insisted, that by virtue of this distinction, that which was called schism by the Catholic prelates, could be changed into orthodoxy by an Irish baronet. This distinction between essential and non-essential, must, therefore, be very beautiful and beautifying. It must be very sublime, as it is very senseless, unless, indeed, he means to tell us, that it contains some secret allusion to our enemies. For example, that the Duke of Richmond affords an instance of the essential, whilst my Lord Manners is plainly non-essential; that Paddy Duigenan is essential in perfection, and the foppish Peel is, in nature, without essence; that Jack Giffard is, surely. of the essential breed, whilst Mr. Willy Saurin is a dog of a different colour. (Hear, and laughter.)

Such, I presume, is the plain English of the worthy baronet's dissertation. Translated thus, it clearly enough alludes to the new commission; but it would be more difficult to show how it

applied in argument against my motion.   I really did not expect
so whimsical an opposition from the honourable baronet.   I.
there be any feeling of disappointment about him for the rejection of the double Veto bill, he certainly ought not to take revenge on the Board, by bestowing on us all the tediousness of
incomprehensible and insane theology.   I altogether disclaim
reasoning with him, and I freely consent that those who relish
his authority as a theologian, should vote against the prelates.

And, now, I address myself to the learned brother of the theological baronet.   He began by taking great merit to himself, and
demanding great attention from you, because he says that he
has so rarely addressed you.   You should yield to him, he says,
because he so seldom requires your assent.   It reminds me of
the prayer of the English offi, er before battle : " Great Lord,
said he, during the forty years I have lived, I never troubled
you before with a single prayer.   I have, therefore, a right, that
you should grant me one request, and do just as I desire, for
this once."   (Hear, hear, and laughter.)   Such was the manner
in which the learned gentleman addressed us ; he begs you wil
confide in his zeal for your interests, because he has hitherto con
fined that zeal to his own (loud and continued cries of hear, hear.
He desires that you will rely upon his attention to your affairs
because he has been heretofore inattentive to them ; and tha
you may depend on his anxiety for Catholic Emancipation, inas
much as he has abstained from taking any step to attain the
measure.   (Hear.)

Quite different are my humble claims on your notice—quite
different are the demands I make on your confidence.   I humbly
solicit it, because I have sacrificed, and do, and ever will sacrifice, my interest to yours—because I have attended to the varying posture of your affairs, and sought for Catholic Emancipation, with an activity and energy proportioned to the great object of our pursuit.   I do, therefore, entreat your attention
whilst I unravel the spider-web of sophistry with which the
learned gentleman has this day sought to embarrass and dis-
figure your cause.

His discourse was divided into three principal heads.   First,
he charged the Catholic prelates with indiscretion.   Secondly
he charged them with error.   And lastly, he charged the Catholics with bigotry ; and with the zeal and anxiety of an hired
advocate, he gratuitously vindicated the intolerance of our oppressors.   I beg your patience, whilst I follow the learned
gentleman through this threefold arrangement of his subject.   I

shall, however, invert the order of his arra gement, and begin with his third topic.

His argument, in support of the intolerants, runs thus. First, he alleges that the Catholics are attached to their religion with a bigoted zeal. I admit the zeal but I utterly deny the bigotry. He seems to think I overcharge his statement; perhaps I do; but I feel confident that, in substance, this accusation amounted to a direct charge of bigotry. Well, having charged the Catholics with a bigoted attachment to their church, and having truly stated our repugnance to any interference on the part of the secretaries of the Castle with our prelates, he proceeded to insist that those feelings on our part justified the apprehensions of the Protestants. The Catholics (said Mr. Bellew) are alarmed for their church; why should not the Protestants be alarmed als for theirs? The Catholic (said he) desires safety for his religion; why should not the Protestant require security for his : When you, Catholics, express your anxiety for the purity of your faith (adds the learned advocate), you demonstrate the necessity there is for the Protestant to be vigilant for the preservation of his belief; and hence, Mr. Bellew concludes, that it is quite natural, and quite justifiable in the Liverpools and Eldons of the Cabinet, to invent and insist upon guards and securities, vétoes, and double vetoes, boards of control, and commissions for loyalty.

Before I reply to this attack upon us, and vindication of our enemies, let me observe, that, however groundless the learned gentleman may be in argument, his friends at the Castle will, at least, have the benefit of boasting, that such assertions have been made by a Catholic, at the Catholic Board.

And, now, see how futile and unfounded his reasoning is: he says, that our dislike to the proposed commission justifies the suspicion in which the plan of such commission originated; that our anxiety for the preservation of our church vindicates those who deem the proposed arrangement necessary for the protection of theirs—a mode of reasoning perfectly true, and perfectly applicable, if we sought any interference with, or control over, the Protestant Church. If we desired to form any board or commission to control or to regulate the appointment of their bishops, deans, archdeacons, rectors, or curates; if we asked or required that a single Catholic should be consulted upon the management of the Protestant Church, or of its revenues or privileges; then, indeed, would the learned gentleman be right in his argument, and then would he have, by our example, vindicated our enemies.

But the fact does not bear him out ; for we do not seek, nor desire, nor would we accept of, any kind of interference with the Protestant Church. We disclaim and disavow any kind of control over it. We ask not, nor would we allow, any Catholic authority over the mode of appointment of their clergy. Nay, we are quite content to be excluded for ever from even advising his Majesty, with respect to any matter relating to or concerning the Protestant Church—its rights, its properties, or its privileges. I will, for my own part, go much further ; and I do declare, most solemnly, that I would feel and express equal, if not stronger, repugnance to the interference of a Catholic with the Protestant Church, than that I have expressed and do feel to any Protestant interference with ours. In opposing their interference with us, I content myself with the mere war of words. But if the case were reversed—if the Catholic sought this control over the religion of the Protestant, the Protestant should command my heart, my tongue, my arm, in opposition to so unjust and insulting a measure. So help me God ! I would in that case not only feel for the Protestant and speak for him, but I would fight for him, and cheerfully sacrifice my life in the defence of the great principle for which I have ever contended— the principle of universal and complete religious liberty. (Loud and repeated cheers.)

Then, can any thing be more absurd and untenable than the argument of the learned gentleman, when you see it stripped of the false colouring he has given it ? It is absurd to say, that merely because the Catholic desires to keep his religion free, the Protestant is thereby justified in seeking to enslave it. Reverse the position, and see whether the learned gentleman will adopt or enforce it. The Protestant desires to preserve his religion free ; would that justify the Catholic in any attempt to enslave it ? I will take the learned advocate of intolerance to the bigoted court of Spain or Portugal, and ask him, would he, in the supposed case, insist that the Catholic was justifiable. No, my lord, he will not venture to assert that the Catholic would be so ; and I boldly tell him, that in such a case, the Protestant would be unquestionably right, the Catholic, certainly, an insolent bigot. (Hear, hear.)

But the learned gentleman has invited me to a discussion of the question of securities, and I cheerfully follow him. And I do, my lord, assert, that the Catholic is warranted in the most scrupulous and timid jealousy of any English, for I will not call it Protestant, (for it is political, and not, in truth, religious) in-

terference with his church. And I will also assert, and am ready
to prove, that the English have no solid or rational pretext for
requiring any of those guards, absurdly called securities, over us
or our religion.

My lord, the Irish Catholics never, never broke their faith—
they never violated their plighted promise to the English. I
appeal to history for the truth of my assertion. My lord, the
English never, never observed their faith with us, they never
performed their plighted promise ; the history of the last six
hundred years proves the accuracy of my assertion. I will leave
the older periods, and fix myself at the Revolution. More than
one hundred and twenty years have elapsed since the treaty of
Limerick ; that treaty has been honourably and faithfully performed by the Irish Catholics ; it has been foully, disgracefully
and directly violated by the English. (Hear, hear, hear.) English oaths and solemn engagements bound them to its performance ; It remains still of force and unperformed ; and the
ruffian yell of English treachery which accompanied its first violation, has, it seems, been repeated even in the senate house at
the last repetition of the violation of that treaty. They rejoiced
and they shouted at the perjuries of their ancestors—at their
own want of good faith or common sense.

Nay, are there not present men who can tell us, of their own
knowledge, of another instance of English treachery ? Was not
the assent of many of the Catholics to the fatal—oh ! the fatal
measure of the Union purchased by the express and written promise of Catholic Emancipation, made from authority by Lord
Cornwallis, and confirmed by the prime minister, Mr. Pitt ?
And has that promise been performed ? or has Irish credulity
afforded only another instance of English faithlessness ? Now,
my lord, I ask this assembly whether they can confide in English promises ? I say nothing of the solemn pledges of individuals.
Can you confide in the more than punic faith of your hereditary
task-masters ? or shall we be accused of our scrupulous jealousy,
when we reject, with indignation, the contamination of English
control over our church ?

But, said their learned advocate (Mr. Bellew), they have a
right to demand, because they stand in need of securities. I deny
the right—I deny the need. There is not any such right—there
exists no such necessity. What security have they had for the
century that has elapsed since the violation of the treaty of Limerick ? What security have they had during these years of
oppression and barbarous and bloody legislation? What security

have they had whilst the hereditary claim of the house of Stuart remained? And, surely, all the right that hereditary descent could give was vested in that family Let me not be misunderstood. I admit they had no right; I admit that their right was taken away by the people. I freely admit that, on the contrary the people have the clear right to cashier base and profligate princes. (Hear, hear.) What security had the English from our bishops when England was invaded, and that the unfortunate out gallant Prince Charles advanced into the heart of England, guided by valour, and accompanied by a handful of brave men, who had, under his command, obtained more than one victory? He was a man likely to excite and gratify Irish enthusiasm; he was chivalrous and brave; he was a man of honour, and a gentleman; no violator of his word; he spent not his time in making his soldiers ridiculous, with horse-tails and white feathers; he did not consume his mornings in tasting curious drams, and evenings in gallanting old women. What security had the English then? What security had they against our bishops or our laity, when America nobly flung off the yoke that had become too heavy to be borne, and sought her independence at the risk of her being? What security had they then? I will tell you, my lord. Their security at all those periods was perfect and complete, because it existed in the conscientious allegiance of the Catholics; it consisted in the duty of allegiance which the Irish Catholics have ever held, and will, I trust, ever hold sacred; it consisted in the conscientious submission to legitimate authority, however oppressive, which our bishops have always preached, and our laity have always practised. (Cheers.)

And now, my lord, they have the additional security of our oaths, of our ever-inviolated oaths of allegiance; and if they had emancipated us, they would have had the additional security of our gratitude and of our personal and immediate interests. We have gone through persecution and sorrow; we have experienced oppression and affliction, and yet we have continued faithful. How absurd to think that additional security could be necessary to guard against conciliation and kindness!

But it is not bigotry that requires those concessions; they were not invented by mere intolerance. The English do not dislike us as Catholics—they simply hate us as Irish; they exhaust their blood and treasure for the Papists of Spain; they have long observed and cherished a close and affectionate alliance with the ignorant and bigoted Papists of Portugal; and now they exert every sinew to preserve those Papists from the horrors of a foreign yoke. They emancipated the French Papists in Canada, and a German Papist is allowed to rise to the first rank in his profession—the army ; he can command not only Irish but even English Protestants. Let us, therefore, be just; there is no such horror of Popery in England as is supposed ; they have a great dislike to Irish Papists; but separate the qualities—put the filthy whiskers and foreign visage of a German on the animal, and the Papist is entitled to high favour from the just and discriminating English. We fight their battles ; we beat their enemies ; we pay their taxes, and we are degraded, oppressed, and insulted —(loud applause), whilst the Spanish, the Portuguese, the French, and the German Papists are courted, cherished and promoted.

I revert now to the learned gentleman's accusation of the bishops. He has accused them of error in doctrine and of indiscretion in practice. He tells us that he is counsel to the college of Maynooth, and, in that capacity, he seems to arrogate to himself much theological and legal knowledge. I concede the law but I deny the divinity; neither can I admit the accuracy of the eulogium which he has pronounced on that institution, with its mongrel board of control—half Papist and half Protestant. I was, indeed, at a loss to account for the strange want of talent —for the silence of Irish genius which has been remarked within the college. I now see it easily explained. The incubus of jealous and rival intolerance sits upon its walls, and genius, and taste, and talent fly from the sad dormitory, where sleeps the spirit of dulness. I have heard, indeed, of their Crawleys and these converts, but where, or when, will that college produce a Magee or a Sandes, a M'Donnell, or a Griffin? When will the warm heart of Irish genius exhibit in Maynooth such bright examples of worth and talent as those men disclose? It is true, that the bigot may rule in Trinity College; the highest station in it may be the reward of writing an extremely bigoted and more foolish pamphlet; but still there is no conflicting principle of hostile jealousy in his rulers; and, therefore, Irish genius does not slumber there, nor is it smothered as at Maynooth.

The accusation of error brought against the bishops by the learned gentleman, is sustained simply upon his opinion and authority. The matter stands thus:—at the one side, we have the most rev. and right rev. the Catholic prelates of Ireland, who assert that there is schism in the proposed arrangement; on the other side, we have the very rev. the counsel for the college of Maynooth, who asserts that there is no schism in that arrangement. These are the conflicting authorities. The rev. prelates assert the one; he, the counsellor, asserts the other; and, as we have not leisure to examine the point here doctrinally, we are reduced to the sad dilemma of choosing between the prelates and the lawyer. (Laughter and cheers.) There may be a want of taste in the choice which I make, but I confess I cannot but prefer the bishops. I shall, therefore, say with them, there would be schism in the arrangement, and deny the assertion of the rev. counsel, that it would not be schism. But suppose his reverence, the counsel for Maynooth, was right, and the bishops wrong, and that in the new arrangement there would be no schism, I then say, there would be worse; there would be corruption, and profligacy, and subserviency to the Castle in it, and its degrading effects would soon extend themselves to every rank and class of the Catholics.

I now come to the second charge which the learned gentleman. in his capacity of counsel to the college of Maynooth, has brought against the bishops. It consists of the high crime of "indiscretion." They were indiscreet, said he, in coming forward so soon. and so boldly. What, when they found that a plan had been formed which they knew to be schismatic and degrading—when they found that this plan was matured, and printed, and brought 'nto parliament, and embodied in a bill, and read twice in the House of Commons, without any consultation with, and, as it were, in contempt of the Catholics of Ireland—shall it be said, that it was either premature or indiscreet, solemnly and loudly to protest against such plan! If it were indiscreet, it was an indiscretion which I love and admire—a necessary indiscretion, unless, perhaps, the learned counsel for Maynooth may imagine that the proper time would not arrive for this protest until the bill had actually passed, and all protest should be unavailing.

No, my lord, I cannot admire this thing called Catholic discretion, which would manage our affairs in secret, and declare our opinions, when it was too late to give them any importance. Catholic discretion may be of value at the Castle; a Catholic secret may be carried, to be discounted there for prompt payment. The learned gentleman may also tell us the price that Catholic discretion bears at the Castle, whether it be worth a place, a peerage, or a pension. (Loud cheering.) But, if it have value and a price for individuals, it is of no worth to the Catholic people. I reject and abjure it as applicable to public officers. Our opinions ought to be formed deliberately, but they should be announced manfully and distinctly. We should be despi-

cable, and deserve to continue in slavery, if we could equivocate
or disguise our sentiments on those subjects of vital importance;
and I call upon you to thank the Catholic prelates, precisely because they had not the learned gentleman's quality of discretion,
and that they had the real and genuine discretion, which made
them publish resolutions consistent with their exalted rank and
reverend character, and most consonant to the wishes and views
of the Catholic people of Ireland. (Hear, hear.)

I now draw to a close, and I conjure you not to come to any
division. Let the amendment be withdrawn by my learned
friend, and let our approbation of our amiable and excellent,
our dignified and independent prelates, be, as it ought to be,
unanimous. We want unanimity; we require to combine in
the constitutional pursuit of Catholic Emancipation; every class
and rank of the Catholics—the prelate and the peer, the country
gentleman and the farmer, the peasant and his priest; our career is to begin again; let our watchword be unanimity, and
our object be plain and undisguised, as it has been, namely,
simple Repeal. (Loud applause.) Let us not involve or embarrass ourselves with vetoes, and arrangements, and securities,
and guards, and pretexts of divisions, and all the implements
for ministerial corruption, and Castle dominion; let our cry be
simple Repeal. (Applause.)

It is well—it is very well that the late bill has been rejected.
I rejoice that it has been scouted. Our sapient friends at Cork
called it a "Charter of Emancipation." You, my lord, called
it so; but, with much respect, you and they are greatly mistaken. In truth, it was no charter at all, nor like a charter;
and it would not have emancipated. This charter of emancipation was no charter; and would give no emancipation. As a
plain, prose-like expression, it was unsupported; and, as a figure
and fiction, it made very bad poetry. No, my lord, the bill
would have insulted your religion, and done almost nothing for
your liberties; it would have done nothing at all for the people
—(loud and repeated cries of hear, hear); it would send a few
of our discreet Catholics, with their Castle-discretion, into the
House of Commons, but it would not have enabled Catholic
peers in Ireland to vote for the representative peers; and thus
the blunder arose, because those friends, who, I am told, took
so much trouble for you, examined the act of Union only, and
did not take the trouble of examining the act regulating the
mode of voting for the representative peers. (Loud cries of
hear, hear.)

The bill would have done nothing for the Catholic bar, save the paltry dignity of silk gowns ; and it would have actually deprived that bar of the places of assistant-barrister, which as the law stands, they may enjoy.   It would have done nothing in corporations—literally nothing at all ; and when I pressed this on Mr. Plunket, and pointed out to him the obstacles to corporate rights, in a conference with which, since his return to Ireland, he honoured me, he informed me—and informed me, of course, truly—that the reason why the corporations could not be further opened, or even the Bank of Ireland mentioned, was, because the English would not listen to any violation of chartered rights ; and this bill, my lord—this inefficient, useless, and insulting bill—must be dignified with the appellation of a " Charter of Emancipation."   I do most respectfully entreat, my lord, that the expression may be well considered before it is used again.

And now let me entreat, let me conjure the meeting to banish every angry emotion, every sensation of rivalship or opposition ; let us recollect that we owe this vote to the unimpeached character of our worthy prelates.   Even our enemies respect them ; and, in the fury of religious and political calumny, the breath even of hostile and polemical slander has not reached them.   Shall Catholics, then, be found to express, or even to imply censure ?

Recollect, too, that your country requires your unanimous support.   Poor, degraded, and fallen Ireland ! has you, and, I may almost say, you alone to cheer and sustain her.   Her friends have been luke-warm and faint-hearted : her enemies are vigilant, active, yelling, and insulting.   In the name of your country, I call on you not to divide. but to consecrate your unanimous efforts to her support, till bigotry shall be put to flight, and oppression banished this land for ever.   (Hear, hear, and loud cheering.)

EMANCIPATION—THE REGENT'S PLEDGE.

At a meeting of the Catholic Board, on the 29th of May, 1813, Mr. O'Connell spoke as follows. upon the Regent's pledge relative to Catholic Emancipation :—

He said, he rose to make the motion of which he had given notice on Saturday last, relative to the recorded opinion of his

Royal Highness the Prince Regent, upon the subject of the Catholic claims.

It was a duty which he felt imposed on him by the present posture of Catholic affairs, to place beyond the reach of controversy, present or future, the various motives which had encouraged the Catholics of Ireland to persevere in pressing their wants on the consideration of parliament. Desirous to obtain Emancipation through the legitimate channels of the constitution, and I would not accept it through any other, I wish to demonstrate to the world, that we have had, and still ought to retain, the highest possible personal encouragement to persevere in the demand of our rights—to show that those rights have been distinctly and unequivocally, deliberately and repeatedly recognized by the very first personage in the state.

This is one great object of my present motion. There is another, and one of some personal and national interest. I wish to justify to the world the enthusiastic effusion of affection with which the first approach to power of his Royal Highness the Prince Regent was greeted by so humble an individual as myself —effusions which were congenial to the sentiments, as they were freely adopted by the deliberate assent of the people of Ireland. I desire to prove, that we were not actuated by the mere delusion of loyalty, nor by the expectations of royal patriotism, originating in our own warmth of hope, or created by the fertility of our own fancy. Our hopes may have been delusive, but they were not irrational.

Allegiance to the sovereign has been long the pride and boast of the Catholic people of Ireland—an allegiance not created by personal kindness, but sustained by a rigid sense of duty. The Catholics were loyal to the ill-fated and oppressive house of Stuart. Even amidst the crimes of that unfortunate family—and towards the Irish they were very criminal—even amidst the crimes and oppressions of that family, the Irish continued faithful; and, in the season of their distress, when the Stuarts deprived themselves of all other friends, the Irish Catholics served them with a zeal and a bravery proportioned only to the wants of their former oppressors. Allegiance then, perhaps, ceased to be a duty and was certainly imprudent; but the Irish heart was not cold or calculating, and it cheerfully spilled its dearest blood in the protection of those very princes, who, in the hour of their prosperity, had insulted and plundered them. Carried too far, it was a mistaken and an absurd principle of action; but the spring nas not lost all its elasticity, and what our fathers had been, the Catholics of the present day were inclined to be.

The Prince of Wales certainly appeared to justify this over-weening propensity to loyalty, and had been brought up in the school of the most manly and honest statesman of the age—Charles James Fox—a man who inherited so much of fervour of liberty, that it glowed in his heart amidst the chilling scenes of parliamentary profligacy, and was never extinguished, even by the cold damps of ministerial corruption. The Prince had been long dear to Ireland. When upon his Majesty's first illness in 1788, Mr. Pitt, that greatest curse that ever providence, in its wrath, had inflicted on England—when Mr. Pitt, in 1788, resolved to alter the constitution, and, in point of fact, disinherited the Prince of his due succession to the regal power, he was applauded by the corrupt tribe of borough-mongers, whose applause he paid for with the public money, and he was supported by, what was then called, the monied interest, with whom he had bartered and sold his country. Mr. Pitt accomplished his purpose in England, and bequeathed his example as no unproductive legacy to the late pious Perceval.

But the Irish parliament judged more rightly; there were borough-mongers in it in abundance. There were corrupt and bribed men in it; but there was an Irish heart in that parliament, that more than once triumphed over all the influence of the minister, and over all the powers of corruption. The Irish parliament decided—and decided justly—that, as upon the personal demise of the King, the regal authority would belong, of unquestionable right to the Prince; so, upon the political and moral decease of the reigning sovereign—for loss of reason is surely moral and political decease—the authority of the crown ought, by the closest and clearest analogy, belong to the same prince.

In the one case, George the Third was, for any of the purposes of the constitution, as much dead as in the other; and the commensurate consequences ought to have followed in one case as in the other. It was thus the parliament of Ireland determined; and the Irish people, with one voice, confirmed that decision.

Who can forget the answers of his Royal Highness—who can forget how he talked of his "affection and gratitude to the generous people of Ireland?"—how he promised to devote his life "to the preservation of their liberties—to the establishment of their happiness!"

When, after a silence of more than twelve years, the Catholic question was revived and brought before parliament in 1805, we had the meanness (pardon me the expression, it is extorted by truth) to apply to Mr. Pitt to present our petition. Mr. Pitt, whose written pledge in favour of Catholic Emancipation, was in our hands—Mr. Pitt, ever consistent in abandoning any principle that might injure his interests, refused to interfere on our behalf, or to perform his promise.

How different was the conduct of Mr. Fox. He well knew that by assisting us, he would increase the number of his ene mies in England, and the difficulty of his attaining power. But he did not hesitate to become our advocate ; he presented the petition, and supported it by one of those powerful bursts of eloquence, the effects of which upon the English mind, still ope rate in our favour. At that period, Mr. Fox was the intimate —the particular friend of the Prince. It required little power of association to combine the wishes of the one with the senti ments of the other. And although the Prince did not attend the House of Peers, when our question was debated—though he neither spoke in the house, nor voted for us, yet his opinions were not concealed.

Shortly after that debate, a letter was written, by the late Earl of Kenmare, to a gentleman still in this town, stating the substance of a communication made to him by the Prince of Wales on the subject of our claims, in which the Prince most distinctly recognized the justice and the expediency of conces sion to us ; excused himself for yielding to the obvious motives of delicacy, which prevented him at that period from taking any public part on our behalf, but added the solemn declaration of his determination to forward our relief so soon as he might have it in his power constitutionally to do so. Such, Mr. Chairman, was the substance of the Prince's pledge, as stated in the letter of the Earl of Kenmare. It contained a request, that the gentleman to whom it was written (a Catholic barrister of family and fortune, and of eminence in his profession.) should show it to many of the Catholic noblemen and gentlemen in Ireland, so as to give it as much publicity as possible, without inserting it in the newspapers.

And, here, I beg leave to correct an error into which I was led on this subject by the perusal of Lord Kenmare's letter. I certainly did understand his lordship to have stated, that the Prince's sentiments were communicated in writing, and were transmitted to the noble earl, by Colonel M'Mahon, at Cheltenham. How I could have been mistaken I know not, but it is quite certain that I was under a mistake ; for, having at a public meeting asserted the existence of such written pledge in the hands of Lord Kenmare, his lordship wrote to me shortly after to say, that he had no written pledge from the Prince—that the declaration made to him by his Royal Highness was not in writing, but was merely verbal. I did then press upon his lordship to allow me to put before the public, in an authentic shape, the particulars of such verbal declaration, and declared, if he would do so, my readiness to contradict the existence of the pledge in writing. But I could not succeed in obtaining from him the publication under his direct sanction, of the precise nature and of the particulars of a communication in which millions are interested.

Since that period the noble lord is no more. With his virtues, his secret, if I may so call it, is buried. Nothing remains of it but the fading recollection of persons who have heard the language of the Prince only from the report of the noble earl. There lives, however, another noble earl, and long may he live for Ireland—the Earl of Fingal (hear, hear,) to whom a similar communication was made by the Prince of Wales. It was not made in any confidence, but expressly for the purpose of being circulated amongst the people of Ireland, and to serve as a soothing balm to assuage the fever of a disappointment created by a rejection of their petition. This declaration of his Royal Highness to the Earl of Fingal contained the same assertion of his having been prevented by motives of delicacy and respect from giving us public support, and of his conviction of the justice of our claims, and his determination to assist, wherever he might be able to afford constitutional assistance.

I am enabled to be thus minute, because the particulars of his communication have been preserved with an accuracy suitable to their importance. The Earl of Fingal, who is placed at the head of the Catholics of Ireland, much more by the unfading lustre of his virtues, than by his exalted rank and ancient honours—Lord Fingal, on the very day of his communication, put the particulars upon paper ; and as Lord Clifden, and the late Lord Petre, were present at the conversation, the paper was shown to them on the same day, and they declared the perfect accuracy of its contents. This it is that I am desirous should come before the public, and remain for ever as an authentic document of the free and unbiassed opinion and judgment of his Royal Highness the Prince of Wales in our favour

I repeat that no delicacy is violated by the disclosure of this fact ; it was communicated to me without any circumstance betokening confidence. I heard it from the noble earl in Fitz-patrick's shop ; there were three or four others present—one of whom was my respected friend Captain Bryan ; and indeed, from its nature, it could not have been intended for any secrecy.

But this was not the only authentic proof we had of the sen-timents of his Royal Highness; there are several gentlemen pre-sent, to whom a similar pledge from the Prince was communi-cated, by his Grace the Duke of Bedford, whilst he was Lord Lieutenant in this country. Indeed, I understand that nothing could be more distinct than the promises held out in that respect by the Duke of Bedford ; and there can be no doubt that his Grace did not so promise without the express authority of his Royal Highness. With these sure grounds of hope—with a re-liance upon the honour and integrity of the Prince—with all the confidence inspired by his declaration, that power was a trust for the people, the Catholics of Ireland viewed his accession to power with the most ardent, the most affectionate demonstrations of loyalty.

That loyalty does, and will ever remain unshaken ; but subse-quent events have damped the ardour of our affections, and turned into the cold observances of duty, those feelings of en-thusiastic attachment with which we were prepared to support a prince who should rule for the good of the people. If those feelings had been encouraged—if their growth had been fostered, what a different scene would Ireland at this day present ! In-stead of detaining an army in her barracks, her entire population, her instinctively martial population, would have furnished ten armies for the public service, and the tranquillity of the land would be secured by an unarmed police constable. Would to God I could contribute to produce such a state of the public mind ! But, if we cannot revive those hopes, let us, at least, save the grounds upon which they stood as an imperishable re-cord of our right to freedom. Our children will, in addition to the arguments in favour of their liberty, be able to adduce the authority of. first, nearly a majority of the House of Lords ; se-condly, of repeated majorities in the House of Commons ; and thirdly, of his Royal Highness the Prince Regent.

Besides, the authentication of this pledge may serve as a check upon the favourites and ministers of his Royal Highness With the knowledge of the existence of these pledges, that pious and very exemplary character, Lord Yarmouth, may cease to infuse

N

scruples into the mind of the Prince. Nothing can be more admirable than Lord Yarmouth's zeal for the Protestant religion ; he is an ornament to the Protestant church, and it is certainly a consolation to the people of Ireland to be able to attribute their sufferings to the hallowed source of that noble lord's piety. But he will not, zealot though he be, he will not advise his royal master to leave those his solemn pledges unredeemed ; neither will any minister attempt to advise the Prince to violate his word. or to enter into an unconstitutional and unbecoming canvass against us, or to hold out promotion in the army as a reward for betraying our rights; neither will any prime minister of the Regent dare to suggest the holding up of any office. such, for example, as that lately held by Lord Ormonde, to auction. to ascertain who could bid most parliamentary interest against the Catholics, as the price of such a place.

Nothing of that kind can occur to the mind of a minister who beholds how solemnly his Royal Highness has promised to us his countenance and protection. I think, therefore, you will not hesitate to accede to my motion. My object is, that it should be carried into effect in the manner most respectful to the Earl of Fingal ; I feel for that noble lord the most profound respect. The Irish people owe him and they cherish for him, the most unbounded gratitude. I shall deeply regret if my motion gives him one unpleasant sensation ; I think it is not calculated, as it certainly is not intended to do so. And should his lordship think that this is not the moment to give to the public the document in question, I shall respect the delicacy that may suggest a decision, which in itself I would consider unfavourable to the just hopes of the Catholics.

Mr O'Connell concluded by moving—

" That the secretary be directed to write to the Earl of Fingal, in the most respectful manner, to request of him to communicate to the Board the contents of the paper, containing the declaration of his Royal Highness the Prince of Wales on the Catholic claims, made to his Lordship, in the presence of Viscount Clifden and Lord Petre."

Major Bryan bore testimony to the accuracy of Mr. O'Connell in the statement he had made relative to Lord Fingal. He (Major Bryan) had been present, as was also Sir Francis Goold, when the noble earl related the entire circumstances of the declaration of the Regent.

Mr. Bagot said he was happy that the result of the learned gentleman's oration was such as to save him the trouble of going over the numerous topics he had introduced, and to render it only necessary for him to give a short opinion upon the expediency of his motion as it respected the personal feelings of Lord Fingal. And as it regarded his lordship's private sentiment he had no hesitation in avowing that it met with his most decided disap

,probation. He knew Lord Fingal would not consent to the request that was about to be
made to him—nay, he had authority for avowing the fact.
Why should he then be placed in an invidious and disagreeable position ?
Mr. Bagot (in the words of the report we quote—viz., the *Dublin Evening Post*) concluded a very dignified and animated speech, by deprecating a warfare with the first
magistrate of these realms, who could do service, and might do injury. Some gentlemen
seemed to consider such a warfare extremely useful in promoting the success of the cause
of Ireland.

Mr. O'Connell said he had but one word to reply to that assertion of Mr. Bagot's, which attributed to the violence and disrespectful conduct of the Catholics, the opposition they had to
encounter from a certain quarter. That gentleman was strangely
mistaken. It was surprising how he could be so very much
mistaken. It was long before the resolutions he alluded to, that
the opposition to the Catholics commenced.

Nay, long before those resolutions, and while the Catholics
were in the midst of their praises of the Regent, and full of their
hopes from him, while they were calling his Royal Highness their
early friend—their best and proudest hope—it was then, even
then, in the full tide of their warm affections that they had been
met by a state prosecution—that they were handed over to the
Attorney-General, and to the Duke of Richmond, and to Lord
Manners, that their delegates were arrested, and their meetings
dispersed !

It was at that period of confidence and affection that the common police justices were sent to arrest the noble earl at their head !

The resolutions to which Mr. Bagot had alluded were *not* the
causes of the opposition to us; they were, on the contrary, the
consequences of that very opposition. They followed as the
effect of that opposition ; they did not precede nor create it. It
was after the prosecution against us had commenced, long after,
that we publicly mourned the "*unworthy witchery*" which had,
with magic touch, blasted our fervent hopes, and blighted our
fairest projects!

It would, seem, too, that Mr. Bagot threatens us with the
alienation of the mind of his Royal Highness from us and from
our cause. He forgets that the Prince is of a very forgiving disposition. Before he attained power, his royal brother, the Duke
of Cumberland, gave him, it is said, no great cause for ardent
affection. They were supposed to be upon no very good terms,
yet he has become, and most deservedly, a prime favourite, so
that, although that royal duke is valiantly serving his country,
and putting down the French, one is surprised he can be spared
at home! (Cheers and laughter.)

Again was there ever so decided an enemy to the Prince as
the man whom he selected as his first and favourite prime minister, the god-like Perceval? What is it, too, that has attached
him to Lord Yarmouth? But I need not press the subject.
Can it be otherwise than clear that his Royal Highness is not
actuated by mere low and selfish motives. He has neither predilection nor resentments!

Mr. Bagot made a brief reply, chiefly in explanation, and the Board then divided :—
For Mr. O'Connell's motion (that Lord Fingal should be written to respecting
the written account of the Regent's declaration to him in favour of the
Catholics) -   -   -   -   -   -   -   -   -   -   - 36
Against the motion -   -   -   -   -   -   -   -   -   - 0
                                                          ————
        Majority in favour -   -   -   -   -   - 30
Major Bryan then moved, pursuant to notice :—

" That the Right Honourable the Earl of Donoughmore be requested
to present the Catholic petition, which had been some time since handed
to him, forthwith, to the House of Lords."

Mr. Hussey suggested some preliminary communication with his lordship. Some diffi-
culty might arise as to the precisely proper course of preferring the application to the
House of Lords.
He did not, however, press his opposition.

Mr. O'Connell said that the motion had his hearty concurrence, and he rose merely to express the full confidence of the
Irish people, in the Earl of Donoughmore. In his family, the
Catholics had found their first and their best advocates—their
sincerest friends. That noble earl would support their cause, as
the cause of a great people ought to be supported. He would
rest it upon the basis of right and justice, and give to every class
of Dissenters the benefit of the principle for which the Catholics
contended—the principle of universal liberty of conscience.

Lord Donoughmore would enter into no compromises unbecoming so great a principle. He would not seek to buy over one
enemy by bartering for his vote part of our liberties; nor would
he seek to purchase another enemy by discounting with him part
of our religion. The Catholics could confide in the Earl of
Donoughmore; in his talents, his integrity, his manliness, and
his devotion to his country, they must repose unlimited confidence. It was in the expression of that confidence, and of their
gratitude, that they might fail; because language was inadequate
to express the fulness of the Irish heart, towards that friend who
had never been even mistaken in his advocacy of their cause.

It was deeply to be regretted that our other friends did not
imitate that noble lord. It was deeply to be deplored that they

had so widely mistaken the proper course. No man could be absurd enough to doubt for one moment the sincerity or the pure patriotism of Grattan. But it was the misfortune of Ireland that his eye, rolling in the fine frenzy of poetic eloquence, was so filled with its own light as to be quite insufficient for the minute details of practical drudgery. No man admires Mr. Grattan more—few admire him so much as I do; and I respect, with bitter sorrow, the errors of his judgment—his heart was never wrong.

I may (said Mr. O'Connell,) be calumniated for speaking the truth to you; but I owe it to my country to express—to express with great respect for our friends—to express my entire disapprobation of the manner in which they have lately conducted our cause. They imagined, perhaps, that they showed impartiality in their scorn of our assistance; or, perhaps, they still entertain—justly perhaps—the notion, that there is in Protestant intellect a natural and moral superiority over that of Papists. at least of Irish Papists, which cannot be surrendered!

But see what the facts are, Mr. Grattan, I understand, took over with him to England a draft of a bill for our relief, drawn in Dublin, last winter, by, I believe, Mr. Wallace, Mr. Burton, and Mr. Burroughs. Not a single Catholic—lay or ecclesiastical—merchant, lawyer, or priest was consulted upon it. Surely we are not quite so dull as not to know what have served us; but no—not one Catholic was consulted. This bill arrived in England, but there, I have heard, was altogether abandoned, and a new bill got up by some worthy English gentleman, who would, I presume, feel something like an insult, if it were suggested to him that we could assist him. Our delegates were in London they were never consulted; they almost obtruded their advice; they were received with courtesy, but all confidence was withheld from them. Well, this bill is at last produced, and it turns out to be just what our enemies could have wished. It is narrow and limited in principle, or rather, it asserts no principle. It is slovenly and untechnical in its language. It is inoperative as to any substantial relief. It is introduced, to be sure, with all the pride, pomp, and circumstance of eloquence, more than human; but the very person who introduced it was only the first victim to it delusion.

There never lived a man less capable of practising any deception than Mr. Grattan; but the very generosity and nobleness of his mind exposes him to the delusions of others. In the meantime an attempt is made to stifle the sentiment of the

Board. We were to have been silenced, lest we should disturb the course of this further relief; and, in the interval, a secret agency was known to be on foot in many quarters amongst us. They thought of sharing the spoils before they could be certain of the victory. Silence was the order of the day: and Mr. Grattan was left in his error, because some amongst us conceived they had an interest in carrying any bill. I have even seen a letter from a Whig baronet in parliament, in which he suggested the Whiggish idea of forming a party in the Board in favour of this bill. Part of that letter was published in the newspapers; but this patriotic idea was suppressed: at length, however, our dissatisfaction began to appear; spite of every restraint, it burst forth; and to close the curious history of this further relief bill, the Right Hon. Mr. Plunkett came over with the assent and approbation of my Lord Viscount Castlereagh, to reconcile all parties to this bill!

Strange mission! What! to reconcile the Catholics to a bill for their relief! What! to entreat of the Catholics to be emancipated? He came over to reconcile everybody—he reconciled nobody; and, in the meantime, this bill met the fate it deserved, and all Ireland rejoiced in its extinction.

I do, therefore, solemnly protest against the course that has been adopted upon this occasion. Grattan, the patriot—Grattan needs but to be informed of your wishes to comply with them. Surely Canning, though a powerful framer of jests, is not the Catholic cause; nor is Castlereagh, though a speeching man, the representative of the Irish sentiment. Let us, of all things, get rid of secret negotiation: our friends are deceived, constantly deceived, by private information. Let us, also, take care to disentangle our cause from the jobbing of the English Catholics; they have just thought fit to signalize their English magnanimity, by sacrificing to their enemies the first of their bishops; and they have humanely attempted to bring the gray head of that venerable prelate in sorrow and disgrace to his grave. They remind one of a band of negro slaves, who, upon the promise of a half holiday, celebrate their joy, by crushing with their chains some unfortunate fellow-slave who presumed to think that black was as good as white, and that colour was no justification of slavery!

Well, be it so. They have censured the agent of our bishops: but, in recompense, they have thanked Lord Castlereagh! Did they never hear that the Irish people were scourged, and picketted, and tortured? Did they never hear that the lash smacked, and the shriek resounded, and the cry of agony was heard, and the yell of the tortured rent the air, and that this full chorus was music to the ear of Lord Castlereagh! Yes, they did hear it all; and therefore it was that these English thanked my Lord Castlereagh, and censured their prelate.

This is a subject I will beg leave to bring again before the Board. We owe it to Ireland to preclude the possiblity of any interference of any English Catholic with our cause. We owe it mainly to one of them that we are still unemancipated. Let me be pardoned for thus trespassing on your time. I need not in conclusion, say, that the motion of my respected friend has my entire approbation.

The resolution was then put from the chair, and carried unanimously

Major Bryan, wishing that the resolution should be conveyed to Earl Donoughmore in the most respectful manner possible, moved—

" That the chairman, Sir Thomas Esmonde, be requested to transmit the same."

This being seconded was carried unanimously.

Mr. O'Connell gave notice of a motion of thanks to the General Assembly of the Church of Scotland, for its recognition, at its late meeting, of the freedom of conscience.

Mr. O'Connell gave notice of a motion of thanks to the Right Rev. Dr. Milner, and the meeting adjourned.

RIGHT REV. DR. MILNER.

UPON the 15th June, 1813, an aggregate meeting was held in Fishamble-street theatre The *Dublin Evening Post*, in its report of the proceedings, says that, when Mr. O'Connell, in the course of reading the resolutions, adverted to the revered name of the persecuted Dr. Milner, he was interrupted by the loudest acclamations we have ever heard. All voices were raised to greet this favoured name. Clapping of hands, beating of feet, &c., were continued and resumed during several minutes, and at three successive intervals.

When, afterwards, he came to move the distinct resolution, the twelfth in order, viz. :—

" Resolved—That the warm approbation and gratitude of the Catholics of Ireland be conveyed to the Right Rev. Dr. Milner, for his manly, upright, and conscientious opposition, in conformity with the Most Rev. and Right Rev. the Catholic Prelates of Ireland, to the ecclesiastical regulations contained in the bill lately submitted to parliament, and purporting to be a bill for the further relief of his Majesty's Roman Catholic subjects,"

the same thunder of applause was repeated, but with peals of, if possible, augmented force and renovated energy.

The whole assembly rose, as if with one impulse. All hats were taken off, and each spectator waved his hat with the loudest demonstrations of pleasure. The ladies came forward, and by courtesies signified their participation in the general feeling

In short, an electric sensation was apparently excited, springing from the reverential
sentiment of merited respect for the Irish prelates, and for their insulted brother, the
Right Rev. Dr. Milner.

The enthusiasm subsided very slowly, and had not wholly disappeared when the assem
bly broke up.

When Mr. O'Connell was allowed to proceed, after the striking demonstration of feeling
thus described by the *Evening Post*—a description strictly according to the fact—he read
the remaining resolutions, viz. :—

" Resolved—That we feel it necessary to repeat our earnest exhortation to all Catholic freeholders throughout Ireland, to register their
freeholds, and steadily to resist the pretensions of any candidates for
their votes, who shall have lent, or are likely to lend, their support to
any administration founded in intolerance, and hostile to the full enjoyment of religious freedom :

" Resolved—That the expenses unavoidably attendant upon the conduct of Catholic petitions, and the defence of the invaded rights of
petitioning, call for the liberal aid of our fellow-countrymen ; and we
confide in the public spirit and zeal of the Catholic body throughout
Ireland, for ample pecuniary support·"

And moved that the entire should be adopted.

Having thus discharged (said he, in continuation,) the duty
imposed on me by the Board, and having come here determined
to address this meeting, I avail myself of this opportunity to
solicit your patience and attention. Let me, in the first place,
congratulate you on the progress which the principle of religious
liberty has made since you last met. It has been greatly advanced by a magnificent discovery lately made by the English
in ethics and upon which I also beg leave to congratulate you.
It is this—several sagacious Englishmen have discovered, in the
nineteenth century, and more than four hundred years after the
propagation of science was facilitated by the art of printing—
several sagacious Englishmen have made this wonderful discovery
in moral philosophy, that a man is not necessarily a worse citizen
for having a conscience, and that a conscientious adherence to a
Christian religion is not an offence deserving of degradation or
punishment. (Hear.)

The operation, however, of this discovery had its opponents ;
like gravitation and the cow-pock, it has been opposed, and, for
the present opposed with success ; but the principle has not been
resisted. Yes, our enemies themselves have been forced to concede our right to emancipation. Duigenan, and Nicholl, and
Scott are laughed at—not listened to ; the principle is admitted
—the right of liberty of conscience is not controverted—your
emancipation is certain—it is now only a question of terms—it

only remains to be seen whether we shall be emancipated upon their terms or upon ours.

They offer you emancipation, as Catholics, if you will kindly consent, in return, to become schismatics. They offer you liberty, as men, if you agree to become slaves after a new fashion—that is, your friends and your enemies have declared that you are entitled to Catholic emancipation and freedom, upon the trifling terms of schism and servitude!

Generous enemies!—bountiful friends! Yes, in their bounty they resemble the debtor who should address his creditor thus:—" It is true, I owe you £100; I am perfectly well able to pay you; but what will you give me if I hand you 6s. 8d. in the pound of your just debt, as a final adjustment?" (Hear, hear.) " Let us allay all jealousies," continues the debtor—" let us put an end to all animosities—I will give you one-third of what I owe you, if you will give me forty shillings in the pound of additional value, and a receipt in full, duly stamped, into the bargain." (Laughter.)

But why do I treat this serious and melancholy subject with levity? Why do I jest, when my heart is sore and sad? Because I have not patience at this modern cant of securities, and vetoes, and arrangements, and clauses, and commissions. Securities against what? Not against the irritation and dislike which may and naturally ought to result from prolonged oppression and insult. Securities—not against the consequences of dissensions, distrusts, and animosities. Securities—not against foreign adversaries. The securities that are required from us are against the effects of conciliation and kindness—against the dangers to be apprehended from domestic union, peace, and cordiality. If they do not emancipate us—if they leave us aliens and outlaws in our native land—if they continue our degradation, and all those grievances that, at present, set our passions at war with our duty; then, they have no pretext for asking, nor do they require any securities; but, should they raise us to the rank of Irishmen—should they give us an immediate and personal interest in our native land—should they share with us the blessings of the constitution—should they add to our duty the full tide of our interests and affection; then—then, say they, securities will be necessary. Securities and guards must be adopted. State bridles must be invented, and shackles and manacles must be forged, lest, in the intoxication of new liberty, we should destroy, only because we have a greater interest to preserve.

And do they—do these security-men deserve to be reasoned with? I readily admit—I readily proclaim Grattan's purity—his integrity—his patriotism; but, in his eagerness to obtain for us that liberty, for which he has so long and so zealously contended, he has overlooked the absurdity which those men fall into, who demand securities against the consequences of emancipation, whilst they look for no securities against the effects of injustice and contumely.

Grattan has also overlooked the insult to our understandings and to our moral feelings which this demand for securities inflicts. Grattan is mistaken upon this topic; but he is the only man who is merely mistaken. The cry for securities has been raised, merely to retard the progress of emancipation. Canning affects to be our friend, because, since his conduct to his colleague, Viscount Castlereagh, he has found it difficult to obtain a niche in any administration. God preserve us from the friendship of Mr. Canning! I have no apprehension of Mr. Canning's enmity: he was our avowed enemy; that is, he always voted against us, from the moment he got pension or place under Pitt, to the time when he was dismissed from office, and rendered hopeless of regaining it. And, as to Lord Castlereagh, rely on it, that, though he may consent to change one kind of degradation for another, he never will consent to your attaining your freedom: and was it to obtain the vote of Lord Castlereagh that Grattan gave up our honour and our religion? Does Grattan forget—does he forgive the artificer of the Union, or the means by which it was achieved? Does not Grattan know that Lord Castlereagh first dyed his country in blood, and then sold her.

But, I repeat it, I have not patience, common patience with those men who cry out for securities, and will not see that they would obtain real security from the generous concession of plain right—from conciliation and kindness; all reasoning, all experience proves that justice to the Catholics ought to be, and has been, in the moments of distress and peril, the first and best security to the state. I will not stoop to argue the theory with any man. I will not condescend to enter into an abstract reasoning to prove that safety to a government ought to result from justice and kindness to the people, but I will point out the evidence of facts which demonstrate, that concession to the Irish Catholics has in itself been resorted to, and produced security to our government—that they have considered and found it to be a security in itself—a safeguard against the greatest evils and calamities, and not a cause of danger or apprehension.

Ireland, in the connection with England, has but too constantly shared the fate of the prodigal's dog—I mean no personal allusion—(a laugh)—she has been kicked in the insolence of prosperity, and she has borne all the famine and distress of adversity. Ireland has done more—she has afforded an abundant source of safety and security to England in the midst of every adversity ; and at the hour of her calamity, England has had only to turn to Ireland with the offer of friendship and cordiality, and she has been rewarded by our cordial and unremitting succour.

Trace the history of the penal laws in their leading features, and you will see the truth of my assertion. The capitulation of Limerick was signed on the 3rd October, 1691. Our ancestors, by that treaty, stipulated for, and were promised the perfect freedom of their religion, and that no other oath should be imposed on Catholics, save the oath of allegiance. The Irish performed the entire of that treaty on their part : it remains unperformed, as it certainly is of force, in point of justice, to this hour, on the part of the English. Even in the reign of William, it was violated by that prince, whose generals and judges signed that treaty—by that prince who himself confirmed and enrolled it.

But he was the same prince that signed the order for the horrible, cold-blooded assassination and massacre of the unfortunate Macdonalds of Glencoe ; and if his violation of the Limerick treaty was confined to some of the articles, it was only because the alteration in the succession, and the extreme pressure of foreign affairs, did not render it prudent nor convenient to offer further injury and injustice to the Irish Catholics.

But the case was altered in the next reign. The power and the glory, which England acquired by her achievements, under Marlborough—the internal strength, arising from the possession of liberty, enabled her to treat Ireland at her caprice, and she accordingly poured the full vial of her hatred upon the unfortunate Catholics of Ireland. England was strong and proud, and, therefore, unjust. The treaty of Limerick was trampled under foot—justice, and humanity, and conscience were trodden to the earth, and a code of laws inflicted on the Irish Catholics, which Montesquieu has well said, ought to have been written in blood, and of which you still feel the emaciating cruelty—a code of laws which still leaves you aliens in the land of your ancestors. Aliens!—did I say? Alas! you have not the privileges of alienage ; for the alien can insist upon having six of his jury of his own nation, whilst you may have twelve Orangemen on vours. (Hear, hear.)

But to return to our own history. The reigns of the First and of the Second George passed away; England continued strong; she persevered in oppression and injustice; she was powerful and respected; she, therefore, disregarded the suffer-ings of the Irish, and increased their chains. The Catholics once had the presumption to draw up a petition; it was presented to Primate Boulter, then governing Ireland. He not only rejected it with scorn and without a reply, but treated the insolence of daring to complain as a crime and punished it as an offence, by recommending and procuring still more severe laws against the Papists, and the more active execution of the former sta-tutes.

But a new era advanced; the war which George the Second waged on account of Hanover and America, exhausted the re-sources, and lessened, while it displayed, the strength of England. In the meantime the Duke of Bedford was Lord Lieutenant of Ireland. The ascendancy mob of Dublin, headed by a Lucas, in-sulted the Lord Lieutenant with impunity, and threatened the parliament. All was riot and confusion within, whilst France had prepared an army and a fleet for the invasion of Ireland. Serious danger menaced England. The very connection between the countries was in danger. The Catholics were, for the first time, thought of with favour. They were encouraged to address the Lord Lieutenant, and, for the first time, their address received the courtesy of a reply. By this slight civility (the more wel-come for its novelty) the warm hearts and ready hands of the Irish Catholics were purchased. The foreign foe was deterred from attempting to invade a country where he could no longer have found a friend; the domestic insurgents were awed into silence; the Catholics and the government, simply by their com-bination, saved the state from its perils; and thus did the Ca-tholics, in a period of danger, and upon the very first application and in return for no more than kind words, give, what we want to give, security to the empire.

From the year 1759, to the American war, England enjoyed strength and peace; the Catholics were forgotten, or recollected only for the purposes of oppression. England, in her strength and her insolence, oppressed America; she persevered in an obstinate and absurd course of vexation, until America revolted, flew to arms, conquered, and established her independence and her liberty.

This brings us to the second stage of modern Catholic history; for England, having been worsted in more than one battle in America, and having gained victories more fatal than many defeats, America, aided by France, having proclaimed independence, the English period for liberality and justice arrived, for she was in distress and difficulty. Distracted at home—baffled and despised abroad, she was compelled to look to Irish resources, and to seek for security in Ireland; accordingly, in the year 1778, our Emancipation commenced; the Catholics were hired into the active service of the state by an easy gratuity of a small share of their rights as human beings, and they in return gave, what we now desire to give, security to the empire.

The pressure of foreign evils, however, returned; Spain and Holland joined with France and America; success in her contest with the Colonies became daily more hopeless. The combined fleets swept the ocean; the English channel saw their superiority; the English fleet abandoned for a while the dominion of the sea; the national debt terrified and impoverished the country; distress and difficulty pressed on every side, and, accordingly, we arrived at the second stage of Catholic Emancipation; for, in 1782, at such a period as I have described, a second statute was passed, enlarging the privileges of the Catholics, and producing, in their gratitude and zeal, that security which we now tender to the sinking vessel of the state.

From 1782 to 1792, was a period of tranquillity; the expenses of the government were diminished, and her commerce greatly increased. The loss of America, instead of being an evil, became an advantage to trade as well as to liberty. England again flourished, and again forgot us.

In 1792, the Catholics urged their claims, as they had more than once done before. But the era was inauspicious to them, for England was in prosperity. On the Continent, the confederation of German princes, and the assemblage of the French princes, with their royalist followers, the treaty of Pilnitz, and the army of the King of Prussia, gave hope of crushing and extinguishing France and her liberties for ever. At that moment the Catholic petition was brought before parliament; it was not even suffered, according to the course of ordinary courtesy, to lie on the table; it was rejected with indignation and with contempt. The head of the La Touche family, which has since produced so many first-rate Irishmen, then retained that Huguenot hatred for Catholics which is still cherished by Saurin, the Attorney-General for Ireland. La Touche proposed that the peti-

tion should be rejected, and it was rejected by a majority of 206
to only 13.

Fortune, however, changed.   The invasion of the Prussians
was unsuccessful; the French people worshipping the name, as it
it were the reality of liberty, chased the Duke of Brunswick from
their soil; the King of Prussia, in the Luttrel style, sold the
pass; the German princes were confounded, and the French
princes scattered; Dumourier gained the battle of Jamappe, and
conquered the Austrian Netherlands; the old governments of
Europe were struck with consternation and dismay, and we arrived at the fourth, and hitherto the last stage of emancipation; for, after those events, in 1793, was passed that act which
gave us many valuable political rights—many important privileges.

The parliament—the same men, who in 1792, would not suffer
our petition to lie on the table—the men, who, in 1792, treated
us with contempt, in the short space of a few months, granted
us the elective franchise.   In 1792, we were despised and rejected; in 1793, we were flattered and favoured.   The reason
was obvious; in the year 1792, England was safe; in 1793 she
wanted security, and security she found in the emancipation of
the Catholics, partial though it was and limited.   The spirit of
republican phrensy was abroad; the enthusiasm for liberty, even
to madness, pervaded the public mind.   The Presbyterians and
Dissenters of the North of Ireland were strongly infected with
that mania; and had not England wisely and prudently bought
all the Catholic nobility and gentry, and the far greater part of
the Catholic people out of the market of republicanism, that
which fortunately was but a rebellion, would, most assuredly,
have been revolution.   The Presbyterians and Catholics would
have united, and, after wading through the bloody delirium of a
sanguinary revolution, we should now, in all likelihood, have
some military adventurer seated on the throne of our legitimate
sovereign.

But, I repeat it, England judged better; she was just and
kind, and therefore she has been preserved.   She sought for security where alone it could be found. and she obtained it.

Thus, in 1759, England wanted security against the turbulence of her ascendancy faction in Ireland, and against the fleet
and arms of France; she was civil and courteous to the Catholics, and the requisite security was the result.

Thus in 1778, England wanted security against the effects of
her own misconduct and misfortunes in America; she granted

some rights of property to the Irish Catholics, and the wanted security followed.

Thus, in 1782, England wanted security against the prodigality and profligacy of her administration—against the combined navies of France, Spain, and Holland; she conceded some further advantages to the Catholics, and she became safe and secure.

Thus, in 1795, England wanted security against the probable consequences of the disasters and treachery of the Prussians—the defeat of the Austrians, and especially against the revolutionary epidemic distemper which threatened the vitals of the constitution; she conferred on the Catholics some portion of political freedom, and the Catholics have recompensed her, by affording her subsequent security.

And thus has Emancipation been in all its stages the effect of the wants of England, but at the same time, her resource in those wants. In her weakness and decay, Emancipation has given her health and strength; it was always hitherto a remedy, and not in itself, a disease; it was. In short, her best protection and security. Away, then, with those idle, those absurd demands for control, and dominion over our mode of faith.

Let Grattan learn the sentiments of the Irish people; let him know that we are ready to give the security of our properties and our lives to the state; but, we will not, we cannot, grant away any part of our religion. Before the Union, no vetoes, no arrangements, no inquisitions over our prelates were required.

If our Protestant fellow-countrymen did not ask them, why should the English suppose we can grant them to their stupid caprice? But we are ready to give them security; we are ready to secure them from foreign foes, and against the possibility of domestic dissension.

Yes, the hour of your Emancipation is at hand; you will, you must be Emancipated; not by the operation of any force or violence, which are unnecessary, and would be illegal on your part, but by the repetition of your constitutional demands by petition, and still more by the pressure of circumstances, and the great progress of events. Yes, your Emancipation is certain, because England wants the assistance of all her people. The dream of delivering the Continent from the dominion of Bonaparte has vanished. The idle romance of German liberty—who ever heard of German liberty! is now a cheerless vision. The allied Russian and Prussian armies may, perhaps, escape, but they have little prospect of victory. The Americans have avenged our outrages on their seamen, by quenching the meteor

; laze of the British naval flag. The war with the world—England, alone, against the world, is in progress. We shall owe to
her good sense, what ought to be conceded by her generosity;
she cannot proceed without our aid; she knows she can command that aid if she will but be just; she can, for liberty, to
which we are of right entitled, command the affections and the
energies of the bravest and the finest people in the world!

Recollect, too, that the financial distress of England accumu-
lates. She owes, including the Irish debt, near a million of millions. Who is there so extravagant as to suppose, but that
there must arrive a period at which it will become impossible
to borrow money, or to pay more interest? Our Irish debt has
already exceeded, by nearly two-thirds, our means? We spend
sixteen millions annually, and we collect, in revenue, about five
millions. Our bank puts a paltry impression on three penny-
worth of silver, and calls it tenpence. In short, with taxes increasing, debts accumulating, revenue diminishing, trade expiring, paper currency depreciating—who is so very blind as not
to perceive, that England does, and must require, the consolida-
tion of all her people in one common cause, and in one common
interest?

The plain path to safety—to security—lies before her. Let
Irishmen be restored to their inherent rights, and she may laugh
to scorn the shock of every tempest; the arrangements which
the abolition of the national debt may require will then be effectuated, without convulsion or disturbance; and no foreign foe
will dare to pollute the land of freemen and of brothers. (Hear.)

They have, however, struck out another resource in England;
they have resolved, it is said, to resort to the protection of
Orange Lodges. That system which has been declared by judges
from the bench to be illegal and criminal, and found by the experience of the people to be bigoted and bloody—the Orange
system, which has marked its progress in blood, in murder, and
in massacre—the Orange system, which has desolated Ireland,
and would have converted her into a solitude, but for the inter-
posing hand of Cornwallis—the Orange system with all its sanguinary horrors, is, they say, to be adopted in England!

Its prominent patrons, we are told, is Lord Kenyon or Lord
Yarmouth; the first an insane religionist of the Welsh Jumper
sect, who, bounding in the air, imagines he can lay hold of a
limb of the Deity, like Macbeth, snatching at the air-drawn
dagger of his fancy! He would be simply ridiculous, but for
the mischievous malignity of his holy piety, which desires to con-

vert Papists from their errors, through the instrumentality of
daggers of steel. Lord Kenyon may enjoy his ample sinecures
as he pleases, but his folly should not goad to madness the people of Ireland.

As to Lord Yarmouth, I need not, indeed I could not, describe
him ; and if I could, I would not disgust myself with the description ; but if Lord Kenyon or Lord Yarmouth have organized the Orange system, I boldly proclaim that he must have
been bribed by the common enemy. Bigotry is not a gratuitous
propensity. Giffard gets money for his calumnies and impudence ;
so does Duigenan. The English Orange patrons must be bribed
by France ; let them appeal to their private lives to repel my
accusation. Can that man repel it, whose life is devoted to the
accumulation of wealth to be added to wealth, already excessive
and enormous?—who never was suspected of principle or honour ?—whose finest feelings were always at market for money !
—who was ready to wed disgrace with a rich dowry, and would
have espoused infamy with a large portion ? If such a wretch
lives, let him become the leader of the Orange banditti. The
patron is worthy of the institution—the institution is suited to
the patron !

You know full well that I do not exaggerate the horrors which
the Orange system has produced, and must produce, if revived
from authority, in this country. I have, in some of the hireling
prints of London, read, under the guise of opposing the adoption of
the Orange system, the most unfounded praises of the conduct of
the Irish Orangemen. They were called loyal, and worthy, and
constitutional. Let me hold them up in their true light. The
first authentic fact in their history occurs in 1795. It is to be
found in the address of Lord Gosford, to a meeting of the magistrates of the county of Armagh, convened by his lordship, as
governor of that county, on the 28th of December, 1795. Allow
me to read the following passage from that address :—

" Gentlemen—Having requested your attendance here this day, it
becomes my duty to state the grounds upon which I thought it advisable
to propose this meeting ; and at the same time to submit to your consideration a plan which occurs to me as most likely to check the enormities that have already brought disgrace upon this country, and may soon
reduce it into deep distress.

" It is no secret that a persecution, accompanied with all the circumstances of ferocious cruelty, which have in all ages distinguished that
dreadful calamity, is now raging in this country. Neither age nor sex,
nor even acknowledged innocence, as to any guilt in the late disturbances, is sufficient to excite mercy, much less to afford protection

o

" The only crime which the wretched objects of this ruthless persecution are charged with, is a crime, indeed, of easy proof; it is simply a profession of the Roman Catholic faith, or an intimate connection with a person professing this faith.   A lawless banditti have constituted themselves judges of this new species of delinquency, and the sentence they have denounced is equally concise and terrible.   It is nothing less than a confiscation of all property, and an immediate banishment.   It would be extremely painful, and surely unnecessary, to detail the horrors that are attendant on the execution of so rude and tremendous a proscription—one that certainly exceeds in the comparative number of those it consigns to ruin and misery, every example that ancient and modern history can supply; for where have we heard, or in what story of human cruelties have we read, of half the inhabitants of a populous country deprived, at one blow, of the means as well as the fruits of their industry, and driven, in the midst of an inclement season, to seek a shelter for themselves, and their helpless families, where chance may guide them ?

" This is no exaggerated picture of the horrid scenes that are now acting in this country "

Here is the first fact in the history of the Orangemen.   They commenced their course by a persecution with every circumstance of ferocious cruelty.   This lawless banditti, as Lord Gosford called them, showed no mercy to age, nor sex, nor acknowledged innocence.   And this is not the testimony of a man favourable to the rights of those persecuted Catholics ; he avows his intolerance in the very address of which I have read you a part ; and though shocked at these Orange enormities, he still exults in his hostility to emancipation.

After this damning fact from the early history of the Orangemen, who can think with patience on the revival of extension of this murderous association ?   It is not, it ought not, it cannot be endured, that such an association should be restored to its power of mischief by abandoned and unprincipled courtiers. But I have got in my possession a document which demonstrates the vulgar and lowly origin, as well as the traitorous and profligate purpose of this Orange society.   It has been repeatedly sworn to in judicial proceedings, that the original oath of an Orangeman was an oath to exterminate the Catholics.   In some years after the society was formed, men of a higher class of society became members of it, and, being too well educated to endure the plain declaration to exterminate, they changed the form of the oath to its present shape, but carefully retained all the persecuting spirit of the Armagh exterminators.   The document I allude to, was printed for the use of the Orange lodges ; it was never intended for any eye but that of the initiated, and

I owe it to something better than chance that I got a copy o
it; it was printed by William M'Kenzie, printer to the Grand
Orange Lodge, in 1810, and is entitled, "Rules and Regulations
for the use of all Orange Societies, revised and corrected by a
Committee of the Grand Orange Lodge of Ireland, and adopted
by the Grand Orange Lodge, January 10th, 1810." I can demonstrate from this document that the Orange is a vulgar, a
profligate, and a treasonable association. To prove it treasonable, I read the following, which is given as the first of their
secret articles:—"That we will bear true allegiance to his
Majesty, his heirs and successors, so long as he or they support
the Protestant ascendancy. (Hear, hear.)

The meaning is obvious, the Orangeman will be loyal just so
long as he pleases. The traitor puts a limit to his allegiance,
suited to what he shall fancy to be meant by the words "Protestant ascendancy." If the legislature presumes to alter the
law for the Irish Catholics as it did for the Hanoverian Catholics,
then is the Orangeman clearly discharged from his allegiance,
and allowed, at the first convenient opportunity, to raise a civil
war; and this is what is called a loyal association. (Hear, hear.)
Oh! how different from the unconditional, the ample, the conscientious oath of allegiance of the Irish Catholic. I pass over
the second secret article, as it contains nothing worthy of observation; but from the third I shall at once demonstrate what
pitiful and vulgar dogs the original Orangemen were. Mark the
third secret article, I pray you—"That we will not see a brother
offended for sixpence or one shilling, (a laugh,) or more if convenient, (a laugh,) which must be returned next meeting if possible." (Much laughter.) Such is the third of the secret Orange
articles. I presume even Lord Yarmouth will go with them
the full length of their liberality of sixpence or one shilling, but
further his convenience may prevent him.

The fourth secret article is quite characteristic—"That we
must not give the first assault to any person whatsoever, THAT
may bring a brother into trouble." (Laughter.) You perceive
the limitation. They are entitled to give the first assault in all
cases, but that in which it may not be quite prudent; they are
restricted from commencing their career of aggression, unless
they are, I presume, ten to one—unless they are armed and the
Catholics disarmed—unless their superiority in numbers and
preparation is marked and manifest. See the natural alliance
of cowardice with cruelty. They are ready to assault you, when
no brother of theirs can be injured; but if there be danger a

injury to one of their brotherhood, they are bound to restrain, for that time, their hatred of the Catholics, and to allow them to pass unattacked. This fourth article proves, better than a volume, the aggressive spirit of the institution, and accounts for many a riot, and many a recent murder. (Hear, hear.) The fifth secret article exhibits the rule of Orangemen, with respect to robbery. "5th. We are not to carry away money, goods, or anything, from any person whatever, except *arms and ammunition*, and those only from an enemy." The rule allows them to commit felony to this extent—namely, the arms and ammunition of any Catholic, or enemy ; and I have heard of a Catholic who was disarmed of some excellent silver spoons, and a silver cup, by a detachment of this banditti. Yes, Lord Gosford was right, when he called them a lawless banditti; for here is such a regulation as could be framed only for those whose object was plunder—whose means were murder. The sixth and seventh secret articles relate to the attendance and enrolling of members ; but the eighth is of great importance—it is this·—"8th secret article—An Orangeman is to keep a brother's secrets as his own, unless in case of murder, treason, and perjury, and that of his own free will." See what an abundant crop of crimes the Orangeman is bound to conceal for his brother Orangeman. Killing a Papist may, in his eyes, be no murder, and he might be bound to conceal that ; but he is certainly bound to conceal all cases of riot, maiming, wounding, stabbing, theft, robbing, rape, house-breaking, house-burning, and every other human villany, save murder, treason, and perjury. These are the good, the faithful, the loyal subjects. They may, without provocation or excuse, attack and assault—give the first assault, mind, when they are certain no brother can be brought to trouble. They may feloniously and burglariously break into dwellings, and steal, take, and carry away whatever they will please to call arms and ammunition. And, if the loyalty of a brother tempts him to go a little further, and to plunder any other articles, or to burn the house, or to violate female honour, his brother spectators of his crime are bound by their oaths to screen it for ever from detection and justice. (Hear, hear.) I know some men of better minds have been, in their horror of revolutionary fury, seduced into these lodges, or have unthinkingly become members of them ; but the spirit, the object, and the consequences of this murderous and plundering association, are not the less manifest.

I do not calumniate them; for I prove the history of their foundation and origin by the unimpeachable testimony of Vis

count Gosford, and I prove their principles by their own secret
articles, the genuineness of which no Orangeman can or will
deny. If it were denied, I have the means of proving it beyond
a doubt.   And when such principles are avowed, when so much
is acknowledged and printed, oh, it requires but little knowledge
of human nature to ascertain the enormities which must appear
in the practice of those who have confessed so much of the criminal nature of their principles.   There is, however, one consolation.   It is to be found in their ninth secret article—"No
Roman Catholic can be admitted on any account." I thank
them for it, I rejoice at it ; no Roman Catholic deserves to be
admitted ; no Roman Catholic would desire to belong to a society
permitting aggression and violence, when safe and prudent, permitting robbery to a certain extent, and authorising treason
upon a given contingency.   (Hear, hear.) And now let me ask,
what safety, what security can the minions of the court promise
to themselves from the encouragement of this association ? They
do want security, and from the Catholics they can readily have
it ; and you, my friends, may want security, not from the open
attacks of the Orangemen—for against those the law and your own
courage will protect you ; but of their secret machinations you
ought to be warned.   They will endeavour, nay, I am most cre-
dibly assured, that at this moment their secret emissaries are
endeavouring to seduce you into acts of sedition and treason,
that they may betray and destroy you.   Recollect what happened little more than twelve months ago, when the Board detected and exposed a similar delusion in Dublin.   Recollect the
unpunished conspiracy which was discovered at Limerick ; unpunished and unprosecuted was the author.   Recollect the
Mayor's Constable of Kilkenny, and he is still in office, though
he administered an oath of secrecy, and gave money to his spy
to treat the country people to liquor and seduce them to treason.
I do most earnestly conjure you to be on your guard, no matter
in what shape any man may approach, who suggests disloyalty
to you—no matter of what religion he may affect to be—no matter what compassion he may express for your sufferings, what
promises he may make ; believe me, that any man who may attempt to seduce you into any secret association or combination
whatsoever, that suggests to you any violation of the law whatsoever, that dares to utter in your presence the language of sedition or of treason, depend upon it—take my word for it, and I
am your sincere friend—that every such man is the hired emis-
sary and the spy of your Orange enemies—that his real object is

to betray you, to murder you under the forms of a judicial trial,
and to ruin your country for your guilt. If, on the contrary,
you continue at this trying moment peaceful, obedient and loyal;
if you avoid every secret association, and every incitement to
turbulence; if you persevere in your obedience to the laws, and
in fidelity to the Crown and Constitution, your Emancipation is
certain, and not distant, and your country will be restored to
you; your natural friends and protectors will seek the redress
of your grievances in and from parliament, and Ireland will be
again free and happy. If you suffer yourself to be seduced by
these Orange betrayers, the members of the Board will not be
bound to resist your crimes with their lives; you will bring disgrace and ruin on our cause; you will destroy yourself and your
families, and perpetuate the degradation and disgrace of your
native land. But my fears are vain. I know your good sense;
I rely on your fidelity; you will continue to baffle your enemies;
you will continue faithful and peaceable; and thus shall you
preserve yourselves, promote your cause, and give security to the
empire.

This speech was received throughout, and greeted at its conclusion, with warm and general applause.

Mr. O'Connell again rose shortly after, and said that there was a matter of very pressing
importance, respecting which he had to move a resolution. His motion would have reference to the important business of the subscriptions. He said—

That it had now become extremely necessary to call upon the
people for procuring aid to counteract the effects of Orange persecution, and to meet the indispensable expenses attendant on
the prosecution of the Petitions.

A resolution like the present had been passed on a former occasion; but means had not been taken to render it extensively
useful. The Board found themselves, in the month of October
last, indebted in a sum of £3,000. He was at that time called
to the management of its financial concerns, and was happy to
say, that the debt he mentioned had been paid off, and a surplus
remained at the present in bank.

It was the object of the Board to create a fund, by carrying
into effect which should be sufficient to provide for the attainment of justice for the Catholic, and which should be equal to
the legal protection of every Catholic peasant in the land from
Orange atrocities. That such a provision had been necessary,
recent events, (particularly those in the county of Monaghan)
clearly prove; and that neither legal protection nor even justice
itself could be obtained free of expense was a fact well known.

He thought it but justice, however, to gentlemen of that profes
sion to which he had the honour to belong, to say, that *Catholic
advocates were no expense to the body*. (Loud applause.)

That money was wanted would not be denied ; and he knew
the Board had only to call upon the people and be supplied.
The Catholics of Ireland were always found willing to grant
more than was required of them; and would be particularly
willing when they knew it was to protect their honest brethren in remote parts of the country from the persecutions of
Orangeism.

He would recommend a general subscription throughout every
parish in Ireland ; but he would wish every man to subscribe
only what he would not miss : and in this way, without bearing
heavy on any individual, would a fund be collected, sufficient to
obtain the objects desired upon any occasion which might happen unexpectedly to call for pecuniary sacrifices.

As he had other subjects of more exciting interest, though
not surpassing that he was now alluding to in practical importance, he would not detain his auditory longer upon it at present, but content himself with moving—

" Resolved—' That the expenses unavoidably attendant upon the conduct of Catholic petitions, and the defence of the invaded rights of petitioning, can for the liberal aid of our fellow-countrymen.

" And that we confide in the public spirit and zeal of the Catholic
body throughout Ireland for ample pecuniary support."

This resolution was carried with the greatest unanimity

DOCTOR MILNER.

Mr. O'Connell rose to propose the resolution of which he had given notice, respecting Dr
Milner

He said there certainly had been some difference of opinion
with regard to it at the meeting of the Board ; but that, from
what he had had the pleasure of observing of the feelings which
pervaded the present highly-respectable and imposing meeting,
he did not, and he could not, for one moment entertain the idea
that any such difference would be found to exist here. There
had been in the Board no division on its merits— it was a mere
division upon form.

That venerable prelate had been expelled by the paltry club calling itself " the Catholic Board of England ?" And the club had perpetrated this upon the very same day upon which they thanked the master of the Flogging and Torturing Club in Dublin —my Lord Castlereagh !

This, indeed, was not an inconsistency which surprised him. Lord Castlereagh's treacheries and cruelties towards the Irish people would never make him less beloved by the English, and that the accident of an Englishman's being a Catholic would have any the slightest effect in inducing him to care more for Ireland, was a proposition which every day's experience demonstrated to be utterly false and absurd.

Indeed, what better illustration could, by possibility, be given of this, than was supplied by the fact, that this venerable agent of the Catholic hierarchy of Ireland was made the sport of the vilest caprice and the most spiteful ill-nature by these English Catholics, as they call themselves—for what crime or offence think you ? Simply for proclaiming that to be schism which the Catholic prelates of Ireland have unanimously declared to be so !

I cannot forget, although the English Catholics would seem to have done so, that this venerable prelate combined the classic elegance of the scholar with the profound learning of the antiquarian and the divine ; that he was one of the first who treated on polemics without forgetting the dictates of politeness and the practices of civility, and bore himself through all the excitements of religious controversy with the temper and manners of a gentleman.

The resolution was warmly supported by Mr. O'Gorman, and was passed amid great cheering.

THE PRINCESS OF WALES.

Upon the same day, Mr. O'Connell had a motion for an address to the much-persecuted Princess of Wales, the unhappy wife of the Regent

Mr. O'Connell, at this as at a later period of the persecution unto death which this unhappy woman underwent, took an active part amongst her defenders.

On this occasion the following was the tenor of his speech :—

He declared he had never, in the whole course of his life, proceeded to address a Catholic, or any other public assembly, with a deeper or more firm conviction in his mind—that he was about

to propose a measure eminently and powerfully recommended by
the best dictates of the judgment, and the noblest feelings of the
heart!

It was a resolution which, he was convinced, would do credit
to their feelings, not only as Catholics and as Irishmen, but as
Christians and as men.   It would procure for them the esteem
of the friends of virtue, and obtain a triumph over the enemies
of goodness.

I am (continued he), I confess, most deeply anxious for the
success of my present motion, as I should be grieved, indeed, to
have any reason to think so poorly of my countrymen, as to
believe that they could, by any possibility, be capable of rejecting it.

I think I can satisfy you by the clearest and most convincing
arguments of the propriety of adopting it.   The proposal is for
an address to her Royal Highness the Princess of Wales.

Loud cheering followed—the entire meeting, as if by an electrical impulse, rose—the
ladies waved their handkchiefs, the men waved their hats. and three distinct shouts of
applause ensued. We have never witnessed such enthusiasm.

Oh, no, (said Mr. O'Connell,) I will not argue the point at all;
I will not enter into any reasoning on the subject: indeed, I
will not.   I leave it to your hearts—to your Irish hearts—to
regulate your conduct. (Loud applause.)

It was, my countrymen, a foul conspiracy; subornation of
perjury, the meanest and most abominable of crimes, and perjury itself, at all times foul and unnatural, but in this, most foul
and most unnatural.   These atrocities were levelled against a
stranger, friendless and alone, in a land of strangers—against a
female, at a distance from her parents, and deprived of her natural protector.   Good God! where is the thing, in human shape,
that can read of these horrors and not join in the shout of execration!—that can behold the triumph of the innocence of this
illustrious lady, and not offer the feeble tribute of applause!

Yet, there have been such beings—there are such monsters!
The Giffards of the Dublin Corporation—and there are many
Giffards, differing in degree, but combining in principle—the
Giffards of the Corporation have refused to say that perjury is a
crime—that persecuted virtue deserves countenance and support.   They have refused to say so, because they do not think
perjury a crime, when employed against an enemy; they do not
deem virtue an object of any admiration; money is their god—
to that they are devoted.

I said I would not enter into any detail or reasoning upon

this subject, and I will keep my promise; but allow me to re-mark upon one circumstance, in the case of this illustrious lady. She becomes a widowed wife soon after her marriage, but by whose default? I do not stop to accuse any person; but this I must say, that even her envenomed and unprincipled enemies have not dared to attribute to her any blame for the separation from her husband. She has never been accused of any fault to cause or justify that separation, and she stands, perhaps, the solitary instance in domestic, or, indeed, in any other quarrel, where one party was confessedly and altogether innocent.

This, I own, has made a strong impression on my mind, and I cannot help thinking that there must have been great purity and great delicacy in the conduct of the lady, who upon such an occasion as this, escaped with her honour not only untouched by any wound, but unsullied by any stain, even in the imagination of calumny itself. For the credit of her sex—for the dignity of human nature, I rejoiced that she so escaped, and the less wonder at the subsequent triumph which the miraculous force of her innocence afforded her, against the vilest and most artful conspiracy that was ever formed against life and honour.

I cannot avoid also taking notice of the absurd pretext which has been lately set up, to cover the real delinquents in this atrocious conspiracy against her Royal Highness. It is said she owes it all to her indiscreet friendship for Lady Douglas; but see how the fact contradicts that assertion; for, in 1804, the year before Lady Douglas gave in her statement, we have seen that the apothecaries were examined, and that Lord Moira—why—oh! why, is poor Ireland doomed to blush at that name, too,—we have seen Lord Moira condescend to shrug and wink at the animated honesty of Esmeade: that scene took place before this miserable Lady Douglas became an actor in the conspiracy: she therefore cannot be considered as the prime mover of the conspiracy: you must go further back to reach at the real author.

Permit me also to remark upon one other circumstance, in the case of this injured and innocent lady. By the testimony of her servants, it now appears that they were placed about her in the double capacity of attendants and of spies. For years she was surrounded with persons employed and anxious to discover in her some fault or some crime. She was quite unconscious of being surrounded by those spies; but she was perfectly safe under the protection of her innocence. She has not been acquitted for the want of evidence. If crime existed, the witnesses stood ready to note it down; nay, so anxious were they to sup-

I, evidence against her, that we find them torturing trivial, unimportant circumstances into evidence of guilt, and directly inventing falsehoods, to give a colour to the conspiracy. She is therefore enabled proudly to feel that she owes her acquittal to her innocence alone; had she been guilty, she must have been convicted.

I close these few observations on this momentous case, by entering my solemn protest as a lawyer, against the species of tribunal before which she was tried, and which, unable, though clearly not unwilling, to convict, dared to censure her whom they had not heard, and could not hear in her defence. A more inquisitorial or unjust proceeding never disgraced the dungeons of the Inquisitions. It is " as false as hell." Permit me to quote one of her judges—" It is as false as hell to pretend that this tribunal was warranted or justified in taking cognizance of the matter at all ; it was a tribunal illegal in its formation, and shamefully disgraceful in its result !"

I repeat it, how dare they to inflict the punishment, the dreadful punishment of censure on the honour of a woman who has not been heard to explain or to defend? (Hear, hear.)

There is, however, another view of this subject which presses strongly on my mind. The Orange lodges are about to be established in England. By this, more may be meant than meets the hearing. We have heard that some Orange lodges in this country had taken an oath of fidelity to the Duke of York. It is about four years since three soldiers were brought up from Belfast, charged, as the newspapers informed us, with swearing in Orangemen to join the Duke of York against the Prince of Wales These men were not punished—they were, probably, privately reprimanded for their indiscretion. I know not, nor do I care if they have been subsequently promoted or rewarded. But it presses very strongly upon my mind, that we are not the sole objects of the English Orange lodges. The Regent is far from being of an active or penetrating disposition. He, of course, would never consent to the disinheriting of his child. *Yet how do we know but that in the secrecy of the Orange association, some plan may be devised and matured to alter succession, and to prevent a female reign?*

Perhaps it is for this that Orangeism, with its conditional allegiance, is now adopted. If it be—if there be any plan for altering the succession in agitation, there is no harm in saying that I am against the Duke, and for the Princess. (Hear, hear.) sneak not to boast, but I have enough of property to make me independent; if I had no property, I have a profession, which, in the kindness of my countrymen, would make me independent, even if I had no property. I easily yield to the delicacy which forbids me to speak of matters of a domestic nature, but I may be permitted to say, that I have those domestic charities about me, which make the cup of life sweet. Oh, sweet; indeed! But I am ready to sacrifice property, and profession, and existence. in the cause of the legitimate successor to the throne ; and if they shall attempt to alter the succession, I will fight against the traitors, and for the young Princess, at your head, or by your side. (Loud cheers.)

Let not these traitors be enabled hereafter to revive these calumnies against her mother ; let them, at least, be met in any such attempts, by the verdict of acquittal pronounced by Catholic Ireland, and recorded in this your address. The fashion of cutting the throats of wives is gone by. Henry the Eighth, the English apostle of the Reformation, had a speedy method of getting rid of a disagreeable wife. He it was that first discovered the errors of the Church of Rome in the fair face of a young lady. In the present day, it is said, that the crimes of the Catholics have been detected in the bloated visage of an ancient matron. This taste of Henry was more correct, but not more laudable. The attempt to destroy female honour, wherever it originated, is, however, as foul, nay, perhaps, more foul, than to take away the female life. The Irish were disgusted by the first experiment ; they cannot refrain from horror at the second; nor can any paltry consideration of personal interest restrain them from expressing that abhorrence.

Our first interest is to be honest, just, and manly. Our first duty is to discountenance and condemn the perjurers and their employers. Our proudest and best feelings are to exalt and praise persecuted innocence. (Loud bursts of applause.) We cannot command success for ourselves ; we cannot coax the Prince Regent, nor bribe the parliament; but it is in our power to deserve to be successful ; to show that we are men—that we are Irishmen, to whom nothing is alien which partakes of justice, dignity, and generosity. (Cheers.)

Yes, let this address injure our cause, yet I would recommend t to your adoption upon that account; because, thus you would have some sacrifice to offer upon the altar of justice and of persecuted innocence. (Loud and repeated applause.)

I do therefore, move that the following address be adopted :—

" The Address of the Roman Catholics of Ireland, to her Royal Highness the Princess of Wales, on her escape from the Conspiracy

" MAY IT PLEASE YOUR ROYAL HIGHNESS.

" We, the Roman Catholic people of Ireland, beg leave to offer our
unfeigned congratulations on your providential escape from the conspiracy which so lately endangered both your life and honour—a conspiracy,
unmanly in its motives, unnatural in its objects, and unworthy in its
means—a conspiracy, combining so monstrous an union of turpitude
and treason, that it is difficult to say, whether royalty would have suffered more from its success, than human nature has from its conception.

" Our allegiance is not less shocked at the infernal spirit which would
sully the diadem, by breathing on its most precious ornament the virtue of its wearer, than our best feelings are wounded at the inhospi-
table baseness which would betray the innocence of a female in a land
of strangers ! !

" Deem it not disrespectful, illustrious lady, that, from a people proverbially ardent in the cause of the defenceless, the shout of virtuous
congratulation should receive a feeble echo. Our harp has been long
unused to tones of gladness, and our hills but faintly answer the unusual
accent. *Your* heart, however, can appreciate the silence inflicted by
SUFFERING ; and *ours*, alas ! feel, but too acutely, that the commisera-
tion is sincere which flows from SYMPATHY.

" Let us hope that, when congratulating virtue in your royal person,
on her signal triumph over the perjured, the profligate, and the corrupt,
we may also rejoice in the completion of its consequences. Let us hope,
that the society of your *only child* again solaces your dignified retire-
ment ; and that, to the misfortune of being a widowed wife, is not added
the pang of being a childless mother.

" But if, madam, our hopes are not fulfilled—if, indeed, the cry of an
indignant and unanimous people is disregarded, console yourself with the
reflection that, though your EXILED DAUGHTER may not *hear* the precepts of VIRTUE from your lips, she may, at least, study the practice of
it in your example." (Cheers.)

The following resolutions were then passed unanimously :—

" Resolved—That the address to her Royal Highness the Princess
of Wales, now read, be adopted, and that the individuals composing the
general board of the Catholics of Ireland, be requested to procure signatures thereto.

" Resolved—That the Catholic delegates, now in London, be requested to present the said address, in the most respectful manner, to
her Royal Highness the Princess of Wales."

REPEAL OF THE UNION.

At the meeting of the 29th of June, in this year, Mr. O'Connell spoke as follows:—

I return you the thanks of my heart for the kindness with which you have this day received me. I am proud of the kindness of my fellow-countrymen. It is the only reward I would accept, as it is the only one I seek; but it is a rich recompense! It consoles and compensates me for the slanders and malignity of those who are *my* enemies, only because they are *your* oppressors!

Nay, in their enmity, too, I feel comfort and delight. I rejoice to have earned their hostility; and I shall deem lightly of myself—most lightly, if the hour shall ever arrive, when the men who enrich themselves and fatten themselves by the degradation and enslavement of Ireland, shall treat me with favour, or even with neutrality.

I complain not of their calumnies; I exult in them. I have lashed the bigot and the tyrant; I have exposed the infamy of those hypocritical pretenders to sanctity, who, in the name of God, plunder and oppress unhappy Ireland!—the men who discount their consciences and obtain money by their pretensions to piety—men, whom I need not name, because you know them at once by description.

These men calumniate me, when it is quite safe so to do, in my absence. I exult in deserving their hatred; I rejoice at their exertions, which only prove that I have, in some measure, revenged my country upon them. I court their bitterest hostility; all I deprecate is, their forbearance or their favour.

Your enemies say—and let them say it—that I wish for a separation between England and Ireland. The charge is false; it is, to use a modern quotation, as "false as hell!" And the men who originated, and those who seek to inculcate it, know it to be a falsehood. There lives not a man less desirous of a separation between the two countries—there lives not a man more deeply convinced, that the connection between them, established upon the basis of one king and separate parliaments, would be of the utmost value to the peace and happiness of both countries, and to the liberties of the civilized world.

Next, your enemies accuse me of a desire for the independence of Ireland. I admit the charge, and let them make the most of it. I *have* seen Ireland a kingdom; I reproach myself with having lived to behold her a province! Yes, I confess it—I will

ever be candid upon the subject—I *have* an ulterior object—
THE REPEAL OF THE UNION, and THE RESTORATION TO OLD IRE-
LAND OF HER INDEPENDENCE. (Loud and repeated cheering, and
acclamations for several minutes.)

I am told that it is indiscreet to avow this intention. It may
be so; but in public affairs, discretion may easily pass into dis-
simulation, and I will not be guilty of it. And if to repeal the
Union be the first service that can be rendered to Ireland, as it
clearly is, I for one, most readily and heartily offer to postpone
our Emancipation, in order to promote the cause of our country. (Loud cheering.)

But let me not be mistaken. It is true, as I declare, that I
desire the restoration of our Irish parliament; I would sacrifice
my existence to restore to Ireland her independent legislature;
but I do *not* desire to restore precisely such a parliament as she
had before. No: the act of restoration necessarily implies a reformation, which would for ever abolish the ridiculous, but most
criminal traffic in the representative privileges. The new Irish
legislature would, of course, be purged of all the close boroughs.
The right to nominate to parliament should no longer be a matter of traffic, or of family arrangement; it should not be, as it is
at present, private property; so much so, that I could name to
you a borough in which a seat in parliament is vested by regular
marriage settlement. I could tell you the date and number of
the registry, in which a judge of the land and a country gentleman, are trustees to raise money upon it, for the benefit of the
younger children of a baronet; this traffic—this most odious and
disgusting traffic, should be abolished at once and for ever, were
our parliament restored to us. (Cheers.)

Desiring as I do the Repeal of the Union, I rejoice to see how
our enemies promote that great object. Yes, they promote its
inevitable success by their very hostility to Ireland; *they delay
the liberties of the Catholic, but they compensate us most amply,
because they advance the restoration of Ireland; by leaving one
cause of agitation, they have created and they will embody and give
shape and form to a public mind and a public spirit.*

Ireland lay in torpor till roused by the call for religious liberty.
She would, I fear and I am convinced, have relapsed into apathy
if liberty of conscience had been speedily conceded. Let them
delay Emancipation but yet a little while, and they will find that
they have roused the sleeping lion of Ireland to awaking activity
which will not permit our further slumber till Ireland is herself
again. (Loud applause.) They may still, perchance, think of ad-

ministering the narcotic of religious freedom, which may tend
to re-establish political lethargy; but only let them allow our
discussions to continue, let them suffer our agitators to proceed
—let the love of country and even the desire of notoriety be permitted to excite fresh agitators, and, above all, let the popular
mind become accustomed to the consideration of public subjects
and to the vehemence of political contest, and they know nothing
of human nature who imagine that they can, with a breath, still
the tempest that they shall have thus excited, or be able to quiet
a people whom they shall have roused to a sense of their wrongs,
and to a knowledge of their own strength and importance!

I repeat it? The delay of Emancipation I hear *with pleasure,*
because in that delay is included the only prospect of obtaining my
great, my ultimate object—the Legislative Independence of my
native land!

I have wandered from my subject; but I have not forsaken
your cause. The very calumnies of your enemies and mine lead
us to the discussion of topics which it is for their own inter st to
bury, if they can, in eternal oblivion! The manner in which I shall
refute their calumnies is, by endeavouring to serve you. I cannot do that better than by tendering to you my humble, but my
honest advice. The present period peculiarly calls for that advice. Emissaries are abroad, agents have been employed, abundance of money and great encouragements are held out to those
who may seduce you from your allegiance. Your enemies cannot put you down, unless you yourselves lend them assistance.
Your cause must triumph, unless you yourselves crush it. You
have the fate of Ireland in your hands—upon you, and upon you
alone does it depend. Alas! for poor Ireland! Her liberties
depend upon the prudence of a people of the most inflammable
passions, goaded almost to madness on the one hand by Orange
insults and oppressions, and exposed at the same time to the
secret seductions of the agents and emissaries of those very
Orange oppressors!

Do you wish to gratify the Orangemen? If you do the way
is before you. You have only to enter into some illegal or traitorous association; you have only to break out into turbulence
or violence, and the Orangemen will be delighted, because it
will afford them the wished-for opportunity of rioting in your
blood!

Do you desire to afflict and disgust your friends? If you do,
the way is open to you. You need only form illegal or seditious
societies. You have only to commit some outrages against the

public peace, and against your sworn allegiance, and your friends must abandon your cause with contempt and abhorrence.

In short, your enemies are on the alert. They throw out the language of irritation, and they adopt every measure of oppression to goad you to a violation of the law—to a departure from your loyalty and peaceable demeanour. But it does not rest there. They send round their agents with money, and with pardon for themselves, to preach in private circles the doctrine of insurrection—to form secret knots and associations—to seduce you into crime and then betray you. These miscreants endeavour to obtain your confidence, that they may sell your lives. In the meantime, the Orangemen stand to their arms, ready prepared, primed, and loaded ; they stand with the triangle and the gibbet, to torture, to plunder, and to massacre !

Alas ! alas ! my countrymen, see you not the fatal snare ? Do you not comprehend the cruel purposes of your betrayers? Yes! my countrymen were never deficient in intellect—they never wanted ready comprehension. They do, and they must perceive that if a single parish—if a single village—nay, if a single individual, exhibits the symptoms of political crime—if a single wish, inconsistent with loyalty, allegiance, peace, be expressed, our enemies will have an excuse, and a justification for their crimes and oppressions ! The Habeas Corpus Act will again be suspended—the reign of torture and of terror will again be renewed, and the cause of Ireland will be lost, and lost for ever.

I am deeply anxious to impress upon those who hear me, or may chance to read a report of what I utter—I am most deeply anxious to impress upon the minds and understandings of every true Irishman, that disloyalty to his sovereign would be double treason to his country ; it would be perjury, aggravated by folly, and followed by the eternal extinction of the liberties of Ireland. And what prospect could there possibly be of aught besides destruction ? You would have no friends—no supporters. We, who now join you in bearing down upon our oppressors—we, who expose the hypocrites that cover their bigotry in the stolen garments of religion—we, who are ready to run every danger, to sustain every calumny, and every loss and personal inconvenience in your cause, so long as you conduct that cause within the limits of the constitution—we, in whom you confide, would, and must, be found, if you violate the law, in the ranks of your enemies, and in arms !

For myself, I will tell you honestly, that if ever that fatal day arrive, you will find me arrayed against you. There will not be

P

so heavy a heart ; but there will not be a more ready hand to
sustain the constitution against every enemy !

Think you that I should thus consume your patience in repeating my cautions, did I not know that at this moment no
means are left untried to seduce the population of this country?
Our enemies have long duped the people of England—indeed,
that was not difficult ; so dishonest and besotted a people as the
English never lived. (Loud cheers.)   Yes ; they *are* dishonest
and besotted !   Individuals—many individuals, and classes
amongst them, I respect and reverence ; but as a nation, I must
say, and I can prove it, that they are most profligate and quite
lost in folly.

For a specimen of their morality, take a few transactions of
this war—a war carried on for the preservation of justice, social
order, and religion !   Well, in this just and religious war, the
English attack, plunder, murder a people with whom they are
then a' peace !   Without a shadow of any provocation, they, in
he midst of peace, steal the Danish fleet, burn the Danish capital, and massacre, even to the infants in her foundling hospital !
Rut this is not all.   This atrocious crime, for which England
will be ever execrated, and will, probably, be punished—this
trocious crime is now followed by a formal treaty with Sweden,
by which England sanctions the robbery of an entire kingdom.
Sweden has no more right to Norway than Napoleon to London ;
yet the English give her Norway !   What would they say if
Napoleon were now to make a present of Ireland?   Sweden is
the good ally of England.   Such good friends ought to make
near neighbours ; and Ireland would, I think, suit Swedish purposes as well as Norway.

Such is the morality of England, that she has afforded tho
xample that would justify the transfer of her own dominions to
foreigners.

As to English stupidity, it is really become proverbial ; it is
treated by her rulers with too little ceremony.   The mercenary
Press which they pay does exhibit, I think, a little too much
contempt for the English understanding.   The *Courier*, for example, begins the week with some egregious lie or other ; the
writers are aware that its falsehood will be discovered by Thursday ; but on Thursday they are prepared with a second lie,
which will last till Saturday, when lie the third is coined ; and
the English—the most *thinking* English—swallow, with the
same unabating credulity, the first, second, and third of these

lies, and are prepared to commence the ensuing week with an unabated appetite for falsehood ! (Cheers and laughter.)

To descend from the nation to an individual. Can anything be more beastly stupid than the conduct of Lord Kenyon, who is now organizing Orange lodges ? Why does not the animal see that the principle of religious exclusion might have prevented him from being a lord !—that he has escaped into sinecure places, property, and a peerage, by the accident of his father's creed ? For example—if his father, who was a common writing clerk to an attorney, if he by accident had been a Papist, the present Lord Kenyon, instead of being a peer, would, most probably, have been a private soldier. or a peasant ; or, at the utmost, by a timely conversion from the errors of Popery, he might have arrived at the dignity of being the first preacher, and highest bouncer, of some society of Welsh "jumpers." (Laughter.) Yes ; my Lord Kenyon, if he had a particle of understanding, would feel that his Orange exertions expose the upstart only to the contempt of a people whom he may oppress, but of whom he would not dare personally to insult the lowest individual !

Such is the state of England ; she is ready to sanction any crime—to credit any delusion.

Her Orangemen calumniate you. They only require of you one single act of sedition and turbulence, and you will confirm and establish their calumnies for ever !

I have, I own, been tedious in the advice I have given you for the regulation of your conduct, but think not that I recommend to you to submit to Orange outrage and insult. Let them go to war with you ; do you content yourself with going to law with them. If they dare to attack the wealthy Catholic—a proceeding they are generally much too prudent to adopt, the wealthy Catholic can protect himself. If they attack the poor, we are bound, and willing, to procure protection for him ; on his behalf the protection of the law shall be exerted. I am able to promise it, because the Catholic Board has the rich treasury of the Irish heart to draw upon, in order to procure the funds necessary to afford this protection.

I repeat it ; no illegal outrage shall be committed with impunity by the Orange banditti upon the poor, or the hitherto unprotected. This is the first duty that we owe to the patient people.

We owe them another. We owe them the home-market ; we owe them the consumption of Irish manufactures—the consumption of *nothing but Irish manufactures*. (Loud cheers.)

Yes; it is a solemn duty imposed upon the Irish Catholics, to give to their own countrymen the priority of their custom. One would imagine that it ought to require no argument to enforce this duty, but the melancholy fact is, that Ireland is debased and degraded; first, and principally, because Irishmen have given a perverse preference to everything that was *not* Irish. We enrich the bigots of England, and we leave our own manufacturers starving, and then we talk of our patriotism! In fact, the clothing districts in England are the most bigoted portions of it. The no-Popery cry commenced last year in the very centre of the cloth manufactory. It commenced with the dealers in cloth, at Pontefract, in Yorkshire; and I need only appeal to the Leeds newspaper, for the absurd virulence with which persecution is advocated in that town.

Why, in that very paper I read about a fortnight ago an account of a fresh rebellion in Ireland—nay, in Dublin!! As none of you heard of it, let me inform you, that it actually took place. (Loud laughter.) I forget the day, but that is not material. It took place in Exchequer-street. The Nottingham regiment covered it with glory! They fought the Popish rebels for two hours; the rebels ascended the houses, fired out of the windows, threw brickbats and large stones from the roofs! Two regiments of horse, three regiments of foot, the Flying Artillery from Island-bridge, and the regiment of Artillery from Chapelizod, all shared in the honour of the day! and, at length, the main body of the rebels retired to the Wicklow mountains, and the residue of them went to bed in town; fortunately no person was killed or wounded, and tranquillity was restored by a miracle. (Loud laughter.)

Do you imagine I jest with you? No; I solemnly assure you that the story is gravely told in the Leeds newspaper. Some of the London journals have copied it, even to the scrap of bad Latin with which Yorkshire dulness has adorned it; and there is not a maker of woollen cloth at Leeds that would not swear to the truth of every sentence, and every word of it!

And are these the men for whom you are making fortunes? Are there not, perhaps, hundreds that have been clothed in the "fabric of these dullest of all malignant bigots?" Probably the wretch who fabricated the lie is himself engaged in the woollen trade, and that Irish Catholics are his customers and consumers. Let us teach these drivellers and dotards that they cannot insult us with impunity. The most sensitive part of an Englishman is his purse; let us apply ourselves to this his organ of sensi-

tiveness, and make him feel in his tenderest part, the absurdity
of rousing an anti-Anglican spirit amongst us; by this will you
punish your enemies; but what is still more delightful, by this
will you encourage and stimulate the industry of your own poor
countrymen. (Cheering.)

Let us leave to the Orangemen the produce of England. The
Orangemen are the sworn enemies of Ireland, and naturally
enough have ratified their alliance with England. But let us
recollect that our own tradesmen are starving; that it is in vain
to preach loyalty and obedience to the laws, if we leave our
people without employment, if we encourage English industry
and thereby promote idleness in Ireland. (Hear, hear.)

For my own part, I have long made it a scrupulous duty, not
to wear anything that was not Irish; and if you will sanction
so humble an example by your imitation, you will confer wealth
and content upon those who, in their turn, will powerfully aid
you in the pursuit of your liberties. I shall move, and I am
confident you will adopt a resolution to this effect. (Hear, hear,
hear.)

I have also one resolution more to propose. It is suggested
to me by my anxiety to obtain an adequate counterpoise from
the law against the weight of misery which the revival of the
Orange system threatens.

I mean to move—

"That the Board should prepare a second petition to the legislature,
to take into consideration the judicial system in Ireland—the administration of the law amongst us."

We all know—and by sad experience we feel—how it is administered. It has been more than once said, quaintly and not
untruly, that voting for the Union did not make a man a good
lawyer. We all know that it did not, but it made many men
judges; and some it made judges who had never held a brief.
But this is not what I complain of at present; it is something
more immediately injurious; it is the profligacy that is induced
by the present state of the law in the mode of selecting *juries!*
I need not remind you of the care with which every Catholic is
excluded from the panel—or at least from the jury—when any
question interesting to us is to be tried. How carefully every
envenomed bigot is congregated, to pronounce a verdict of conviction by anticipation. Our petition must state these facts,
and we will offer to prove them in their details. For example—
we will offer to prove, that a man in the class of bank director

has been heard to declare in public company, that he wanted no money—not he, from government—all he asked was, that when they should have a Papist to try, that they should put him on the jury!! (Cries of shame.)

I tell you that this is a fact—a fact which we are able distinctly to prove—nay, more, that his request was complied with, or, at least, that he *was* put on a Papist's jury!!!

We will also furnish the instance of the present sheriffs of Dublin—Morgan and Studdart; they were elected for no other reason but for their hostility to the Catholics.

The facts are public—Mr. Warner was entitled by the courtesy usually adopted in the corporation, to be sheriff. He was called on by Giffard (what a sense of justice this being must have!)—he was called on by Giffard to pledge himself against the Catholics. Mr. Warner who is a man that does honour to your city, finally refused to give any such pledge. Messrs. Morgan and Studdart cheerfully gave it. What was the consequence? Why, Mr. Warner was instantly rejected—Morgan and Studdart instantly appointed. The tenure of their office was a pledge against us—they have faithfully redeemed that pledge.

How many gentlemen, too, have been refused the office of sheriff, for signing a petition in our favour? I need not go to Carlow for instances! How many have been appointed for their hostility to us? I need not go to Kilkenny for instances! In short, my object is simply this: at present the law treats the Catholics as aliens and strangers in their native land. All I require is, that if we are to continue aliens and strangers in Ireland, we may have the privilege of aliens and strangers; not only the Frenchman, but the Turk, the Jew, and the negro, are entitled to this privilege, that if they are indicted for robbery, or killing an Irishman, the jury shall not be all Irish, but that one-half must be foreigners.

The privilege of the Jew, or the Turk, or the barbarous negro, is all I ask for the Catholic. Let not Mr. Attorney-General be enabled to get up a mocking of a trial, and array his bigots in support of the falling cause of bigotry.

I will conclude with a motion to this effect: but let me first recal to your recollection the situation of one of your earliest advocates, the Rev. Steel Dickson. He dared to be honest and independent, when it had ceased to be a fashion. At one time, the Presbyterians of Ireland stood the very foremost amongst her children. They it was who principally forced a free trade from England, in 1778—they it was who, in 1782, insisted in arms

that Ireland should have a free constitution ; and a free constitution she instantly obtained—they it was who were the enthusiastic friends of every liberty.   But, alas, how fallen ! Lord Castlereagh, Doctor Black, and the *regium donum* have converted
them into Orangemen.   As Orangemen, they brought about the
Union ; and now they are persecuting this Christian priest, this
preacher of the Most High God, because, forsooth, he has presumed to preach peace, and charity, and good-will to all men.

Allow me to say one word of myself.   I want to read my recantation. (A laugh.)   I have been accused by the public papers
of having spoken slightingly of Grattan.   I do not think I did
so ; but if I did, I shall only say, that I retract and renounce
my error.   Grattan if he be mistaken, must ever be beloved by,
and a pride to, every Irish heart. (Cheering.)

Mr. O'Connell concluded by moving the resolution respecting
Irish manufacture, and also that for adopting and forwarding a
second Catholic petition, during the current session of parliament."

THE KING *v.* JOHN MAGEE.

THE long remembered case of the government prosecution of .Mr. John Magee, proprietor
of the *Dublin Evening Post*, furnished occasion for Mr. O'Connell's next speech ; as well as
for another which we shall presently give, and which was perhaps the most powerful of all
his forensic efforts.

On this occasion Mr. Magee was being prosecuted for an alleged libel upon the Duke of
Richmond, then Lord Lieutenant of Ireland.

On Wednesday, the 8th of July, 1813, the case was called on, when Mr. Finlay applied
for a postponement until some day in the following Michaelmas term; on the ground of
the absence of several parties, without whose attendance the defendant was advised that
he could not safely proceed to trial, viz.—

Sir Charles Saxton, late Under-Secretary at the Castle,

Right Hon'ble William Wellesley Pole, late Secretary for Ireland,

Robert Peel (or *Peele*, as then spelled), then Secretary for Ireland ; and

Right Hon. William Fitzgerald (since Lord Fitzgerald and Vesci), Chancellor of the Irish
Exchequer

With Mr. Finlay were Messrs. O'Connell, Wallace, Hamilton, and Charles Phillips

The counsel against Magee were—Saurin, the Attorney-General, Bushe, the Solicitor-
General (late Chief Justice Queen's Bench), Sergeants Moore (late Judge Moore), Ball and
M'Mahon (late Sir William M'Mahon, Master of the Rolls).

The Attorney-General strongly resisted the application, which he characterized as "idle
and silly."

After a good deal of personal invective against the defendant, he said—"My lords, you
will be shocked to hear that the defendant is indicted and charged, by this indictment,
with charging his Grace of Richmond with being a murderer."

Mr O'Connell—I must, my lords, interrupt Mr. Attorney-General, intending him to dis respect. He now purports to state matter which is contained in the indictment, but he has not given any notice of using it upon this motion. So that we are not prepared to correct, by the attested copy, any misstatements that he may choose to make of its contents.

The Chief Justice allowed the Attorney-General to proceed.

The latter urged that it was idle to expect Sir Charles Saxton and Mr. Wellesley Pole to return to Ireland, they having no private affairs, nor fixed residence here, and being out of office.

That if Mr. Peele and Mr. Fitzgerald were not arrived on the day he had fixed for the trial, he would consent to a postponement until the 20th instant; and if they were not in reland even by that day, it would, of course, be in the hands of the Court to postpone until November.

Mr. O'Connell said, that as leading counsel for Mr. Magee, it was his duty to reply to the Attorney-General.

I am, indeed, said he, at a loss to discover what it is I am to reply to!

I have heard from him abundance of confident and unfounded assertion, but a total want of anything resembling reason or argument; with his style, it is beneath me to quarrel; but with the manner in which he has treated my client and the Court, I have just reason to be dissatisfied.

Against every principle of law and reason he pronounces my client guilty before trial; he anticipates conviction, and exults in the prospect of inflicting punishment with as much gratification as if he were, at the moment, in the actual enjoyment of so doing. And he has dictated to the Court that which involves direct contradiction of its former decisions.

I did interrupt him, my lords, and I was right to interrupt—first, because he made use of a document, namely, the indictment, of which, in point of form, he could make no use on this motion, because of not having given any notice of using it. Secondly, because he wilfully misstated and misrepresented that indictment.

He has told me that my assertion is absurd. It is not a polite mode of reply, but he does say that my assertion is absurd. I wish to be lenient to him, but I am compelled to prove that his assertions are disgraceful to him, because directly contrary to the fact!

He has told you that Mr. Magee is indicted as the printer of a newspaper. My lords, the fact is otherwise. Mr. Magee is *not* indicted as the printer of any newspaper. He has told you that Mr. Magee is indicted as the proprietor of a newspaper. My lords, the fact is otherwise. Mr. Magee is not indicted as the proprietor of any newspaper. And the Attorney-General has also told you that Mr. Magee is indicted for charging the Duke of Richmond with being a murderer. The truth is not so—the truth is otherwise. Mr. Magee is *not* indicted for charging the Duke of Richmond with being a murderer.

Will it then be said, that it is absurd to endeavour, by interruption, to prevent the Court from being imposed upon by so glaring and disgraceful a misrepresentation of the facts? If so, this is an absurdity which I am proud of committing.

After this preface, extorted from me by the arrogant manner of the Attorney-General, I beg to call the attention of the Court to the motion.

It is really a motion of course, if the documents be sufficient. Now, upon the 13th of May last, the Court decided upon debate; and, notwithstanding the opposition of the Attorney-General, that those documents *were* sufficient. That determination was founded upon good sense, and upon admitted principles of law. The ingredients of a motion to postpone a trial are these :— First, that it be sworn that witnesses are material and necessary; secondly, that they have been served with process to compel their attendance ; thirdly, that they are prevented from attending by reasons of a temporary nature ; and, fourthly, that there is a reasonable expectation and a prospect of their attending upon a future day. All these ingredients belong to the present motion.

1. It is sworn that the four witnesses are material and necessary.

2. That they have been served with process.

3. That they are detained in England by parliamentary duty, and appear to be protected in their absence by their parliamentary privilege.

4. And that there is every reason to expect their attendance by the first day of next term.

Upon these grounds, common sense tells you that a trial ought to be postponed ; and upon these grounds the law says it must be postponed.

Has any man denied that this is the law? Will any man presume to deny that this is the law? if he do, my lords, I will cite a case directly in point to sustain my allegation. I will not search for it in the blue-paper books of stupid reports, which every packet brings us—the English Court of King's Bench contradicting their Court of Common Pleas, and each of those courts most impartially contradicting itself—reports that involve present litigants in an inextricable maze of controversy, and will entail upon posterity the curse of still more uncertain and more interminable litigation. I cite not any of these cases, I cite the case of *the King against Magee*. The identical case decided by your lordships on the last day of last term. Upon the very documents which I use now, you then decided that it was the duty of the Court, and the right of the party, to have the trial postponed. Then, as now, the Attorney-General exerted himself to have Mr. Magee tried in the absence of his witnesses—then, as now, he gave you assertion instead of argument—abuse instead of logic.

Does he expect that this Court will contradict itself? Shall it be said, that the highest criminal court of justice in the land has decided the same question in two different ways?—that on the 31st of May, they decided on the same documents and between the same parties, that the trial should be postponed; and on the 7th of July, upon those very documents and between those very parties, that it should *not* be postponed? Does the Attorney-General expect that the Court will involve itself in this plain and manifest contradiction—that it will this day decide one thing, and to-morrow decide exactly the reverse?

In his unfeeling, unjust, and unconstitutional anxiety to try Mr. Magee at a time when his witnesses are absent, the Attorney-General cares little for the character and dignity of the Court, His only object is the gratification of a malignant spirit of revenge, which the Court will, as it ought, feel a pleasure in counteracting, when at the same time it vindicates its own consistency.

But, my lords, there is, in fact, a difference between the present application and the last, precisely because our case is stronger in the present instance than in the former. Then, my lords, we could have made but one attempt to procure the attendance of those witnesses. Now we show you many exertions to procure their attendance. Our diligence was less on the former occasion —it is now greater; and is it possible to conceive anything more absurd than to expect that the Court will, at the request or upon the dictation of the Attorney-General, now refuse that to a stronger case, which the Court, on the last occasion, conceded to a weaker and less powerful case. The administration of justice would fall into great disrepute, and the law would be a mockery, if that which was deliberately decided on the 31st of May should, by the same judges, upon a stronger and a better case, be reversed on the 7th of July.

I feel, my lords, that it is impossible that such an example of inconsistency and want of principle in decision, can be sanctioned for one moment by the Court, however ardently sought for by the Attorney-General. Thus stands the case upon our affidavits.

You decided with us before; we only require a repetition of your decision.

But, it is said the case is different now—that there is now an affidavit made on the part of the Crown, which will warrant the Court in departing from its former rule. This I must altogether deny; and I am prepared to show you, first, that you cannot read that affidavit at all; secondly, that even if it were read, it would furnish no grounds for resisting our motion. This affidavit cannot be read, because the person who makes it shows no connection with the court or the parties. He furnishes no description of himself—no reason to account why he should throw an affidavit on your files; he calls himself James Murphy, of the city of Dublin; but which of the thousands of Jemmy Murphys who people Dublin, you have no means to ascertain; whether he belong to Channel-row or Kildare-street, you cannot conjecture; if he be gentleman, esquire, knight, or baronet, attorney, doctor, grocer, or merchant—all this is concealed from the Court: he states himself to be "James Murphy," of the city of Dublin, and no more. This affidavit has been made deliberately and advisedly. It has been filed by the active and intelligent Solicitor for the Crown. It has been advised, of course, by some or all of the wise, grave, and learned phalanx of counsel for the prosecution. Why, then, is the swearer concealed? Let them give us a reason for introducing a nondescript to the court. Oh! he is safe—this James Murphy is! How can we detect—how can we punish him for perjury? Where shall we look for him? How shall we identify him? If the Court receives this affidavit, it holds out an indemnity to perjury—a protection against discovery, to fabrication and forgery.

The prosecutors have not, however, the merit of invention; they only imitate. The original example of setting at defiance was given them by the contrivers of a public document, presented to an honourable assembly, subscribed in many a forged and fictitious name, by rendering detection difficult by its uncertainty: to that document were affixed four-and-twenty Armstrongs, all "of the city of Dublin." Thus may every species of imposition, of perjury, and of forgery be committed, if not without disgrace, at least without punishment. This affidavit cannot be read, because it is the affidavit of a nondescript. The rules of the court require the particular description of every man who comes forward to give his written testimony on oath. Here is no description; you must, therefore, reject this affidavit.

Again, it is a ruled case that no affidavit can be read, unless the person shows some acknowledged connection with the court or the cause. Thus, in the case of Sullivan *v.* Margill, reported in 1st Hen., Black. 637, an affidavit was made to postpone a trial. The affidavit stated quite a sufficient case for that purpose, and the trial would have been postponed accordingly, but that it was discovered to have been made by the clerk of the defendant's attorney, describing himself as such. My lords, the affidavit was rejected, and the motion refused *on that account.* It was rejected and refused, because the Court would not recognise any connection between the attorney's clerk and the court, or the cause entitling him to make an affidavit in the cause. See how much a stronger case the present is for rejecting this affidavit. There the man who made the affidavit was an ascertained person, and actually employed as the assistant of the attorney of the defendant. Here the affidavit-maker is unknown, and does not appear to have any connection whatsoever, even with the attorney. If the Court in that case, which has ever since been recognised as law, refused to hear a person who certainly had some, though a remote connection with the cause and the parties, how can you hear a mere volunteer, who has no connection, remote or otherwise, either with the court or the parties?

It follows, in point of convenience, good sense, precedent, justice, and law, that this affidavit must be rejected. But let me concede that notwithstanding all those, it may be read. What advantages can it afford? What difference can it make in the case? You may, then, see what it is that James Murphy, whoever he be, and I care not who he be, swears. He tells you, upon his oath, that he believes that Saxton, who has sought and won the unpurchaseable suffrages of the ancient and loyal corporation of Cashel, does not intend to grace Ireland again with his presence; that Mr. Wellesley Pole, the representative of the Queen's County, does not, as this worthy Jemmy Murphy believes, possess any residence in Ireland, nor does he intend, as the said Murphy believes, to return here; and he then swears that he believes Mr. Robert Peele intends to come back, and that Mr. William Fitzgerald intends to revisit Ireland shortly. And can this ludicrous—this nonsensical affidavit—this affidavit, that in every re-statement of it excites the laughter and contempt of every person who hears it—can it be gravely urged, as affording a shadow of excuse for requiring of you to change your pronounced and solemn opinion on the subject of this trial?

It is, my lords, worse than no excuse; it tends to render the administration of justice ridiculous, to urge it, or to argue upon it. But the Attorney-General is so very desirous to have this trial take place before the witnesses for Mr. Magee can attend, that I must be indulged in a short comment on this affidavit. One can easily perceive that it is a bungling and slovenly attempt to produce some similarity between his case and the case of the King *v.* the Chevalier D'Eon, the 3rd Bur. 1514; and as, in that case, the Court refused to postpone the trial, although the witnesses were absent; so it is hoped that your lordships will, on the authority of it, refuse to postpone this trial. But examine the facts, and you will see that case cannot furnish any rule to govern this. In D'Eon's case the witnesses were natives of France, and resident there; they were in the service of the crown, and as the French court was interested in the prosecution, they would not even be permitted, if they were willing, to come over. There was no probability, therefore, of their future attendance; on the contrary, there was a certainty that postponement of the trial must be useless, as those witnesses could never attend.

One regrets, indeed, that Lord Mansfield suffered himself to be swayed even by so plain an argument, when the case afforded a principle upon which the trial might, and ought to have been postponed. It was this: The French king was, in fact, the prosecutor; it was at his instance the prosecution was instituted yet he it was who detained the witnesses. It seems that it would have required but little of the indignant spirit of liberty, which the constitution requires from its judges, to have enabled Lord Mansfield to have decided that he who prosecuted should not be permitted to prevent a fair trial; that if he detained the witnesses, the Court would postpone the trial, so as to attain justice —not as our Attorney-General desires to go on, merely to procure punishment. No; Lord Mansfield was not a man calculated to disappoint power of its prey, and he refused to postpone the trial.

Let the Attorney-General, then, make the most of his precedent. D'Eon's case does not resemble ours—the witnesses were in France, out of the jurisdiction; ours are in England, within the jurisdiction of the authority of your process. His witnesses were beyond the reach of punishment for any disobedience of the process of the English courts; our witnesses are liable to punishment if they disobey your process. His witnesses could not be compelled to attend; our witnesses can, and when parliament rises, will be compelled to attend. His witnesses would not be

permitted to leave France ; no man can prevent our witnesses
from leaving England and coming here.   The Duke of Richmond,
who, one may venture to hope, has no anxiety to prevent a fair
trial, and Mr. Attorney-General, who clearly does wish to prevent
a fair trial, cannot exclude our witnesses from Ireland, nor detain
them in England.   In D'Eon's case, the postponement he required would have been nugatory ; he had no prospect of procuring his witnesses, even if the time he asked had been granted.
In our case, the postponement gives us a certainty of procuring
the attendance of our witnesses.   D'Eon's case can, therefore, fur
nish no rule to regulate this case ; which, so far from being like
D'Eon's. is precisely the reverse.   •

Mr. Justice Day—The cases, certainly, are not alike, as you put them : and your distinction is founded, if you can show us how you can compel the attendance of English witnesses here.

Mr. O'Connell.—There is no difficulty in that, my lord.   Their
attendance can be compelled, under the provisions of the 45th
of the King, c. 84.   An act passed for the amendment of Judge
Johnson's Act.   In Judge Johnson's case, the gross and glaring
inconvenience and injustice which would manifestly arise from
taking a man from the place where he had really done any act
to a place where he had offended only constructively—to a place
where, though he might be transported himself, he could not
compel the attendance of his witnesses.   This injustice was so
forcibly felt, that the legislature interfered, and softened, in some
degree, the injustice of the first statute, by the act of the 45th
of the King, which gives a power to the Irish and English courts
of criminal justice reciprocally to enforce the attendance of witnesses from one kingdom into the other.   The provisions of the
statute are express, and include all cases.

And thus, my lords, by your lordship's confession, I have distinguished this case from the authority of D'Eon's case.   There
is, therefore, not a shadow of reason, authority, or law for refusing this postponement, until we can procure our witnesses.   Even
the Attorney-General admits it, when he concedes that the trial
shall stand over until Mr. Peele and Mr. Fitzgerald shall arrive.
So far he cannot controvert our request.

But, as to Sir Charles Saxton and Mr. Pole, he says the case
is different.   In what is the case different ?   Simply and singly
in this, that the Attorney says so—in nothing else.   Oh ! but,
perhaps Mr. Peele is a man after Mr. Attorney-General's own
heart, and that Mr. Pole is not.   I know of no other difference ;

and I really disdain to argue a topic in which I have not a particle of common sense to contend against, and nothing to oppose but the *ipse dixit* of the Attorney-General. Mark the sapient, the admirable distinction of this wise and grave personage. He tells the Court that the trial ought to be postponed till Mr. Peele and Mr. Fitzgerald arrive; but that it ought not to be postponed till Sir Charles and Mr. Pole arrive. What am I to combat? Upon what is the Court to act?—Upon the high will and pleasure of the Attorney-General? Really, my lords, I should fear to insult your understandings by detaining you in exposing the idle and extravagant nonsense which attempts to distinguish between two of the witnesses, for whom it is admitted the trial must wait, and for two others of them for whom it is insisted that it shall not wait. It would be better to decide upon avowed caprice, or the hazard of a die, than upon this wretched distinction, without the shadow of difference.

I conclude, my lords, by merely stating to the Court what it is we want. It is merely to postpone the trial until the termination of the session of parliament shall have deprived our witnesses of all excuse for non-attendance. It is not suggested, even upon the faith or the credulity of this James Murphy, that Mr. Magee has any intention of eluding a trial or of preventing the due course of justice. Murphy's paltry affidavit does not presume to suggest that which is so manifestly contrary to truth.

Mr. Attorney-General, indeed, of his own authority, tells us that we desire to postpone the trial *under the pretence* of wanting witnesses, whilst in fact we do not want them. I tell him he mistakes or misrepresents. We do not seek to put off the trial *under any pretence.* We desire to put it off *for the purpose* of procuring a fair and impartial trial, and a full investigation of all the facts of our defence. We desire a fair trial; the Attorney-General requires a trial in the absence of our witnesses. The Court will decide between us; it will decide as it has already done and, perceiving that as great injustice and oppression must follow from complying with the Attorney-General's request, whilst no unfair advantage can be obtained by our motion, it will again decide that the trial shall be postponed, until the cause of the absence of our witnesses is removed

The Solicitor-General rose and said, that it was possible all the witnesses might be able to attend on the 20th; that he did not desire any order inconsistent with a full, fair, and impartial investigation of the merits—God forbid he should! He would, therefore, propose that the trial should now stand postponed generally till the 20th; and if then it should appear that *any* of the witnesses were prevented from attending, the Judge at Nisi Prius would, and he admitted ought to, postpone the trial till the next term.

Mr. O'Connell declared his perfect satisfaction at what had fallen from the learned Solicitor-General, and a rule was pronounced accordingly. Thus has the object of the motion
been completely obtained.

PERSONAL ATTACKS.

On the 10th of July, in the Catholic Board, letters were handed in from certain absent
members, which were understood to contain personal attacks
On this ground, Mr. Mahon objected to their being publicly read.

Mr. O'Connell said, that if the fact was as had been stated
(but he was very loth to believe that these letters of Sir Francis
Goold and Mr. James O'Gorman contained attacks upon individuals), they ought not to be published without having under-
gone a previous inquiry. For Mr. O'Gorman he had a very sincere
regard, and claimed his friendship ; but on a general principle
ne made this objection. The principle was this, that if any person were at liberty to attack others by letter, it might be done
with impunity. A person in India, for example, might thus
assail either of those gentlemen, the learned baronet or Mr.
O'Gorman, or any other member of the Board. The individuals
thus attacked would have no opportunity of righting themselves
oy inflicting that chastisement which an unfounded and insolent
etter might merit. (Applause.) It was on this principle, and
without any allusion to the present letters, that he would support Mr. Mahon's motion.

Mr. O'Connell took the present opportunity to state a fact
which had just come to his knowledge. The question of religious
liberty had been debated in the Presbyterian Synod of Ulster a
few days back ; it was introduced by that venerable and enlightened advocate of liberty of conscience, the Rev. Steele Dixon ;
and, after a full and ample discussion, it was carried with the
most perfect triumph.

One hundred and thirty of the clergy and elders of the Presbyterian Church, loudly and unanimously declared themselves
in favour of extending religious freedom to every man ; eight
only opposed it, and those eight have since expressed their regret,
that motives of respect and deference for the opinions of some
noble lords, &c., (motives with them) had been the occasion of
their opposition, but that in sentiment they fully accorded with
the majority. Therefore, the transactions of that day must be
considered a great and signal triumph, not simply for the cause

of the Catholics, but for that of all those who suffer for a conscientious adherence to the creed they believe best.

He would prefer giving notice of a motion of thanks to the Synod to be passed next Saturday, to proposing it at the present moment, though he was certain if he were to do so, it would be carried with acclamation, and no person found to enforce the standing order; but he chose to postpone it till next meeting, that it might come with that dignity and weight, which a regular notice and a week's deliberation would bestow upon it. (This notice was received with the loudest approbation.)

HENRY GRATTAN.

Mr. M'Donnell brought forward an address to Henry Grattan.

Mr. O'Connell fully agreed in the principle of gratitude to Mr. Grattan which the address conveyed; but at this moment above all others, it was necessary that they should be distinctly understood. He said it came highly recommended when offered by the most respectable gentleman who had proposed it, but still there were some phrases in it which, he was bound to say, he could wish to see altered.

We could not (he continued) be sufficiently profuse in the expressions of gratitude and veneration for that distinguished character. It was impossible to do justice to a name which was the boast and glory of every Irishman. (Hear, hear.)

The splendour of Grattan's talents had been eclipsed by the noble integrity of his heart; and he was the brightest ornament of his native land, which he had so eminently served. If she had fallen again, and had again to commence the career of national freedom, no fault could be attributed to Henry Grattan, who had waked her first to independence, and fought the manly and the good fight for her liberties. His eloquence could never have been equalled; but if the other anti-Unionists had equalled him in other points—if they had caught one spark of his valour Ireland would not now be a province, nor would stupidity and heavy ignorance have battled their way to judicial station, and profited by the extinction of our country!

With these sentiments warm and glowing in my breast, I have at the same time another duty—a more sacred duty—the duty I owe to Ireland.

Q

It consists in having her cause—for the cause of religious liberty is her cause—brought forward in the only manner that can be deemed compatible with our interest, and with our honour. I do, therefore, with great respect, beg leave entirely to controvert the assertion of my friend Mr. M'Donnell. I beg leave to *deny* that Mr. Grattan has done the best he could for us, during the present session.

Was it the best to agree to the double Veto? Was it the best to consent, that the secretary's-clerk at the Castle should have the nomination of the hitherto, and now venerated and venerable prelacy of Ireland? Was it the best to talk of securities? To countenance that insult alike to our understandings, and to our hearts—that insult which says, that in subjection and in degradation, the Catholics will continue faithful, but that from participation in the benefits of the constitution, disloyalty is to ensue—and hence, that "securities" are requisite ! !

I will not follow this exasperating topic; but I will say, that the sacred duty that I owe to this "*mine own, my native land,*" impels me to say, that Henry Grattan was greatly and grievously mistaken in this session of parliament.

I only require that we should reconcile these concurrent duties. Let us thank Grattan with all the veins of our hearts, but let us not use a single expression which can, by any construction whatsoever, be tortured into any approbation of the late very mistaken and mischievous bill. I do not require, nor would I consent, that any trace of ill-humour or reproach should be found in our address; but I would wish that you should suggest to him his former glories in the cause of " SIMPLE REPEAL," * and entreat of him again to adopt for the motto of his country, and her watchword in the war of parliament, " SIMPLE REPEAL !" Cheers.)

I am anxious to infix this truth on the minds of all our parliamentary friends, that it is for the great principle of religious liberty that we contend, and not for individual advantages to the Catholic body. Let the sentiment be the main idea of every address, as well as of every petition; and though we may be defeated, we shall never again be disgraced !

* Alluding to the discussions of 1782, when the question was, whether the Irish parliament would consider its independence sufficiently vindicated, and asserted by the mere repeal of the Act of the English parliament in the sixth year of the reign of George the First, by which the latter claimed and usurped legislative authority over Ireland, or whether an express renunciation of this usurped legislative authority should be insisted on.
Grattan was for "*simple Repeal*," Flood for the *express renunciation.* The first was obtained in 1782, and the second the year after, viz. 1783, by the 23d George III., chapter 28, declaring our legislative and judicial independence " ESTABLISHED FOR EVER !"

I would, under these circumstances, earnestly press upon my esteemed friend to postpone the address to Mr. Grattan for the present; to consent to have it referred to the sub-committee, in order to have it modelled upon the principle and in the manner that I suggest. It will not be the less complimentary to Mr Grattan for being the work of deliberation, and it clearly will be more useful and more honourable to ourselves.

Upon this subject let us not have—I trust we shall not have —any division. Our country has suffered for centuries from degradation and oppression, brought on her, and perpetuated by her internal divisions. First, the Irish were divided amongst themselves; then the English were divided from the Irish; then followed the long-cherished divisions between the Catholics and the Protestants; and now yet another division is encouraged by the government. Every individual in the Catholic body, whom the administration can influence, either directly or indirectly, is separated from the Catholic prelates and the people. An endeavour was made to control us; it failed, and now the plan is secession. For my part, I rejoice at the secession of those who desire to gratify themselves, and not to serve their country.

But whom do we miss? I do not perceive the deficiency. Our meetings, as it appears to me, have never been so crowded with the health, and strength, and independence of the body, as since the last and poorest attempt to stay our majestic onward course towards the temple of concord and freedom. (Cheers.)

Let us, then, concur in the two leading features of this address —gratitude—eternal gratitude to Grattan; fidelity—unalterable fidelity to our country. To combine both, I move that the address which has been this day brought forward and read by Mr. M'Donnell, be referred to the sub-committee to report upon this day week.

IRISH MANUFACTURE.

Mr. O'Connell brought forward his promised motions on this subject.

The first resolution is, that no member be allowed to speak or vote at the Board, after the 1st of August, who shall not be clothed in Irish manufacture.

The second, that the ladies of Ireland be entreated to encourage the wear of their native manufacture, and not to introduce any other.

The third, that a committee of seven be appointed, for the purpose of calling upon the Protestant gentlemen of the country to form "*An Association for the encouragement of consumption of Irish Manufacture.*" The resolutions were all received with loud applause and were passed by acclamation."

The following gentlemen were then appointed upon this committee :—

Mr. O'Connell,   Counsellors O'Gorman and
Mr. Richard O'Gorman,   Finn, and
Doctor Sheridan,   R. O'Bryan, Esq.
E. Cox, Esq.

Mr. O'Connell then moved that his resolutions should be printed in the liberal papers as Dublin, and in the liberal prints of Limerick, Cork, Waterford, Kilkenny, and Clonmel, and in a Belfast paper.

This was also agreed to, and the meeting adjourned.

On Tuesday, the 20th July, Mr. Saurin moved the Court of King's Bench, "that the case of the King against Magee, in consequence of the continued absence of Messrs. Fitzgerald, Pole, Peele, and Sir Charles Saxton, witnesses for the defendant, should stand over to Monday, the 26th," which was accordingly granted.

ADDRESS TO HENRY GRATTAN.

On the preceding Saturday, the 17th of July, the address to Mr. Grattan was reported to the Catholic Board, by its original proposer, Mr. M'Donnell.

In the course of his speech on this occasion, he alluded to the continued absence of several members of the Board, who had formerly been constant attendants, and had taken an active part in its proceedings. This allusion had reference chiefly to the parties who had made themselves prominent in opposing the vote of thanks to the Catholic bishops, and who, since the triumphant carrying of that motion in aggregate meeting, had secluded themselves in high dudgeon at their well-merited discomfiture.

The adoption of the address, which had been altered, as agreed upon, at the preceding meeting, and, therefore, while highly complimentary to Mr. Grattan, contained nothing that could be held to involve any species of tolerance towards the "*securities*" of his "Relief" Bill, was seconded by Mr. O'Connell.

He said, that in seconding this address, he did not think it necessary to take up one moment in recommending it to the Board. He relied upon its being carried with the most perfect unanimity; and when he rose to second it, he only meant to give it all the strength which his individual expression of the gratitude due by Ireland to Mr. Grattan could impart.

No man in the community felt more sensibly the great debt which we all owe to Mr. Grattan than he did ; and he was happy that he could make ample acknowledgment of its justice and magnitude, without conceding either his religion or the steady principle of simple repeal, upon which alone the Catholics were determined to stand. The clauses, the arrangements, the details, the provisions, the enactments, the restrictions, which would deprive the Irish people of the one, and which were totally inconsistent with the other, were not of Mr. Grattan's invention. These subjects were not now touched upon with any retrospective view. The address speaks prophetically. It tells Mr. Grattan that he has always had the hearts of the Irish people and that in future he shall have their full judgments.

It was immaterial whether their petition should succeed in the next session or not ; the cause was proceeding with a rapid and steady pace, gaining daily additional strength as it went along. He was sorry that he could not agree with his most respectable friend, Mr. M'Donnell, in any part of the late bill. It was unnecessary, after the very powerful manner in which that gentleman had condemned the interference with the clergy, to say anything upon that part of the bill ; the sentiments expressed by Mr. M'Donnell were only those of the public in general, and any feeble cry that has been attempted to be raised in favour of the clauses, only made the expression of this feeling the more marked. But he was bound to say, that none, even of the political enactments of the bill, deserved approbation.

He entreated his respected friend to permit the legal men of the Board, merely as barristers (if not lawyers), to declare their opinion upon it, as upon matter of law. And this opinion he unequivocally declared was, that the bill, had it passed into law, would have been totally inefficient—would have done nothing. In the House of Commons and in the higher ranks of the army, some trifling benefit might have accrued from it to a few ambitious Catholics, but in respect to the great mass of the people, they would have gained nothing by it. Taxation without representation, and the numerous other crying grievances which they endure, would have been left wholly unaffected by its operation. This he asserted as the opinion of the barristers of the Catholic Board, and if it shall be contradicted by anything like argument in the public papers, he pledged himself to support the assertion.

There was now upon the table an abstract of the bill, which had been prepared by Mr. Charles Butler for the emancipation of the Catholics : and he felt himself bound to say, that he had never met anything which appeared to have been drawn up in more complete ignorance of the penal laws which aggrieve the Catholics of Ireland, and that if it had passed into a law, it would have been totally useless. Mr. Butler (he said) is an expert penman, who writes a great deal, and if he shall contradict in print his (Mr. O'Connell's) assertion, he will, for the information of the gentleman and the public, quote the statutes which would render his bill a nullity.

He (Mr. O'Connell) spoke this that the people might know

that bad bills had been prepared ; and for the purpose of inform-
ing any known person who took an interest in the affairs of the
Catholics, that if a bill for their emancipation was wanted, and
the Board were to be called upon to produce one, the frame of
such a bill was ready, and should be instantly produced.

THE SYNOD OF ULSTER.

THE pressure of prior business at the meeting of the 17th of July, compelled a postponement of the motion of Mr. O'Connell, relative to the Presbyterian Synod of Ulster. On the
succeeding Saturday, he, however, brought it forward.

He said he had to call on the Board to carry out their intention of thanking that very important body, the Synod of Ulster.
for the late vote of the members composing it, in favour of religious liberty. The learned gentleman (say the reports of the
Post and Freeman,) prefaced the motion by a speech of some
length, and delivered it with his wonted eloquence. He touched
upon a variety of topics, having reference to or bearing u pon
the subject matter of his motion. The late decision of the Synod
of Ulster he considered perfectly unanimous, for the eight individuals who had opposed, have since that time declared, that in
sentiment and feeling, they were in perfect accordance with the
majority.

He looked upon it as one of the most important, auspicious,
and gratifying events which had occured for a considerable
period. Divisions had ever been the ruin of Ireland ; they yet
pursued and scourged her ; but the declaration of the Synod of
Ulster, in favour of religious liberty, was an earnest he hoped,
for the banishment of them from amongst us in future. It was
not to be expected, however, that an evil, which had not only
been suffered to exist, but had actually been encouraged, and, in
consequence, had grown to a melancholy extent indeed, should
be all at once overcome.

The Synod of Ulster had done their part. They had set a
noble example ; let it be met by a corresponding spirit, and be
imitated throughout the country.

The enemies of Ireland having had long experience of the
efficacy of divisions in forwarding their purposes, had never lost
sight of promoting them. There were two sorts of divisions
which were peculiarly fatal, and should be guarded against with

the utmost care. One—the lesser kind—was, divisions amongst the Catholics themselves; the other—and the greater—was, that which would separate the Presbyterian, the Quaker, and all the other numerous classes of Dissenters from the Catholics, and from each other.

With respect to the first kind of division, he was proud to say, that the great body of the Irish Catholics were unanimous in their determination to knock at the gate of the temple of liberty, and temperately, but firmly, and with the port of men, demand admittance. Knowing this to be the spirit which animated the body, he was prepared to say, that if any Catholic, no matter what were his rank and property, seceded from them, he only made an outlaw of himself, and inflicted no injury upon the cause.

And with respect to the second kind of division, the declaration of the Synod of Ulster was a gratifying proof, that good sense, reason, and patriotism were beginning to triumph over the distractions which had so long disfigured Ireland.

It was with pain he found himself compelled to say that many of the clergy of the Established Church were very hostile to the just claims of their fellow-countrymen and fellow-Christians, who sought liberty to worship God according to the dictates of their consciences. This was particularly observable during the late elections. Wheresoever a gentleman, whose principles were tolerant, appeared as a candidate, he was sure to be encountered by a host of the votes of the clergy. Dr. St. Lawrence and that galloping, preaching gentleman, his son, were proofs of this when, at Cork, they strenuously opposed Mr. Hely Hutchinson. It was true, there were many illustrious exceptions which only proved the general rule.

It was gratifying, however, to remark, that this illiberality was confined to the clergy, and even amongst them to the beneficed ones. The laity—the respectable and uninfluenced laity—were all favourable to the rights of their fellow-men and fellow-subjects; but, while this afforded matter for warm congratulation, it was impossible to avoid regretting, that the practice of the Established clergy should be so widely different from those doctrines of peace and charity which they are so liberally paid for teaching. He was willing to hope, notwithstanding all that could be done, their efforts and the efforts of those who set them in motion, would prove ineffectual; that every odious distinction would be obliterated; and that every man in this country would be ambitious for one title, and one title only, that of IRISHMEN! (Loud cheering.)

The Synod of Ulster talks of the constitution. He perfectly agreed with the Synod, in what it had said in that respect. All he required, all the Catholics required, was *Emancipation to the extent of the constitution !*—*Emancipation agreeable to the principles of the revolution !* Those principles were plain, indisputable, and well understood—they were liberty to the people to choose their own religion and their governors. The Catholics merely seek religious freedom. The revolutionists changed their king, because he was not of the religion of the people, and refused to be governed by any person who would not adopt that religion. The Catholics, however, seek no such change, and nothing beyond what he had said.

He had but one observation more. The great object of his life, and that which he had in view at present, was to defeat and put down any man who should attempt to excite discontent, or disloyalty, or disunion amongst the people. Union and harmony were the great and healing balsams which he wished and hoped to see applied to the wounds of his country.

TRIAL OF JOHN MAGEE.

On Monday, the 26th of July, the case of the King *v* Magee was again called on.
Mr. O'Connell addressed the Court at its sitting.

TRIAL OF JOHN MAGEE,

Proprietor of the *Dublin Evening Post*, for a libel against his Grace the Duke of Richmond.

King's Bench, July 26, 1813.

The court of King's Bench was yesterday morning crowded at an early hour, by the interest excited in this case, which had been twice postponed, on account of the absence, as the affidavits of the traverser stated, of witnesses material to his defence. The Chief Justice entered the court soon after eleven o'clock, and the Clerk of the Crown was proceeding to call over the panel, when Mr. O'Connell, one of the traverser's counsel, rose and spoke as follows:—

My lord, I am to apply to your lordship to postpone this trial to the first *nisi prius* day of next term, in consequence of the absence of two witnesses material for the traverser's defence; and I can undertake to state, with confidence, that if your lordship grant this application, those witnesses will be in attendance at that time; my application is grounded on three affidavits, and is opposed by one on the part of the Crown, by which I find there is the same anxiety to try Magee in the absence of his witnesses, as prevailed on the former occasions; in the affidavits of

Mr. Magee, one of the 28th of May, and the other of the 5th of July, it was stated that Mr. W. Pole, Sir C. Saxton, and Mr. Fitzgerald were important witnesses; the latter gentleman is in attendance, but the two former not; and if the Court before agreed to postpone, on account of their absence, the same cause now operates, and we come now with stronger documents than before; for we have the affidavit of service of two *subpœnas ad testificandum,* and the affidavit of the English agent will be produced to prove he transmitted £30 British, as viaticums for Mr. Pole and Sir Charles Saxton.

And what says the affidavit of the Crown Solicitor? Why that a letter was received from C. Saxton, stating that he had not received his viaticum. How frivolous is it to talk of £15 preventing a high-minded gentleman doing justice between party and party; it is sworn by the process-server that he believes it was sent to the lodging-house in which Sir C. Saxton lived and where he learned that Sir Charles had set off for Ireland; the viaticum would have been personally paid if there had been personal attendance. Mr. Magee further swears that he will apply to the Court of King's Bench in England, for attachments for not obeying your lordship's process.

Chief Justice—That attachment issues on certificate from this Court that a viaticum was tendered.

Mr. O'Connell.—The only certificate, I believe, my lord, required, is a certificate of non-attendance. The process-server was informed that Sir Charles had set out for Ireland, and if his servant told a falsehood, why should Mr. Magee suffer? Mr. Kemmis makes affidavit of a letter from Sir Charles, and only presents us with a fragment of it; is it not strange he did not write to Mr. Magee's agent instead of the agent for the prosecution? The letter is written not to the person who wanted his evidence, but to the person that did not. Mr. Fitzgerald did not send his excuse, but wrote to the agent of the traverser. Were we to hunt all over England for Sir Charles to give him his viaticum personally? We have the letter of the English agent who is now in court, whose affidavit will be sworn before this trial shall have proceeded, and in which he states that he believes the viaticum was received. Consider, my lord, the great severity it would be to try a man in Ireland, while his witness is in England.

Mr. W. Pole, it is true, has no residence in Ireland, although here presents an Irish county, and I am sure (said Mr. O'Connell) ne would not peddle about fifteen pounds; if there had been any negligence upon the part of the traverser, his application would come with a bad grace, but he has done everything in his power to induce the attendance of his witnesses; two fresh subpœnas have been served; and I should hope the case of the Chevalier D'Eon, reported in Burrowes, will not be here debated; in that case the witnesses were in France, and no chance of their coming over; but the obstacle to the attendance of our witnesses is now done away; they were, at the time of former applications, attending their duty in parliament; but that cause, which I allow a legal one, is now done away; up to Thursday last, their absence is accounted for, and we can now proceed to enforce their attendance, so that there is little doubt of their being present on the day this trial will stand for, if your lordship grant this application. Being now in possession of Sir Charles Saxton's last excuse, the non-receipt of the viaticum, that shall be obviated, and that it has not been caused by the default of Mr. Magee, Mr. Menzie's affidavit will clearly evince. And as former postponements took place on weaker grounds, I should hope this application will be allowed. Mr. Kemmis cannot say he believes Mr. Magee intends to escape from justice; he sets out a letter of Sir C. Saxton, and does not swear that he believes it; by the postponement, a failure of justice cannot ensue, but great injustice may be done if traverser be obliged to go to trial, in the absence of his witnesses.

Chief Justice.—Do you consent. Mr. Attorney-General?

Attorney-General.—By no means, my lord; two of the persons formerly absent are now present, and further postponement would be but a mockery of justice.

Mr. Wallace.—There is nothing to justify the expressions of a mockery of justice; this is not an application to postpone the punishment, but one to the discretion of the Court to postpone the trial. Mr. Magee may be guilty of the libel, but until proved so, he is to be considered innocent; the Crown cannot suffer by the delay, for judgment cannot be had till next term.

Chief Justice.—Let me see the affidavits.

Mr. Wallace.—I am glad your lordship has looked into the affidavits; they contain the usual ground for postponing the trial, that justice cannot be done if the trial proceeded in the absence of traverser's witnesses; and am I not at liberty to assume that Sir C. Saxton is a material witness, when it has not been contravened by the affidavit on the other side? It would be miserable special pleading to say, that because the money was not actually put into Sir C. Saxton's pocket, although he was on his way to Ireland, that, therefore, he is justified in acting as if no viaticum at all had been sent to him. I am sorry he conceived a viaticum at all necessary. Two of the witnesses, the Attorney-General states, have arrived, but we made no compromise to go to trial in the absence of the others. I shall not trouble your lordship at greater length; but the cardinal fact in our case is, we have the best grounded hope that he will attend on the day we have applied to fix the trial for.

Chief Justice.—This case comes before me like any other cause at *nisi prius*, and I will act in it as I would on circuit. The Judge cannot say I will not try it; let the party prosecut' ing proceed at his peril; because two postponements have taken place before the Court, is it to be argued that, therefore, a third shall? There is no fact either stated in the affidavit or by counsel, by which the Court can judge of the materiality of the absent witness; one of them says he would have attended if he had received a proper viaticum; that which is spoken of would not be sufficient to bring persons of their rank half way. I cannot consent to postpone the trial, but let the prosecutor proceed at his own risk.

Mr. Townsend cited the case of the King against Finney, which afterwards went to the twelve judges, and in that case there was no postponement.

Mr. O'Connell—Mr. Attorney-General will proceed, if he please; but it would be a mockery of justice to consent to go on in the absence of our witnesses.

Attorney-General.—My lord, it is most important that jurors should attend when summoned.

Chief Justice—They have been called on £50 fines. Here a long delay took place for want of jurors.

Mr. O'Connell—I am desired by Mr. Magee to state, that if the postponement shall be allowed, proper viaticums shall be sent.

Attorney-General—I cannot consent, as I feel confident delay is the only object in view.

Mr. O'Connell—We differ in opinion with Mr. Magee; we do not wish to appear if the trial proceed, but we yield to his wish that we should. A further delay took place.

Mr. Finlay, in a very nervous manner, then said—My lord. I think it extremely unreasonable, since they won't wait for *our* witnesses, that we should wait for *their* jury. (A general laugh.)

Mr. Attorney-General—My lord, there are but eleven jurors in attendance, we, therefore pray *a tales*; we would, however, rather have the panel, if your lordship will wait a short time.

Mr. O'Connell—My lord, I am to pray to quash the panel. This is a trial by *nisi prius* and yet the panel is different from the *nisi prius* one; there are but twenty-four names instead of thirty-six, and the 29th of Geo. II., cap. 6, includes the case of the King against Magee, as well as other trials at *nisi prius*; the third section enacts, that any sheriff or other officer, shall annex the Christian names, &c., of the persons returned, who shall be in number thirty-six, and that they shall try all the cases at *nisi prius*; the sheriff has here returned the *venire*, and has not returned thirty-six names; twenty-four only being returned; the words of the statute are express; the only doubt is, whether criminal cases are included; it may be said that party and party include the King; the third section is a positive enactment; the first section has these words, "*per medietatem lingua*," which is only applicable to criminal cases, as there is no such thing in civil cases.

Chief Justice—This appears, reading the statute, to apply to the assizes.

Mr. O'Connell—And *nisi prius* also

Chief Justice—I don't think it applies to the city of Dublin.

Mr. O'Connell—Then your lordship will make a note of our motion to quash the panel. Now, my lord, we object to the array; there has been a misdirection of the *venire*; before the statute the proceedings were by *distringas alias*, and *pluries distringas*; the *venire* issued in this case has been returned, and remains amongst the records of the court. There are, at present, two *venires*. The Attorney-General can appoint triers to try the fact.

Attorney General—They allege there are errors on the record. Your lordship is not sitting here to try the plea roll, but the issue knit between the parties. If there be error on the record, a writ of error will lie, or a motion may be made to arrest the judgment.

Mr. O'Connell—The *nisi prius* roll will exhibit the ground of our objection.

Mr. Wallace—We could have no opportunity to challenge the array, if we did not know of the second panel.

Chief Justice—The record is now before me, and I do not see the second *venire*.

Mr. Townsend—All objections to the array are against the officer himself, but this is for the Court above, and not to be considered as *nisi prius*.

Attorney-General—If there be any error on the record, this is not the place to amend it

Mr. Wallace—We contend for it; we are not to be tried by the second jury

The Clerk of the Crown then read from the record, the objections put in by the traver-sor's counsel; they were put in as pleas, and were substantially: in the first place, that the panel was returned by the sheriffs, under the denominations (nominations) of the Attorney-General; that the panel did not contain truth; and that a *distringas* did not issue on the first *venire*. The Attorney-General then, *ore tenus*, joined issue on the first and second plea, and demurred to the third. Triers were then appointed—Messrs. Heyland and Hamilton.

WILLIAM GOFF, Esq., examined by Mr. O'Connell

Do you know Joseph Goff?

I do.

Is he not one of the persons returned on this panel?

I believe so.

Mr. O'Connell—My lord, we are going to prove that this person, not having any other favour to ask of the government, expressed a wish to be always employed as a juror in cases where the Crown was a party; such expressions would warrant a conclusion that his name now appeared on the panel in consequence of his own wishes, and in violation, there-fore, of the impartiality necessary in the formation of juries. The reason why we did not produce the person himself, is upon the general principle that no man is bound to crimi-nate himself. If Crown influence be proved, it will affect the Attorney-General, as identi-fied with the officers of the Crown.

This challenge was, after some discussion, disallowed, as the Court would not admit hear-say evidence on the point.

The following were the jury, as finally sworn.

Leland Crosthwaite,	Martin Keene,
Thomas Andrews,	Benjamin Darley,
Bladen Swiney,	William Watson,
Richard Palmer,	William Walsh,
Thomas Rochfort,	Richard Cooke,
Alexander Montgomery,	Edward Clibborne.

Mr. Kemmis then opened the indictment, and the Attorney-General followed.

The nature of his speech will be readily gathered from Mr. O'Connell's reply, which has been generally considered one of his greatest bar efforts, and which we now proceed to give.

It was on Tuesday, 27th July, the second day of the proceedings, that he was called upon to speak. We quote the ample report of the *Evening Post*.

At eleven o'clock, the *Chief Justice* took his seat in the court, which was crowded from an early hour, public expectation being much excited and interested, with respect to the proceedings and issue of the day.

Mr. O'Connell rose and spoke as follows:—

I consented to the adjournment yesterday, gentlemen of the jury, from that impulse of nature which compels us to postpone pain; it is, indeed, painful to me to address you; it is a cheer-less, a hopeless task to address you—a task which would require all the animation and interest to be derived from the working of a mind fully fraught with the resentment and disgust created in mine yesterday, by that farrago of helpless absurdity with which Mr. Attorney-General regaled you.

But I am now not sorry for the delay. Whatever I may have lost in vivacity, I trust I shall compensate for in discretion. That which yesterday excited my anger, now appears to me to be an object of pity; and that which then roused my indignation, now only moves to *contempt.* I can now address you with feelings softened, and, I trust, subdued; and I do, from my soul, declare, that I now cherish no other sensations than those which enable me to bestow on the Attorney-General and on his discourse, pure and unmixed compassion.

It was a discourse in which you could not discover either order, or method, or eloquence; it contained very little logic, and no poetry at all; violent and virulent, it was a confused and disjointed tissue of bigotry, amalgamated with congenial vulgarity. He accused my client of using Billingsgate, and he accused him of it in language suited exclusively for that meridian. He descended even to the calling of names: he called this young gentleman a " malefactor," a " Jacobin," and a " ruffian," gentlemen of the jury; he called him "abominable," and " seditious," and "revolutionary," and "infamous," and a " ruffian" again, gentlemen of the jury; he called him a "brother keeper," a "pander," "a kind of bawd in breeches," and a "ruffian" a third time, gentlemen of the jury.

I cannot repress my astonishment, how Mr. Attorney-General could have *preserved* this dialect in its native purity; he has been now for nearly thirty years in the class of polished society; he has, for some years, mixed amongst the highest orders in the state; he has had the honour to belong for thirty years to the first profession in the world—to the only profession, with the single exception, perhaps, of the military, to which a high-minded gentleman could condescend to belong—the Irish bar. To that bar, at which he has seen and heard a Burgh and a Duquery; at which he must have listened to a Burston, a Ponsonby, and a Curran; to a bar which still contains a Plunket, a Ball, and despite of politics, I will add, a Bushe. With this galaxy of glory, flinging their light around him, how can he alone have remained in darkness? How has it happened, that the twilight murkiness of his soul, has not been illumined with a single ray shot from their lustre? Devoid of taste and of genius, how can he have had memory enough to preserve this original vulgarity? He is, indeed, an object of compassion, and, from my inmost soul, I bestow on him my forgiveness, and my bounteous pity.

But not for him alone should compassion be felt. Recollect, that upon his advice—that with him, as the prime mover and instigator of those rash, and silly, and irritating measures, of the last five years which have afflicted and distracted this long suffering country have originated—with him they have all originated. Is there not then compassion due to the millions, whose destinies are made to depend upon his counsel? Is there no pity to those who, like me, must know that the liberties of the tenderest pledges of their affections, and of that which is dearer still, of their country, depends on this man's advice?

Yet, let not pity for us be unmixed ; he has afforded the consolation of hope ; his harangue has been heard ; it will be reported—I trust faithfully reported ; and if it be but read in England, we may venture to hope that there may remain just so much good sense in England as to induce the conviction of the folly and the danger of conducting the government of a brave and long-enduring people by the counsels of so tasteless and talentless an adviser.

See what an imitative animal man is ! The sound of ruffian —ruffian—ruffian, had scarcely died on the Attorney-General's lips, when you find the word honoured with all the permanency of print, in one of his pensioned and well-paid, but ill-read newspapers. Here is the first line in the *Dublin Journal* of this day :—" The ruffian who writes for the *Freeman's Journal.*' Here is an apt scholar—he profits well of the Attorney-General's tuition. The pupil is worthy of the master—the master is just suited to the pupil.

I now dismiss the style and measure of the Attorney-General's discourse, and I require your attention to its matter. That matter I must divide, although with him there was no division, into two unequal portions. The first, as it was by far the greater portion of his discourse, shall be that which was altogether inapplicable to the purposes of this prosecution. The second, and infinitely the smaller portion of his speech, is that which related to the subject matter of the indictment which you are to try. He has touched upon and disfigured a great variety of topics. I shall follow him at my good leisure through them. He has invited me to a wide field of discussion. I accept his challenge with alacrity and with pleasure.

This extraneous part of his discourse, which I mean first to discuss, was distinguished by two leading features. The first, consisted of a dull and reproving sermon, with which he treated my colleagues and myself, for the manner in which we thought fit to conduct this defence. He talked of the melancholy exhibition of four hours wasted, as he said, in frivolous debate, and he obscurely hinted at something like incorrectness of professional conduct He has not ventured to speak out, but I will. I shall say nothing for myself; but for my colleagues—my inferiors in professional standing, but infinitely my superiors in every talent and in every acquirement—my colleagues, whom I boast as my friends, not in the routine language of the bar, but in the sincerity of my esteem and affection; for my learned and upright colleagues, I treat the unfounded insinuation with the most contemptuous scorn!

All I shall expose is the utter inattention to the fact, which in small things as in great, seems to mark the Attorney-General's career. He talks of four hours. Why, it was past one before the last of you were digged together by the Sheriff, and the Attorney-General rose to address you before three. How he could contrive to squeeze four hours into that interval, it is for him to explain; nor should I notice it, but that it is the particular prerogative of dulness to be accurate in the detail of minor facts, so that the Attorney-General is without an excuse, when he departs from them, and when for four hours, you have had not quite two. Take this also with you, that we assert our uncontrollable right to employ them as we have done; and as to his advice, we neither respect, nor will we receive it; but we can afford cheerfully to pardon the vain presumption that made him offer us counsel.

For the rest, he may be assured that we will never imitate his example. We will never volunteer to mingle our politics, whatever they may be, with our forensic duties. I made this the rigid rule of my professional conduct; and if I shall appear to depart from this rule now, I bid you recollect that I am compelled to follow the Attorney-General into grounds which, if he had been wise, he would have avoided.

Yes; I am compelled to follow him into the discussion of his conduct towards the Catholics. He has poured out the full vial of his own praise on that conduct—praise in which, I can safely assure him, he has not a single unpaid rival. It is a topic upon which no unbribed man, except himself, dwells. I admit the disinterestedness with which he praises himself, and I do not envy him his delight, but he ought to know, if he sees or hears a word of that kind from any other man, that that man receives or expects compensation for his task, and really deserves money for his labour and invention.

My lord, upon the Catholic subject, I commence with one assertion of the Attorney-General, which I trust I misunderstood. He talked, as I collected him, of the Catholics having imbibed principles of a seditious, treasonable, and revolutionary nature! He seemed to me, most distinctly, to charge us with treason!

There is no relying on his words for his meaning—I know there
is not.   On a former occasion, I took down a repetition of this
charge full seventeen times on my brief, and yet, afterwards, it
turned out that he never intended to make any such charge ;
that he forgot he had ever used those words, and he disclaimed
the idea they naturally convey.   It is clear. therefore, that upon
this subject he knows not what he says ; and that these phrases
are the mere flowers of his rhetoric, but quite innocent of any
meaning !

Upon this account I pass him by, I go beyond him, and I content myself with proclaiming those charges, whosoever may make
them, to be false and base calumnies!   It is impossible to refute
such charges in the language of dignity or temper.   But if any
man dares to charge the Catholic body, or the Catholic Board, or
any individuals of that Board with sedition or treason, I do here,
I shall always in this court, in the city, in the field, brand him
as an infamous and profligate *liar !*

Pardon the phrase, but there is no other suitable to the occasion.   But he is a profligate liar who so asserts, because he must
know that the whole tenor of our conduct confutes the assertion.
What is it we seek ?

Chief Justice—What, Mr. O'Connell, can this have to do with the question which the
jury are to try ?

Mr. O'Connell.—*You heard the Attorney-General traduce and
calumniate us—you heard him with patience and with temper—
listen now to our vindication !*

I ask, what is it we seek ?   What is it we incessantly and, if
you please, clamorously petition for ?   Why, to be allowed to
partake of the advantages of the constitution.   We are earnestly
anxious to share the benefits of the constitution.   We look to
the participation in the constitution as our greatest political
blessing.   If we desired to destroy it, would we seek to share it ?
If we wished to overturn it, would we exert ourselves through
calumny, and in peril, to obtain a portion of its blessings ?   Strange
inconsistent voice of calumny!   You charge us with intemperance
in our exertions for a participation in the constitution. and you
charge us at the same time, almost in the same sentence, with a
design to overturn that constitution.   The dupes of your hypocrisy may believe you ; but base calumniators, you do not, you
cannot believe yourselves !

The Attorney-General—"*this wisest and best of men,*" as his
colleague, the Solicitor-General. called him in his presence—the

Attorney-General next boasted of his triumph over Pope and Popery—"I put down the Catholic Committee; I will put down at my good time, the Catholic Board." This boast is partly historical, partly prophetical. He was wrong in his history—he is quite mistaken in his prophecy. He did not put down the Catholic Committee—we gave up that name the moment that it was confessedly avowed, that this sapient Attorney-General's polemical-legal controversy dwindled into a mere dispute about words. He told us that in the English language "pretence" means purpose;" had it been French and not English, we might have been inclined to respect his judgment, but in point of English we venture to differ with him; we told him " purpose," good Mr. Attorney-General, is just the reverse of "pretence." The quarrel grew warm and animated; we appealed to common sense, to the grammar, and to the dictionary; common sense, grammar, and the dictionary decided in our favour. He brought his appeal to this court, your lordship, and your brethren, unanimously decided that, in point of of law—mark, mark, gentlemen of the jury, the sublime wisdom of law—the court decided that, in point of law, "*pretence*" *does mean* "*purpose.*"

Fully contented with this very reasonable and more satisfactory decision, there still remained a matter of fact between us : the Attorney-General charged us with being representatives; we denied all representation. He had two witnesses to prove the fact for him ; they swore to it one way at one trial, and directly the other way at the next. An honourable, intelligent, and enlightened jury disbelieved those witnesses at the first trial—matters were better managed at the second trial—the jury were better arranged. I speak delicately, gentlemen ; the jury were better arranged, as the witnesses were better informed ; and, accordingly, there was one verdict for us on the representative question, and one verdict against us.

You know the jury that found for us ; you know that it was Sir Charles Saxton's Castle-list jury that found against us. Well, the consequence was, that, thus encouraged, Mr. Attorney-General proceeded to force. We abhorred tumult, and were weary of litigation ; we new-modelled the agents and managers of the Catholic petitions; we formed an assembly, respecting which there could not be a shadow of pretext for calling it a representative body. We disclaimed representation ; and we rendered it impossible, even for the virulence of the most malignant law-officer living, to employ the Convention Act against us—that, even upon the Attorney-General's own construction, requires representation as an ingredient in the offence it prohibits. He cannot possibly call us representatives ; we are the individual servants of the public, whose business we do gratuitously but zealously. Our cause has advanced even from his persecution—and this he calls putting down the Catholic Committee !

Next, he glorifies himself in his prospect of putting down the Catholic Board. For the present, he, indeed, tells you, that much as he hates the Papists, it is unnecessary for him to crush our Board, because we injure our own cause so much. He says that we are very criminal, but we are so foolish that our folly serves as a compensation for our wickedness. We are very wicked and very mischievous, but then we are such foolish little criminals, that we deserve his indulgence. Thus he tolerates offences. because of their being committed sillily ; and, indeed, we give him so much pleasure and gratification by the injury we do our own cause, that he is spared the superfluous labour of impeding our petition by his prosecutions, fines, or imprisonments.

He expresses the very idea of the Roman Domitian, of whom some of you possibly may have read ; he amused his days in torturing men—his evenings he relaxed in the humble cruelty of impaling flies. A courtier caught a fly for his imperial amusement—"Fool," said the emperor, "fool, to give thyself the trouble of torturing an animal that was about to burn itself to death in the candle !" Such is the spirit of the Attorney-General's commentary on our Board. Oh, rare Attorney-General !—Oh, best and wisest of men ! ! !

But, to be serious. Let me pledge myself to you that he imposes on you, when he threatens to crush the Catholic Board. Illegal violence may do it—force may effectuate it ; but your hopes and his will be defeated, if he attempts it by any course of law. I am, if not a lawyer, at least, a barrister. On this subject I ought to know something, and I do not hesitate to contradict the Attorney-General on this point, and to proclaim to you and to the country that the Catholic Board is perfectly a legal assembly—that it not only does not violate the law, but that it is entitled to the protection of the law, and in the very proudest tone of firmness, I hurl *defiance* at the Attorney-General !

I defy him to allege a law or a statute, or even a proclamation that is violated by the Catholic Board. No, gentlemen, no ; his religious prejudices—if the absence of every charity can be called anything religious—his religious prejudices really obscure his reason, his bigoted intolerance has totally darkened his understanding, and he mistakes the plainest facts and misquotes the clearest law, in the ardour and vehemence of his rancour. I disdain his moderation—I scorn his forbearance—I tell him he knows not the law if he thinks as he says ; and if he thinks so, I tell him to his beard, that he is not *honest* in not having sooner prosecuted us, and I challenge him to that prosecution.

It is strange—it is melancholy, to reflect on the miserable and mistaken pride that must inflate him to talk as he does of the Catholic Board. The Catholic Board is composed of men—I include not myself—of course, I always except myself—every way his superiors, in birth, in fortune, in talents, in rank. What! is he to talk of the Catholic Board lightly ? At their head is the Earl of Fingal, a nobleman whose exalted rank stoops beneath the superior station of his virtues—whom even the venal minions of power must respect. We are engaged, patiently and perseveringly engaged, in a struggle through the open channels of the constitution for our liberties. The son of the ancient earl whom I have mentioned cannot in his native land attain any honourable distinction of the state, and yet Mr. Attorney-General knows that they are open to every son of every bigoted and intemperate stranger that may settle amongst us.

But this system cannot last ; he may insult, he may calumniate, he may prosecute ; but the Catholic cause is on its *majestic march ;* its progress is rapid and obvious ; it is cheered in its advance, and aided by all that is dignified and dispassionate —by everything that is patriotic—by all the honour, all the integrity of the empire ; and its success is just as certain as the return of to-morrow's sun, and the close of to-morrow's eve.

"*We will—we must soon be emancipated*, in despite of the Attorney-General, aided as he is by his august allies, the aldermen of Skinner's-alley. In despite of the Attorney-General and the aldermen of Skinner's-alley, our emancipation is certain, and not distant.

I have no difficulty in perceiving the motive of the Attorney-General, in devoting so much of his medley oration to the Catholic question, and to the expression of his bitter hatred to us, and of his determination to ruin our hopes. It had, to be sure, no connection with the cause, but it had a direct and natural connection with you. He has been, all his life, reckoned a man of consummate cunning and dexterity ; and whilst one wonders that he has so much exposed himself upon those prosecutions, and accounts for it by the proverbial blindness of religious zeal, it is still easy to discover much of his native cunning and dexterity. Gentlemen, he thinks he knows his men—he knows you; many of you signed the no-Popery petition; he heard one of you boast of it; he knows you would not have been summoned on this jury, if you had entertained liberal sentiments; he knows all this, and, therefore, it is that he, with the artifice and cunning of an experienced *nisi prius* advocate, endeavours to win your confidence, and command your affections by the display of his congenial illiberality and bigotry.

You are all, of course, Protestants; see what a compliment he pays to your religion and his own, when he endeavours thus to procure a verdict on your oaths; when he endeavours to seduce you to what, if you were so seduced, would be perjury, by indulging your prejudices, and flattering you by the coincidence of his sentiments and wishes. Will he succeed, gentlemen? Will you allow him to draw you into a perjury out of zeal for your religion? And will you violate the pledge you have given to your God to do justice, in order to gratify your anxiety for the ascendancy of what you believe to be his church? Gentlemen, reflect on the strange and monstrous inconsistency of this conduct, and do not commit, if you can avoid it, the pious crime of violating your solemn oaths, in aid of the pious designs of the Attorney-General against Popery.

Oh, gentlemen! it is not in any lightness of heart I thus address you—it is rather in bitterness and sorrow; you did not expect flattery from me, and my client was little disposed to offer it to you; besides, of what avail would it be to flatter, if you came here pre-determined, and it is too plain that you are not selected for this jury from any notion of your impartiality?

But when I talk to you of your oaths and of your religion, I would full fain I could impress you with a respect for both the one and the other. I, who do not flatter, tell you, that though I do not join with you in belief, I have the most unfeigned respect for the form of Christian faith which you profess. Would that its substance, not its forms and temporal advantages, were deeply impressed on your minds! then should I not address you in the cheerless and hopeless despondency that crowds on my mind, and drives me to taunt you with the air of ridicule I do. Gentlemen, I sincerely respect and venerate your religion, *but* I despise and I now apprehend your prejudices, in the same proportion as the Attorney-General has cultivated them. In plain truth, every religion is good—every religion is true to him who, in his due caution and conscience, believes it. There is but one bad religion, that of a man who professes a faith which he does not believe; but the good religion may be, and often is, corrupted by the wretched and wicked prejudices which admit a difference of opinion as a cause of hatred.

' The Attorney-General, defective in argument—weak in his cause, has artfully roused your prejudices at his side. I have, on the contrary, met your prejudices boldly. If your verdict shall be for me, you will be certain that it has been produced by nothing but unwilling conviction resulting from sober and satisfied judgment. If your verdict be bestowed upon the artifices of the Attorney-General, you may happen to be right; but do you not see the danger of its being produced by an admixture of passion and prejudice with your reason? How difficult is it to separate prejudice from reason, when they run in the same direction. If you be men of conscience, then I call on you to listen to me, that your consciences may be safe, and your reason alone be the guardian of your oath, and the sole monitor of your decision.

I now bring you to the immediate subject of this indictment. Mr. Magee is charged with publishing a libel in his paper called the *Dublin Evening Post*. His lordship has decided that there is legal proof of the publication, and I would be sorry you thought of acquitting Mr. Magee under the pretence of not believing that evidence. I will not, therefore, trouble you on that part of the case; I will tell you, gentlemen, presently, what this publication is; but suffer me first to inform you what it is not—for this I consider to be very important to the strong, and in truth, triumphant defence which my client has to this indictment.

Gentlemen, this is *not* a libel on Charles Lennox, Duke of Richmond, in his private or individual capacity. It does not interfere with the privacy of his domestic life. It is free from any reproach upon his domestic habits or conduct; it is perfectly pure from any attempt to traduce his personal honour or integrity. Towards the man, there is not the least taint of malignity; nay, the thing is still stronger. Of Charles Duke of Richmond, personally, and as disconnected with the administration of public affairs, it speaks in terms of civility and even respect. It contains this passage which I read from the indictment:—

" Had he remained what he first came over, or what he afterwards professed to be, he would have retained his reputation for *honest open hostility*, defending his political principles with firmness, perhaps with warmth, but without rancour; the supporter and not the tool of an administration ; a mistaken politician, perhaps, but an honourable man and a respectable soldier."

The Duke is here in this libel, my lords—in this libel, gentle men of the jury, the Duke of Richmond is called an honourable man and a respectable soldier! Could more flattering expressions be invented? Has the most mercenary Press that ever yet existed, the mercenary Press of this metropolis, contained in return for all the money it has received, any praise which ought to be so pleasing—"an honourable man and a respectable soldier?" I do, therefore, beg of you, gentlemen, as you value your honesty, to carry with you in your distinct recollection, this fact, that whatever of evil this publication may contain, it does not involve any reproach against the Duke of Richmond, in any other than in his public and official character.

I have, gentlemen, next to require you to take notice, that this publication is not indicted as a seditious libel. The word seditious is, indeed, used as a kind of make-weight in the introductory part of the indictment. But mark, and recollect, that this is not an indictment for sedition. It is not, then, for private slander, nor for any offence against the constitution, that Mr. Magee now stands arraigned before you.

In the third place, gentlemen, there is this singular feature in this case, namely—that this libel, as the prosecutor calls it, is not charged in this indictment to be "false."

The indictment has this singular difference from any other I have ever seen, that the assertions of the publications are not even stated to be false.

They have not had the courtesy to you, to state upon record, that these charges, such as they are, were contrary to the truth. This I believe to be the first instance in which the allegation of falsehood has been omitted. To what is this omission to be attributed? Is it that an experiment is to be made, how much further the doctrine of the criminality of truth can be drawn? Does the prosecutor wish to make another bad precedent? or is it in contempt of any distinction between truth and falsehood, that this charge is thus framed; or does he fear that you would scruple to convict, if the indictment charged that to be false, which you all know to be true?

However that may be, I will have you to remember, that you are now to pronounce upon a publication, *the truth of which is not controverted.* Attend to the case, and you will find you are not to try Mr. Magee for sedition which may endanger the state, or for private defamation which may press sorely upon the heart, and blast the prospects o a pri ..e amily; and tha the subject matter for your decision is not characterized as false, or described as untrue.

Such are the circumstances which accompany this publication, on which you are to pronounce a verdict of guilt or innocence. The case is with you; it belongs to you exclusively to decide it. His lorship may advise, but he cannot control your decision. and it belongs to you alone to say whether or not, upon the entire matter, you conceive it to be evidence of guilt, and deserving of punishment. The statute law gives or recognises this your right, and, therefore, imposes this on you as your duty. The legislative has precluded any lawyer from being able to dictate to you. The Solicitor-General cannot now venture to promulgate the slavish doctrine which he addressed to Doctor Sheridan's jury, when he told them, "not to *presume* to differ from the Court in matter of law." The law and the fact are here the same, namely—the guilty or innocent design of the publication.

Indeed, in any criminal case, the doctrine of the Solicitor-General is intolerable. I enter my solemn protest against it. The verdict which is required from a jury in any criminal case has nothing special in it—it is not the finding of the fact in the affirmative or negative—it is not, as in Scotland, that the charge is proved or not proved. No; the jury is to say whether the prisoner be guilty or not; and could a juror find a true verdict, who declared a man guilty upon evidence of some act, perhaps praiseworthy, but clearly void of evil design or bad consequences?

I do, therefore, deny the doctrine of the learned gentleman; it is not constitutional, and it would be frightful if it were. *No judge can dictate to a jury*—no jury ought to allow itself to be dictated to.

If the Solicitor-General's doctrine were established, see what oppressive consequences might result. At some future period, some man may attain the first place on the bench, by the reputation which is so easily acquired by a certain degree of church-wardening piety, added to a great gravity, and maidenly decorum of manners. Such a man *may* reach the bench—for I am putting a mere imaginary case—HE may be a man without PASSIONS, and THEREFORE without VICES; he may, my lord, be a man superfluously RICH, and, therefore, not to be BRIBED with MONEY, but rendered PARTIAL by his BIGOTRY, and CORRUPTED by his PREJUDICES; such a man, INFLATED by FLATTERY, and BLOATED in his dignity, may hereafter use that character for SANCTITY which has served to promote him, as a sword. to hew down the struggling liberties of his country ; such a judge may interfere before trial ! and at the trial be a PARTISAN !

Gentlemen, should an honest jury—could an honest jury (if an honest jury were again found) listen with safety to the dictates of such a judge ?   I repeat it, therefore, that the Solicitor-General is mistaken—that the law does not, and cannot, require such a submission as he preached ; and at all events, gentlemen, it cannot be controverted, that in the present instance, that of an alleged libel, the decision of all law and fact belongs to *you*.

I am then warranted in directing to you some *observations* on the *law of libel*, and in doing so, I disclaim any apology for the consumption of the time necessary for my purpose.   Gentlemen, my intention is to lay before you a short and rapid view of the causes which have introduced into courts the monstrous assertion —*that truth is crime !*

It is to be deeply lamented, that the art of printing was unknown at the earlier periods of our history.   If, at the time the barons wrung the simple but sublime charter of liberty from a timid, perfidious sovereign, from a violator of his word, from a man covered with disgrace, and sunk in infamy—if at the time when that charter was confirmed and renewed, the Press had existed, it would, I think, have been the first care of those friends of freedom to have established a principle of liberty for it to rest upon, which might resist every future assault.   Their simple and unsophisticated understandings could never be brought to comprehend the legal subtleties by which it is now argued, that falsehood is useful and innocent, and truth, the emanation and the type of heaven, a crime.   They would have cut with their swords the cobweb links of sophistry in which truth is entangled ; and they would have rendered it impossible to re-establish this injustice without violating the principle of the constitution.

But in the ignorance of the blessing of a *free Press*, they could not have provided for its security.   There remains, however, an expression of their sentiments on our statute books.   The ancient parliament did pass a law against the spreaders of FALSE rumours. This law proves two things—first, that before this statute, it was not considered a crime in law to spread even a false rumour otherwise the statute would have been unnecessary ; and, secondly, that in their notion of crime, falsehood was a necessary ingredient   But here I have to remark upon, and regret the strange propensity of judges, to construe the law in favour of tyranny, and against liberty ; for servile and corrupt judges soon decided, that upon the construction of this law, it was immaterial whether the rumours were true or false, and that a law made to punish false rumours, *was equally applicable to the true.*

This, gentlemen, is called CONSTRUCTION; it is just that which, in more recent times, and of inevitable consequence, from purer motives, has converted "*pretence*" into "*purpose.*"

When the art of printing was invented, its value to every sufferer—its terror to every oppressor, was soon obvious, and means were speedily adopted to prevent its salutary effects. The Star-Chamber—the odious Star-Chamber, was either created, or at least, enlarged and brought into activity. Its proceedings were arbitrary—its decisions were oppressive, and injustice and tyranny were formed into a system. To describe it to you in one sentence, it WAS A PREMATURELY PACKED JURY. Perhaps that description does not shock you much. Let me report one of its decisions which will, I think, make its horrors more sensible to you—it is a ludicrous as well as a melancholy instance.

A tradesman—a ruffian, I presume, he was styled—in an altercation with a nobleman's servant, called the swan, which was worn on the servant's arm for a badge, a goose. For this offence —the calling a nobleman's badge of a swan, a goose, he was brought before the Star-Chamber—he was, of course, convicted; he lost, as I recollect, one of his ears on the pillory—was sentenced to two years' imprisonment, and a fine of £500; and all this to teach him to *distinguish swans from geese.*

I now ask you, to what is it you tradesmen and merchants are indebted for the safety and respect you can enjoy in society? What is it which has rescued you from the slavery in which persons who are engaged in trade were held by the iron barons of former days? I will tell you; it is the light, the reason, and the liberty which have been created, and will, in despite of every opposition, be perpetuated by the exertion of the Press.

Gentlemen, the Star-Chamber was particularly vigilant over the infant struggles of the Press. A code of laws became necessary to govern the new enemy to prejudice and oppression—the Press. The Star-Chamber adopted, for this purpose, the civil law, as it is called—the law of Rome—not the law at the periods of her liberty and her glory, but the law which was promulgated when she fell into slavery and disgrace, and recognised this principle, that the will of the prince was the rule of the law. The civil law was adopted by the Star-Chamber as its guide in proceedings against, and in punishing libellers; but, unfortunately, only part of it was adopted, and that, of course, was the part least favourable to freedom. So much of the civil law as assisted to discover the concealed libeller, and to punish him when discovered, was carefully selected; but the civil law allowed truth to be a defence, and that part was carefully rejected.

The Star-Chamber was soon after abolished. It was suppressed by the hatred and vengeance of an outraged people, and it has since, and until our days, lived only in the recollection of abhorrence and contempt. But we have fallen upon bad days and evil times; and in our days we have seen a lawyer, long of the prostrate and degraded bar of England, presume to suggest an high eulogium on the Star-Chamber, and regret its downfal; and he has done this in a book dedicated, by permission, to Lord Ellenborough. This is, perhaps, an ominous circumstance; and as Star-Chamber punishments have been revived—as two years of imprisonment has become familiar, I know not how soon the useless lumber of even well-selected juries may be abolished, and a new Star-Chamber created.

From the Star-Chamber, gentlemen, the prevention and punishment of libels descended to the courts of common law, and with the power they seem to have inherited much of the spirit of that tribunal. Servility at the bar, and profligacy on the bench, have not been wanting to aid every construction unfavourable to freedom, and at length it is taken as granted and as clear law, that truth or falsehood are quite immaterial circumstances, constituting no part of either guilt or innocence

I would wish to examine this revolting doctrine, and, in doing so, I am proud to tell you, that it has no other foundation than in the oft-repeated assertions of lawyers and judges. Its authority depends on what are technically called the *dicta* of the judges and writers, and not upon solemn or regular adjudications on the point. One servile lawyer has repeated this doctrine, from time to time, after another—and one overbearing judge has re-echoed the assertion of a time-serving predecessor, and the public have, at length, submitted.

I do, therefore, feel, not only gratified in having the occasion, but bound to express my opinion upon the real law of this subject. I know that opinion is but of little weight. I have no professional rank, or station, or talents to give it importance, but it is an honest and conscientious opinion, and it is this— that in the discussion of *public subjects*, and of the administration of *public men*, *truth* is a duty and not *a crime*.

You can, at least, understand *my* description of the liberty of

the Press. That of the Attorney-General is as unintelligible
as contradictory. He tells you, in a very odd and quaint phrase,
that the liberty of the Press consists in there being no previous
restraint upon the tongue or the pen. How any *previous* restraint could be imposed on the tongue it is for this wisest of
men to tell you, unless, indeed, he resorts to Doctor Lad's prescription with respect to the toothache eradication. Neither
can the absence of previous restraint constitute a free Press, unless, indeed, it shall be distinctly ascertained, and clearly defined, what shall be subsequently called a crime. If the crime
of libel be undefined, or uncertain, or capricious, then, instead of
the absence of restraint before publication being an advantage,
it is an injury; instead of its being a blessing, it is a curse—it
is nothing more than a pitfall and snare for the unwary. This
liberty of the Press is only an opportunity and a temptation
offered by the law to the commission of crime—it is a trap laid
to catch men for punishment—it is not the liberty of discussing
truth or discountenancing oppression, but a mode of rearing up
victims for prosecution, and of seducing men into imprisonment.

Yet, can any gentleman concerned for the Crown give me a
definition of the crime of libel? Is it not uncertain and undefined; and, in truth, is it not, at this moment, quite subject to
the caprice and whim of the judge and of the jury? Is the
Attorney-General—is the Solicitor-General disposed to say otherwise? If he do, he must contradict his own doctrine, and adopt mine.

But no, gentlemen, they must leave you in uncertainty and
doubt, and ask you to give a verdict, on your oath, without furnishing you with any rational materials to judge whether you
be right or wrong. Indeed, to such a wild extent of caprice
has Lord Ellenborough carried the doctrine of crime in libel,
that he appears to have gravely ruled, that it was a crime to
call one lord "a stout-built, special pleader," although, in point
of fact, that lord was stout-built, and had been very many years
a special pleader. And that it was a crime to call another lord
"a sheep-feeder from Cambridgeshire," although that lord was
right glad to have a few sheep in that county. These are the
extravagant vagaries of the Crown lawyers and prerogative
judges; you will find it impossible to discover any rational rule
for your conduct, and can never rest upon any satisfactory view
of the subject, unless you are pleased to adopt my description.
Reason and justice equally recognise it, and believe me, that
genuine law is much more closely connected with justice and
reason than some persons will avow.

Gentlemen, you are now apprised of the nature of the alleged libel; it is a discussion upon the administration of public men. I have also submitted to you my view of the law applicable to such a publication; we are, therefore, prepared to go into the consideration of every sentence in the newspaper in question.

But before I do so, just allow me to point your attention to the motives of this young gentleman. The Attorney-General has threatened him with fine and a dungeon; he has told Mr. Magee that he should suffer in his purse and in his person. Mr. Magee knew his danger well. Mr. Magee, before he published this paper, was quite apprised that he ran the risk of fine and of imprisonment. He knew also that if he changed his tone— that if he became merely neutral, but especially, if he went over to the other side and praised the Duke of Richmond—if he had sufficient gravity to talk, without a smile, of the sorrow of the people of Ireland at his Grace's departure—if he had a visage sufficiently lugubrious, to say so, without laughing, to cry out "mournfully, oh! mournfully!" for the departure of the Duke of Richmond—if at a period when the people of Ireland, from Magherafelt to Dingledecouch, are rejoicing at that departure, Mr. Magee could put on a solemn countenance and pick up a grave and narcotic accent, and have the resolution to assert the sorrow of the people for losing so sweet and civil a Lord Lieutenant—why, in that case, gentlemen, you know the consequences. They are obvious. He might libel certain classes of his Majesty's subjects with impunity; he would get abundance of money, a place, and a pension—you know he would. The proclamations would be inserted his paper. The wide-street advertisements, the ordnance, the barrack-board notices, and the advertisements of all the other public boards and offices—you can scarcely calculate how much money he sacrifices to his principles. I am greatly within bounds when I say, at least, £5,000 per annum, of the public money, would reach him if he was to alter his tone, and abandon his opinions.

Has he instructed me to boast of the sacrifices he thus makes? No, gentlemen, no, no; he deems it no sacrifice, because he desires no share in the public plunder; but I introduce this topic to demonstrate to you the purity of his intentions. He cannot be actuated, in the part he takes, by mean or mercenary motives; it is not the base lucre of gain that leads him astray. If he be mistaken, he is, at least, disinterested and sincere. You may dislike his political opinions, but you cannot avoid respecting the independence of his principles.

Behold, now, the publication which this man of pure principles is called to answer for as a libel. It commences thus:—

"DUKE OF RICHMOND.

" As the Duke of Richmond will shortly retire from the government
of Ireland, it has been deemed necessary to take such a review of his
administration, as may at least, warn his successor from pursuing the
errors of his Grace's conduct.

" The review shall contain many anecdotes of the Irish court which
were never published, and which were so secret, that his Grace will not
fail to be surprised at the sight of them in a newspaper."

In this paragraph there is nothing libellous; it talks of the
errors, indeed, of his Grace's administration; but I do not think
the Attorney-General will venture to suggest, that the gentle
expression of "errors," is a libel.

To err, gentlemen, is human: and his Grace is admitted, by
the Attorney-General, to be but a man; I shall waste none of
your time in proving, that we may, without offence, treat of his
"errors." But, this is not even the errors of the man, but of
his administration; it was not infallible, I humbly presume.

I call your particular attention to the second paragraph; it
runs thus:—

" If the administration of the Duke of Richmond had been conducted
with more than ordinary talent, its errors might, in some degree have
been atoned for by its ability, and the people of Ireland though they
might have much to regret, yet, would have something to admire; but
truly after the gravest consideration, they must find themselves at a loss
to discover any striking feature in his Grace's administration, that
makes it superior to the worst of his predecessors."

The Attorney-General dwelt much upon this paragraph, gentlemen, and the importance which he attached to it furnishes a
strong illustration of his own consciousness of the weakness of
his case. What is the meaning of this paragraph? I appeal to
you whether it be more than this—that there has been nothing
admirable in this administration—that there has not been much
ability displayed by it. So far, gentlemen, there is, indeed, no
flattery, but still less of libel, unless you are prepared to say,
that to withhold praise from any administration deserves punishment.

Is it an indictable offence not to perceive its occult talents!
Why, if it be, find my client guilty of not being a sycophant
and a flatterer, and send him to prison for two years, to gratify
the Attorney-General, who tells you that the Duke of Richmond
is the *best* chief governor Ireland ever saw.

But the mischief, I am told, lies in the art of the sentence.
Why, all that it says is, that it is difficult to discover the striking features that distinguish this from bad administrations.   It
does not, gentlemen, assert that no such striking features exist,
much less, does it assert that no features of that kind exist, or
that such features, although not striking are not easily discerni-
ble.   So that, really, you are here again required to convict a
man for not flattering. He thinks an administration untalented
and silly ; that is no crime ; he says, it has not been marked
with talent or ability—that it has no striking features; all this
may be mistaken and false, yet there is nothing in it that resembles a crime.

And, gentlemen, *if it be true*—if this *be* a foolish administration, can it be an offence to say so? If it has had no striking
features to distinguish it from bad administrations, can it be
criminal to say so? Are you prepared to say, that not one word
of truth can be told under no less a penalty than years of a dungeon and heavy fines?

Recollect, that the Attorney-General told you that the Press
was the protection of the people against the government. Good
Heaven! gentlemen, how can it protect the people against the
government, if it be a crime to say of that government that it
has committed errors, displays little talent, and has no striking
features?   Did the prosecutor mock you, when he talked of the
protection the Press afforded to the people? If he did not insult
you by the admission of that upon which he will not allow you
to act, let me ask, against what is the Press to protect the people?   When do the people want protection?—when the government is engaged in delinquencies, oppression, and crimes.   It is
against these that the people want the protection of the Press.
Now, I put it to your plain sense, whether the Press can afford
such protection, if it be punished for treating of these crimes?

Still more, can a shadow of protection be given by a Press
that is not permitted to mention the errors, the talents, and the
striking features of an administration?   Here is a watchman admitted by the Attorney-General to be at his post to warn the
people of their danger, and the first thing that is done to this
watchman is to knock him down and bring him to a dungeon,
for announcing the danger he is bound to disclose. I agree with
the Attorney-General, the Press is a protection, but it is not in
its silence or in its voice of flattery.   It can protect only by
speaking out when there is danger, or error, or want of ability.
If the harshness of this tone be complained of, I ask, what is it

the Attorney-General would have? Does he wish that this protection should speak so as not to be understood; or, I again repeat it, does he mean to delude us with the name and the mockery of protection? Upon this ground, I defy you to find a verdict for the prosecutor, without declaring that he has been
guilty of an attempt to deceive, when he talked of the protection
of the Press against errors, ignorance, and incapacity, which it
is not to dare even to name. Gentlemen, upon this second
paragraph, I am entitled to your verdict, upon the Attorney-
General's own admission.

He, indeed, passed on to the next sentence with an air of triumph, with the apparent certainty of its producing a conviction;
I meet him upon it—I read it boldly—I will discuss it with you
manfully—it is this:—

"They insulted, they oppressed, they murdered, and they deceived."

The Attorney-General told us, rather ludicrously, that they,
meaning the Duke's predecessors, included, of course, himself.
How a man could be included amongst his predecessors, it would
be difficul. to discover. It seems to be that mode of expression
which would indicate, that the Attorney-General, notwithstanding his foreign descent, has imbibed some of the language of the
native Irish. But our blunders arise not like this, from a confusion of idea; they are generally caused by too great condensa-
tion of thought; they are, indeed, frequently of the head, but
never—never of the heart. Would I could say so much for the
Attorney-General; his blunder is not to be attributed to his cool
and cautious head; it sprung, I much fear, from the misguided
bitterness of the bigotry of his heart.

Well, gentlemen, this sentence does, in broad and distinct
terms, charge the predecessors of the Duke, but not the Duke
himself, with insult, oppression, murder, and deceit. But it is
history, gentlemen : are you prepared to silence the voice of
history? Are you disposed to suppress the recital of facts—
the story of the events of former days? Is the historian, and
the publisher of history, to be exposed to indictment and punishment?

Let me read for you two passages from Doctor Leland's History of Ireland. I choose a remote period, to avoid shocking
your prejudices, by the recital of the more modern crimes of the
faction to which most of you belong. Attend to this passage,
gentlemen.

" Anno 1574.—A solemn peace and concord was made between

the Earl of Essex and Felim O'Nial. However, at a feast, wherein the Earl entertained that chieftain, and at the end of their good cheer, O'Nial, with his wife, were seized; their friends, who attended, were put to the sword before their faces. Felim, together with his wife and brother, were conveyed to Dublin, where they were CUT UP IN QUARTERS."

How would you have this fact described ? In what lady-like terms is the future historian to mention this savage and brutal massacre. Yet Essex was an English nobleman—a predecessor of his Grace; he was accomplished, gallant, and gay; the envied paramour of the virgin queen ; and, if he afterwards fell on the scaffold, one of the race of the ancient Irish may be permitted to indulge the fond superstition that would avenge the royal blood of the O'Nial and of his consort, on their perfidious English murderer.

But my soul fills with bitterness, and I will read of no more Irish murders. I turn, however, to another page, and I will introduce to your notice another predecessor of his Grace the Duke of Richmond. It is Grey, who, after the recal of Essex, commanded the English forces in Munster. The fort of Smerwick, in Kerry, surrendered to Grey at discretion. It contained some Irish troops, and more than 700 Spaniards. The historian shall tell you the rest :—

"That mercy for which they sued was rigidly denied them. Wingfield was commissioned to disarm them, and when this service was performed, an English company was sent into the fort.

"The Irish rebels found they were reserved for execution by martial law.

"The Italian general and some officers were made prisoners of war : but the garrison *was butchered in cold blood;* nor is it without pain, that we find a service so horrid and detestable, committed to Sir Walter Raleigh."

"The garrison was butchered in cold blood," says the historian. Furnish us, Mr. Attorney-General, with gentle accents and sweet words, to speak of this savage atrocity ; or will you indict the author? Alas ! he is dead, full of years and respect—as faithful an historian as the prejudices of his day would allow, and a beneficed clergyman of your church.

Gentlemen of the jury, what is the mild language of this paper compared with the indignant language of history? Raleigh—the ill-starred Raleigh—fell a victim to a tyrant master, a corrupt or overawed jury, and a virulent Attorney-General; he was baited

at the bar with language more scurrilous and more foul than
that you heard yesterday poured upon my client. Yet, what
atonement to civilization could his death afford for the horrors
I have mentioned?

Decide, now, gentlemen, between those libels—between that
defamer's history and my client. He calls those predecessors of
his Grace, murderers. History has left the living records of their
crimes from the O'Nial, treacherously slaughtered, to the cruel
cold butchery of the defenceless prisoners. Until I shall see the
publishers of Leland and of Hume brought to your bar, I defy
you to convict my client.

To show you that my client has treated these predecessors of
of his Grace with great lenity, I will introduce to your notice one,
and only one more of them; and he, too, fell on the scaffold—
the unfortunate Strafford, the best servant a despotic king could
desire.

Amongst the means taken to raise money in Ireland, for James
the First, and his son Charles, a proceeding called "a commission
to inquire into defective titles," was invented. It was a
scheme, gentlemen, to inquire of every man what right he had
to his own property, and to have it solemnly and legally determined
that he had none. To effectuate this scheme required
great management, discretion, and integrity. First, there were
4,000 excellent horse raised for the purpose of being, as Strafford
himself said "good lookers-on." The rest of the arrangement
I would recommend to modern practice; it would save much
trouble. I will shortly abstract it from two of Strafford's own
letters.

The one appears to have been written by him to the Lord
Treasurer; it is dated the 3rd December, 1634. He begins with
an apology for not having been more expeditious in this work of
plunder, for his employers were, it seems, impatient at the
melancholy waste of time. He then says—

" Howbeit, I will redeem the time as much as I can, with such
as may give furtherance to the king's title, *and will inquire out
FIT MEN TO SERVE UPON THE JURIES.*"

Take notice of that, gentlemen, I pray you; perhaps you
thought that the "packing of juries" was a modern invention—
a new discovery. You see how greatly mistaken you were; the
thing has example and precedent to support it, and the authority
of both are, in our law, quite conclusive.

The next step was to corrupt—oh, no, to interest the wise and
learned judges. But commentary becomes unnecessary, when

S

read for you this passage from a letter of his to the King, dated the 9th of December, 1636 :—

"Your Majesty was graciously pleased, upon my humble advice, to bestow four shillings in the pound upon your Lord Chief Justice and Lord Chief Baron in this kingdom, fourth of the first yearly rent raised upon the commission of defective title, which, *upon observation, I find to be the best given that ever was.* For now they do intend it, with a care and diligence, such as if it were their own private, and most certain gaining to themselves ; every four shillings once paid, shall better your revenue for ever after, at least five pounds."

Thus, gentlemen of the jury, all was ready for the mockery of law and justice, called a trial.

Now, let me take any one of you ; let me place him here, where Mr. Magee stands ; let him have his property at stake ; let it be of less value, I pray you, than a compensation for two years' imprisonment ; it will, however, be of sufficient value to interest and rouse all your agony and anxiety. If you were so placed here, you would see before you the well-paid Attorney-General, perhaps, malignantly delighted to pour his rancour upon you ; on the bench would sit the corrupt and partisan judge, and before you, on that seat which you now occupy, would be placed the packed and predetermined jury.

I beg, sir, to know what would be your feelings, your honour, your rage ; would you not compare the Attorney-General to the gambler who played with a loaded die, and then you would hear him talk, in solemn and monotonous tones, of his conscience ! Oh, his conscience, gentlemen of the jury !

But the times are altered. The Press, the Press, gentlemen, has effectuated a salutary revolution ; a commission of defective titles would no longer be tolerated : the judges can no longer be bribed with money, and juries can no longer be —— I must not say it. Yes, they can, you know—we all know they can be still *inquired* out, and "packed," as the technical phrase is. But *you*, who are not packed, *you*, who have been *fairly* selected, will see that the language of the publication before us is mildness itself, compared with that which the truth of history requires—compared with that which history has already used.

I proceed with this alleged libel.

The next sentence is this—

"The profligate, unprincipled Westmoreland." I throw down the paper and address myself in particular to some of you. There are, I see, amongst you some of our Bible distributers, " and of our suppressors of vice." Distributers of Bibles, sup-

pressors of vice—what call you profligacy ? What is it you
would call profligacy ? Suppose the peerage was exposed to
sale—set up at open auction—it was at that time a judicial
office—suppose that its price, the exact price of this judicial
office, was accurately ascertained by daily experience—would
you call that profligacy ? If pensions were multiplied beyond
bounds and beyond example—if places were augmented until
invention was exhausted, and then were subdivided and split
into halves, so that two might take the emoluments of each, and
no person do the duty—if these acts were resorted to in order
to corrupt your representatives—would you, gentle suppressors
of vice, call that profligacy ?

If the father of children selected in the open day his adulterous
paramour—if the wedded mother of children displayed her
crime unblushingly—if the assent of the titled or untitled wittol
to his own shame was purchased with the people's money—if
this scene—if these were enacted in the open day, would you
call that profligacy, sweet distributers of Bibles ? The women of
Ireland have always been beauteous to a proverb ; they were,
without an exception, chaste beyond the terseness of a proverb to
express ; they are still as chaste as in former days, but the depraved example of a depraved court has furnished some exceptions, and the action or criminal conversation, before the time
of Westmoreland unknown, has since become more familiar to
our courts of justice.

Call you the sad example which produced those exceptions
— call you *that* profligacy, suppressors of vice and Bible distributers ? The vices of the poor are within the reach of control ;
to suppress them, you can call in aid the churchwarden and the
constable ; the justice of the peace will readily aid you, for he is
a gentleman—the Court of Sessions will punish those vices for
you by fine, by imprisonment, and, if you are urgent, by whipping. But suppressors of vice, who shall aid you to suppress
the vices of the great ? Are you sincere, or are you, to use your
own phraseology, whitewashed tombs—painted charnel-houses ?
Be ye hypocrites ? If you are not—if you be sincere—(and, oh,
how I wish that you were)—if you be sincere, I will steadily require to know of you, what aid you expect, to suppress the vices
of the rich and great ? Who will assist you to suppress those vices ?
The churchwarden !—why he, I believe, handed *them* into the
best pew in one of your cathedrals, that they might lovingly hear
Divine service together. The constable ! !—absurd. The justice
of the peace !—no. upon his honour. As to the Court of Ses-

sions, you cannot expect it to interfere ; and my lords the judges
are really so busy at the assizes, in hurrying the grand juries
through the presentments, that there is no leisure to look after
the scandalous faults of the great.   Who, then, sincere and candid
suppressors of vice, can aid you ?—*The Press ;* the Press alone
talks of the profligacy of the great ; and, at least, shames into
decency those whom it may fail to correct.   The Press is your,
but your only assistant.   Go, then, men of conscience, men of
religion—go, then, and convict John Magee, because he published
that Westmoreland was profligate and unprincipled as a lord
lieutenant—do, convict, and then return to your distribution of
Bibles and to your attacks upon the recreations of the poor,
under the name of vices !

Do, convict the only aid which virtue has, and distribute your
Bibles that you may have the name of being religious ; upon
your sincerity depends my client's prospect of a verdict.   *Does*
he lean upon a broken reed ?

I pass on from the sanctified portion of the jury which I have
latterly addressed, and I call the attention of you all to the next
member of the sentence—

" The cold-hearted and cruel Camden."

Here I have your prejudices all armed against me.   In the
administration of Camden, your faction was cherished and triumphant.   Will you prevent him to be called cold and cruel ?
Alas ! to-day, why have I not men to address who would listen
to me for the sake of impartial justice !   But even with *you* the
case is too powerful to allow me to despair.

Well, *I do* say, the cold and cruel Camden.   Why, on *one circuit,* during his administration, there were ONE HUNDRED
INDIVIDUALS TRIED BEFORE ONE JUDGE ; OF
THESE NINETY-EIGHT WERE CAPITALLY CON-
VICTED, AND NINETY-SEVEN HANGED !   I understand
one escaped ; but he was a *soldier* who murdered a *peasant,* or
something of that TRIVIAL nature—NINETY-SEVEN victims
in one circuit ! ! !

In the meantime, it was necessary, for the purposes of the
Union, that the flame of rebellion should be fed.   The meetings
of the rebel colonels in the north were, for a length of time,
regularly reported to government ; but the rebellion was not
then ripe enough ; and whilst the fruit was coming to maturity,
under the fostering hand of the administration, the wretched
dupes atoned on the gallows for allowing themselves to be deceived.

In the meantime the soldiery were turned in at free quarters amongst the wives and daughters of the peasantry !!!

Have you heard of Abercrombie, the valiant and the good—he who, mortally wounded, neglected his wound until victory was ascertained—he who allowed his life's stream to flow unnoticed because his country's battle was in suspense—he who died the martyr of victory—he who commenced the career of glory on the land, and taught French insolence, than which there is nothing so permanent—even transplanted, it exhibits itself to the third and fourth generation—he taught French insolence, that the British and Irish soldier was as much his superior by land, as the sailor was confessedly by sea—he, in short, who commenced that career which has since placed the Irish Wellington on the highest pinnacle of glory. Abercrombie and Moore were in Ireland under Camden. Moore, too, has since fallen at the moment of triumph—Moore, the best of sons, of brothers, of friends, of men—the soldier and the scholar—the soul of reason and the heart of pity—Moore has, in documents of which you may plead ignorance, left his opinions upon record with respect to the cruelty of Camden's administration. But you all have heard of Abercrombie's proclamation, for it amounted to that; he proclaimed that cruelty in terms the most unequivocal; he stated to the soldiery and to the nation, that the conduct of the Camden administration had rendered "the soldiery formidable to all but the enemy."

Was there no cruelty in thus degrading the British soldier? And say, was not the process by which that degradation was effectuated cruelty? Do, then, contradict Abercrombie, upon your oaths, if you dare; but, by doing so, it is not my client alone you will convict—you will also convict yourselves of the foul crime of perjury.

I now come to the third branch of this sentence; and here I have an easy task. All, gentlemen, that is said of the artificer and superintendent of the Union is this—"the artful and treacherous Cornwallis." Is it necessary to prove that the Union was effectuated by artifice and treachery? For my part, it makes my blood boil when I think of the unhappy period which was contrived and seized on to carry it into effect; one year sooner, and it would have made a revolution—one year later, and it would have been for ever impossible to carry it. The moment was artfully and treacherously seized on, and our country, that *was* a nation for countless ages, has dwindled into a province, and her name and her glory are extinct for ever.

I should not waste a moment upon this part of the case, but that the gentlemen at the other side who opposed that measure have furnished me with some topics which I may not, cannot omit. Indeed Mr. Magee deserves no verdict from any Irish jury, who can hesitate to think that the contriver of the Union is treated with too much lenity in this sentence; he fears your disapprobation for speaking with so little animosity of the artificer of the Union.

There was one piece of treachery committed at that period, at which both you and I equally rejoice; it was the breach of faith towards the leading Catholics; the written promises made them at that period have been since printed; I rejoice with you that they were not fulfilled; when the Catholic trafficked for his own advantage upon his country's miseries, he deserved to be deceived. For this mockery, I thank the Cornwallis administration. *I rejoice, also, that my first introduction to the stage of public life, was in the opposition to that measure.*

In humble and obscure distance, I followed the footsteps of my present adversaries. What their sentiments were then of the authors of the Union, I beg to read to you; I will read them from a newspaper set up for the mere purpose of opposing the Union, and conducted under the control of these gentlemen. If their editor should be gravely denied, I shall only reply—" on cease your funning."*

The charge of being a Jacobin, was at that time made against the present Attorney-General—him, plain William Saurin—in the very terms, and with just as much truth as he now applies it to my client. His reply shall serve for that of Mr. Magee. I take it from the anti-Union of the 22nd March, 1800.

" To the charge of Jacobin, Mr. Saurin said he knew not what t meant, as applied to him, *except it was an opposition to the will of the British minister.*"

So says Mr. Magee; but, gentlemen, my eye lights upon another passage of Mr. Saurin's, in the same speech from which ι have quoted the above. It was in these words :—

" Mr. Saurin admitted, that debates might sometimes produce *agitations,* but that was the PRICE *necessarily paid for liberty.*"

Oh, how I thank this good Jew for the word. Yes, agitation is, as Mr. Saurin well remarked, the price necessarily paid for liberty. We have paid the price, gentlemen, and the honest man refuses to give us the goods. (Much laughing.)

' A pamphlet under this title was published by the Solicitor-General; it was full of wit and talent.

Now, gentlemen, of this Mr. Saurin, then an agitator, I beg leave to read the opinion upon this Union, the author of which we have only called artful and treacherous. From this speech of the 13th March, 1800, I select those passages :

"Mr. Saurin said he felt it his duty to the crown, to the country, and to his family, to warn the minister of the dreadfu. consequences of persevering in a measure which the people o. Ireland *almost unanimously disliked.*"

And again—

'He, for one, would assert the principles of the glorious revolution, and boldly declare in the face of the nation, that when the Sovereign power dissolved the compact that existed between the government and the people, that moment the right of resistance accrues.

"Whether it would be prudent in the people to avail themselves of that right, would be another question. But if a legislative union were forced on the country, against the will of its inhabitants, it would be a *nullity,* and resistance to it would be a *struggle* against *usurpation,* and not a *resistance* against law."

May I be permitted just to observe, how much more violent this agitator of the year 1800, than we poor and timid agitators of the year 1813. When did we talk of resistance being a question of prudence? Shame upon the men who call us intemperate, and yet remember their own violence.

But, gentlemen, is the Attorney-General at liberty to change the nature of things with his own official and professional prospects? I am ready to admit that he receives thousands of pounds by the year of the public monies, in his office of Attorney-General—thousands from the Crown-Solicitor—thousands, for doing little work, from the Custom-house ; but does all this public booty with which he is loaded, alter the nature of things, r prevent that from being a deceitful measure, brought about by artful and treacherous means, against which Mr. Saurin, in 1800, preached the holy doctrine of insurrection, sounded the tocsin of resistance, and summoned the people of the land to battle against it, as against *usurpation ?*

In 1800, he absolves the subjects from their allegiance—if the usurpation, styled the Union, will be carried—and he, this identical agitator, in 1813, indicts a man, and calls him a ruffian, for speaking of the contrivers of the Union, not as usurpers, but as artful, treacherous men. Gentlemen, pity the situation in which he has placed himself ; and pray, do not think of inflicting punishment upon my client for his extreme moderation.

It has been coarsely urged, and it will, I know, be urged in the splendid misrepresentations with which the Solicitor-General can so well distort the argument he is unable to meet—it will, I know, be urged by him, that having established the right to use this last paragraph—having proved that the predecessors of the Duke were oppressors and murderers, and profligate, and treacherous, that the libel is only aggravated thereby, as the first paragraph compares and combines the Duke of Richmond with the worst of his predecessors.

This is a most fallacious assertion ; and here it is that I could wish I had to address a dispassionate and an enlightened jury. You are not, you know you are not, of the selection of my client. Had he the poor privilege of the sheep-stealer, there are, at least, ten of you who should never have been on his jury. But the jury he would select is not such a jury in his favour, as has been impanelled against him ; he desires no favour ; he would desire only that the most respectable and unprejudiced of your city should be selected for his trial ; his only ambition would be perfect impartiality ; he would desire, and I should desire for him, a jury whose verdict of conviction, if they did convict h u, would produce a sense of error and feeling more painful to his mind of being wrong than a star-chamber sentence.

If I had to address such a jury, how easily could I show them that there is no comparison—no attempt at similitude. On the contrary, the object of the writer is clearly to make a contrast. Grey murdered ; but he was an able statesman ; his massacre was a crime in itself, but eminently useful to his employers ; it contributed mainly to secure the forfeiture of the overgrown territories of the House of Desmond. Essex was a murderer, but his extreme of vice was accompanied by great military services ; he was principally instrumental in effectuating the conquest of Ireland—even his crimes served the cause of his royal mistress, and the territory of the slaughtered O'Nial became shire land ; he had terrific cruelty to answer for, but he could give it some answer in the splendour and solidity of his services. So of Strafford—he was an eminent oppressor, but he was also eminently useful to his royal master.

As to the Duke of Richmond, the contrast is intended to be complete—he has neither great crimes nor great virtues. He did not murder, like Essex and Grey, but he did not render any splendid services. In short, his administration has been directly the reverse of these. It has been marked by errors and not crimes. It has not displayed talents as they did ; and it has no striking features as they had. Such is the fair, the rational, and the just construction which a fair, rational, and just jury would put upon it.

Indeed, the Attorney-General seems to feel it was necessary for him to resort to other topics, in order to induce you to convict upon this part of the case. He tells you that this is the second time that the Duke of Richmond has been called a murderer. Gentlemen, in this indictment there is no allegation that the Duke is styled a murderer by this publication; if there had, he should be readily acquitted, even for the variance; and when the Attorney-General resorts to Barry's case, he does it to inflame your passions, and mislead your understandings—and then what has the Irish Magazine to do with this trial?

Walter Cox, with his Irish Magazine, is as good a Protestant as the king's Attorney-General, and probably quite as sincere in the profession of that religion, though by no means as much disposed to persecute those who differ from him in religious belief. Indeed, if he were a persecutor of his countrymen, he would not be where he is—in prison; he would probably enjoy a full share of the public plunder, and which is now lavished on the stupid journals in the pay of the Castle—from the versatile, venal, and verbose correspondent, to the equally dull and corrupt *Dublin Journal*.

It is, however, not true, that he is in gaol because he published what is called a libel. The Attorney-General talked with a gloating pleasure of the miseries poor Watty Cox endures in gaol—miseries that seem to give poignancy and zest to the enjoyments of his prosecutor. I will make him happy; let him return from this court to his luxuries, and when he finds himself at his table, surrounded with every delicacy, and every profusion, remember that his prisoner Walter Cox is starving. I envy him not this relish, but I cannot suffer him to mislead you. Cox is not in goal because he published a libel; he is there because he is poor. His time of imprisonment expired last February, but he was condemned to pay a fine of £300, and having no money, he has since remained in goal. It is his poverty, therefore, and not his crime, that detains him within the fangs of the Attorney-General—if, indeed, there be any greater crime in society than being poor.

And, next, the Attorney-General makes a beautiful eulogium on Magna Charta. There we agree. I should, indeed, prefer seeing the principles of that great charter called into practical effect, to hearing any palinode however beautiful, said or sung

on its merits.   But what recommendation can Magna Charta
have for poor Cox ?   That charter of liberty expressly provides,
that no man shall be fined beyond what he can pay.   A very
simple and natural provision against political severity.   But Cox
is fined £300, when he is not worth a single shilling.   He appealed
to this court for relief, and quotes Magna Charta.   Your lordship
was not pleased to give him any relief.   He applies to the Court
of Exchequer, and that Court, after hearing the Attorney-General against him, finds itself unable to give any relief; and, after
all this, the unfortunate man is to be tantalized with hearing that
the Attorney-General contrived to couple his case with the praise
of the great charter of liberty—a most unlucky coincidence—
almost enough to drive him, in whose person that charter is violated, into a state of insanity.

Poor Watty Cox is a coarse fellow, and, I think, he would be
apt to reply to that praise in the profane and contemptuous
rhyme of Cromwell ; most assuredly he has no reason to treat
this useless law with great reverence.   It would, indeed, appear
as if the prosecutor eulogized Magna Charta only to give more
brilliancy to his triumph, which he has obtained in the person
of poor Cox over it.

The next topic of the Attorney-General's triumphant abuse
was the book entitled, "The Statement of the Penal laws."   He
called it a convicted book.   He exulted that the publisher was
in prison ; he traduced the author, and he distorted and misrepresented the spirit and meaning of that book.   As to the publisher, he is, I admit, in prison.   The Attorney-General has had
the pleasure of tearing a respectable citizen, of irreproachable
character and conduct, from his wife and the little children who
were rendered comfortable by his honest, persevering industry,
and he has immured him in a dungeon.   I only congratulate him
on his victory.

As to the author, he is just the reverse of what the Attorney-
General would wish him to be; he is a man of fortune; he is an
able lawyer—a professional scholar, an accomplished gentleman
—a sincere friend to his country, which he has ornamented and
served.   As to the book, it is really ludicrous to an extreme degree of comicality to call it a convicted book.   There are about
400 pages in the work : it contains an elaborate, unexaggerated,
and, I think, softened detail of the laws which aggrieve the Catholics of Ireland, and of the practical results of those laws.   Such
a system, to which the Attorney-General is wedded, as much as
to his own emolument, must have excited no small share of irri-

tation in his mind. It produced a powerful sensation on the entire party to which he belongs. Abundant attempts were made to answer it: they were paid for out of the public money; they totally failed, and yet if the book had been erroneous, there could be nothing easier than its confutation.

If that book had been mistaken in matter of law, or exaggerated in matter of fact, its refutation would have been found, where we have found and proved its perfect accuracy, in the statute book and in the daily experience of every individual in Ireland. Truth, you are told by the prosecutor, is no defence in case of libel; but certainly this book was much the more provoking for being true; and yet, gentlemen, with the most powerful incentives to prosecute this book, the Attorney-General has been compelled, most reluctantly, to space every word of the 400 pages of text and margin, and has been unable to find any pretext for an indictment, save in a paltry note containing eight lines and a half, and three marks of admiration.

My lords, I address your lordships particularly on the three notes of admiration, because they formed a prominent ground in your lordship's learned argument, when you decided that the passage was a libel *per se*. Yes, gentlemen, admire again, I pray you, the solidity and brilliancy of our law, in which three marks of admiration are of wonderful efficacy in sending a man to prison. But with the exception of the note of eight and a half lines, the book has borne the severest criticism of fact and of law. It has defied, and continues to defy, the present Attorney-General and his well-assorted juries; and, as to the note which he indicted, it contained only a remark on the execution of a man who, whether innocent or guilty, was tried in such a manner, that a gentleman of the Irish bar, his counsel, threw up his brief in disgust; and when the judge who presided at the trial ordered the counsel to remain and defend Barry, that counsel swore, in this court, that he rejected the judge's mandate with contempt.

What a mighty triumph was the conviction proved against this note on Barry's case! And may one be permitted mournfully to ask, whether the indignation, which might have produced indiscretion in speaking of Barry's fate, was a very culpable quality in a feeling mind, prone to detest the horrors with which human blood is sometimes shed under the forms and mockery of trial? But that conviction, although it will erase the note, will not stay the demand which an intelligent public make for this valuable work. Already have two valuable edi tions of it been sold, and a third edition is loudly called for, and about to appear.

What, in the meantime, has been the fate of the answers? I see two booksellers amongst you; they will tell you that the answers are recollected only by the loss they have produced to them, and by the cumbering of their shelves. Such is the result of the loyal triumph of his Grace the Duke of Richmond's administration. May such in every age be the fruits of every prosecutor of free discussion, and of the assertion of political truth!

I have followed the Attorney-General through his discussion upon Walter Cox. and "The Statement of the Penal laws," without being able exactly to conjecture his motives for introducing them. As to Cox, it appears to be the mere gratification of his delight at the misery to which that unfortunate man is reduced. As to "the book." I can only conjecture that his wish is to insinuate to you that the author of "the book" and of this publication is the same. If that were his design, it may be enough to say, that he has not proved the fact, and, therefore, in fairness, it ought not at all to influence your decision. I go further and tell him, that the fact is not so; that the author is a different person; that the writer of this alleged libel is a Protestant —a man of fortune—a man of that rank and estimation, that even the Attorney-General, were I to announce his name, which my client will never do, or suffer his advocate to do, that name would extort respect, even from the Attorney-General himself.

He has, in his usual fashion, calumniated the spirit and object of "The Statement of the Penal Laws." He says it imputes murder and every other crime to persons in high stations, as resulting from their being Protestants. He says that it attributes to the Lord Lieutenant the committing murder on a Catholic, because he himself is a Protestant. Gentlemen, I wish you had read that book; if you did, it would be quite unnecessary for me to contradict those assertions of the Attorney-General. In fact, there never were assertions more unfounded: that book contains nothing that could warrant his description of it; on the contrary, the book seeks to establish this position, that the grievances which the Irish Catholics suffer, are not attributable to the Protestant religion—that they are repugnant to the spirit of that religion, and are attributable, simply and singly, to the spirit of monopoly, and tone of superiority, generated and fostered by the system of exclusion, upon which the Penal Code rests.

The author of that book is confessedly a Catholic; yet the book states, and the Attorney-General heard the passage twice read in this court, that "if Roman Catholics were placed, by unjust laws, in the situation in which the Irish Protestants now are placed, they would oppress and exclude precisely as the Protestants now ..o." In short, his statement and reasonings are founded on this, that it is unjust to give any religion exclusive political advantages; because, whatever that religion may be, the result will necessarily prove oppressive and insulting towards the less favoured sect. He argues not exclusively against any particular religion, but from natural causes operating on human beings. His book may be a libel on human nature, but it is no more a libel on the Protestant than on the Catholic religion. It draws no other inference than this, that Catholics and Protestants, under similar circumstances, would act precisely in the same way.

Having followed the prosecutor through this weary digression, I return to the next sentence of this publication. Yet I cannot —I must detain you still a little longer from it, whilst I supplicate your honest indignation, if in your resentments there be aught of honesty, against the mode in which the Attorney-General has introduced the name of our aged and afflicted sovereign. He says, this is a libel on the king, because it imputes to him a selection of improper and criminal chief governors. Gentlemen, this is the very acme of servile doctrine. It is the most unconstitutional doctrine that could be uttered: it supposes that the sovereign is responsible for the acts of his servants, whilst the constitution declares that the king can do no wrong, and that even for his personal acts, his servants shall be personally responsible. Thus, the Attorney-General reverses for you the constitution in theory; and, in point of fact, where can be found, in this publication, any, even the slightest allusion to his Majesty. The theory is against the Attorney-General, and yet, contrary to the fact, and against the theory, he seeks to enlist another prejudice of yours against Mr. Magee.

Prejudice did I call it? oh, no! it is no prejudice; that sentiment which combines respect with affection for my aged sovereign, suffering under a calamity with which heaven has willed to visit him, but which is not due to any default of his. There never was a sentiment that I should wish to see more cherished —more honoured. To you the king may appear an object of respect; to his Catholic subjects he is one of veneration; to them he has been a bountiful benefactor. To the utter disregard of your aldermen of Skinner's-alley, and the more pompous mag-

nets of William-street, his Majesty procured, at his earnest solicitation from parliament, the restoration of much of our liberties.
He disregarded your anti-Popery petitions. He treated with
calm indifference the ebullitions of your bigotry ; and I owe to
him that I have the honour of standing in the proud situation
from which I am able, if not to protect my client, at least to pour
the indignant torrent of my discourse against his enemies, and
those of his country.

The publication to which I now recal you, goes to describe the
effects of the facts which I have shown you to have been drawn
from the undisputed and authentic history of former times. I
have, I hope, convinced you, that neither Leland nor Hume
could have been indicted for stating those facts, and it would be
a very strange perversion of principle, which would allow you
to convict Mr. Magee for that which has been stated by other
writers, not only without punishment, but with applause.

That part of the paragraph which relates to the present day is
in these words :—

" Since that period the complexion of the times has changed
—the country has advanced—it has outgrown submission, *and
some forms, at least, must now be observed towards the people.*"

The system, however, is still the same ; it is the old play
with new decorations, presented in an age somewhat more enlightened ; the principle of government remains unaltered—a
principle of exclusion which debars the majority of the people
from the enjoyment of those privileges that are possessed by the
minority, and which must, therefore, maintain itself by all those
measures necessary for a government founded on injustice."

The prosecutor insists that this is the most libellous part of
the entire publication. I am glad he does so ; because if there
be amongst you a single particle of discrimination, you cannot
fail to perceive that this is not a libel—that this paragraph cannot constitute any crime. It states that the present is a system
of exclusion. Surely, it is no crime to say so ; it is what you
all say. It is what the Attorney-General himself gloried in.
This is, said he, exclusively a Protestant government. Mr. Magee
and he are agreed. Mr. Magee adds, that a principle of exclusion, on account of religion, is founded on injustice. Gentlemen,
if a Protestant were to be excluded from any temporal advantages upon the score of his religion, would not you say that the
principle upon which he was excluded was unjust? That is precisely what Mr. Magee says ; for the principle which excludes
the Catholic in Ireland, would exclude the Protestant in Spain

and in Portugal, and then you clearly admit its justice. So that, really, you would condemn yourselves, and your own opinions, and the right to be a Protestant in Spain and Portugal, if you condemn this sentiment.

But I would have you further observe that this is no more than the discussion of an abstract principle of government ; it arraigns not the conduct of any individual, or of any administration ; it only discusses and decides upon the moral fitness of a certain theory, on which the management of the affairs of Ireland has been conducted. If this be a crime, we are all criminals; for this question, whether it be just or not to exclude from power and office a class of the people for religion, is the subject of daily—of hourly discussion. The Attorney-General says it is quite just; I proclaim it to be unjust—obviously unjust. At all public meetings, in all private companies, this point is decided different ways, according to the temper and the interest of individuals. Indeed, it is but too much the topic of every man's discourse ; and the gaols and the barracks of the country would not contain the hundredth part of those whom the Attorney-General would have to crowd them, if it be penal to call the principle of exclusion unjust. In this court, without the least danger of interruption or reproof, I proclaim the injustice of that principle.

I will then ask whether it be lawful to print that which it is not unlawful to proclaim in the face of a court of justice ? And above all, I will ask whether it can be criminal to discuss the abstract principles of government ? Is the theory of the law a prohibited subject ? I had understood that there was no right so clear and undoubted as that of discussing abstract and theoretic principles, and their applicability to practicable purposes. For the first time do I hear this disputed ; and now see what it is the Attorney-General prohibits. He insists upon punishing Mr. Magee; first, because he accuses his administration of "errors ;" secondly, because he charges them with not being distinguished for "talents ;" thirdly, because he cannot discover their " striking features ;" and fourthly, because he discusses an "abstract principle !"

This is quite intelligible—this is quite tangible. I begin to understand what the Attorney-General means by the liberty of the Press ; it means a prohibition of printing anything except praise, respecting "*the errors, the talents, or the striking features*" of any administration, and of discussing any *abstract principle of government.* Thus the forbidden subjects are errors, talents,

striking features, and principles. Neither the theory of the
government nor its practices are to be discussed; you may, indeed, praise them; you may call the Attorney-General "the best
and wisest of men;" you may call his lordship the most learned
and impartial of all possible chief justices; you may, if you
have powers of visage sufficient, call the Lord Lieutenant the best
of all imaginable governors. That, gentlemen, is the boasted
liberty of the Press—the liberty that exists in Constantinople—
the liberty of applying the most fulsome and unfounded flattery,
but not one word of censure or reproof.

Here is an idol worthy of the veneration of the Attorney-
General. Yes; he talked of his veneration for the liberty of the
Press; he also talked of its being a protection to the people
against the government. Protection! not against errors—not
against the want of talents or striking features—nor against the
effort of any unjust principle—protection! against what is it to
protect? Did he not mock you? Did he not plainly and palpably delude you, when he talked of the protection of the Press?
Yes. To his inconsistencies and contradictions he calls on you
to sacrifice your consciences; and because you are no-Popery
men, and distributers of Bibles, and aldermen of Skinner's-alley,
and Protestant petitioners, he requires of you to brand your
souls with perjury. You cannot escape it; it is, it must be perjury to find a verdict for a man who gravely admits that the
liberty of the Press is recognized by law, and that it is a venerable object, and yet calls for your verdict upon the ground that
there is no such thing in existence as that which he has admitted,
that the law recognises, and that he himself venerates.

Clinging to the fond but faint hope that you are not capable
of sanctioning, by your oaths, so monstrous an inconsistency, I
lead you to the next sentence upon this record.

"Although his Grace does not appear to know what are the qualities
necessary for a judge in Canada, or for an aid-de-camp in waiting at a
court, he surely cannot be ignorant what are requisites for a lord lieutenant."

This appears to be a very innocent sentence; yet the Attorney-
General, the venerator of that protection of the people against a
bad government—the liberty of the Press—tells you that it is a
gross libel to impute so much ignorance to his Grace. As to the
aid-de-camp, gentlemen, whether he be selected for the brilliancy
of his spurs, the polish of his boots, or the precise angle of his
cocked hat, are grave considerations which I refer to you. Decide upon these atrocities, I pray you. But as to the judge in

Canada, it cannot be any reproach to his Grace to be ignorant of his qualifications. The old French law prevails in Canada, and there is not a lawyer at the Irish bar, except, perhaps, the Attorney-General, who is sufficiently acquainted with that law to know how far any man may be fit for the station of judge in Canada.

If this be an ignorance without reproach in Irish lawyers, and if there be any reproach in it, I feel it not, whilst I avow that ignorance—yet, surely it is absurd to torture it into a calumny against the Lord Lieutenant—a military man, and no lawyer. I doubt whether it would be a libel if my client had said, *that his Grace was ignorant of the qualities necessary for a judge* in Ireland—for a *chief judge*, my lord. He has not said so, however, gentlemen, and true or false, that is not now the question under consideration. We are in Canada at present, gentlemen in a ludicrous search for a libel in a sentence of no great point or meaning. If you are sapient enough to suspect that it contains a libel, your doubt can only arise from not comprehending it ; and that, I own, is a doubt difficult to remove. But I mock you when I talk of this insignificant sentence.

I shall read the next paragraph at full length. It is connected with the Canadian sentence :—

" Therefore, were an appeal to be made to him in a dispassionate and sober moment, we might candidly confess that the Irish would not be disappointed in their hopes of a successor, though they would behold the same smiles, experience the same sincerity, and witness the same disposition towards conciliation.

" What, though they were deceived in 1795, and found the mildness of a Fitzwilliam a false omen of concord ; though they were duped in 1800, and found that the privileges of the Catholics did not follow the extinction of the parliament, yet, at his departure, he will, no doubt, state good grounds for future expectation ; that his administration was not the time for Emancipation, but that the season is fast approaching ; that there were "existing circumstances," but that now the people may rely upon the virtues even of an hereditary Prince ; that they should continue to worship the false idol ; that their cries, must, at least, be heard ; and that, if he has not complied, it is only because he has not spoken. In short, his Grace will in no way vary from the uniform conduct observed by most of his predecessors, first preaching to the confidence of the people, then playing upon their credulity.

He came over ignorant—he soon became prejudiced, and then he became intemperate. He takes from the people their money ; he eats of their bread, and drinks of their wine ; in return, he gives them a bad government, and, at his departure, leaves them more distracted than ever. His Grace commenced his reign by flattery, he continued it in

T

olly, he accompanied it with violence, and he will conclude it with
falsehood."

There is one part of this sentence, for which I most respectfully solicit your indulgence and pardon. Be not exasperated
with us for talking of the mildness of Lord Fitzwilliam, or of
his administration. But, notwithstanding the violence any
praise of him has excited amongst you, come dispassionately, I
may you, to the consideration of the paragraph. Let us abstract the meaning of it from the superfluous words. It certainly does tell you, that his Grace came over ignorant of Irish
affairs, and he acquired prejudices upon those subjects, and he
has become intemperate. Let us discuss this part separately
from the other matter suggested by the paragraph in question.
That the Duke of Richmond came over to Ireland ignorant of
the details of our domestic policy cannot be matter either of
surprise or of any reproach. A military man engaged in these
pursuits which otherwise occupy persons of his rank, altogether
unconnected with Ireland, he could not have had any inducement to make himself acquainted with the details of our barbarous
wrongs, of our senseless party quarrels, and criminal feuds ; he
was not stimulated to examine them by any interest, nor could
any man be attracted to study them by taste. It is, therefore, no
censure to talk of his ignorance—of that with which it would
be absurd to expect that he should be acquainted ; and the
knowledge of which would neither have served, nor exalted, nor
amused him.

Then, gentlemen, it is said he became " prejudiced." Prejudiced may sound harsh in your ears ; but you are not, at least
you ought not, to decide upon *the sound*—it is *the sense* of the
word that should determine you. Now what is the sense of the
word " prejudice" here ? It means the having adopted precisely
the opinions which every one of you entertain. By "prejudice"
the writer means, and can mean, nothing but such sentiments as
you cherish. When he talks of prejudice, he intends to convey
the idea that the Duke took up the opinion, that the few ought
to govern the many in Ireland ; that there ought to be a favoured,
and an excluded class in Ireland ; that the burdens of the state
ought to be shared equally, but its benefits conferred on a few.
Such are the ideas conveyed by the word prejudice ; and I fear
lessly ask you, is it a crime to impute to his Grace these notions
which you yourselves entertain ? Is he calumniated—is he
libelled, when he is charged with concurring with you, gentlemen of the jury ? Will you, by a verdict of conviction, stamp

your own political sentiments with the seal of reprobation ! If
you convict my client, you do this ; you decide that it is a libel
to charge any man with those doctrines which are so useful to
you individually, and of which you boast ; or, you think the
opinions just, and yet that it is criminal to charge a man with
those just opinions. For the sake, therefore, of consistency, and
as an approval of your own opinions, I call on you for a verdict
of acquittal.

I need not detain you long on the expression "intemperate ;"
it does not mean any charge of excess of indulgence in any enjoyment ; it is not, as the Attorney-General suggested, an accusation of indulging beyond due bounds in the pleasures of the
table, or of the bottle ; it does not allude, as the Attorney-General says, to midnight orgies, or to morning revels. I admit—I
freely admit—that an allusion of that kind would savour of libel,
as it would certainly be unnecessary for any purpose of political
discussion. But the intemperance here spoken of is mere political intemperance ; it is that violence which every man of a
fervid disposition feels in support of his political opinions. Nay
the more pure and honest any man may be in the adoption of
his opinions, the more likely, and the more justifiable will he be
in that ardent support of them, which goes by the name of intemperance.

In short, although political intemperance cannot be deemed
by cold calculators as a virtue, yet it has its source in the purest
virtues of the human heart, and it frequently produces the
greatest advantages to the public. How would it be possible to
overcome the many obstacles which self-interest, and ignorance,
and passion throw in the way of improvement, without some of
that ardour of temper and disposition which grave men call intemperance ? And, gentlemen, are not your opinions as deserving of warm support as the opinion of other men ; or do you
feel any inherent depravity in the political sentiments which the
Duke of Richmond has adopted from you, that would render him
depraved or degraded by any violence in their support ! You
have no alternative. If you convict my client, you condemn,
upon your oaths, your own political creed ; and declare it to
be a libel to charge any man with energy in your cause.

If you are not disposed to go this length of political inconsistency, and if you have determined to avoid the religious inconsistency of perjuring yourselves for the good and glory of the
Protestant religion, do, I pray you, examine the rest of this paragraph, and see whether you can, by any ingenuity, detect that

nondescript a libel in it.   It states in substance this : that this administration, treading in the steps of former administrations, preached to the confidence of the people, and played on their credulity ; and that it will end, as those administrations have done, in some flattering prophecy, paying present disappointment with the coinage of delusive hope.   That this administration commenced, as usual, with preaching to the confidence of the people, was neither criminal in the fact, nor can it be unpleasant in the recital.

It is the immemorial usage of all administrations and of all stations, to commence with those civil professions of future excellence of conduct which are called, and not unaptly, "*preaching to the confidence of the people.*"   The very actors are generally sincere at this stage of the political farce ; and it is not insinuated that this administration was not as candid on this subject as the best of its predecessors.   The *playing on the credulity of the people* is the ordinary state trick.   You recollect how angry many of you were with his Grace for his Munster tour, shortly after his arrival here.   You recollect how he checked the Mayor of Cork for proposing the new favourite Orange toast ; what liberality he displayed to Popish traders and bankers in Limerick ; and how he returned to the capital, leaving behind him the impression that the no-Popery men had been mistaken in their choice, and that the Duke of Richmond was the enemy of every bigotry—the friend to every liberality !   Was he sincere, gentlemen of the jury, or was this one of those innocent devices which are called—playing on the people's credulity ?   Was he sincere ?   Ask his subsequent conduct.   Have there been since that time any other or different toasts cheered in his presence ?   Has the name of Ireland and of Irishmen been profaned by becoming the sport of the warmth excited by the accompaniment to these toasts ?   Some individuals of you could inform me.   I see another dignitary of your corporation here (said Mr. O'Connell, turning round pointedly to the lord mayor)—I see a civic dignitary here, who could tell of the toasts of these days or nights, and would not be at a loss to apply the right name—if he were not too prudent as well as too polite to do so—to that innocent affectation of liberality which distinguished his Grace's visit to the south of Ireland.   It was, indeed, a play upon our credulity, but it can be no libel to speak of it as such ; for see the situation in which you would place his Grace ; you know he affected conciliation and perfect neutrality between our parties at first ; you know he has since taken a marked and decided part with you.

Surely you are not disposed to call this a crime, as it were, to convict his Grace of duplicity, and of a vile hypocrisy. No gentlemen, I entreat of you not to calumniate the Duke ; cal this conduct a mere play on the credulity of a people easily deceived—innocent in its intention, and equally void of guilt in its description. Do not attach to those words a meaning which would prove that you yourselves condemned, not so much the writer of them, as the man who gave colour and countenance to this assertion. Besides, gentlemen, what is your liberty of the Press worth, if it be worthy of a dungeon to assert that the public credulity has been played upon ? The liberty of the Press would be less than a dream, a shadow, if every such phrase be a libel.

But the Attorney-General triumphantly tells you that there must be a libel in this paragraph, because it ends with a charge of falsehood. May I ask you to take the entire paragraph together ? Common sense and your duty require you to do so. You will then perceive that this charge of falsehood is no more than an opinion, that the administration of the Duke of Richmond will terminate precisely as that of many of his predecessors has done, by an excuse for the past—a flattering and fallacious promise for the future. Why, you must all of you have seen, a short time since, an account of a public dinner in London, given by persons styling themselves " Friends to Religious Liberty." At that dinner, at which two of the Royal Dukes attended, there were, I think, no less than four or five noblemen who had filled the office of lord lieutenant of Ireland. Gentlemen, at this dinner, they were ardent in their professions of kindness towards the Catholics of Ireland, in their declarations of the obvious policy and justice of conciliation and concession, and they bore ample testimony to our sufferings and our merits. But I appeal from their present declarations to their past conduct ; they are now full of liberality and justice to us ; yet, I speak only the truth of history, when I say that, during their government of this country, no practical benefits resulted from all this wisdom and kindness of sentiment ; with the single exception of Lord Fitzwilliam, not one of them even attempted to do any good to the Catholics, or to Ireland.

What did the Duke of Bedford do for us ? *Just nothing* Some civility, indeed, in words—some playing on public credulity—but in act and deed, nothing at all. What did Lord Hardwicke do for us ? Oh, nothing, or rather less than nothing ; his administration here was, in that respect, a kind of negative quality; it was cold, harsh, and forbidding to the Catholics; lenient, mild, and encouraging to the Orange faction; the public mind lay, in the first torpor caused by the mighty fall of the Union, and whilst we lay entranced in the oblivious pool, Lord Hardwicke's administration proceeded without a trace of that justice and liberality which it appears he must have thought unbefitting the season of his government, and which if he then entertained, he certainly concealed; he ended, however, with giving us, flattering hopes for the future. The Duke of Bedford was more explicit; he promised in direct terms, and drew upon the future exertions of an *hereditary Prince*, to compensate us for present disappointment. And will any man assert that the Duke of Richmond is libelled by a comparison with Lord Hardwicke; that he is traduced when he is compared with the Duke of Bedford? If the words actually were these, "the Duke of Richmond will terminate his administration exactly as Lord Hardwicke and the Duke of Bedford terminated their administrations;" if those were the words, none of you could possibly vote for a conviction, and yet the meaning is precisely the same. No more is expressed by the language of my client; and, if the meaning be thus clearly innocent, it would be strange, indeed, to call on you for a verdict of conviction upon no more solid ground than this, that whilst the signification was the same, the words were different. And thus, again, does the prosecutor require of you to separate the sense from the sound, and to convict for the sound, against the sense of the passage.

In plain truth, gentlemen, if there be a harshness in the sound, there is none in the words. The writer describes, and means to describe, the ordinary termination of every administration repaying in promise the defaults of performance. And, when he speaks of falsehood, he prophecies merely as to the probable or at least possible conclusion of the present government. He does not impute to any precedent, assertion, falsehood; but he does predict, that the concluding promise of this, as of other administrations, depending as those promises always do upon other persons for performance, will remain as former promises have remained—unfulfilled and unperformed. And is this prophecy —this prediction a crime? Is it a libel to prophecy? See what topics this sage venerator of the liberty of the Press, the Attorney-General, would fain prohibit. First, he tells you, that the crimes of the predecessors of the Duke must not be mentioned —and thus he forbids the history of past events. Secondly, he informs you, that no allusion is to be made to the errors, follies.

or even the striking features of the present governors ; and thus he forbids the detail of the occurrences of the present day. And, thirdly, he declares that no conjecture shall be made upon what is likely to occur hereafter ; and thus he forbids all attempts to anticipate future acts.

It comes simply to this; he talks of venerating the liberties of the Press, and yet he restrains that Press from discussing past history, present story, and future probabilities; he prohibits the past, the present, and the future; ancient records, modern truth, and prophecy, are all within the capacious range of his punishments. Is there anything else? Would this venerator of the liberty of the Press go further? Yes, gentlemen, having forbidden all matter of history past and present, and all prediction of the future, he generously throws in *abstract principles*, and, as he has told you, that his prisons shall contain every person who speaks of what was, or what is, or what will be, he likewise consigned to the same fate every person who treats of the theory or principles of government; and yet he dares to talk of the liberty of the Press! Can you be his dupes? Will you be his victims? Where is the conscience—where is the indignant spirit of insulted reason amongst you? Has party feeling extinguished in your breasts every glow of virtue—every spark of manhood?

If there be any warmth about you—if you are not clay-cold to all but party feeling, I would, with the air and in the tone of triumph, call you to the consideration of the remaining paragraph which has been spread on the lengthened indictment before you. I divide it into two branches, and shall do no more with the one than to repeat it. I read it for you already ; must read it again :—

 "Had he remained what he first came over, or what he afterwards professed to be, he would have retained his reputation for *honest, open hostility*, defending his political principles with firmness, perhaps, with warmth, but without rancour ; the supporter, and not the tool of an administration ; a mistaken politician, perhaps, but an honourable man, and a respectable soldier."

Would to God I had to address another jury! Would to God I had reason and judgment to address, and I could entertain no apprehension from passion or prejudice! Here should I then take my stand, and require of that unprejudiced jury, whether this sentence does not demonstrate the complete absence of private malice or personal hostility. Does not this sentence prove a kindly disposition towards the individual, mixing and min gling with that discussion which freedom sanctions and requires, respecting his political conduct? Contrast this sentence with the prosecutor's accusation of private malignity, and decide between Mr. Magee and his calumniators. He, at least, has this advantage, that your verdict cannot alter the nature of things; and that the public must see and feel this truth, that the present prosecution is directed against the discussion of the conduct towards the public, of men confided with public authority; that this is a direct attack upon the right to call the attention of the people to the management of the people's affairs, and that, by your verdict of conviction, it is intended to leave no peaceful or unawed mode of redress for the wrongs and sufferings of the people.

But I will not detain you on these obvious topics. We draw to a close, and I hurry to it. This sentence is said to be particularly libellous:—

" His party would have been proud of him ; his friends would have praised (they need not have flattered him), and his enemies, though they might have regretted, must have respected his conduct ; from the worst quarter there would have been some small tribute of praise ; from none any great portion of censure ; and his administration, though not popular, would have been conducted with dignity, and without offence. This line of conduct he has taken care to avoid · his original character for moderation he has forfeited ; he can lay no claims to any merits for neutrality, nor does he even deserve the cheerless credit of defensive operations. He has begun to act ; he has ceased to be a dispassionate chief governor, who views the wickedness and the folly of faction with composure and forbearance, and stands, the representative of majesty, aloof from the contest. He descends ; he mixes with the throng ; he becomes personally engaged, and having lost his temper, calls forth his private passions to support his public principles ; he is no longer an indifferent viceroy, but a frightful partisan of an English ministry, whose base passions he indulges—whose unworthy resentments he gratifies, and on whose behalf he at present canvasses."

Well, gentlemen, and did he not canvass on behalf of the ministry? Was there a titled or untitled servant of the Castle who was not despatched to the south to vote against the popular, and for the ministerial candidates? Was there a single individual within the reach of his Grace that did not vote against Prittie and Matthew, in Tipperary, and against Hutchinson, in Cork. I have brought with me some of the newspapers of the day, in which this partisanship in the Lord Lieutenant is treated by Mr. Hutchinson in language so strong and so pointed, that the words of this publication are mildness and softness itself, when compared with that language I shall not read them for

you, because I should fear that you may imagine I unnecessarily identified my client with the violent but the merited reprobation poured upon the scandalous interference of our government with those elections.

I need not, I am sure, tell you that any interference by the
Lord Lieutenant with the purity of the election of members to
serve in Parliament, is highly unconstitutional, and highly criminal; he is doubly bound to the most strict neutrality; first,
as a peer, the law prohibits his interference; secondly, as representative of the crown, his interference in elections is an usurpation of the people's rights; it is, in substance and effect, high
treason against the people, and its mischiefs are not the less by
reason of there being no punishment affixed by the law to this
treason.

If this offence, gentlemen, be of daily occurrence—if it be frequently committed, it is upon that account only the more destructive to our liberties, and, therefore, requires the more loud,
direct, and frequent condemnation : indeed, if such practices be
permitted to prevail, there is an end of every remnant of freedom; our boasted constitution becomes a mockery and an object of ridicule, and we ought to desire the manly simplicity of
unmixed despotism.   Will the Attorney-General—will his colleague, the Solicitor-General, deny that I have described this
offence in its true colours?   Will they attempt to deny the interference of the Duke of Richmond in the late elections?   I
would almost venture to put your verdict upon this, and to consent to a conviction, if any person shall be found so stocked with
audacity, as to presume publicly to deny the interference of his
Grace in the late elections, and his partisanship in favour of the
ministerial candidates.   Gentlemen, if that be denied, what will
you, what can you think of the veracity of the man who denies
it?   I fearlessly refer the fact to you; on that fact I build.
This interference is as notorious as the sun at noon day; and
who shall venture to deny that such interference is described by
a soft term when it is called partisanship?   He who uses the
influence of the executive to control the choice of the representatives of the people, violates the first principles of the constitution, is guilty of political sacrilege, and profanes the very sanc-
tuary of the people's rights and liberties; and if he should not
be called a partisan, it is only because some harsher and more
appropriate term ought to be applied to his delinquency.

I will recal to your minds an instance of violation of the constitution, which will illustrate the situation of my client, and

the protection which, for your own sakes, you owe him. When,
in 1687, King James removed several Protestant rectors in Ireland from their churches, against law and justice, and illegally
and unconstitutionally placed Roman Catholic clergymen in
their stead, would any of you be content that he should be simply called a partisan! No, gentlemen, my client and I—Catholic
and Protestant though we be—agree perfectly in this, that partisan would have been too mild a name for him, and that he
should have been branded as a violator of law, as an enemy to
the constitution, and as a crafty tyrant who sought to gratify
the prejudices of one part of his subjects that he might trample
upon the liberties of all. And what, I would fain learn, could
you think of the Attorney-General who prosecuted, or of the
judge who condemned, or of the jury who convicted a printer
for publishing to the world this tyranny—this gross violation of
law and justice? But how would your indignation be roused,
if James had been only called a partisan, and for calling him a
partisan a Popish jury had been packed, a Popish judge had been
selected, and that the printer, who, you will admit, deserved applause and reward, met condemnation and punishment.

Of *you*—of *you*, shall *this story be told*, if you convict Mr.
Magee. The Duke has interfered in elections; he has violated
the liberties of the subject; he has profaned the very temple of
the constitution; and he, who has said that in so doing, he was
a partisan, from your hands expects punishment.

Compare the kindred offences: James deprived the Protestant
rectors of their livings; he did not persecute, nor did he interfere with their religion; for tithes, and oblations, and glebes, and
church lands, though solid appendages to any church, are no
part of the Protestant religion. The Protestant religion would,
I presume—and for the honour of human nature I sincerely hope
—continue its influence over the human mind without the aid
of those extrinsic advantages. Its pastors would, I trust and
believe, have remained true to their charge, without the adven-
titious benefits of temporal rewards; and, like the Roman Catholic Church, it might have shone forth a glorious example of firmness in religion, setting persecution at defiance. James did not
attack the Protestant religion; I repeat it; he only attacked
the revenues of the Protestant Church; he violated the law and
the constitution, in depriving men of that property, by his individual authority, to which they had precisely the same right with
that by which he wore his crown. But is not the controlling
the election of members of parliament a more dangerous violation

of the constitution ? Does it not corrupt the very sources of legislation, and convert the guardians of the state into its plunderers ?
The one was a direct and undisguised crime, capable of being redressed in the ordinary course of the law, and producing resistance by its open and plain violation of right and of law ; the other disguises itself in so many shapes, is patronised by so many high examples, and is followed by such perfect security, that it becomes the first duty of every man, who possesses any reverence for the constitution, or any attachment to liberty, to lend all his efforts to detect, and, if possible, to punish it.

To any man who loved the constitution or freedom, I could safely appeal for my client's vindication ; or if any displeasure could be excited in the mind of such a man, it would arise because of the forbearance and lenity of this publication. But the Duke is called a frightful partisan. Granted, gentlemen, granted. And is not the interference I have mentioned frightful ? Is it not terrific ? Who can contemplate it without shuddering at the consequences which it is likely to produce ? What gentler phrase—what lady-like expression should my client use ?
The constitution is sought to be violated, and he calls the author of that violation a frightful partisan. Really, gentlemen, the fastidiousness which would reject this expression would be better employed in preventing or punishing crime, than in dragging to a dungeon the man who has the manliness to adhere to truth, and to use it. Recollect also—I cannot repeat it too often—that the Attorney-General told you, that " the liberty of the Press was the best protection of the people against the government." Now, if the constitution be violated—if the purity of election be disturbed by the executive, is not this precisely the case when this protection becomes necessary ? It is not wanted, nor can the Press be called a protector, so long as the government is administered with fidelity, care, and skill.
The protection of the Press is requisite only when integrity diligence, or judgment do not belong to the administration ; and that protection becomes the more necessary, in the exact proportion in which these qualities are deficient. But, what protection can it afford if you convict in this instance ? For, by doing so, you will decide that nothing ought to be said against that want of honesty, or of attention, or of understanding ; the more necessary will the protection of the Press become, the more unsafe will it be to publish the truth ; and in the exact proportion in which the Press might be useful, will it become liable to punishment. In short, according to the Attorney-General's doctrine

when the Press is "best. employed and wanted most," it will be most dangerous to use it. And thus, the more corrupt and profligate any administration may be, the more clearly can the public prosecutor ascertain the sacrifice of his selected victim. And call you this protection? Is this a protector who must be disarmed the moment danger threatens, and is bound a prisoner the instant the fight has commenced?

Here I should close the case—here I should shortly recapitulate my client's defence, and leave him to your consideration; but I have been already too tedious, and shall do no more than recal to your recollection the purity, the integrity, the entire disinterestedness of Mr. Magee's motives. If money were his object, he could easily procure himself to be patronised and salaried; but he prefers to be persecuted and discountenanced by the great and powerful, because they cannot deprive him of the certain expectation, that his exertions are useful to his long-suffering, ill-requitted country.

He is disinterested, gentlemen; he is honest; the Attorney-General admitted it, and actually took the trouble of administering to him advice how to amend his fortune and save his person. But the advice only made his youthful blood mantle in that ingenious countenance, and his reply was painted in the indignant look, that told the Attorney-General he might offer wealth, but he could not bribe—that he might torture, but he could not terrify! Yes, gentlemen, firm in his honesty, and strong in the fervour of his love of Ireland, he fearlessly awaits your verdict, convinced that even you must respect the man whom you are called upon to condemn. Look to it, gentlemen; consider whether an honest, disinterested man shall be prohibited from discussing public affairs; consider whether all but flattery is to be silent—whether the discussion of the errors and the capacities of the ministers is to be closed for ever. Whether we are to be silent as to the crimes of former periods—the follies of the present, and the credulity of the future; and, above all, reflect upon the demand that is made on you to punish the canvassing of abstract principles.

Has the Attorney-General succeeded? Has he procured a jury so fitted to his object, as to be ready to bury in oblivion every fault and every crime, every error and every imperfection of public men, past, present, and future—and who shall, in addition, silence any dissertation on the theory or principle of . legislation. Do, gentlemen, go this length with the prosecutor and then venture on your oaths. I charge you to venture to

talk to your families of the venerable liberty of the Press—the
protection of the people against the vices of the government.

I should conclude, but the Attorney-General compels me to
follow him through another subject ; he has told you, and told
you truly, that besides the matter set out in the indictment—
the entire of which, gentlemen, we have already gone through—
this publication contains severe strictures upon the alleged inde-
licacy in the Chief Justice issuing a ministerial warrant, in a
case which was afterwards to come before him judicially, and
upon the manner in which the jury was attempted to be put together in Doctor Sheridan's case, and in which a jury was better
arranged in the case of Mr. Kirwan. Indeed, the Attorney-General seemed much delighted with these topics ; he again burst
out into an enraptured encomium upon himself; and, as it were
inspired by his subject, he rose to the dignity of a classical quotation, when he exclaimed, " *me me, adsum, qui feci.*" HE *forgot to add the still more appropriate remainder of the sentence,
" mea fraus omnis !"*

YES, *gentlemen*, he has avowed with more manliness than discretion, that he was the contriver of all those measures. With
respect to the warrant which his lordship issued in the stead of
the ordinary justices of the peace, and upon a charge not amounting to any breach of the peace, I shall say nothing at present.
An obvious delicacy restrains me from entering upon that subject ; and as the interest of my client does not counteract that
delicacy, I shall refrain. But I would not have it understood
that I have formed no opinion on the subject. Yes, I have
formed an opinion, and a strong and decided opinion, which I
am ready to support as a lawyer and a man, but the expression
of which I now sacrifice to a plain delicacy. But I must say,
that the Attorney-General has thrown new light on this business ; he has given us information we did not possess before.
I did not before know that the warrant was sought for and procured by the Attorney-General ; I thought it was the sponta-
neous act of his lordship, and not in consequence of any private
solicitation from the Attorney-General. In this respect, he has
set me right—it is a fact of considerable value, and although
the consequences to be deduced from it are not pleasing to any
man, loving, as I do, the purity of justice, yet, I most heartily
thank the Attorney-General for *the fact—the important fact.*

His second avowal relates to Dr. Sheridan. It really is comfortable to know how much of the indecent scene exhibited upon
his trial belonged to the Attorney-General. He candidly tells

us, that the obtrusion of the police magistrate, Sirr, as an assistant to the Crown-Solicitor, was the act of the King's Attorney-General. "*Adsum qui feci*," said he. Thus he avows that he procured an Orangeman—*I do not exactly understand what is meant by an Orangeman—some of you could easily tell me*—that he caused this Orangeman to stand in open court, next to the Solicitor for the Crown, with his written paper, suggesting who were fit jurors for his purpose, and who should be put by. Gentlemen, he avows that this profligate scene was acted in the open court, by his directions. It was by the Attorney-General's special directions, then, that such men as John Lindsay, of Sackville-street, and John Roche, of Strand-street, were set aside ; the latter, because, though amongst the most wealthy and respectable merchants in your city, he is a Papist ; and the other, because, although a Protestant, he is tainted with liberality —the only offence, public or private, that could be attributed to him. Yes, such men as these were set aside by the Attorney-General's aid-de-camp, the salaried justice of the police office.

The next avowal is also precious. This publication contains also a commentary on the Castle-list jury that convicted Mr. Kirwan, and the Attorney-General has also avowed his share in that transaction ; he thus supplies the only link we wanted in our chain of evidence, when we challenged the array upon that trial. If we could have proved that which the Attorney-General, with his "*adsum qui feci*," yesterday admitted, we should have succeeded and got rid of that panel. Even now, it is delightful to understand the entire machinery, and one now sees at once the reason why Sir Charles Saxton was not examined on the part of the crown, in reply to the case we made. He would, you now plainly see, have traced the arrangement to the Attorney-General, and the array must have been quashed. Thus in the boasting humour of this Attorney-General, he has brought home to himself personally, that which we attributed to him only in his official capacity, and he has convicted the man of that which we charged only upon the office.

He has, he must have a motive for this avowal ; if he had not an adequate object in view, he would not have thus unnecessarily and wantonly taken upon himself all the reproach of those transactions. He would not have boasted of having, out of court, solicited an extra-judicial opinion, in the form of a warrant from his lordship; he would not have gloried in employing an Orangeman from the police office to assist him in open court, with instructions in writing how to pack his jury ; still less would he have suffered it to believed that he was a party at the Castle, with the acting Secretary of State, to the arrangement of the jury that was afterwards to try a person prosecuted by the state.

He would not have made this, I must say, disgraceful avowal, unless he were influenced by an adequate motive. I can easily tell you what that motive was. He knew your prejudices—he knew your antipathy—alas! your interested antipathy—to the Catholics, and, therefore, in order to induce you to convict Protestant of a libel for a publication, innocent, if not useful in itself, in order to procure that conviction from your party feel ings and your prejudices, which he despaired of obtaining from your judgments, he vaunts himself to you as the mighty destroyer of the hopes of Popish petitioners—as a man capable of every act within, as out of the profession, to prevent or impede any relief to the Papists. In short, he wishes to show himself to you as an active partisan at your side; and upon those merits he who knows you best, claims your verdict—a verdict which must be given in on your oaths, and attested by and in the name of the GOD of the Christians.

For my part I frankly avow that I shudder at these scenes · I cannot, without horror, view this interfering and intermeddling with judges and juries, and my abhorrence must be augmented when I find it avowed, that the actors in all these sad exhibitions were the mere puppets of the Attorney-General, moved by his wires, and performing under his control. It is in vain to look for safety to person or property, whilst this system is allowed to pervade our courts; the very fountain of justice may be corrupted at its source, and those waters which should confer health and vigour throughout the land, can then diffuse nought but mephitic and pestilential vapours to disgust and to destroy. If honesty, if justice be silent, yet prudence ought to check these practices. We live in a new era—a melancholy era, in which perfidy and profligacy are sanctioned by high authority; the base violation of plighted faith, the deep stain of dishonour, infidelity in love, treachery in friendship, the abandonment of every principle, and the adoption of every frivolity and of every vice that can excite hatred combined with ridicule—all—all this, and more, may be seen around us; and yet it is believed, it is expected, that this system is fated to be eternal. Gentlemen, we shall all weep the insane delusion; and in the terrific moments of alteration you know not, you cannot know, how soon or how bitterly the ingredients of your own poisoned chalice may be commended to your own lips.

With these views around us—with these horrible prospects lying obscurely before us—in sadness and in sorrow party feelings may find a solitary consolation. My heart feels a species of relief when I recollect that not one single Roman Catholic has been found suited to the Attorney-General's purpose. With what an affectation of liberality would he have placed, at least, one Roman Catholic on his juries, if he could have found one Roman Catholic gentleman in this city capable of being managed into fitness for those juries. You well know that the very first merchants of this city, in wealth as well as in character, are Catholics. Some of you serve occasionally on special juries in important cases of private property. Have you ever seen one of those special juries without many Catholics?—frequently a majority—seldom less than one-half of Catholics. Why are Catholics excluded from these state juries? Who shall venture to avow the reason? Oh, for the partisan indiscretion that would blindly avow the reason! It is, in truth, a high compliment, which persecution, in spite of itself, pays to independent integrity.

It is, in fact, a compliment. It is intended for a reproach, for a libel. It is meant to insinuate that such a man, for example, as Randal M'Donnell—the pride and boast of commerce—one of the first contributors to the revenues of the state, and the first in all the sweet charities of social life—would refuse to do justice, upon his oath, to the Crown, and perjure himself in a state trial, because he is a Roman Catholic. You, even you, would be shocked, if any man were so audacious as to assert, in words, so foul a libel, so false a calumny; and yet what does the conduct of the Attorney-General amount to? Why, practically, to just such a libel, to precisely such a calumny. He acts a part which he would not venture to speak, and endeavours silently to inflict a censure which no man could be found so devoid of shame as to assert in words. And here, gentlemen, is a libel for which there is no punishment; here is a profligate calumny for which the law furnishes no redress; he can continue to calumniate us by his rejection. See whether he does not offer you a greater insult by his selection; lay your hands to your hearts, and in private communion with yourselves, ask the reason why you have been sought for and selected for this jury—will you discover that you have been selected because of admitted impartiality?

Would to God you could make that discovery! It would be one on which my client might build the certain expectation of a triumphant acquittal.

Let me transport you from the heat and fury of domestic politics; let me place you in a foreign land; you are Protestants, with your good leave, you shall, for a moment, be Portuguese, and Portuguese is now an honourable name, for right well have the people of Portugal fought for their country, against the foreign invader. Oh! how easy to procure a similar spirit, and more of bravery, amongst the people of Ireland! The slight purchase of good words, and a kindly disposition, would convert them into an impenetrable guard for the safety of the Throne and the State. But advice and regret are equally unavailing, and they are doomed to calumny and oppression, the reality of persecution, and the mockery of justice, until some fatal hour shall arrive, which may preach wisdom to the dupes, and menace with punishment the oppressor.

In the meantime I must place you in Portugal. Let us suppose for an instant that the Protestant religion is that of the people of Portugal—the Catholic, that of the government—that the house of Braganza has not reigned, but that Portugal is still governed by the viceroy of a foreign nation, from whom no kindness, no favour has ever flowed, and from whom justice has rarely been obtained, and upon those unfrequent occasions, not conceded generously, but extorted by force, or wrung from distress by terror and apprehension, in a stinted measure and ungracious manner; you, Protestants, shall form, not as with us in Ireland, nine-tenths, but some lesser number, you shall be only four-fifths of the population; and all the persecution which you have yourselves practised here upon Papists, whilst you, at the same time, accused the Papists of the crime of being persecutors, shall glow around; your native land shall be to you the country of strangers; you shall be aliens in the soil that gave you birth, and whilst every foreigner may, in the land of your forefathers, attain rank, station, emolument, honours, you alone shall be excluded; and you shall be excluded for no other reason but a conscientious abhorrence to the religion of your ancestors.

Only think, gentlemen, of the scandalous injustice of punishing you because you are Protestants. With what scorn—with what contempt do you not listen to the stale pretences—to the miserable excuses by which, under the name of state reasons and political arguments, your exclusion and degradation are sought to be justified. Your reply is ready—"perform your iniquity

U

—men of crimes (you exclaim) be unjust—punish us for our
fidelity and honest adherence to truth, but insult us not by supposing that your reasoning can impose upon a single individual
either of us or of yourselves." In this situation let me give you
a viceroy; he shall be a man who may be styled—by some person disposed to exaggerate, beyond bounds, his merits, and to
flatter him more than enough—"an honourable man and a respectable soldier," but, in point of fact, he shall be of that little-
minded class of beings who are suited to be the plaything of knaves
—one of those men who imagine they govern a nation, whilst,
in reality they are but the instruments upon which the crafty
play with safety and with profit. Take such a man for your
viceroy—Protestant Portuguese. We shall begin with making
this tour from Tralos Montes to the kingdom of Algesiras—as one
amongst us should say, from the Giant's Causeway to the kingdom of Kerry. Upon his tour he shall affect great candour and
good-will to the poor suffering Protestants. The bloody anniversaries of the inquisitorial triumphs of former days shall be for
a season abandoned, and over our inherent hostility the garb of
hypocrisy shall, for a season, be thrown. Enmity to the Protestants shall become, for a moment, less apparent ; but it will be
only the more odious for the transitory disguise.

The delusion of the hour having served its purpose, your
viceroy shows himself in his native colours ; he selects for office,
and prefers for his pension-list, the men miserable in intellect,
if they be but virulent against the Protestants ; to rail against
the Protestant religion—to turn its holiest rites into ridicule—
to slander the individual Protestants, are the surest, the only
means to obtain his favour and patronage. He selects from his
Popish bigots some being more canine than human, who, not
having talents to sell, brings to the market of bigotry his impudence—who, with no quality under heaven, but gross, vulgar,
acrimonious, disgustful, and shameless abuse of Protestantism
to recommend him, shall be promoted to some accountant-gene-
ralship, and shall riot in the spoils of the people he traduces, as
it were to crown with insult the severest injuries. This viceroy
selects for his favourite privy councillor some learned doctor,
half lawyer, half divine, an entire brute, distinguished by the unblushing repetition of calumnies against the Protestants. This
man has asserted that Protestants are perjurers and murderers
in principle—that they keep no faith with Papists, but hold it
lawful and meritorious to violate every engagement, and commit
every atrocity towards any person who happens to differ with

Protestants in religious belief. This man raves thus, in public, against the Protestants, and has turned his ravings into large personal emoluments. But whilst he is the oracle of minor bigots, he does not believe himself, he has selected for the partner of his tenderest joys, of his most ecstatic moments—he has chosen for the intended mother of his children, for the sweetener and solace of his every care, a Protestant, gentlemen of the jury.

Next to the vile instruments of bigotry, his accountant-general and privy councillor, we will place his acts. The Protestants of Portugal shall be exposed to insult and slaughter; an Orange party—a party of Popish Orangemen, shall be supposed to exist; they shall have liberty to slaughter the unarmed and defenceless Protestants, and as they sit peaceably at their firesides. They shall be let loose in some Portuguese district, called Monaghan; they shall cover the streets of some Portuguese town of Belfast with human gore; and in the metropolis of Lisbon, the Protestant widow shall have her harmless child murdered in the noon day, and his blood shall have flowed unrequited, because his assassin was very loyal when he was drunk, and had an irresistible propensity to signalise his loyalty by killing Protestants. Behold, gentlemen, this viceroy depriving of command, and staying the promotion of, every military man who shall dare to think Protestants men, or who shall presume to suggest that they ought not to be prosecuted. Behold this viceroy promoting and rewarding the men who insulted and attempted to degrade the first of your Protestant nobility. Behold him in public, the man I have described.

In his personal concerns he receives an enormous revenue from the people he thus misgoverns. See in his management of that revenue a parsimony at which even his enemies blush. See the paltry sum of a single joe refused to any Protestant charity, whilst his bounty is unknown even at the Popish institutions for benevolent purposes. See the most wasteful expenditure of the public money—every job patronised—every profligacy encouraged. See the resources of Portugal diminished. See her discords and her internal feuds increased. And, lastly, behold the course of justice perverted and corrupted.

It is thus, gentleman, the Protestant Portuguese seek to obtain relief by humble petition and supplication. There can be no crime surely for a Protestant oppressed, because he follows a religion which is, in his opinion, true, to endeavour to obtain relief by mildly representing to his Popish oppressors, that it is the right of every man to worship the Deity according to the dictates of his own conscience; to state respectfully to the governing powers that it is unjust, and may be highly impolitic to punish men, merely because they do not profess Popery, which they do not believe; and to submit, with all humility, that to lay the burdens of the state equally, and distribute its benefits partially, is not justice, but, although sanctioned by the pretence of religious zeal, is, in truth, iniquity, and palpably criminal. Well, gentlemen, for daring thus to remonstrate, the Protestants are persecuted. The first step in the persecution is to pervert the plain meaning of the Portuguese language, and a law prohibiting any *disguise* in apparel, shall be applied to the ordinary *dress* of the individual; it reminds one of *pretence* and *purpose.*

To carry on these persecutions, the viceroy chooses for his first inquisitor the descendant of some Popish refugee—some man with an hereditary hatred to Protestants; he is not the son of an Irishman, this refugee inquisitor—no, for the fact is notorious, that the Irish refugee Papists were ever distinguished for their liberality, as well as for their gallantry in the field and talent in the cabinet. This inquisitor shall be, gentlemen, a descendant from one of those English Papists, who was the dupe or contriver of the Gunpowder Plot! With such a chief inquisitor, can you conceive anything more calculated to rouse you to agony than the solemn mockery of your trial. This chief inquisitor begins by influencing the judges out of court; he proceeds to inquire out fit men for his interior tribunal, which, for brevity, we will call a jury. HE selects his juries from the most violent of the Popish Orangemen of the city, and procures a conviction against law and common sense, and without evidence. Have you followed me, gentlemen? Do you enter into the feelings of Protestants thus insulted, thus oppressed, thus persecuted—their enemies and traducers promoted, and encouraged, and richly rewarded—their friends discountenanced and displaced—their persons unprotected, and their characters assailed by hired calumniators—their blood shed with impunity—their revenues parsimoniously spared to accumulate for the individual, wastefully squandered for the state—the emblems of discord, the war-cry of disunion, sanctioned by the highest authority, and Justice herself converted from an impartial arbitrator into a frightful partisan?

Yes, gentlemen, place yourselves as Protestants under such a persecution. Behold before you this chief inquisitor, with his prejudiced tribunal—this gambler, with a loaded die · and now say what are your feelings—what are your sensations of disgust, abhorrence, affright? But if at such a moment some ardent and enthusiastic Papist, regardless of his interests, and roused by the crimes that were thus committed against you, should describe, in measured, and cautious, and cold language, scenes of oppression and iniquity—if he were to describe them, not as I have done, but in feeble and mild language, and simply state the facts for your benefit and the instruction of the public—if this liberal Papist, for this, were dragged to the Inquisition, as for a crime, and menaced with a dungeon for years, good and gracious God! how would you revolt at and abominate the men who could consign him to that dungeon! With what an eye of contempt, and hatred, and despair, would you not look at the packed and profligate tribunal, which could direct punishment against him who deserved rewards! What pity would you not feel for the advocate who heavily, and without hope, laboured in his defence! and with what agonized and frenzied despair would you not look to the future destinies of a land in which perjury was organized and from which humanity and justice had been for ever banished!

With this picture of yourselves in Portugal, come home to us in Ireland, say is that a crime, when applied to Protestants, which is a virtue and a merit when applied to Papists? Behold how we suffer here; and then reflect, that is is principally by reason of your prejudices against us that the Attorney-General hopes for your verdict. The good man has talked of his impartiality; he will suppress, he says, the licentiousness of the Press. I have, I hope, shown you the right of my client to discuss the public subjects which he has discussed in the manner they are treated of in the publication before you, yet he is prosecuted. Let me read for you a paragraph which the Attorney-General has not prosecuted—which he has refused to prosecute:

"BALLYBAY, JULY 4, 1813.

"A meeting of the Orange Lodges was agreed on, in consequence of the manner in which the Catholics wished to have persecuted the loyalists in this county last year, *when they even murdered some of them for no other reason than their being yeomen and Protestants.*"

And, again—

"It was at Ballybay that *the Catholics murdered one Hughes, a yeoman sergeant for being a Protestant, as was given in evidence at the assizes by a Catholic witness.*"

I have read this passage from the *Hibernian Journal* of the 7th of this month. I know not whether you can hear, unmoved,

a paragraph which makes my blood boil to read; but I shall
only tell you, that the Attorney-General refused to prosecute
this libeller. Gentlemen, there have been several murders committed in the county of Monaghan, in which Ballybay lies. The
persons killed happened to be Roman Catholics; their murderers are Orangemen. Several of the persons accused of these murders are to be tried at the ensuing assizes. The agent applied
to me personally, with this newspaper; he stated that the obvious intention was to create a prejudice upon the approaching
trials favourable to the murderers, and against the prosecutors.
He stated what you—*even you*—will easily believe, that there
never was a falsehood more flagitiously destitute of truth than
the entire paragraph. I advised him, gentlemen, to wait on the
Attorney-General in the most respectful manner possible; to
show him this paragraph, then to request to be allowed to satisfy
him as to the utter falsehood of the assertions which this paragraph contained, which could be more easily done, as the judges
who went that circuit could prove part of it to be false; and I
directed him to entreat that the Attorney-General, when fully
satisfied of the falsehood, would prosecute the publisher of this,
which, I think, I may call an atrocious libel.

Gentlemen, the Attorney-General was accordingly waited on;
he was respectfully requested to prosecute upon the terms of
having the falsehood of these assertions first proved to him. I
need not tell you ne refused. These are not the libellers *he* pro-
secutes. Gentlemen, this not being a libel on any individual,
no private individual can prosecute for it; and the Attorney-
General turns his Press loose on the Catholics of the county of
Monaghan, whilst he virulently assails Mr. Magee for what must
be admitted to be comparatively mild and inoffensive.

No, gentlemen, he does not prosecute this libel. On the contrary, this paper is paid enormous sums of the public money.
There are no less than five proclamations in the paper containing
this libel; and, it was proved in my presence, in a court of justice, that, besides the proclamations and public advertisements,
the two proprietors of the paper had each a pension of £400 per
annum, for supporting government, as it was called. Since that
period one of those proprietors has got an office worth, at least,
£800 a year; and the son of the other, a place of upwards of
£400 per annum: so that, as it is likely that the original pensions continue, here may be an annual income of £2,000 paid
for this paper, besides the thousands of pounds annually, which
the insertion of the proclamations and public advertisements

cost. It is a paper of the very lowest and most paltry scale of talent, and its circulation is, fortunately, very limited; but it receives several thousands of pounds of the money of the men whom it foully and falsely calumniates.

Would I could see the man who pays this proclamation money and these pensions at the Castle. [Here Mr. O'Connell turned round to where Mr. Peele* sat.] Would I could see the man who, against the fact, asserted that the proclamations were inserted in all the papers, save in those whose proprietors were convicted of a libel. I would ask him whether this be a paper that ought to receive the money of the Irish people?—whether this be the legitimate use of the public purse? And when you find this calumniator salaried and rewarded, where is the impartiality, the justice, or even the decency of prosecuting Mr. Magee for a libel, merely because he has not praised public men, and has discussed public affairs in the spirit of freedom and of the constitution. Contrast the situation of Mr. Magee with the proprietor of the *Hibernian Journal;* the one is prosecuted with all the weight and influence of the crown, the other pensioned by the ministers of the crown; the one dragged to your bar for the sober discussion of political topics, the other hired to disseminate the most horrid calumnies! Let the Attorney-General now boast of his impartiality; can you credit him on your oaths? Let him talk of his veneration for the liberty of the Press; *can you* believe him in your consciences? Let him call the Press the protection of the people against the government. Yes, gentlemen, believe him when he says so. Let the Press be the protection of the people; he admits that it ought to be so. Will you find a verdict for him, that shall contradict the only assertion upon which he and I, however, are both agreed?

Gentlemen, the Attorney-General is bound by this admission; it is part of his case, and he is the prosecutor here; it is a part of the evidence before you, for he is the prosecutor. Then, gentlemen, it is your duty to act upon that evidence, and to allow the Press to afford some protection to the people.

Is there amongst you any one friend to freedom? Is there amongst you one man, who esteems equal and impartial justice, who values the people's rights as the foundation of private happines, and who considers life as no boon without liberty? Is there amongst you one friend to the constitution—one man who hates oppression? If there be, Mr. Magee appeals to his kindred mind, and confidently expects an acquittal.

* Chief Secretary to the Lord Lieutenant.

There are amongst you men of great religious zeal—of much public piety. Are you sincere? Do you believe what you profess? With all this zeal—with all this piety, *is* there any conscience amongst you? *Is* there any terror of violating your oaths? Be ye hypocrites, or does genuine religion inspire ye? if you be sincere—if you have conscience—if your oaths can control your interests, then Mr. Magee confidently expects an acquittal.

If amongst you there be cherished one ray of pure religion—if amongst you there glow a single spark of liberty—if I have alarmed religion, or roused the spirit of freedom in one breast amongst you, Mr. Magee is safe, and his country is served; but if there be none—if you be slaves and hypocrites, he will await your verdict, and despise it.

And slaves, hypocrites, and bigots they proved themselves, by finding a verdict for the Crown

CORK CATHOLIC MEETING.

August 30, 1813.

We now approach the period when the noted "Veto" controversy began to rage in Ireland. The next speech of Mr. O'Connell's was delivered during the progress of a species of *agitating circuit* through the South of Ireland, to rally opinion there against the measure in question. The "Catholic Board of the City and County of Cork" was understood to contain several parties favourable to giving the Government control over the nomination of our bishops, by means of this proposed Veto; and in order a little to illustrate the divisions in the Catholic body generally upon the measure, we give, not only Mr. O'Connell's speech itself, but also much of the newspaper report of the circumstances under which it was delivered:—

The most numerous and respectable meeting of our Catholic countrymen that has ever been witnessed in this city, was held on last Monday (30th August). Pursuant to the appointment of the Board, the place of meeting was changed from the Patrick-street Theatre to the Lancasterian School; and accordingly, at twelve o'clock, upwards of ten thousand persons attended At this hour, the members of the Board proceeded to take their station in the School-room. The chair was placed upon a small table, and no hustings raised, which created great inconvenience. There were no seats prepared, except within a paling intended for the accommodation of the Board and their select friends. This total neglect of arrangement, and the evident insufficiency of the room to contain the thousands who crowded to the meeting, gave rise to a general cry of adjournment, which no exertions of the gentlemen near the chair could induce the meeting to suppress. At length James Roche, Esq., proposed John Galway, of Lota, to fill the chair; and Mr. Galway having immediately complied with this invitation, a general outcry was raised against the propriety of placing that gentleman in the chair. He, however, persisted in holding his place, and the opposition of the meeting continued equally determined. Mr. Roche frequently endeavoured to satisfy the meeting of the fitness of Mr. Galway to fill that station, an recommended them at least to try him, but the general complaint against the vote given by that gentleman at the General Board in Dublin, in opposition to the motion of thanks to the prelates, was repeated in several charges, as replies to Mr. Roche's request. In the midst of this confusion, Counsellor O'Regan took out from his pocket a sheet of paper with some writing upon it, which, as well as we could collect, contained the resolutions intended to be proposed by the Board for the adoption of the meeting, and was proceeding to read them, when he was interrupted by Counsellor Mac Donnell, who called upon him not to endeavour to pass his resolutions in such a manner, and at such a moment. Mr. O'Regan did not then proceed, but Mr. Roche again renewed his endeavours to reconcile the meeting to Mr. Galway as their chairman, but they would not consent; and the opposition having continued unabated for a very considerable period of time, Mr. Mac Donnel' suggested to the Board the prudence of substituting another chairman. No answer being given to this, Mr. Mac Donnell addressed the chair, and moved that Mr. Roche should take the chair. This motion was sanctioned by almost the unanimous voice of the meeting, but the question was not put, and consequently the confusion continued.

Mr. Mac Donnell then proceeded to the place where the Board were assembled, and after some conversation between Mr. Roche and other members of the Board with that gentleman, Mr. Roche again addressed the meeting, and begged they would allow the Board to consider among themselves for a few minutes, and that he could assure them all their reasonable desires should be complied with. This proposition of Mr. Roche was loudly cheered and the Board proceeded to deliberate for about ten minutes, when Richard Barry, of Barry's Lodge, Esq., one of the Board, exclaimed, in a very loud voice, " Will you suffer the proceedings of the day to go on ?" Some persons from the crowd replied, "No; not until you have another chairman ;" upon which the Board retired from the meeting. This secession excited great agitation and disgust. Mr. Mac Donnell entreated the gentlemen present to observe strict temperance, as he assured them they could not more gratify the enemies, than by a violation of good order. He suggested the propriety of appointing another chairman at once, as the members of the Board had thought proper to withdraw. He recommended for their choice a gentleman who had done more for their city than any one of those who had then left them—Mr. Timothy Mahony, of Blackpool. This proposition was received with loud plaudits, and in the meantime Counsellor O'Connell made his appearance, and was immediately cheered by the greetings and benedictions of the meeting. He was conducted to the chair, and when the uproar of patriotic exultation which his presence had created had somewhat subsided he addressed the meeting. He told them that the success of their cause depended on the unanimity of their body : and illustrated in a most happy strain of eloquence, the advantages of union, and the evils of division. These propositions were cheered by unanimous applause, and Mr. O'Connell then finding the public feeling to be so well disposed, he quitted the room for the purpose of seeing the Board. When Mr. O'Connell had retired, Mr. Mac Donnell again proposed Mr. Mahony as chairman, and the cry for Mr. Mahony became general; but owing to the pressure of the crowd in the room, that respectable gentleman had found it necessary to retire. On this being ascertained, Counsellor O'Leary was proposed by Mr. Mac Donnell, and called to the chair by the unanimous voice of the meeting, and, being conducted thereto, the most perfect order prevailed. By this time the heat and pressure in the room became insupportable, and several thousands, who could not gain admittance, became clamorous for an adjournment, which was agreed to unanimously ; and the meeting adjourned, accordingly, to an extensive open plain, immediately adjoining the School room. When Counsellor O'Leary had taken the chair at this adjourned place of meeting, Timothy Mahony, Esq., addressed him and the meeting, stating that in declining the very high honour they were kind enough to offer him, he was not influenced by any unwillingness to contribute his humble mite to the support of the great cause they were assembled to advance ; but, conscious of his own feeble abilities to fill so exalted a station, he willingly and gratefully resigned the chair to the highly able and respectable gentleman who had so properly been called to it.

Several most respectable Protestant gentlemen being observed at a distance, there was a general expression of wishes for their accommodation, when

Counsellor Deuris advanced to the chair, and addressed the meeting to the following effect:—

"Mr. Chairman and Gentlemen—I beg to make one observation: I am at this moment honoured with being the mouth-piece of those good and worthy Protestant gentlemen who have assembled here to sanction by their presence, and assist by their voices, the great, the glorious, and the just cause in which ye and ourselves are embarked. Gentlemen, wo are distinctly and deservedly your friends—the friends of justice and of truth, because we are the friends of the Irish people, of Irish Catholics, the best and the most virtuous men upon the face of the earth. But, gentlemen, we lament to behold anything like a division between you; your great object should be conciliation; it is the desire of your Protestant friends; they have no wish to indulge in any but that of general conciliation, because they know that if you do not draw together, you give the triumph to your bitter and irrecon tilcable enemies. But when I look round and behold this immense and respectable meet. ing, there can be no doubt of success. Gentlemen, as your dissenting party were retiring from you, they entreated of us, your Protestant friends, to accompany them, but we cfused, because we would not identify ourselves with any party in the Catholic body; you must allow us to act in the same manner towards you. No, those steady and long-trie, friends to your cause—Stawell, Beamish, Crawford—will not attach themselves to any party, but go with the unanimous voice of the Irish Catholics. Having stated thus, allow me to mention the resolution we have come to; we will retire for the present in the hope of an arrangement between yourselves. Allow me, for the present, to depart; accept my warm and ardent feeling—be firm, be united, be unanimous amongst yourselves and your enlightened, liberal, and patriotic friends will be at their post."

Counsellor Mac Donnell then addressed the meeting:—

"Mr. Chairman and Gentlemen—We have heard the statement of Counsellor Dennis— the statement of that good and amiable friend. It is true we have a division, but we have no right to complain of the principle which occasions this division. Gentlemen, under our circumstances, our Protestant friends have taken a high and an exalted stand; they have not descended to connect themselves with that feeble party which have occasioned this internal division; but the very circumstance of their explanation proves the respect they bear to you; as they would not condescend to any explanation with you, if they did not espect you, and they are entitled to our warmest thanks. But, gentlemen, without observ- ing upon the conduct of those persons who have deserted your great cause; yet it is a duty we owe to ourselves, pointedly to mark the conduct which brought about this divi- son. We are called unanimously to pronounce upon the conduct of those arrogant men who will not condescend to act with us, unless suffered to lead and drive the people as they may choose; but yet, under all these circumstances, I will call upon you to give up resentment—to forget the injuries they have done you, and I would even still reach out the glive, rather than flourish the laurel. Would they were now within my hearing, that they might return and discharge the duty—the imperative duty which they owe the great cause they are engaged in, how freely would we forgive and forget our injuries; nay, to the very last moment we will be ready to receive them. But I fear a disappointment; however, we know the principle upon which we act, and we will be firm to our duty. They fancied they could assemble a party in that building, and carry their wishes with a high hand against the general voice of the people. Gentlemen, was that a fit hole to drive this im- mense assembly into?—(cries of "no, no.") No, it was not; and even if it had been filled, certain death would have been the consequence to some. Look at the immense concourse of persons in every direction about—Protestant and Catholic—and see if that was a fit place, without air, seats, or any accommodation whatever! Yet this was the place selected in despite of every remonstrance; and what was the precious reason given by those gen- tlemen to the earnest and repeated solicitations made to them? why, gentlemen, a reason which no Orangeman would have dared to have offered, or dared to have insulted your ear with—"*tho' they were disinclined to enter a chapel, as they were afraid of the clergy.*"

Why, gentlemen, at this day, are wo forgetting all duty, forgetting all obligation, forgetting all truth, constancy, and honour? are we to allow ourselves to be the slaves of such coarse and vulgar bigotry, "that they were afraid of the clergy?" The Catholic clergy have never yet betrayed or neglected their duty, they are above the slanders of their calumniators. Gentlemen, under the guidance and direction of several Catholic gentlemen of this great county and city of Cork, I will proceed to submit some few resolutions for your adoption; but before I proceed, give me leave to observe upon some suggestions which were laid before the committee, by their own desire, nearly a fortnight ago, for the purpose of their framing resolutions founded upon those suggestions: and, gentlemen, read those suggestions now to you, in order to satisfy you that neither I, nor the respectable gentlemen with whom I had the honour to act, ever interfered until their interference became actually necessary; the following are the suggestions as delivered to them:—

"SUGGESTED PROCEEDINGS FOR THE NEXT AGGREGATE MEETING.

" 'Meeting to be held in the North or South Chapel; the keys to be delivered to James Roche, Esq., previous to the meeting.

" ' Determination to petition for unconditional Emancipation.

" ' Direct condemnation of ecclesiastical arrangements in the late bill.

" ' Approval of, and gratitude to the prelates for their general conduct, and particularly for their late address and resolutions.

" 'Thanks to Dr. Milner for his opposition to the late ill, and faithful discharge of his duties as agent to the Irish bishops.

" 'Thanks to the members of the Church of Scotland and Synod of Ulster.

" ' Approbation of the conduct of the General Board.

" ' Declaration of the expiration of the term for which the Cork Board was appointed and appointing persons who shall co-operate in Dublin with the General Board in presenting the petition, &c.; the object being to suspend for the present the sittings of a local Board. No resolution to be proposed of either approval or disapproval of the conduct of the Cork Board.

" ' Adoption of general petition. .

'Thanks to Donoughmore and friends in Lords. Grattan having been thanked at last meeting, *quere* propriety of repetition of thanks to him, as Donoughmore was not then named?

" 'Thanks and gratitude to John Magee, Esq., for his undeviating support of Catholic interests.'

"Gentlemen, here is one more which this late committee did not think worthy of being treated even with common politeness; it is a suggestion for a vote of thanks to that best of men, and worthiest of Irishmen, Counsellor O'Connell. This suggestion was scouted with disregard, and flung from them with contempt, thus refusing the empty tribute of a simple vote of thanks to the man who had devoted his life to our service. I will read the suggestion:—

" 'Thanks and gratitude to Counsellor O'Connell, to be expressed in the most animated and affectionate terms.'

The other suggestions were as follows:—

" 'Determination not to vote for any candidate who will not pledge himself to be a friend: and a recommendation to the Catholics of county and city to register freeholds.

" 'Determination to prefer Irish manufacture, and encourage its prosperity'

Now, gentlemen (continued Mr. Mac Donnell), it is my duty to proceed to read the resolutions; in doing so I have the concurrence of respectable gentlemen of both the city and county."

Here Mr. Mac Donnell was interrupted by the appearance of Counsellor O'Connell, who had returned from the meeting of the Board, who had retired. When he reached the chair, ho addressed the meeting to the following effect:—

Mr. Chairman and Gentlemen—Before my highly and valuable friend, Counsellor Mac Donnell, proceeds to read those resolutions. I have a proposal to make, which, if it meets your sanction, may, under Providence, have the full effect of bringing about a general reconciliation. Gentlemen, nothing can be of more benefit to us than unanimity ; and therefore it is I would propose, that before you proceed to establish a new Board, or whatever other mode you may think proper to pursue, that you give the seceders another opportunity of returning to their post and their duty. Do not conceive that I mean to insinuate that their presence is necessary to establish the justness of your proceeding. —No, no, gentlemen, I insinuate no such matter ; on the contrary, it is a fact, a strong fact, that the moment the aggregate meeting assembled, their power was dissolved—you have not again elected them, and they are as nothing without your support. But I am induced to this, that I might be the happy means of effecting unanimity in this great county and city ; my only hope is that of doing good for my poor country. It is this feeling for the good of old Ireland that is forcing me forward in this instance—and also, because I think we shall be successful. I think those gentlemen have seen their error ; they begin to find they are nothing. I saw them a few moments back, a few scattered individuals, in a corner of a yard. I addressed them, because, though small, very small indeed in their numbers, yet, as individuals, they are respectable, and I wished to undeceive them of their errors. I asked them if they were Roman Catholics, and could they talk about securities ? I told them to leave securities to the minions of the Castle—to the pensioned hirelings of the state—aye, and to the Orange Papists too ; but let not them, as honest, honourable, worthy Roman Catholics, insult the public ears with so discordant a sound. I told them, that we had only one security to offer, and that we were willing to surrender our heart's blood, our lives, our properties, our persons, in the front of the battle. Away, then, with faction, with party and division—give us Emancipation, and we, in return, will give every security in our persons, lives, and properties. Then let faction raise its head, we will put it down, spring from what quarter it may. Then let the foreign foe pollute our shores, and we will prove our sincerity and our attachment to that constitution, which we are now seeking to receive the benefits of, by driving them before us. At present how are we treated ? Something in the nature of mad dogs, which they will not let loose without first tying up one of their legs ; so by us, they will give us Emancipation, after we give them security that we will be slaves. Let us then go after those people—let us endeavour to effect, if possible, an understanding between the anti-vetoists and the Board. We will endeavour to find out the sound and the perfect. Send your independent and honourable chairman, Counsellor O'Leary, for one of the deputation—let my esteemed and worthy honest friend, Counsellor Mac Donnell, be another—let the Rev. Mr. England be a third ; he is too sincere, upon a good cause, to deny his aid. Fill up the list to the number of ten. I promise you, if we gain no honour in this affair, we shall lose none.

I do therefore move, Sir, that a deputation of ten persons be appointed to wait upon the committee, and commune with them on the present differences ; and that they do return in one hour with their reply.

After some discussion, Mr. O'Connell's motion was acceded to and he, with the follow-ng gentlemen, were deputed to communicate with the Board :—

Counsellor O'Leary,	Timothy Mahony, Esq.
Counsellor Mac Donnell,	Nicholas Murphy, Esq.
Rev. Mr. England (the late much	Edmond O'Flaherty, Esq.
esteemed Right Rev. Dr England,	James N. Mahon. Esq.
Catholic Bishop of Charleston,	Maurice Hoare, Esq.
South Carolina,)	Jeremiah Murphy, Esq.
Francis J. Moloney, Esq.	

This deputation accordingly proceeded, and were admitted to an interview with the Board in a *bed-chamber!* To this dignified *hall of council* the body in question had to re-ire, from the hootings of the people, who were becoming exceedingly dissatisfied with their proceedings. After two hours' delay the deputation returned, and Counsellor O'Con-nell addressed the meeting.

He informed them that there had been an unanimous agree-ment come to on resolutions perfectly without qualification of any kind, and unequivocally demanding "*simple repeal,*" as it was phrased—that is, the unconditional abrogation of the penal code.

He further stated, that the same unanimity had prevailed with regard to a vote of thanks to the Catholic bishops—and similar votes to Grattan, Donoughmore, and the Dukes of Kent and Sussex.

He added that the Board, obedient to the manifestations of popular feeling that day witnessed, would now consider their office at an end ; and their body, as hitherto constituted, entirely dissolved ; but that they offered themselves for re-election as members of a Board to consist of double the number of that to which they had belonged ; the latter having been 34, the new Board would therefore, of course, be 68.

He thus concluded :—

These gentlemen are now coming back repentant, and seeking

y^ur favour; will you refuse it to persons repenting their
errors?

" No," said some persons in the crowd; " *we forgive them, and
may heaven forgive them!*"

Aye, you follow that—the pure feeling of our Irish Catholics!
How I love to hear such sentiments—the effusions of honesty
bursting from the heart! Oh, that such sentiments pervaded
the country—then had we no need of meetings! But *prove*
your forgiveness. The Board bring with them the chairman,
whom you, this day, would not allow to preside—but he now
comes like the prodigal child! Oh, will you not receive him
into your bosoms, and prove yourselves Christians?

Is it because he has once done wrong, that you should spurn
him through life?

If he *did* vote against the motion of thanks to our bishops,
still he is now sorry for it; no doubt it was the error of his
judgment; but he sees this error in common with others; receive him and them cordially, then; let Mr. Galwey take the
chair, and we shall have unanimity, that most desirable of all
objects under heaven.

As Counsellor O'Connell was speaking (says the *Cork Mercantile Chronicle*, from which
we quote), the Board made its appearance. and Mr. Galwey addressed the meeting.

He congratulated the meeting on their prospects of unanimity, and announced that a set
of resolutions were now to be proposed—twelve certainly, with the full concurrence of
those with whom he acted—but that any beyond that number should be dealt with as mere
individual suggestions open to discussion and opposition.

The following resolutions were accordingly read by James Roche, Esq., who acted as
secretary upon the occasion :—

" Resolved—That having confidently anticipated that the beneficent
interposition of the legislature would have, ere now, relieved us from
the necessity of a further expression of our complaints, we cannot but
lament the disappointment of our just and reasonable expectations.

" Yet, however acutely we may feel even the temporary postponement
of our success, we consider it a matter of real consolation to have found
that an actual majority of the 658 members, who compose the House
of Commons, have declared themselves favourable to our relief.

"Resolved—That firmly relying on the immutable justice of our cause,
on the wisdom of the legislature, and on the distinguished liberality of
our Protestant brethren, we will persevere in every constitutional endeavour to obtain the repeal of those oppressive and impolitic laws by
which we are aggrieved.

"And that we do, therefore, in concert with our fellow-citizens
throughout the kingdom, renew our earnest applications for their TOTAL
AND UNQUALIFIED REMOVAL.

" Resolved—That we do adopt the petition of the Catholics of Ireland
and that it be referred to the gentlemen now composing the Catholic

Board for this county and city (in conjunction with the following names which are added to the Board), to prepare and forward it at such time, and in such manner, as shall seem to them most conducive to their success :—

Thomas Coppinger,	Luke Shea,
Counsellor O'Leary,	Edward Reardon,
Philip Harding,	Bartholomew Foley,
Pierce Nagle, jun.,	John Morrogh,
Dr. Pigott,	Nicholas Murphy,
Jeremiah M'Carthy,	Dr. Donegan,
Daniel Clanchy,	Denis Richard Mayland,
John Shinior,	Francis Molony,
Anthony O'Connor,	Frederick Shanahan,
Counsellor Mackey,	Alexander M'Carthy,
Garrett Nagle,	Timothy Mahony,
Timothy Donovan,	Francis Molony,
Dr. Balwin,	Jeremiah O'Leary
Michael Callaghan,	John Cremin, jun.,
Patrick Russell,	James Nicholas Mahon,
Maurice O'Connell (of Darrynane,)	Edmond Hore.

" Resolved—That the said Board does not consist of any representatives of the people, or of any part of the people, and that their sittings be open and public.

"Resolved—That reposing the most implicit confidence in our revered prelates, a grateful confidence to which their pastoral and personal virtues so eminently entitle them, we can never accept of any legislative relief, however unlimited in its political operation, encumbered as on a late occasion, with restrictions which they shall declare contrary to the doctrines or discipline of our Church.

"Resolved—That among the many able supporters of our cause in parliament, pre-eminent and unrivalled stands the immortal name of Henry Grattan. The splendour of his talents, the extent of his services, and the unabated ardour of his zeal, in the advocacy of our cause, have justly exalted this illustrious patriot to the foremost place in our estimation and gratitude.

"Resolved—That their Royal Highnesses the Dukes of Kent and Sussex, by their zealous and honourable exertions in our behalf, have proved themselves the true supporters of those principles which placed the House of Hanover on the throne, and have received our attachment and gratitude.

"Resolved—That the most lively thanks of the Catholics of the county and city of Cork are eminently due, and hereby given to the Right Honourable Earl Donoughmore, and the illustrious family of Hutchinson. for their uniform, manly, and hereditary support of our rightful cause.

"Resolved—That we are deeply indebted to the General Assembly of the Church of Scotland as well as to the Synod of Ulster, for the liberality with which they have respectively declared themselves on the subject of our claims.

" Resolved—That the zealous and unwearied exertions of the Earl of

Fingal and the General Board of Ireland, in the cause of Catholic liberty, claim our cordial thanks.

"Resolved—That it is a primary and indispensable duty to obtain for ourselves that constitutional weight which the elective franchise confers, and to acquire for our parliamentary friends, that legislative importance which can best ensure the success of our cause.

" And we trust our body will carry this into effect.

"Resolved—That to relieve the necessities, and increase the industry of a numerous class of our distressed fellow-countrymen, we most earnestly recommend to our countrymen, the exclusive use of IRISH MANUFACTURE."

The foregoing resolutions were proposed by the Board. Here follow the resolutions partly objected to.—

"Resolved—That the warmest expression of our gratitude is due, and hereby offered, to that venerable and indefatigable Catholic prelate, the Right Rev. Dr. Milner, as well for those mighty labours which his great mind has suggested, as for that faithful discharge of the high trust reposed in him, as agent for the prelates of Ireland, who have sanctioned his struggles by their public and grateful approval.

" And, that we confidently trust he will proceed in his exertions for our religious preservation and political redemption, unshaken by the hostility of false friends, or false brethren, who have not the good sense to estimate, or the spirit to approve, his generous attachment to our cause and our country.

" And, that we feel particularly indebted to that excellent prelate, for his manly, upright, and conscientious opposition to the ecclesiastical arrangements, submitted to parliament during the last session, in the bill purporting to provide for the further relief of his majesty's Roman Catholic subjects.

"Resolved—That our most grateful thanks are imperatively due, and cheerfully offered to that invaluable Irishman, John Magee, Esq., proprietor of the *Dublin Evening Post*, for his undeviating support of our cause, and manly exposure of the bigotry and profligacy of our enemies of every rank and degree.

"Resolved—That the Roman Catholics of the county and city of Cork most gratefully admire the merits, and approve the worth of that great and good Irishman, the strong pillar of our cause, and the pride of our land, *Counsellor O'Connell*—who, in the spirit of constitutional independence, often has undauntedly stood foremost in the fight, whenever the interests of Ireland were to be defended, her rights demanded, or her enemies confounded.

" And that we consider him particularly entitled to our most glowing gratitude as Catholic Irishmen, for his virtuous motion in support of our hierarchy, proposed in the General Board on the 29th day of May last, and triumphantly carried by a glorious and patriotic majority.

" Resolved—That Counsellor Mac Donnell, the patriotic editor of the *Mercantile Chronicle*, the vigilant sentinel of our rights, the undaunted and incorruptible advocate of Catholic claims and religious freedom, has well merited, and continues to obtain the entire confidence, sincere gratitude, and cordial thanks of this meeting, and that he be appointed a member of the Board.

"Resolved—That the cordial thanks of the meeting are eminently due, and hereby given to Messrs Stawells, Beamish, senior and junior, Crawford, Cuthbert, Blennerhasset, Yates, and many other Protestant gentlemen whose presence, and Major Torrens, Counsellor Dennis, and Mr. Jackson Reid, whose eloquence have shed so bright a lustre on the proceedings of this day.

"JOHN GALWEY, jun., Chairman.
"WILLIAM J. SHEEHY, Secretary."

"As chairman and secretary of the meeting of the Roman Catholics of the county and city of Cork, assembled yesterday, we have considered it our duty to authenticate the proceedings by our signatures. But lest it should be thence inferred that they had received our approbation, we do hereby declare our utter dissent from, and do protest against the proceedings there adopted.

"J. GALWEY, jun., Chairman.
"WILLIAM J. SHEEHY, Secretary."

We have given the resolutions in their advertised form, with the Chairman and Secretary's protest appended; and now revert to the period of the meeting when they were brought forward, to give in detail the proceedings which were had upon them, and which gave rise to this protest, as well as to other occurrences which shall be noticed in due order.

After the Chairman's announcement that the Board had "*sanctioned*" only the first twelve of these resolutions, and after the three which related to Right Rev. Dr. Milner, to John Magee, and Mr. O'Connell, had been brought forward, read, and proposed by Mr Mac Donnell

Mr. R. Moylan came forward.

He protested against the resolutions just proposed by Mr. Mac Donnell—dealing thus with the three :—

"My first objection is to Dr. Milner!

"His *tergiversation* is known. He deceived and disappointed our friends in England, and deceived us all; and his tergiversation is *known* and *acknowledged* by *all !*—(Loud cries of disapprobation.)

"And upon the second point I fear not to express my disapprobation of any vote of thanks to Mr. Magee—a man generally known and acknowledged to stand a CONVICTED LIBELLER!!!"

At this moment, (says the newspaper report,) the shouting against Mr. Moylan became very great; and several Protestant gentlemen, who were near the Chairman, were seen to be withdrawing.

Order, however, was restored, with some difficulty; and Mr. Moylan was allowed to proceed.

"With respect to the third motion, viz., that of thanks to Counsellor O'Connell—no man respects his private worth more than I do—but if I grant him a vote of thanks, it will be approving his public conduct; therefore I cannot give my consent to any vote of thanks to him.

"As an amendment to Mr. Mac Donnell's motion, I therefore move the following, which I am about to read :—

"Resolved—That no spirit of conciliation has been; or ever shall be wanting on our part; and that we are ready to make every concession to our Protestant brethren, consistent with the safety, integrity, and essential discipline of our Church."

Mr. Eugene M'Sweeney, of Mary-street, seconded Mr Moylan's amendment.

Counsellor Dennis remonstrated, as a Protestant, against this proceeding of Mr. Moylan's in particular against the use of such epithets to such a person as that gentleman had applied to John Magee.

"Is he, for his virtuous consistency, to have his character profaned, and himself termed a convicted libeller!! . . . . . Have you never heard of juries being packed, and truth being made a libel? Oh, reflect! beware!—remember the times you live in, and th scenes you have lately passed through! . . . . . Feel as Irishmen *should* feel Lov in your hearts the hero who gloriously falls in a great public cause!" ' . . . .

A ter an eloquent address in this strain, he concluded with an exhortation to temper moderation &c., and the meeting was then addressed by—

COUNSELLOR O'CONNELL—Mr. Chairman and Gentlemen, offer myself to your notice this moment with feelings it is impossible to assume. I offer myself in support of two resolutions and most decidedly adverse to the third.

It is wrong of you to think of bestowing thanks to one o yourselves, who, in his exertion in common with yourselves, can do no more than merely his duty—to fight and struggle in a good cause. But besides all this, there is no man worthy of what is said in that resolution—no man alive could deserve the warmth of approbation so expressed ; and, therefore, I do entreat of you, as it entirely regards my person, to dismiss it from your notice as one unworthy of occupying your attention. (No, no, pass the resolution.)

But, gentlemen, it is objected to that enlightened prelate, Dr. Milner, that he at one time agreed to the veto, but that after he changed his opinion !

Oh! would to God that any man who finds himself in error would act thus nobly, and that, believing he might be wrong, would not go about misleading others, but, like the great and good divine, whom they charge with tergiversation, renounce their errors and permit the public mind to repose in peace.

Who are those men who charge tergiversation ? Why, they are persons who change hourly—such among them who have opinions to change; for the majority of them possess no opinion at all. Who are those independents, who have so lately started up amongst you ? or what is their title to the character of independent ? For my part, I declare I do not know in what their independence can exist, except it be that no person can depend on them. (Excessive laughter for a long time.)

But yet, these are the persons to come forward and charge upon an high-minded and deeply-respected divine, "tergiversation," because upon a point of vital and most essential importance, where his great mind was awakened to a sense of the threatening danger by the honest remonstrance of his virtuou' brethren, he calmly listens to the dictates of conscience— .. considers, and finding his error. openly, honestly, and man' ily avows it !

He did not allow his illumined mind to be obscured by the doctrines of this world. No selfish vanity, no worldly pride, prevented him from retracting his errors : he did so ; and like a man, whose kingdom was not of this world, as publicly as he had erred, were his sorrow and his regret. And, gentlemen, what is Doctor Milner after all but a man ? Can you expect more of him than you will allow to all other men ? It is the lot of human nature to err ; but it is only in the greatness of virtue to retract and feel regret. (Cheers.)

But look at the erudite politicians; it is really surprising how modest, meek, and humble those enlightened independents are ; the population of Ireland declare against *all* vetoism, under *all* and *every* shape and form, and these two youths came forward, the one to propose, the other to second a resolution, for what ? For *provisional* securities ! That is, you have declared against *vetoism ;* now under the other name of *provisional securities*, grant it ; and thus you become tergiversators ?

They come forward to give one proposition, which they turn into an adjective, and the other into a substantive, and which substantive cannot support the adjective ; and this is the doctrine and precious argument upon which you are called upon to defame the character and wound the feelings of one of the most learned and able men in England ! A prelate who is now opposed in England by a vile faction, more disgraceful, and possessing worse passions, than the infuriated anarchial faction which desolated and laid waste the happiness of society in France. The latter were a faction which have brought their country under a wicked military despotism that has ended in subverting the liberties and privileges of mankind. But the faction in England are still more wicked, because they are the determined enemies of everything virtuous, liberal, honest, and enlightened ! And this is the vile faction which would seek to bow his gray head in sorrow to the grave. They endeavoured to cast him down ; but Ireland met him in his fall, and upheld him. (Cheers.)

How glad I should be to know those people who are here disposed to act against reason and good sense ! How gladly would I labour to convince them of their error. But why should I

lose time? Who are they? What are they? Where are their
numbers? Is there another man in this immense meeting to
join these two youths? Oh, that they could count our numbers
this day? Will they call for a division? Oh, for tellers to
enumerate our majority? Oh, what an appearance those dissenters would exhibit! What! a minority of two or four to
countless thousands? And what do they dissent from? From
the very principle now laid down by the Board itself. Mr.
Roche just told us, the simple repeal was the defined intention
of the Board; nay, it is one of the resolutions which you have
just now carried; yet those dissenters talk of an *amendment of
the securities.* Mr. Roche is the identical gentleman who has seconded this motion of thanks introduced by Mr. Mac Donnell, to
Dr. Milner, yet, this young gentleman would tell you to reject it.
They talk of securities; some of the Board were satisfied with
the late bill, and voted against your bishop in Dublin; and upon
this it is, perhaps, that those gentlemen dare to talk of security:
but your Board have retracted from that conduct, and they have
found favour.

We will make no charges of tergiversation, nor will we blame
those unreflecting young gentlemen, if they now retract their
errors. But I will tell those people that are satisfied with the
late bill, that so far as being a bill of relief, it was anything else
than a charter for emancipation. Oh! how proud I am of the
unanimity I perceive upon this great point; it will be a delightful consolation to the already tortured feelings of the good old
prelate! He has broken no faith with you; there has been no
breach of contract; he has watched with a guardian's care over
our interests; he is too honest, too sincere, too virtuous to deceive Ireland; he possesses a combination of all the qualities,
and all the excellences which should compose the aged prelate,
and amongst all these great qualifications and virtues, there is
but one thing bad about him, he has for us, perhaps, too much
of the Englishman about him.

But, gentlemen, when I turn my thoughts on the other branch
of Mr. Moylan's speech, what are my feelings? Oh! for the
pensioned minions of the Castle! Oh! for the Attorney-General and the prosecutors of Catholics to stand up here to-day and
behold a Catholic rise up in a Catholic Assembly, and pronounce
JOHN MAGEE a convicted libeller!!! If you would reflect
upon the thousands of which you are daily deprived, to bestow
upon the wretched hireling prints of the day; if you could know
the sums lavished upon the dull and stupid *Patriot*—upon the

vile and proverbially profligate *Correspondent*, to abuse, revile. and condemn the people—to blazon forth a bigoted ministry— you would soon discover that the enlightened and patriotic writer of the *Dublin Evening Post*, which has the confidence of the people, and a circulation throughout the empire, would have been gladly and eagerly purchased up! How might then such a young gentleman, so educated, so enlightened, be received at the Castle! how he might have made his way among the minions of a court, instead of his being calumniated as a convicted libeller' Oh, for a packed jury in some trying case, where Mr. Moylan's feelings or interests were concerned, to make him know the effects of courtly influence!

If this Mr. Moylan had seen the masters of Orange lodges sitting upon the jury of *John Magee*, he could not long have hesitated to decide that John Magee would have been declared a convicted libeller. If Mr. Moylan had been placed under such circumstances, however innocent his conduct, he too would have been declared a convicted libeller. But of what was he convicted? That he truly described the character of the Duke of Richmond's administration. Is it not in all your recollections, that this great duke dined at the mayor's feast in this very city? —that he on that occasion refused to drink the toast proposed of "the glorious and immortal memory?"—and yet, is it not a fact, that this great duke did actually pardon Hall, the Orangeman, the murderer of the only son, and only support of a poor aged widow? Did this noble duke bring to punishment the murderers of the Catholics at Curruginsheega? No. And yet this noble duke, with the Attorney-General at his elbow, brings a prosecution bravely into a court of law, to defend the purity of his administration in Ireland; a jury of Orangemen are empannelled; they find truth is a libel; and they find that John Magee is the libeller.

Let this noble duke enjoy the fame he has reaped in this great exploit. I tell him, John Magee is happier in his mind, confined within the dungeon of a prison, than that lord duke is now in his palace, and that when the memory of that lord duke shall be forgotten in our land, or only recollected with disgust and horror, the name of Magee, the independent proprietor of the *Dublin Evening Post*, shall be hailed as the proud and stern advocate of a nation's rights, and the glorious victim of persecution and proscription. To be sure he is now in Kilmainham prison; but he feels no pain for himself; he only feels for his country— for you my Catholic countrymen; but yes, he will feel pain when he hears that at a meeting of the Catholics at Cork, a Catholic Irishman rose up and called him a convicted libeller!

But I call on this young man, not to discredit his name and his family by this transaction; I call upon him to retract; it is the only means left him.

[Mr. Moylan here said he would not, and one person said he could not, as he was pledged to persevere in it.]

Well then, there is no way left but to divide upon it; but how can it be accomplished? Well, is it not provoking that we cannot see what majority they will have against a vote of thanks to John Magee? There he is in Kilmainham, in the bloom of youth, with a head clear and intelligent, his genius bright and brilliant, his heart virtuous and incorruptible. Yes, my countrymen, his head is as clear as his heart is honest; he is a true Irishman, and I pride myself in calling him my friend. He is ardently, really, honestly attached to his country; he has cause to be so; he is deeply interested in her peace, tranquillity and glory. He would call out to her aid, and to the aid of the state, an unbought army of Irishmen, and for these virtues he is sentenced to linger out two years in a dungeon!

When it will be imparted to Mr. Magee that this vote of thanks passed this meeting, his honest heart will rejoice; but what will be his pleasure when he is informed, that if there were an objection he will see that it only called out the greater spirit in the people, he will see that it gave more gravity, more weight, more consequence to the measure. (Cheering.)

My good friends, guard yourselves against division; be watchful of those that seek to divide you; these divisions have put down Ireland—a continuance of them will destroy the finest and fairest country in the world. We have no intense heat in summer to dry up the earth; we have no chilling colds in winter to freeze us; we are the most light-hearted people upon any shore; for seven hundred years our spirit has continued unsubdued. We were never beaten in any battle; on one occasion we submitted to an agreement, a compact, and that compact was broken not by us, but by those who pledged themselves solemnly to its fulfilment. Why, then, should we be abused? Why insulted? Why doubted in our honour, in our integrity? At all events, why quarrel among ourselves? (Cheers.)

If it were not for these cursed divisions, Ireland would be the paradise of the world. (Cheers.)

With respect to the third motion before you, I shall be short, particularly as it regards myself. When I direct my attention to the great cause I am engaged in, I could not but anticipate the assaults which would be made against me: yet, I set out with a fixed determination, that though I may be deprived of abilities to serve, yet, I knew I had a heart to feel, and thus emboldened, I trusted more to the excellence of our good cause, than the talent of the advocate; and if I have in any degree been conducive to the great interests of Catholic Ireland, I rejoice; nor shall the slanders, or the vile malignities of my enemies deter me.

I WILL GO ON, *and the more I am maligned, the more will I be pleased, and hope for the prospect of success, nor will I ever doubt myself, until I shall hear those wretched hirelings of corruption teem forth odious praise to me!* Then doubt me, but not till *then.*

Externally and internally I will fight the enemies of us all; they are sometimes to be found nearer to us than we can suspect, and they are the more dangerous for that. I have continued to labour, and will continue so to do. But, adopt not this exaggerated praise offered to me here to-day; it is not possible I could, or any man could be deserving of it. I give up this point to Mr. Moylan; I make Mr. Moylan a present of his motion, and let him give us the rest. (Loud and persevering cries of no, no! we will not, we will not!)

Then, beforehand, I thank you, sincerely and honestly I thank you; it encourages, it cheers me on; I here want language to express my feelings; *I will stand by you while I live;* I WILL NEVER FORSAKE POOR IRELAND.

When the enthusiasm of the auditory, after the foregoing speech, subsided enough to give him a hearing, Mr. James Roche again came forward and seconded Mr. O'Connell's protest against Moylan's amendment.

After some further speaking, Mr. Moylan's amendment to Mr. Mac Donnell's three resolutions was put, with the following result, according to the calculations of the newspapers:—

For the amendment
For the votes of thanks to the Right Rev. Dr Milner John
Magee, and Daniel O'Connell, Esqrs.   10 000

MEETING OF THE CORK CATHOLIC BOARD.

September 3rd, 1813.

THE report of the above meeting, which is from the *Cork Mercantile Chronicle,* states that a mistake having delayed the attendance of the press, they found Mr. O'Connell speaking.

He proceeded to say that in whatever point of view he con-

sidered the protest, signed by several of the Roman Catholics o.
the county and city, the resignation of several members of the
Board, and the consequent division between them and the body
at large, he would say it was to him a source of regret, because
he was well assured, and well convinced, that unanimity was
strength, and division weakness.

Ireland would never have fallen from the pinnacle of grandeur
upon which she stood as a nation, but for the division of her
children ; and it was often said—he hoped, not truly—that if
any Irishman were put to the torture, another would be found
to turn the wheel.   He did not, even upon reviewing these divisions and distractions, and the steps taken by the protestors, yet
give up the idea of beholding a spirit of conciliation pervade the
Catholics of the county and city of Cork ; he sincerely hoped
they would see the necessity of union and harmony, and that
every man would discharge his duty by his country ; and if the
seceders obstinately refused to return to their post, he knew the
gentlemen composing the present Board, having the confidence
and support of the people, would transact the affairs of the great
body of the Catholics, and discharge the great trust reposed in
them, with honour, dignity, and integrity ; and the public would
not ultimately have to regret either the secession of supposed
friends or real enemies.

Amongst the signatures to the requisition of the Board, and
to those of the protest he was alluding to, he saw those of several
of the most respectable and enlightened men of the county and
city ; and why those characters have seceded from the general
wish was yet to be ascertained.

Was it because they objected to the 13th resolution, passed at
the aggregate meeting ?   No, it could not be ; because this resolution, which was one of thanks to Doctor Milner, was seconded
by James Roche, one of the most independent members of the
late Board.

Was it, then, on account of the 14th resolution, which was
one of thanks to Mr. John Magee, the independent proprietor of
the *Dublin Evening Post*, and offering himself the consolation of
the public sympathy ?   No ! for this resolution met the support
of several members of the Board.   They could not refuse their
sympathy to the sufferings of a man who had, for a series of
years, devoted his talents and his fortune in fighting their battles, and supporting their right to freedom—a man who had embarked his fame on the success of their cause, and for which he
ultimately brought upon himself the vengeance of the govern

ment. The smallest opposition to such a resolution from one of that body would afford him more real pain than the imprisonment of two years, to which he has been consigned.

Was it, then, in consequence of the 15th resolution, adopted at Monday's meeting? He could not conceive it was. That resolution was seconded by Mr. T. Denehy, one of the Board, and supported by several other members of that body. This vote was one of compliment to himself. He considered that indeed it should be flattering that his poor exertions in the cause of his country met the approbation of the meeting; but much as he valued that sentiment, he would freely forego the pleasure it afforded him, if it tended in the smallest degree to create any division or disunion among the Catholic body.

For himself, he wished for freedom much; for his children, he wished for it more; but he sought and wished for that blessing much more for his enslaved and afflicted country. For this grand object he fought unceasingly and unremittingly, and encountered obstacles and difficulties that could, most probably, have dismayed a man of a less ardent or sanguine mind. (Great cheering.)

He would ask, was it to the 16th resolution the Board and protestors so strongly objected? This certainly was one of the reasons that induced the resignation of the Board; and he would not have presumed to say so, but that it was publicly avowed by the majority of that body. They declared they would not act with Counsellor Mac Donnell. He, as well as the other members of the Board, was appointed by the only legitimate authority—that is, by the voice of the people, at the aggregate meeting; and they had no right to question that appointment; neither had they the power to resign that authority with which they were invested, until they did so to the people at the next aggregate assembly. Therefore there was no legal resignation of the Board; they were still in existence as members of that body; and he still entertained the fond hope that they would surrender any irritated, disappointed, paltry feeling, at the shrine of conciliation, and as men of honour, give credit to the public voice, and return to the post they would appear to have deserted.

He would like to meet the members among the protestors who were security-men, and those who considered themselves *not* security-men, and who might have signed that document from other causes, in fair reasoning and argument. He would wish to give any man credit for the purity and honesty of his motives and as a diversity of opinion existed among them, it was perfectly natural, among men exercising their own free judgments upon great national and political questions, in which all were equally interested ; while he would pay his tribute of respect to their opinions, even though erroneous, he would endeavour to correct, by calm discussion and plain truths, the fallacy of their judgments and opinions.

He hoped there was some person present that would convey to those security-men the reasons why those securities cannot be complied with ; because it would be entrusting to the hands of men who were no judges of their religion—either of its tenets or discipline—and who could feel no anxiety in its support or preservation, but the contrary, the management of its affairs, and the appointment of its hierarchy ; and even though we were disposed to join the Orangemen in giving up our religion into such hands, we would not do so without the previous consent of the Pope. This the Bishops have unanimously declared ; and it is out of the nature of things that the Pope could be consulted at present—and when he could, it was impossible to tell.

Unfortunately the Pope is under the power of Bonaparte. It is the interest of that military despot that the divisions and animosities existing in the empire should be kept alive and continued. He is proud that the Roman Catholic millions of this country should be kept in slavery, knowing that the power of England is thereby weakened ; and though we did offer the securities required, we cannot, from Bonaparte's conduct hitherto, suppose him the dupe of such extreme absurdity and folly as to suffer any communication with the Pope which would tend to heal the divisions amongst the people of the empire.

It was absurd to think of the idea ; and it was equally absurd to press those securities (which could not be given, though we were satisfied to do so) as a bar to the freedom of a brave, loyal, and suffering people.

There are (said Mr. O'Connell) fourteen Roman Catholic dioceses at present vacant in this country ; and it is impossible to appoint bishops to them, because there can be no communication had with the Pope. His approbation is absolutely necessary ; and will it be contended that those bishoprics would be continued thus vacant, if the Pope's approbation in the appointment could be dispensed with ? It is a part of the discipline of the Catholic Church that cannot be given up ; and however those security-men may pant for freedom, the great body of the Catholics would not accept it in barter for their religion.

"But," say those who clamour for those securities, " if the present Pope died, Bonaparte would undoubtedly raise to the

Papal chair his uncle, Cardinal Fesch." Be it so. He was willing to meet them upon every fair ground. They say, if Cardinal Fesch was the Pope, he would be the creature of Bonaparte, and subject to his control; and having the nomination of the Catholic Bishops of Ireland, he would only appoint such men to that dignity as would be disaffected to the British government, and who would best suit the views of Bonaparte.

Cardinal Fesch! who is *in disgrace* with his nephew, and *in exile, because he opposed,* and would not *sanction* his *marriage* with his *present wife!*

Was the man who thus opposed Bonaparte, and refused to lend himself to his ambitious or capricious views, likely to degrade and disgrace the Papal chair, by submitting to his will in the appointment of bishops for this country? In time of war, he could not be at all consulted for that purpose; and if peace were brought about previous to Catholic emancipation, who would expect the attainment of that measure from the British ministry?

There were *thirty-four* bishoprics vacant in France at present, because, *that same Cardinal Fesch would not submit that his nephew should have the least control in their appointment.* He would not suffer that one of them should be filled by any of his creatures; and if this be the principle by which the cardinal is governed in the country where Bonaparte rules with despotic sway, is it to be supposed that when this country shall be at peace with France, he will act upon a different principle in the appointment of bishops for this country, in which Bonaparte can have then no interest whatever?

Yet the British ministry demand those securities which were attached to the bill almost passed in the house of parliament—and these prepared by men who did not understand our religion; yet they undertook to regulate that which they knew nothing about, without consulting one Roman Catholic prelate, clergyman, or layman. And this was called, in this city, a charter of Emancipation!!

We cannot surrender our religion into the hands of such men. If we were disposed, we could not do so. We will give them security, however. We will share with them our prosperity and our blood; and if they want a precedent for enacting a charter of Emancipation, and for their redeeming their brethren and country from slavery and bondage, we will give them the precedent of the Diet of Hungary, who were exclusively Roman Catholic. That independent body, in 1791, granted, without veto or securities, the privileges of the state to Protestants, and every other religionists, and embraced their countrymen as brethren. This passed only twenty years ago, and it was a noble example set to other nations. Let the British act towards Irishmen with the same spirit of freedom and conciliation, and they would be found to live in the hearts of a proud, brave, and enthusiastic nation.

It was remarkable that amidst all the agitation of the Catholic question throughout Ireland—and he felt pride in stating it—no spirit of disaffection was to be traced amongst its people; that though they called aloud for Emancipation, they pursued their legitimate object loyally and constitutionally. At the different assizes throughout the country for the last circuit, not an individual was charged with being disaffected to the government. No; not a single person was even tried upon the Whiteboy Act, and this argued the quiet and undisturbed state of the country; and this fact he would throw in the face of the hirelings who would attempt to charge the agitators of the Catholic question with disaffection. The people of the country caught at the sympathy offered them by their agitators, and in this sympathy was peace and harmony preserved.

He would again revert to the protestors. He could not well divine their meaning; and amongst the rest, there was one protestor who stood alone—he meant, Mr. John Boyle. Neither could he well tell what was intended by his protest. All he would say of him was, that he considered him a man endowed with talent; and if he had a little ballast with the sail, he thought he would prove a respectable and useful Irishman.

If those protestors succeeded to the utmost, they might form a body of one, or two, or three hundred persons—they were certainly, in point of prosperity, men of consequence and respectability, but in point of numbers, insignificant indeed; if they continue their desertion of the popular feeling, they will be opposed to five millions of their fellow-slaves—and they will be spoken of through Ireland with contempt—they will appear as if fighting against their country. At one period, Lord Fingal, and several of the most respectable persons seceded from the general and popular feeling, and in a very short time they found they had a sacred duty to perform, and they returned.

He did hope that the seceders in Cork would be found to act with the like good sense—that they would return; the present members of the Board invited them to join in the sacred cause in which all were alike interested, and have pointed out the baneful effects of disunion upon the country, at other periods of her history.

If, however, they persevered in the desertion, he said he was convinced that the Board would hereafter be governed by th spirit of harmony towards all their brethren, that was breathed throughout the resolutions then passed; that they would watch the interests of their cause, aided by the voice of the people by whom they were chosen, with firmness and temper, and that the protestors would be found only as flies on the wheel in its motion.

Mr. O'Connell then read the first, second, third, fourth, fifth, and sixth resolutions, which were put by the chair and carried unanimously.

On the sixth being put, Mr. O'Connell said he hoped he would be excused saying a few words. It was not necessary to arouse the people of Cork to a sense of the obligations they owed, in unison with every Irishman, to the illustrious family of the Hutchinsons; the last elections called their particular attention to the registry of freeholders, and they have acted upon it; the resolutions then read would still operate as a further stimulud upon them for exertion. If the late Board had made or adopted proper arrangements previous to the election, and if a spirit of apathy had not seized them, this great and commercial city would not be represented by Dumley Longfield—nor robbed, as it was now, of its true and honest representative, the patriotic Christopher Hely Hutchinson. (Cheers.)

Mr. T. S. Coppinger and Counsellor Mac Donnell spoke strongly on the subject of Irish Manufacture; and the latter suggested that the preference of everything Irish to English should be urged on those parents who sent their sons to *England for education*.

Counsellor O'Connell thought that would be doing much; the sure way of doing business was to do a little at a time.

He did condemn, as much as his learned friend, the absurd practice of sending children to be educated in England. Since the Union he knew, out of fifteen young gentlemen who had got an English education, one only to be a man of talent; seven broke their fortunes, and others were engaged in every species of dissipation and folly. So much for the advantage of an English education. He would not have this topic form part of the resolution, as in a very short time he was convinced the evil must remedy itself.

There was another branch of trade that deserved the notice and encouragement of the Board—he meant the cotton trade. At one period it flourished, and it was now as much depressed as any other branch of trade. The English sent over some cords and velveteens, and undersold the Irish manufacturer; the fact was, that though the Irish goods were sold at a higher price, it

was by no means dearer than the English.   It was found at the
end, to be more lasting, and give much more wear than the
other, yet the people were led away by the appearance of the
English article and the smaller price, and therefore gave it the
preference ; thus this branch of trade was completely ruined.

It only required a proper spirit amongst the people to put an
end to this monopoly; let them be taught what was of real advantage to their country, and it must flourish.   It was the finest
country under heaven—indented with the finest harbours, and
inhabited by the bravest men in the world—and it only required
the cordial co-operation of all her sons to make it the happiest
country in the globe.   (Cheers.)

He concluded by reminding the Board, that the day-notes
would inform them who it was that imported goods from England.

This was one of the many occasions in Mr. O'Connell's life, when he laboured in the good
cause of the deserving, hard-working, and most skilful artizans of Ireland.   We shall have,
unfortunately, to note the failure of several such efforts—as all such *must* fail, till the
vitality of industry be restored with the money and rich consumers of the country, by the
repeal of the emaciating Act of Union

LIEUTENANT O'CONNELL.

As we have been speaking of relatives of Mr. O'Connell, the following brief notice of one
towards whom he cherished a strong affection, will find an appropriate place here, from
the *Dublin Evening Post* of Saturday, September 25, 1813 :—

"The successful storming of St. Sebastian (31st August), from the nature of the obstacles
opposed by a scientific enemy, confessedly ranks first, in point of military achievement on
the part of the allies.   Many of our countrymen distinguished themselves most conspicu-
ously upon that memorable occasion.   The relatives of the fallen heroes, though under the
influence of national or Spartan pride, must notwithstanding feel heart-rending grief, 'not
loud but deep,' for the irreparable loss sustained in their domestic society.

"In no instance, perhaps, will this adversity be more poignantly felt than in the family
of Lieutenant John O'Connell, of the 43rd Regiment, a near relative of the Counsellor of
that name, a brave and promising youth, whose talents as a soldier would indubitably, one
day or other, do honour to his country, when those disabilities under which the greater
part of his Majesty's Irish subjects labour should have been removed.

"He volunteered on the forlorn hope at the ever-memorable siege of Badajoz, where he
was severely wounded ; and on the attack on St. Sebastian. he sought a post of danger
where he gloriously fell in the arms of victory.

"The meritorious death of this young officer leads the writer of this to take notice of a
circumstance well worthy of remark in the Irish character—that although a difference of
political principles at home may prevail for a time, yet when their country demands their
aid, every sentiment is abandoned but those of loyalty and union.   Party is regarded as
subordinate, or as the 'reverie of an idle dream ;' all prejudice is abandoned, and nothing
appears but a desire to defend the king, the country, and the constitution—thus refuting
the base calumnies of some, who would say that a difference of religious opinions consti-

turus a difference of loyalty; and who would cloud the imagination of the young soldier with mistaken ideas, tending only to mislead his opinions, and throw an insuperable barrier in the path of his military career."

Mr. O'Connell's affection for this gallant young man, which had been manifested in more than words—having extended to the equipping and furnishing him with all necessary matters, when joining the army—was most fervidly and devotedly reciprocated by its object.

What a condition was that of the Irish Catholic soldier at the time in question! He might fight; nay, he *did* fight, bleed, die for England—in England's wars; and the chains of his fellow-Catholics, and of his country, were all the more firmly rivetted by his sacrifices!

During the progress of the autumn, Catholic meetings were held in various parts of Ireland besides those already noticed; and resolutions similar in substance to what had been passed elsewhere, were universally adopted.

Mr. O'Connell's conduct, therefore, in respect of the Veto question, at the trial of Magee, and all other occasions that he had come before the public, was stamped with the seal of general approbation and concurrence.

Late in October he returned to Dublin, in time to attend the second meeting of the Catholic Board, after its re-assembling for the winter "*campaign.*'

On Saturday, October 20, 1813, Mr. O'Connell proposed a resolution for general adoption by the Catholics of Ireland, declaring against the introduction of any measure into Parliament, affecting in any way Catholic discipline, without previous examination and approval of it by the Catholic prelates.

His object was to endeavour to smoothen the way to the mistaken "*security*"-men to return to Catholic agitation; and so to effect a restoration of entire harmony in the Catholic body. But a violent opposition having arisen to the resolution, on the ground that it might be interpreted as an indirect approval of some form of "securities," Mr. O'Connell, though unconvinced of its having any such tendency, withdrew it, and so had to abandon for a season the hope of restoring unanimity to the popular councils.

THE KILKENNY RESOLUTIONS.

TRIAL OF JOHN MAGEE.

On the 19th of November, the unfortunate John Magee was brought up in custody to plead at the King's Bench to an indictment for publishing the resolutions of the Kilkenny Catholics, in which, while complimenting him and his counsel, they assailed the Duke of Richmond.

The Attorney-General strongly opposed Mr. O'Connell's motion to the court, that Mr. Magee, who had entered his plea of "not guilty," should be allowed to "traverse in prox," in the usual way.

Mr. Justice Day ineffectually suggested to the Attorney-General the fitness of acceding, if for no other reason than the advanced state of the term, and pressure of business.

Attorney-General (Saurin)—My lord, I certainly will not consent. If counsel for the traverser can show, that in point of law he has the right, I shall bow with submission; but if not, I consider it most material, as well to the public justice of this country as to the administration of the law, that the trial be proceeded on as speedily as possible.

MR. O'CONNELL—It is clearly the right of the subject, in cases of misdemeanour, to traverse *in prox;* and Mr. Justice Day will

please to recollect that at the last summer assizes of the county
of Monaghan, where he presided as judge, several persons who
had been indicted for a riot and assault, availed themselves of
the right we now contend for, and had their trials postponed till
the next assizes.

The case of "the King v. M. O'Connor," indicted for a misdemeanour, before the Chief Baron, was another recent instance
where the practice was recognised and adopted.

It is laid down in the 4th vol. of "Blackstone's Commen-
taries," that it is usual to try all felons immediately, or soon after
their arraignment ; but it is not customary, nor agreeable to the
general course of proceedings—unless by consent, or where the
defendant is actually in gaol—to try persons indicted for smaller
misdemeanours at the same court in which they have pleaded not
guilty, or traversed the indictment.

Mr. Justice Blackstone does not say that it *may* not be done
—but he declares that it was not customary nor agreeable to the
course of legal proceedings.   It is for the counsel for the crown
to show that there exists a legal distinction in the practice between the term and the assizes—both being, in contemplation of
law, considered only as one day.

Mr. Perrin, in support, cited the "great Anglesea case," in which one of the witnesses
having been indicted for perjury, Baron Mountenay held that though justice required an
immediate trial, yet the traverser, being indicted for a misdemeanour, had a *right* to post
pone

Mr. O'Connell—It would be impossible for his client to be prepared.   Mr. Townshend
had said the Court might issue its *precipe*, and order a jury to be returned in five minutes·

Mr. Townshend begged the learned gentleman's pardon—*he said no such thing*.   What he
had said was, that the Court might issue its *precipe*, and direct a jury to "be returned
instanter !"

Mr. O'Connell would not argue the point of distinction between the great space of time
of *instanter* and *five minutes*; but he would contend that the crime of *wilful and corrupt
perjury* was more atrocious than that of a supposed libel for publishing resolutions, which
he presumed the traverser had never seen until they were in print.

Mr. Justice Day and Mr. Justice Osborne considered that the practice applied only to
assizes or quarter sessions ; and the Attorney-General then pressed that Wednesday, the
24th of the month, should be fixed.

Mr. O'Connell—There are no less than eleven counts contained in the indictment—eleven
distinct offences charged in it.   The transaction arising in Kilkenny, at a considerable distance from town, it will be quite impossible for Mr. Magee to be prepared on so short a
notice.

Remonstrance, however, was useless—the Attorney-General persisting in his appointment.

Mr. Magee's appearance the day on which the foregoing proceedings took place, was
much remarked upon.   His confinement had evidently impaired his health; and might
have induced some feeling of mercy in the breast even of an ordinarily hard-hearted man.
But they were tigers that managed Irish affairs then, and nothing but hunting their vic
tims down to the death could allay their savage appetites.

We postpone Catholic meetings, proceedings, &c., to follow out the history of the hunt.

On Wednesday, the 24th November, the traverser was duly brought up again, for the purpose of taking his trial for the alleged libel on the Duke of Richmond, in the Kilkenny resolutions of the 4th of August; *and also*

"To hear the judgment of the Court on the motion made to set aside the verdict in the former prosecution:"

The latter scent was first harked upon; and the leading blood-hound, the Chief Justice, delivered, at considerable length, the opinion of the Court—that the verdict ought to stand; and ordered the traverser (who had been in Kilmainham since the preceding term) to be brought up on the next Saturday, to receive sentence.

A conversation then occurred as to affidavits in mitigation, on the one side, and aggravation on the other, of the impending sentence; and the Attorney-General,

"Still cheering on the prey,"

strongly urged that the very next day should be fixed for bringing his victim up.

Some glimmerings of humanity, or more likely of shame, awoke in the Chief Justice's breast, at the earnest appeal of Mr. O'Connell, against the unfairness of not allowing some little time to the prisoner to answer the affidavit of the prosecution; and the *great* indulgence was conceded of *two days* for that purpose.

Mr. O'Connell then addressed himself to the argument respecting the traverser's right to *traverse in prox* in the matter of the indictment for the Kilkenny resolutions.

The court of King's Bench, he said, had, from the earliest period recognised the practice as the right of the subject—a right never violated but once, during the reign of James II.; and restored again early in the reign of his successor, William III. The instance he alluded to was the celebrated case of the seven bishops.

The Chief Justice interposed, that if the Court had decided the question the previous day, it ought not now to be re-opened.

Mr. Justice Osborne set him right as to the fact of its not having been decided and said the counsel had then seemed unprepared, and that the motion was fully open to further discussion.

Mr. O'Connell in continuation:—

In Chief Baron Gilbert's "History of the Common Pleas," chap. 4, p. 143, your lordships will find it thus laid down.

This was plainly the ancient practice; because there was no continuance from the appearance day to the time of declaring; there being no precedent of *libertas narrandi;* therefore the declaration must be of the same term. But in the King's Bench, when a defendant comes in on a criminal process, which is supposed to issue on a complaint to, and by examination of, the Chief Justice, the defendant is not discharged till the second term after his appearance; for in the first term, all parties concerned might possibly not have notice.

When a man comes in on criminal process, he had liberty to *traverse in prox* (it is strange said Mr. O'Connell, here pausing in his reading—it is strange how Lord Chief Baron Gilbert could have used this phrase, which the Attorney-General lately stig-matised as so *vulgar!)* on all bailable offences, because he might not be prepared for trial with his witnesses; but it was otherwise in capital cases, because there was oath of the crime, &c., &c.

He (Mr. O'Connell) admitted that the case of the seven bishops was contrary to these principles; but even then one of the judges, Mr. Justice Powel, differed with the rest of the court and preserved his integrity during that infamous and depraved reign, when every case between the king and the subject was decided by the other three judges against the liberty of the subject.

There was another case, in 2nd Salkeld, page 515, to which he would call their lordships' attention:—"King's Bench, Michaelmas Term, 1st of William and Mary.—If a man be bound by recognizance to appear on the first day of term, and is charged on his appearance with an information, in case the information be laid in Middlesex, the party has time to plead during all that term, so that it cannot come to trial in the term; but in case it be laid in any *other county,* the party shall have time to plead till the next term; for he is as much concerned to defend himself in those cases as in any civil action; and since the law allows him counsel, the law likewise allows him time to consult with them: *for not to allow the means of defence,* is to take away the *subject's defence.* Otherwise it is in *capital* cases; but note —in these cases there are no counsel, &c., &c. (Decided *per curiam,* contrary to the case of the seven bishops.)

Mr. O'Connell then cited the 37th Geo. III. c. 30, to the same point; and concluded by observing that both the common and the statute law "had recognized the right of the subject, *in vulgar epithets*—according to the Attorney-General—to *traverse in prox.*"

The Attorney-General replied, citing cases in support of his position.

He failed, however, even with that court; and the trial was ordered to stand over to Monday, the 31st day of January, 1814.

But the victim was not to escape. The other matter came on at the appointed time. The following is a brief account:—

The Attorney-General commenced with referring in strong terms to the whole course of the defence of Mr. Magee, since the beginning of the prosecutions—or rather *persecutions* —most particularly Mr. O'Connell's speeches in defence, which he characterised in the most violent terms. He urged in aggravation of sentence Mr. Magee's publication of the speech in question, and declaration of approval of it.

The Attorney General did his utmost also to enlist the personal feelings of the Chief Justice, by drawing his attention to Mr. O'Connell's scarcely-indirect charges against him on the occasion mentioned. The following was Mr. O'Connell's reply:—

COURT OF KING'S BENCH.

SATURDAY, 27TH NOV., 1813.

The Attorney-General's Motion in Aggravation of Sentence on Mr. Magee, for Publishing a Report of the Trial of THE KING *at the Prosecution of* HIS GRACE THE DUKE OF RICHMOND *against* JOHN MAGEE, *Proprietor of the " Dublin Evening Post."*

Mr. O'CONNELL.—I am sure, my lords, that every gentleman present will sympathise in the emotions I now experience. am sure no gentleman can avoid feeling the deepest interest in a situation in which it is extremely difficult to check the strongest resentment, but quite impossible to give that resentment utterance in the severity of language suited to its cause and provocation. Yet, even here, do I yield in nothing to the Attorney-General. I deny, in the strongest terms, his unfounded and absurd claim to superiority. I am his equal, at least, in birth—his equal in fortune—his equal, certainly, in education ; and as to talent, I should not add that, but there is little vanity in claiming equality. And thus meeting him on the firm footing of undoubted equality. I do rejoice, my lords—I do most sincerely rejoice—that the Attorney-General has prudently treasured up his resentment since July last, and ventured to address me in this court in the unhandsome language he has used ; because my profound respect for this temple of the law enables me her to overcome the infirmity of my nature, and to listen with patience to an attack which, had it been made elsewhere, would have met merited CHASTISEMENT.

Justice Daly—Eh! What is that you say?

Justice Osborne, with much apparent emotion—I at once declare, I will not sit here to listen to such a speech as I have seen reported. Take care of what you say, sir.

Mr. O'Connell—My lord, what I say is, that I am delighted at the prudence of the Attorney-General, in having made that foul assault upon me here, and not elsewhere, because my profound respect for the bench overcomes now those feelings which, elsewhere, would lead me to do what I should regret—to break the peace in chastising him.

Justice Daly—*Chastising!* The Attorney-General! If a criminal information were applied for on that word, we should be bound to grant it.

Mr. O'Connell—I meant, my lords, that elsewhere thus assailed, I should be carried away by my feelings to do that which I should regret—to go beyond the law—to inflict corporal punishment for that offence, which I am here ready, out of consideration for the Court, to pardon.

Justice Osborne—I will take the opinion of the Court whether you shall not be committed.

Chief Justice—If you pursue that line of language, we must call upon some other of the counsel at the same side to proceed.

Justice Day—Now, Mr. O'Connell, do not you perceive that, while you talk of suppressing those feelings, you are actually indulging them? The Attorney-General could not mean you offence in the line of argument he pursued to enhance the punishment, in every way of your client. It is unnecessary for you to throw off, or to repel, aspersions that are not made on you.

Mr. O'Connell—My lord, I thank you—I sincerely thank you. It relieves my mind from a load of imputation when I hear such high authority as that of your lordship kindly declaring that it did not apply to me. And yet, my lord, what did the Attorney-General mean when he called a question a senseless and shameless question? What did he mean when he—he, my lord—talked of low and vulgar mind? What did he mean when he imputed to the advocate participation in the crime of the client? This he distinctly charged me with. All I require from the Court is the same liberty to reply with which the Attorney-General has been indulged in attack. All I ask is, to be suffered to answer and repel the calumnies with which I have been assailed.

Justice Daly—You shall have the same liberty that he had; but the Court did not understand him to have made any personal attack upon you.

Justice Osborne—We did not understand that the Attorney-General meant you, when he talked of a participator in the crime of your client.

Attorney-General—I did not, my lords I certainly did not mean the gentleman. To state that I did would be to misrepresent my meaning, which had nothing to do with him.

Mr. O'Connell—Well, my lords, be it so ; I rejoice, however, that this charge is thus publicly disavowed, and disavowed in the presence of those who heard his words originally, and who have heard me repel any attack made upon me. I rejoice to find that your lordships have interposed your opinion that no personal attack has been made upon me, and thus have rendered unnecessary any further comment on what had flowed from the Attorney-General. I am, therefore, enabled at once to go into the discussion of the merits of my client's case.

And now let me first solemnly and seriously protest against the manner in which the Attorney-General seeks to aggravate the punishment. It is by introducing into the affidavit of the attorney for the prosecution, passages from the speech of counsel at the trial. These, perhaps, are times in which it may be desired by him, as it certainly is safe for him, to make bad precedents. But against this precedent I enter my earnest, my honest, my independent protest. My protest may, for the present, be disregarded; but it will accompany the precedent in future times, and if not destroy, perhaps mitigate, its evil effects. I therefore do protest against it, on behalf of the bar, and on behalf of the public.

What ! is the Bar of Ireland to be thus degraded, that it shall be permitted to the inferior branches of the profession, to every attorney in the hall, to drag into affidavits the names of counsel, and their discourses for their clients? If it be permitted against a defendant in a criminal case, it must be equally, or rather more liberally, allowed to civil suits. There will, in future, be no motion for a new trial without introducing the name of counsel, and his exertions for his client, and perhaps his politics—perchance his religion! We shall be subject to a commentary upon the Oath of Attorneys. The debate on motions will not be what the pleadings state, or what the witnesses swore, or what law was laid down by the judge; but the discussion will turn upon the speech of the counsel, what it was he said, what he thought. A meaning will be affixed, by an attorney's swearing, upon every sentence of the counsel, and he shall not dare to describe crime or to portray criminality, lest the general description of offence may be transmuted by the oath of an attorney into particular and powerful individuals; and whilst he ought to have his mind at complete liberty to look for all the topics to serve the cause of his clients, and to confute the arguments of his adversary, he will in future be fettered and encumbered by the dread of exposing himself to the imputations of the adverse attorney, and the compliments of the bench. I do not think any gentleman ought to condescend to advocate a cause under such circumstances, or that he could continue high-minded and worthy of his rank in society, if he were to submit to such degradation.

Against this practice now, for the first time, attempted to be introduced—against the first but mighty stride to lessen the dignity of an honourable profession, I proclaim my distinct, unequivocal, and solemn dissent. But the privileges of the bar, however interesting to a numerous and respectable class of men, sink into insignificance when contrasted with the rights of the public. The public have a right to the free, unbiassed, and unintimidated exertions of the profession. If the bar be controlled—if the bar be subjugated—if the profane hand of the Attorney-General may drag the barrister from the high station of responsibility in which he is at present placed, and call for censure on the client for the conduct of the barrister, then indeed will it be quite safe for power to oppress and to plunder the inhabitants of the land; in vain shall the subject look for a manly advocate, if he is to be exposed to the insolent mockery of a trial of himself in the shape of an attack upon his client. How are the powerful to be resisted? How are the great to be opposed when they menace injustice? Certainly not by the advocate who fears that whilst he endeavours to serve his client he shall injure himself; certainly not by the barrister who has reason to apprehend that his language, being distorted in an attorney's affidavit, will expose him to censure from those to whom he cannot reply.

It is the first interest of the public that the bar shall be left

free. No inconvenience can result from this freedom, because
it is always subject to the discretion of the judge who presides
at the trial. He has it in his power to stop any proceeding inconsistent with propriety · but if he does not interfere at the
trial when the advocate could defend himself and assert his
right, what authority has been found to warrant an appeal to a
future court, in order to punish that which ought not to have
been prevented? In short, the public are deeply interested in
our independence; their properties, their lives, their honours,
are entrusted to us, and if we, in whom such a guardianship is
confided, be degraded, how can we afford protection to others?
Lessened in our own esteem, habituated to insult, we shall dwindle in talent as in character; and, if the talent may remain, it
will be simply useless to the oppressed, greatly serviceable to
the oppressor. For the public, therefore, who may easily be enslaved, if the bar be debased, I again enter my solemn protest
against this bad precedent.

For myself, I have scarce a word to say; talents I do not
possess, but I never will yield the freedom of thought and of
language —I never will barter or abandon the independence of
the profession. It may injure me; I know it will injure me,
and I care not; but as long as I belong to the Irish bar, I will
be found open, decided, manly, independent. Unawed by the
threats or frowns of power, holding in sovereign contempt the vile
solicitations of venality, and determined to do my duty in despite of every risk, personal and public—the enemy of every oppression and fraud—the unalterable friend to freedom. I have
a fault—I know it well—in the eyes of the Attorney-General.
The spirit that invented the inquisition exists in human nature;
that there was an inquisition proves the existence in nature of
an inquisitorial spirit. Nature is not calumniated when she is
charged with all the atrocity of bigotry in design and action;
and towards me that design has an object that is easily understood. To check the Popish advocate may, in the eyes of the
Attorney-General, be a work equally pious and prudent; but
the proudest feelings of contempt may defeat his intention and
place me above the reach of malevolence.

From myself and from this strange precedent, I come to the
case of my client. It is my duty to show your lordship that
the matters stated for aggravation ought not to affect my client.
It would be unjust—it would be cruel—it would be atrocious to
punish him by reason of the controversy into which I have been
driven; that, I am sure, the court ought not, and therefore will

not do. Neither can you punish him for publishing his trial. It is admitted that his report is a true report of the trial; the truth of the report is not even controverted; and having this fact admitted, that he has given a true report, the law is clear; it is clear no indictment or information, nor any criminal process can be maintained against a person who publishes a true report of our proceedings in our courts, nor does any civil action lie for such report.

It is laid down in 2 Hawk. 354, that nothing is a libel, or can become the subject matter of a criminal prosecution as such, which occurs in the course of proceeding in a court of justice; and the case of *Astley* v. *Young* in 2 Burr. has settled that no civil action will lie for anything that so occurs; there is but one case in the books where a contrary doctrine was held, and that case is just one of those bad precedents which, though triumphantly established at the time, are soon rendered obsolete and unavailing by the abhorrence of every rational man. It is the case of the *King* v. *Williams* in 2 Show. It was an indictment against Sir William Williams, for having published, by order of the House of Commons, *"Dangerfield's Narrative of the Meal-Tub Plot."* Such was the horror which the wise people of England entertained of the Pope in his proper person; or at least some conspiracy to re-establish his authority had been discovered close concealed in a meal-tub, and the House of Commons catching and propagating the delusion, ordered the narrative of this terrific plot to be printed and circulated throughout the country. It was for this publication that Sir William Williams, the speaker of the Commons, was indicted in the first year of King James. If your lordships take the trouble of looking into the report, you will find that the counsel for the defendant, Mr. Pollexfen, a man who deserves the admiration of posterity, for he, at that despotic period, had the courage to attempt to stem the torrent of unrelenting persecution at the bar, and overbearing and iniquitous intolerance of the bench; he, the counsel for the defendant, was interrupted by the bench, and not suffered to defend his client as his case merited to be defended.

I admit that the case of Sir William Williams determined that the high court of parliament itself had no right to sanction the publication of any part of its proceedings which contained matter in itself libellous. But fortunately the authority of that case has been completely exploded, even by the modern Court of King's Bench in the time of Lord Kenyon, in the case of *The King* v. *T. Wright*, in 8 Term Reports, 293: it was a favourable

circumstance; that was an application on behalf of the late Mr.
Horne Tooke. Mr. Tooke, in 1794, had been acquitted of high
treason, and yet, in 1799, the House of Commons adopted the
report of a committee, and ordered it to be printed, stating in
substance, that although Mr. Tooke had been acquitted, yet that
the evidence adduced at his trial showed him to be guilty. The
order of the house, however, was, that the report should be
printed for the use of the members. Wright, the defendant,
printed it for public circulation, and he therefore had no protection from the order of the house but the general protection which
every man has, to publish the written documents laid before that
house. For this publication, grossly reflecting on Mr. Tooke,
and accusing him of a crime, of which a jury of his country acquitted him, he applied to the King's Bench for a criminal information, relying on the case of *The King* v. *Williams*, as only
not in point, because much stronger. The court refused the information, and *declared the case of* The King and Williams *not
to be law*. Judge Grose, upon that occasion, said these words:—
"The case of Williams occurred in the worst of times, and is a
disgrace to a court of justice ;" and Judge Laurence declared,
"that no information could be granted for publishing a true
statement of the proceedings in a court of justice, although it
may in itself contain a libel—and no matter of law, for," said he,
"it is of vast importance to the public that the proceedings of a
court of justice should be universally known. The general advantage to the country in having those proceedings made public
more than counterbalances the inconvenience to individuals."
Such is the law—such is the doctrine laid down by a court which
could not be reproached with any overweening propensity to
popular rights or popular opinions.

Nor is this case shook, or its authority weakened by the case
before Lord Ellenborough, reported in 7th East, 493, under the
fictitious names of *Nokes* v. *Styles ;* on the contrary, the principle
is distinctly recognised and admitted, and that case was decided as an exception, by being beyond the principle, and not a
true report of judicial proceedings. I do, therefore, lay it down
as clear law, that no indictment or information, or action could
be sustained for publishing this report of the trial ; which report the Attorney-General seeks to convert into an aggravation
of punishment, that is, of course, an increase of punishment—
that is, a double punishment : punishment for the original libel
for which the defendant has been found guilty, and punishment
for this report, of which not only has the defendant not been

found guilty, but for which he could not legally be put on any trial.
It is no offence, in point of law, yet the defendant is to be
punished, in point of fact, for it. In point of law, the Attorney-
General could not prosecute him for this publication. If he indicted him, I would demur to the indictment; and still for this
report, upon which he could obtain no conviction or judgment,
does he call on the court to inflict a sentence! No jury could
convict the defendant of this publication; but the Attorney-
General requires a vote of the court to be substituted for the
verdict of a jury, and sentence to be pronounced upon that
vote, when no verdict could sustain a judgment. It is abhorrent to law, and detestable to common sense, that a man
should suffer twice for one crime; but this is a case in which it
is sought that Mr. Magee should suffer twice—once for what is
in law a crime, and once for what is not a crime in law or in fact
—that is, he is to be punished in the second instance, although
the law admits his innocence. It is not that detestable thing.
double punishment for one offence—it is this greater atrocity
that is sought for by the Attorney-General, a punishment for no
offence. This court is bound, by every principle and every feeling, to resist the solicitation of the Attorney-General, and not to
punish a man for that which the law has sanctioned.

But suppose I am wrong, and that this report is, in itself, a
libel; then let the Attorney-General indict for it; and if he can
convict, let him call for sentence. If it be indictable, the consequence may be, first, that he procures an increase of punishment for it in this instance; and secondly, that he afterwards,
upon an indictment, procures a sentence for the same publication! Out of this dilemma the court cannot be relieved. If
this be no offence, you have no right to punish for it; if it be
an offence, you ought not to leave it in the power of the Attorney-General to punish twice for it.

It is, perhaps, unnecessary to follow the Attorney-General
through the matter which the affidavit of the attorney for the
prosecution contains; and I do it slightly, and merely to show
how little my client has to answer for with regard to those.
The affidavit sets out three passages from my speech in the defence of Mr. Magee: the first relates to the Attorney-General
directly and by name; the second consists of a passage addressed
to the jury, upon their impartiality; and the third, the attorney
who made the affidavit swears he believes alluded to one of your
lordships. It is said that Mr. Magee ought to have made an affi-

338

dávit to contradict that of the prosecutor's attorney ; how could he contradict that affidavit ? The attorney swears he believes the passage has a certain meaning ; and how could any person swear that the attorney does not so believe ? If he had given us the reasons of his belief, he might be possibly contradicted in fact, or confuted in reasoning. But look unto the passage, and you will find that it expressly states an imaginary case ; and wretched indeed must be the state of the bar and the client, if the paintings of the imagination of counsel are to be reduced in shape and form, and embodied into an array against the client. I disdain being a party to any such degradation ; I should feel disgraced if I were to offer an explanation upon this topic. Then with respect to the passage relative to the jury : it was my duty, and my client's interest, to speak to them candidly ; and the passage in question does not hinge more than merely to state what would be the conduct of an impartial and unbiassed jury upon such an occasion, and to contrast that conduct with what we had to apprehend from a jury of a different complexion. I will not, indeed, condescend to vindicate the passage. The manner of procuring the attention of a jury to the defence of the client, is the privilege as well as the duty of the counsel, and the client was never yet made responsible for the mode in which counsel effectuates that purpose. The remaining passages relate to what was said of the Attorney-General himself. He has read for you that part in which, as counsel for Mr. Magee, I proclaimed (after an apology for the coarseness of the expression), any man who charged the Catholic people of Ireland with treasonable or revolutionary sentiments, to be *a liar*. You will, upon reading the entire of the passage, find that it is a reply to what fell from the Attorney-General—it is a mere answer to his speech. He ndulged in extraneous topics, and, as counsel for the defendant I felt it my duty to follow him.

Justice Day—You have no affidavit for the defendant stating that the Attorney-General went into extraneous topics.

Mr. O'Connell—We have not, my lord ; nor is it necessary we should : for those passages purport of themselves to be a reply to such extraneous topics—to be a reply to the Attorney-General using those topics. If those passages are to be resorted to, they must be taken altogether, and resorted to for what they purport upon the face of them to be. They purport, then, to be a reply to the Attorney-General ; and I ask your lordships in what language such charges ought to be refuted ? The jury was composed of what are called outrageously loyal men. It was the interest of my client, who had long been the advocate of the Catholics of Ireland, to stand well with that jury; it was his interest that his counsel should stand well with them.

Besides, there was a higher and more imperative duty on the advocate—as the Catholics are, by their oaths and their allegiance to the constitution—feeling for myself the pride of disinterested loyalty—that loyalty which is the result of judgment and of principle, not the mean and abject speculation of personal gain—that loyalty which would equally maintain the safety of the throne and the liberty of the people, and not that canting, peculating loyalty which seeks to enrich itself by cringing submission to the powerful, and insulting oppression to the weak and humble. With the fire of genuine and constitutional loyalty about me, I did brand with the harsher expressions known to the language, the man who should presume to impeach the allegiance of the Irish Catholic, or mine own; and I will even proclaim as a liar, the man who makes that charge, whether he boldly and directly charges it, or contents himself with mean insinuation of its truth.

Thus much I have said rather for myself than for the defendant, for in the extravagant shape of the present proceeding, I have the air of being on my trial and not my client; and I confess there is some justice in this. It was I who spoke the speech—it was I who urged these topics of defence—why should my client be punished for it? It was I who commented freely on the Attorney-General, and addressed the jury as I deemed best—why should Mr. Magee suffer for my acts?—why should he be punished for the boldness of my language? Is it because he sat in silence, and did not interrupt me? Why, his lordship, the Chief Justice, who presided at the trial, saw me there—he heard me, I presume, as well as Mr. Magee; the counsel for the crown heard me, and did not interrupt me; your lordship heard me, and did not interrupt me—I beg pardon, you did interrupt me once, and then I was able easily to satisfy your lordship of my right to reply to the Attorney-General. If there were any objection to what was said—if the line of reasoning or comment I pursued was objectionable or faulty, the trial was the time to have noticed it—it was the time peculiarly and exclusively suited for such notice; and it is due as well to the traverser as to the prosecutor, to take that and no other time for the investigation of the propriety of the defence.

It is *then* that the counsel for the defendant can be best prepared to vindicate the line for defence. The assertions of the antagonist, his conduct at the trial, are then fresh in the recollection of the counsel and the court—all the subject is in the possession of the counsel for the traverser. The judge himself can then best determine—the counsel for the traverser can then best maintain his right—a doubtful or ambiguous sentiment can then be easily explained, and made to bear only its precise and proper meaning ; in short, every view of the case will clearly show that the trial is the proper, and indeed the only proper place to investigate the rights of the parties, the privileges of the counsel, and, in fact, the duties of the judge.

But, suppose it otherwise—suppose there does lie some new appeal to a future court—yet, surely, Mr. Magee is not to blame. There is no appeal to him from the Chief Justice ; he is not bound, under peril of punishment, to be a better judge of the propriety of a defence and of the privileges of counsel than his lordship. Was it ever heard of that a private person was required, for his own safety, to avoid an increase of punishment, demanded to superintend the conduct of the bench, and to become a censor of the judge ? Must Mr. Magee be punished because he, fortified by the example of the court, listened in silence to the topics which I urged ! The Attorney-General is, therefore, quite unreasonable, when he requires of the court to increase the punishment of Mr. Magee for not interrupting the discourse of his counsel.

It has, however, been relied on, that Mr. Magee afterwards in his newspaper, approved of and applauded the defence set up for him, and avowed it. My lords, I pray you see to what this amounts. In the first place, it can be nothing more than would necessarily be implied from his silence. The client is presumed to avow that defence which is made in his presence ; the public avowal of it can, therefore, make no difference. Whether he speaks of it or not, the defence is his ; the public avowal is no aggravation. But in the next place, see, I entreat of you, what Mr. Magee has avowed thus publicly ; he has avowed the " topics of this defence ;" that is the extent of his avowal. Now, the speech of his counsel—my speech, my lords, was distinctly and emphatically divided into two distinct series of topics : the latter, and lesser part, related to the defence of Mr. Magee ; the former, and far greater part regarded the extravagant attack made by the Attorney-General on the Catholic population of Ireland. All the passages in the affidavit, taken from those extraneous topics, arose between the Attorney-General and myself

personally ; none of the passages in the affidavit relate to the
series of topics in the defence, properly so called. The avowal
and approbation of Mr. Magee are referrible only to the topics of
defence, and not to the matters contained in the affidavit to aggravate the punishment.   To his *defence* no objection has been
stated ; and beyond what is purely his defence he ought not, in
any view of his case, be made responsible.

I recapitulate, for Mr. Magee, his publication of the trial is no
crime—no offence cognizable by any public tribunal ; it is an
act to which the law declares that no punishment is attachable.
Besides, here it is sought to make him answer for what could be
the fault, if fault at all, only of his counsel.   And, good God!
what a precedent will be established, if you do so!—if you punish him for that which the zeal of his counsel urged perhaps in-
discreetly—I would concede, for argument sake, improperly ;
but not for this ought the client to be punished ; and then any
approbation given by him is confined expressly to the "topics of
defence ;" so that upon any view of the subject, he cannot be
confounded with his counsel.   In short, the object—the plain
object of the present proceedings is, under pretence of seeking
punishment on the client, to attack the counsel.   Your lordships
have said that nothing personal to me was meant by the Attorney-General ; but welcome should any attack he may choose to
make on me be, so you, my lords, spare the client, innocent, at
least, of this default.   I put his case, in this respect, on your
sense of right and common justice.

I conclude by conjuring the court not to make this a precedent
that may serve to palliate the acts of future, and, perhaps, bad
times.   I admit—I freely admit—the Utopian perfection of the
present period.   We have every thing in the best possible state ;
I admit the perfection of the bench—I concede that there cannot
be better times, and that we have the best of all possible prosecutors—I am one of those who allow, that the things that be could not
be better.   But there have been heretofore bad times, and bad times
may come again—there have been partial, corrupt, intemperate
ignorant, and profligate judges—the bench has been disgraced by
a Bilknap, a Tressilian, a Jeffers, a Scroggs, and an Alleybown.
For the present there is no danger, but, at some future period,
such men may arise again, and if they do, see what an advantage
they will derive from the precedent of this day, should it receive
your lordships' sanction.

At such a period it will not be difficult to find a suitable Attorney-General—some creature—narrow-minded, mean, calum-

nious, of inveterate bigotry, and dastard disposition, who shall prosecute with virulence and malignity, and delight in punishment. Such a man will, with prudent care of himself, receive merited and contemptuous retort. He will safely treasure up his resentment for four months. His virulence will, for a season, be checked by his prudence until, at some safe opportunity, it will explode by the force of the fermentation of its own putrefaction, and throw forth its filthy and disgusting stores to blacken those whom he would not venture directly to attack. Such a man will, with shameless falsehood, bring sweeping charges against the population of the land, and afterwards meanly retract and deny them; without a particle of manliness or manhood, he will talk of bluster, and bravado, and courage; and he will talk of those falsely, and where a reply would not be permitted.

If such times arrive, my lords, the advocate of the accused will be sure not to meet what I should meet from your lordships this day were I so attacked; he will not meet sympathy and equal liberty of speech. No, my lords, the advocate of the accused will then be interrupted and threatened by the bench, lest he should wipe off the disgrace of his adversary—the foul and false calumnies that have been poured in on him! The advocate then will not be listened to with the patience and impartiality with which, in case of a similar attack, your lordships would listen to me. The then attorney-general may indulge the bigoted virulence and the dastard malignity of an ancient and irritated female, whose feelings evaporate in words; and such judges as I have described will give him all the protection he requires; and although at present such a dereliction of every decency which belongs to gentlemen would not be permitted, and would rouse your indignation, yet in such bad times as I have described, the foul and dastard assailant would be sure, in court and beyond it, to receive the full protection of the bench, whilst the object of his attack would be certain of meeting imprisonment and fine, were he to attempt to reply suitably.

My lords, you who would act so differently—you who feel with me the atrocity of such a proceeding—you, my lords, will not sanction the attempt that has been made this day to convert the speech of counsel against the client, lest by doing so, you should afford materials for the success of any future attorney-general, as I have endeavoured to trace to you. Before I sit down, I have only to add, that I know the reply of the Solicitor-General will, as usual, be replete with talent, but I also know it will be conducted with the propriety of a gentleman, for he is a gentleman—an Irish gentleman ; but great as his talents are they cannot, upon the present document, injure my client. With respect to his colleague, the Attorney-General, I have only to say that whatever relates to him in my speech, at the trial, was imperatively called for by his conduct there. As to him I have no apology to make. With respect to him I should repeat my former assertions. With respect to him I retract nothing. I repeat nothing. I never will make him any concessions. I do now, as I did then, repel every imputation. I do now, as I did then, despise and treat with perfect contempt every false calumny that malignity could invent, or dastard atrocity utter whilst it consi dered itself in safety."

It was after the close of this speech of Mr. O'Connell's that Mr. Magee's repudiation o him was made.

Mr. Wallace, as counsel for the prisoner, requested to be heard before the Solicitor-General's reply; and his request being acceded to, he delivered a long and laboured argumen. —contending that Mr. Magee was not to be held responsible for his counsel's speech ; and that even if he were, his adoption of it by the publication in his paper and as a pamphlet should be held as a separate offence, separately to be adjudicated upon, and not to be taken, without trial, as an aggravation of the former.

In the course of his speech, Mr. Wallace having said :—

"I am solicitous to avoid, in any degree, implicating the case of my client, Mr. John Magee, with the merit or the demerit of his counsel's speech.

"If my learned colleague have fallen into any error or impropriety in the speech which he delivered, he has the manliness and candour, I am confident, to avow it, and to take upon himself the responsibility."

Mr. O'Connell—I do not admit that I have been guilty of any impropriety.

Mr Wallace—I am misunderstood if it be supposed that I mean to charge any impropriety upon Mr. O'Connell. I say only that if such impropriety had been committed, &c.

Notwithstanding this retractation, Mr. Wallace, in discharge, it is to be supposed, of the duty his client had imposed upon him, suffered himself to be betrayed into rough language afterwards, using such expressions as " the sins and crimes of counsel," "abuse of the forensic robe," &c., and even calling on the bench to punish Mr. O'Connell for the speech, and not Mr. Magee.

There was no want of will on the part of those he addressed to punish the former as well as the latter. Neither was there, as may well be supposed, any disinclination on the part of counsel for the prosecution to press for such a course.

But prosecutor and judges well knew that Mr. O'Connell was prepared for every emergency ; and that no submission was to be expected from him. In their consciousness of the truth and justice of even the most violent portions of his address, they shrunk from exercising the somewhat doubtful power of the court in such a conflict with a fearless and a determined man. In short, to use a homely proverb, the expressiveness of which will plead its excuse, they were fearful of " catching a Tartar."

Mr. Solicitor-General accordingly refused to draw the distinction argued for by Mr Wallace, between counsel and client; and solacing himself with some foul language, for having to forego the direct attack upon Mr. O'Connell, called for the rigour of the court against Mr. Magee, for his original offence and its aggravation—his adoption, by a printed avowal in his own paper, of the philippic of counsel.

The Solicitor-General's example was imitated by the bench. Lord Chief Justice Downes, indeed, went so far as to indulge in a ludicrous expression of penitence for not having himself stopped Mr. O'Connell in mid-career.

Mr. Justice Day, in delivering judgment, had the powers of face to defend, and praise the Lord Chief Justice and the jury!

And he crowned the whole by a eulogium upon the court—as a "sober, *unimpassioned*, and *dignified* tribunal!!!"

It is, indeed ludicrous at the present day to find such epithets applied to the whole or any portion of the Irish bench for many years after the Union. Men the most notoriously incompetent, the most notoriously partizan, disgraced that bench; placed there by the infamous governments that, under the auspices of Castlereagh and Sidmouth, afflicted poor Ireland.

The following was the sentence passed on Mr. Magee:—

THE SENTENCE—BY JUSTICE DAY.

"The sentence of the court is—That you, John Magee, do pay a fine of £500 to his Majesty; that you be imprisoned for the space of two years in Newgate, to be computed from the day of conviction, and that you do find security for your good behaviour for seven years, yourself in the sum of £1000, and two sureties in the sum of £500 each; and that you be further imprisoned until such fine be paid, and such security given.'

THE VETO QUESTION.

THE unhappy question of the "VETO," or according to its almost equally-noted designation of "securities," (*i. e.*, securities professedly sought for under the insulting pretence that the loyalty of our clergy required to be attested under oath; but really intended for the, if possible, more insulting purpose of securing government control over our religious institutions and discipline,) began now to mix with and embitter every discussion of the popular party. To sow dissension and division among the latter was, no doubt, one of the collateral objects of those with whom the project originated, and in this respect, and luckily in this respect alone, did they eventually obtain a triumph.

Amongst the divisions and differences of opinion and feeling alluded to, one of a serious nature occurred between the Catholic Board and its parliamentary friends and advocates. The Board, alarmed at the progress which the "veto" or "securities" question seemed to have made in England, and the apparent acquiescence in it of the English Catholics, had passed a resolution pledging themselves and requesting of their friends not to entertain any question of the kind, without the previous knowledge and full approbation of the Catholic prelates. The Earl of Donoughmore, who, in accordance with the then liberal politics of his family (the Hutchinsons), was the leading advocate of the Catholics in the Upper House, and Mr. Grattan—*the* "Henry Grattan"—who filled the same position in the Lower, refused to continue in communication with the Catholic Board in this matter, on the basis proposed by the latter—namely, that no "securities" should be embodied in any future "Relief" Bill, without the previous knowledge and approbation of the Catholic prelates.

Both accused the Board of at least the appearance of an intention to invade the privileges of parliament, and to dictate to it by, as Lord Donoughmore worded it, "leaving a naked affirmative or dissent, as their only remaining sphere of action, to the representatives of the people and the hereditary counsellors of the crown."

Mr. O'Connell at a meeting of the 20th of November remarked, that these letters gave the opportunity to explain the *real* views and motives of the Board; and "to show that their conduct was sanctioned by the constitution, and warranted by necessity—that it was temperate and respectful: but always firm and dignified."

He then referred to the previous meeting to show that the tenor of the resolutions had been mistaken by the noble and right honourable writers of the letters just read—that from a desire to obviate every objection, no matter how little weight in their eyes, they had

given up the intention of submitting a *draft of a bill*, confining themselves to mere suggestions, and that they did not wish in the least to interfere with the dignity, or control the
judgment of those whom they addressed.

He thus continued :—

But I beg Mr. Chairman, to go one step further, and to contend that there is *no* dictation implied in the drawing up of a bill
to be afterwards submitted to the consideration of a member of
parliament.

Who spoke of dictation when Mr. Charles Butler, last year,
prepared the frame of a bill ? Lord Castlereagh, who now professes to be our ardent friend, did not call *that* dictation. No ;
he called for the draft of a bill, and I believe acted upon it. Is
the privilege reserved for Mr. Butler, and are the Catholics of
Ireland to be excluded ?

Who spoke of dictation when Mr. Grattan procured the frame
of a bill to be prepared by Mr. Burrowes, by Mr. Burton, and by
Mr. Wallace ? If the frame of a bill carry dictation in its train,
why did our illustrious advocate risk our cause by getting that
draft prepared in Ireland ?

Or am I, in sober sadness, to inquire whether it be the Irish
Popish touch that pollutes the deed, and renders that which was
lauded by the minister in England, and practised by the Protestant patriot in Ireland, an act of dictation and crime in us !

Mr. O'Connell concluded with a motion for another communication to be addressed to
the noble lord and Mr. Grattan, respectfully pointing out to them their mistake as to the
intentions of the Board.

Mr. O'Gorman (after two or three speakers had been heard to the same effect as Mr.
O'Connell) opposed the motion ; and in deference to a point of form, it was withdrawn for
the day, notice being given that it would be brought forward again at the next meeting.

On that occasion (27th November) Mr. O'Connell accordingly moved it, in an altered and
modified shape—namely as "for a committee to prepare answers" to the letters in question.

He alluded to some of his former arguments ; and cited the cases of Lord Melville and
Mr. Pitt's conduct towards the Catholic delegates on two occasions, to show that there
would be nothing derogatory in their being listened to by private members of either house.

It was not to be expected (he continued), that any one should
be able so well to unravel the labyrinth, whose intricacy had
caused the defects of former bills, as men whose interests and
feelings had led them to make it the study of a great part of their
lives, and who had been continually in the habit of answering, as
counsel, the applications of persons aggrieved by these compli-
cated laws.

In short, a recurrence to the information in the hands of
Catholics was the only means to prevent the same unhappy catas-
trophe which destroyed the fruits of last year's exertions. . .

How lamentable if the Irish people should be deprived of results almost within their grasp, by internal dissension, or by a secession from each other, which, if it were not really dissension, inflicted all the consequences of such a calamity!

What! shall an attorney-general be able to boast, as he did to me *this day* (Mr. O'Connell had just come from the scene of Mr. Magee's renewed persecution) that there is a party of the Catholics of Ireland attached to him! To HIM—their continual, their unwearied persecutor!!! And have there been appearances in our behaviour to each other which could give the colour of truth to such an assertion; and shall we continue to authorize it?—Shall we not rather sacrifice every difference of opinion, every individual prejudice, and unite at once to spurn away the contumely with which it stains us?

For my own part, I have heard that some gentlemen are kept away by a fear that I may recur to the subject of an alleged promise to the Prince Regent. I utterly disclaim such an intention. I never will recur to it. In the name of my esteemed and patriot friend, George Bryan, I can also state, that he never again will mention it. Let every Irishman offer up his sacrifice on the altar of unanimity; her omnipotent spirit will receive our incense with gladness, and will guide us irresistibly through every danger, to the goal of triumph and success!

. . . .

There are but two causes that can retard our success—disunion and distrust among ourselves; and the continuance of that unworthy prejudice among others, which degrades the Catholic to comparative insignificance in the scale of intelligent beings.
. . . . Is it not thought high insolence in a Popish writer to be talented?—in a Popish mechanic to exercise his profession with ingenuity? And from what other source could it arise were Catholic assistance to be refused in the formation of a bill to relieve us? Did not Mr. Wilberforce consult with the Negroes on the subject of their slavery, receive information from them, and bring the answers of the African to the bar of the House o Commons? And is the Catholic alone to labour under the stigma of mental degradation, without asserting the rights of his nature?

The motion was carried with some discussion, but no opposition; and Lord Ffrench, who was in the chair, Mr. O'Connell himself, and Messrs. Dromgoole, Mahon, Bryan, Scully Finn, Owen O'Connor, Finlay, and Sir T. Esmonde appointed of the committee.

On Wednesday, December 1st, after some general business, Mr. O'Gorman called Mr. attention of the Board to the attacks on Mr. O'Connell, for his conduct as counsel for the Magee.

Nicholas Mahon warmly concurred in the opinion of Mr. O'Gorman, that it was the duty of the Catholics to come forward and repel the attacks made upon Mr. O'Connell, "by some solid and lasting memorial, which he could hand down to his latest posterity." He further styled him the "best and dearest friend of his country."

Mr. Plunkett had so imperatively felt that every Catholic in the land was bound to come forward and support the undaunted, incorruptible, and inflexible supporter of the Catholic people; that, although not a member of the Board, he had attended that day for the sole purpose of declaring his determination to support him at the hazard of his life and fortune.

He felt that upon this subject his powers of expression were altogether inadequate to do justice to his feelings; but he would venture to assert, without fear of contradiction, that the man of whom he spoke was the first of Irishmen—that he lives more in the affections of the people than any other who could be named! And it would be wonderful indeed o, the fact were otherwise, for it had been his unceasing ambition to expose, at the risk of his person and fortune, the errors and corruptions of the enemies of Ireland, and to rally a genuine spirit, which had long lain dormant in this country, and which he had at length so effectually accomplished, that it would take the minister, with all his power, and the treasury at his back, full fifty years to overcome it, even if the glorious career of its first mover were at this moment to be stopped.

His object had ever been to rally men of all persuasions, parties, and habits, under one title—that of Irishmen: and Mr. Plunkett thought the Board should come to some immediate resolution indicative of their conviction of his merits.

Mr. O'Conor (the chairman) regretted that it should be thought necessary to delay such a measure.

Counsellor O'Gorman wished to give every member an opportunity of doing justice to transcendant desert.

Mr. Scully pronounced, a speech in which he dwelt upon the many claims of Mr. O'Connell on the gratitude of his country, the total failure of any attempts to injure him in his profession, (if indeed such attempts were made at all), and declared his warm approbation of the notice respecting the testimonial of the feeling of the Board towards him. He said it was a fact notorious, that not even one late Sergeant Ball (before he got a silk gown) had more extensive practice, more general business than Mr. O'Connell enjoys at this moment: and those who visit the courts, and the agents and clients who employ him, know best with what excellence that business is done.

Yet, with all this, he contrived to devote more time to the public good, and to indulge the native excellence of his disposition in acts of private benevolence, than almost any other man! As to the alleged secession, he did not think it would be becoming the dignity of the Board to entertain any specific measure upon it; and he drew a long picture of the unpleasant situation in which, he presumed, the persons said to have seceded must be placed.

MR. O'CONNELL said it had been suggested to him not to speak; but it was impossible to listen to such language as he had just heard without emotions indescribable, and still more impossible would it be to listen to it and remain silent.

When first he had volunteered as the advocate of his country's rights, he did conceive that he had embarked in the service of an insolvent ingratitude, but never was a man more completely mistaken. He had met rewards equal to the most brilliant services, when, in fact, all he would lay claim to was good intention. No form of words could convey an idea of what he felt, when he heard his name coupled with encomiums so disproportioned to any thing he could effect—he would not attempt an impossibility.

In returning thanks to his friend, Mr. Plunkett, for the kindness of his expressions towards him, he wished to say, that in any personal controversy in which he might happen to be engaged, he required neither aid nor seconding. If he required assistance other than his own arms could afford him, he would not deserve to receive it. If a miscreant, clad in the robes of an alderman, had dared to introduce a personal quarrel of his into a public transaction, he owed his protection to his cloak and his secrecy.

Was he (Mr. O'Connell) to meet him in the street, he would proclaim him a coward.

With respect to his profession, he was only surprised at the perseverance with which clients committed their cases to him. The progress he had made had been effected in despite, in contempt of favouritism; and if his professional career were stopped by any conspiracy, he should not be astonished at it! As to an attack that was made upon him, and which came from a quarter that could not be replied to, if emancipation was carried, it should be brought before the proper tribunal. A scene which must surprise the British parliament would, in that case, be unfolded.

REPLY TO MR. RICHARD L. SHEIL.

On Wednesday, the 8th of December, occurred an almost first meeting, and collision of opinion between Mr. O'Connell and Mr. Sheil.

The Board met at the Shakspeare Gallery, in Exchequer now Wicklow-street—a place given for the purpose by, strange to say, one of the old corporation. a good-humoured, well-natured individual, of somewhat eccentric character, named Stephenson. Lord Ffrench was in the Chair.

The proceedings commenced with a notice by Mr. O'Connell, of an intended address to the Northern Catholics, warning them from joining Ribbon Societies, or suffering themselves in any way to be betrayed into criminality by the provocations of the Orangemen.

Doctor Dromgoole next brought forward a motion, for some time on the books, and postponed from meeting to meeting, for a positive and unqualified declaration on the part of the Catholic body against "*securities*" of any kind. description, or degree; and against even entertaining any proposition under any circumstances, which could be at all construed into a suggestion of them.

The motion was ably seconded by Dr. Sheridan.

Mr. Sheil then rose in opposition. The *Evening Post* thus treats of his speech :—

"We shall not pronounce upon certainly one of the most brilliant harangues ever delivered in a public assembly. Mr. Sheil has taken a part contrary to that recommended by us. and finally contrary to that adopted by the Catholic Board; but we feel great satisfaction in giving circulation to a correct and faithful copy of his speech. It is an honour to his country, although we cannot help thinking it directed against his country's dearest interests."

Mr. Shell concluded amid very warm cheering.
Mr O'Connell rose immediately in reply :—

My lord, whilst the meeting is yet dazzled and warmed with
the brilliant and glowing language—"the thoughts that breathe,
and words that burn"—of my young friend, I rashly offer myself
to your consideration.

I rashly interpose the cold, dull jargon of the courts—the un-
animated and rough dialect of the pleader ; but the cause of
freedom and of my country will enable me, even me, to unravel
the flimsy web of sophistry which is hid beneath the tinsel
glare of meretricious ornament. Unsound reasoning may be so
adorned by the flowers of the imagination, and the corruscation
of fancy, as to dazzle for a moment and mislead, but it requires
only the sober voice of plain sense—it asks only the sacred name
of liberty and our native land, to break the spell, to dissolve the
enchantment, and to expose the genuine deformity of the unpa-
triotic advocacy.

Let me not be misunderstood ; I admire, no man can more
admire, the splendid talents of my young friend ; I appreciate
them at their full value—I hold them higher than he does himself. They were bestowed on him for the highest purposes—they
are suited to the greatest and best purposes—to relieve and adorn
his country. He does not do justice to his own genius when he
confines it to the advocacy of a sect or party. Let it never be
reproach that—

> ' Born for the universe, he narrowed his mind,
> And to party gave up what was meant for mankind.'

Oh, no! Let him raise his soul to the elevation of his talents,
and not take the puny and pigmy ground of party or division.
Let him devote himself to his country ! God and nature have
been bountiful to him. Let him, in recompense, as bountifully
give, by consecrating to the service of liberty and Ireland all
the fascinations of his fancy, and all the brilliant glories of his
genius. See how mistaken he must be, when I can exhibit myself his superior. I own I am his inferior in talent, but the cause
I advocate sustains me, and my eloquent young friend sinks beneath the cause which he has espoused.

I must regret that he has given utterance to sentiments which
every sense of duty commands me to condemn. The doctrines
of slavery, which he has preached, I must censure. He has told
us that the Catholics have nothing to do with questions of freedom or the constitution—that their object should be to place

themselves on a level with the Protestants, and he is indifferent whether this equality be obtained by pulling down the Protestant or elevating the Catholic. In direct terms he has preferred the dead level of despotism to our present situation of comparative inferiority.

My lord, I object to those assertions, I protest against those principles of action. Many of the topics which have been urged by the eloquent gentleman do not bear on the present subject of debate. It is unnecessary to reply to them. To much more of his discourse it is needless to reply, because he did himself give the most powerful and the best answer to the arguments that might be used against the motion of Dr. Dromgoole. But it is incumbent on every friend to freedom, and to the constitution, to confute the slavish doctrine we have just heard. I am ready to meet him on this topic plainly, directly, and unequivocally.

The proposed resolution goes to declare that either as Irishmen, or as Catholics, we never will consent to allow to the crown, or the servants of the crown, any interference in the appointment of our bishops! I support this motion upon both grounds: —First, as an Irishman, that this interference would be injurious to public liberty. Secondly, as a Catholic, that it would be destructive of the Catholic religion. The manners of society—the state of the public press, fettered and in chains though it be— the decency and decorum of modern habits, the progress of the human mind, and many other causes, render the constitution secure from open and direct attack. Absolute power is not likely to be obtained, nor even sought after by direct force and plain violence. But who is there so blind as not to see the inroads that have been made upon our rights and liberties by the effect of corroding influence? Who is so sunk in apathy—who is so degraded in stupidity, as not to perceive how unconditional and unlimited the power is that may be obtained indirectly and by corruption? In truth, the only danger that menaces the constitution, the only chance of rendering that constitution a mere name, arises from the spread of influence and corruption, which, like a cancer on a fair face, disfigures and destroys the beautiful fabric of public freedom!

He is no friend to liberty—he knows not how to appreciate freedom—he is fitted for slavery, who can behold unmoved the progress of this terrific disease in the state—influence! I support the present motion because I dread and detest that influence, and should deem myself unworthy to seek for any liberty, could I consent to increase the influence of the servants of the crown. The young gentleman has argued, that this influence is already so great, that the appointment of our bishops would not add to the evil, and he has underrated much the value, even in a pecuniary point of view, of the office of Catholic bishops. Let the servants of the crown then be content with the patronage they have It is sufficient for their purpose, and if this addition be but small, let them leave us this small independence, for this little is our all—and great it is in fact.

The state is secure already of the allegiance of the Catholic bishop, he is bound to the state by his repeated and solemn oaths; but, not content with this, the ministers want to have him become their political agent—they want to have him in the subservient management of electioneering politics : if they succeed in obtaining the power to appoint a Catholic bishop, they will, without doubt, take good care to stipulate with him for the selection of priests devoted to their patrons ; and at the ensuing elections we shall see the courtly sheriff become insignificant— the castle bishop will canvass the diocese, the parish priest will ransack the different districts of the county, and you will have a Vereker, or a Bagwell borne on the shoulders of a duped people, in the room of a Glentworth or a Matthew.

I do, therefore, meet the eloquent young gentleman upon this ground first, and insist that we should be unworthy of emancipation should we adopt his doctrines. Emancipation ! My lord, the word would cease to have its appropriate meaning—the thing would cease to have any value. By emancipation I mean a participation in the free constitution of this country—not a chance of sharing in the public plunder. By emancipation I understand a right as a freeman to constitutional liberty, not a participation in the servitude of slaves—not a share in the authority of a despot.

Besides, I beg to bring your minds to the second motive for adopting this resolution :—The injury your religion must sustain if the minister of the day appoint our prelates. The minister is and will continue a Protestant as far as a minister of state may be said to have any religion. If he be sincere, as a Protestant his choice of a bishop will be governed by his sincerity, and he will appoint as Catholic bishop the man least likely to serve the Catholic religion—most likely to injure and degrade that religion.

But suppose him insincere, as a Protestant, there will be no doubt of his attachment to power as a statesman. As a statesman, then, who will he appoint as bishop ? The man who can purchase the situation—perhaps for money—certainly for service. And does any man imagine that the Catholic religion will prosper in Ireland, if our prelates, instead of being what they are at present, shall become the servile tools of her administration. They would then lose all respect for themselves; all respectability in the eyes of others; they would be degraded to the station of excisemen and gaugers; and the people, disgusted and dissatisfied, would be likely to join the first enthusiastic preacher of some new form of Methodism, that might conciliate their ancient prejudices, and court their still living passions.

The ministerial bishops of Ireland would become like the constitutional bishops of France, one of the means of uncatholicising the land. I beg to remind the young gentleman of the description he himself has given of the English; he has told us they were sunk in prejudice, and overcome by groundless and irrecoverable antipathy to Irish Catholics. And if this be so, and much of his argument was founded on the assumption of this as a fact, if this be so, who in his senses would think of confiding to these English the government of the Catholic Church in Ireland, and the appointment of her bishops. He who would confide to England this sacred duty, demonstrates that she is unfit for it. Surely he cannot be prepared to sacrifice all religion and country, for the name and shadow of a useless and degrading emancipation.

I therefore call on this meeting, as they are Catholics, and value the religion which they have inherited and believe; as they are Irishmen, and idolize their native land and her liberties, to reject the splendid fascinations of my youthful friend, and to adopt the proposed motion.

Let us show that we value freedom, and therefore deserve to be free! Let us prove that we respect the constitution, and therefore merit to partake of its blessings. Let us resist, not increase, an already overgrown influence, which may be so fatal to liberty, to justice, to happiness!

But I go further; for my part, I hold my Protestant fellow-countrymen in no animosity; I view them with no jealousy: I wish—I sincerely wish to elevate, not to degrade them. They are Irishmen, as I am, and I am anxious for their liberties; even should I not increase my own, I should be delighted to promote theirs. My desire is directly the reverse of that of Mr. Sheil; he prefers the equality of slavery, to the having one class depressed and the other elevated. For my part, if I could not elevate the Catholic, I wish not to depress the Protestant. I would advance both if I could; I would depress neither; and if the Catholic be still a slave, it is some comfort to my mind that the Irish

Protestant has some share of freedom; and here I answer the question of my young friend. He asks am I content to be a slave, that others may be free? The question relates to myself personally; I answer it at once. If I can procure freedom for my country, I am content with torture—death—with what is worse than either, with slavery!

He then asks, if I consent that my children should be slaves for the sake of my country? I readily answer—no. For myself, I can submit to slavery, but not for them. It is, indeed, to confer the blessings of liberty on *the nestlings of my heart (my children)*, that I struggle against obloquy, conspiracy, and calumny—I can sacrifice myself, but not them; but it is my dearest duty so to educate them in the love of Ireland, that each for himself will be ready to make the sacrifice of his all for Ireland.

Let me in my turn put a question or two to the eloquent young gentleman. Knows he not how delightful it must be to suffer for our country? Does he not feel how sweet pain, and reproach, and death would be for Ireland? Has he not a monitor within that tells him it requires no heroism to prefer his native land to self, and that the first transport of existence must be to contribute, by any sacrifice, to his country's liberties? If he have any, why did he question me? if he have not, let me assure him, compassion must give way to admiration; and I must pity even whilst I admire his poetic strains.

I stop here for one moment, to protest against one sentence of the learned doctor, on which I trust I mistook him. He spoke of the thousand sects that nestle under the wing of Protestantism, and he spoke in terms that appeared to me to imply disrespect. For my part, I shall never, in silence, listen to any language trenching on the freedom of religious opinion, or implying disrespect to any man who follows the dictates of his own conscience; if, instead of a thousand sects of Protestants, they have the same right to choose for themselves that the learned doctor has; and it would little become him, struggling for freedom of conscience for himself, to reproach the effort of that liberty in others. Any man who worships the Deity in the form which his unbiassed conscience prescribes, is worthy of respect; he may be in error, but his error can only deserve compassion not reproach.

Doctor Dromgoole here interposed by disavowing any disrespect to any sect of Christians.

From this digression, my lord, I come back to the arguments of the eloquent young gentleman, Mr. Sheil.

He intimates, that he has at length found out the grand secret for obtaining emancipation ; and he insinuates that we have hitherto misconducted the cause, and postponed freedom. I shall follow him upon both topics—first, his secret for obtaining emancipation ; and, secondly, his discovery of our mistakes in that pursuit. His secret to emancipate is thus disclosed : the English, he said, are prejudiced against us, vilely prejudiced— their prejudice is inveterate, and cannot by any means be cured ; it must therefore be yielded to, and gratified, if you would be emancipated ; but the only method of gratifying their proud prejudice, is by sacrificing to it some share of the discipline at least, if not of the doctrine of the Catholic Church.

My lord, nothing can be more clear or distinct than this reasoning ; but I contend for it, that it is built on untrue premises ; and even if it were true in all its terms, it should be rejected from higher considerations. But I deny the premises ; admitting, however, that the English are ignorant—grossly ignorant of us, and therefore blindly prejudiced against us. I admit this fact, and the causes of that prejudice have been given by Mr. Sheil. The genius of misrepresentation has presided over their historians, from the splendid romance of the unbelieving Hume to the stupid and malignant fictions of the credulous Musgrave. It is by misrepresentation that the English have become prejudiced ; facts have been distorted and falsified ; truth has been violated ; individuals have been calumniated ; tenets abhorrent from our judgment, our reason, and our religion have been imputed to us, and continue to be imputed to us!

Hence this prejudice—hence this evil ; and here also is the remedy to be found. It is by constant and unwearied application to the causes of disease. It is by explaining away misrepresentation ; by vindicating the truth of history ; by demonstrating the falsehood of calumnies ; by the public rejection of the abominable tenets imputed to us, and the plain and manly exposition of our real and genuine opinions. It is not sufficient once, or twice, or ten, or fifty times to meet this enemy of falsehood, or vindicate our friend, truth. The English have become prejudiced by the force of repetition of calumny. We shall set them right, by means of the repetition of the vindication.

Will the gentleman contend, that falsehood and delusion are all-powerful—candour and truth vain and impotent ? In the first encounter, they may be defeated by proud and overbearing and stupid prejudice, I admit ; but candour and truth have in them a reviving principle ; and returning again and again to the contest, they must ultimately prevail. I do therefore rely on the force of the truth—on the repetition of our vindication, as the means of overcoming English prejudice.

He says you should sacrifice some of the discipline of your Church to this English Dagon. I deny that the idol is worthy of such a sacrifice. I deny that you could conciliate the monster by any sacrifice short of your entire religion, discipline, doctrine and all. If you offer to prejudice this sacrifice, you, by your actions, though, perhaps, not in words, admit the justice of the prejudice. When you offer to English prejudice part of the discipline of your Church, you admit, at least in the opinions of the prejudiced, the truth of their suspicions and their fear. But it is in the nature of suspicion and fear never to be satisfied ; and the first sacrifice will justify and stimulate them to demand more.

You come before the legislature, admitting the propriety of their taking away something from you ; and they, acting upon your admission, will be ready enough to take away all. You cannot bribe their prejudice with a share of your religion : it will not—it cannot—indeed, it ought not to be satisfied with the part you offer. But thus, admitted by yourself into your camp, prejudice would not be consistent, unless it insisted upon converting all your property into spoil, and rendering itself for ever secure, by extinguishing for ever its enemy. Away, then, with this base and vile traffic—this bribing of a prejudice, which Mr. Sheil has so powerfully proved to be absurd. Away with this bartering with absurd prejudice—this traffic of so much of your religion for so much of their privileges—this exchange of certain lots of your discipline or doctrine, for a specific quantity of emancipation. We never can succeed in this peddling and huxtering speculation. They are ready to take all and give none. We are entitled gratuitously to our freedom, or rather we have already purchased it by our allegiance, our treasure, and our young blood. We are entitled to it as a right. Reason, justice, and nature are at our side. Let us preserve our integrity and our honour, as well as our religion ; and be emancipated as our forefathers desired—as Catholics, or not at all.

I now come to the discovery which my talented friend obscurely intimated that he has made, namely, that we, agitators, have retarded the progress of emancipation.

I have heard this charge made repeatedly out of this Board ; I have heard it said that by our violence, our intemperance, and what not, we have put back emancipation for fifty years. Against these calumnies, too, I appeal to the fact : the fact furnishes me with an answer—a triumphant answer—I could scarcely desire any reply more complete, more decisive.

The agitation of the Catholic question commenced in 1805 and nothing could be weaker or of less effect than our commencement. In 1807, the Grenville administration attempted to do something for us—they attempted to pass a law to enable Catholics to be officers in England as they are in Ireland. That was all they could attempt—but did they succeed? No ; the attempt cost them their places; and Mr. Perceval, seated on the shoulders of the "no-Popery" mob, was borne into power in triumph ; the "no-Popery" cry was raised, and all England was shook from the centre to the extremities. The war-whoop of religious bigotry resounded throughout the land, and in the pride and folly of its prejudices, it deemed the Catholic claims extinguished for ever.

Well, what has followed? We continued our agitation—our *violence* as it has been called—our *intemperance*. We passed our strong, our "*witchery*" resolutions. We exposed the vices and the secret motives of the insolent and venal beings who opposed our emancipation. I myself was in the habit of painting, in their native colours, the creatures who, for pay, insulted my native land, a practice which I have given up rather from lassitude and disgust than from any opinion of its being injurious to our cause. Amidst all this violence and intemperance, what was the consequence? Why, that in 1813, a bill was near to pass. intending and purporting to give us all. Our enemies themselves consented to give us everything except seats in parliament. They consented to give us situations and command in the army and navy, places at the bar and on the bench, corporate offices and dignities, places in the excise and customs ; all, all except parliament—they consented to all. Mr. Abbott, our leading adversary, consented to everything except parliament.

Now, place the two undoubted and indisputable facts together : in 1807 our friends could not procure for us even so much as the military rank in England ; in 1813 our enemies offered us the station of sheriffs, mayors, admirals, generals, judges and chancellors. Compare the two periods—contrast the two situations, and then let me see the man who will say that the Catholic cause has receded, or been driven back during that period I demand of the candour of my young friend to admit that the Catholic cause has advanced during the last seven years of agitation ; I do not ask of him the sacrifice of admitting that it has advanced by that agitation ; but it comforts my own mind, and rheers my secret soul to see the natural effect result from the plain, manly, uncompromising course we have steered.

I return one moment to English prejudice, so happily described by Mr. Sheil ; and I ask him whether this very alteration be-tween the opinions of the English in 1807 and in 1813 does not prove to demonstration that prejudice is best met by reason and argument. During the last seven years we made no degrading sacrifice ; and yet the repetition of our arguments, and the dis-play of truth have advanced our cause. Let my young friend meditate on these facts, before he again envelopes in poetry the cause of despotism, and the triumph of prejudice !

My lord, I have combated this eloquence advocating the in-fluence of the crown—I have ventured to oppose it supporting the prejudices of England ; I will now briefly allude to another argument, or rather assertion, of his ; he says the present reso-lution implies a censure on our prelates !

What, my lord, can it be censure to declare that we are so pleased and proud of our prelates, who have been appointed without any interference of the crown, that we never will consent to any such interference ? The Board censure the bishops! The Board, my lord, has always expressed its respect, its veneration for the bishops. Our enemies, indeed, would be delighted, if they could establish any division between the Board and the Catholic hierarchy. But, no ; that is impossible. Instead of the present resolution implying censure, it directly and justly speaks praise and approbation. We approve and applaud—and it would be difficult, indeed, not to approve and applaud our prelates as they are. We seek no change—nor will we consent to any change that would be likely to place different men in high offices. The prelates, too, I may venture to add, approve of the course pursued by the Board : they see, they easily see that however anxious we are for freedom, we are still more anxious for the purity of our religion—they know that though we are desirous not to remain slaves, we are determined to continue Catholics ; and that ardently as we love liberty, we will not purchase it as the price of schism.

It is, therefore, impossible, to separate the prelates from the Board, or the Board from the prelates. We interfere only upon subjects belonging to our province. Any connexion between the crown and the Catholic hierarchy in Ireland must, of course, be of a political nature ; and against such, we have a right to pro test, and do protest ; but if the revered and venerable prelates of our Church, exercising their discretion as to that which belong

to them exclusively—the details of discipline—shall deem it right
to establish a system of domestic nomination, purely and exclusively Irish; if, I repeat, our prelates deem it right to establish a system of domestic nomination—of a nomination purely
and exclusively Irish; if our prelates deem it right, in their wisdom and piety, to establish any such arrangement, the Board,
my lord, will not interfere with such arrangement, because it has
no right whatsoever to interfere with it; but it will certainly applaud and grateful.y receive any such decision.

Before I conclude, let me avow the pleasure I feel that my resolution on this subject was negatived—not because I think it was
an improper resolution in the sense I meant it—but because it
was, I find, so capable of being misunderstood. I never complained of its being rejected—all I complained of was, that it
was not understood. I attributed the fault to others, I now see
it was my own; for the sense which Mr. Sheil has put on that
resolution convinces me that there was an ambiguity in it which
alone merited condemnation. I do, therefore, myself condemn it as
mischievous, because equivocal, and cheerfully submit myself to
the censure that may follow the man who uses, on a delicate subject, ambiguous language.

This great question is now fairly before the Board. We, who
support the resolution, call for emancipation, without making
our bishops the slaves or the instruments of the ministry—and
require our liberties, to which we are entitled as our birthright,
without any sacrifice of the doctrine or discipline of our Church.
We humbly petition parliament to assure us freedom, but we ask
it as Catholics—we respectfully require of them liberty, but we
wish for it with perfect safety to our religion. We have given
them the security of our allegiance—we have sealed their sincerity with our oaths, and confirmed it with our blood; all we require in return is the privilege of worshipping God as our forefathers worshipped him. We are ready to ensure, with our
dearest interests, the integrity of the state—all we ask in return
is, the integrity of our religion!

Those who agree with me, that we are entitled to emancipation,
without compromise, will support this resolution; all who agree
with my eloquent friend, that our emancipation should be purchased by some undefined concessions of doctrine, or, at least, of
discipline, to absurd prejudice—for so he proved it; all those
who think they can bargain with absurd prejudice, upon the
capital of their faith, will reject the present resolution with Mr.
Sheil.

He has, indeed, been unfortunate in the side he has selected ;
he has not been lucky in his allusion. It was not the Catholic
barons of the reign of John that crouched beneath Papal usurpation. It was a profligate, faithless, unprincipled prince, who
used the Pope's then authority to enable him to enslave a Catholic people.

I am of the faith of the Catholic barons, who with their swords
extorted the great charter of liberty ; I am of the religion of the
Catholic parliament that passed the statute of provisors ; firm
in my attachment to her ancient faith, ardent in the pursuit of
liberty. Let my young friend join this standard, and soon shall
he become a leader. To the superiority of his talent we shall easily
cheerfully yield, and give him that station in his country's cause
to which his high genius entitles him. Let him devote himsel.
to the uncompromising advocacy of Ireland—glory will await him,
and the sweeter satisfaction of serving his country ! Let him
reject party and adopt Ireland, who, in her widowhood, wants
him ; and in her service let his motto be—" God, and our native
land."

The tone of the meeting was taken from this speech, and Dr Dromgoole's motion carried with acclamation.

MR. FINLAY'S ADDRESS.

On the 11th December a meeting of the Board occurred, at which, in Mr. O'Connell's
absence of course, a splendid tribute of Catholic feeling was paid to him for his exertions
in the Catholic and national cause. The tribute was not confined to words, warm and
kindly even to enthusiasm as they were ; but a service of plate was voted, and shortly
afterwards given to him, under the following resolution, moved in a most kind speech by
Nicholas Purcell O'Gorman, Esq., the present assistant-barrister for the county of Kilkenny

" At a meeting of the General Board of the Catholics of Ireland,
held at the Shakespeare Gallery, Exchequer-street, Dublin, on Satur
day, the 11th December, 1813—Owen O'Conor, Esq., in the Chair

" Resolved—That a service of plate, value one thousand guineas, be
presented to Daniel O'Connell, Esq., on the part of the Catholic people of Ireland, as a small tribute of their gratitude for the unshaken
intrepidity, matchless ability, and unwearied perseverance, with which
in despite of power and intolerance, he has uniformly asserted the
rights, and vindicated the calumniated character of his Catholic fellow
countrymen.

" That the following noblemen and gentlemen do compose a committee for the purpose of carrying the above resolution into effect, viz.
the Viscount Netterville, the Lord Ffrench, Nicholas Purcell O'Gor-

man, Owen O'Conor, George Bryan, Henry Edmond Taaffe, Nicholas Mahon, Randal M'Donnell, Esqrs.

> "OWEN O'CONOR, Chairman.
> "EDWARD HAY, Secretary."

There was one speech made upon this occasion, which, although it cannot rightly be considered as coming within the scope of the present collection, we cannot forbear to give. It was that of an old, fast friend of Daniel O'Connell's—a man most estimable in every relation of life, and one who is yet living, and likely to live many a day yet, encircled as he deserves by "a troop of friends." We speak of Mr. Finlay, or, as he is best known, of honest John Finlay—true and honest in the worst of times, when there was every temptation for a young struggling barrister of the dominant persuasion (Mr. Finlay is a Protestant) to ally himself with the oppressors of the people and the assailants of their advocates

Between him and Daniel O'Connell there was ever an old and warm friendship. A congeniality of mind first produced it, and closer acquaintance fast ripened it into the warm est and most enduring vigour. Most truly indeed may it be said that no sincerer friend Mr. O'Connell ever had; and none did he more sincerely recognize and endeavour to repay the attachment.

Mr. Finlay's speech bears strong evidence of that talent and power of intellect which, if nature had given him the same taste for the agitator's life of unceasing activity and toil that animated his friend, would have rendered him "*facile princeps*" at least of far the greater number of those who have been prominent in the struggle for Irish rights.

The following was his address on this occasion:—

" When a man steps forth from the ranks of tranquil life, and devotes his time to public interests, he avows that he employs himself in that which is equally the business of all. Thus the public, in whose service he starts a volunteer, are placed in censorship over his words and actions; and the members of the community protect themselves from self-reproach of civic inexertion, by scrutinizing his motives with all possible doubt, and accounting for his acts with the least possible charity.

" This caution, though sometimes unfair, is seldom unreasonable; it is frequently justified by the event, and always allowable, under the principle that no class of men should be more suspected than patriots, because no class has produced more impostors.

" But this suspicion, like everything else, should have its limits; and there is a length of time—a quantity of fidelity beyond which jealousy or suspicion cannot exist without injustice to its object. Time is the ordeal of patriotism. To preserve a patriot's purity, it is not expected that he should be always *right*, because he cannot be always *wise;* but it is necessary that his acts should be always well-intended, because he may be always honest.

" Therefore when time has assayed and established the fairness, not of his acts, but of his intentions, his exertions, his talents, and his purpose, it then becomes the duty of the people to repay, by an increased portion of their gratitude, for those doubts which their caution compelled them to entertain.

" Ten years have tried the fidelity of O'Connell; and you stand now indebted to him in the article of gratitude, not only for the quantity of service conferred, but the time during which the trial has been protracted, and the expression of your collective gratitude deferred.

" This line of reasoning applies to every free country, but it applies in a more particular manner to Ireland. In Ireland there is one simple division of its inhabitants—Catholic and Protestant; religion, in truth, makes no part in the political results which flow from this distinction Protestant is another word for the possessor or expectant of place ; Catholic, another word designating whom the law excludes. Thus power, place, patronage, and a large portion of franchise being, in fact, denied to the great majority, and confined to a few, they become real property in the hands of their possessors; and, unless their possessors be endowed with no common portion of disinterestedness, they have every motive derivable from self to examine with severity, and interpret without charity, the motives and conduct of those men who would destroy that property, by the generality of its diffusion.

" Therefore, the advocate of Catholic emancipation appears in greater or less degree of hostility to every Protestant in this country who has not the virtue to dismiss the calculations of self; therefore, the advocate most efficient, prominent, and persevering presents an aspect of political hostility, varying its phases exactly in proportion to the degree of self-love which sways the motives of those Protestants to whom he is an object of observation ; and for this reason Daniel O'Connell is hated by some, disliked by many, and cannot, in the nature of things, depend for approbation on any Protestant not purely disinterested ; therefore, he must suffer from calumny exactly as long as you must suffer from injustice, and the amount of injury in this way inflicted is the exact measure of reparation which mere justice should prompt you to compensate.

" The permanency of his country's affection is the only species of remuneration to which he ever looked forward. The vulgar value of the certifying instrument is a matter of indifference to him, and should not be a subject of deliberating economy with you.

" Such are the disadvantages, moral and political, which, *for a time*, must always operate to obstruct the actions and obscure the motives of him who struggles for the public good. The moral disadvantage applies to all countries; but the moral and political unite in Ireland.

" There is a third disadvantage, if the patriot be a lawyer, which I shall call a professional disadvantage. The bar is an educated, enlightened community. It has been truly said that the pursuit of the law exercises, in its study, the noblest faculties of the mind, and engages, in its practice, the cardinal virtues of the heart. Ambition is a passion suitable, perhaps essential, to a barrister ; but, in the mind of all who are not great or good, envy is the inseparable handmaid of ambition. In the barrister's career to professional success, the course is so narrow, the competition so violent, and the prize so important, that all praise is rigorously denied except when extorted by unquestionable desert. Thus, then, where a man happens to unite the characters of a patriot, an Irishman, and a barrister, there is a threefold censorship imposed o'er his conduct, which nothing but eminent virtue can sustain, and which, sustained, cannot well be over-rated.

" EMINENT AND PROMINENT IN THESE THREE RELATIONS, *history will describe* DANIEL O'CONNELL *spotless in the relations of private life, matchless in the duties of private friendship, beloved by every man who knows him, esteemed by all who have not a prejudice or an interest in disliking him; with manners that instantly disarm hostility, there never yet was a man introduced to him for the first time, under prepossessions to 'his disadvantage, that did not feel his dislikes hastily evaporating, and depart from the conference a convert to esteem!*

"At five in the morning you will find him in his study; at five in the evening you will probably find him still labouring in the public service; if you cannot find him thus employed, you may be almost certain of finding him at home. I never knew any man of equal industry; I never thought that any man could be so industrious. No man at the bar *labours more* in his profession, and no man at the Board labours *so much* in politics; but to labour *so much*, and to labour *so well*, far exceeds the common notions of human capability.

"*Social and sober—polite and unceremonious—cheerful, affable, candid, and sincere—proud with the haughty, and meek with the humble; his frown rebukes arrogance to inferiority, and his smile lifts humility to his own level. His virtues cannot be indifferent to you; they should be objects of your care, for they have been agents of your interest.*

"Such a man, in difficult times, volunteered as the advocate of press and people. The apathy that followed the measure of the Union had depressed the nation to political indifference. Lord Clare had declared, in the British House of Peers, that the Catholic people felt uninterested in the question of emancipation. It became necessary to correct the error or the fact. The two great pillars on which emancipation could be raised were, the exercise of a free press, and the exercise of the right of petition. *O'Connell* started the advocate of both; and here commenced the political hostility between the interested advocate for the governor, and the disinterested advocate for the governed; that is, between Mr. Saurin and Mr. O'Connell.

"Those two pillars of emancipation were assaulted alternately by the Attorney-General. A new and severe tax was imposed on the press, in the expectation that men would be discouraged from embarking their property in a speculation in an enterprise so unprofitable as an independent journal. The experiment failed; the press was not weakened—it was strengthened; and those who had been the friends became the enemies of the Irish government.

"This attempt against the Press was made during the ministry of Mr. Foster; the next attempt was against the people, and made in the ministry of Mr. Pole. A proclamation was issued against the manner in which the people exercised the right of petition. A circular was issued, which every magistrate in Ireland felt it his duty to disobey. It appears by the declaration of Mr. Pole, that this circular was the suggestion of Mr. Saurin. It appears, by the highest law authorities in England, that it was a composition of which a lawyer should be ashamed. *Ex-officio* informations were poured in abundance against the Catholic peers and gentlemen who presided at the Catholic meetings. The convention act, enacted many years before, was called into action against the people.

"The next attempt was against the Press. The Press was attacked by every mode of attachment, information, and indictment. The most objectionable mode was first resorted to—*attachment*. The cry became .oud ; and the less objectionable mode of information was next resorted o ; and as the cry became louder still, this usual and more constitu-.ional mode of indictment was finally fixed upon.

"Mr. Saurin, ambitious of a character for lenity, has lately declared, on his motion for an aggravation of punishment, that he had not prose-cuted more than *three*. Of his Majesty's Attorney-General I should not wish to speak *without deliberation*. It might be unbecoming—it might be unsafe. I am not inclined to speak disrespectfully, *or other-wise*. I must not, in politeness or in prudence, contradict ; but when he states as a fact, that of the Press he never yet prosecuted but *three*, I may be permitted to say, without offence, that this is an assertion which, consistently with a good conscience, I dare not to affirm.

" It is certainly true that he did prosecute the *Irish Magazine* for the article called ' *The Painter Cut ;*' secondly, Mr. Fitzpatrick, for the Statement of the Penal Laws ;' and, thirdly, Mr. Magee, for the arti-cle against the Duke of Richmond : these are *three*. But it is equally true that he did prosecute the proprietor of the *Freeman's Journal*, by that most objectionable mode of prosecution, an attachment, and that he did obtain that attachment ; and that Mr. Harvey, under the appre nension of its execution, was for a year confined to his own house. a can say this is true, for I was present at these motions. This reckons *four*.

" It is equally true that he moved for another attachment against each of two proprietors of the *Evening Herald*, and although the Court of King's Bench unanimously pronounced the libel to be NONSENSE, they however, granted him the attachment, with their opinion that he ought not to execute it. This I know, for I was counsel in the cause. Then reckoning this prosecution against two as but one prosecution, I say this makes *five* prosecutions.

"It is equally true that he at the same time filed an *ex-officio* against the *Herald*. This I know, for I was counsel in the cause. This reck-ons *six*. It will not be denied that he also issued *ex-officio* informations against the *Correspondent* and *Freeman*. These make *eight*. He also .ssued, of late, two *ex-officio* informations against two Kilkenny papers for publishing the resolutions of public bodies. These make *ten*. He says *three*—I say *ten*. Does he mean to say that he only prosecuted three to *conviction?* The fewer he prosecuted to conviction compared with the number that he did prosecute, shows his want of ability rather than of will, and gives no claim to the character of lenity ; but even reckoning those that he prosecuted to conviction, he does not reckon fairly. He only reckons, even in this sense of prosecuting, Cox for one. I say he prosecuted Cox for THREE, and obtained conviction for TWO. Thus, taking prosecutions for CONVICTIONS, he is not right, and taking prosecutions in its proper sense, he should have said TWELVE instead of THREE.

" In addition to this   am informed that he issued *ex-officio* informations against almost all of the publishers of Dublin, on the subject of the 'Statement of the Penal Laws.' Then where is the ground of his boast of lenity? Finally, the Irish Attorney-General, after having produced one sleeping statute against the Press, brought forth another against the people—the Convention Act against the people—the Stamp Act against the Press—both enacted in bad times: neither of them were enacted in England—neither of them before used in Ireland. The operation of this Stamp Act was to extinguish the property itself, or at least wrest it from the owner's hand. Mr. Magee was obliged to part with his property; but though an unprecedented act of power tore his property from him, he took care that it should not be torn from the service of the country.

"Mr. Saurin having so far succeeded, by every usual and unusual mode of prosecution against Press and people, finally *attacked the advocate of both.* His speech for his client was the ground of complaint An attempt was made, by the partizans of power, to injure his professional character, by insinuating that *he had* injured his client by his defence; and the unbecoming rumour was spread abroad, that the manner of the counsel should be the measure of mercy—that had Mr. O'Connell been more merciful to Mr. Saurin, Mr. Saurin would have been more merciful to Mr. Magee; but this insinuation lost its force —it was very well known to every one, and to no one better than to Mr. Magee, that tenderness was not among the weaknesses of his prosecutor.

"The object of the *motion in aggravation* was, in truth, to punish the advocate for the defence. Mr. Saurin insinuated ulterior proceedings, *and the benchers* were sounded on the subject of stripping the *advocate* of *his gown!* Many severe philippics had been pronounced at the bar before. Such a measure was never attempted Lord Clare has been compelled to look at a portraiture of his own vices, presented to his eye by an immortal advocate, but he never dreamt of punishing the advocate by law. He has spoken in the severest terms in the House of Lords respecting the philippic on the trial of Finnerty; but he never thought of any proceeding of this description. The Solicitor-General admitted it was a most extraordinary proceeding; and his apology for this most extraordinary proceeding was, that it was an extraordinary speech: but what was the amount of blame imputable to the speech? I omit the appeal to the passions of the Chief-Justice—an appeal which in decency should not have been made, and which never could be made with decency. This being omitted, what is the amount? The composition of that jury, and the distribution of justice in this country. As to the distribution of justice, I shall be very cautious in speaking on that subject: it appears to give particular offence. I do not wish to lose my gown: I cannot afford it as well as O'Connell: but I hope I may say this much without losing my gown—that a considerable prejudice exists on the subject.

"I lately heard a peasant say—' *Oh, Sir, it requires a great deal of* INTEREST *in this country for a poor man to get a* LITTLE JUSTICE !' This prejudice is very widely spread I do not boast of a particular strength of mind, and, therefore, plead guilty to the infirmity of being occasionally affected by this prejudice myself.

" As to the business of selected juries, the fact cannot be denied, that the religion of a Catholic operates as a challenge to exclude him from juries in every criminal case of importance. The juries, without one exception, have had no Catholic in any crown prosecution in which the Attorney-General has been engaged. These two topics were the objectionable parts, for I cannot suppose that extracts from history constitute crime. These two topics were the ground of offence; so that, in future, it will be safe, perhaps necessary, to *believe* that the juries are selected equally and indiscriminately, and that every judge and every juror is beyond all exception. ''Tis unsafe to blame them,' says one public accuser; 'and it is more unsafe to praise them,' said the other. ' They have a right to be angry with their libeller,' said Mr. Saurin; 'and they have a greater right to be angry with their panegyrist,' said Mr. Bushe God help us! How are we to speak of them ? Act upon both opinions : say nothing at all upon the subject.

" I lament that this discussion has arisen here ; for notwithstanding Mr. Saurin's reliance on the respectable Catholics, I don't see any Catholic, respectable or otherwise, who appears here disposed to defend him, although some are of opinion that he requires some defence. Therefore I am sorry that his conduct is discussed, but he challenged you to it. He sent you an issue, and it becomes necessary for you to return him his verdict. Why should he rely on the Catholics ? He has used against the press and the people every species of prosecution, legal and severe, common and uncommon. He has brought forth two statutes—one against the press, the other against petition—both unused before—both strangers to the law of England ; he has issued circulars and summonses to his own house, both rebuked by high law authorities in England, and he is the first Attorney-General who ever made a motion in aggravation in Ireland. Was it just that his Stamp Act should tear from John Magee the property of a paper which he had convicted? —and if it was, is it just that it should also deprive him of the property of another paper, which *was not convicted ?* Are these the grounds of his reliance ? Why, then, he rests upon a broken reed.

" As he asks, give him a verdict, and express your condemnation of his conduct, by the honours which you pay to the object of his persecution.

" It is your duty to hold up O'CONNELL. It has been said with some truth that no man ever yet yoked his fortunes to the fate of Ireland, who was not ruined by the connexion. The Catholic cause is of considerable weight, but it is said its weight has often operated rather to sink than float its adherents. Contradict those imputations. Give me now, in the instance of O'Connell, a practical proof that this rumour is untrue, and in doing so I make not this an occasion to express your respect for the virtue of economy ; parsimony at best is amongst the minor virtues ; it is a personal attribute, it should make no part of a people's character when developing their affections to a great man for great services in a great cause If you do exercise it upon this occa-

sion, it may be said in fact, as it must be said in law, you do not represent the benevolent purposes of my generous countrymen.

" Power has attempted to put down *O'Connell ; it is the* people's interest to hold him up. *What would you do without him ? Who would
you get like him ?*

" In his political and forensic capacities, his enemies allow he possesses two qualities always essential, not always combined—an *intrepid
Advocate, an* HONEST *Patriot,* a clear head, an honest heart, and a
manly purpose, are seldom united—are united in him, and necessary
for you. He resembles Mr. Whitbread in that every-day working talent,
which does the business of practical usefulness, and which in both, curious to say, is compatible with eminence of talent—a sort of talent
that does not work itself down—that, like the memory, gathers vigour
from its toil—and, like the Bridge of Cæsar, acquires strength and solidity from the very weight of its burden. Therefore Whitbread, in
real usefulness, is worth half of the opposition—he is, in fact, an opposition in himself; and so it is with O'Connell.

" Compared with such a man, what are the dozens of periodic orators
who, like myself, occasionally come forth with a holiday speech, decked
in the finest trappings of our eloquence. Give me the man who is not
afraid to lose character by every-day work—who will speak well to-day
and ill to-morrow. Every man who speaks often, must sometimes
speak ill. Health, indisposition, constitution, fits of dulness, many
things may cause it ; but give me the man who will not avoid speaking
when necessary, because he may speak with less effect ; who will not
deem it necessary to let the soil lie fallow in order to give value to the
future production ; who in truth is more anxious for the public service
than his own fame, and who, in public attention, rests upon facts and
not upon phrases !

" This power of continual exertion falls to the lot of very few ; for
my own part, in my humble exertions, I have found occasional periodic
exertion more than enough; and I have often been surprised and astonished at the powers of uninterrupted and successful exertion which
exist in Whitbread and O'Connell, and do not at all exist in the same
degree in two other men in these countries.

" These talents are now yours ; you should prize the highly gifted
honest owner, fighting the battles of his country, he stands exposed to
the shafts of angry power. Let Hibernia, in whose cause he acts and
suffers, cover her patriot with her ample shield—

> " ' Let him but stand in spite of power,
> A watchman on the lonely tower
> His thrilling trump will rouse the land,
> When fraud or danger is at hand
> By him, as by the beacon light,
> The pilot must keep course aright.'

" But if he, like many others, should be fated to endure the ingratitude of the country—if he should be placed in the midst of useless
friends and implacable enemies—if his enemies should gratify their
purpose against him.—

" ' *Then* is the stately column broke,
The beacon-light is quenched in smoke,
The trumpet's silver sound is still,
The warden silent on the hill !' "

This passage with its poetic quotations, was cited last in the declining days of the Repeal Association, some months after Daniel O'Connell's death, by poor—poor—"Tom Steele !" The effect was *then* most thrilling; what the effect would be if now cited in a popular assembly, and whether the prediction it embodies would be held to have come true, it is not for the editor of these speeches to say.

Mr. O'Connell's acknowledgment of the great compliment paid him at the meeting of the Catholic Board, last mentioned, was made on the succeeding Saturday, 18th December, 1813, at their next meeting—Owen O'Conor, Esq., again in the chair.

To you personally, Sir (said Mr. O'Connell to the chairman), I trust I need not apologize for not having answered your communication. I have the honour of calling you my friend ; and I hope the high value which you know I entertain for your public and private worth, will convince you that I could not have intended anything disrespectful to you personally, by not acknowledging your letter.

With respect to the public, my reason for not answering the communication is either the best or the worst in the world. It is literally this—I was unable to do it ! I did frequently attempt to commit to paper the expression of my feelings, but my powers of language sunk beneath the effort. I was utterly unacquainted with any form of words that could give utterance to the sensation which throbbed at my heart. I could guess at no terms which could even impart an idea of the gratitude which swelled in my bosom for so unmerited an honour, conferred by such a people, and on so humble an individual.

The feelings to which this unexampled kindness gave rise, were not to be expressed in any form of words. My gratitude is too big for language, and I leave it to kindred spirits to recognize and appreciate sentiments too ecstatic and too refined for utterance.

But should I not have seized this opportunity to make professions of attachment, of zeal, of affection for the ill-starred land of my birth ? Should I not endeavour to repay your exceeding kindness, by declaring that your approbation would increase that attachment—enliven that zeal, animate that affection ? No, Sir. I will not make any such profession. They would be untrue, and I scorn them. No, Sir, even your applause—and who can describe how much I value your applause—even your applause will not, because it cannot, increase the devotion with which I have consecrated my existence to Ireland. I have already devoted all the faculties of my soul to the pursuit of the liberties of my country; and humble as my capabilities are, i had already given them all to my native land.

Alas! the gift was small, but it included certainly purity of design, sincerity of intention, perseverance of exertion, contempt of personal danger, neglect of personal advantage, and finally, incorruptible integrity and truth.

You cannot increase my zeal—my devotion, but you have recompensed them beyond measure, and beyond reason. I have been unable to serve my country—I am a zealous but a useless servant; and you have thrown away upon mere zeal that high recompense of your approbation which ought to be reserved for actual services. However flattering to myself, still I cannot but blame the prodigality of your kindness. I know I owe much of it to private friendship, and I avow I have been delighted and gratified beyond measure by the proofs of friendship which your resolution has been the means of calling forth. It has satisfied me that I may rank amongst my friends those persons whose virtues and patriotism must render their favourable opinion an object of the highest consideration to every man, and whose friendship must reflect honour upon any individual whom they shall distinguish by it!

I am glad that it was introduced, because it elicited those proofs of friendship; and I am grateful to my enemies, who gave occasion for an exhibition of the feeling which was that day witnessed here. I am glad that the enemies of my country, who are my enemies because they are hers, have so completely identified me with the Catholic cause, and have proved that they attack me only when they commit still greater attacks upon Ireland.

But there is another and a higher consideration—a consideration which gives me pure and unmixed pleasure—it is that afforded by the stimulus you hold out to the patriotism of others, when you bestow honours thus liberally upon plain and unserviceable honesty. The man who dedicates himself to the cause of his country must calculate on meeting the hostility and calumny of her enemies—the envy and falseheartedness even of or friends. He must reckon on the hatred and active malignity of every idolator of bigotry—of every minion of power—of every agent of corruption. But that is little; he will have to encounter the hollow and treacherous support of pretended friends —of those interested friends respecting whom he will in vain exclaim—"God protect me from my friends, I can guard myself from mine enemies!"

What is to cheer and to recompense him in his exertions?—
The richest and best of rewards— your applause !

You have, then, done wisely to grant that precious recompense
to one so little deserving as myself, because you have thereby
held out a prospect to higher minds of what' they may expect
from you.   You have fanned the flame of pure patriotism, and
I trust enlisted in your service the juvenile patriots of the land
with talents superior—oh! beyond comparison—to my pretensions.   (Mr. O'Connell here turned to Mr. Sheil who sat near
him.) [Hear, hear.]

And he and others will be roused to serve and adorn their
widowed country.

Of your traducer I shall say nothing.   You have refuted his
calumnies.   For myself I need not tell you that, in the struggle
for the liberties of Ireland, every peril, personal or political, is
to me a source of pleasure and gratification.   For myself I can
only once more repeat that any language I am acquainted with
sinks beneath the sensations with which a reward so disproportioned to the only merit I can lay claim to (that of good intention) inspires me.

I have heretofore loved my country for herself—*I am now her
bribed servant, and no other master can possibly tempt me to
neglect, forsake, or betray her interests !*

Forty years have elapsed since this protestation: nearly seven since the death of him
who made it. Let Ireland now calmly review his life and acts, and say did he not keep
his word

At the meeting of the 18th, at which Mr. O'Connell thus spoke, there were read preliminary to the business of the day, communications from the Earl of Donoughmore and
Henry Grattan, in answer to the explanatory address of the Board, passed some meeting
previous.

The tone of these letters was not improved, continuing to savour very much of captious
superciliousness; but the ground which the writers took at the beginning of the correspondence was so far lowered, that they consented to receive, *as suggestions*, the statement
of Catholic opinion which they had before so stiffly refused, and endeavoured to stigmatise
as an attempt at dictation.

After a few words from Mr. O'Connell and others, the consideration of them was post
poned to a future day

CATHOLIC BOARD.

Saturday, December 24th, 1813.

EDWARD BLAKE, of Frenchfort, in the Chair.

We close the record of Catholic proceedings in the eventful year 1813, with their meeting
of Saturday, December 24th, on a matter that had given rise to considerable excitement
and discussion—it was the speech of Dr Dromgoole, when proposing his motion of entire

repudiation of securities; and the whole affair can be best explained by a brief account of some of the occurrences at it.

On the chair being taken, Dr. Dromgoole rose and said he had, on the last day of meeting, intimated that it was his intention to take an early opportunity of replying to the animadversions made on his speech. It had borrowed its importance, not so much from anything to be found in the speech, as from the mutilation of the paragraphs. As he meant to have it printed in a correct form, accompanied with a vindication of his statements and opinions, he trusted the Catholic Board would, until then, give him a short respite of opinion.

Mr. O'Gorman immediately got up, with the *Dublin Evening Post* in his hand, containing Dr. Dromgoole's speech, and a sheet of paper, containing the heads of the objections which he (Mr. O'G.) intended to urge.

Mr. O'Connell and others urged the propriety of granting the delay desired.

After some discussion, Mr. O'Gorman being called upon proceeded:—

"Sir, this is a question of too vital and important a nature to be stifled or suppressed. It resolves itself, in fact, to this point: whether the Catholics of Ireland shall silently submit to have themselves considered as participators in the folly and guilt of a speech which amounts to a complete verification of all the calumnies imputed to us by Dr. Duigenan, Mr Giffard, or Sir Richard Musgrave—for silence is, in this instance, acquiescence.

"The objectionable passages of that speech which were heard, were rebuked on the spot both by my learned friend (Mr. O'Connell) and myself; those were the passages in which he described different descriptions of sectaries, as nestling under the wings of Protestantism; and in which he alluded to the improbable, nay, almost impossible case of a Catholic becoming the king of those realms."

Mr. O'Gorman then went on to review the speech, *seriatim*, and concluded thus:—

"I have felt it a paramount duty to disclaim, both on my own part and that of the body, doctrines so unwise, so injurious, so dangerous, so unjust, and so unchristianlike; and I trust the disclaimer will be adopted by this meeting.'

Mr. Finn followed, and entered his solemn protest against the doctrines contained in the speech imputed to Dr. Dromgoole.

Mr. O'Connell said, that before the question was put, he, too, was anxious to deliver his sentiments; and although he concurred with the resolution, and was desirous to redeem the Catholic Board from the novel charge of bigotry, yet he was still more anxious to rescue his excellent friend, Dr. Dromgoole, from the load of much unmerited calumny.

In despite of that calumny, he would call and consider Dr Dromgoole his excellent friend; he had qualities meriting that name, both as a public and a private man. As a public man, he was zealous, talented, honest, incorruptible, persevering, indefatigable; as a private man, he was kindly, sincere, unaffected —with as little of the oppressive bigot disposition about him— with a disposition as contrary to bigotry and oppression as any human being.

In public, you all know him—in private, I know him well; and a man more abhorrent of any violence or constraint upon any religious opinion whatsoever, however repugnant to his own, cannot exist. I have, therefore, to complain, that so much clamour has been raised against him upon the report of a speech which, he tells you, is not correctly reported—and which we,

who were present when he spoke, all know cannot possibly be
correctly reported. I do but justice to my friend in this description; and although there is no calumny I fear so little as a
charge against me of bigotry—because even my enemies know
that I am the devoted advocate of the principle of religious liberty—yet I must do myself the justice to say, that no man can
reject and condemn, more distinctly or emphatically than I do
whatever of intolerance, or of harshness, or of bigotry, may be
found in the speech published as that of Dr. Dromgoole.

But I do not condemn that publication upon any ground of
impolicy; policy does not seem to me to be the ground upon which
our censure should be placed; I know of no policy that could
justify, or ought to palliate the suppression of every man's real
opinions; for my part I have no desire to enter into the pale
of the constitution under any disguise—I have no wish to filch
away any part of the constitution. My sentiments are frank and
avowed: I am a Roman Catholic from conviction, as well as in
consequence of my birth and education—I am firmly attached
to the Catholic persuasion, because it appears to my mind the
best; and whilst I admit, cheerfully, to others a similar right to
selection and preference, I disclaim and reject any emancipation
but that which shall be granted to me as a Catholic.

If this declaration be displeasing to our enemies—if it have
not sufficient of accommodation and conciliation for our kind
and condescending friends, let them reject my claim, for I never
will condescend to offer that claim otherwise than as a Catholic.

Speaking, therefore, of the speech, not as spoken here by Dr.
Dromgoole, but as published for him, I have no hesitation in
saying, that it is not because of its impolicy I find any fault with
it, but upon that principle of mutual toleration and respectful
courtesy towards each other, which ought to govern the speeches
and publications of all sects of Christians.

Perhaps we are justified in treating the bigotry of a Catholic
with more harshness than the same quality in a Protestant, just
as the injury one suffers from a friend is more unpardonable
than the extreme of outrage from an enemy; yet I am grieved
to see that those very persons who behold, with perfect indifference, the Catholic religion and Catholic people of Ireland outraged and insulted in the most scandalous and infamous manner,
exhibit all the violent and frantic irritation of a diseased and
morbid sensibility at the lesser offences comprised in the speech
published by Dr. Dromgoole. I do complain that this morbid
sensibility should exhaust its violence upon the speech attributed

to the learned doctor ; and whilst I do not justify, but reprobate every harsh and narrow-minded passage in that publication, I do not, I cannot forget the beastly and brutal bigotry towards us which is daily exhibited in the newspapers in the pay of the government, and which is sanctioned by the laws themselves.

This clamour, which has been excited respecting the learned doctor's speech, brings with it one source of gratification. I am pleased to find our Protestant friends and enemies so alive to the evils of bigotry. It seems to me as if they had made a new discovery, and they show a zeal and freedom which does honour to their feelings, and is proportionate to the goodness of the cause in which they are engaged—that of hostility to bigotry. I have ran before them—in this hostility to bigotry I now most heartily join them, friends and enemies—I most cheerfully join them in their hatred of bigotry ; all I require of them is to allow this holy animosity to be impartial and just—to suffer it to be applicable and applied to all parties and religious persuasions.

Let it not be exhausted and spent upon Dr. Dromgoole's speech ; but let, at least, a little of it be reserved for the bigotry of those who attack the Catholics of Ireland.

I have had lately occasion to refer to Dr. Duigenan's pamphlets ; and I thought to select some passages to show how much bigotry may be borne by modern liberality, provided it were bigotry directed against the Catholics. But it was vain to endeavour to select—there is but one idea in the entire of his works, that Irish Catholics are perjurers in principle, traitors from choice, and murderers by religion.

During the Richmond administration in Ireland, this man was made a privy councillor, for no other reason but his calumnies against us, and yet these detestators of bigotry—these men who are now in such a ferment against illiberality—these accusers of Dr. Dromgoole were silent, or applauded the promotion of Duigenan ! If, however, I have not been able to make any selection from amongst the calumnious rhapsodies of Duigenan, I have collected a few flowers from the government newspapers of the last six weeks—I will not disgust you with the reading of more than two of them.

Under the date of the 18th of last November, a newspaper in the pay of the Castle has the following tirade, upon the occasion of the seat called Castle-Brown, in Kildare, having been, as it asserts, purchased by Jesuits :

" Ireland stands in imminent danger. If Popery succeeds, her fairest plains will once more witness days worthy of bloody Mary (

and the walls of Derry shall again become the lamentable bulwarks against Popish treachery and massacre !"

Well, this from men who hate the expression of any kind of bigotry ! who are in a rage at Dr. Dromgoole for using the word "novelty" in a disrespectful sense; it is, one would think, rather uncivil. " Papist treachery and massacre" are perhaps nearly as bad as " Protestant novelty."

But this is a mere jest, compared with a paragraph which I found in a government newspaper of the second of this present December. Hear it with patience :—

" The letter of Cranmer (alluding to a letter inserted in that paper), shows that times respectively, when each of the fundamental tenets of Popery were invented, viz., the power of the Pope to dispense with oaths, and depose sovereign princes, by absolving subjects from their oaths of allegiance, the nullity of oaths to heretics, their extirpation as a religious duty."

Recollect that it is not a mere isolated individual—it is a man patronized and salaried by the administration—a man paid with our money, that has the effrontery to traduce us thus. To attribute to us, as fundamental tenets, doctrines of perjury, murder, and treason—doctrines which, if they were those of the Church of Rome, I would not belong to her communion for an hour—doctrines which shock anity, and would make religion the most cruel and the most absurd mockery!

Where is now that fever of zeal and fever of liberality that induced the public press to strain all its energies on the attack of Dr. Dromgoole? Whom did his published speech accuse of perjury, of murder, and treason ? What ! shall it be said that, like the eels in the story, we Catholics are so accustomed to be skinned alive, that we do not feel it, but that the sensibility of every other sect deserves the highest protection—that of the Catholic people none ? Are, then, the Catholics, in the opinion of their friends, in such a state of moral degradation, that it is quite unimportant how they are treated ? Alas! I much fear there are too many who think so; and, miserable slaves that we are, our own dissensions encourage and justify the opinion.

But that opinion has a higher source still. The law—the barbarous and calumniating spirit of legislation—has consecrated the contempt in which we are held. No Protestant can hold office in Ireland without being obliged to swear :—

" That the invocation of the saints, and the sacrifice of the mass, *as they are now used in the Church of Rome*, are superstitious and idolatrous !"

Take notice, it is not any abstract notion that may be formed of these practices, but the practices themselves, "*as they are actually* used," are idolatrous.

Thus our Protestant relatives, kinsmen, friends, are to swear solemnly, to attest to the ETERNAL BEING, that we are IDOLATERS! Hence, then, with the partial and corrupt irritability that seeks for causes of censure in the language of an unavowed individual Catholic, and forgets the paid, the salaried, the authorized, alas! the sworn calumnies, the bigotry of our adversaries.

But do I justify the speech given to the learned doctor? Oh, no; certainly not. I do not think calumny and bigotry can or ought to be set off, the one against the other; or that the Catholic could or ought to compensate himself for the intolerance of his enemies by being himself intolerant. No; I condemn both —I condemn equally—I condemn the paid bigot and his employer, as well as the volunteer bigot and his approvers. I would if I could silence both, and establish in the place of hatred, bigotry, and recrimination, a heart-cheering system of affection, toleration, and mutual cordiality; and I would call upon all the liberal press of Ireland—a press which has such a paper as the *Dublin Evening Post* at its head—not to exhaust all the thunders of my friend Dr. Dromgoole, but to reserve enough of its fire and fury to blast and destroy all the enemies of perfect freedom of conscience.

Let me not be for one moment mistaken. Much as I regard Doctor Dromgoole, I never shall conceal my decided disapprobation of some of the topics contained in his printed speech. I heard one of them here; and, respecting my friend as I sincerely do, I distinctly reprobated that topic, and insisted that reproachful language should not be used of any sect or persuasion. Doctor Dromgoole will also give me credit to believe, that if I had heard any where other topics of the printed speech, I would equally have disclaimed them at the moment.

But there is much exaggeration in the censure I heard this day—the meaning is shamefully mistaken—I had almost said, distorted; but there is one thing quite clear, that this Board is the most unfit theatre in the world for polemical divinity. It is bad enough any where—here it is abominable. The Protestant divines assert their system commenced with the Christian era, and was disfigured by the idolatrous errors of Popery for centuries. The Catholic divines assert, that our system commenced with the apostles, and has been continued since, in uninterrupted and unbroken succession and that our adversaries

have embraced human inventions in the stead of truth. The in-
fidel will be apt to exclaim, "*Sottise des deux parts !*"—and the
sober layman will leave the discussion to the divines at both
sides.

Doctor Dromgoole seems to think that the word Protestant,
which has been in use for near three hundred years, is a novelty.
The word seems to have caused great anger and violent indignation. I really am not aware of its insulting quality. If it be
true, why not use it? If it be untrue, what harm can this unimportant falsehood do? But the fact is that those subjects, one
and all, are unfit for our discussion here. The mutual assertions
of polemics cause irritation and enmity, and never can induce
conciliation or conviction. No man is ever converted from his
opinions by persecution or abuse. Let all those subjects be for
ever banished from amongst us, and let us set the glorious example of preaching and practising the doctrines of that Christianity
which is founded in fraternal affection, and best evinced by fraternal charity.

Eight years have now elapsed since our agitation commenced.
During that period we have had meetings of every class; we have
had speakers of every age, of every occupation, of every profession; we have spoken in the hour of hope; we have talked in
disappointment; we have been heard in the long intervals of
doubt—almost of despair; during this period our active, zealous,
and indefatigable enemies have watched us well. The secret spy,
the avowed hireling, the treacherous friend, have attended to all
our discourses, and yet they have been unable to detect one sin
gle phrase of bigotry, a single expression of illiberality, a single
idea of harshness to other sects, or a single indication of that
mind which would retaliate oppression upon the oppressors.

We could not have kept a secret so long. We could not have
suppressed our real sentiments. Why has there, to the present
period, been no bigotry discovered? For one reason only, because it did not exist; and those who boast that they have at
length discovered it in Doctor Dromgoole's speech—those who
exhibit such joy at the discovery, do, in spite of themselves, by
their very triumph at the discovery of bigotry in one individual
pay the Catholics at large the compliment of admitting that
the discovery was unexpected—that bigotry was rare amongst
us, and the finding of it, therefore, a triumph to our enemies.
In this very triumph is found the finest eulogium that could be
paid to the long-oppressed and mildly-suffering people of Ireland. It is the voice of a bitter enemy in its joy proclaiming

its astonishment that a cause of reproach could be found to
exist in any one individual of the Catholic body.

I conclude by giving my concurrence to the motion.   For my
own part I have devoted much of my time to the Catholic cause
—a time of little value, alas! to my country, but of great value
to myself; but I would not give up one hour of that time, or a
single exertion of my mind, to procure the mere victory of any
one sect or persuasion over the others!   No, my object is of a
loftier and different nature.   I AM AN AGITATOR WITH
ULTERIOR VIEWS!—I wish for liberty—real liberty!

But there can be no freedom any where without perfect
liberty of conscience.   That is of the essence of freedom in
every place.   In Ireland, it is eminently, almost exclusively
the hope of liberty.

The emancipation I look for is one which would establish the
rights of conscience upon a general principle to which every
class of Christians could equally resort—a principle which would
serve and liberate the Catholics in Ireland, but would be equally
useful to the Protestant in Spain—a principle, in short, which
would destroy the Inquisition and the Orange Lodges together,
and have no sacrilegious intruder between man and his Creator!
I esteem the Roman Catholic religion as the most eligible.   All
I require is that the Protestant, the Presbyterian, the Dissenter,
the Methodist, should pay the same compliment to his own persuasion, and leave its success to its own persuasive powers, without calling in the profane assistance of temporal terrors, or the
corrupt influence of temporal rewards.

With these views, with these sentiments, I concur in the resolution proposed, and, I am encouraged to concur in it because
it does not appear to me that my friend, Doctor Dromgoole,
thinks it ought, in its present shape, to be opposed, or if I find
any difficulty in acceding to it, that difficulty arises from my
great contempt for that hireling clamour, excited by the vilest
bigots, against a very feeble imitation of their own practice, and
to which clamour you appear to me to offer a tribute which it
does not deserve to obtain.

This senseless and magpie accusation of bigotry is raised
against us by the very creatures who are daily trafficking themselves in bigotry.   The Orangemen arraigning religious prejudices!   Oh, for a sermon in favour of chastity, to be preached
by the venerable keeper of a brothel!   Yet to this goddess is
the tribute of this vote offered.   Think you that you will conciliate those who raised this uproar?   Do you imagine that

light from heaven would convince them? No, no ; they have an immediate interest in traducing you, and, right or wrong, they must give their allotted portion of bigotry.

I do dislike this motion on that account, and it does require the knowledge that Doctor Dromgoole himself will not oppose the motion, to bring me over to his support.

There is another principle of opposition, too, which I meant to take, and if I did, it would, I imagine, be irresistible—it is the precedent which this vote will leave. I solemnly protest against it as a precedent. I would not have the Board made re sponsible for the speeches of any individual. I protest against such responsibility. I would not have the Board deemed answerable for the speeches of my learned friend, Mr. O'Gorman, nor for my nearer friend, Mr. Finn ; still less would I have you held responsible for my discourses. And yet if we disavow Doctor Dromgoole's speech, what will be the obvious consequences? Why, that the hirelings will exclaim at every sentence that sounds harsh to their servile ears, "Why, this is the sentiment of the Catholic Board." It will be in vain to answer, " No, it is the sentiment but of an insignificant individual"—I allude to my own case—the reply will in future be decisive. It must be the opinion of the entire Board, otherwise they would disavow it, as they disavowed Doctor Dromgoole.

Thus the present motion, originating as it has done with men whose errors can be attributed only to mistaken patriotism, will for ever afford our enemies an argument and a proof that the opinions of each individual are authorized by the Board, because not disavowed.

Yet I will not divide the Board, but vote for this motion, because it gives me another opportunity of reprobating bigotry and religious rancour in general, and of pouring my execrations on the causes of that feud which changed the inhabitants of this land from countrymen and brothers, and made them aliens to each other, and mortal enemies ; that feud which has struck down the ancient kingdom of Ireland from her rank as a nation, leaving her nothing but the name of the paltry and pitiful province, in which we vegetate rather than live !

After Mr. O'Connell. Dr Dromgoole spoke, and the resolution passed.

2 B

COURT OF KING'S BENCH.

THE KING *at the Prosecution of the* DUKE OF RICHMOND *v.* MAGEE.

We revert once more to the year 1813, to give another act of the Magee melo-orama.

MR. O'CONNELL said he was instructed to move the Court to set aside the verdict of conviction obtained by the prosecutor against Mr. Magee. These were the reasons assigned by the defendant, upon which the verdict ought to be set aside :—

"First—That the jury was not regularly empannelled, ballotted, and sworn.

"Second—That the jury was unduly returned upon a second *venire* after a former *venire* had been issued and returned.

"Third—That there was not evidence to go to the jury of a publication of the alleged libel in the county of the city of Dublin, and for the misdirection, in that particular, of the learned judge."

To raise these objections in law, it would be necessary to examine the facts, and these facts were brought before the court by the affidavit of Mr. Magee, which stated that notice of trial had been served on him on the 17th of May last ; that a writ of *venire facias* had issued, tested the 5th of May, and returnable on the Monday next after the Morrow of the Ascension, which had been returned with a panel annexed ; that he heard and believed that a writ of *distringas* had issued, grounded on that *venire.*

The affidavit further stated, that the trial having been postponed, it did not take place till the 26th of July; that a new writ of *venire facias*, bearing test the 31st of May, and returnable in three weeks from the Holy Trinity, had issued and was returned with a panel annexed ; and that in the panel annexed to the second *venire*, there were some names different from those in the panel annexed to the first *venire.*

Such were the facts disclosed by Mr. Magee's affidavit. There had been abundant time given to the crown-solicitor to answer this affidavit, and to rectify any mistake or misapprehension ; no answer had been given, and, therefore, for the purposes of the present motion, it must be taken for granted that the facts were as Mr. Magee stated them to be ; in other words, the defendant's affidavit must be taken to be true.

Chief Justice—We will not look to any affidavit—these are matters of record. We will consult the officer of the court upon them · this is the time to have the facts ascertained by him. Mr. Bourne, how is the fact ?

Mr. Bourne, the clerk of the crown, said that on the 5th of May a *venire* issued returnable on the 31st, being the last day of term, on which day the court had postponed the trial. The *venire*, however, had been returned in the usual way, with the panel annexed by the sheriff, on the 30th of May, but no *distringas* issued on that *venire*. On the 31st of May a second *venire* issued, returnable on the morrow of three weeks of the Holy Trinity and on this *venire* a *distringas* issued, and the trial was had.

Mr. O'Connell asked if the names inserted in the second panel were not different from those inserted in the first?

Mr. Bourne said that there were *some* of them different.

Mr. O'Connell—Now, my lords, we are agreed as to all the facts, except one. We are agreed that two *venires* issued, and were returned with a panel annexed to each, and that those panels were different from each other. The only fact we can dispute about is the issuing of the *distringas* on the first *venire*. Now the affidavit states that such *distringas* issued. The crown-solicitor, who must know the fact positively, as it belonged to him alone to issue it, is silent. The fact being uncontradicted by him, who alone could positively contradict it, must be taken for admitted, because not denied. I am, therefore, at liberty to assume, for the purposes of my argument, that there were two writs of *distringas* as well as two writs of *venire*.

Chief Justice—No such thing. The officer declares that there was but one *distringas*, and we will take his certificate as conclusive.

Mr. O'Connell—My lord, the officer cannot certify any such thing. He does, I admit, declare it, but he cannot certify it, because a negative certificate to that effect would be in the nature of an *alibi*, lasting from the 5th to the 31st of May. If the officer was for one moment out of the office during that period, the *distringas* might have issued without his knowing anything about the matter; for it is not to be supposed that he can possibly recollect all the writs he signs for a month. Now the practice is to issue the *venire* and *distringas* together. You will find it so laid down in Tidd's Book of Practice, 5th edition, page 795. The assertion of the officer is therefore of no weight in the matter. The only way to contradict our affidavit would be by the affidavit of the crown-solicitor, who must know the fact, or a negative certificate out of the seal-book.

Justice Day—If the *distringas* had issued, it would have been returned to the office, and we should find it with the officer, along with the *venire*.

Mr. O'Connell—No, my lord, you could not find it with the officer; it is never returned to the office; it cannot be returned to the office, because it is not a returnable writ; nor is it ever brought in, unless there be a trial, and then it comes to the officer, together with the *postea*.

Justice Day—Why, it is impossible that *distringas* could have issued. The *venire* was returnable on the 31st of May, the *distringas* could not issue until the next day, and upon the 31st the court postponed the trial.

Mr. O'Connell—Is it your lordship's opinion that the *venire* being returnable the 31st May, the *distringas* could not be tested or issue until the 1st of June?

Justice Day—Certainly; that is my opinion. I am quite clear that the *venire* being returned on the 31st of May, the *distringas* must bear test next day.

Mr. O'Connell—Then, my lord, that would be error; that precisely would make the Record erroneous. The identical point was determined in Tutchin's case, 2nd Lord Raym 1061, and 14th Cobbett's State Trials, 1095. There the *venire* was returnable the 23rd of October—the *distringas* bore test the 24th, and it was held to be a discontinuance, and the judgment was arrested.

Chief Justice—*Well, Sir, we are all of opinion that the report of the officer must be taken conclusive; and you are bound to argue the case as if no distringas had issued. We will not hear the matter debated after the declaration of the officer.*

MR. O'CONNELL—Well, my lords, I must take it so; and really it does not weaken the case of my client. The law is as clearly in his favour as if it was admitted that the *distringas* had issued;

although, until controlled by the court, I did not feel at liberty to give up even a point of no great importance.

Let me, before I go into the argument of the case, take the precaution (probably a superfluous precaution) of showing that the court can, and may set aside verdicts had against any person charged with a crime. When the party accused is acquitted, then, indeed, the court cannot set aside the verdict; but it is otherwise when a verdict of conviction was given. In 2 Hawkins, 628, it is said to be settled, that "the court cannot set aside a verdict which acquits a prisoner, but they may a verdict that convicts, as contrary to evidence, or the directions of the learned judge, or any other verdict whatsoever for a mis-trial." This authority is express, that a verdict of conviction may be set aside; so it seems may any verdict, which I understand to mean even a verdict of acquittal in the case of a mis-trial.

Now, my lords, this is an application to set aside a verdict of conviction, and in the strongest possible case—a case of mistrial. There was, I contend, a mis-trial for two reasons:—

First, because the jury was not regularly empannelled and balloted for according to the provisions of the act, called the Balloting Act; and

Secondly, by reason of the second *venire*.

The third point—the want of legal evidence—belongs rather to the class of cases upon improper verdicts, than as a ground of mis-trial.

Upon the first point, the fact appears on the record that there were but twenty-four jurors returned. If the case be within the Balloting Act there should have been at least thirty-six. The fact also is, that the jury were sworn as they appeared; but if the case be within the Balloting Act, they should have been drawn by lot. Now I contend for it that this case is within the Balloting Act. That act is the 20 Geo. II. c. 6. It is entitled "An Act for the better regulating Juries." The recital of this act is general, that many evil practices had been used in corrupting of jurors returned to try issues before justices of assize, or at nisi prius, and expressly to prevent the like practice the remedy is applied by the legislature.

The first section prescribes the amount of property, which shall be a necessary qualification for jurors, for the trial of issues between party and party before justices of assize or nisi prius, save upon trials *per medietatem linguæ*. I entreat of the court to carry the exception in its recollection, as trials *per medietatem* can occur only in criminal cases. The 3rd and 4th sections of

the statute are those the construction of which is now in controversy; they enact that, after the 1st of May, 1756, every sheriff
or other officer, to whom the return of the *venire*, or other process, for trial of causes before the justices of assize or nisi prius,
doth belong, shall annex a panel thereto containing not less than
thirty-six, nor above sixty names of jurors, and that those names
need not be entered in the *distringas*, but the panel referred to ;
and the statute then enacts, that those names shall be written
on separate slips of paper or parchment, and put into a box or
glass, and drawn out by some person appointed by the court for
that purpose ; and that the first twelve names so drawn shall
constitute the jury, unless in case any person be set aside on a
challenge when another name is to be drawn, and so on in every
case of challenge until the jury is complete.

My lord, if the case of Mr. Magee come within this statute,
there has been a mis-trial, because the proper number thirty-six
were not returned, and because there was no ballot, or drawing
of the names. But it will be contended for, on the other side,
that this act of parliament is applicable solely to civil causes,
and does not extend to criminal causes ; and this position is sustained upon the legal rule that the king is bound by no act of
parliament, unless specially named or necessarily implied. I
admit, my lords, the fact, that the king is not expressly named
in this act. I admit also the rule, as a general rule, but it has
exceptions, and I think I shall be able to demonstrate that this
act binds the king, and extends to criminal cases. I shall establish that this act includes criminal as well as civil causes upon
three grounds :—

First—Upon the ground that this is one of those acts of parliament which, upon general principles, bind the king without
his being specially named.

Secondly—Upon the construction of the act itself taken sepa
rately.

Thirdly—Upon the construction of this act, as induced and
forfeited by a comparison with other statutes made in *pari ma-
teria*.

I have admitted the rule, that the king is not bound by any
statute unless specially named. I insist there are exceptions
to that rule. The very first authorities in the law prove those
exceptions. The words of Lord Coke, in the 2nd Inst., 681, are
these—" Whenever a statute is intended to remedy a wrong, as
the statute 32 Henry VIII., to prevent a discontinuance by the
husband of his wife's estate, the king is bound by it, though not

specially named." I beg also to refer the court to 5th Co. 14—
letters A and B, called the "Case of Ecclesiastical Persons." It
is expressly laid down "that all statutes to suppress wrong—to
take away fraud—to prevent the decay of religion—bind the
king, though not named in them." And in the case of the king
against the Archbishop of Armagh, reported in 1st Stra. 516, it is
decided, that the king is bound, without being named, by all
statutes for the advancement of religion or of learning. Thus,
then, we have exceptions to the rule that the king is not bound
by a statute unless expressly named. The king is bound, though
not named by all the statutes made to remedy wrong, to suppress wrong, to take away fraud, to prevent the decay of religion,
to advance religion, to advance learning.

Does the statute in question come within any of those exceptions, is the only remaining question. It is an "act expressly
to prevent the evil practices of corrupting jurors, and to procure a fair and impartial trial." Is not that to remedy wrong?
Is not the suppression of the corrupting of jurors a suppression of
a wrong? Is it not a fraud to corrupt jurors, and does not this
act take away a fraud? I may go further and say, that it is an
act to prevent the decay of religion, because in the corruption
of jurors perjury is necessarily implied, and surely, where perjury
prevails religion must decay. But this may be a forced construction, and I need not rely on it. It is quite plain, that this is a
statute which remedies a wrong, suppresses a wrong, and takes
away a fraud ; it suppresses and gives a remedy for a wrong
of the most grievous, scandalous, and abominable kind, the corrupting of jurors; it takes away a fraud of the most mischievous
and dangerous description, the corrupting of jurors.

Is the court prepared solemnly to determine that to corrupt
jurors is no wrong, nor any fraud ? Look at the instance put by
Lord Coke of a wrong, for the suppression of which the king is
bound without being named. A discontinuance by the husband
of the wife's estate—a mere inquiry to individual property ; and
can it be imagined that the corrupting of jurors, which renders
all property, life, and honour insecure —the corrupting of jurors,
which destroys the very foundation of our laws, and renders
civilized society worse than barbarism—the corruption of jurors,
including judicial robbery and murder ; that all this is so light
and trivial a nature as to be no wrong, no fraud, and not to be
compared in importance with the invasion by a husband of the
rights of his wife to her freehold estates.

I feel that I consume time unnecessarily when I press this

point.   It is impossible that this evil should not be admitted to
be a wrong and a fraud ; as the authorities which I have cited
cannot be overturned, I look with confidence to your decision.
that this statute of the 29th of George II. is one which binds
the crown, although not specially named ; but the case is still
stronger, because even if the Court decided the question against
me on the general principle, yet this particular statute is so
framed as to bind the king.   He is bound by the first section.
That section enacts, that in the trial of all issues joined between
party and party in the courts above or at Nisi Prius, no person
shall be a juror unless he have a certain property, except on
trials *per medietatem linguæ,* and also except in counties of cities
and towns.   Now, if ever the exception proved the rule, this is
a case where it does so.   The exception is of a trial *per medietatem ;* but that trial can be had in criminal cases only.   It can
be had in the one case alone where the king is a party.   The
legislature have excepted this species of trial.   If they had not
expressly excepted it, it would have been included, or this absurdity must follow, that the legislature, by express words, excepted that which was not included at all in the enactment.

To this dilemma is the Court reduced, it must decide either
that the general enactment of the first section includes criminal
cases, and then this exception is sensible and rational, or that
the first section does not include criminal cases, and then this
exception, introduced by the legislature, is absurd and nonsensical.   Either my construction of the statute is the right one, or
the legislature has enacted gross and childish nonsense.

Which construction will the Court adopt ?   Assuredly that
construction which I put on the statute, and which gives to the
entire of it good sense and plain meaning, and the Court will at
once reject that interpretation which converts the act into a
jumble of absurdities and contradictions.

Having thus established upon the constitution of the first section of the statute that criminal cases are included in it as well
as civil, I come to the third and fourth sections ; and here the
matters appear quite plain : those sections speak of any sheriff
or other officer having the return of the *venire* or other process,
for the trial of causes (those are the words of the act), before
justices of assize or *Nisi Prius* in any county.   The words are
general, they apply to all sheriffs and officers, to all jury process,
to all causes, and to all counties.   There is no exception here
as in the first section of trials *per medietatem.*   There is no exception here as in the first section of counties, and cities, and

towns.   Let it be recollected that I have established that the
first section applies to criminal as well as civil cases, and then
have only to contend for it, that the other sections, which are
more extensive in the words of enactment, are at least equally
extensive in meaning.

The state of the argument is this; I have proved that the
first section, though more limited in phrase and language, extends
to criminal as well as civil cases, and all that remains is to show
that the third and fourth sections, which are more extensive in
phrase and language, are equally extensive in meaning.   But
the very terms of the proposition are self-evident, otherwise this
absurdity would follow, that when the legislature said *less* it
meant *more*, and when it said *more* it meant *less*.   And now, my
lords, to decide the construction of the statute against my client
will be to introduce inextricable confusion and absurdity into
our statute law, and render language of no avail but to confound
all meaning and understanding.   It may, perhaps, be answered
as I have before heard the assertion made, that the king is never
included under the description of a party to a cause.   My answer
will be the words of the 10th Charles I. c. 13, an act which I
will have again to refer to.   It enacts :—

" That in all cases where a full jury does not appear, then
either party may pray *a tales*, as well where the *king is a party*
as otherwise."

I cite this act to show that the legislature, under the description of party to a cause, has included the king, thus giving a
legislative meaning to the word which precludes the necessity of
any argument to show its legal meaning.   I have thus obviated
the only objection that I conceive can be raised to my construction of this statute.   I have thus I hope successfully contended, that this statute should be construed to extend to criminal as well as civil cases, but I deem it right to confirm this construction, by pointing the attention of the Court to statutes
made for the same purposes—the procuring of fair and impartial
jurors.   Statutes made in aid of the *same purpose* have been always used to aid the construction of each.   The courts consider
the entire as one system of law, each part of which should serve
to support and illustrate the rest.

Let us see then how the present statute can be best considered
to form part of the same system, with the 10th Charles I. ; it is
the 13th chapter of the 2nd session of that year.   The section
I would particularly call the attention of the Court to is the
third ; it is entitled :—

"An Act concerning the Appearance of Jurors at Nisi Prius."
The first section relates to the qualification of jurors and regulates the *venire ;* the second regulates the *distringas ;* and the third provides for the appointment of *a tales,* for default of the jurors named in the panel "in all actions as well where the king is a party as where he is not."

Now take those two statutes together, you will find the king included in the first, which purports to regulate the jurors at Nisi Prius ; you will find him included as a party, and you will find criminal cases (for none other can be meant) comprised in the words "all actions." See, then, whether it be possible to exclude the king from the second statute. That statute is part of the same system with the first, and both are made with the same object ; the intention of the legislature is the same in both—to procure a fair and impartial trial. As in the third section of the statute of the 10th of Charles I., so in the first section of the 29th of George II., criminal cases are plainly included.

Can the Court perceive all this, and not feel the monstrous absurdity of attempting to disjoint the two statutes—to break up the system of law into fragments, by giving to one statute a different construction from the other ? And why should this be done ! Why should the Court make the legislature thus capricious and contradictory ? Why should it make the first statute differ from the second ? Why should the Court make the first section of the second statute contradict the third and fourth sections of the very same statute ! Surely the mischief which the legislature desired to remedy is as great in criminal as in civil cases.. It is as easy to corrupt jurors in criminal as in civil causes. Nay, it is more likely to be done. The temptation to corrupt—the temptations to be corrupted are much stronger in criminal than in civil causes. The evil consequences are as great, really much greater, in the criminal causes. Why then shall the Court adopt a construction of the statute, which, against the words and plain intention of the legislature, must confine the remedy and relief intended by parliament to crimes of minor mischief and more difficult perpetration, and exclude the cases of greater evil and more easy commission.

My lords, I confess I am anxious to succeed upon this part of the case. If the Court will give my construction to the act, they will go far to prevent any odious and atrocious attempt to pack a jury. The subjects of the land will have the same chance of fair and impartial juries in criminal cases tried at Nisi Prius, as they have in civil suits, and the law upon this subject will be consistent with itself, and conducive to justice.

Let it not be said that the practice of returning but twenty-four jurors has fixed a judicial construction upon this act. I deny that any practice can alter the law, and besides practice in civil cases (and the practice has been confined merely to civil cases) cannot have been considered as of any importance. It is a practice that could not be controlled by the parties, because under the statutes of Isofailes, the error is cured by verdict, and therefore, there has been no person interested in civil cases to bring this practice in review before the court. It would be of no avail to a party in a civil suit to go to the expense of calling on the court to decide upon the construction of this act after verdict, when he was stopped from taking any advantage of the error.

I do, therefore, firmly rely on it, that the practice in civil cases cannot afford any assistance in construing this statute. *The statute itself must decide the question*, and to that I with confidence appeal.

If this statute, the 29th George II., be held to extend to criminal cases, there is an end to all question, and the verdict must be set aside. If, on the contrary, the court shall decide that this statute does not extend to criminal cases, then our second objection must prevail—that of the two *venires;* because it is only that statute which allows a second *venire* after the first is returned. The prosecutor is reduced to this dilemma—either the 29th of George II. c. 6, extends to criminal cases (and then there has been a mis-trial for want of sufficient return of jurors, and of a ballot), or that act does not extend to criminal cases, and then there has been a mis-trial, because of the second *venire.*

My lords, neither at common law, nor under any other statute could a second *venire* issue after the return of the first ; even in civil cases no second *venire* could issue at common law. The case of *Pretious* v. *Robinson*, 2 Vent. 173, proves that there could be no second *venire* at common law. It was an action in which issue was joined in Hilary Term, in the second year of William and Mary; the *venire* was awarded and issued in that term. In Easter Term a second *venire* issued, upon which a trial and verdict were had ; the jury returned *was precisely the same upon both venires*, yet the verdict was set aside upon the grounds of its being a mis-trial. The court said all the proceedings were void, there being no authority for the second *venire*. This, my lords, is a case in point, though a weaker case than ours ; for the jury

in that was the same—in ours, different. The case of *Pretious*
v. *Robinson* appears, however, to have been the cause of the interference of the legislature. The inconvenience of continuing
the same jurors from term to term, until it should suit the convenience of the parties to go to trial; to continue the jury for
years in attendance, was felt, in civil cases, to be a great inconvenience to suitors as well as to jurors themselves, and therefore
the legislature interfered. But you see from the case I have
cited, that at common law there could have been but one *vehire*,
even in civil cases; and the practice was to continue the jury
by issuing a *distringas*, then an *alias*, and then a *pluries distringas*, and so on until the case was tried, see Tidd's Prac. 789. The
first statute in England that altered the law in this respect was
the 7th and 8th of Will. III. c. 32, which was amended and extended by the 3rd Geo. II. c. 25. In Ireland, the statutes that
relate to the *venire* are, first, the act of the 10th Chas. I., st. 2, c.
12; it enacts, that any mis-awarding of a *venire*, or defect in its
return, shall be cured by verdict; but in this act there is an express exception of criminal cases.

Second—The act of 7 Will. III. c. 25; it enacts, that want of
fifteen days between the test and the return of the writ of *venire*
shall not be deemed error; but in this act there is also an express exception of criminal cases.

Third—The act of the 6th of Anne, c. 10; it enacts, that a *venire*
may be directed to the body of the county, and not to any particular ville, but criminal cases are excepted.

These, my lords, are the only statutes in Ireland which altered
the common law, with respect to the writs of *venire facias*, before
the act of the 29th Geo. II. c. 6. But in the three former acts
criminal cases were excepted, so that unless the last act, the 29th
of Geo. II. applies to criminal cases, the writ of *venire* in those
cases must be regulated by the common law, and then the authority of *Pretious* v. *Robinson* is in point to show that there could
not have been a second *venire*.

But this doctrine does not rest upon the authority of that solitary case. The law is distinctly laid down in the case of the
King v. *Franklin*—a case which occurred in the 5th of Geo. II.
the year 1731, and of which a full report is given in 5th T. Rep.
453, in the case of the *King* v. *Perry*. In Franklin's case it was
material for his counsel to show that there *ought* to have been a
second jury under the English Special Jury Act; but they failed
upon the construction of that act, and they were compelled to
admit that at common law there could not have been a *venire de*

novo. Lord Raymond, then Chief Justice, is indeed express upon the point. "The statute of William and Mary," said he, "does not extend to criminal cases ; and, therefore, in criminal cases there cannot be a second *venire.*" Such is the express decision of the court in Franklin's case, in 1731; and that case is adopted as clear law in 1793, by the unanimous opinion of the Court of King's Bench, in the *King* v. *Perry.* The same law that, after one *venire* returned, there could not issue at common law a second *venire,* is expressly laid down by all the books of practice; you will find it in Tidd, 5th Ed. 1792, in Gilb. Comm. Pleas, 92, and laid down very distinctly in the case of the *King* v. *Haire and Mann,* in 1st Stra. 267.

In that case there was a *scire facias,* at the suit of the crown, to repeal letters patent. One of the defendants pleaded to the facts—the other demurred in law. The Attorney-General applied for a trial at bar. It was resisted until after the argument of the demurrer ; because if that were determined against the crown, any trial of the fact would be superfluous. The Attorney-General, however, said that the *venire* was returned and filed, so that if the trial was put off, there would be a discontinuance. But the court said, "there is no danger of a discontinuance if the *venire* be filed, the proper entry is that the jury *ponitur in respectu ;* if it be not filed, you may enter a *vice comes,* not *misit breve,* and either will prevent a discontinuance."

So that upon all these authorities—*Pretious* v. *Robinson, The King* v. *Franklin, The King* v. *Perry, The King* v. *Haire and Mann,* and from all the books of practice, I draw this undeniable conclusion, that after one *venire* is returned and filed, there cannot be a second *venire* without a discontinuance and a mis-trial, unless under the authority of the statute of the 39th of Geo. II. But the prosecutor, in the present case, cannot rely on that act, because if this case be within its provisions, then there was a mis-trial for the other reasons adduced.

Perhaps some flimsy attempts may be made to distinguish this case from those I have cited, upon the idle allegation that the first *venire* was not filed. My lord, this distinction would be so very senseless, that I conjecture it would be resorted to only because there is no other possible mode of escaping from the dilemma to which the prosecution is reduced. But I disdain to argue upon so unfounded a distinction. The *venire* is produced in court from amongst your records ; it is produced, together with the rest of the record, and as part of the entire. Nothing is filed unless this *venire* be filed ; and I believe it would be impossible to show any authority to distinguish between records that are filed and records that are not. I dismiss the objection with the perfect conviction that it cannot be seriously attended to, and does not deserve a serious reply.

Thus, then, stands the case; there are two *venires*, both returned and filed. The first is totally abandoned, and, although in the office, yet a false suggestion entered of *vice comes* not *nisit breve*. There was, therefore, a discontinuance, there was, therefore, a mis-trial.

There was a discontinuance because the first *venire* was not followed up in regular course. The entry should have been a respite of the jury—*ponitur in respectu*—*respectus* being the law Latin for a respite; but instead of that entry a new *venire* is awarded, and upon that the trial is had. The first *venire* is abandoned, and completely discontinued; any the slightest interruption in the progress of the process is a discontinuance. In Tuchin's case, which I have already cited to the court, the *venire* was returnable the 23rd of October; to continue the process regularly, the *distringas* should have borne test on that day; it bore test the next day, the 24th, and this was held to be a discontinuance or interruption of the process; yet, as the law knows no fraction of a day, the process was well continued by the *venire* until the last moment of the 23rd of October, and the *distringas* carried it on from the first moment of the 24th. There was therefore, no discontinuance, no interruption of the process, save for the ideal instant that may be supposed to separate the last moment of the 23rd, from the first moment of the 24th of the same month; but the law recognising the existence of that ideal instant, as making a separation between the *venire* and *distringas;* and the *venire* being completely run out *before* the *distringas* commenced, the court decided that there was a want of connexion between them, which prevented a regular continuance of process, and the judgment was arrested, and Tuchin escaped punishment, although he had been convicted by a jury.

But see how much—how infinitely stronger Mr. MAGEE'S case is; the first *venire* was returned the 30th of May last; on the 31st its return was out; from that day to this there have been no further proceedings on it; it has been abandoned, not for an ideal instant, but for many months, and altogether; there is no man who can contend but, under those circumstances, a discontinuance has occurred in the cause.

I may, my lords, be greatly mistaken, but I confess it seems to me to be impossible to get over these objections. The prosecutor has discontinued his first *venire*, and therefore. the subsequent proceedings are void.   He has tried Mr. MAGEE upon a second *venire* and a new panel, and therefore the proceedings are void ; or if he shall resort to the statute, which enables parties in civil cases to abandon the first and issue a second *venire*, then, my lords, his proceedings are equally void for want of the ballot and the proper number of jurors which that statute requires.

The third point relates to the evidence.   I feel the case so strong upon the two views of it, that I am disposed to abandon the third to the exertions of my learned colleagues.   In fact, the only evidence given of a publication in Dublin of the matter alleged to be libellous was the paper left at the stamp office. Now, the purpose of its being left there was merely to have the stamp duties calculated and paid.   It was not left there for any other purpose of information—not that the columns should be read or communicated to others.   Can this be called a publication ?   I admit it proves proprietorship ; but suppose—and upon the present evidence you are bound to suppose—that only the one paper which was sent to the stamp office to have the duties ascertained, was printed, could you call that a publication of a libel in Dublin ?   I submit that would be carrying the doctrine of constructive publication farther than it has yet been ; and the court will not, I trust, make, in a criminal case, any decision so unfavourable to the liberty of the subject.

I conclude with conjuring the court not to sanction the proceedings of the Attorney-General in this case ; for, supposing and admitting that it did not originate in improper motives, it may lead to improper conduct in future law officers.   I mean not to make an unnecessary charge upon the present law officers of the crown ; but if the court determines this case against my client, they will enable a future attorney-general to change his jury as often as he pleases, until he shall procure one suited to his purposes : whilst, by the same construction, the subject will be deprived of all chance of a fair and impartial trial, by being deprived of the large number to select from—the knowledge of their character and situations in life in time to prepare his challenges, and the fair chance of having the best men in the panel on the jury ; all precious advantages, to which every subject who has property to the amount of £10 at stake is clearly entitled.

PRESENTATION CUP TO MR. O'CONNELL.

In reference to the subject of popular compliments to Mr. O'Connell, it will save time to insert here the following publication from the *Dublin Evening Post* of January 18, 1814:—

" Daniel O'Connell, Esq., at his house in Merrion-square, was this day, January 14, 1814, presented with a silver cup, accompanied with the following

"ADDRESS.

" ' SIR—Please to accept from the manufacturers of the Liberty of the City of Dublin, a silver cup as a token of their confidence and esteem. It is but the widow's mite;— yet they hope not less acceptable, as it overflows with their affections.

" ' They value equally your private worth, and public transcendant bilities, evinced on all occasions for the good of our common country.

" ' May your days be long and happy in your honourable professional pursuits—so as your children's children may unite in greeting you with ours, for having handed down to posterity, unsullied, those virtues and talents which we all so much admire.

" ' We are, with respect, your faithful humble Servants,

" ' J. TALBOLT.
" ' C. DOWDALL.'

"ANSWER.

" ' FELLOW-COUNTRYMEN.—You make me very proud ; you make me very vain. You call this the token of your esteem and your confidence : you offer it as the pledge of your affections ! ' My Irish heart swells with grateful acknowledgments. It prizes your gift beyond all that princes or powers could bestow.

" ' How fondly do you overrate me ! I have not talents—I have not services—but I have a heart devoted to the civil and religious liberties of our common country. Your kindness confirms and exalts that devotion ; and sooner shall my heart cease to vibrate than forsake the cause of conciliation and cordiality, or abandon the wish and the hope for the re-establishment of the independence of Ireland.

" ' You compare the situation of your manufactures to the widow's state. Alas ! your country is widowed too! Manufactures and freedom equally require a resident and national legislature. Before 1782 Ireland had neither manufactures nor freedom. Legislative independence gave her both ; and as they were created by the genius of the Irish constitution, so they can revive only under the same powerful influence.

" ' My gratitude to the manufacturers will be best evinced if I can awake the people of Ireland to hope for a REPEAL OF THE UNION ! If they once entertain hope, success will be neither remote nor difficult. The nations of Europe are bursting their bondage. Shall Ireland alone remain accursed ? Yes! she is accursed in the insane dissensions of her inhabitants. But she may become a nation again, if we all sacrifice our parricidal passions, prejudices, and resentments on the altar of our country. Then shall your manufactures flourish and Ireland be free

" ' To hold a place in your esteem, confidence, and affection, and to merit it by the honesty of my wishes for the welfare of our country, is the first ambition, fellow-countrymen, of your devoted and grateful Servant,

" ' DANIEL O'CONNELL.' "

The cup in question is a very handsome one, and reflects great credit upon the taste and skill of the Irish artist and fabricators.

On the occasion of receiving it, Mr. O'Connell, in allusion to the then subsisting custom of toast-giving, declared that no toast should ever be drunk out of it save

" THE REPEAL OF THE UNION !"

It is a melancholy thing to reflect upon, that low and poverty-stricken as was the condition of that extensive district entitled "The Liberty" of Dublin City, it has long since fallen much lower, and, indeed, declined into utter ruin. The time is many years ago gone by, when such a presentation could be repeated as that which we record; and, "The Liberty" which, during the Irish Parliament, was the focus of active and most remunerative manufacturing employment of various descriptions, is now, and has for a long time been known, only as the focus of the last and uttermost wretchedness and helpless destitution.

ILLEGAL SOCIETIES.

The following speech of Mr. O'Connell's, was delivered on the very last day of the year .618 :—

At a meeting of the Catholic Board, at the Shakspeare Gallery, Friday, 31st Dec., Mr. O'Gorman in the Chair,

MR. O'CONNELL rose to make his promised motion on the subject of illegal associations. He said that the importance of the subject he had to introduce should serve as an excuse for want of method. The miseries of Ireland pressed too heavily on the heart not to exclude every other consideration.

It required no authority to prove that Ireland had been wretched almost beyond the lot of humanity. Her sufferings were known where they were not felt—in England. The present Lord Sidmouth, then Mr. Addington, in one of the Union debates, had said, "that in the six hundred years since the reign of Henry II., there had been more unhappiness in Ireland than in any other civilised nation not actually under the visitation of pestilence or internal war. There was neither prosperity, nor tranquillity, nor safety." Such was the representation made before the Union, and it was now confessed by everybody, that the Union had not diminished our calamities.

It was beyond the present question to consider the causes of the miseries of Ireland. They were either too remote, or too obvious, to justify any lengthened commentary. But the effects of her wretchedness were daily exhibited in various wild and frightful forms.

Amongst these effects stood prominent the tendency of the people to form combinations and secret associations. The law of nature which, during evaporation, gave a form to the crystal, was not more powerful than the moral influence that tended to connect in bonds almost indissoluble the children of misfortune. Under various fantastic denominations, the Irish people classed themselves together in societies, some of which still exist, but many had left little trace, save their names, their crimes, and the graves of their victims.

There had been, or were, " White Boys," and " Right Boys" —" Caravats" and " Shanavests"—" Thrashers" and " Carders" —" Hearts of Steel "—" Peep-o'-Day Boys"—" Defenders"— "Orangemen" and "Ribbonmen"—and, above and different from all, " United Irishmen."

The immediate causes that had produced those associations were of two different kinds. The associations had two distinct characters. The first cause and character were to be traced to the oppressions of tithe-jobbers and land-jobbers ; and to this class belonged the " White Boys," " Right Boys," " Caravats," " Shanavests," " Thrashers," and " Carders." The second cause and character were easily discerned in religious animosity and rancour, and to this class belonged the " Hearts of Steel," " Peep-o'-Day Boys," " Defenders," " Orangemen," and " Ribbonmen." The last, and the " Defenders," were exclusively Catholic—the other three exclusively of the different Protestant persuasions.

As to the United Irishmen, they were not peculiar to either sect, but endeavoured to embrace all sects, and to include the partizans of all classes, and amongst the United Irishmen there had been found men, led away by the vain desire of republican institutions—men who, however mistaken, may be admitted, now that the storm has long since ceased, to have been actuated by pure, though erroneous, love for Ireland.

The evils which created the first class belong not to any of the objects for which this Board assembles. They, however, deserve and require the greatest attention from the legislature and government : they exist in the actual state of society in Ireland —in the exactions of the tithe-farmers and tithe-proctors—*in the natural rapacity of land-owners, excited by a limited market, and a multitude of bidders.*

These evils are aggravated, too, by the laws which enable the landlord to dispense with any personal confidence in the tenant. *The statute law has done much to aggravate the evil ; the laws were made by landlords : they have improved the proceedings in replevin and ejectment, until the landlord may, with perfect ease, first strip the tenant, who has assumed too high a rent, of all his property, and then evict him from the land.*

To restore the common law in these particulars would much tend to quiet the country ; but no efficient remedy will ever be adopted by a distant, and ill-informed and mis-informed legislature ; and these evils will continue until Ireland shall have a resident parliament, instructed in the facts, and interested in the results. Perhaps the period of such a parliament is remote, but in it are centred all my hopes of permanent tranquillity for Ireland.

The class of combinators on the score or under the pretence of religion is that which should engage our attention at present ; these religious animosities are terrible and degrading, but they bring with them this consolation, that they are easy of remedy. They exist only at the pleasure of the administration : the government, when it pleases, can terminate their course, and it will remain at the discretion of the ministry to put a period to religious dissensions, unless, indeed, the Orange faction shall be so long fostered as to grow too strong for the persons who have nourished it, and to become too powerful for the legitimate authorities of the state. That period is still distant ; and now by the expression of a single wish, the government could extinguish religious factions in Ireland for ever. The Orange system exists only because it has the countenance of the administration, and if that system ceased, religious animosities would vanish.

To understand the nature of the associations on the score of religious differences, it is necessary to recur briefly to their history.

The " Hearts of Steel" and " Peep-o'-Day Boys" were Protestant associations for the oppression of the Roman Catholics. They existed only in the northern province. The " Peep-o'-Day Boys" associated principally in the county of Armagh ; their first object was to prevent the Roman Catholics from having arms. They attacked the houses of Roman Catholics early in the morning—taking name from this circumstance—and deprived the Catholics of arms. When the arms were quietly surrendered, the assailants usually did no further injury, but any resistance provoked vengeance ; and resistance was natural, and, being sometimes successful, became frequent ; thence bloodshed, and the repetition of attacks and outrages.

The Roman Catholics, assailed by the " Peep-o'-Day Boys," without the slightest colour of law, and without any original provocation on their parts, formed themselves into counter as-

sociations, under the descriptive name of " Defenders;" and from
the year 1791 to the year 1795, a village warfare, a feud of un-
mitigated barbarity, pervaded a great part of Ulster, between
the two rival and illegal parties—the " Peep-o'-Day Boys" and
the " Defenders."

In the year 1795 a material alteration took place in one of
the parties. Several battles had taken place in that year, in
which the "Peep-o'-Day-Boys," though inferior in numbers, were
infinitely superior in discipline and arms, and were consequently
successful. Their views enlarged : the total extirpation of the
Catholics from Armagh, if not from Ulster, became a probable
expectation ; and the name of " Peep-o'-Day-Boys" yielded its
place to the system, regularity, and superior station of "Orangemen." A regular organization was planned and effectuated by
bigots of a superior rank and order. A feeble imitation of free-
masonry lent something of mysticism, and much of regularity, to
the Orange lodges.

I had from a militia officer, a friend of mine, the detail of the
initiation of an Orangeman. The gentleman I allude to was
allowed, by mistake, to be present in an Orange lodge, in the
county of Wexford, when two Orangemen were *made*. The ceremony contained an analogy to the facts related in the seventh
and eighth chapters of Judges, and the password was, "The sword
of the Lord and of Gideon !"

The Orangemen were the 300 selected by divine inspiration
from the immense multitude—the 32,000 who originally formed
the camp of the Israelites ; and as those 300 were composed, by
the directions of the Most High, of the men who lapped water
out of their hands, without kneeling to drink at the running
stream, so this chosen few of the Orangemen were designated as,
" the men who lap and do not kneel !" And distinct allusions
were made to a different liquor for Orangemen than water—a
liquor to be furnished by the kneeling and superstitious Papists !
The oaths were administered with much solemnity, and the secret
signs communicated : and the newly-initiated were reminded that,
with so small a number, Gideon had brought confusion and destruction on the numerous host of the Midianites ! The Orange
men became thus the chosen of the Lord, and the Papists were
the Midianites doomed to destruction.

I have, I confess, sometimes been amused at the happy apti-
tude of the hideous allegory. The chosen few, with Gideon,
were successful, not by force or bravery, but because they introduced discord and dissension in the camp of their enemies. The

Midianites turned against each other their own swords, and thus
the Orangemen excite strife and dissension among the Catholics,
*and place their best hopes of success in our wretched differences
and squabbles !*

And there are some Catholics, perhaps, who would co-operate
in the hateful purpose; but the number is few, and the Orangemen must be disappointed, because there never was a period in
Irish history when so much congenialty of sentiment prevailed
amongst the Irish Catholics.

The first design of the Orangemen was the extirpation of the
Catholics from Ulster : nor was this design confined to mere
speculation.   Out of the county of Armagh alone, more than
seven hundred families were banished by the Orangemen ;—
their properties were destroyed; their houses levelled or burned;
the lives of all endangered ; some of them murdered, and the
survivors driven from their farms, and compelled to quit the
province.   Had they committed any crime ?   Had they been
guilty of any offence ?   Yes, they had : they were Roman Catholics.   Nothing more ; but that was sufficient : they were
Roman Catholics.

This is the first grand fact in the history of the Orangemen
In the audacity of falsehood, this fact may be denied, and the
person who asserts it may be treated as a calumniator.   But
this is a fact of which there is, fortunately, the most unquestionable evidence.   There is the testimony of Lord Gosford, the
governor of the county of Armagh—testimony given publicly at
a meeting of the magistrates of that county, convened by him on
the 28th of December, 1795.   He there stated, " that this banditti," as he called them, "had commenced and carried on a persecution of atrocious cruelty ; that they spared neither age, nor
sex, nor innocence ; that neither ancient nor modern history
could supply an example of the ruin and misery inflicted by the
Orangemen ; and he added—let this, I pray, be marked well—
" that the only crime of the wretched objects of this ruthless persecution was, a profession of the Roman Catholic faith, or an intimate connexion with a person of that faith !"

Such was the testimony of a Protestant nobleman, resident on
the spot, an eye-witness of what he described ; and he, too, a man
of strong anti-Catholic feelings.   The evidence of Mr. Grattan,
also, at the same period, may be adduced.   In parliament, he
painted the origin of Orangeism—he detailed the first persecution
of the Catholics by the Orangemen—" Those insurgents," said Mr.
Grattan, "call themselves Orangemen, or Protestant Boys—that

is, a banditti of murderers, committing massacre in the name of God !" Such was the language of Mr. Grattan—such was the evidence of Lord Gosford ; and thus is the cardinal fact of the commencement of Orangeism, and its mischievous and murderous origin, placed beyond a doubt.

From such a beginning the spirit of the Orange institution may be easily collected. Its history in Ireland is written in letters of blood, from its first murders in Armagh to its innocent and almost praiseworthy manslaughter of the present year in the streets of Belfast.

It is said that the original plan of extermination was soon abandoned—that it was softened down to perpetual slavery and degradation ; that Catholics are to be allowed to live, provided they are quiet and tractable slaves. The rebellion in which the United Irishmen had engaged drove some men of a milder tone and temper into the Orange associations, and they are said to have assumed something less of persecution ; but the living principle of exclusion and reproach still remains, and cannot but bring forth fruits of bitterness and oppression.

In 1800, a new organization of the Orange lodges took place, and, with more regularity, less zeal was exhibited. The system languished after the Union, and was decaying fast, and strong hopes were entertained that it would sink into oblivion, when, in an ill-starred hour, Ireland was handed over to the legal advisers of the secretaries to the Duke of Richmond, and in the year 1808, Orangeism, patronised and revived again, displayed its horrid front, to affright and desolate the land. The great patron of this revival was made a privy councillor—the Orange processions, insults, tumults, and murders ensued. I need not remind you of the unpunished massacre of Caharnashegagh ; need not recal to recollection the introduction of this system into the county of Donegal, where it had been theretofore unknown. But I am compelled to lead you to that fact, because it is there that the origin of the Ribbonmen is to be found.

The county of Donegal is one of the most Catholic counties in Ireland : almost all the peasantry in that county are Catholics. Like the other two greatest Catholic counties, Galway and Kerry, neither disaffection nor disturbance were found there during the rebellion ; and, as in the latter counties, so in Donegal, the Orange institution was unknown until the year 1809, when, in the Richmond administration, it was introduced into that county, one scarcely knows why, unless as part of a general plan. Orange processions were established ; the people, insulted and outraged, were easily induced to apprehend greater evils: they saw no reason why, during a profound and long-continued tranquillity, their religion should be vilified and insulted, and their persons exposed to danger and outrage. They imagined that the Orange Society was sanctioned by the law, as they saw it remain unrestrained and unpunished. They resolved to form a counter-association, similar in plan and form to the Orange Association, to be exclusively of Roman Catholics, and to be confined merely to the purposes of defence against the attacks of the Orangemen. The Roman Catholics of the county of Donegal did therefore associate under the denomination of Ribbonmen; and several anti-Orange or Ribbon Societies were soon formed.

The Ribbonmen, like the Orangemen, were bound together by oaths of secrecy and co-operation. Like the Orangemen, they had their secret articles annexed to their oaths; like the Orangemen, they were organized in lodges, having a master and a deputy-master, a secretary, and three committee men to each lodge. The Orangemen, have, indeed, five committee men to each regular lodge—the Ribbonmen were content with three. As the Orange violences in the counties neighbouring to Donegal became more frequent, the Ribbon Societies extended. About two years ago they formed a regular Grand Lodge, still imitating the Orangemen, which was composed of nine grand officers, and held its sittings in Derry. From this Grand Lodge, there were, I am told, more than ninety lodges affiliated; and it is said that in the space of six months upwards of twenty thousand men between the ages of eighteen and forty, had been sworn in as members of this association! Such was, as I am informed, the state of the Ribbon Society in the month of June, and it was then rapidly extending itself into the more southern counties of Ulster.

I have great pleasure in adding, that the address published by the Catholic Board, in June last, had the most powerful effect in putting a stop to the meeting, and, I am assured, it induced the Grand Lodge of the Ribbonmen to resign its functions. Those who were before the most active partizans of the system have since exerted themselves with energy and success to suppress its lodges. The system has been broken up, and unless the renovated activity of Orangeism shall give it new life (of which there is much reason to be apprehensive), the Ribbon Society will shortly be at an end for ever.

I have not stated the oaths by which this society was bound Those oaths were, I understand, three times uttered At first the Ribbonmen's oath commenced with a direct, positive, and unconditional oath of allegiance. They also swore to assist in the defence of the Catholic clergy and laity against the attacks of Orangemen, and an oath of secrecy as to what was to be privately communicated to them was added. This oath was soon altered; and in its place was substituted an oath resembling almost exactly the Orange oath. It began with an oath of allegiance to the king, his heirs and successors, so long as he and they should protect the Catholic clergy and laity of Ireland from the illegal violence of schismatics, heretics, and Orangemen; and it then continued and concluded as the former oath. The third oath and that latterly adopted, was different from the former in nothing else, as I am informed, than in omitting altogether the part that related to allegiance to the king.

Such, according to my information, is the short history of the Society of Ribbonmen. This society owed its origin to the Orangemen. Its decay was the work of the Board. But the Orangemen are again on the alert. The resemblance in colour and name, for in nothing else are they like to the patriots in Holland, has filled the Irish bigots with fresh hopes and renovated fury. In the north, they indulge in excesses almost as ridiculous as they are illegal. A festival of three days, an Orange boven of half a week, has been lately celebrated in Derry. Under the ludicrous pretence that it was necessary to bless, with the Orange flag, the first stone of a new court-house, a three-days' festival was celebrated, sufficient to remind the poor Catholics of Derry of the Spartan solemnities, during which it was permitted to inflict every cruelty on the wretched helots.

The consequences of this most absurd carnival, at which baronets and bishops, sheriffs and clergymen, magistrates and mobs joined in revelry, may be a revival of the Ribbon lodges. Attempts have been made, I am told, to revive them, even before this festival; and unless a strong impression be now made of the illegality and impolicy of those lodges, there is reason to apprehend that they will once more multiply.

The people will readily listen, however, to us, as they have done before. They know we are actuated by no motive but the pure and disinterested desire to obtain for them relief, in the only way that relief can or ought to be obtained—according to the constitution. We who are honoured with popular confidence, only because we have deserved it—we will easily persuade the people to avoid violating the law, or exposing themselves, as they must do, if they continue in those associations, *o the treachery of their pretended friends, and to the persecutions of their open enemies. We will point out to the people that these illegal societies expose them to certain punishment ; that no useful result can possibly arise from them ; that the individuals who belong to them will be prosecuted, and the Catholic body disgraced by their continuance, whilst the very existence of those societies will serve as a pretext and excuse for the Orangemen to continue their outrages. It will gratify their appetite for vengeance, and disappoint the hopes and wishes of the individuals of this Board, who are looking for Emancipation through the legitimate channels of the constitution. In short, the Orangemen will be gratified and delighted by the continuance of those associations ; whilst the real friends of Ireland, who, amidst danger and calumny, have continued to advocate the Catholic cause, must retire in disgust and despair, if the people will not abandon all illegal societies.

That the Ribbon Society is illegal is easily proved by a reference to the statute book. The statute of the 50th of the King, chapter 102, includes almost every possible case of an association bound together by any solemn oath or engagement. The oath is illegal, if the person taking it be bound to any association, brotherhood, committee, society, or confederacy whatsoever, formed, or to be formed, for any seditious purpose, or to disturb the peace, or to injure persons or property, or to obey any commander, officer, or leader, or to obey any committee, or the orders, rules, or commands of any committee, or other body of men, or to assemble at the desire or command of any such person or persons, or not to give evidence against any brother associate, or for various other purposes mentioned in the statute.

Now, it is very clear that an organised association such as the Ribbonmen, must be bound, by import of its engagement, to assemble at the command of some superior, and to obey some rules or orders. The Ribbonmen are, therefore, liable to punishment under this statute. The Orangemen by the sixth rule in their secret articles, are bound to assemble at any time when summoned by the master, getting ten hours' notice, or, if possible, at any other time. They are also bound to obey all the rules contained in the ten secret articles. It is, therefore, equally clear that the Orangemen are within the statute of the 50th of the King. And upon an indictment, properly framed under that statute, if the evidence of the facts that really exist could be given, there is no doubt that for every Ribbonman and Orangeman sworn since the year 1810, the person who administered the oath could be transported for life, and the Orangeman or Ribbonman who took it could be transported for seven years.

I am aware that the Orangemen run no great risk of being prosecuted. But the impunity of the Orangeman affords no great protection to the unfortunate Ribbonman. The Ribbonman will be only the more certainly prosecuted because of the indulgence held ont to the Orangemen. Would to God I could see an administration in Ireland that would equally and impartially hold out protection and punishment, according to law and not otherwise, to both parties.

I am very ready to believe ; nay, it is the conviction of my soul, and I loudly proclaim it, that if Lord Whitworth was apprised of the real state of those facts, he would fulfil the pledge he has so distinctly given—of an equal and impartial administration of justice. But Lord Whitworth is surrounded by men who are deeply interested in deceiving him. The facts are concealed from him. The truth is disguised. The Catholics are represented as desiring the overthrow of the constitution—the Orangemen as its supporters. But the truth is, that the Catholics most anxiously wish to see the constitution placed beyond the possibility of danger ; they are, to a man ready to die for the integrity of the empire and of the constitution. The Orangemen, on the other hand, seek to control the legislature, and to oppress their fellow-subjects, and perpetuate their slavery; they would continue Irishmen as slaves, in the name of a constitution that gave us freedom as a birthright.

To return to the illegality of these associations. The Ribbonmen are liable to be indicted under another statute, by the 15th and 16th of the King, chap. 21, it is declared to be a high misdemeanour, punishable by fine, by imprisonment, by whipping, for any persons to assemble, by day or night, with any unusual badge, or to assume any particular name or denomination. The Ribbonmen are liable to punishment under this statute ; they assemble with a badge—a green ribbon ; they assume the denomination of Ribbonmen. For either offence they may be indicted and punished. It is true that the Orangemen come expressly within the provisions of the same statute—they assemble with badges of orange—they assume a particular denomination —Orangemen. Under this statute they may and ought to be indicted ; nay, I can answer for it they will be indicted, if the Catholics enable us, as I am sure they will enable us, to put together the funds necessary for carrying on those prosecutions. But even the impunity of the Orangemen affords no prospect of safety for the Ribbonmen. The Ribbonmen of the North, like the Whiteboys of the South, will experience the rigour of the statute, although the Orangemen may be allowed to escape without punishment, notwithstanding the plain violation of the law!

The duty of the Board, under those circumstances, is to expose to the Catholics of Ulster the criminality and the folly of engaging in any secret association. It may be suggested that the people are driven, in their own defence and by persecution, into those combinations. The answer is ready—the people need not be driven to any such extremity, because for the outrages of the Orangemen legal redress may be obtained; and if the individuals attacked be too poor to procure that redress for themselves, the Board will readily enable them to bring their cases before the public and the courts of justice. We will enable them to seek for and obtain all the redress that the law can give in such case; but no man shall partake of our assistance who will continue any longer a member of any illegal confederacy whatsoever.

Let what will become of the Ribbonmen, from us they can never expect countenance or support. But the poor Catholics who have the good sense to avoid any such association shall be certain of meeting pecuniary and professional assistance. We will not go to war with the Orangemen, however able and willing we may be to do so; but we will go to law with them, and expose their absurd pretensions and atrocious cruelties to contempt and punishment.

By adopting my motion for another address to the people, you will have an opportunity of again cautioning them against being the dupes of their own passions, or of the artifices of their enemies. You will call upon them to confide in the laws, and you will enable them to secure all the protection that law can give.

Mr. O'Connell concluded by moving—That a committee should be appointed to prepare an address to the people cautioning them against illegal associations.

Motion agreed to and the meeting adjourned.

"ADDRESS TO THE PEOPLE.

"FELLOW COUNTRYMEN AND FELLOW SUFFERERS!—The General Board of the Catholics of Ireland, to whom you have confided your petitions to the legislature, once more address you. They claim the continuance of your confidence only because they feel that they deserve it by the zeal and purity of their intentions and exertions in the cause of your religion and your country.

"Fellow-Countrymen, the object of your petitions is sanctioned by justice; it is enforced by wisdom; it *must* be attained, unless the artifices of your enemies shall triumph over justice and wisdom! We say their *artifices*, because their arguments have failed, and their calumnies are forgotten or despised.

"Amongst their artifices we dread but one—it is that which has been tried with success on former occasions—it is one to which you are exposed by your situation, your sufferings, and your feelings. *Your enemies wish to betray you into illegal associations and combinations!* They wish to bring upon you punishment, aggravated by its being merited; and they still more earnestly desire to ruin your cause and that of Ireland!

"Their emissaries, become more cautious from former detection, are likely to assume deeper disguise. It is our duty to expose to you the evils which must ensue to yourselves and the Catholic cause if you enter into any illegal or secret combination.

"Repeated acts of parliament have pronounced associations and combinations, for almost any imaginable purpose, to be *illegal*. A recent statute, called the 50th of Geo. III. chap. 102, besides more associations which are plainly criminal, as for seditious purposes, or to disturb the public peace, has declared every association, brotherhood, committee, or society whatsoever to be unlawful, if formed to injure any person, or the property of any person—*or to compel any person to do, or omit, or refuse to do, any act whatsoever.* That statute has also declared any oath or engagement to be illegal, which imports to bind any person to obey the rules, or orders, or commands of any committee or body of men not lawfully constituted; or of any captain, leader, or commander not appointed by the king; or binding any persons to assemble at the command of any such captain, leader, commander, or committee, or of any person not having lawful authority; or binding any person not to inform nor give evidence; or not to reveal nor discover having taken any illegal oath, or having done any illegal act, or to conceal any illegal oath hereafter to be taken.

"For inducing or procuring, by any means, the taking of any such oath or engagement, the punishment is transportation for life. He who takes any such oath is liable to transportation for seven years; and it will not be received as an excuse that the party has been compelled, by force or menace, to take such oath.

unless he make full discovery to a magistrate within seven days.

"By another act of parliament, called the 15th and 16th of the King, chap. 21, it is made a high misdemeanour, punishable by pillory or whipping, to wear any particular badge or dress, or to assume any particular name or denomination of party.

"Recollect, too, we entreat of you, that not only is it unlawful and punishable to assume the name, or wear the colours or badge of such an association, or to take or induce any person to enter into engagement or oath to belong thereto; but that almost every act, in pursuance of such oath or engagement, is made by various acts felony of death. Even to assault a dwelling house (strangely as the phrase may sound), is a capital felony in Ireland. And to raise the arm, even without a blow, is an assault in law.

"So that he who, in pursuance of the plans of any such association, raises his unarmed hand against a dwelling house, may, for that offence, be capitally convicted and suffer death!

"We select this instance to show you the extent to which capital punishments are applicable by law to the consequences of illegal associations.

"Transportation for seven years is the doom of him who enters into any illegal association.

"Transportation for life is visited upon him who induces another to enter into an illegal association.

"And finally—death is the punishment of him who does any one act in pursuance of the designs of an illegal association.

"Such, fellow-countrymen, are the punishments which the law denounces against illegal associations—whether they be called White Boys or Right Boys, Thrashers or Carders, Ribbonmen or Orangemen, they *all are liable to punishment*, and all deserve condemnation.

"It is quite true that some delinquents may escape; but do not flatter yourselves that you can be of the fortunate number. If you transgress the law, you will meet, as you will deserve, all the zeal and activity of prosecution.

"Reflect upon these serious subjects for your consideration. If you offend against the laws, what favour can you hope for? what favour have you any grounds for expecting?

"Reflect, also, upon the *inutility* of these associations. What utility—what advantage of any description has ever been derived from them? None—none whatsoever! No redress has ver been obtained by their means. They have been quite usuless! Nay, worse, they have always produced crimes!—robbery, outrage, murder!!!

" And they have uniformly been followed by numerous executions, in which the innocent have been often taken for and confounded with the guilty!

" Do you require any other arguments to induce you to refrain from these associations? Perhaps you are careless of your own lives? You cannot be insensible to the blood of the innocent!

" There is, however, another inducement to refrain: your enemies—the men who would deny you the poor privilege of worshipping your God as your forefathers have worshipped—these men, all these men, anxiously desire that you should form criminal combinations and confederations; they want but a pretext for framing laws still stronger and more sanguinary; they want but a pretext to lay the heavy hand of power upon your country and your religion!

" Your enemies seek to seduce or to drive you into illegal associations. Your friends, the Catholic Board, ardently desire to prevent your forming any such association. They conjure you, if you confide in them, to hearken to advice which can be dictated only by their affectionate attachment to you. They conjure you to respect the laws—to live in peace—to offer no outrage nor injury to any man—to seek legal redress alone for every injury and outrage inflicted on you.

" *That redress is and shall be*, within your reach.

" They beseech you to look for relief from your grievances only through the lawful channel of petitioning parliament.

" And they confidently promise you, that the wisdom of parliament will speedily extend that relief, if you continue, by peaceable and dutiful conduct, to deserve it; to gratify your friends, and disappoint your enemies.

" So will you afford us the happiness of seeing your religion rescued from the calumnies and inflictions of centuries of persecution, and your countrymen of all classes and persuasions reconciled, coherent, and finally free!"

CATHOLIC BOARD.

Saturday, January 8

SHAKESPEARE GALLERY, EXCHEQUER-STREET,

MR. SHERLOCK in the Chair.

Secretary read proceedings of former meeting.

Mr. O'Connell, from the committee appointed to prepare an address to the northern Catholics concerning *illegal societies*, stated the address was not ready, and, on motion, got leave to sit again till the next Saturday.

Mr. Lawless asked the secretary if the resolution for printing Mr. Lidwell's speech had been acted on.

Secretary replied it had not.

Mr. Lawless having said he would move for the printing.

Mr. Mahon saw no necessity for the motion.

Mr. O'Connell suggested to Mr. Lawless the appointment of a committee to have the speech printed. It was the best speech he had ever heard, and a copy ought to be in the hands of every member of parliament before the end of the long adjournment.

Suggestion adopted, and a committee of five named.

Lord Donoughmore and Mr. Grattan's letters having, on Mr. O'Connel.'s motion, been read.—

MR. O'CONNELL said, he trusted those letters had made, and would continue to make, a deep impression on the minds of the Catholics of Ireland.

He should judge of the moral fitness of the Catholic population of the land for freedom, by the sensation those letters had created and should continue to create. Deep, but not loud, should be the feelings of men deserving liberty. It belonged to the spirit of philosophic inquiry to trace out the causes of which the temper and tone of those letters were the natural results : but it belonged to the dignity of philosophic patriotism to bear with this temper and tone in patient, and, he may add, unrelenting calmness.

For my part (said he) I may, perhaps with the greatest justice, be denied the praise of either philosophy or patriotism ; but in treating of the subject of those letters, and especially of that of the Earl of Donoughmore, I have another guide ; it consists in perfect respect for the purity of his intentions, and great gratitude for his manly, uncompromising, unconditional, unqualified advocacy of emancipation. He did not talk of entering into any traffic between a portion of the liberty of the constitution and a fragment of the discipline of our Church. He did not insult his enslaved countrymen by supposing or admitting, that though we were quiet whilst we were kept in thraldom, we should become riotous, and ought to be put upon "*our securities*" the moment

we were liberated. No, Sir; the advocacy of Lord Donoughmore was precisely that which the great people whose cause he
was to support, wished and wanted. It took right and justice
for its lofty ground, and scorned traffic, and barter, and compromise.

I repeat, therefore, that Lord Donoughmore so entirely commands my respect and gratitude, that I am in no danger of suggesting any course respecting his letter inconsistent with those
feelings.

As to the other letter—that of Mr. Grattan—it is not my
intention to introduce, with respect to it, any proceedings for
the present; and I am the more inclined to refrain, lest what I
have said of Lord Donoughmore should suggest any unpleasant
contrast. If such contrast arises, let me not be accused for it—
I make no comparisons; and if, in the nature of the facts, any
contrast arise, let the blame be flung on the facts, and not on
me, who am bound by every argument supplied by my judgment,
and by every affection of my soul, to prefer—greatly to prefer,
and to praise, indeed to praise exclusively, the unconditional,
unqualified, uncompromising advocacy of our rights.

Such has been the support given to the Irish people by the
Earl of Donoughmore, and for that he deserves and possesses our
warmest hearts.

With these sentiments towards our advocates we are not to
forget ourselves. Indeed those letters not only make it impossible to forget, but they open a new view of the state of the
Catholics of Ireland; they have led me to a discovery of some
magnitude—they have shown me distinctly the cause of many
appearances that I reckoned most monstrous and unnatural; they
have reconciled me to Duigenan, to Musgrave, and to Giffard;
they have disclosed to me the source and secret of their abuse.
Vulgar it is, and coarse; but then vulgarity and coarseness are
scarcely the fault of the individuals; it is to be attributed to their
education, and habits, and tempers. Had they the education and
temper of gentlemen they would treat us differently; we should
have a better style and more courtly condescension in their reproach, and even in the calumny of their advice; but the principle would not be different from that which they act on at present.

It is a principle discoverable and discovered by me, for the
first time, in those letters. It consists simply in the natural and
moral superiority which the law imposes upon the Protestant over
the Irish Catholic. It is to be found in the natural and moral in-

feriority to the Protestant, which the law inflicts on the Irish Catholic. A century of persecution commenced by the grossest violation of the faith of treaties that ever disgraced the page of history, authentic or fictitious. A century of legal degradation has so lessened and brought down the Irish Catholics in the eyes of their Protestant neighbours, that we are in the scale of humanity but dwarfs compared with those social giants.

I was long aware that such was the estimate of us in which our enemies indulged ; but this correspondence was necessary in order to convince me that the same prejudice lurked in the minds of our friends. I flattered myself that we had risen in their estimation ; I did imagine we had ceased to be whitewashed negroes, and had thrown off for them all traces of the colour of servitude ; but this correspondence has, I confess, done away the delusion.

Perhaps they are themselves unconscious of this claimed superiority—indeed I believe that they perceive it not—being a matter of habit, and having arisen before reflection, and unaided by reasoning, it may well happen, and I believe it does happen, that our friends are themselves unaware of the judgment of inferiority which has been tacitly passed upon us ; and that when they announce, as those letters announce, a plain superiority— a superiority not as of any assumption but as of clear right, our friends are themselves ignorant of the assertion of any such superiority. In short, my conviction now is, that the inferiority of the Irish Catholic resembles a species of innate idea in the minds of our Protestant friends, which remains there unaccompanied by any distinct consciousness of its existence.

Do the Catholics really deserve this opinion of inferiority ? I think not—I think both their enemies and their friends will soon acknowledge their just claims to equality, if the Catholics continue to look to themselves and to their own exertions, for their first and best claim of success.

Conceding this superiority for the present, and cautiously avoiding to hurt its national pride, or to provoke any other exhibition of its inherent dignity, there is yet one passage in the letter of the Earl of Donoughmore which requires a reply from the Board, and one passage only. It is that which relates to representation —it is that in which the noble lord seems to charge upon us having assumed or exercised a representative capacity. I feel at once that this charge could have originated simply and singly in the mistake or misapprehension of the noble lord. It cannot have any other source whatsoever than from some misrepresentation of the mode of our association, or of our conduct when associated.

But, admitting and proclaiming the purity of the motive of making this charge ; it is, however, even upon that account, the more imperative upon us to set his lordship right upon the subject. We owe it to him to afford him accurate information on this interesting subject. We owe it to ourselves to prevent the possibility of the continuance of mistake or misapprehension of this important subject.

I am confident I need use no other argument to induce the Board to adopt my motion for giving the noble lord precise nformation with respect to our association, than the manifest propriety of giving our advocate a true view of our situation. We have too much respect for him to allow him to remain in error.

But there is another and a pressing motive for disclaiming the imputed representation. It is to be found in the construction put on the convention act by our adversaries. They have procured, by their arguments, the decision that " pretence" and " purpose" are synonymous, and that any persons who meet, no matter under what " pretence"—no matter for what " purpose" —commit a crime if they really be, or assume to be, representatives. This decision establishes that the crime prohibited by the statute, consists in " representation," but in " representation" alone. The pretence or purpose is immaterial. The only thing, said the Attorney-General, and say the judges of the King's Bench, to be inquired into is, representative or not. This decision suited the purposes of the prosecutor at the time it was pronounced, but it has now become inconvenient to him, and is certainly at this moment the protection of the Board from his attacks. Our construction of the statute would have limited the Catholic committee to the exclusive consideration of a petition. The only *purpose* should, according to our construction, have been petition, leaving us, perhaps, the empty honour of claiming an useless and almost ridiculous title to a representative capacity ; and then, upon our own showing, and with our own assent, the Attorney-General would have a right to put down the committee the moment it departed from the strict line of mere petitioners.

But our construction was overruled ; the Attorney-General was too wise to adopt it, though it was manifestly the most convenient, as well as the most constitutional view of the subject.

2 D

He did not foresee that we would divest the select meeting of the Catholics of all representative capacity, and that getting rid of representation, we should, upon the Attorney-General's own showing, and upon the authority of the Court of King's Bench, be entitled to discuss other subjects with as full and strong a right as that of petition.

The result of the prosecution of Doctor Sheridan and Mr. Kirwan, has, therefore, been highly beneficial to us. It has been infinitely more useful to the Catholic body than if we had succeeded in obtaining a judgment of the court. Then our committee must have been confined within the narrowest limits of preparing and forwarding petitions, but now we run no risk of any indictment on the Convention Act, whatever extent our deliberations may have.

There is, however, one precaution—it is simply this, that we are not to be, nor pretend to be, representatives.

Allow me here to protest against being understood to say that, as a lawyer, I conceive the construction put on the statute by the Court of King's Bench right. No ; I certainly think the court was mistaken ; and I hope the first possible opportunity of bringing that construction in review before a superior tribunal will be taken ; but, until it is reviewed, until it is altered, it is our duty to submit to it, and to acquiesce in it. I do, therefore, cheerfully submit to the decision, although not convinced of its accuracy : as the court has no claim to infallibility, it is liable to error.

But, submitting to its present opinion, it became necessary to avoid not only the reality, but all appearance of representation. We are not constituted upon any scheme of representation. We never claimed any representative capacity ; on the contrary, we always disclaimed it ; and having it now charged upon us by the Earl of Donoughmore, we are bound again to disclaim it, because our silence, under such a charge, might be construed into an admission of its justice. Yes, upon legal principles, silence would now be an admission of this legal crime; and it is scarcely necessary to remind the meeting that the same law officer who plunged the Richmond administration into a warfare of litigation—nor a very wise one, I imagine, with the Catholic people—has every motive of resentment, of passion, of prejudice, and even of interest to induce him, if he can, to involve the present administration in a similar silly contest.

The historian of human nature has admirably described his state physician as presenting similar remedies for all diseases

He prescribed bleeding and warm water for all his patients, with uniform success. They all died. The Sangrado of the law is as uniform in his prescription : it is simply a state prosecution, as a remedy for all evils. Prosecute, prosecute, is ever on his lips.

He has not, indeed, been uniformly successful ; nor has the learned and grave doctor effected any great political cures. But he is as sanguine as ever in his opinion of the efficacy of his prescriptions ; and if this letter of Lord Donoughmore remain unanswered, it will afford the Attorney-General a fair pretext for what he delights in—a new prosecution.

He will be able to read, as part of his speech, two paragraphs from the letter; and we should have the mortification of finding the language of our friend and advocate rendered useful to the most bitter and unrelenting of our enemies—the only one of our enemies, indeed, who actively, and zealously, and from his heart opposes us—the single individual whose passions and whose conscience—such is the force of early and hereditary prejudice—drive him to seek for any prosecutions that may impede our progress. It would be melancholy—it would be deplorable, that such a man should be furnished with arguments against us by the Earl of Donoughmore ! The authority of that noble lord ought to have great weight with any jury ; and it is possible—recollect that I only say it is possible—that the Attorney-General may find in the city of Dublin a jury sufficiently disposed to convict us on the authority of Lord Donoughmore.

I speak with great reverence of Dublin juries. It is boasted that they do their duty gratuitously ; but duty is done as well and as zealously for love as for money ; and we ought to avoid giving them gratuitous trouble. For the ease of these juries, and for our own protection, let us respectfully, but distinctly, disclaim the imputation of representation which the noble lord has, by mistake, cast upon us.

I conclude by again referring this correspondence to the serious consideration of the people of Ireland. Let them weigh it well. If it meet disapprobation amongst us, it has had more than enough of praise from our enemies. There is not a public writer enlisted against the Catholics, that has not been decided in his approbation of it. It is certainly our duty to reply to this paragraph. There our epistolary intercourse will end, for our suggestions ought to be so framed as not to require any reply.

Would to God that I could revive in the mind of Mr. Grattan his former feelings for the Catholics of Ireland !—that I could rouse him to that energy with which he formerly advocated our cause.

What securities did he ever speak of in the Irish Parliament? What apprehension was about him for the Established Church, in the year 1793, when he obtained so much for us? Where were his alarms *then?* and yet that, if ever, was the period in which the Established Church might have been in danger. What is there in the English air to alter the mental vision, so that it shall behold gorgons, and hydras, and chimeras dire, where before it saw nothing but the pleasant prospect of amity, strength, and social security?

Would I could conjure up the ghosts of the illustrious dead who so often aided him in his battle for his then own Ireland; and amid the group I would call up the phantom of departed Ireland herself to remind him of what he was, and what he ought to be, unsophisticated by the delusions of English politics.

In the sacred names of the mighty dead, I would conjure him, to return to the grand and simple principle of the right to perfect liberty of conscience! Whether he succeed or fail in that pursuit his ancient glories will brighten in the rays of these his later honours; and he will singly sustain, in degenerate days, the consistency, as well as the splendour of the first models of Grecian and Roman virtue!

An incident occurred just after the termination of this speech. that, trifling in itself would yet supply the key, were such wanting, to the policy that has pervaded and marked the public life of the subject of this work.

One of the members of the Board present, Mr. B. Coyle, drew Mr. O'Connell's attention to a person who was taking notes of the proceedings, at a place different from the usual seats of the reporters; being below the kind of "bar" formed by a railing at the end of the room. This person Mr Coyle said he believed to belong to the police-office.

The individual thus made the object of general attention, admitted that he was employed by the police authorities, and said "that he acted solely by the command of his superiors, and sincerely hoped he should not be held to have thereby forfeited the regard of others."

"Mr. O'Connell," continues the report, "said that was all perfectly fair, and that he expected by the next meeting to have a desk or table, at which two or three, or as many more as the police should think fit, might be accommodated comfortably."

Thirty or forty times at least, during the course of his agitation, similar occasions have arisen for similar steps upon his part—greatly to the disappointment and discomfiture of the authorities. he showed such readiness to oblige.

It would have been the most agreeable news at the Castle, during any period of that long course of agitation, to have word brought that Mr. O'Connell had caused to be turned out, or obstructed. or even shown a disinclination to the attendance of the police reporters, at any of his thousand-fold meetings.

When in a few years after the period at which our sketch has arrived, the Catholic Association arose, and almost from its birth began to give symptoms of how far it would surpass all former popular gatherings in its giant mutual/, two reporters, and of a class much superior to the police news carriers who had hitherto been usually employed in the duties of watching and communicating all proceedings of the Catholics at their meetings were delegated to attend. Both acknowledged subsequently that they had come to Ireland (they were English by birth) with the most rueful and despondent feelings, fully impressed with the conviction that they were doomed men, in being selected not only to go to that turbulent and throat-cutting country, Ireland, but to attend the consultations of the terrible confederacy acting under the orders of the arch-rebel, O'Connell!

Being fair-minded and well-disposed men, they very soon learned to laugh at their fancied terrors, and freely acknowledged the highly favourable impressions they received from the general tone of the proceedings at the Association. One of them indeed became quite fiery in his partizanship in favour of Mr. O'Connell and his Association.

Mr. O'Connell was ever careful, as his words already quoted indicate, to provide the fullest and the amplest accommodation to parties thus sent; and their generally inoffensive, and highly creditable conduct made him the more anxious to convenience and oblige them. There have been but two or three instances in which his attention has been at all badly repaid; and these are scarcely of moment sufficient to be mentioned at all.

CATHOLIC "SECURITIES."

The year 1814, with which we have now to occupy ourselves, was one of a very eventful nature. The "veto," or "securities" discussion was hottest in that year, and the opposition to it the most earnest, and in its results the most effective.

Some vantage ground had been given to the advocates of the "veto" by the general promulgation of the fact that, in 1799, a portion—but a very small one, being not one-third—of the Irish Catholic hierarchy, had, under the extreme pressure of the sad and difficult circumstances of that time of terror, and with great limitations and reservations, in some degree entertained the proposition of "securities."

Making the most, however, of the concessions which they were at all inclined to consider they amounted to no more than an expression of readiness to allow of some species of guarantee being held out against the possible appointment to high ecclesiastical office in Ireland of persons who might be known to be inimical to the connexion between Great Britain and Ireland.

This was the entire effect and purport of the document which was said, and with truth, to have been drawn up in 1799.

This document (according to the account afterwards given of it by the celebrated Dr Milner, the distinguished and most learned vicar apostolic of the Midland District in England, and for several years the agent of the Irish Catholic bishops) was signed by the small proportion mentioned of the Irish hierarchy, while under a delusion as to the fair intentions of the government, but was soon after attempted to be suppressed by themselves, as far as possible, when they began to see through their delusion.

Such a document, however, was far too precious to the enemies of the Catholics, and of their religious independence, not to be preserved; and indeed undue pains were taken to preserve it by the parties to whom it would have appeared strange to apply that designation. The English Catholics procured copies of it to be printed and privately circulated; and when in 1808, the question of veto was first distinctly taken up by the Government, some of these copies were found in the ministers' hands.

Catholics on this side of the water were also found to involve themselves in this terrible mistake. The honoured name of Lord Fingal was unfortunately to be reckoned amongst them; and the part he took was sufficiently active. It procured for him the distinction, such as it was, of a special letter from Lord Grenville, explaining the views of the British Cabinet in proposing the 'securities.'

"Ministers," said the letter, "must have an effectual control over the appointment of Catholic priests, for the security of the religious establishments of this country."

That was to say, that in order to preserve the temporalities of the Protestant Church in England (and of course in Ireland,) it was necessary that Catholic priests should if possible, be made the creatures and tools of the government.

A strange inducement and recommendation to Catholics of the proposed measures!

Dr. Milner was summoned to an interview with Mr. Ponsonby, on Saturday, 21st of May, 1808; when being introduced by Lord Fingal, he was questioned as to what likelihood there was of inducing "his constituents," the Irish bishops, to favour the "veto," or some equivalent security.

His reply (as stated by himself in a letter of February 19th, 1811, to the *Freeman's Journal*, answering and commenting on some statements with regard to his conduct in the matter, made in an article in the thirty-third number of the *Edinburgh Review*, was to the following effect:—

"That he had *no instructions* from the Irish prelates relative to their admitting of a regal interference in the appointment of their future colleagues; and that, therefore, he *could give no pledge whatever on their behalf*: that he well knew they could not admit of any *positive interference* in this business on the part of the *uncatholic government*;—nevertheless, that he himself was persuaded there was a disposition in them to admit of such a limited negative interference as might give the proposed additional pledge with respect to the loyalty of episcopal candidates. Finally, that in consequence of his undecisive answer, he was directed by the right honourable gentleman to write to Ireland for instructions, which he did, in letters to five different prelates."

The answers which he received to these communications were, however, of such a nature, in the majority of instances, as to make evident to him his mistake; and he accordingly took immediate steps to make it known equally to all whom it concerned.

The rest of the discussion, so far as our sketch has to do with it, will be noticed as we proceed.

On the 3rd of February, the *persecution* of Magee recommenced in the Queen's Bench with the indictment against him for the Kilkenny resolutions of August last.

It is quite enough to say that the Attorney-General had, in this case as in all others he pleased, his own pet picked jurymen in the box; and the fact of the traverser having been found guilty follows as an inference of course.

The sentence was, a fine of £1000, with imprisonment for six months from expiration of his former sentence. Subsequent securities for the peace to be given, in £1000 for himself, and two sureties of £500 each.

However desirous to avoid, henceforward, delays of any length upon particular years, we cannot omit a speech of Mr. O'Connell's, towards the end of March, at a Catholic meeting in the county Clare, on the noted subject of the "securities," as mixed up with the differences between the Catholic Board and Lord Donoughmore and Mr. Grattan.

Mr. Woulfe, the late Chief Baron, a man of singular intellect and ability, made a splendid oratorical effort on this occasion, to induce the Catholics to falter and hesitate in their hitherto decided course of open opposition to the fraudulent and ruinous schemes of the government, relative to Catholic matters. His talents enabled him to make a powerful impression upon the meeting, and it was necessary for Mr. O'Connell to leave no stone unturned to remove that impression.

For this purpose he made use, in the beginning of his speech, of the fair party weapon of ridicule, protesting that the proceedings of the day had strongly brought to his memory one of the old fables he had learned in childhood—that of the sheep consulting whether they should not manifest their faith in the good words of their ancient enemies, by getting rid of the guardianship of the dogs who usually attended them.

After amusing his auditory for some time by his description of the sage counsels of an old patriarch of the flock, who warned them against the course they were about to adopt, Mr. O'Connell, perceiving that he had tuned the meeting up to the proper pitch, suddenly raised his eyes to the gallery, from which part of the chapel in which they were assembled the previous speaker had addressed them, and

"At this critical moment, when the voice of prudence was beginning to be heard, a WOLF (Woulfe) came forward to *the front of the gallery*," &c.

As he spoke the words, he pointed to Mr. Woulfe, and an uproarious and universal shout of laughter did more than fifty long speeches could have done to destroy the effect of that gentleman's eloquent harangue.

The rest of Mr. O'Connell's address was in a graver spirit, and effectually carried with it the meeting.

MR. O'CONNELL said that he did not rise to oppose the motion, as it was now modified by Mr. Woulfe. He did not, and never should resist any tribute of Catholic respect and Catholic gratitude to the Earl of Donoughmore. He should never forget how much the Catholics owed to that noble lord. In his illustrious family they had found their best supporters. The Hutchinsons of the present day had their fathers' and their own claims upon our gratitude. At a time when liberality to Papists was little short of crime, their revered father broke the bondage of bigotry, and stood forth, single and alone, the advocate of his enslaved country. The cause which he espoused was zealously and faithfully pursued by his sons. The Earl of Donoughmore has unremittingly pursued it upon every occasion; in every discussion he stood prominent in our cause. No enemy of religious liberty was too humble to escape his contempt; no profligate deserter of religious freedom would be too exalted to escape his dignified reprobation. (Loud applause for many minutes.) And then he had a brother, too—the very first of patriots—the most disinterested, the bravest, the truest Irishman living;—a man who could be described, in the language of truth, only by adopting a familiar phrase, but certainly not a disrespectful one, and calling him the finest fellow that breathes—CHRISTOPHER HELY HUTCHINSON. (Shouts of applause.) To his family more was due than ever could be repaid; but alas for poor fallen Ireland!—when, instead of combining in the expression of those sentiments, attempts were made to use the name of one of that house as an instrument of dissension. But Mr. Woulfe is mistaken; there cannot be any dissensions conjured up under the auspices of that name.

The learned gentleman, Mr. Woulfe, has indeed endeavoured to excuse himself from an attempt to convert his motion into a tocsin of discord. He says that he has been unfairly dealt with—that your resolution to confine the business of this day to the petition itself has unjustly deprived him of other opportunities of dissension, and that he is, therefore, driven to this effort, in order to disturb, if he can, your unanimity

What, Sir, will the gentleman then avow that discord and dis
scusion are of themselves such mighty blessings that their absence
is to be regretted? Is he in love with disorder and disunion?
Does he think unanimity an evil, and cordial combination a
curse? If such be his opinions—if there be the sentiments of
the gentlemen with whom he says he acts, and who have taken
the names of seceders—oh! long may they secede from Catholic counsels, and never may they return!

But what is the justice of Mr. Woulfe's complaint? A select
meeting held before we came here, consisting of a large number
of that respectable class of Catholic gentry in your county, who
have hitherto been most active in your cause, concurred in this
sentiment, that irritation and division amongst the Catholics
ought now particularly to be avoided, and therefore, they agreed
to submit to this assembly that resolution which Mr. Mahon has
moved, and you have adopted.

At the select meeting, division had at length but one supporter: with the exception of one, the meeting agreed to forbear
from all discordant topics. Here, indeed, Mr. Woulfe has had
two persons to vote with him against Mr. Mahon's motion.

[Here a gentleman exclaimed that there were three besides Mr. Woulfe, for he, too, had
voted with him.]

Well, said Mr. O'Connell, there were three—might minority!
—there were just three in this assembly—three against the hundreds here met ; and if the twenties and thirties of thousands of
Catholics whom your county contains were all here assembled,
the minority would not be increased by a single individual. (Applause.) Well, with this glorious minority of three, the learned
gentleman proceeds. He first moves that the name of the Earl
of Donoughmore be substituted for that of Earl Conyngham.
Sir, however we respect the former, that was a motion which
could not be acceded to. Earl Conyngham, even if he did not
support your claims, possesses a species of affectionate popularity
in this country which would protect his name from any slight.
The best reward of that rare character in Ireland—an excellent
landlord and a steady friend—Earl Conyngham deservedly possesses in the respectful affections of his countrymen. There
never was a more vain attempt than that to displace him amongst
the Catholics of the county of Clare. (Applause.)

This difficulty was felt by Mr. Woulfe. He felt that he could
not succeed in erasing the name of Lord Conyngham from your
resolution. He, therefore, substituted a motion confined to a
compliment to Lord Donoughmore. This motion was instantly

acceded to. Every individual present cheerfully, readily, cordially agreed to it. The resolution must pass unanimously.

Was Mr. Woulfe satisfied? His motion met unanimous support. Was he content? No, Sir, he was not satisfied—he was discontented. Unanimity even upon his own proposition displeased him. The motion was a *pretence;* his purpose was disunion and discord ; and accordingly, without an assignable motive, or rational cause—quite *apropos des bottes*, as the French say—he pronounced a long harangue against the Catholic Board, full of sound and fury, but in plain truth signifying little if anything. In good set terms he railed at the Board. I regret that the points of accusation were so indistinct that it is difficult to follow or understand them. But as far as I could comprehend them, this volunteer harangue of accusation shall not pass without reply.

Yet I first must proclaim my delight at the manner in which this attack was received. I am glad he made it. I am glad that a "seceder" should thus have had ocular demonstration of the unpopularity of his own opinions. You first heard him in silence. The disapprobation which soon followed marked your sentiments, and amidst the expressions of your decided disapprobation, which accompanied the close of his speech, he has learned how justly you prize the honest exertions of your General Board. (Loud and continued applause.)

Yet an object has been attained. One purpose is effectuated. The philippic you have heard will appear in print ; it will grace the columns of the hireling press—the vile, the scandalous corruption, the base-born slaves of venality will rejoice to publish it, and some shallow and false friends will give it double circulation. It will appear uncontradicted and unaccompanied by that indignant reproof which you have poured upon it ; and the seceders, joined in an holy alliance with the Orange Bovens of Derry, and with the paltry persecutors of Wicklow, with the Wingfields and Stratfords, conscientious supporters of religion! God bless the mark! Yes, the "seceders" and the persecutors will rejoice in chorus, for the Catholic Board has been attacked by both ; and the speech you have heard this day will be quoted with equal delight by Protestant and Papist Orangemen. (Applause.

Let me, however, here, where I can be heard, proudly vindicate the Catholic Board from the aspersions of the learned gentleman. I am, indeed, proud to be the advocate of the Board— doubly proud, because such advocacy requires nothing but the

simple statement of facts to make it triumphant. For of what
does he accuse us?—of what do his four charges consist? I shall
separate the four counts in his indictment, to speak technically,
and you will soon perceive how idle and absurd is the accusation.
It charges the Board—

First—With acting in such a manner as enables our enemies
to misrepresent our actions.

Secondly—With this, that the Earl of Fingal and Sir Edward
Bellew, by name, and the learned gentleman himself, and several
other important persons, calling themselves " seceders," have separated from the Board.

Thirdly—With having made an unnecessary and virulent attack on Lord Donoughmore and Mr. Grattan ; and—

Fourthly—With having been guilty of a——pun. (Laughter.)

Such, Mr. Chairman, are the grave and portentous charges
brought by Mr. Woulfe against the Board. I shall plead to
them, but reversing the order and continuing the phrase of my
profession, I shall plead not guilty to the two latter counts, and
tender a justification to the two former.

The last charge is that with which I begin, namely, that the
Board has committed a pun. This has the merit of comicality
and of novelty. It has been gravely stated by Mr. Woulfe; but
I am unable to attempt, with gravity, to refute the charge, otherwise than by denying the fact, and regretting that some worthy
seceder has not furnished the Board with a collection of approved
jests and moderate witticisms, that could suggest nothing bold
or dangerous. A public body accused of a joke! a public body
charged with being miserably witty! Oh! most wise, most sapient accusers! But, let the fact be known. One gentleman of
the Board, Mr. Lawless, used the unfortunate witticism now reprobated. He, Mr. Lawless, talked of the " *knockloftiness*" of the
style of a certain letter ; but besides, that the Board is scarcely
responsible for the jests of an individual, the fact is, that the one
in question did not originate with him ; he found it in "*The
Belfast Magazine*," and retailed it to the Board at second hand.

Let " *The Belfast Magazine*," and not the Board, bear the
blame ; and there never was a work that could better sustain an
attack ; it is a work that does honour to Irish genius, taste, and
talent ; it is a work consecrated to Irish liberty ; it glows with
every noble sentiment of religious and civil freedom ; and dull
must be the understanding, and cold must be the heart it could
fail to enlighten and to warm in the cause of Ireland. The con-
ductors of it are Protestants and Presbyterians ; would to God

the Catholic Board contained many—would that it contained any such men.

To return from the digression which a very silly charge against the Board bid me indulge, I now take up the next proposition to which I have, for the Board, pleaded not guilty. It is, Sir, the solemn accusation, "that the Board has made an unnecessary and violent attack on Lord Donoughmore and Mr. Grattan!"

This charge I totally and entirely deny. The gentleman has not supported it with a single proof; but as it involves us in the base sin of ingratitude, I shall reply to an improved charge; and by merely stating the facts, demonstrate the plain injustice of the accusation. The facts are these; attend to them I pray you; they are of importance to every Irishman, no matter what may be his mode or form of faith.

Last year a bill was brought into parliament, purporting to be for the relief of the Roman Catholic body. There was no deliberation on that bill. Lord Donoughmore was scarcely consulted with at all; but it was prepared principally under the auspices of Mr. Canning, one of the foremost in that class of statesmen who raise their own interests whilst they despise public liberty and political principle, and laugh in private at the dupes, by whose confidence they rise to wealth and power. Mr. Canning was the chief framer of the bill, and it was quite suited to a patriot of his description.

It was the duty of the members of the Catholic Board diligently and carefully to examine the principle and contents of a proposed law, in which, as Catholics and as Irishmen, we were all so deeply interested. We found it to be erroneous in principle; defective, and almost entirely useless in its details respecting our religion; indeed, it might have been said to contain no principle at all; or, rather, it contained a direct negative of the great object of our pursuit—the principle that would declare conscience free, and religion a question between man and his Creator. (Applause).

Then, with respect to our religion, it went to place our Church, the appointment of our bishops, and the consequent control over our clergy, in the hands of three privy councillors, to consist perhaps, of Dr. Duigenan, Sir Richard Musgrave, and the acting clerk or secretary at the Castle, generally some conceited and ignorant English coxcomb. Such were the men who were to preside over our Church; to whose fostering care our religion was to have been confided; to whose tender mercies the holiness of our faith was to be entrusted. Is there in the Catholic body any man s stupid as to imagine, that the Catholic religion could exist fifty years under such control ?

It has survived persecution ; built upon a rock, it has defied the storms of force and violence.   But this Emancipation Bill would have undermined the Church, and the rock on which it is founded ; and in the fall of both, the credulous people would be crushed to death and destruction.

This to you is enough.   Canning's Emancipation Bill would have destroyed your religion.   No man could expect to be appointed a bishop after it passed, for any other reason than because he did not deserve that sacred office.   Piety and learning, and holy zeal, and blessed charity, which we now see so often combined in our venerated prelates, would all be passed over and carefully rejected ; and in their room the men would be selected, who were subservient, and subtle, and flattering ; the men who could sacrifice their consciences to the interest of their patrons.   A good electioneering agent would deserve a mitre by ardency in the bribery and corruption of a contested election ; and the patronage of the Catholic Church would become a constant, as it would be a valuable article of ministerial traffic and barter.

Add to this the hereditary hatred which so many cherish against the Irish Catholics ; and when you have placed the Irish Catholic Church under the combined control of bigotry and interested profligacy, I would fain learn whether there be any seceder so confident as to assert, that the Catholic religion in Ireland could survive under that domination.

But this is not all : the last ray, the remaining spark of liberty in Ireland would have been extinguished by the same process which had put out your religion.   The quantity of influence which the minister would have procured by means of Mr. Canning's bill is obvious : there would be placed in every diocese, and then in every parish in Ireland, a ministerial dependant, obliged to support the minister by the tenure of his ecclesiastical office ; and then the expectants of the offices would, as is usual, be under the necessity of using double diligence in the service of the friends of the ministry.   Thus Canning's bill would have given a more extensive and formidable patronage and support to every succeeding administration ; it would have brought more numerous, better disciplined, and more effective recruits into the ranks of corruption than any one political measure ever yet invented or even imagined.

I repeat it, that then, public liberty would be a shadow, and th simple and the unpretending despotism of a Turkish province would be a subject for admiration and regret. (Applause.)

See what has already occurred in the Presbyterian Church in Ireland. The Irish Presbyterians were remarked and admired for their love of liberty; their hatred of oppression; their manly and noble spirit of independence. The republican portion of our mixed constitution; that part of our constitution which is essentially necessary for the preservation of the liberties of the people, had, in the Irish Presbyterians, vigilant guardians, active, zealous, informed, and enlightened supporters. The Presbyterians first felt that the true interests of Ireland required a cordial co-operation of all the Irish people; and demanded the extinction of religious animosities, and the glow of mutual benevolence. The Irish Presbyterians, accordingly, sacrificed their prejudices on the altar of Ireland; they made the first advances to conciliation; and met even the half-way advances of the Catholics, to a cordial combination of effort in the cause of freedom. They were always the friends of civil liberty; and, for the sake of that darling object, they became the friends of religious liberty also.

But in an evil hour, when the clergy accepted salaries from the state, the "*Regium Donum*" was introduced; their clergy became familiar with the Castle; the natural consequences followed: their leading gentry fell off, and joined the more courtly and fashionable worship of the Established Church; their lower classes deserted, and joined the ranks of the Methodists, and sought untried preachers amongst other sectarians; and there remains now to remind us of the ancient glories and worth of the Irish Presbyterians, only just such a residue as must convince us what they would have been, and what she would have done for Ireland, if the Church had not been corroded and almost annihilated by the blighting breath of ministerial influence and corruption.

With this example before us of a religion almost destroyed, and a watchfire of liberty almost extinguished, could we feel otherwise than indignant at Canning's attempt to destroy the Irish Catholic Church? We are attached to the Catholic Church firmly and conscientiously; we are attached to liberty ardently and devotedly; and we could not behold with indifference our religion and our liberties devoted, under the name of relief, to decay and ruin. We had not, we confess, sufficient coldness and discretion to see those prospects, and remain unmoved. Our venerable prelates joined in our fears; they condemned Canning's clauses; we expressed our gratitude, and here secession

Legan. The "seceders" thought the bill right, and the bishops wrong; and from the day on which we thanked our prelates for their care of the Catholic Church—from that day the great era of secession is dated, and the party of whom, for the first time, a boast is made at a public meeting, commenced its history; but of this party I shall say more presently.

The relief bill, I have told you, was defective in its details. After having pointed out its natural and necessary tendency to destroy religion and liberty, it may be deemed quite superfluous, or worse, to notice its details; but I cannot avoid pointing out a few of its most prominent defects. At present it is said that the Catholics of Ireland cannot found any school, nor establish any charity for Catholics. Catholic schools and Catholic charities are, they say, forbidden by law; nay, the law is much worse; for there is a commission, consisting principally of Protestant bishops, with Dr. Duigenan at their head, whose duty it is to look for illegal—that is, Catholic—charities; then to employ an attorney, who, *in all events*, is to be paid out of the charitable fund attacked. Whether they succeed or not, their attorney is entitled to his plunder—his full costs from the defendants; and it is the duty of those commissioners, thus amused with litigation, at the expense of their adversaries, to lay hold of all property destined for Catholic schools and charities, and to convert it to the purposes of Protestant charities and schools!

All charitable bequests for Catholic purposes, the executors are bound to divulge, under severe penalties. Besides, concealment is impossible; for the wills must remain in the Ecclesiastical Court, and thus a complete inquisition is established over every source of charitable relief, and every fund for the education of Catholics. Besides, the very collections of your charity sermons may be swept away by any common informer, but that such species of profligacy is restrained and controlled, in despite of the law, by the execration of mankind.

Perhaps you imagine that the late relief bill would have reduced those evils, and rescued your schools and charities from the Protestant inquisition. You are mistaken if you think so. The bill would have left the inquisition precisely as it found it.

I shall particularise but one more defect. A Catholic priest is at present subjected by law to capital punishment if he happens to marry a Catholic to a Protestant, or to a person who was a Protestant at any time within twelve months before the marriage. It is immaterial whether the priest know the fact, or he ignorant of it. Let it be so studiously concealed from him that he cannot possibly discover it, still he is guilty of a capital felony; and I will venture to assert that there is not a single priest in any of the large towns in Ireland who has not repeatedly been rendered liable to the punishment of that offence. But the law is not content with directing the priest to be hanged, even for a mistake; the cruel folly of the penal code went further; and lest the priest should be unreasonable enough not to be contented with hanging, another statute has, in addition, imposed a penalty of £500. Thus, a priest may, by law, be first hanged, and secondly fined £500 for one and the same offence; and the construction was, in the year 1802, expressly admitted, in my hearing, by the late Lord Kilwarden, pronouncing the unanimous opinion of the Court of King's Bench.

The relief bill would have left the law, in this particular also, as it found it; and if the charter of emancipation, as it was ludicrously called in Cork, had passed, the priests of that city would have continued liable, for a mere mistake, to death, with a superadded fine.

I will not delay you to particularise many other defects in the relief bill; I will not point out to you the omission to give votes to Catholic peers at the election of Irish representative peers; of the insertion of civil and military officers, without adding naval and judicial, although the distinction between naval and military officers is pointedly recognized by the statute law, and the difference between naval and military officers has already been effectually relied on to exclude the Catholic from the latter. Neither shall I detain you with pointing out the insufficiency of the relief bill to procure the Catholics their rights in corporations.   You well know the advantages derived from the freedom of corporate cities; you know by experience what vexations freemen of cities escape. Corporate rights are now become of inestimable value in the neighbouring city of Limerick; and if there be spirit and independence amongst you, they may also soon become valuable in the town of Ennis.

All these, and many more wants were in the relief bill of last year. The Catholic Board would have ill-deserved the confidence of their oppressed countrymen, if they had not sagacity to discover, and manliness to expose those defects. The course to be pursued appeared plain and simple. Lord Donoughmore was certainly in no manner responsible for the relief bill; and Mr. Grattan, who had supported its civil enactments, was, we are convinced, unacquainted with the particulars in which that bill was defective. Under these circumstances, the Board so

licited respectfully a communication with those illustrious personages. Something like offence appears to have been taken
at our solicitation ; we were replied to in a style of superiority,
better suited, perhaps, to periods when the Catholics were more
depressed, the Protestants more elevated. What was the cause
or reason of the error—for so I must pronounce it—into which
these, our great advocates, fell ? The Board treated it with perfect respect, and replied to it in terms of perfect civility. The
rejoinder was, perhaps, more unbending than the first answer.
Lord Donoughmore did not think it right to descend from his
lofty attitude.   Mr. Grattan took the same ground, and even
condescended to lecture the Board. But the Board never swerved
from its determined respect. It was the prototype of humility
personified ; and it did not, for one instant, forget what it owed
to the former services of the noble lord and right honourable
gentleman.   It did not even enter into any expostulation, much
less into any reproof. But it submitted in silence to a claim of
superiority which the law conferred, and, perhaps, nature had
confirmed ; nor was that silence the less meritorious for the
thousand heart-breaking recollections which legal superiority
rouses and perpetuates. (Loud and continued applause.)
    Such are the facts ; I defy Mr. Woulfe, or any other gentle-
man to contradict any one of them.   Where, then, is the attack
on Lord Donoughmore ?   Where, then, is the violence or intemperance of the Board ?   For my part, I felt and found blame,
for another and a very different reason. I apprehended that the
Board would have met censure and reprobation for the excess of
its tameness and submission. "Bold measure men," as the hirelings of the administration call us, would have acted otherwise.
"Bold measure men," if such there really were, would have put
an earlier period to the correspondence, by respectfully, but
firmy, declining future support. But we thought and judged
differently ; and therefore can securely laugh to scorn those who
would accuse us of intemperance, or disrespect to Lord Donoughmore or Mr Grattan. (Much applause.)
    Little must be said on the other topics of accusation. It is
rather ludicrous to charge us with the course that Lord Fingal,
and Sir Edward Bellew, and the learned gentlemen have seceded
or that our enemies misrepresent us.   I cheerfully admit the
private worth and high rank of the noble lord ; I readily concede
the great wealth and respectability of the worthy baronet ; but
after all, what are they when put in contact with the people of
Ireland ? Lord Fingal is not the Catholic cause. nor is Sir

Edward Bellew the Catholic strength. That cause may proceed in its native and inherent strength without them. Whilst I lament their absence, and should rejoice at their exertions, I cannot consent to think that the liberty of the people depends on their presence or secession. The seceders of 1792 were as high in rank, and were sixty-eight in number; yet the people pressed on their cause, and were eminently successful. I say this to show you, that even if Mr. Woulfe be right, and that this secession has taken place, yet the people may, if they please, again triumph. Let Mr. Woulfe too, recollect, that the Board contains other noble lords and honourable baronets, who have not seceded: and that the families of those who remain are as free from the intercourse of placemen and pensioners as those who are alleged to have seceded.

One word, then, as to the charge that we give room for misrepresentation. My answer is ready:—If our actions were mischievous or improper, our enemies would have no occasion to misrepresent. They pay a compliment to our integrity when they resort to misrepresentation; they tacitly admit that the fact would not serve their purposes, when they distort it, in order to injure us.

And, after all, who can stay the progress of misrepresentation? We have open and avowed enemies. We have equally tried enemies, who pretend to be our friends; for their daily pay they must calumniate and misrepresent; and for my own part, I should as soon be angry with the winds for shifting to an unpleasant point, as I would with any of those pitiful creatures, whose rancour is paid by the day, and who, perhaps, for smaller pay, certainly for greater, would calumniate the subjects of their present eulogies. But while the people of Ireland listen to the dissemination of discord and dissension, does Mr. Woulfe and his "seceders" imagine that the people will never learn the wisdom of union and concord? Have seven centuries of misery and misfortune not taught Ireland the source of her woes?—is she now to learn that it was by division she was first conquered?—that it was by the dissension of her sons she was often plundered—and that it was by their discord she was finally erased from the rank of nations, and reduced to the form of a province?

Yes, Mr. Chairman; our enemies did, our enemies can at all times succeed in Ireland. The curse of the country is in that spirit which leads Irishmen to prefer a contest with one and the another, to the attack of the foes of their religion and liberty. It is quite characteristic of this ill-fated land to have Mr. Woulfe

exhaust thateloquence in a sally against the Catholic Board,
which might be better employed upon the opponents of his faith.
and country.   Why does he play the Roman fool, and turn his
sword upon his fellow-slaves, whilst 'oppressors are allowed by
him to escape with impunity?   Let him expose one bigot—let
him desert and reprobate one prejudice, and then, perhaps, he
may be entitled to war with his fellow-labourers; but if he prefer
to take the same side with the persecutors, and to strike at those
who strike at them, let him not wonder if he be mentioned amongst
the enemies of his country.

How often has Ireland been taken to the market, and sold by
the corruption of her own children!—how often has she been betrayed by the folly of her own sons!   But a better day opens,
I trust, to her view.   Her Catholic Board will remain firm at its
post until religious liberty is attained.   It is cheered and rewarded
by your confidence; and the "seceders" themselves will, I trust,
soon learn, that unqualified emancipation is our undoubted right,
as the active pursuit of it is our first duty; and in that sacred
cause let the watchword be—UNANIMITY FOR OLD IRELAND!"

Well was it that the Catholic mind was thus again excited against the detestable " secu
rities;" as in a very few weeks after, the afflicting intelligence was announced, that the
prelates appointed to administer ecclesiastical affairs at Rome, during the captivity of the
Pope, had not only assented to, but approved of the' " securities" in the parliamentary bill
the preceding year.

The document itself which conveyed this disastrous assent, and which bore the signature
'Monsignor Quarantotti, Vice-Prefect of Rome," was immediately published, in extenso-
ly all the journals of the United Kingdom; and exceeding was the jubilee of the enemies
of the *religion* of the Catholics—*friends* of their political claims, as many of them were.
Corresponding was the grief and dismay of every Catholic of sound judgment and sound
heart; but in an equal measure was their determination not even yet to abandon their
opposition to the ruin of their religious independence.

A very few brief extracts from the letter of " An Irish Priest," which appeared in the
Dublin Evening Post the day after Quarantotti's document had been given, will show the
spirit in which the latter was met at once.—

" The ferment spread like wildfire through every gradation of society: and the very
lowest order of people felt its influence.   Some cursed—others moaned—all complained
Early this morning my old servant-maid, without waiting for any commands of mine, ac-
costed me abruptly with these words:—'Oh, sir! what shall we do?   Is it—can it be true
that the Pope has turned Orangeman?!!"

" I must beg to correct two material mistakes of yours. . . . . . .   The document
is *not* from his Holiness Pius VII. . . . . . .   Nor is there a word to indicate any
sort of consent or approbation from him, or any one of his cardinals.   Quarantotti refers to
no authority but his own. . . . . . .   A clerk to the Congregation of Propaganda.
presumes to decide on a subject of the greatest magnitude, and which would require the
deliberation not only of the whole Congregation and of the Pope himself, with his whole
College of Cardinals, but of an entire Œcumenical Council.   Nay, as it appertains to local
discipline, that Œcumenical Council itself could not compel us to submit—much less an
understrapper of Propaganda!"

After severe criticism on the *Latinity* of the document, the writer thus proceeded to another point of attack—the channel through which an announcement of such importance to Ireland was made: through an English Vicar Apostolic! instead of, at least, being addressed to the Irish regularly constituted Hierarchy. We pass over this and other points strongly and warmly put and expressed, to give the concluding sentence, applicable to the circumstances of the present day, with the single alteration of substituting the words ' self-styled *liberal* Catholics" for the last word here given :—

" Every attempt to weaken the Catholic Church in Ireland shall, in the end. prove fruitless ; and as long as the shamrock shall adorn our island, so long shall the faith delivered to us by St. Patrick prevail ; in despite of kings, parliaments, Orangemen, and *Quarantottis.*"

Almost the next newspaper contained a stirring protest and address of clergymen against this rescript by Quarantotti (or " *Mister Forty-Eight,*" as the irrepressible tendency to Justing, in the Irish Catholic, had already christened him, in allusion to a wild story about the derivation of his patronymic, said to have been from the number of a lucky lottery. ticket that had made his father's fortunes). As the first clerical move we give it in full, with the names annexed ; foremost among them, as our readers will gladly recognize. the honoured name of the revered and admirable present Bishop of Dromore, the Right Rev. Dr. Blake.

Others too, names of dearly loved and respected members of the priesthood of Dublin at the present day, will also be gladly and warmly recognised—and affectionate regrets will be again awakened at seeing the names of others who have, at various periods of the long interval since this act of true-hearted patriotism and unerring religious fidelity, gone to receive the reward of their virtues.

·RESOLUTIONS

"OF THE PARISH PRIESTS AND CLERGYMEN OF THE ARCHDIOCESE OF DUBLIN,
" BRIDGE-STREET CHAPEL, THURSDAY, MAY 12

We, the undersigned parish priests and clergymen of the archdiocese of Dublin. feel it as a duty that we owe to GOD, and to our flocks, to make the following public declaration.—

" Resolved- ' That we consider the document or rescript signed " *Quarantotti,*" as non-obligatory upon the CATHOLIC CHURCH IN IRELAND, particularly as it wants those authoritative marks, whereby the mandates of the HOLY SEE are known and recognized and ESPECIALLY THE SIGNATURE OF THE POPE.

" That we consider the granting to an anti-Catholic government any power, either direct or indirect, with regard to the appointment and nomination of the Catholic bishops in Ireland, as at all times inexpedient.

" That, circumstanced as we are in this country, we consider the granting of such a power not only inexpedient, but highly detrimental to the best and dearest interests of religion, and pregnant with incalculable mischief to the cause of Catholicity in Ireland.

' That such arrangements of domestic nomination can be made among the clergy of Ireland, as will preclude that foreign influence against which those securities, so destructive to religion, are called for by the parliament.

" We, therefore, most humbly and .respectfully do hereby supplicate our venerable archbishop, and we do hope that the Catholic clergy and laity of all Ireland will join us in praying, that he and the other Irish prelates will, without delay, remonstrate against this document, and represent to his holiness and the sacred college of cardinals, now happily re-instated at Rome, the peculiar situation of the Catholic Church in Ireland, and the tremendous evils which we apprehend would inevitably flow from the adoption of the principles laid down in the said document.

" Michael Blake, P.P., and President of the Meeting.
Miles Mac Pharlan, P.P.
Andrew Lube, P.P.
Morgan D'Arcy, P.P.
John Joseph Smyth, P.P.
Joseph Ham, P.P.
Barnaby Murphy, Econome of Townsend-street Parish.
John Fitz Harris, Townsend-street.
John Barret, Francis-street Chapel.
Patrick Corcoran, Superior of Church-street Chapel.

C. G. O'Rielly, Provincial O.D.C.
Patrick Doyle, Liffey-street Chapel.
G. Staunton, Ex-Provincial O.S.A., S.T.M.
Edward Armstrong, Liffey-street Chapel.
Denis Farrell, O.S.D.
L. S. Phelan, Curate of St. James'
Patrick Brady, Meath-street Chapel.
— Prendergast, Curate of St. Audeon's.
J. Pearson, Curate of SS. Michael & John's
J. J. Callan, Curate of St. James'.
Miles O'Connor, Curate of St. Audeon's.
Joseph Joy Dean. Principal of Blanchardstown Academy

William Yore, Curate of St. James'.
J. Kavanagh, Curate of Francis-st. Chapel.
James Reynolds, O.S.F.
Patrick Purcell, Curate of St. Audeon's.
M. Doyle, Curate of SS. Michael & John's.
Alexander Roche,   do.   do.
Thomas Coleman,   do.   do.
M. Keogh, Curate of Meath-st. Chapel.
Patrick Corr, Mary's-lane.
M. B. Corr,   do.
John C. Kearney Francis-street Chapel.
Stephen Dowdall, O.S.F.
Francis Joseph L'Estrange, O.D C., Clarendon-street Chapel.
Joseph O'Hanlon,   do.   do.
Charles Boyle, Curate, Clontarf.
Joseph Sheridan, Church-street Chapel.
Michael Nowlan, James'-street Chapel.
Nicholas Malone, Church-street Chapel.
Walter Miler, Curate of Liffey-st. Chapel.
Hugh Daly, SS. Michael & John's.
James Campbell, Meath-street Chapel.
Richard Fannin, John's-lane Chapel.
Daniel Costigan, Liffey-street Chapel.

John Martin O'Donovan, Chapman to the House of Industry.
Michael P. Kinsela, O.S.F.
Peter Wade, Mary's-Lane Chapel.
John Madden, John's-lane Chapel.
John Devereux, Church-street Chapel.
Andrew Ennis, Liffey-street Chapel.
John Francis Roche, Clarendon-st. Chapel
John Murray, Swords.
Anthony Gulfoyle, O.S.A. Adam and Eve.
L. Plunkett, O.S.D.
James Carey, P.P. Swords.
James P. Kenny, Church-street.
J. Leonard, O.C.E., Church-street.
John Grace, Townsend street Chape..
Simon M'Carthy, French-street Chapel.
Denis M'Feeley, Portmarnock.
Patrick Caffrey, Church-street Chapel.
Patrick Callaghan,   do.   do.
B. J. M'Dermott, S. Ord. Prædm. Curate of Francis-street Chapel.
Joseph Glinn, Liffey-street Chapel.
James M'Keon, P.P., Finagh.
Denis Gahan, O.S.A., Curate St. Catherine's."

The *Evening Post* announced that the names thus appended included all the clergymen at that moment in the city of Dublin, and ends its remarks upon the address with

"DEO IN EXCELSIS!"

Meantime the Catholic and liberal newspapers, with but one exception, were blazing out in indignation against the scheme, and all connected with it; and their own articles were accompanied and, as it were, sanctioned by letters from clergymen. &c., full of the same denunciations and protests.

The venerable Dr. Coppinger, Catholic Bishop of Cloyne, was first in the field, of his order, at this crisis. In a letter of his that appears in the *Dublin Evening Post*, of May 14' he styled "*Mr. Quarantotti's decree*" a "*very mischievous document*," and added:—

"In common with every real friend to the integrity of the Catholic religion in Ireland, I read it with feelings of disgust and indignation!"

In similar strong terms the Catholic Bishop of Dromore, the Right Rev. Dr. Derry, followed a few days later.

Right Rev. Dr. O'Shaughnessy:—

"The result of this pernicious document, if acted upon, would be fatal to the Catholic religion; therefore I hasten to protest against it, and while I have breath in my body will continue to do so."

What we have given were the first—almost instantaneous demonstrations. It would be utterly impossible to give even a summary of those which rapidly and in overwhelming numbers and increasing strength followed them.

On Thursday, May 19th, an aggregate meeting took place at the Farming Repository, Stephen's-green, Thomas Wyse, jun., Esq., in the Chair (the present member for Waterford city), to consider the rescript of Quarantotti, and other Catholic business.

The following were the pith and marrow of the resolutions which were unanimously passed on this occasion:—

"Resolved—That we deem it a duty to ourselves and to our country, solemnly and distinctly to declare, that any DECREE, MANDATE, RESCRIPT, OR DECISION WHATSOEVER OF ANY FOREIGN POWER OR AUTHORITY, RELIGIOUS OR CIVIL, ought not, and cannot of right, assume any dominion or control over the political concerns of the Catholics of Ireland.

"Resolved—That the venerable and venerated the Catholic PRIESTS of the arch-diocese of Dublin have deserved our most marked and cordial gratitude, as well for the uniform tenor of their sanctified lives, as in particular for the HOLY ZEAL AND ALACRITY with which at the present period of general alarm and consternation, they have consoled the people of Ireland, by the public declaration of their sentiments respecting the *mischievous document*, signed B. QUARANTOTTI, and dispose them to await with confidence the decision of our revered prelates at the approaching synod.

"Resolved—That we do most earnestly and respectfully beseech our revered prelates to take into consideration, at the approaching synod, the propriety of for ever precluding any public danger either of MINISTERIAL or FOREIGN influence in the appointment of our prelates.

Mr. O'Connell's speech at the aggregate meeting is given in evidently a very imperfect shape indeed. It had three chief points:—first, a protest against the recent steps taken in favour of the veto; next, a vindication of the conduct of the clergy of the archdiocese of Dublin, who had so nobly come forward against that measure, and an expression of confidence that the hierarchy would soon fulminate against it; and finally, a contemptuous and indignant comment upon some peculiarly bigoted and peculiarly absurd anti-Catholic resolutions of several county grand juries.

The bishops' protest was as follows, agreed to on the 27th of May, after two days' conference at Maynooth:—

"Resolved—That a congratulatory letter be addressed to his Holiness Pius VII., on his happy liberation from captivity.

"Resolved—That having taken into our mature consideration the late RESCRIPT of the VICE-PREFECT of the PROPAGANDA, we are fully convinced that it is not *mandatory*.

"Resolved—That we do now open a communication with the HOLY SEE on the subject of this document; and that, for this purpose, two PRELATES be forthwith deputed to convey our unanimous and well-known sentiments to the CHIEF PASTOR, from whose wisdom, zeal, and tried magnanimity, we have reason to expect such decision as will give general satisfaction.

"Resolved—That the two last resolutions be respectfully communicated to the Right Honourable the EARL OF DONOUGHMORE, and to the Right Honourable HENRY GRATTAN, with an earnest entreaty, that when the question of Catholic Emancipation shall be discussed in Parliament, they will exert their powerful talent in excluding from the bill intended for our relief, those clauses which we have already deprecated as severely penal to us, and highly injurious to our religion."

We must hurry on our summary of the fast-crowding events of this stirring year, with as little of comment as is possible, consistent with preserving the slender thread of our narrative.

The unsatisfactory correspondence between the Catholic Board and Lord Donoughmore and Mr. Grattan continued in the same mixed style of compliment and remonstrance until early in June, when, without warning to those who had entrusted him with the Catholic petition to the lower House, and without consultation with any one, Mr. Grattan, when presenting the petition, announced that it was *not* his intention to bring forward the Catholic claims that session.

The Catholic Board was instantly summoned to consider this unexpected event, and decide on what steps it might be proper to take under the circumstances, when suddenly the following proclamation made its appearance.

" WHITWORTH.

" Whereas an assembly, under the denomination of the Catholic Board has for a considerable time existed in this part of the United Kingdom, under pretence of preparing petitions to parliament on behalf of the Catholics of Ireland.

" And whereas, under the provisions of an act made in the parliament of Ireland, in the thirty-third year of the reign of his present Majesty, intituled—' An act to prevent the Election or Appointment of Unlawful Assemblies, under the pretence of preparing public petitions or other addresses to his Majesty, or to the parliament'—The said assembly is an unlawful assembly.

" And whereas, great artifice has been employed in order to persuad the public generally and his Majesty's Roman Catholic subjects in Ireland in particular, that such an assembly is lawful and necessary to the exercise of the right of petitioning.

" And whereas, the law hath hitherto not been enforced against the said assembly, in the expectation that those who had been misled by such artifice would become sensible of their error ; and in the hope that the said assembly would be discontinued without the necessity of legal interposition.

Now we, the Lord Lieutenant, by and with the advice and consent of his Majesty's Privy Council, being satisfied that the permanence, or the further continuance of the said assembly can only tend to serve the ends of factious and seditious persons, and to the violation of the public peace,

" Do hereby strictly caution and forewarn all such of his Majesty's subjects as are members of the said assembly, that they do henceforward abstain from any further attendance at or in the said assembly

" And do hereby give notice .

" That if, in defiance of this our proclamation, the said assembly shall again meet after the date hereof, the said assembly and all persons acting as members of the same, shall be proceeded against according to law.

Given at the Council Chamber in Dublin, this third day of June, 1814.

CHARLES MANNERS, (Lord Chancellor).	FRANKFORT.
CHARLES CASHEL.	J. M'MAHON.
DROGHEDA.	G. HEWETT.
WESTMEATH.	G. KNOX.
MAYO.	J. ORMSBY VANDELEUR.
ERNE.	WILLIAM SAURIN.
CHARLES KILDARE.	S. HAMILTON."
CASTLE COOTE.	

It will thus be seen that the Catholics had their hands pretty full ! The unauthorised capitulation with the British Government as to Irish ecclesiastical independence, by Quarantotti ; the folly and treachery that were backing him in Ireland ; the extraordinary abandonment (as, at least for the current session of parliament, it was) of their cause by its old parliamentary advocates ; and now the renewed activity of hostility on the part of the government—all this might well have been expected to dismay the faint-hearted, and chill the hopes of the brave.

But the cause was *not under the* guidance of a faint heart ; or of one whose bolder conceptions needed fair skies and summer weather to ripen them into action A meeting was immediately held in Mr. O'Connell's house, in Merrion-square, at which it was resolved, of course, to submit to the government, in so far as the abstaining from assembling at that moment the Catholic Board; but at the same time to summon at once another aggregate Catholic meeting, to consider the most advisable course to be pursued at so important and difficult a juncture.

As any work dealing with the public life of Daniel O'Connell, must necessarily partake, more or less, of the character of a political history of Ireland during his time, we cannot think it out of place to insert here a "charge" made by the late Baron Fletcher, to the county Wexford grand jury in the year 1813—a charge which astonished every one by the boldness and directness with which it went to the very roots of the social evils of Ireland; and which to this day is applicable in many parts, and deeply interesting to all.

The learned judge said :—

"In my circuits through other parts of the kingdom, I have seen the lower orders of the people disturbed by many causes, not peculiar to any particular counties; operating with more effect in some, but to a greater or less extent in all. I have seen them operating with extended effect in the north-west circuit—in the counties of Mayo, Donegal, Derry, Roscommon, &c., &c.

"These effects have made a deep impression on my mind. My observations certainly, have been those of an individual; but of an individual seeing the same facts coming before him, judicially, time after time; and I do now publicly state that never, during the entire period of my judicial experience (comprising sixteen circuits), have I discovered or observed any serious purpose, or settled scheme, of assailing his Majesty's government, or any conspiracy connected with internal rebels or foreign foes. But various deep-rooted and neglected causes producing similar effects throughout this country, have conspired to create the evils which really and truly do exist.

*   *   *   *   *   *   *   *   *

"In the next place, the county has seen a magistracy, over-active in some instances, and quite supine in others. This circumstance has materially affected the administration of the laws in Ireland. In this respect, I have found that those societies called ORANGE SOCIETIES have produced most mischievous effects, and particularly in the north of Ireland. They poison the very fountains of justice : and even some *magistrates, under their influence have, in too many instances, violated their duty and their oaths.* I do not hesitate to say that ALL associations, of every description, in this country, whether of ORANGEMEN or RIBBONMEN—whether distinguished by the colour of *orange* or of *green*—all combinations of persons, bound to each other by *the obligation of an oath*, in a league for a common purpose, endangering the peace of the country, I pronounce them to be *contrary to law*. And should it ever come before me to decide upon the question, I shall not hesitate to send up bills of indictment to a grand jury, against the individuals, members of such an association, wherever I can find the charge properly sustained.

"Of this I am certain, that so long as those associations are permitted to act in the lawless manner they do, there will be no tranquillity in this country, and particularly in the north of Ireland. There those disturbers of the public peace, who assume the name of Orange yeomen, frequent the fairs and markets, with arms in their hands, under the pretence of self-defence or of protecting the public peace, but with the lurking view of inviting the attacks from the Ribbonmen confident that, armed as they are, they must overcome defenceless opponents, and put them down. Murders have been repeatedly perpetrated upon such occasions; and though legal prosecutions have ensued, yet such have been the baneful consequences of those factious associations, that, under their influence, petty juries have declined (upon some occasions) to do their duty.

*   *   *   *   *   *   *   *   *

" Gentlemen, that moderate pittance which the high rents leave to the poor peasantry, the large county assessments nearly take from them. Roads are frequently planned and made, not for the general advantage of the county, but to suit the particular views of a neighbouring land-holder, at the public expense. Such abuses shake the very foundation of the law; they ought to be checked.

" Superadded to these mischiefs are the permanent and occasional absentee landlords, residing in another country, not known to their tenantry, but by their agents, who extract the utmost penny of the value of the lands. *If a lease happens to fall in, they set the farm by public auction to the highest bidder. No gratitude for past services; no preference of the fair offer; no predilection for the ancient tenantry; be they ever so deserving; but if the highest price be not acceded to, the depopulation of an entire tract of country ensues.*

"*What, then, is the wretched peasant to do? Chased from the spot where he had first drawn his breath, where he had first seen the light of heaven, incapable of procuring any other means of existence, vexed with those exactions I have enumerated, and harassed by the payment of tithes, can we be surprised that a peasant of unenlightened mind, of uneducated habits, should rush upon the perpetration of crimes, followed by the punishment of the rope and the gibbet?*

" Nothing, as the peasantry imagine, remains for them, thus harassed, and thus destitute, but with strong hand to deter the stranger from intruding upon their farms; and *to extort from the weakness and terror of their landlords, (from whose gratitude or good feelings they have failed to win it) a kind of preference for their ancient tenantry.*"

*   *   *   *   *   *   *   *   *

The learned judge next turned to the evils not even yet quite abated—the jury laws. It is to be recollected that the grand juries were entirely (and are still, in many instances) in the hands of the ascendancy faction.

" Gentlemen, another deep-rooted cause of immorality has been the operation of the *county presentment code* of Ireland—abused as it has been for the *purpose of fraud and peculation*, will you not be astonished when I assure you that I have had information judicially from an upright country gentleman and grand juror, of unquestionable veracity in a western county, that in the general practice, not one in ten of the accounting affidavits was actually sworn at all ! Magistrates have signed and given away printed forms of such affidavits *in blank*, to be filled

up at the pleasure of the party. This abuse produced a strong representation from me to the grand jury; and had I known the fact in time,
I would have made an example of those magistrates who were guilty of
so scandalous a dereliction of duty.   Another source of immorality
may be traced in the registry of freeholders.   The tenantry are driven
to the hustings, and there, collected like sheep in a pen, they must poll
for the great undertaker, who has purchased them by his jobs, and this
is frequently done with little regard to conscience or duty, or real value
of the alleged freehold.

"Another source of immorality lay in the hasty mode of pronouncing
decrees upon civil bills, which was common before assistant-barristers
were nominated for the several counties.   All these concurring causes,
however, created such a contempt for oaths, that I have often lamented
it to be my painful lot to preside in a court of justice, and to be obliged
to listen to such abominable profanations."

*   *   *   *   *   *   *   *   *   *   *   *

The next matters touched upon in this admirable address come upon us like an echo
from the debates on Ireland of no very remote date; instead of, as the recital of words uttered in a time barely within the memory of the present generation.

" But, gentlemen, is there no method of allaying those discontents of
the people, and preventing them from flying in the face of the laws?
Is there no remedy but act of parliament after act of parliament, in
quick succession, framed for coercing and punishing?   Is there no cor-
rective but the rope and the gibbet?   Yes, gentlemen; the removal of
those causes of disturbance which I have mentioned to you will operate as the remedy!

" I should imagine that the permanent absentees ought to see the
policy (if no better motive can influence them) of appropriating liberally
some part of those splendid revenues which they draw from this country—which pay no land-tax or poor's rate, and of which not a shilling
is expended in this country!   Is it not high time for those permanent
absentees to offer some assistance, originating from themselves, out of
their own private purses, towards improving and ameliorating the condition of the lower orders of the peasantry upon their great domains,
and rendering their lives more comfortable.   Indeed, I believe that
some of them do not set up their lands to auction.   I know that the
Earl Fitzwilliam, in one county (Wicklow), and the Marquis of Hertford,
in another (Antrim), act upon enlightened and liberal principles; for
although their leases generally are only leases for one life, and twenty-
one years, the tenant in possession well knows that, upon a reasonable
advance, merely proportionate to the general rise of the times, he will
get his farm without rack-rent or extortion.   But I say that the permanent absentees ought to know that it is their interest to contribute
every thing in their power, and within the sphere of their extensive influence, towards the improvement of a country from whence they derive such ample revenue and solid benefits.   Instead of doing so, how
do many of them act?   They often depute their manager upon the
grand jury of the county.   The manager gets his jobs done without

question or interruption; his roads, and his bridges, and his park walls —all are conceded.

"For my part, I am wholly at a loss to conceive how those permanent absentees can reconcile it to their feelings or their interests to remain silent spectators of such a state of things, or how they can forbear to raise their voices in behalf of their unhappy country, and *attempt to open the eyes of our English neighbours, who, generally speaking, know about as much of the Irish as they do of the Hindoos* Does a visitor come to Ireland to compile a book of travels? What is his course? He is handed about from one country gentleman to another, all interested in concealing from him the true state of the country; he *passes from squire to squire,* each rivalling the other in entertaining their guest—*all busy in pouring falsehoods into his ears touching the disturbed state of the country and the vicious habits of the people.*

"Such is the crusade of information which the English traveller sets forward, and he *returns to his country with all his unfortunate prejudices doubled and confirmed, in a kind of moral despair of the welfare of such a wicked race, having made up his mind that nothing ought to be done for this lawless and degraded country.* And, indeed, such an extravagant excess have *those intolerant opinions* of the state of Ireland attained, that I shall not be surprised to hear of some political projector coming forward, and renovating the obsolete ignorance and the prejudices of a Harrington, who, in his 'Oceana,' calls the people of Ireland an untameable race, declaring that they ought to be exterminated, and the country colonized by Jews; that thus the state of this island would be bettered, and the commerce of England extended and improved.

"Gentlemen, I will tell you what these absentees ought particularly to do. They ought to promote the establishment of houses of refuge, houses of industry, and schoolhouses, and set the example, upon their own estates, of building decent cottages, so that the Irish peasant may have at least the comfort of an 'English sow;' for an English farmer would refuse to eat the flesh of a hog so lodged and fed as an Irish peasant is.

"Are the farms of an English landholder out of lease, or his cottages in a state of dilapidation? He rebuilds every one of them for his tenants, or he covenants to supply them with materials for the purpose But how are matters conducted in this country? Why, if there is a house likely to fall into ruins upon an expiring lease, the new rack-rent tenant must rebuild it himself; and can you wonder if your plantations are visited for the purpose, if your young trees are turned into plough handles, spade handles, or roofs for their cabins? They are more than Egyptian task-masters, who call for bricks without furnishing a supply of straw. Again, I say, that those occasional absentees ought to come home, and not remain abroad, resting upon the local manager, a species of '*locum tenens'* upon the grand jury. They should reside upon their own estates, and come forward with every possible improvement for the country.

"I do not suppose that you should expect any immediate amendment or public benefit from the plans suggested for the education of the poor. It is in vain to flatter yourselves that you can improve their minds if you neglect their bodies. Where have you ever heard of a people desirous of education, who had not clothes to cover them, or bread to eat? I have never known that any people, under such circumstances, had any appetite for moral instruction.

"So much, gentlemen, for landlords, permanent and occasional abtentees. You should begin the necessary reformation. You now enjoy comforts and tranquillity, after seasons of storm, and fever, and disturbance. The comparative blessings of this contrast should make you anxious to keep your county tranquil. If your farms fall out of lease, set them not up to be let by public auction—encourage your tenantry to build comfortable dwellings for themselves—give them a property in their farms, and an interest in the peace of the county. These are the remedies for the discontents of the people; they will be found much better than the cord and the gibbet.

*　　　*　　　*　　　*　　　*　　　*　　　*　　　*　　　*

"Gentlemen, this subject brings me to a consideration of the magistracy of the county. Of these I must say that some are over zealous; others too supine. Distracted into parties, they are too often governed by their private passions, to the disgrace of public justice, and the frequent disturbance of the country.

"Here let me solicit your particular attention to some of the *grievous mischiefs flowing from the misconduct of certain magistrates; one is occasioned by an excessive eagerness to crowd the jails with prisoners, and to swell the calendars with crimes.* Hence, the amazing disproportion between the number of the committals and of the convictions—between accusation and evidence—between hasty suspicion and actual guilt. Committals have been too frequently made out, in other counties, upon light and trivial grounds, without reflecting upon the evil consequences of wresting a peasant (probably innocent) from the bosom of his family—immuring him for weeks or months in a noisome jail, amongst vicious companions. He is afterwards acquitted, or not prosecuted, and returns a lost man in health and morals, to his ruined and beggared family. This is a hideous but common picture.

"Again, fines and forfeited recognizances are multiplied, through the misconduct of a magistrate. He binds over a prosecutor, under a heavy recognizance, to attend at a distant assizes, where it is probable that the man's poverty or private necessities must prevent his attending. The man makes default; his recognizance is forfeited; he is committed to the county jail upon a green-wax process; and, after long confinement, he is finally discharged at the assizes, pursuant to the statute; and from an industrious cottier, he is degraded, from thenceforth, into a beggar and a vagrant.

"Other magistrates presume to make out vague committals, without specifying the day of the offence charged, the place, or any other particular, from which the unfortunate prisoner could have notice to prepare his defence. This suppression is highly indecorous, unfeeling and unjust; and it deserves upon every occasion, a severe reprobation of the magistrate, who thus deprives his fellow-subject of his rightful opportunity of defence.

"There are parts of Ireland, where, from the absence of the gentlemen of the county, a race of magistrates has sprung up, who ought never have borne the king's commission. The vast powers entrusted to those officers, call for an upright, zealous, and conscientious discharge of their duty.

* * * * * * * *

"Gentlemen, the judge whose duty it is to pass the presentments can be of little service towards detecting a 'job.' He has no local knowledge; he knows not the distances, the rates, the state of repairs, or the views of the parties. He may, indeed, suspect the job, and tear the suspected presentment; but he may tear inadvertently that which is useful, and let the job pass. Therefore for the sake of the county, do as Mr. Bagwell did at Clonmel. Begin the reformation, and discountenance firmly all parcelling of 'jobs.'

"Gentlemen, when I visited the House of Industry at Clonmel, which is liberally and conscientiously conducted by an association, consisting of persons of every religious persuasion, with the Protestant parson and the Catholic priest at their head, never did my eyes witness a more blessed sight. I immediately asked: 'What do you pay to the matron and to the manager?' The sum was mentioned: it was small. 'I suppose,' said I, 'it is no object of a county job?' Mr. Grubb—the benevolent Mr. Grubb—smiled, and said, 'You have hit it, my lord—that is the fact!'

"*But there is one remedy that would, in my estimation, more than any other, especially contribute to soothe the minds of the discontented peasantry, and thereby to enable them patiently to suffer* the pressure of those burthens which cannot, under existing circumstances, be effectually removed—I mean the *equal and impartial administration of justice*—of that justice which the rich man can pursue until it be attained but which, that it may benefit the cottager, should be brought home to his door. *Such an administration of justice would greatly reconcile the lower orders of the people with the government under which they live; and at no very distant period, I hope, attach them to the law, by imparting its benefits and extending its protection to them in actual and uniform experience.*

"Gentlemen, if you ask me, 'How may this be accomplished?' I answer, 'By a *vigilant superintendence of the administration of justice at quarter sessions, and an anxious observance of the conduct of all justices of peace.*' Perhaps the commission of the peace in every county in the kingdom should be examined. In seasons of popular commotion, under chief governors, all acting, unquestionably, with good intentions, but upon various principles and different views, it is not improbable that many men have crept into the commission, who, *however useful they might occasionally have been*, ought not to remain. *The needy adventurer; the hunter for preferment; the intemperate zealot; the trader in false loyalty; the jobbers of absentees*:—if any of these various descriptions of individuals are now to be found, their names should be expunged from the commission; and if such a mode of proceedings should thin the commission, vacancies might be supplied, by soliciting every gentleman of property and consideration to discharge some part of that debt of duty, which he owes to himself and the country, by accepting the office of justice of peace. Should their number be inadequate to supply the deficiency, clergymen long resident on their benefices—more inclined to follow the precepts of their divine Master, by feeding the hungry and clothing the naked Catholic (although adhering to the communion of his fathers, he should conscientiously decline to receive from him spiritual consolation); not harassing and vexing him by a new mode of tithing, and an increase of tithes; not seeking to compensate the dissentients from the communion for the income he derives from their labour by showing a regard for their temporal welfare; attached to their Protestant flocks by a mutual interchange of good offices, by affection and by habit. Such a man, anxiously endeavouring not to distract and divide, but to conciliate and reconcile all sects and parties, would from his education, his leisure, his local knowledge, be a splendid acquisition to the magistracy, and a public blessing to the district committed to his care. Men of this description are retired and unobtrusive; but I trust, if sought after, many such may be found.

" *Persons there have been of a sort differing widely from those I have described. These men identify their preferment with the welfare of the Church; and if you had believed them, whatever advanced the one, necessarily promoted the other.* Some clergymen there may have been, who, in a period of distraction, perusing the Old Testament with more attention than the New; and, admiring the glories of Joshua, the son of Nun, *fancied they perceived in the Catholics the Canaanites of old; and, at the head of militia and armed yeomanry, wished to conquer from them the promised glebe.* Such men, I hope, are not now to be found in that most respectable order; and if they are, I need scarcely add, they should no longer remain in the commission."

*　　　*　　　*　　　*　　　*　　　*　　　*　　　*

The necessity of hastening with our task compels the omission of several details of the anti-veto agitation, and reduces us to the summary statement of the proceedings on this subject.

In July, an address, pompously announced as from the Catholics of England, to His Holiness the Pope, made its appearance in the public papers. Its tenor was unhappy and unworthy, containing, as it did, unequivocal manifestations of the spirit of compromise and surrender, and landing, in unmeasured rescripts, the spirit of Quarantotti.

Almost at the same moment came the intelligence of the disclaimer of the rescript by the authorities in Rome. Cardinal Gonsalvi, deputed by the Pope, drew up and published this disclaimer, denying the authority of Monsignor Quarantotti to issue it; and announcing his dismissal, and that of his colleagues in the act.

The late venerable and much-beloved Archbishop of Dublin, Doctor Murray—then coadjutor to his predecessor in the see, the Most Reverend Doctor Troy—was at the time upon a mission in Rome, on matters relative to this subject, in company with the Right Reverend Doctor Milner.

The latter justly-eminent prelate had, as we have seen, both by word and deed, long before made the most ample and abundant *amends* for the temporary mistake into which ne had been led by the surreptitiously-published resolves of the terrified little meeting of Irish prelates in 1799. He had, as wo have also seen, carried his anxiety to make reparation so far as to have brought upon himself the bitter and scandalously-irreverent hostility of the English retoisus, but did not consider he had yet done enough. Accordingly, he had joyfully assented to the joint mission to Rome; and, when there, laboured indefatigably to undo the miserable intrigues of which some of the high ecclesiastical dignitaries in that city had become the victims.

Meantime, whatever differences han at first existed among the prelates at home, as to the terms in which their rejection of Quarantotti's rescript, and the "*arrangements*" it involved, should be finally made known, were fast disappearing, as the Catholic body, led by the clergy, protested more and more energetically against the observance of any measure in dealing with the obnoxious and detestable propositions. The year 1815, on which we are now entering, saw an end for the time to the base hopes entertained by the bitter enemies of Irish ecclesiastical independence.

MEETING AT LORD FINGAL'S.

The year 1814 closed amid considerable gloom, in so far as related to the political prospects of the Catholics. The Board had been put down; and though some rash heads had suggested resistance to the illegal and unconstitutional act of the Lord Lieutenant in proclaiming against it, the wiser leaders declined entering into what could be at best only a bootless struggle with an unscrupulous and powerful government, and might easily become one of sad disaster and bloodshed. No thing, however, was farther from their minds than to desist from all exertion; and the autumn and winter were passed by them in attending meetings in the provinces, and half-private consultations on Catholic affairs in Dublin.

Their firmness was, however, sorely tested by the faint-heartedness of many, and the false-heartedness of some, amongst the men who had hitherto been prominent with them in Catholic affairs. Nor did the conduct of those who had taken on themselves to be the patrons of the Catholics in parliament by any means tend to lighten the heavy pressure of impending difficulties. The unworthy quibblings and cavillings of these parties—the undeserved and somewhat arrogant taunts and reproaches in which they indulged—and, finally, their miserable coquetting for popular applause, after first wantonly affronting popular opinion, made the Catholics consider any assistance derived from them as dearly and sorely purchased indeed.

The Dublin meetings were but of a few persons in a drawing-room of Lord Fingal's residence in Dublin. The press not being admitted, nor, indeed, anything like general access given, they speedily received a *nickname*, being designated as the "*Catholic Divan*." Mr. O'Connell, however, succeeded in procuring a mitigation of the rule of exclusion, during the brief period that the "*Divan*" survived his return to town for the winter season.

On the 10th January, 1815, at one of these little snug meetings Mr. Shiel brought forward a long, and, so far as language went, a well-written form of petition to be adopted by the Catholics. Mr. O'Connell, however, took several objections to it, and an animated and somewhat sharp discussion ensued.

Mr. O'Connell's objections began with the very first paragraph, in which there was much laudation of the "*generosity and liberality*" of the British parliament. The exhibition, or existence of these attributes, he totally and entirely denied; and would oppose the petition if on this ground alone.

But far weightier reasons for objection remained behind. In a subsequent paragraph, Mr. Shiel would have made the Catholics declare that, "in seeking capabilities for constitutional distinctions, they must proportionally come within the sphere of constitutional influence and control," and when pressed for explanation of his exact meaning, admitted he meant to allude to the power the government might acquire by distribution of patronage among the Catholics.

This paragraph was indignantly scouted at by Mr. O'Connell and others present.

Another, equally objectionable, met the same fate. Its tenor was confessed by Mr. Sheil to have been directed towards the leaving of a loophole open; for the proposal, at some future time, of "*security*" measures of one kind or another.

A statement that Pitt had been favourable to Catholic claims, was flatly contradicted, and, finally, the petition as a whole being put to the vote, was negatived, and Mr. O'Connell and some others requested to act on a committee to provide a substitute fit for general adoption.

On the 17th there was another meeting at Lord Fingal's.

MR. O'CONNELL said that it was his duty to report to the sub-committee, to whom the various petitions had been submitted. It was easy matter to make the report, as it consisted in the simple statement, that they had rejected all the petitions, and were unable to agree on any other. Indeed, there appeared to be a radical and decisive difference of sentiment between the members of the sub-committee, which evinced itself upon a point of vital importance. It was one upon which, for his part, he never could make any concession.

Having failed in coming to any agreement on the subject of a petition, the sub-committee directed its attention to the other part of their duty—the preparing resolutions to be submitted to the aggregate meeting; but here, in the very first step, dissension was introduced; although, for my part (said Mr. O'Connell), I have taken every possible precaution to obviate the cause of any difference of opinion.

The first resolution which I have to propose is one that has been already four times adopted; it is—

"That we do renew our earnest petitions to the legislature for the total and unqualified repeal of the penal statutes, which aggrieve and degrade the Catholics of Ireland."

I now offer this resolution to this meeting, and I should merely state, that it is one in which every individual present, including you, my lord, has publicly and repeatedly concurred—that it has been the preface to all our petitions since 1808. I should content myself with this statement, but that my friend, Mr. Sheil, has already announced his intention of opposing this resolution, unless the word "unqualified" be omitted, and has announced, as if with effectual authority, that a new secession will take place, unless we agree to alter the language of our petition and resolutions. This object is plain and undisguised. It is by changing our language we evince to the legislature that our sentiments are altered, and thus most significantly call on them to enact for our religion, I know not what vetoistical arrangements.

If we refuse, and refuse we certainly shall, he has pronounced our punishment, a new secession.

Allow me, therefore, to justify the gentlemen with whom I have acted, and let me show that, if this resolution creates a new secession, it will only betray the inconsistency of those who secede. In our endeavour to promote conciliation, and procure unanimity, it became necessary to ascertain the causes of the secession. I found, my lord, that the Catholics had acted together until the summer of 1813. It was then the secession commenced. The cause of that secession was alleged to be the introduction of extraneous topics—topics unconnected with our petition. I have your express authority, my lord, in stating *this* to be the cause of secession. We had all gone together to a certain point ;—that point was the introduction of extraneous topics in 1813.

Taking, then, this open and only avowed cause of secession, it seemed easy to produce unanimity. The seceders had agreed with us upon certain subjects. We readily consented to confine all our present proceedings to those subjects on which all parties had before agreed. To this we have pledged our faith : let us see whether a similar fidelity will be observed towards us.

The resolution which I propose was adopted in substance in 1809. In 1810 we unanimously agreed—all parties agreed, and published the resolution—

"That, as Irishmen and as Catholics, we never would consent to any interference on the part of the Crown, or the servants of the Crown, with the nomination of our bishops."

You, my lord, and all the seceders, went with us in 1809 and in 1810. In 1811, the identical resolution which I now propose was passed at an aggregate meeting. You, my lord, were in the chair. It has the sanction of your approbation. You and the seceders continued to act with us. In 1812 this resolution was again passed. You, my lord, and the seceders continued to act with us. This resolution passed again in 1813. You, my lord, and the seceders continued to act with us for many months afterwards; and until the memorable vote of thanks to the bishops. At all those times this resolution passed unanimously ; and now, because we wish to repeat the usual form ; because we repeat a resolution so often unanimously adopted ; there is to be a secession again ;—that is, you will all secede because we use your own language for the fifth time—you having already used it four times !

It is better to be manly at once. Let the truth be told : the acceders were not candid when they resolved on unqualified emancipation. They then desired the veto: they still desire it. Let the pretences of extraneous topics and of intemperance of language be laid aside; let the fact be avowed: we will meet it boldly. We are ready to give up every matter of form; we are ready to sacrifice every thing except principle. We most ardently desire unanimity; but if the late seceders will retract their words for the sake of the veto, and claim only a qualified emancipation, the sooner they secede again the better, and the division must be perpetual; for we, at least, will be consistent AND NOW, AND FOR EVER, SHALL REJECT ANY PARLIAMENTARY BOON FOR THE SACRIFICE OF OUR RELIGION AND LIBERTY!

I do therefore move the resolution as unanimously adopted—the Earl of Fingal in the chair—on the 9th of July, 1811.

Mr. Power, of county Waterford—"Do you mean to say that you will not accede to any ecclesiastical arrangements?"

Mr. O'Connell—"Certainly. I mean to ask for our emancipation without any qualification of our religious opinions."

Mr. Power—"Then I will not agree with your resolution."

Earl Fingal—"I agreed to these meetings on the supposition of an honourable understanding between us, that no religious subjects should be introduced, but that we should confine ourselves solely to a petition for our civil immunities."

Mr. O'Connell—"My lord, that is exactly what I wish. I desire that we shall receive emancipation without reference to our religious opinions, and without subjecting our religion to the control of a Protestant parliament."

After some general observations from several gentlemen on this part of the subject,

Mr. Sheil addressed the meeting at considerable length against the introduction of the words "unqualified emancipation."

His views, which may be gathered from the statement we have given of the nature of the leading paragraphs in the petition he had seen rejected at the preceding meeting, were supported eagerly by some, and as warmly opposed by others.

Some of those who agreed with Mr. O'Connell having repeated his exhortations to end these unpleasant and irritating discussions by some steps towards that union of sentiment, the want of which would paralyse their efforts in the cause,

Mr. Sheil said it rested with Mr. O'Connell and his friends to procure that union. Would they give up that solitary word, "unqualified," and then there would be a certainty of union?

Mr. O'Connell—"So, then, the only chance the gentlemen would give us for obtaining union rests upon our abandoning a word which has been used at every Catholic meeting in Ireland."

He accordingly entirely refused to omit the word so obnoxious to Mr. Sheil, and, soon after, the meeting came to a division, when there appeared nine for Mr. O'Connell's view of the case—Messrs. Segrave, N. Mahon, M'Manus, O'Brien, O'Hara, Blake, and Lyons, with himself, and three against it, viz., Messrs. Shiel, R. M'Donnell, and Lube.

Another committee was then named, and the meeting adjourned.

On the 21st of January, Mr. O'Connell reported to a meeting at Fitzpatrick's in Capel-street, that all that had been done was to pass a resolution, that a petition should be presented, leaving it open to discussion what that petition should be, and also the point as to who should be called upon to present it to parliament.

Considerable discussion ensued upon the latter point, some being for again entrusting it to Lord Donoughmore in the Peers, and Mr. Grattan in the Commons, while others agreed that the Duke of Sussex should be chosen in the Lords, and that in the Commons one or the three following, viz..—Whitbread, Romilly, and Horner, ought to be selected, as more steady, considerate, and kind towards the Catholics, than their Irish friends among the members had of late shown themselves.

It was nearly resolved that the choice should be made as last mentioned, when Mr. Lidwill, a Protestant gentleman of property in the county of Tipperary, and a long time a zealous labourer in the cause, made a long and effective speech, advocating the entrusting the petition to the same hands as before.

Those whom his reasoning did not convince, gladly yielded out of compliment to him, and withdrew their opposition to Lord Donoughmore and Mr. Grattan.

On the 24th of January the following scene occurred:—

"The aggregate meeting of the Catholics of Ireland was held on Tuesday last, in Clarendon-street chapel.

"Shortly after one o'clock, the chair was taken by the lineal descendant of the last monarch of Ireland, Owen O'Connor (O'Conor Don.)

"Lord Fingal appeared at the meeting, and was offered the honour of sitting in the chair. His lordship, however, declined it, stating that he did not conceive the tenor of the resolutions conformable to the plan of proceeding laid down on his re-uniting himself with the body.

"It was, he imagined, agreed that no topic should be introduced touching on spiritual matters, as the result of the mission to Rome had not yet been known. The resolutions, as far as he understood them, little accorded with this determination. It would not then, he contended, be doing justice to his own opinions, if he had been a party to the proposition or adoption of those resolutions.

"That he might be able to give this explanation personally, he obtruded himself on the meeting. He thought, in fact, that his name should not have been signed to a requisition calling a meeting, at which he did not wish to act, without some description of eclaircissement. He hoped he need not assure the assembly, that whether he decided erroneously or not, he, at all events, acted with good intention. Without doubt, he could be most proud of the honour of filling their chair; but he could never think of accepting it, if the act were not sanctioned by a sense of what he owed to his own consistency

"After this there was a pause of several seconds, as all thought that the noble lord intended to take the chair.

"At length Mr. Mahon rose, and in an address which did great credit to his head and his heart, he conjured the noble lord to alter his opinion, and concede to the unanimous wishes of the whole assembly.

"He could not be persuaded that there was anything in the resolutions which could clash with his lordship's sentiments. It was true that he opposed an intermeddling with spiritual matters. 'But, good God, said Mr. Mahon, 'what has a simple demand of unqualified emancipation to do with theological controversy?'

"Lord Fingal protested that his mind was made up upon this matter, and begged that he may not be pressed further. He was not wedded to any particular mode of emancipation —he was not pledged one way or the other—but he thought it was agreed that nothing should be said on questions of church discipline, until some official communication was had from Rome; and as he conceived that gentlemen did not recognize this arrangement by the measures they proposed, he thought he was called upon to remain neutral."

Mr. O'Connell said, that so much had fallen from Lord Fingal both now and on a former occasion, respecting a contract or compact, that as a party to the late proceedings, he felt himself bound to make a few observations on that subject.

And first he must distinctly and emphatically deny that he ever was a party to any compact which could directly or indirectly tend to sanction any alteration by parliament in our ecclesiastical concerns. He never heard that any such compact existed.

For my part, said he, the understanding which I conceived to exist was, that we should so petition parliament, that we should not, neither should the legislature, if we could prevent them, enter into any arrangements respecting the discipline of our Church ; but that we should either be emancipated, just such Catholics as we are, or continue in our present state, as in both religion and rights.

For this purpose, and to exclude discussion, I took up a resolution which prefaced all our petitions for seven years ; a resolution adopted, sanctioned, and confirmed repeatedly by the noble lord himself.   It was a resolution to ask for *unqualified* emancipation.   The noble lord and his friends immediately dissented ; they said that resolution meant a rejection of the veto, and they insisted it should be so altered, and so modelled as to strike out the word " unqualified," and let in " vetoism ;" and then, mark what must appear a strange mistake, they *most consistently* accused us of having started a discussion upon this forbidden subject !

First, they objected to the usual language of our petitions ; and then they accused us of creating the discussion which their own objection produced ! !

This dilemma was immediately produced.   We asked for unqualified emancipation, as we had always hitherto done.   By doing so, said Lord Fingal, you introduce ecclesiastical subjects, and break the compact.   Next, his lordship would alter the usual course, and ask for emancipation, leaving to, and thereby inviting, the parliament to qualify it ; that is a direct introduction of ecclesiastical subjects, and the alleged compact is thereby plainly broken.   So that this alleged compact amounts to this— that, in either cases, it must be violated.   There are but two courses, and in either of those courses, this compact, as understood by Lord Fingal, must be broken.   That is infallible.   If we use the old words, with the old meaning, his compact is broken ; if he uses new words, he must clearly have a new meaning, and then his compact is equally broken.   There is but one way of avoiding the violation of his lordship's contract, that is, either by finding out words to use in our petition, which have no meaning, cr to petition without using any words at all.

Having then shown how impossible, it was for us men, having some small share of that acuteness so necessary for our profession, to understand the implied compact on which we met, as his ordship understood it, I will state to the public what I conceived was our agreement.

We agreed to abandon all intemperance, though, God knows, it is not easy for those who feel for Ireland's wrongs to keep their temper. We agreed, first, to substitute mildness for any intemperance ; secondly, to forget the wanton attacks of our enemies, and not to retort by any personal abuse ; thirdly to confine ourselves to our petition, to the exclusion of all other topics ; and fourthly not to agitate religious subjects.

The last point was the only one difficult to be managed. We were sure we had overcome the difficulty, for we adopted the noble lord's own words, his often repeated words :—" My God ! how can we have differed with him !" Here are his own words ! Yes, he objects, he dissents, and he threatens to secede. Why ? because we use his own words. By what ingenuity—by what magic could we procure unanimity ? We sacrifice everything. We submit to imputations which I cannot but say are unfounded, and adopt the language of the noble lord himself, and our return is a new dissension.

He who runs may read the truth—*a purchase of emancipation*, AS THE PRICE OF RELIGION, is the plain object.

It may be disguised, but it now obtrudes itself too forcibly not to be visible to the dullest eye. I *desire unanimity, I have endeavoured to obtain it, but I now disclaim it for ever*, IF IT BE NOT TO BE HAD WITHOUT THIS CONCESSION.

I will for ever divide with the men who, directly or indirectly, consent to VETOISM OF ANY DESCRIPTION.

After this distinct avowal, will the noble lord be pleased to accept the chair ? Let him only recollect, that he is most important, most valuable, whilst he remains at his natural post—the head of the Catholics. But if he choose to give our enemies this triumph, let him refuse, and, although we know his value, and shall regret his refusal, the Irish Catholic people are too great to feel the loss.

Lord Fingal declared himself distressed at being obliged to declare that he would outrage his own feelings if he consented to take the chair, under all the circumstances of the case. He did not presume to say he was right, but he could not surmount the difficulties which his opinions had thrown in his way.

Lord Fingal departed from the assembly, and the O'Conor Don remained, therefore, in the chair. A letter was read from Lord Donoughmore, the tone and sentiments of which met high approbation.

Some other gentlemen having spoken, Mr. Lidwill (before mentioned) rose and delivered a very able speech, entirely acquiescing in Mr. O'Connell's views. When he had concluded, the latter came forward to speak again :—

He began by declaring, that he never addressed any auditory

with so much depression of heart. He felt chilled to the very soul at the mournful contrast this day exhibited between the Protestant and the Catholic. The Protestant gentleman who had just spoken, the Protestant nobleman whose letter had been read, were both deeply anxious for the character and liberty of the Catholics—whilst the Catholic nobleman coldly departed from the cause of his children and his country, because his fellow-labourers would not consent to that which Lord Donoughmore so gently called *a degrading stipulation!*

But the mental inferiority of the Catholics was easily accounted for—they are slaves. The Protestant superiority was easily traced to the share which he had in the British constitution. Whilst the Catholic crouched in thraldom, the Protestant tasted the air of freedom, and his mind acquired the energy and elevation which liberty alone can bestow!

This was a source of many a bitter reflection; the scene that had taken place there that day, the new dissension announced and carried into effect, the war proclaimed against Ireland and her people—all conspired to weigh him down with sorrow. Yet, there does (said he) exist some consolation; I derive some comfort from these melancholy events. One of the two great objects I had in view has completely succeeded; the cause of Catholic division is now manifest. My first object was to procure unanimity; that indeed has failed, after I had made every effort to attain it, except the sacrifice of principles. My second great object was, that if we were to remain divided, the cause of our division should be plain, clear, and simple.

The division, the secession has been attributed to our violence, our personal sarcasms, our introduction of extraneous topics. I myself believed, that these were, at least, partly the real causes; but all these were cheerfully, readily, and at once abandoned by us; and the cause of secession is now, as I anxiously desired it, should be, plain, clear, and simple.

That cause is our seeking UNQUALIFIED EMANCIPATION. Here, now, is the single cause. If we expunged the unqualified, if we consented to take qualified emancipation, we should have no secession, no division; my Lord Fingal would preside in that chair; there would be unanimity. The quarrel is reduced to a single word—but, certainly, a word pregnant with meaning— *unqualified.*

Now, I rejoice that all the pretences upon which division was justified, have thus vanished. The truth is at length told. When the seceders recommended to us *moderation,* the English of moderation was *the veto;* when they accused us of *violence,* they meant that *we scorned a barter of our religion!* And when they charged us with "*agitating extrinsic topics,*" they mean that we had too strongly resolved *never to allow a hostile inter-ference with our Church.* The seceders have now thrown off all disguise, and though some of them may deceive themselves, no other honest man can longer be the dupe of their artifices. We have now parted with the seceders on principle, and unless they return to that principle, may their secession be perpetual.

I must blame the want of candour of those gentlemen. They are for qualified emancipation. To *qualify,* is a technical word of familiar meaning. In Mr. Shaw Mason's book, one worthy divine boasts he was so powerful a theologian in his youth, that no less than 136 Papists *qualified* under his auspices in five years ; but that since 1778, he lost his talent for controversy, and not one Papist could, since the statute of that year, be prevailed on to qualify. This reverend gentleman is still living, and ready to give *qualified* emancipation to all our seceders. Let them betake themselves to him, and leave us to seek the only emancipation to which, as Catholics, or as Irishmen, we will ever consent—UNRESTRICTED, UNQUALIFIED, UNCONDITIONAL.

If the veto, if the interference of the Crown with our religion, were a question exclusively religious, I should leave it at once to the bishops. But it is infinitely interesting as a political measure. It is an attempt to acquire, without expense, an influence greater than any the minister could purchase for millions. Who is there that does not feel the vital, the pressing danger to liberty that results from ministerial influence? We owe it to ourselves, and to the Protestants equally, to resist this contagious interference ; and every duty that can urge a man to a public disclosure of facts, interesting to every class in the state, calls on me to declare that there exists a conspiracy against the religion of the Irish Catholics, and in its efforts, against the liberties of all the Irish people!

I state it as a fact, which I have from such authority as leaves no doubt in my mind, that a negotiation is going on between Lord William Bentinck, Lord Castlereagh, and Cardinal Gonsalvi, one result of which is intended by the two former to be, the concession to the minister of the British crown of an effectual supremacy over the Catholic Church in Ireland; and there is every reason to dread that the cardinal waits only to get what he considers an *adequate compensation,* before he accedes to the measure.

The restoration of part of the Pope's territories, still withheld, is said to be the price offered by Lord Castlereagh; but it is not so clear that he has it in his power to make the payment. Besides, I do not think so unworthily of the Pope, as to believe easily that he who resisted the favour of Napoleon will yield to the seductions of Lord Castlereagh.

The danger, however, appears much increased, when we recollect the exaggerated praises of England contained in the letter from our prelates to the Pope. Can his holiness doubt the sincerity of our prelates? I know they regarded that passage as the unmeaning language of compliment; and if they had considered it as a serious assertion of fact, they would have died before they signed it. But, indeed, the lightness with which such language was used by them increases much our peril; as it must inspire the Pope with that confidence in the English government which he ought *not* to have. This danger, too, is still augmented when we see the plain proof of the existence of this conspiracy amongst ourselves. It can be defeated only by vigilance, activity, and the animated and loud expression of our abhorrence of the proposed measure.

Let our determination never to assent reach Rome. It can easily be transmitted there; but even should it fail, I am still determined to resist. I am sincerely a Catholic, but I am not a *Papist*. I deny the doctrine that the Pope has any temporal authority, directly or indirectly, in Ireland; we have all denied that authority on oath, and we would die to resist it. He cannot, therefore, be any party to the act of parliament we solicit, *nor shall any act of parliament regulate our faith or conscience.*

In spiritual matters, too, the authority of the Pope is limited; he cannot, although his conclave of Cardinals were to join him, vary our religion, either in doctrine or in essential discipline, in any respect. Even in non-essential discipline the Pope cannot vary it without the assent of the Irish Catholic bishops. Why, to this hour, the discipline of the general Council of Trent is not received in this diocese. I do, therefore, totally deny that Gonsalvi, or Quarantotti, or even the Pope himself, can claim the submission which the seceders proclaim that they are ready to show to their mandates; and my confidence is great in the venerated prelates of Ireland. They fill their sees in a succession unbroken for an hour since the days of St. Patrick and his companions; they have resisted for more than a thousand years fraud and force; and they will preserve in its native purity, in contempt of persecution and in despite of treachery, that religion committed to their care, which commenced with the first, and is destined to continue immutable, to the second coming of our blessed Redeemer!

Yes; as our former prelates met persecution and death witl. out faltering, the bishops of the present day will triumph ovei the treachery of base-minded Catholics, and insidious ministers of government!

Even should any of our prelates fail, which I do not and cannot believe, there is still resource. It is to be found in the unalterable constancy of the Catholic people of Ireland. If the present clergy shall descend from the high station they hold, to become the vile slaves of the clerks of the Castle—a thing I believe impossible—but should it occur, I warn them in time to look to their masters for their support; for the people will despise them too much to contribute. (Great applause followed this sentiment.)

The people would imitate their forefathers; they would communicate only with some holy priest who never bowed to the Dagon of power; and the Castle clergy would preach to still thinner numbers than attend in Munster or in Connaught the reverend gentlemen of the *present* Established Church.

Those are evils which we shall never witness. It would be preposterous folly in any statesman to grant an emancipation, which, instead of conciliating and quieting, would only alienate and disgust still more the minds of the people. Indeed such an emancipation could be thought of only in this age of deliverance. At present there was a rage for delivery; every thing and every body, except poor Johanna Southcote, was delivered. Spain was delivered to the beloved Ferdinand and the odious inquisition; Saxony was delivered to the King of Prussia; the faithful Poles were delivered to the magnanimous Alexander; and Catholic Ireland is to be delivered to Duigenan, Saurin, and Peel!!!

The process by which this last deliverance is to be effectuated is various, according to the tempers of the deliverers. There is a Scotch plan—an English plan—and *the old Irish plan.* The Scotch plan has been announced by the Earl of Selkirk, and some other worthies of Edinburgh, in advertisements containing the most insulting calumnies. That earl and his associates proposed to deliver the "wild Irish" by a plan of "*education;*" and in order that such a plan should infallibly succeed, the earl magnanimously subscribed half-a-guinea to carry it into effect (laughter).

The English plan was still a wiser one; they formed missionary societies ; they had a mission to the islands of the South Sea ; they had, as the perfection of human absurdity, a mission to convert the Jews ; and they have lately established a mission to convert the idolaters in Ireland !

But, notwithstanding the prudence of the Scotch, and the boasted wisdom of the English, their plans have totally failed. The only efficient plan was the old Irish one ! It was simple as it was effectual ; it consisted merely in *dissension ;* its only operation was to *divide* the people, and success was the certain result. It had been successful for more than seven hundred years in Ireland. Irish dissension had hurled your ancestors, Sir, from a throne ; it had reduced the chieftains and lords of the soil to the state of vassals and slaves, and it continued their descendants the inferiors, in this, their own—their native land, of every foreigner that would perform the only condition required—the swearing that the religion of Ireland was idolatry. This fatal dissension was never to end—nay, it was proclaimed anew ; and this very day the Earl of Fingal commenced a new secession.

(Here the Chairman interrupted by saying, that he was quite convinced, that whatever Lord Fingal's conduct might be, his motives were pure).

Mr. O'Connell resumed—I attributed no motives at all to the noble lord. I merely stated a fact ; and in his absence, as I could not discover any thing in his motives to praise, I should think it quite unfair to censure. I stated the fact that my Lord Fingal has again seceded from us. It is a melancholy thing to see those wretched divisions perpetuated ; it is melancholy that the few will not submit their judgment, upon matters of form at least, to the many—for it is a matter of form that has taken from us the noble lord ; because he, too, could accept, without violating any principle, unqualified emancipation.

I know we are threatened with a renewal of the scenes of 1792 ; but the men who would now contend against unqualified liberty will never again muster sixty-eight ; they may muster some solitary dozen, but, perhaps, not so many. The noble lord, respected as he is in private life, when he retired from this meeting, took with him just the number of Falstaff's recruits—only three and a-half—(laughter)—and what are three and a-half in contrast with five millions ?

Apathy and indifference can alone injure a cause sustained by the wants and wishes of a people. Indifference in this case is a crime—apathy is sacrilege. There exists abroad a conspiracy against your religion and liberties ; at home, beware of treachery.

Let us recollect that our pursuit is a real not a fictitious freedom—that our objects are not the paltry and personal emoluments of place and power, but liberty for our country and our posterity.

Let us ask this blessing as Catholics ; and spurn it if offered in any other form. Dissension, which weakens our strength, should increase our zeal and exertions. I now confidently call on every man who refuses to enter into a base traffic of his religion for place or power, to come forward in this cause ; and I feel and know, that throughout the land the voice of the people will be heard—the compromisers will sink into insignificance—and WE SHALL HAVE THE GLORY OF ACHIEVING OUR LIBERTIES, WITHOUT FORSAKING THE WORSHIP OF OUR FATHERS !'"

As upon this occasion, so throughout the many similar junctures of his eventful career Mr. O'Connell showed that he, however anxiously, earnestly, and unwearingly he could and did labour to put an end to dissensions, and bring conflicting parties in the popular body to at least an outward unanimity, sufficient to prevent interruption or damage to the common cause, he never allowed his anxiety for this end to carry him too far ; but boldly met the difficulty in front, and quelled it with a firm hand, when milder measures had not been successful.

THE CATHOLIC ASSOCIATION.

We now come to the formation a "*Catholic Association*," thus announced in the journals of the day :—

"There was a meeting in Capel-street on Saturday, and some of the most distinguished and opulent members of the Catholic community proceeded to act upon the resolution passed at the aggregate meeting, which declares the necessity of forming some association to undertake the management of such petitions or appeals to the legislature as may be demanded by the continuance of the disqualifications which still so grievously harass the body at large.

"The ceremony of organization was very simple, and we trust fully consistent with every real or imaginary provision of the Convention Act. No chair was taken—no proposition submitted—no instructions offered—no *speechification* even indulged in ; but every gentleman who chooses entered his name in a book, which Mr. Secretary Hay held open (and will continue to keep open from eleven till three each day,) and the rites and solemnities of installation were then complete and ended.

"The first meeting of the Association will, we understand, take place on Saturday."

One of the first acts of this new body was to appoint a committee to take certain steps relative to the "Veto" question, which will be best described in the following report, presented by them to the Association, at its meeting on Thursday 16th February, 1815 :—

REPORT OF THE
COMMITTEE OF THE CATHOLIC ASSOCIATION.

Appointed February 14th, 1815, to wait upon the Most Rev. Doctor Murray, in order to ascertain from him the facts respecting any negotiation that has existed, or does exist, respecting any arrangement of Catholic discipline in Ireland, as connected with the Crown, or the ministers of the Crown.

"The Most Reverend Doctor MURRAY, having appointed the hour of three o'clock in the afternoon of Wednesday, 15th February, as the most convenient hour for meeting the deput tation of the Catholic Association, your committee waited upon his grace accordingly at the appointed hour.

"His grace was pleased to open the interview by stating that he had received the letter of the chairman, Owen O'Conor, Esq., intimating the objects of the deputation; that he felt every disposition to give any information in his power; at the same time that he felt it necessary to observe, that he could not admit that the Catholic Association could claim his compliance with their desire as a matter of right, or that they possessed any authority to demand from him any account of his conduct.

"He proceeded to Rome as the delegate of the Catholic bishops, not of the Catholic Association; and he felt himself accountable only to the prelates for his conduct on that mission, to which they deputed him. He thought it necessary to state thus much, to prevent the present case being made a precedent on any future occasion. He, however, felt that in the present times all matters of form and ceremony should be waived, and that all classes of Irish Catholics should co-operate together in support of the great cause in which they were engaged.

"Your committee most distinctly informed his grace, that there did not exist in their minds, or in the minds of those who had deputed them, the most distant disposition to press upon his grace's consideration any subject which he did not feel himself perfectly disposed to entertain.

"They did not, by any means, desire or intend to ask of his grace that he should enter into any account of his conduct, as they felt fully sensible of the justice of his grace's observations; they merely desired to receive from his grace any information which he should consider worthy or fitting to be communicated to the Catholic body, and would feel indebted to his grace if he should please to grant such information, which they would receive as a favour, without pretending to demand it as a right.

"His grace was pleased to express himself perfectly satisfied with this explanation; and proceeded to say, that he did not consider himself called upon to refer to any negotiations which may have existed prior to his having been deputed to proceed to Rome, such as the negotiations in 1799.

"To this your committee assented.

"His grace then stated, that he proceeded to Rome as delegate from the Irish prelates for the sole purpose of remonstrating against the rescript of Quarantotti; that that rescript had been recalled by the Pope, on the principle that it was issued without due deliberation in the absence of his holiness and the sacred college; that the matters contained in that rescript had been referred by his holiness to a special congregation, composed of the most exalted and incorruptible characters in Rome. His grace further expressed his complete conviction that the opinions of that council would be formed upon principles purely of a spiritual character; and he was also satisfied that when the opinion of the council should be referred to his holiness, who had reserved to himself the right to pronounce definitively on the subject, the sovereign pontiff would be influenced in his determination solely by a regard for the spiritual welfare of the Catholics of Ireland, for whom he felt strong affections; and his grace felt satisfied that neither the interference of the British ministry, nor any other temporal consideration whatever, would affect that determination of his holiness.

"His grace could not anticipate when the determination of his holiness could be expected.

"In answer to a question from your committee, his grace further stated, that, exclusive of the objections to the rescript for informality and want of authority, the see of Rome felt other and most serious objections to the subject matter of the rescript; and that *affair* *stood now exactly in the same state as if that rescript had never existed*—the whole matter being referred, *ab integro*, to the congregation appointed by his holiness, and their report to be subject to his revision and determination. The last accounts received by his grace from Rome, came down to the 24th December, at which time no decision had been formed.

"In answer to your committee, his grace stated, that his holiness had been put in full possession of the feelings of the Catholic clergy and laity of Ireland relative to the rescript, and that copies of all the documents considered well calculated to communicate information of those proceedings, were laid before his holiness and the congregation, to whom the whole matters were referred.

"Your committee inquired whether any deputation from the English Catholic Board, or any other portion of the English Catholics had reached Rome? To which his grace was pleased to reply, that *Dr. Macpherson had presented a memorial to the Pope from some portion of the English Catholic body, which he inclined to believe was the English Catholic Board. This memorial prayed his holiness to confirm the rescript of Quarantotti*; it reached Rome some time in November last, and after the rescript had been recalled.

"Dr. Milner protested against Mr. Macpherson being the English agent; and also against the English Board being considered as the English Catholics. In answer to another question from your committee, whether or not the memorial of the English Catholics was supported by the British cabinet, his grace replied, that he could not speak positively on this subject; he had heard it mentioned. He was pleased, however, to repeat the assurance of his conviction, that the decision of his holiness would be influenced solely by spiritual considera

"Your committee further prayed his grace to inform them, whether Cardinal Gonsalvi had been authorised by his holiness to confer or negotiate with Lord Castlereagh on the subject of the rescript. His grace observed, that he could not answer for the truth or falsehood of every rumour; he felt certain, however, that if any such instructions were given to Cardinal Gonsalvi, he must have been limited by certain defined principles, which he could not violate or trespass upon; and that any measures resolved on between him and any English minister would be ultimately submitted to the decision of his holiness, who would be influenced in that decision solely by spiritual considerations, which would not be affected by any opinions or desires of the British minister, or by any other temporal influence.

"Your committee expressed unaffected reluctance in intruding so long upon his grace, who was pleased to assure your committee, in the most gracious and confidential terms, that he felt sincere pleasure in communicating any information in his power to the Catholic body; and the more particularly as it was not probable that there would be a meeting of the prelates at an early period. His grace concluded by assuring your committee that he would be always ready to communicate such information as he may possess on any other subject upon which the Catholic body would please to consult him.

"Your committee cannot conclude their report without recording their testimony of the very kind and courteous language and deportment of his grace during the whole of their interview; and further, they deem it their duty humbly to suggest, that his grace is pre-eminently entitled to the thanks and gratitude of his Catholic countrymen, for the readiness which he evinced in meeting the desires of this Association."

"Thursday, 16th June, there was an adjourned meeting of the Catholics of Ireland held at Clarendon-street chapel. At one o'clock the chair was taken, at the universal call of the meeting, by Owen O'Conor, Esq. The chairman opened the proceedings of the day, by stating, that in consequence of the resolution to that effect passed at the late aggregate meeting, he had solicited an answer from Lord Donoughmore and Mr. Grattan, to the question accompanying the petition of the Catholics of Ireland."

The letter of Lord Donoughmore was couched in terms that demonstrated a great anxiety to meet the wishes and forward the views of the Catholics.

Mr. Grattan's letter was, unfortunately, not of the same tenor, as will be gathered from the speech we are about to give. No circumstance could have given Mr. O'Connell more severe pain than to find himself compelled to speak with censure of such a man as Henry Grattan. But the Catholic body should be vindicated at all hazards and all cost

MR. O'CONNELL rose, and begged leave to read to the meeting a second time, the letter from the chairman to Mr. Grattan, and the reply of Mr. Grattan. He then spoke to the following effect:— I have, said he, a painful duty to perform; but it is my duty and I shall not shrink from the performance of it, however painful. The course to be pursued is sufficiently obvious; and it is necessary to recapitulate the facts, merely to place beyond any cavil the propriety of those measures which the honour as well as the interests of the Catholic body demand.

Mr. Grattan took charge of our petition last year; he presented it to the house, but he refused to discuss its merits. No reason was given for this refusal, other than the reason that silences, though it cannot satisfy, the slaves of despots. It consisted singly of the phrase "*Stet pro ratione voluntas.*" We were deeply impressed with the conviction that the discussion of our grievances and claims in the last session—indeed, every session, could produce nothing but advantages. Our cause is founded on eternal justice and plain right; therefore, so long as there remains one particle of common sense amongst men, discussion must advance that cause. The Catholic Board called on Mr. Grattan to bring forward our question; he again refused. The Board a second time entreated of him to do so; he once more refused. We then called another aggregate meeting, and that meeting requested from Mr. Grattan a discussion. Strange to say, he still persevered in his refusal—a perseverance unexampled in the history of parliament.

It must be recollected that this unrelenting refusal on the part of Mr. Grattan to move on our petition, was one adopted without any consultation or concert with our best friends. Lord Donoughmore was in London, and yet he was not consulted. It was determined by Mr. Grattan to postpone, as long as he could, for one session, any chance of relief; and he came to this resolution without the advice, or even the knowledge of our other chosen advocate Lord Donoughmore. Thus, without concert, without co-operation, we were doomed by Mr. Grattan to another year of slavery, and also without the poor pleasure of rattling our chains in the hearing of our oppressors. Allow me here, as an humble freeholder of the city of Dublin, solemnly to protest against this refusal. I do not dispute nor question the integrity of Mr. Grattan nor his high honour; but I dispute his judgment; and, humble as I am in talents and in station when compared with him, yet I am ready to demonstrate that he is mistaken.

I am ready to show that a member of the House of Commons is, by the constitution, bound to receive and attend to the instructions of the constituents. I can show precedents where this duty has been recognized even by the bitterest enemies, as it has been always hitherto asserted by the best friends of liberty. I mean not to dispute the right of the representative to exercise his judgment respecting the instructions of his constituents; but I can prove that those instructions have been hitherto received and attended to as their acknowledged duty, by the members of the House of Commons.

Thus, then, has Mr. Grattan, finally rejected you. You offered him your petition upon this condition, that he would agree to discuss your grievances this session. He refuses to enter into any such agreement. He therefore rejects your petition. You may, indeed cringe and fall before him. The Catholic people may submit and, with Christian meekness, seek another blow. The thousands who hear me, and who were right in demanding this condition, may retract and degrade themselves; but there is no other course, if you would have Mr. Grattan to present your petition. He has taken his high station; he will neither descend nor bend.

It remains for us to seek another advocate—an advocate less brilliant in eloquence, but more suited to our views and wishes. At this period it is doubly incumbent on us to make a prudent choice. Mr. Grattan differs from us on the veto. He assented to Canning's clauses, though he did not introduce them. If he had accepted our petition, it would have been necessary to give him information of the disgust and abhorrence produced by those clauses. We should owe to ourselves and our religion, emphatically to announce the detestation in which we hold any intermeddling with our Church. This and more would be necessary, had Grattan been our advocate; but if this meeting were now to retract, and to abandon their own judgment, and to select Mr. Grattan, notwithstanding his letter, the consequences are obvious. He would refuse to receive any suggestions whatsoever; and then you who desire unqualified emancipation, would have your advocate calling, in your name, for an emancipation which, in your judgment, would only increase your slavery.

Good God! can any man imagine that Mr. Grattan would find it possible to listen to us upon these matters of importance, when he declares it impossible to answer us upon a mere question of time? The question we put to him was as simple as, "What is it o'clock?"—his reply, "It is impossible for me to answer!" Well, if he cannot condescend to answer as to the hour of the day, what prospect is their of his being able to reply to more weighty questions? In short, he has taken his stand; he will answer no questions; he will receive no instructions; he rejects all stipulations; and he disclaims the condition upon which you offered, and the Earl of Donoughmore accepted, your petition.

There cannot, therefore, be found in this crowded assembly any Catholic sufficiently hardy to propose that we should retract, and again offer our petition without a condition. (A general cry of "no, no!" for many minutes.) I know that no person would hazard such a proposition, whatever powers of effrontery he may possess; nor do I accuse any man of entertaining such an idea.

You must have a new selection made; you must have a man selected who *will* consent to lay your grievances before parliament this session; who will consent to receive your instructions; who, in short, will seek to obtain for the Catholics of Ireland that which the Catholics of Ireland deserve, and not get up a plan of his own, in which he may be the principal figure, and the Catholics secondary objects.

The advocate we want is a man who will require from parliament an emancipation that would quiet and content the people of Ireland, and extinguish the heart-burnings and animosities which at present rage in this country—not an emancipation which would create more jealousy and disaffection, and embitter our feuds, and increase our rancorous hostility to each other:— an advocate, in fine, who would, from his heart prefer the emancipation of Ireland to the emancipation of Mr. Grattan and Mr. Canning. Such is the advocate we want; and such an advocate may, I know, be found; but alas! we must, I much fear, go to England to seek for him. We must seek for an Englishman, for I know of no Irish member to whom you can now commit your petition.

Let me not be taunted with this preference. I do not prefer an Englishman as such. Oh, no! My preference and my prejudices are altogether Irish. My heart, my soul, my feelings are all—all Irish. My patriotism is almost exclusively Irish; and I remember the wrongs England has inflicted on my wretched country, with a hatred doomed to be immortal and unrelenting.

But there is now no choice. Ireland was, in the last session, abandoned by all the Irish members. She was flung at the feet of Peel, to insult and to trample upon her as he, in his majestic forbearance and wisdom, should think fit; and, lastly, our Irish patriots have found out that he is an Alfred—nothing less! (Much laughing.)

Oh, it is sorrowful mirth; but this is true; Ireland was defended only by Englishmen. There remained amongst them the still unextinguishable flame of liberty, and they made a generous effort to protect Ireland. May the best blessings of heaven be poured upon them. Whitbread, and Horner, and Romilly, and Grant, and others, fought for Ireland. We will find amongst them an advocate suited to our purpose; the cause and the principle of civil and religious liberty will never be scorned by them.

I cannot conclude without deprecating any declamation on the merits of Mr. Grattan. No man can be more sensible of those merits than I am.

I recal to mind his early and his glorious struggles for Ireland. I know he raised her from degradation, and exalted her to her rank as a nation. I recollect, too, that if she be now a pitiful province, Grattan struggled and fought for her whilst life or hope remained. I know all this, and more : and my gratitude and enthusiasm for those services will never be extinguished.

But I know, too, that, to use his own phrase of another, "he was an oak of the forest, too old to be transplanted."

I see with regret, that except his services in our cause, he has, since the Union, made no exertions worthy of his name and of his strength.   Since he has inhaled the foul and corrupt atmosphere that fills some of the avenues to Westminster, there have not been the same health and vigour about him.   He seems to have forgotten his ancient adorations.   He supported the Insurrection Bill, and every future Peel has the authority of his name to aid in outlawing Ireland.   He accused his fallen countrymen of cherishing a French party.   Alas ! he ought to have distinguished between the strong anti-Anglican spirit which centuries of oppressive government created and fostered, and any attachment to the enemy of freedom.   The very party whom he was induced to traduce, hated despotism as much in France as in Russia or in England; and it assuredly had nothing French about it.

But above all, Mr. Grattan has mingled the support of our cause with the procuring for a Protestant ministry the patronage of our Church.   These recollections mitigate the sorrow I feel at his having now disclaimed our petition.   I feel for him unfeigned respect ; but he has refused to accept the petition upon our terms.   I shall, therefore, move—

"That the Catholic Association be requested to send a delegation to London, in order to procure a member of the House of Commons to present our petition, and apply for unqualified Emancipation."

Some members having interfered to request a postponement of the resolution, on various grounds, but chiefly in order to have more time for considering it, Mr. O'Connell withdrew his resolution, on the grounds of an unwillingness to create a difference of opinion, and the sincere wish that he had for unanimity ; but he would wish that if it should be given into the hands of the Association, that they should report to an aggregate meeting to be held on Thursday, the 23rd instant.

A resolution was then put and carried to that effect

PATTISON JOLLY, Steam-press Printer, 22, Essex-st. West Dublin.